BETHLEHEM'S CHILDREN

A NOVEL

JOHN INDERMARK

Copyright @ 2020 John Indermark

All Rights Reserved

Cover Photo: @iStock.com/Vladimir Zapletin

DEDICATION

To J.K.I.
For encouraging all along

To the W.G.
For years of listening and supporting

To R.M.P.
For the assignment that got this underway

PROLOGUE

Dawn broke uneasily over the hills outside Bethlehem. A wind stirred from the southeast, lofting hints of sulphur and bitumen from the Salt Sea. The people and animals of the village favored the prevailing westerlies that swept from the Great Sea across the coastal plain, before ascending the highlands in which Bethlehem nestled. These winds blew with a regularity depended upon for seasons of growth and cycles of time. They brought a sharp edge to winter's chill and a soft respite from summer's heat. Their clouds bore the early and latter rains that watered crops and filled cisterns. Flocks and fields thrived on the west wind.

On occasion, though, an east-originating *khamsin* scorched the landscape. For unfortunates caught in the wilderness of the Jordan, the *khamsin's* sand and dust choked throats and stung eyes. Stories swirled of salt collectors surprised by these winds beside the Salt Sea. Those whose survival skills combined with good fortune escaped with skin chafed and mouth burnt by the wind's abrasive heat. The dried remains of those not so blessed might be found when the wind relented, if the jackals didn't find them first.

All cursed the *khamsin*, even when it arrived at its expected time to herald the onslaught of summer's heat. This was still spring, the first day of Nisan, when west-borne rains and cooling breezes should prevail for a month or more. But that was not to be this day in the town of Bethlehem.

When such winds blew, village life came to a standstill. Only activity deemed critical was carried on outside of home. A jug of water might be filled, a portion of food might be obtained, but little else. Canvas stretched tight across windows to keep sand from flying in. If the khamsin and its heat lingered more than a few hours, the window canvas would be soaked with water to cool and filter the air.

Elias the carpenter didn't try to work in his open-sided shop this morning. But rather than waste the whole day, he brought two small unfinished carvings, along with a bronze cutting blade given him by his father, back to the house. Elias was sculpting figurines from scrap blocks of olive, one for each of his sons. For Saul, the older boy, a wolf emerged from the raw wood. For Levi, not quite a year and a half old, a lamb took shape from the working of Elias' knife.

Saul and Levi loved to listen to their father tell them Isaiah's story of a wolf and a lamb, and a little child who led them. The two often played out the story as Elias recited the tale. His narration often broke into laughter at the sound of fierce wolf growls and soft lamb bleats coming from the two boys. Elias poured his heart into these objects. He even whispered a prayer of thanks for this wind that provided excuse to spend a day on the nearly finished carvings.

"Husband, have we become so rich that you spend your hours whittling toys?" Rebekah's voice spoke the annoyance an adult might have with the dawdling of a child.

"Why Rebekah," he offered in mock resentment, "have we become so poor I can't indulge my sons? If God gave Sabbath to enjoy the Almighty's company, surely he understands setting aside a day now and then for the children given us. Or maybe, I could indulge my wife!"

The attempt at humor escaped Rebekah, as she shook off a playful grasp at her waist intended to pull her into his lap. "Oh, Elias! If you choose to squander your day, so be it. But there's work to be done in this house, and it appears I must be the one to do it."

Elias saw that further attempts to distract her were useless. He'd grown accustomed to her occasional disappointment with him. Rebekah had brought her family's lost wealth to his attention with greater frequency of late. It was not as if Elias had slackened in his work. As the village's master carpenter, Elias prospered even after he brought his friend Joseph into the shop. Still, the manner of life Elias' craft provided fell short of Rebekah's youthful experience. She looked with envy on some of her cousins, married to wealthy families in Jerusalem and Jericho. A less secure man might have been resentful. In his love for Rebekah, Elias offered himself as he was: carpenter, commoner, lover. He hoped Rebekah would find that enough.

On this day, though, Elias gave his wife free rein in her busyness while he focused on making intricate cuts to draw out the grain of the olive wood. All that remained were curved incisions on the lamb's back to replicate tufts of wool, and some delicate notching on the wolf's teeth. The boys sat alongside him, watching their father's hands shape the wood. Elias leaned over to them and whispered: "See to it you pick up the shavings that fall, or your mother will take the broom to the three of us for turning her fine floor into a woodshop stall." With a wink and a tousle of their heads, Elias resumed carving while the boys picked up the scraps. A slice here, a scrape there. The boys practiced wolf howls and lamb bleats. Between those sounds and the wind's gusting, they didn't notice the first faint strains of other noises echoing off the walls in Bethlehem. A new khamsin swept from the northwest, bearing down on the village. Its scorching originated not in the valley of a dying desert sea, but in the jealousies of a mortally ill king.

Elias abruptly stopped the movement of his knife. When the boys looked up to see why shavings no longer fell, he put a finger to his mouth. Rebekah also became very still. Initially, there was nothing to hear so much as feel. A rumbling of the ground, a rattling of Elias's carved plates hung on the wall. Then, off in the distance, a shout, what sounded like a scream, then more. Clangs of metal, doors opening and slamming – the noises drew closer.

"Rebekah, we've got to go!"

"What is it, Elias? I can't make anything out of the sounds. Shouldn't we wait – "

"Not now, woman. Do as I say!" Elias' uncharacteristic

shout shocked her and the children. Tears started down the faces of his sons. Elias hugged them. "No need to worry. We're just going to the cave Joshua uses for a stable."

The idea of going to the cave comforted the boys. It was a special place, where they played and where Levi's friend Yeshua had been born. There would be straw to jump in and animals to pet. Still, trembling hands and reddened eyes betrayed fear.

Elias reached down, picked up the carvings, and gave them to his sons. "When we go to the cave, you take good care of these – maybe they're nervous, too." Having someone to care for made the boys feel older, and braver. On his way out, Elias paused to grab the bronze carving blade and tuck it inside his belt.

The family slipped into the street: Levi in his father's arms, Rebekah holding Saul's hand. Though the wind had relented, they saw dust swirling over houses to the north. Worse yet, the sounds rang sharper and clearer. Elias glanced at Rebekah. The screams grew stronger. Some mournful. Some painful. As they hurried through alleyways and alongside rock walls, the wave of sound continued to crest. There could be no doubt. The metallic sounds belonged to swords. The earth rumbled beneath horse hooves pounding on bedrock and cobbled stones. The glimpse of a red-plumed helmet revealed the truth: Romans were creating this havoc.

The heat and confusion heightened Elias' mounting fury. Why here, why Bethlehem? Why did swords strike shepherds and farmers? Damn those Roman bastards – why us! Reaching Joshua's home, he pounded on the door. "Joshua, Naomi! It's Elias!" Joshua opened the door, ashen faced and mute. Naomi and their three children arrayed behind him.

"We're headed to your stable. It's the Romans – I don't know why, but there's trouble. Bring your family, now! And Joseph's as well." Joshua stood speechless. Packing the twins on her hip, Naomi stepped beside her husband.

"Joshua, we have to go. We can't stay here any longer."

Joshua muttered something unintelligible, then started out the door ahead of the others.

Rebekah called out for Mary, but Naomi interrupted. "They're not here. We didn't notice until this morning. They must have left in the middle of the night."

Rebekah and Naomi stared at each other. Their friendship with Mary made her and Joseph's abrupt disappearance out of character. No goodbyes, especially when the next day...

"Women, come! We have no time!" Elias' shout tore them back to the street. Simeon, the oldest child of Joshua and Naomi, had already set out after his father. Naomi followed with Hannah and David in her arms, trying to keep up.

It wasn't far to the cave Joshua had converted into the inn's stable. They could only hope the soldiers wouldn't bother searching inside it.

"You there! Stop!" The voice came from a Roman officer astride his horse. Alongside him stood four soldiers on foot, swords drawn. Just short of the cave, Joshua stopped at the command and stepped back into the circle of the two families. Without a clear plan, Elias placed Levi in Rebekah's hands and approached the one whose uniform was that of a centurion.

"Excellency, I beg you to allow our family to pass. We've done nothing."

Some who remained in surrounding houses peered out from behind doors and curtains narrowly cracked. They had no desire to be noticed by the Romans and jeopardize themselves.

"Hand over your youngest boys to my men, then return to your home."

The face of Elias flushed red. "Excellency, what use could your army have with children? They're barely out of infancy, too young for any crime against Rome."

Rebekah recognized the defiance spilling into Elias's voice.

"Stand aside, Jew, if you value your own life."

"Surely there can be some arrangement made if we..."

"Enough! Guards, take the youngest boys." The four soldiers advanced.

Looking back at the families, Elias determined no other choice remained. When the soldiers marched past him, Elias pivoted and drove the carving blade deep into the side of one guard. "Run! Joshua, protect them!"

For a moment, it appeared the diversion might work. As the wounded man slumped to the ground, the other three legionnaires stared in amazement at a Jew who dared to publicly attack a soldier of Rome. The families made a frenzied dash toward the cave.

As quickly as the opportunity came, it closed. The officer spurred his horse and cut off their escape. Though Joshua might have thrown himself against the horse and perhaps unseated its rider, he froze as he had at the doorstep.

The three remaining guards moved to avenge their comrade's attacker. One lunged quickly, his sword piercing the abdomen of Elias. Sensing only seconds remained, Elias leaned into the thrust so he could slash his blade across the man's throat. Another guard swiftly delivered the kill stroke. The screams of Rebekah and his sons were the last sounds Elias heard.

Saul broke away from his mother's hold and threw himself on the Roman who had just killed his father. He bit and slapped before being kicked away, and then a bloodied sword took aim. "You miserable little Jew! I, Lucius, should kill you!" The Roman's mouth twisted into a sneer. "But you're not important enough to kill, not the right age." A slap across Saul's face sent the boy sprawling atop his father's lifeless body. The son clung to his father, pressing the smooth wood of the wolf upon the death wound, as if it were a talisman capable of returning life.

The centurion backed the women and children against a wall. The remaining two soldiers wrested Levi from Rebekah's arms. Even her shock at Elias' death did not prepare her for what ensued. Instead of taking the child away, the guard named Cassius took his sword and ran the boy through, then dropped him to the ground like a discarded doll.

Naomi barely had time to take in the obscenity just inflicted before Lucius ripped David and Hannah from her arms. Their screaming scream roused Joshua from his stupor. He lunged, taking the Roman by surprise. As they tumbled to the ground, Joshua drew a knife from beneath his robe. Lucius took hold of his own dagger. On their knees, eyes locked on each other. Both knew that at this range, neither could avoid being stabbed. Joshua's frequent boasts in the inn of fighting the Rome occupiers pounded inside his head. Yet, with his son's life hanging in the balance, Joshua felt the imminence of death. Kill this soldier, and his own life was forfeit.

Lucius held no such qualms, and he recognized advantage in the hesitation of his opponent. For this Jew, who had wrestled him to the ground before his commander, death would not be punishment enough. Standing slowly, the soldier's dagger still pointed in Joshua's direction, a far more brutal execution than Elias' unfolded.

"Go ahead, Jew, use your knife. USE IT!" Joshua's hand trembled, but did nothing. The guard twisted the knife from his hand. Lucius sheathed his own dagger. He turned to Cassius, who had seized David during the struggle while letting go of Hannah once he saw she was a girl. Taking the boy from Cassius, Lucius looked at Joshua, looked through Joshua, then slit the child's throat with the just-surrendered knife of his father. Naomi collapsed. Joshua retched.

David's killer dropped the knife in front of Joshua: "Pick up the knife, coward. Take revenge on your son's killer!" Joshua made no move. Seeing the poorly hidden faces of neighbors peering at the scene, Lucius completed the humiliation. "See this noble father of Bethlehem! Whose own knife sends his son to the pit, afraid to lift a hand lest he join him. What spirited blood you have in this disgusting place! Herod was wrong: no king could ever arise from such a town! Perhaps we should have killed your daughters."

"Lucius, enough!" The centurion interrupted, not to save this Jew from further degradation but to expedite the remaining chores of this day's assignment. "You and Cassius take the bodies of Demetrius and Marcus back to the square." With that, the three soldiers left the site of but one of that day's many atrocities.

Rebekah revived Naomi. Her anguish at David's lifeless and bloodied body was exceeded only by her revulsion toward Joshua. Hannah, David's twin sister, sobbed and sobbed, unable to wake her brother. Saul clung to Elias' body. And Simeon... Simeon walked slowly to his father. He picked up the knife thrown back to Joshua by the Roman, the knife that could have avenged David. Joshua searched for a word, but none came. Simeon spoke first – and last.

"My brother died. Why didn't you?"

The khamsin stirred again, blowing hot with salt and sulphur: salt to burn wounds that would last a lifetime, sulphur whose stench was lilac compared to the odor of shame filling Bethlehem's streets. Some said the wind howled into the night. For most, however, the khamsin's sound could not be heard above the wails of Bethlehem's grieving for her lost innocents . . . a grieving whose origins traced nearly two years before, to a very different night marked by very different cries.

BOOK ONE

"BEGINNINGS"

CHAPTER I

The birth cries of three women pierced a clear night sky that canopied Bethlehem.

Nervous relatives in the house of Elias awaited the birthing shout of Rebekah. Banished from the room by the midwife Rachel, Elias retreated to his carpentry shop to busy himself with more familiar work. Within moments of arriving, hands normally deft slipped as he pushed a cutting blade along an aged block of olive wood. Elias returned to the house, looking for a strip of cloth to staunch the blood dripping from his thumb. Levi, the father of Rebekah, patted Elias on the shoulder and stifled a smile.

"Ah, what a thoughtful son-in-law. He feels such sympathy for my daughter's pain that he slices himself with a knife!"

Elias laughed, but only for a moment.

"Have the two of you no sense of dignity for this moment? Or does my daughter labor so father and husband may find some amusement?"

Levi recognized the sharp edge in his wife's voice. "Let me see if I can find some wrapping for that thumb of yours," he said, leaving Elias and Salome alone.

Salome thoughts focused in the room where her only child, Rebekah, struggled to bring new life into the world. Salome had raised Rebekah for a life far more refined than a carpenter's wife. Levi had once provided such affluence. A series of misfortunes in the caravans with which he traded brought an end to their wealth.

Rebekah's marriage to Elias issued from that change.

Though born to a family undistinguished in heritage, Elias prospered in his carpentry. Levi reckoned Rebekah would never want for food or shelter with such a husband. He also perceived Elias to be a man of honor, who would be shamed if his wife's family lived in poverty. So Levi arranged the marriage. Salome acquiesced: never forgiving Levi, never accepting Elias.

Louder groans from her daughter startled Salome. Elias joined her by the door, as did Levi. The sounds reminded them all of the scene outside this same room two years before when Rebekah birthed her first child, Saul. Elias' parents had taken Saul to their home when Rebekah's labor had begun. No one needed a toddler underfoot today.

The pitch of the midwife's voice leapt high, matching a rise in Rebekah's shrieks. "Now, child! Push, PUSH!" A cry burst from Rebekah's throat as spasms thrust the child from her womb. After some minutes, Rachel opened the door. "Elias, come see the son which the Almighty, blessed be His Name, has given to you and Rebekah!"

Led by Elias, the family stepped through the narrow door. The newborn nestled in the snug wedge formed by Rebekah's left arm and breast. In the lamp's glow, Elias could trace the sweat from her brow mingling with tears. He kissed Rebekah's eyelids. Stroking back her hair and cooling her forehead with a moistened cloth, Elias added his own salty tears to Rebekah's.

"You've a fine son-in-law in Elias," Rachel whispered to Salome. "I've swaddled the child in the wrappings you prepared. Any needs he has now, his mother will meet."

"And Rebekah? Was her labor difficult?"

"No, not at all. She's a strong young woman, as you and I once were. If you need me, I'll be at the inn. Naomi's birthing time is also near." With that, the midwife hurried away.

Rachel did not like to leave a mother and child so quickly. She savored the moments following birth. The wondrous looks, every mother's beauty, the adoration of each newborn in these hours: Rachel could conceive of no better vocation than her own. Still, her vocation doled out its share of painful times. Times when her best efforts proved vain, and a child drawn out by her hands never breathed. Times when the mother forfeited her own life. Such thoughts hastened her steps. The last time she mid-wifed at the home of Naomi and Joshua, the town's inn-keeper, the child perished and the mother barely survived. The feel of Naomi's abdomen during Rachel's last visit convinced the midwife of twins within. Perhaps the ease of Rebekah's birthing augured well for Naomi. Two births occurring on the same day was unusual for a small village like Bethlehem. Rachel clung to that hope as she reached the inn's courtyard.

The inn adjoining the house was relatively quiet, with only a few voices coming from the tables. Rachel came to an abrupt halt when she heard the nasal tone of Joshua whining:

"I must be blessed with the luck of Job! A census that would fill this inn comes when Naomi lies flat on her back, leaving me to tend this place alone. It just isn't fair. Plus, there's that butcher-of-a-midwife. If she'd known what she was doing the last time, we'd be toasting our third child to-night – or fourth, if she's right about twins, though right is not something she's often been. To make matters worse – " The sight of Rachel bursting through the door cut off Joshua in midsentence. She strode to the table where he had been airing his complaints. Eyes wide open and face flushed, Rachel leaned across the table at her bewildered target:

"Joshua, I've brought more children into this life than you will ever know! No one grieved the stillbirth of your second son more than me. No one fought harder to save Naomi's life than me, so don't EVER speak that way about me again!" Rachel whirled round and exited, leaving Joshua to endure the barely muffled laughter of his companions at this humiliation.

Halfway across the courtyard, Rachel stopped. A

mother in labor depended on the midwife to set the mood. Naomi did not need a birthing companion piqued with anger. After several deep breaths and a prayer for calm, the midwife entered the house.

Unlike the spacious home of Elias, which had the luxury of a separate room for sleeping, the dwelling of Joshua and Naomi consisted of a single large room. On one side, a shelf used for food hung low from the wall. Next to it, a two-handled cooking pot sitting on a small clay oven spewed a thin trail of steam. A straw sleeping mat stretched across the floor on the other side of the room. Deborah, Naomi's mother, knelt beside the mat and supported her daughter. Naomi sat on a birthing stool. Its smooth curved seat and rounded back supported the mother during the wrenching hours of labor. Not all availed themselves of its benefits. Some regarded it as a Gentile intrusion on the purity of birth. But not Rachel. She judged that the relief it provided, particularly during hazardous childbirths, overrode any superstitions. Anything that conserved the strength and protected the mother's life, Rachel reasoned, must be a gift from the Almighty.

"Deborah, may God be praised you sit with your daughter tonight." Rachel joined her words with an embrace of Deborah, then the daughter. "And Naomi, you look strong."

Rachel spoke to encourage the mother-to-be, whose face was unusually flushed, even for a woman soon to give birth. She struggled to pant as Rachel advised during the waves of intense pain. But Naomi's severe trembling between those periods troubled the midwife most.

"Deborah, drape another blanket around Naomi." Rachel brushed a strand of hair from Naomi's eye. "I'm going to see how far along you are." More with hands than eyes, Rachel examined her. The earlier suspicions of twins proved true. One child poised close to birth.

"Rachel – can you tell – if the twins – are they alive?"

Gasps punctuated her question, as did worry from her last attempt at childbirth.

"Don't worry, child. The twins are well positioned, and the time shouldn't be long. Just remember your breathing when the pain swells. Don't push until I say. Everything will be fine."

Evening turned to night. Rachel and Deborah knelt by Naomi as she randomly passed between fear and confidence, pain and near-unconsciousness. Gradually, Rachel's worries began to subside. Naomi held her own as the time between contractions shortened. The worrisome tremors ceased. Even though the pain intensified, her panting had the desired effect. Deborah clung to Rachel, as if mother could give daughter the endurance her agony required.

At one moment, Rachel thought she glimpsed Joshua's face outside through the narrow window slits. There was too much to be done with Naomi to determine if it was him. But since husbands typically avoided these events, Rachel briefly allowed Joshua a kind thought for wanting to see how Naomi fared. Perhaps some decency dwelt in him after all.

When the time came, Naomi birthed the twins without complication. The second child, a boy, came literally at the heels of his older sister. The squeals of life brought Joshua's face again in the window, the light from the room illuminating his smile.

Naomi kept to her chores of cutting and knotting the umbilical cords and cleansing the children. With the washing complete, Rachel applied salt to the newborns. Some believed salt protected a child from demons. Rachel, like the midwife who taught her, gave greater credence to salt's cleansing abilities. At last, Rachel swaddled the twins in fresh linen strips of cloth.

Naomi, after birthing, had been cared for by her mother. Deborah first cleaned her daughter: wiping away the blood and mucus from her thighs and abdomen, washing the tears and sweat from her face, brushing her hair with the same long slow strokes she used when Naomi was a young girl. Afterwards, Deborah helped her daughter into a new robe, then eased Naomi on to the sleeping mat, softened by the addition of a dry fleece blanket. Rachel brought the twins to their mother, gently laying them within Naomi's caress like two fresh-picked flowers. When all was ready, the women beckoned Joshua, who now knelt beside his wife.

Rachel leaned close to Naomi. "You are twice blessed this night. Take care of them, and yourself. You'll need your sleep. May the Lord keep you, child."

Naomi took her hand. "Did Joshua speak with you yet?"

A glance toward Joshua revealed a look of shock. "Only a brief conversation. Why?"

"Visitors came to the inn this morning. A guest sent them here, as Joshua was looking in on me. The man asked for a place to stay, saying his wife was with child and in need of rest."

Joshua interrupted. "Naomi's being kind to me, I'm afraid. I turned them down, being the rooms were all filled. Then Naomi, she felt sorry for the poor girl. And in truth, she was quite young. And quite pregnant. Naomi suggested we could let them stay in the stable. So they'd be out of the cold. Last I saw them was before supper. Maybe if you could check on them..."

"Would you, Rachel? The girl looked so frightened and bewildered."

Moved as much by Joshua's admission as Naomi's plea, Rachel consented. Joshua lent her a small lamp so she could find her way to the stable – a cave, actually. Located on the town's southeast slope, it was used to hold the animals owned by the inn and its guests.

On her way, Rachel's thoughts turned toward the stabled couple. Sleeping in a cave would not be the best of lodgings. Odors collected against damp rock walls. Then there'd be the livestock. Still, a bed of straw bettered the hardscrabble rock covering much of Bethlehem's terrain. The faint sound of an infant's cry reached Rachel's ears. The sound sped her pace when she realized it came not from the inn but the stable.

When she reached the cave's mouth, a man inside bolted upright and stood alongside a feeding trough. Inside the trough, a tiny bundled figure cooed. The girl mentioned at the inn stretched out in one of the stalls, whose usual bovine resident crowded together with several sheep in another stall further back in the cave. The man stepped forward.

"My name is Joseph. What do you want here?"

Rachel barely glanced at him as she walked past and held her light above the child.

"I am Rachel, Bethlehem's midwife. I was told your wife was with child, but not so close to delivery as this!"

"Joseph, who is that with you?"

"A midwife, Mary. God continues to watch over us."

Rachel's brief check of the child pleased her. "The Almighty has had good help from the two of you. You've done a fine job of swaddling. Was he cleansed with salt?"

"Yes. Before Mary gave birth, I found some kept here for the animals. I dug around to find the cleanest bits, then Mary and I used them after we'd washed our son."

"Yes, you've done well." Rachel left the side of the trough and stepped to the girl reclining in hay. "And you, child, how have you fared?" The midwife shone her lamp close to the face of the new mother. "I'd venture this was your first."

"It was, midwife. The pain came as my mother warned, but Joseph stayed by me. And by our son, when I drifted into sleep."

"Can I do anything for you?"

"Right now, I just want to rest."

"As well you should, Mary." Rachel stroked her forehead, then moved the blanket to cover over her shoulders.

"This is an unusual night. I'd already attended two women giving birth in this village. And now I come upon you. I've never seen three birthings in a single day here."

Her comment regarding "unusual" sparked quick glances between Mary and Joseph. As though they, too, knew this night to be unusual.

CHAPTER II

Grey clouds blanketed Jerusalem the next morning. The abrupt change in weather didn't surprise those who trod its streets in the day's first light. The month of Marcheshvan typically brought the early rains upon which the next harvest depended. Folk in the countryside rejoiced at the rain's return. But for some in the city, who'd abandoned the ways of the land for urban comforts, the joy was lost. Cobblestone walks sprouted no stalks when puddles formed. The great stone buildings grew cold and damp without the sun's steady heat on their walls.

Treading along the Street of David, Nathaniel drew his cloak tightly over his shoulders. Open sandals provided his feet no protection from the drops splattering the stones beneath. Everywhere he looked, grey dominated. Street, sky, the wall that once formed Jerusalem's northern limit but now bisected its expanding precincts – all appeared a dull, wet, lifeless grey.

Nathaniel thoughts drifted to his home in Bethlehem. As a child, he reveled in these rains and their greening of the landscape. Its arrival in fall infused the slopes with new life, providing fresh pasture for the sheep. Nathaniel remembered joining his father and brother, both shepherds, on such days in the wet green of the land. Nathaniel's heart, however, thrived in the class led by Bethlehem's rabbi. The lad excelled in reading and writing and Torah memorization. The rabbi spoke to Nathaniel's parents about the boy's gifts, telling them of a school in Jerusalem that could provide education and opportunity not accessible in the village. The decision was made. The rabbi enrolled Nathaniel at the age of thirteen in the Jerusalem academy.

Nathaniel's aptitude soon attracted the notice of Jerusalem's elite, leading to an apprenticeship as scribe for the Sanhedrin. Visits to Bethlehem became more infrequent, even as the rigors of shepherding took their toll on his family. His father died one especially bitter winter. Some attributed the death of Nathaniel's mother the following year to grief that eroded her will to live. His brother died in a fall when seeking to rescue a lamb trapped on a ledge. Nathaniel's only family now was his widowed sister-in-law Deborah and her daughter Naomi.

Nathaniel dutifully offered to marry Deborah, even though she was ten years his elder. Deborah politely declined, professing her desire to remain in Bethlehem. In truth, Deborah distrusted her brother-in-law. She didn't understand how a scribe trained in Torah could be so consumed with ambition, a common theme in his conversations. For his part, Nathaniel never understood how she could turn down such a practical offer. Still, he accepted Deborah and Naomi as a family burden to be borne. Every month, Nathaniel sent a small stipend to them.

Walking along the Street of David, Nathaniel dismissed these rambling thoughts. An appointment at the Temple spurred him through this chilling shower. He was to meet with the High Priest Simon and Saripheus, who held the office of *Sopher Kohen Gadol* – Scribe to the High Priest. The Sopher served publicly as advisor and secretary to the High Priest. Privately, the Sopher worked behind the scenes as intermediary between Jerusalem's religious and political leaders. In this way, the High Priest could avoid the appearance of any contact with the Gentile Romans and the similarly disdained members of Herod's entourage. At the same time, through the Sopher, the high priest could conduct necessary business with them.

"Greetings, Nathaniel, on this disagreeable morning."

The voice belonged to Saripheus. He stood in the western portico, just inside the gate that brought the Street of David into the temple precincts. The silver hair and beard of Saripheus gave him the look of a scholar that he in fact was. His lectures on Torah never failed to draw enthusiastic crowds.

"Saripheus, it's honor enough to meet with you and Simon. You humble me more by meeting me outside in this weather."

"I thought we should talk before our time with Simon. The demands on the High Priest fill his days. I try to make his conversations pass swiftly and to the point."

The two men walked through the empty outer courts of the temple and into the Court of the Women, on their way to the High Priest's chamber situated within the Court of Israel. Worshippers and pilgrims would fill these courts later in the morning.

"You've shown yourself to be an excellent apprentice, Nathaniel. Many follow your advance within the Sanhedrin: some with envy, some with anticipation."

"And how have you followed it, sir?" The question brought their strides to a halt underneath a covered porchway. Saripheus studied the eyes of his younger companion. They betrayed no hint of weakness or fear in raising such a blunt question.

"If I were younger, Nathaniel, you can be sure I'd mark your progress with envy. But I've lived most of my years already. So I look upon you with anticipation. Which leads us to why you've been summoned here today."

As the two men climbed the steps of the Nicanor Gate, the Sanctuary's immense facade came into view. Golden vines clustered with grapes strung across the top of the two-story structure. Thick tapestries embroidered with stars and other designs hung in front of the doors. A few priests could be seen readying for the morning sacrifices. At the top of the steps, Saripheus headed left toward the High Priest's chamber. Nathaniel hoped the Sopher would speak further of his anticipation and the meeting's purpose. When silence followed, Nathaniel took the initiative.

"Sir, you mentioned `anticipation.' I'm not sure I understand your meaning."

Saripheus stopped, resting his hand rested on the bronze handle of a huge oak door. "I once stood where you do now and asked my predecessor the same question. So I tell you the response given me. It has been decided to prepare you for the office of Sopher, if you are willing. You possess a quick mind, and the ability to interpret and conform the words of our tradition to the demands of these times. You've also been overheard to express certain thoughts as to the relationship between this temple and the authorities of Rome and Herod. Your perceptions run close to my own. And, unlike me, you've no family to divide time or energy. On the other side of this door is apprenticeship to be Sopher under my guidance. When I die, the office will be yours. But you must be willing to give yourself totally to this office. If you're not prepared to accept such sacrifice, or unwilling to submit to my instruction: turn around now and resume the life you lead. Our conversation will never have occurred. But if you would be Sopher, follow me inside!"

Saripheus swung open the door and entered, taking his place by Simon. Inhaling deeply, Nathaniel entered the chamber.

"Come forward, my son." The voice of the High Priest Simon echoed off the room's stone walls. Nathaniel dared lift his eyes only enough to walk directly to the chair where the High Priest sat. Never before had he been in private audience with the High Priest.

"Saripheus speaks very highly of you, as do members of the Sanhedrin. Your work is valued. Do not fear, then, to lift your face before me. I am your priest, not your judge."

As Nathaniel raised his head, he saw the whitehaired priest smiling at him. Simon didn't wear the elegant vestments and robes worn at the Sanhedrin or in Temple appearances. Here in this chamber, warmth was more the concern. Simon's clothing consisted of a plain white tunic wrapped with a thick fleece cloak. It reminded Nathaniel of garments used by his father and brother to warm themselves against the chill on Bethlehem's hills. Had Nathaniel not seen this man preside over the Sanhedrin, he might have taken him for one of Jerusalem's traders.

"Nathaniel, is it in your heart to become apprentice to Saripheus?"

"Yes, though I question my worthiness for such an office."

"Scribe, your perception is not at issue. Had we not deemed you worthy, you'd not be before the High Priest this morning." The words of Saripheus came calm and even, but full of force. "The High Priest seeks to learn of your desire for such an office."

Desire for such an office, thought Nathaniel, sustained him through tedious years of reading and writing the words of others. The limitation imposed upon a scribe were words already composed, already authored, already spoken. Nathaniel yearned to create and speak his own words that others would heed and follow.

"My lord Simon, be assured I want nothing more than to serve you and our people wholeheartedly. I have sought to do that as scribe, and I will seek to do so as Sopher."

"You shall, my son. Saripheus will be your mentor and guide. Watch him, and learn how others should come to view you. Heed him, and discover how others should listen to you. Walk with him, and understand how others should follow you. May the Lord bless you, Nathaniel."

Simon stood and embraced Nathaniel, then motioned the two of them to depart.

Leaving the chamber, Saripheus led Nathaniel toward the Temple's inner courts. "You spoke well, Nathaniel. A more aggressive approach might have given him pause. That's an important lesson in your work as Sopher: never let your ardor give others reason to distrust you."

The words surprised Nathaniel. "But you raised the question of my desire?"

"I did – and for the very reason of which I spoke. You will need as Sopher to be prepared for persons who will test you, who try to draw out your weaknesses. Not that I see ambition as weakness. But Simon might have. Contrary to some of the previous High Priests appointed by Herod, Simon is a pious man. He and those like him view ambition with suspicion, especially when it involves religious office. In the Sanhedrin, you'll relate to many who are so minded."

Nathaniel began to understand more deeply the respect given to the Sopher. "Saripheus, since we will be working together, may I ask you a personal question?"

The pace of the Sopher noticeably slowed. "I would not make a habit of personal questions. But if it relates to our work, let me hear it."

"My own assumption had been that your son, Judas, would succeed you. He has a following in the city, especially among the scribes now finishing their training."

Saripheus walked on in silence. Nathaniel took the lack of response to mean there'd be no answer to his question. They walked through the Court of Israel, then turned right to approach a small tower that Nathaniel knew to be prohibited to all but high-ranking officials. Temple guards allowed them entrance through its barred doors. Once inside, Nathaniel heard the wooden bars slide back into place outside. With the doors secured, Saripheus drew a key from a small pouch that hung from his belt and unlocked a door leading into a seemingly empty storeroom.

"Pay close attention, Nathaniel." Saripheus grasped a torchholder on the wall inside the door and pulled it to the left. Holding it there, he closed the door. A loud crack sounded as a trapdoor in the floor dropped open.

"Herod built this tower to provide secret entrance into the temple from the Tower of Antonia. As Sopher, you'll use it for meetings involving the Romans and Herod's representatives. But you must never, for any reason, mention the existence of this to anyone. We use it today so that I may introduce you to others with whom you will work."

Nathaniel stood awestruck. He never imagined such a connection existed between the temple and the Antonia. He understood Saripheus' instruction to maintain secrecy. The temple was Judaism's most sacred site, while the Antonia with its Roman garrison its most hated. The two shuffled through a torchlit tunnel. As they approached a stairway leading to another trapdoor, Saripheus stopped to face Nathaniel.

"You asked before of my son. I've now taken you where I once longed to take him. As you say, he boasts a great following. But a Sopher cannot have a following. A Sopher mediates between those with followings, whether priest or king, governor or rebel. Those who wave their own banner to attract the crowd's devotion will also plot to obtain or deter the disciples of others. A Sopher, to survive, must never be a rival to any. Even in the name of a cause. Judas refused to learn that lesson. If you would be Sopher, you must. For the sake of our people."

In spite of the passageway's chill, Nathaniel wiped perspiration now dampening his forehead. After years of waiting, things were moving fast. The words of Saripheus spun in his head. Nathaniel the scribe wanted to mull over this morning's conversation, time to decipher the text and discern its meaning. But time escaped him. Nor was Nathaniel a mere scribe any longer. Stairs were taken. Another door opened.

Two Roman guards, swords drawn, awaited the pair emerging from the passageway. One of the guards, Lucius, held a torch to their faces.

"Saripheus, we were told this morning you would come. But who is this fellow?"

"His name is Nathaniel. Study his face well. He'll be returning with me from now on, and eventually in my stead."

The other guard, Antioch, stepped to the room's only other door. It had no handle or key slot. Antioch knocked twice, then called out: "Visitors for Julius and Alexas." Wood slid across metal and the door opened.

Nathaniel saw it to be at least four inches thick, with iron rods crisscrossing both sides. Anyone trying to storm through it would find the task arduous. Even if successful, the time required would allow the hallway to fill with legionnaires stationed in the Antonia. Herod's architects had gone to great lengths to ensure the safety of this way.

Saripheus now stood in the hallway with two other guards. "Demetrius and Cassius, this is my companion, Nathaniel."

Nathaniel tilted his head slightly to acknowledge the pair.

"He has the permission of the High Priest to accompany me."

Cassius led Nathaniel and Saripheus to a corner stairway at the end of the hallway. The stairway wound upwards. As they ascended it, Nathaniel noted it had ventilation slits rather than windows as its only openings. At last, they reached what Nathaniel presumed to be the top.

Walking down a lengthy hallway, Nathaniel caught several glimpses of the Temple from windows along the way. The builders allowed for more openings here, as scaling the wall would be suicidal. In addition, the windows afforded easy views to spy the courtyard of the Temple below. The crowd had grown since he and Saripheus passed through it. From this height, what he remembered of the view from Bethlehem's hills seemed insignificant.

"The chamber for your audience, sirs." Cassius opened a door for Saripheus and Nathaniel. Nathaniel's eyes widened at the sight. Marble panels and bright-colored mosaics decorated the room's walls. A balcony filled with plants and statuary overlooked the inner courtyard of the

Antonia. Velvet-covered couches enclosed three sides of a table laden with fresh fruit. A charcoal brazier blazed with glowing coals.

Saripheus addressed two men walking in from the balcony. "Alexas and Julius, this is the scribe, Nathaniel, whom I've told you about."

While never having met the pair before, Nathaniel had certainly heard of them. Julius was a Roman centurion assigned to the Jerusalem cohort. Though other Romans of higher rank served in Palestine and Jerusalem, his reputation for knowing the land and its people was known and respected even by the Jews in the Sanhedrin. And Alexas, this was the brother-in-law to King Herod! While Alexas held no official post, rumors had it that he was one of the few family members Herod trusted. In contrast to the stern athletic features of Julius, Alexas was a rotund figure sporting the curls of hair and beard in fashion among devotees of Hellenism. To Nathaniel, he looked soft and pliant. But anyone who managed to remain Herod's ally for so many years surely possessed an instinct for survival.

"Nathaniel, this is the centurion Julius. And Alexas, a member of the Herodian family. They are the two with whom I work most. You'll have much to learn from them."

"Would that my father had lived to see the honor I am given by working with you," Nathanial began as he bowed before Alexas. "I am humbled in your presence."

"Don't deprecate yourself, Nathaniel," Alexas replied. "Do the philosophers not advise us to 'know thyself?' Why, even my brother-in-law Herod is eager to have an individual with your talents preparing to assume the role of Sopher."

Nathaniel didn't believe for a moment the king possessed such eagerness, nor that he even knew a mere scribe. The words, however, reminded Nathaniel that a man in Alexas' position would need to be a daily practitioner of flattery to stay in Herod's good graces. And why not? The proverbs of Solomon, after all, teach that *"Pleasant words are like the honeycomb."*

Julius stepped up to Nathaniel. He didn't offer a hand-shake, knowing the traditions proscribing Jews from physical contact with Gentiles. "Give heed to Saripheus. He serves well the interests of your people and Rome. I hope you prove yourself to do the same."

"The hope is mine as well, Centurion."

"One more thing. When we meet here, and a meeting stretches long, you'll not offend me if you don't eat while I'm in the room. I'm aware of your table customs, and I don't need or seek your friendship. Only your service." With that Julius walked away and out of the room.

"Don't be offended by his manner," Saripheus began. "You can be sure his informants briefed him on you thoroughly. If he didn't believe you could work together, he would have told you to your face. Julius is simply aware that some of our practices present difficulties. As a Roman, I'm sure he laughs at them. As a soldier, I'm equally sure he doesn't want to risk the blood of his men on them. For him and for us, peace entails compromise."

"Besides," added Alexas, "many of us have come to see the folly of some of these old ways. If dining with Gentiles results in peace for Jews, who cares what's eaten? Or with whom?"

Such a statement from someone other than Herod's brother-in-law normally would have stirred Nathaniel's argumentative side. But, he found himself thinking, a Sopher does have not the luxury of taking sides. And, after all, there was an odd logic to Alexas' practicality.

CHAPTER III

Elias and Rebekah arranged the last wooden platter with goat cheese, bread, and figs. The family of Joshua and Naomi, along with the strangers they were bringing from the inn, had been invited for the evening meal. The midwife Rachel had urged such a gathering take place, still amazed at the birth of four children on the same night in the village. And now it was to be.

The meal fell on the day following the traditional week of uncleanness for the mothers, a ritual state brought about by the flow of blood during birthing. During those seven days, Rebekah and Naomi and Mary had only limited contact with family members besides their newborns. The meal would provide a welcome end to this time of separation.

In addition, the meal commemorated an age-old ceremony of Israel's faith. The eighth day also meant the rite of circumcision for the newborn sons. Earlier, the town's rabbi brought the same stone blade used in Bethlehem for generations in this ritual. After intoning the solemn words of Abraham's covenant with God from Genesis, the rabbi slit off the child's foreskin as his father watched. Three times the scene repeated itself in Bethlehem that day: an infant son cried out, and a father lifted his child into the air to thank God for this new son of Abraham's covenant.

"Rebekah, I think that may be Joshua's voice." The couple stepped toward the window and listened. Soon they heard the distinct shrill tone of Bethlehem's innkeeper.

"You're right. Joshua must be regaling the Nazarenes

with one of his stories."

"He does have a way of going on sometimes."

"He could bore a corpse, Elias: talk of taxes, talk of Romans, talk of what he'd do if he sat on Herod's throne. Really, that friend of yours is going to wear out his tongue, or our ears!"

Elias smiled. "Joshua means no harm by it. He just likes to hear the sound of his own voice. But for me, I'm less for talk and more for action!" Elias wrapped his arms around her waist and pulled Rebekah close. "Moses might not have given the law of husbands and wives remaining separate a week after birth, had he longed to hold you."

Rebekah marveled at how tender the rough hands of Elias could feel. But the duties of a household about to welcome guests caused her to pull away.

"One shouldn't speak of Torah that way, husband. Why don't you go out and meet them at the gate? I'll see if the boys still sleep."

As he opened the door, Elias saw the guests had already passed the gate and were inside the yard. Joshua and Naomi each carried one of the twins, while little Simeon, almost five years old now, walked between his parents. The couple from the stable followed behind.

"Naomi, Joshua, welcome. And who is this!?" Elias leaned over to peer at Simeon, tousling the boy's hair. "This young man cannot be Simeon? He's too tall and broad-shouldered!" Elias raised the young boy in his arms and spun him in a circle.

"Elias, God's blessing upon you and your house. And let me introduce our companions. This is Joseph of Nazareth, his wife Mary. And the son, they have named Yeshua."

Elias set down Simeon and stepped forward to greet the newcomers. Shaking the hand of Joseph, Elias felt it as calloused as his own. Joseph's grey hair and face showed the effects of far more years than the twenty-eight Elias had thus far seen. When Elias turned to Mary, the contrast took him aback. She was but a girl, seventeen years at most, likely younger. Raven-black hair crowned her head, falling softly to her shoulders. Her dark complexion seemed as smooth as a fine grain of olive wood. Her slight stature was dwarfed by Elias, yet he felt humbled.

"Joseph and Mary, and Yeshua, this home and those in it welcome you."

Rebekah came to the door, laying out the mat upon which to place sandals. Young Saul hid behind his mother's dress, while Levi squirmed in Rebekah's left arm. She greeted each one as they entered, bowing slightly to the men, touching cheeks with the women and Simeon.

A low wooden table crafted by Elias sat in the middle of the room. Platters heaped with food covered the table, along with stoneware plates and cups, and pitchers of wine and water. Cushions and mats spread on the floor provided seating. The infant twins of Naomi and Joshua remained asleep, so several cushions were pushed together in a corner of the room for them. Levi and Yeshua nestled in the arms of their mothers. The meal ready, Elias offered the blessing:

> *King of the Universe: You give seed for grain and sun to ripen vines; you give life from a mother's womb and children to lighten our faces. So receive our thanks. This day we have kept your word given to Father Abraham for the circumcision of our sons. Keep them in your ways and your covenant all their lives long. This day we offer thanks for the daughter Hannah, borne to our friends Naomi and Joshua. Pray keep her in your commandments and covenant as a true daughter of Sarah. Bless this food, which You give us. Bless us who are gathered here to enjoy the fruits of Your hands.*

Elias paused, as if ready to close the prayer. He opened one eye ever so slightly, and caught sight of the couple from the stable. Elias continued.

And we thank you for those newly come to us, Mary and Jo-

seph, and their son Yeshua. Bless the friendship about this table, that it may nourish us as surely as this food. We pray to your Holy Name. Let it be.

Rebekah poured wine into the cups of the adults, then a mixture of water and wine for Saul and Simeon. Elias raised his cup and offered: "For sons and daughters who brighten our lives, for wives and mothers who give them birth, may the Almighty be praised!"

"May the Almighty be praised!" echoed the others, and the meal began.

As feared by Rebekah, Joshua dominated the initial conversation. The others didn't mind at this point, since listening left mouths free to savor the food set before them. In time, however, Elias found an opportune break in Joshua's monologue and seized upon it.

"Joseph, all I know from Joshua's introduction is that you come from Nazareth. Are
you here for the numbering?"

"Yes. My grandfather's family came from Bethlehem. He left to work as a carpenter in Nazareth when his wife's father died, leaving no son to continue his trade there."

"From Bethlehem, really? Joshua may not have told you, but I am Bethlehem's carpenter. Perhaps I've heard of your grandfather. What was his name?"

Joseph paused, then replied, "Matthan."

The name startled Rebekah. "You don't mean Matthan, son of Eleazar?"

"Eleazar was my great-grandfather's name."

"Why, Joseph, my father spoke of him often. Eleazar descended from the royal family, the last of David's line to live in this village. No one heard what became of Matthan, his only child, once the family left here."

Now it was Elias's turn to become excited. "No wonder Rachel thought these births a favorable omen. We have a member of David's house back in Bethlehem!"

"And we've stuck him in a stable," lamented Naomi. "Can you ever forgive us, Joseph? If only we'd known – "

"There's no need for forgiveness," interjected Joseph. "When we found no shelter, you gave us what we needed." Then, in a lowered voice: "These days, it's not prudent to claim kinship with David too loudly, what with Herod's paranoia." At her husband's words, Mary drew Yeshua closer to her bosom.

Agreeing with Joseph's judgment and noting Mary's reaction, Elias spoke: "So be it. No one at this table will reveal your lineage. You have my word. Joshua?"

The innkeeper swirled the wine in his cup. "I suppose. But the grandson of Matthan shouldn't have to hide in the shadows like a common criminal. Herod and the Romans are the criminals. In my opinion, Joseph should let it be known exactly who he is. There's enough of the old families left to give him the respect and protection he deserves." Joshua finished his wine and set the cup down hard on the table. "And if Herod and his Syrian mercenaries come 'round to cause some trouble, we can just give them a taste of steel for their efforts. Why, I know of – "

"Joshua, Joseph believes knowledge of his family could compromise their safety. That's his to judge, not ours. But since this knowledge came out in our home and at this table, I must ask for your word of silence on the matter. Do you give it or not?"

Without lifting his eyes, Joshua mumbled a begrudging assent. A tense silence reigned over the table for some moments, broken only by an infant's cooing and food being eaten.

Finally, Mary restored the conversation. "Elias, I couldn't help noticing the workshop alongside the house. Did you fashion these platters and this table?"

"They're pieces from a while back. As carpenter for this village, I hardly have time for personal projects these days."

"You've a hand for fine craft," Joseph added, passing his fingers over the carvings on one platter. "My carpentry tends toward larger work: yokes and ploughs, or construction. I admire such detail work as this. My hands were never deft enough."

"Joseph, would you like to go out and have a look at my shop?"

Mary laughed. "You needn't ask. When we turned the corner onto this street, the first thing he saw was the shop. And when Joshua told him it belonged to our host, my husband joked if he suddenly disappeared from the meal, I'd know where to find him."

"Joshua, let's give our Nazarene friend a tour. And Simeon, maybe we can find some blocks of wood for you to play with. You too, Saul – up on the shoulders you go!"

Hoisting his eldest son on his back, Elias led the men and Simeon out to the workshop. The women rearranged their cushions into a semicircle, with the infants in front of them.

After freshening their cups with wine, Rebekah turned to Mary. "Are you, like your husband, from a family of Bethlehem?"

"No, my family has been in Nazareth for generations. My father Joachim served as a priest until his death."

Naomi hesitated, then went on. "Mary, forgive my curiosity, but there seems a great difference in age between you and Joseph. Was your marriage arranged quite early?"

"When my father died, mother wanted to insure my well-being. So, she and the rabbi arranged the agreement with Joseph when I was fifteen. But then, we had little time after the promises of betrothal. . ." Her voice trailed off.

Naomi wondered if she sensed sadness, or something else. "Joseph seems like a fine man. Sometimes the older ones can be very caring."

"Oh, he is an exceptional man. I could not want a better husband for me or father for Yeshua. A man of humility and sincere love. He is dear to me."

As the conversation stretched on, Naomi and Rebekah felt drawn to Mary. She truly possessed an affection for this man whose age placed him nearly a full generation from her own. Mary's wistfulness intrigued them. There seemed far more to her than youthful features alone.

* * *

Nathaniel received word only yesterday of the birth of twins to his niece Naomi. He planned to purchase gifts for mother and children this day at the bazaar along the Street of David. Instead, Nathaniel and Saripheus hastened to the Antonia for an abruptly called meeting with Alexas and Julius. Without speaking, they traversed the underground passage linking Temple to fortress. The pair at last entered the same chamber used for their meeting the week before. Beads of sweat dotted the round face of Alexas, while Julius sat rigid beside him on the couch's edge.

Saripheus offered with a bow. "We came as quickly as we could."

"We appreciate the haste, Sopher," the centurion replied. "I didn't think we'd meet again so soon, Nathaniel. The fates conspire to accelerate your learning of the Sopher's duties."

"I've spent much time at his side this week, trying to do just that. And I'm grateful for the opportunity to be included today."

"You may want to hold your gratitude till after Alexas informs you why we meet."

Nathaniel glanced toward Saripheus, hoping for some reassuring look that would indicate his mentor knew of the situation. The Sopher only furrowed his eyebrows and fixed his gaze upon Herod's brother-in-law. After taking a deep breath, Alexas spoke.

"Two developments at the palace bode ill for us all. First, the rumors you may have heard of Herod's illness are true. His physicians tell him there's no immediate danger.

But they don't know what to make of his condition, much less its treatment. And rather than admit ignorance and risk Herod's anger, they give him useless prescriptions. The pain only heightens the suspicions of my brother-in-law. The danger of that can be seen in his ordering the arrest of Alexander and Aristobulus, his two sons by the late queen. He's charged them with sedition."

"They'll die, guilty or innocent," muttered Julius.

Alexas nodded. "A trial's been scheduled, as a formality. But Herod will see to their execution, just as he arranged their mother's death. So until this illness of his ends in cure or death, anyone Herod views as a threat is in imminent danger."

The four sat in silence. Assassinations and poisonings littered palace life since the king's enthronement thirty-one years ago. Herod's increased instability weighed on them all.

Walking to the balcony, Julius scanned the courtyard of the fortress. Several legionnaires practiced sword and dagger thrusts. Keeping his eyes on them, he spoke to the three in the room. "Herod is a favored client of Rome. He enjoys the protection of our cohort, a gift to him from Augustus. Neither my tribune nor I can stand between Herod and those he conjures to be his enemies." Julius turned back to face the room. "Everything possible must be done to maintain order. The calmer the streets, the calmer Herod will be. What of the palace, Alexas?"

"A few insist on a fair trial for the two sons, to their own peril. The rest of us understand the two are dead already, so we assure Herod of his prudence. Salome and I have made pains to applaud his decisiveness in public, knowing his spies are everywhere."

The centurion nodded, understanding the necessity of Alexas' toadying. But it was time to move on to why Saripheus and Nathaniel had been summoned. "Alexas, tell them about one of the wives of Herod who is clamoring for a fair trial, putting herself and her family at risk."

Alexas looked directly at Saripheus. "It sorrows me to say that Mariamme, the daughter of the High Priest Simon, speaks for the young men."

The face of Saripheus flushed red. "That foolish – doesn't she know the jeopardy she places her father in? Herod already broke tradition by investing him as High Priest in order to marry Mariamme. If the marriage collapses, Simon stands to be removed in retaliation."

Alexas nodded. "You're right, Sopher. My own feeling is that Mariamme's maternal instincts for her own son were stirred by the fate of these other sons of Herod. Salome and I can no longer protect Mariamme's standing, nor Simon's."

Saripheus interlaced his fingers and rubbed his palms together. "I shall see that word is spread about the High Priest's outrage against sons who plot against their father. Perhaps this may deflect Herod's resentment. Maybe I can persuade Simon to meet with Herod and offer his support for the king's action, stressing his daughter does not speak for him on this matter."

"If I might suggest," Nathaniel added, "why not approach Simon with the scroll of Samuel? The story of Absalom's rebellion against his father David may be incentive for interpreting God's hand in Herod's punishment of rebellion."

The lips of Saripheus cracked in a brief smile. "Julius, our young apprentice shows promise. A wise suggestion, Nathaniel."

Julius stood up and walked next to Saripheus. "I don't know this scripture of which Nathaniel speaks, Saripheus. But let me give you advice as a friend regarding fathers and sons. Another person for whom Herod's mood bodes ill is your son. Judas."

Saripheus stiffened. Julius had never spoken Judas' name to him before.

The centurion continued. "My informants say he critiques the lack of Torah observance by the royal family.

Were Judas just another Pharisee, his words would fade into countless other accusations abroad these days. But Judas carries the crowd's attention, by virtue of his oratory and a father who is Sopher. And you can be sure: if my contacts hear these things, so do Herod's. Speak to your son, Saripheus. And not only for his sake. If Judas oversteps the bounds, your position will be compromised, no less than Simon by Mariamme. You know that."

Saripheus slowly stood. "Yes, I know that. But my son long ago stopped listening to one he judged stained by compromise. Like his young devotees, he's a purist."

"All I'm saying," concluded Julius, "is that his pursuit of purity may undermine you."

"I thank you for the warning and will do what I can. But for now, we must go, Nathaniel. There's work to be done for the sake of the High Priest."

Julius wondered if Saripheus might be better to consider what must be done for his sake. The Roman had come to deeply respect the Sopher in their labors to maintain peace and order in Jerusalem during his assignment here. He didn't want that to change.

After closing the door to the chamber on their way back to the temple, Saripheus stopped and placed his hand on Nathaniel's shoulder. "This is why I saw your lack of family as an asset. As Sopher, you must have no one so close you cannot set them aside, if need be."

* * *

An hour or more passed before the men returned from the shop. Simeon carried several wooden blocks of various shapes, which he proceeded to set on the floor and stack. Saul slept in the arms of Elias. As Rebekah made a place for Elias to lay Saul, the men rejoined their wives on the cushions. Except for Joseph.

Joseph took Mary's hands and lifted her to her feet. "Excuse us, but I need a word with my wife." The two stepped outside. A cool breeze descended from the western hills.

"Mary, what would you think of remaining here in Bethlehem?"

"Here? How could we do that? Our home, your business, wait in Nazareth?"

"Elias proposed I join him in his shop. He said there's far more work than one carpenter can manage. And Joshua offered us a room in exchange for work on needed repairs."

Mary brought her hands together, the tips of her fingers just below her lips. "Joseph, do you think we could? Naomi and Rebekah were so kind. They didn't pry or ridicule, as many in Nazareth have of late. But again, what of our life in Nazareth?"

"I'm sure Abinadad will crow with delight to find himself the sole carpenter in town. I'd only need to take the donkey back to pack up my tools and our few furnishings. As to our room by the shop, I could tell the leader of the synagogue to use it as might be needed until we choose to return. Besides, I think such a move a wise one at the moment. Too many in Nazareth know my grandfather's lineage."

"Then let it be done, Joseph! Elias and Joshua pledged silence about your family. Perhaps the angel of the Almighty will give us leave to share what's been revealed of Yeshua."

"If He does, so be it. But for now, we'll find joy enough in finding a new home for ourselves and Yeshua." Joseph kissed Mary, then the two walked back into the house.

Apparently, the topic of conversation around the table had been related to the one that occurred outside. For as Mary and Joseph re-entered the room, Elias rose from beside the table. "Do you need to give our offer more time?"

"I think not," said Joseph, "our decision is made. We stay in Bethlehem."

At that, the men came forward and shook Joseph's hand while the women hugged Mary. It was Naomi who noticed Mary starting to cry. "Mary, you aren't sad about staying, are you?"

"No, no. I'm glad to be. More than I can say."

Naomi brushed away the tears on Mary's cheek, then gave her another hug. "You are welcome here, child. You are with friends."

CHAPTER IV

Rebekah, Naomi and Mary talked the next day about how the three families might make pilgrimage to Jerusalem together for the purification sacrifices. The plan's only uncertainty involved the twins borne to Naomi, one of whom was a girl. The Levitical laws required new mothers to offer sacrifices following the time of their purification. For those giving birth to sons, the ritual came at the end of forty days. Those who bore daughters faced a wait of eighty days. Did Hannah's birth take precedence, or her brother's?

After the noonday meal, Joshua went to Bethlehem's synagogue to seek the counsel of its rabbi, Hananiah ben Johannan. A wooden ark, the repository for the Torah scrolls, stood at the front wall. Two carved tablets depicting the Ten Commandments embellished the ark's front. The two men sat on one of the rows of plank benches facing the ark.

"Rabbi ben Johannan, thank you for the time you take to see me."

"We take no time, but what God gives. How are your wife and children?"

"All fine. Naomi proved stronger this time. Already she's able to assist me at the inn."

"I see." The rabbi cleared his throat. "You indicated a question you had."

"It's about Naomi. We hope to accompany the families of Elias and Joseph to Jerusalem for the purification rites. But we're unclear as to whether it is permitted for Naomi to do so yet."

"Because one of the twins born was a girl?"

"Yes. We're unsure what Moses taught in such a case."

"Moses left no words on this particular matter. Even though the Torah tells several stories of twins, this question is not answered."

"What, then, do the rabbis teach?"

"Freshen my memory, Joshua. Your daughter was born first, correct?"

"Yes. So her birth takes precedence for Naomi's purification?"

"That would be the expected answer, but the Almighty does not always take the predictable path." Hananiah offered, fingering his beard. "Many rabbis, myself included, view the matter in this light. The gender of the last child to have left the mother's womb determines the time needed for purification. Since Naomi's lastborn was a boy, she requires but forty days."

Joshua's smile revealed bits of bread stuck in his teeth from lunch. "That is good news, rabbi. We wanted to make this journey with the others. And with Hanukkah falling so closely after the fortieth day, we'll share the Great City with many pilgrims."

"I wish you well on your journey, Joshua." Both men stood and shook hands. As Joshua turned to leave, the rabbi spoke again.

"Before you go, I would ask a favor."

"Certainly."

"Shortly after I came here, I taught Naomi's uncle, Nathaniel. In fact, I arranged his placement in the scribal academy of Jerusalem. If you see him during your visit, please send him my greetings. It's years since I heard from him."

"It will be done, Rabbi. In fact, we hope to lodge with him. The festival could make it difficult to find public rooms available. Even for an innkeeper's family!"

"I trust the Lord will provide for you. May the blessings of God rest on your journey."

"Thank you, rabbi, and blessings to you as well."

*　*　*

Nathaniel didn't know this Joseph whose signature ended the letter, but its contents pleased him. Sent from his niece Naomi, it told of plans to come to Jerusalem with her family for the sacrifice of purification. Would it be possible for them to stay with him? Two other families would journey with them. "Would my uncle be able to arrange a place for them to lodge, too?

Nathaniel smiled at the timing. His family had no knowledge he apprenticed to the Sopher Kohen Gadol, nor of the change in fortune it involved. The new position brought with it a large home, befitting the future counselor to the High Priest and intermediary with Rome and Herod. A cook and house servant came with it, along with a generous food allowance. The idea of hosting the remnant of his family pleased Nathaniel. What stories they would take back to Bethlehem: a shepherd's son who lived among Jerusalem's nobility! It occurred to Nathaniel the letter mentioned nothing of Deborah, Naomi's mother, who had turned down his marriage offer. He decided his return letter, extending hospitality to his niece and the others, should also include an invitation for Deborah. Let her eyes see the folly of spurning his marriage proposal. Nathaniel wrote his response and dispatched it immediately.

*　*　*

The pilgrims left Bethlehem for Jerusalem on the 23rd day of Chislev. Dawn came without a cloud to be seen. The road wound its way to the north and east through fields freshly greened. While the last of the olives had been picked when the rains began, other crops glistened in the sun. Newly emerged barley daubed brown furrows with green speckles. The earth sparkled from the dew, in contrast to the same land browned by summer heat and autumn drought. The brightness of the sun enhanced the colors of life returned by the rains.

Unlike the roads descending into the wasteland to

the east, this one presented no danger of steep-walled desert canyons nor the brigands who raided there. The route from Bethlehem to Jerusalem followed the highland plateau. Herod's soldiers regularly patrolled this way to ensure the safety of merchants and pilgrims and their often-sizable purses.

Joshua headed the procession, leading two dun oxen harnessed to a wagon. The three mothers and four infants rode in the wagon along with Deborah. Simeon took turns walking with Joshua and riding in the wagon, while Saul rode on the shoulders of his father. Elias and Joseph trod alongside the wagon, leading Joseph's donkey on a tether. Were it not for the steep Hinnom valley to Jerusalem's south, half a mile could be saved. But no road crossed the Hinnom, except at its far eastern corner. The Bethlehem road continued north close to half the length of the city before turning east to enter Jerusalem through the Corner Gate.

Where the road veered east, Joshua brought the oxen to a halt. Pilgrims arriving early for Hanukkah filled the gate. The going would slow considerably, and the vista of the city at that juncture was impressive. Three massive stone towers built by Herod overlooked this entry through the western wall. The sight of the towers served as a stark reminder that the Holy City was also an armed camp. South of the towers stood the white-stoned palace built by Herod. The families from Bethlehem shared bread and cheese by the roadside before pressing into the city in search of the house of Nathaniel.

* * *

In a small room in the Antonia, where the passageway from the Temple made its entry, the centurion Julius spoke with four guards as they finished their noonday meal.

"Over the next two weeks, pilgrims will fill the city for their winter festival. Three of you have served long enough here to know that means extra vigilance. This festival recalls a rebellion which pried the Temple from the Syrians, which feeds the Jews' resentment of us. So be on alert. Any sounds in this tunnel when none are expected, secure the room and send for help."

The Syrian legionnaire Antioch spoke. "Centurion, some campwomen spoke last night of rumors concerning the sons of Herod, that they were executed."

"True enough. Strangled, I understand, in front of their loving father's eyes." Julius held his tongue, lest he let slip with even more of his disgust for Herod.

"Will the Judeans do nothing to bring down such murderer?" asked Cassius.

"That is exactly why Herod tolerates our presence here, to keep him safe."

"Tell me, centurion", said Lucius, "why do these Jews call us barbarians, when their king spills the blood of his own kin? It seems they, not we, are the brutal race."

"Don't mistake their king for a Jew, Lucius. He's a Jew only when it's convenient. The Temple crowds despise him – yet most understand, were it not for Herod, a Roman procurator would rule in his place. And they hate us more."

A new recruit, Demetrius, sat silently in a chair atop the trapdoor entrance. He recently arrived from Tarsus to replace a soldier whose term of service had ended. Unlike the others in that room, Demetrius had yet to use his gladius beyond the training grounds. "Centurion, when will we rotate with others in the cohort? I expected to see duty with more excitement than this."

"Keep your ear to that floor, legionnaire! You'll have excitement enough if some fanatic bursts through, wishing to celebrate Hanukkah by slashing a Roman throat. Your duty is what I say it to be! Be glad you've got boredom now. You'll get your share of action soon enough."

The soldiers saluted the centurion as he left, then resumed their duties. Cassius and Antioch flanked the barred door in the hallway. The other two sat inside the room.

Demetrius drew out his gladius and felt the blade's

edge. "You said you've been here nearly ten years, Lucius. Has the centurion lost his nerve for fighting?"

"Watch your tongue, boy. You'd want no finer man to lead you in battle. He's just had to mop up too many of Herod's bloody intrigues. And unlike many of his rank, he holds the well-being of his men in high regard. That's why he studies these Jews and their ways. He wants any knowledge that might get some advantage and save our skins. Course, for old foot soldiers like me, bloodletting is a specialty – long as it's the blood of others!" With a wink, Lucius stood up and slapped Demetrius on the back. "Don't worry, boy, your time'll come."

* * *

"My lord, your guests have arrived." The servant delivered the news as Nathaniel stood in the courtyard. How perfect, he thought. A servant to greet them at the door, a wait as the master of the house was fetched, a few moments to apprise the stately household that would serve as their home for the next week. Nathaniel strode confidently to the colonnaded porch.

"Deborah, Naomi, it has been so long!" Nathaniel politely hugged the women of his family. "All of you, welcome to my home."

Joshua stepped forward to offer his hand, and admiration. "We thought we came to the wrong house, Nathaniel. I never knew scribes lived so well. With a servant!"

"I too, Joshua, sometimes cannot believe how gracious the Almighty has been. In the words of the Psalmist, `The lines have fallen to me in pleasant places.'"

"Husband, my uncle needs introduction to our companions."

"Why yes, forgive me. You may remember Elias, carpenter of Bethlehem, and his wife Rebekah? She carries their new son Levi, while their other boy Saul still sleeps in the wagon."

"Elias, it is good to see you again. And Rebekah."

Joshua waved the second couple forward. "And this is Joseph of Nazareth, and his wife Mary. The little one is Yeshua."

"Joseph, it is a privilege to meet you. Would you be the one who wrote the letter for my niece? If so, you must have trained as a scribe."

"My trade is carpentry. But my father believed I should know not only Hebrew for the synagogue, but Aramaic for the market, and the writing of both."

"A wise man, I would say."

"Finally, Nathaniel, your grandnephews and grand-niece. Simeon rests with Elias' boy Saul in the wagon. Naomi holds Hannah, while I have David."

"Ah, let me have a look." Nathaniel lifted the shawl covering David's head. "He looks well and healthy. And Hannah, as pretty as her mother. Don't you agree, Deborah?"

Naomi's mother stood back from the others, observing the scene before her, measuring Nathaniel's words against her remembrance of him. "Yes, both of my new grandchildren are beautiful. It's more than kind of you to provide us your home for our pilgrimage, Nathaniel."

"What is more important in life than family and attending to their needs?"

Deborah remembered questioning similar words. Then, Nathaniel uttered them as part of his marriage proposal to her after the death of her husband, his brother. Deborah also recalled Nathaniel's absence in his mother's grief and dying, and how he never set eyes on Simeon, now three years old. It seemed to her Nathaniel attended to the family's needs only as it suited him. Today it did. Deborah wondered why.

CHAPTER V

Masses of Hanukkah pilgrims swelled Jerusalem's population nearly threefold. Winding streets clogged with carts and pedestrians passing to and from the Temple. The coarse sounds of bazaar hawkers mingled with pungent scents wafting from market stalls. Aromas of spices and dung and roasting meats saturated the air. The greatest crowds milled about the Court of the Gentiles, the Temple's extensive outer plaza. The Temple managed the sale of unblemished animals for sacrifice there that met the Torah's requirements. Less stringent was oversight of the money-changers. Since only Jewish shekels could be used to pay the Temple tax and monetary offerings, pilgrims from other regions needed a place to exchange foreign currency. With no fixed rate, prudence had to be exercised in choosing with whom to deal.

Nathaniel had arranged for servants to care for the families' children. The three couples, along with Nathaniel and Deborah, made their way to the Temple. Nathaniel led them to a stall presided over by a tiny stooped man. His white turban banded by a piece of black cloth left only a shock of grey hair protruding from the front. A tunic hung loosely from his shoulders, while a coarse brown cloak wrapped his upper body. Dark blue eyes sparkled in recognition.

"Scribe Nathaniel, the blessings of Hanukkah rest upon you and your house. Is there something I may provide you with today?"

"Yes, Benjamin. I come with family and friends from

Bethlehem. These women are here to offer the sacrifices for purification."

"Ah, may the Almighty be praised for the wonder of birth! As you can see, I have the finest of lambs for such a sacrifice."

As Benjamin called his assistant to bring forward several lambs, Joseph spoke up. "Merchant, my wife and I require only two of your turtledoves. A lamb is beyond our means."

"The same is true with us," added Naomi. "A pair of turtledoves will serve – "

"A moment, please, Benjamin." Nathaniel turned his back to the stall and faced the small gathering. "Niece, you and your friends are my guests. God has blessed me with good fortune. I shall be pleased to purchase the lambs for the sacrifice."

"Uncle, that's too much. We already stand in your debt."

Joshua interrupted. "Naomi, such a gift honors your uncle. It's not our place to deny him such a gesture." Turning to Nathaniel, "Our thanks for the lamb you provide to Naomi."

"You're most welcome, Joshua."

"Nathaniel," Joseph interjected, "I don't wish to appear ungrateful, but I insist we pay for Mary's sacrifice, as this is our firstborn. The offering is more privilege than duty to us."

"And Nathaniel," added Elias, "there's no need for you to provide a lamb for Rebekah. The Lord has prospered our home as well as yours."

"I respect your wishes, though reluctantly." Nathaniel pivoted to face Benjamin: "We've need of two lambs and a pair of turtledoves. You're finest of both, mind you."

"An excellent choice, Scribe." Benjamin handed Nathaniel two short cords, each leashing a lamb, and then lifted a small cage in which the doves roosted. "The lambs are two shekels apiece; the doves cost a denarius. The best price available in the city."

Though the same animals could be had for half to a third of that price in the countryside, Benjamin spoke truthfully. Still, a denarius represented the daily wage of a common laborer, while two shekels came to nearly a week's earnings. The pricing enabled merchants like Benjamin to earn their living and provided the Temple with added income. Few in the city protested this arrangement, since their own coffers depended upon the monies of pilgrims.

With animals in tow, the families entered the Temple proper. A low wall encircled the Temple building to separate it from the Court of the Gentiles. Above the entrance known as the Beautiful Gate stood a warning sign inscribed in Latin and Greek. Its message: *any Gentile passing beyond this point does so under penalty of death.*

Once inside, Nathaniel led the others through the Court of the Women. This would be as far as the mothers and Deborah could go. Nathaniel disappeared for a moment into the crowd milling at the next gate, emerging with a priest who would take the animals. After pronouncing a blessing upon the three mothers, the priest and the husbands walked through the Nicanor Gate into the Court of the Israelites. The priest alone continued into the Court of the Priests, waiting his turn by the altar along with other priests offering sacrifices that day.

As the three women waited on their husbands, Deborah and Nathaniel returned to the outer plaza. After some innocent words, the discussion took a more serious tone.

"Nathaniel, you shouldn't have purchased the lamb for Naomi."

"Naomi is my only niece, Deborah. I see all of you too rarely. And we both know I can well afford such a gift."

The intimation of wealth irritated Naomi. "It's not a matter of money, or even kinship. It's tradition for the husband to provide the sacrifice for a woman's purification."

"Many things are a tradition among our people, and not all go heeded. For example, a man's marriage of his widowed sister-in-law."

Nathaniel's words aggravated an old wound. "There's no need to visit my decision upon my daughter's family, Nathaniel."

"She is my niece, Deborah." Nathaniel halted, drawing Deborah close by her arm and then speaking in a lowered voice. "She might have been as my own daughter, had you allowed reason to influence your decision. Look at this life that would have been yours."

Deborah bit her tongue. She judged Nathaniel the same as ten years before. If anything, his years in Jerusalem only magnified ambitions and manipulations under a veneer of piety.

"Brother-in-law, we've said all this before. Nothing's to be gained from revisiting the past. I only ask that you not seek to punish me by disrupting Naomi and her family."

"Really, Deborah, I don't see where this idea of punishment enters your mind. A little generosity and hospitality is all I offer to Naomi and Joshua ... and to you."

"You are far better at words than I, Nathaniel. Let's end them now."

"As you wish, Deborah. Silence toward me always has been your way." With that, the pair turned and walked to rejoin the others. Nathaniel acknowledged the occasional bows of deference directed his way from Temple guards and sellers. Deborah couldn't be sure, but she thought a smile crossed his face at each such encounter. A smile, in her mind, of immense satisfaction in who he had become – and, perhaps, in rebuke for who she had rejected. A rejection for which she now silently thanked Adonai Elohim.

* * *

"Nathaniel, Deborah!" Joshua cried out. "Over here!"

It took some jostling through the crowd to reach the others. Nathaniel gave his guests a brief tour of the Temple precincts joined to a narration of his rise to apprentice of the Sopher Kohen Gadol before they continued back to his home.

"This is where Saripheus first spoke to me that morning, beside these colonnades. Can you imagine? A humble son of Bethlehem, met in the rain by so great a scribe?"

"It must have seemed like a dream, uncle. Weren't you afraid why the Sopher Kohen Gadol requested you to meet?"

Joshua cleared his throat. "Wife, is that any way to talk to your uncle?"

"Naomi is right, Joshua. I had no idea why Saripheus and the High Priest himself wanted to see me. I first thought I must have said something ill-advised at the Sanhedrin. But to be asked to apprentice under Saripheus and learn his office? It's still a wonder."

Elias placed a hand on Nathaniel's shoulder. "Rebekah and I congratulate you. You honor Bethlehem. If only I'd spent more time heeding the rabbi's words instead of daydreaming about woodwork, maybe I'd be the one giving the tour today and you'd be worrying about a work bench that sags under the weight of unfinished projects." Glancing at Joseph, Elias added, "Though with my friend working the bench with me, the load is much easier."

"Am I to understand, Joseph," Nathaniel began, eyebrows slightly raised, "that you partner with Elias? I thought you lived in Nazareth."

"We did, but the census brought us to Bethlehem. Elias offered a share in his shop's work, while Joshua and Naomi opened one of the inn's rooms to us."

"Living here for so long, I'd forgotten how hospitable the villages can be to strangers."

"But these are not really strangers. Nathaniel. Would you believe that Joseph's family not only once resided in Bethlehem, but that Matthan son of Elea – "

"JOSHUA!" Elias's voice boomed in anger, startling the entire group.

A suddenly dry throat made Joshua's stammering reply even more belabored. "I, I saw no reason not to confide in Nathaniel. He's family. He'd never say anything."

"This has nothing to do with Nathaniel. This has to do with your word. Given to me!"

Before emotions rose any higher, Joseph stepped between the two men and then turned to face Nathaniel. "My apologies, Sopher. The fault here is mine. At one time, I overstated needless concern over distant family connections. Please, everyone, let's put this aside."

Nathaniel smiled at Joseph. "As far as I am concerned, the incident never occurred. A good noon meal and rest with the children awaits us at home."

Nathaniel's dismissal, linked with Joseph's minimizing, broke the tension. The ensuing conversations on the return to Nathaniel's home unfolded innocently enough. The women marveled at silks and linens available in the bazaar. Joshua rambled on about how much money an inn in Jerusalem might profit over the festival. Joseph and Elias admired the woodwork and carvings displayed in several of the market stalls.

No one noticed how silent their host became. Nathaniel's quiet issued not from disinterest, but deep thought. Had the last of David's line in Bethlehem not been Matthan, son of Eleazar? Had the town storytellers not said that Matthan left to work as a carpenter in his wife's hometown of Nazareth? And why would Elias demand silence from Joshua about Joseph's Nazarene family, if no importance attached to his kin? No need to press the matter for the time being. A few discreet inquiries later, perhaps through the contacts of Julius and Alexas, and Joseph's background would be clear. If Joseph did have David's blood coursing his veins, it might provide a bit of useful information someday.

CHAPTER VI

During their decades in Israel, the Romans had learned the eight days of Hanukkah demanded caution. The old stories of deliverance sometimes emboldened firebrands to lash out at Rome and its Herodian allies. The cohort assigned to Jerusalem remained on alert. This year had not seen any serious incidents. A few patrols had an occasional rock thrown in their direction, but there had been no assaults or knifings as in previous years to escalate tensions.

The last evening of Hanukkah was traditionally the quietest of the nights. Visitors staying with family in Jerusalem enjoyed one final meal together before departing the next day. Pilgrims took to sleeping mats early, as morning's first light signaled time to travel home. As such, the eighth night evolved into a celebration within the Roman garrison. It marked a return to normalcy, an easing of the alert during which the tribune allowed no leaves.

The tribune of the Roman cohort in Jerusalem, Gaius Maximus, invited his centurion Julius to dine with him this night. Gaius, gifted more in the martial than diplomatic arts, trusted Julius for his discernment of the Jewish mind and spirit. The tribune depended upon the centurion's advice in dealing with this baffling culture. That dependency grew all the more pronounced as Gaius neared his time of retirement and life back in Rome. Gaius' anticipations of gardened villas and leisurely days dominated their mealtime conversation. Only later did talk shift to matters more immediate.

"Julius, have we ever known a Hanukkah so peaceful in our time here? Could it be these Jews at last accept the reality of our rule?"

"I wish I could believe that. If Roman rule alone confronted them, I'd be more optimistic. The empire's become more adept at handling subjects. The Greeks vie for our favor and friendship. Their treaties negotiate not for freedom, but the privilege of Roman citizenship."

The tribune laughed. "You don't think these Jews will come around to such thinking!"

"Again, if it were simply our rule, the issue would be far simpler. The problem is, if I may speak bluntly, Herod."

The face of Gaius tightened. Peering into his chalice wine as if looking for something, he answered. "You and I are soldiers, Julius, not politicians. The Senate, not to mention Augustus himself, considers Herod a friend and client. For men like us, mere officers in the legion, Herod provides an unpleasant fact of life." Gaius set his chalice upon the table. He stretched his body, stiffened from too many hours in the Antonia's cold walls, then reclined as was the Roman custom for dining. After a deep sigh, Gaius added: "And he is a fact of life we cannot change."

"I agree. All I meant is, the most likely scenario for the Jews to turn on us would be through some vendetta of Herod's. He'd force us to back him, then let us swing for the crime."

"But what can be done? The emperor's personal regard for Herod ties our hands. The observations we make across this table tonight have to stay here."

Julius sat up and leaned in Gaius' direction. "But isn't there the possibility of informing Augustus of Herod's illness, and the volatility it creates? Augustus doesn't want a crisis requiring more troops pulled from the German frontier. And that's what could happen!"

"Your thoughts race ahead of your judgment, Julius. There's no report we could send to Rome that would escape Herod's notice. He's more spies than we do, and no hesitation to send his assassins and poisoners our way. We can only hope the disease works quickly."

"His illness may be our ally in the long run," Julius responded, "but it makes him more dangerous now. A wounded animal is always apt to lash out. And who will get the blame if Herod chooses a Roman hand to plunge in his knife?"

The tribune sneered. "Who always gets the blame for the folly of kings, but those dutybound to carry out their work? Julius, you and I swore to uphold the wishes of our emperor. Right now, Augustus calls Herod a friend of Rome. As men of honor, we fulfill our obligation to Augustus. But in a few more years, the gods be willing, I'll be back in Rome and never again be troubled with the likes of Herod."

Julius refilled his chalice and Gaius', then stood. "Then this year, a toast to Hanukkah and its peace. May next year bring a toast to our dear but dead Herod, if the gods show favor. Or at least a bit of justice." The two chalices struck together with a dull metallic clank.

* * *

"Judas, this is a night meant for joy, not pain. Can't you and your father set aside this running battle you both seem to relish for one evening?"

Miriam's fingers nervously laced her hair into the braid to be wrapped atop her head as she worried about tonight's dinner with Saripheus. Meals between father and son had become rare. Over the past ten years, Judas viewed his father with growing disdain. He felt Saripheus discredited the office of Sopher by compromising the Torah's demands to Roman and Herodian dictates. For Judas, his father no longer possessed the fire of Moses' law in his heart. And with that loss of fire came a loss of respect and love.

"You know my father! He enjoys belittling my devotion to Torah, if only to excuse his own neglect of it. The nights of Hanukkah are to honor Torah, and how the Maccabees risked all to purify our Temple from foreign pollution."

Miriam did not look forward to the evening. Too

many table conversations had devolved into shouted accusations. Securing her braid with hairpins made of bone, Miriam offered another plea for the sake of peace at the table. "I don't ask you to sacrifice your convictions, Judas. Only that you and your father set aside your differences for one night. For one meal."

"Miriam, I won't introduce any animosity into my father's house. But if he suggests – "

"Judas, enough." The last pin now in place, Miriam turned on the stool and stood. "I know what follows if your father upsets you. But please, try to keep the table a place of shalom."

Miriam's plea for concord held uneasily through the meal. Judas and Saripheus spoke as stiffly as they sat, but each man took care not to set off the other. When Saripheus excused himself and left for a moment, Miriam squeezed Judas' hand and whispered a soft thank you. But after the servants cleared the platters and Saripheus returned, the truce began to unravel.

"Miriam, there are matters about which I need to speak privately with my son."

"As you wish, father-in-law."

"There's a fire in my reading room to sit by. It shouldn't be too long before we join you."

With a parting kiss on her husband's brow and a brief bow in the direction of Saripheus, Miriam left the room. Saripheus moved directly opposite his son.

"Thank you for breaking bread with me. I know it wasn't an easy decision, given the outcome of our recent meals."

"Hanukkah is a night for our people to celebrate. Why shouldn't we be able to do so?"

Saripheus sensed sarcasm, but chose to ignore it. "I do have reason for us to speak."

With Miriam gone, Judas felt free to play the cynic. "And what would that be, father? Some plan hatched by the

Sanhedrin to help us appreciate our Herodian lords? Or have my lectures on Torah breached some finer point of Temple etiquette?"

"Judas, this doesn't come any easier for me than I suspect for you. Please, hear me out."

Judas said nothing, only nodding his head ever so slightly. Saripheus resumed.

"You're partially right, about the lectures. No one questions your beliefs or sincerity. You may not be aware of it, or choose to take any delight in it, but I take pride in the way you expound on the Law and the Prophets. That so many attend your words and those of your colleague Matthias shows a genuine hunger for the Torah in the land."

His father's words caught Judas off-guard. "I seek only to do what a scribe is meant to do, father. Open the way of God taught us by Moses."

"And you do that well, better than any of the other teachers at the Temple."

"I appreciate your words. But what urgency is there to congratulation?"

"As I said, the difficulty does not come in your theology. You're a gifted teacher. Many listen closely to your words. Most to learn – but a few, to gain evidence."

"Gain evidence?" Judas' voice faltered momentarily, not so much from fear as surprise. "Why these riddles? Come now, father, speak bluntly to me. You always have!"

"Very well. Your words concerning Herod have not gone unnoticed. The crowds may delight in this, but his spies do not sit at your feet for entertainment."

"Whatever critique I make of Herod's plague on us derives solely from keeping Torah. The demands of the Law must be taught, especially when those who rule make a mockery of it."

"Judas, the Herodians don't make neat distinctions between political critics and religious critics. They find both subversive, enemies of the king."

The arms of Judas rose into the air, as if to support some unseen weight. They then dropped partway, so that his hands hit the top of his head before returning to the table. "What do you want me to do? Teach that the Law of Moses concerns only ordinary people, not those on thrones or their sycophants? Or do you desire that I water down the Torah and become one of Herod's kept scribes. That is, after all, an option for which you have ample expertise!"

Saripheus's face flushed. "That will be enough, Judas! I respect the Torah as much as you. I care for this people as much as you! You have a knack for turning phrases, but you deal with words alone. As Sopher, I must move beyond pious phrases to protect our freedom to follow the Torah. Neither Rome nor Herod will have the terms of their rule dictated to them. Scribes with your views couldn't teach at the Temple without give and take on both sides."

"Forgive me for not praising this noble compromise! It never dawned on me to protect the Torah by ignoring Herod's daily trespass of it. What a courageous idea!"

A deep groan issued from the chest of Saripheus. The two stared at one another for a minute that weighed like an hour. Finally, Saripheus arose and walked to a window. "Judas, how many years has it been since we've spoken as father and son? If she were alive, your mother's heart would break to hear us as we speak now." The hollowness of Saripheus' voice betrayed a weariness of soul, as if each word drained life from him. "Believe what you will of my work. But if there is any trust of me left in your heart, heed this: there are those who attend to your words out of a desire to build a case against you." Saripheus turned back to face his son. "Your life is in genuine jeopardy. I've no wish to lose my only son. And if that means nothing to you, I've no wish for Miriam to be widowed. That is how serious your message has become."

Judas walked up to Saripheus, their faces only inches apart. The son's voice swelled with emotion, controlled by a slow and deliberate pronouncement of his words: "Torah is to be kept, father. Herod calls himself a Jew, so he must observe the Law. It is as simple as that. Don't ask me to turn my back on God." Judas turned to leave, then paused. Without looking back, he spoke. "I may be your son, but by the Almighty I will not become as you."

Judas strode into the reading room to get Miriam. They left the house without further word. In the light of the Menorah candles, Saripheus watched his hands tremble uncontrollably. The one who advised High Priests and princes and tribunes now stood shaking in an empty room, powerless to sway his own son. His stomach convulsed in a wave of nausea. The meal he'd hoped might dissuade Judas from his precarious course spewed up through his throat, filling his mouth with its sourness before splattering his robe and the cold stone of the floor. Saripheus slumped down and knelt in his retchings, too weak to lift himself. David's words from the Samuel scroll flashed through his mind: "My son, my son, would I had died instead of you."

But they were just words, and work needed to be done. Unsteadily, Saripheus rose to wash himself, don a fresh robe, and put this night – and his son – behind him.

CHAPTER VII

"Goodbye uncle." Naomi pressed her face against the side of Nathaniel's. His closely trimmed beard felt scratchy against her cheek. "Thank you for lodging us during the Festival."

"My pleasure, child. And don't let so much time pass before you visit again. Bethlehem isn't that far."

"Nor is Jerusalem from us," interjected Deborah. "I'm sure Joshua could spare a room should you wish to visit."

"If only I had the time to journey your way. Apprenticing to the Sopher ties me to the Temple, as you can imagine. But a place always awaits you here. All of you."

The other families thanked Nathaniel for his hospitality before taking to the road. Unlike the pleasant day on which they came to Jerusalem, this day's weather proved blustery and rainy. Joshua and Deborah walked ahead, leading the oxen, while the mothers huddled with the children in the wagon to keep as warm and dry as possible. Elias and Joseph followed behind, leading the donkey that once carried Mary to Bethlehem.

The party plodded along the Street of David and out the Corner Gate, until it intersected the north-south road known as the King's High Way. While the others turned south to Bethlehem, the two carpenters took the donkey and headed for Nazareth, eighty-five miles distant. Once there, they would secure a cart to load the tools and household goods of Joseph and Mary. With both sharing the work, they might be back in Bethlehem in under two weeks.

Less than two miles from Bethlehem, a contingent of

legionnaires marched sullenly in the rain past Joshua and the others. Joshua recognized them as the detail assigned to the census in Bethlehem. Several evenings, they had descended on his inn for food and wine. Then, Joshua was more than happy to speak favorably of the emperor and the Pax Romana. Now, safely out of earshot, his spine stiffened in patriotic fervor.

"There, Deborah, go the reasons for our nation's poverty. They take our taxes, then force us to house and feed them. I think the Sicarii are right: draw blades across Roman throats."

"The Sicarii are thieves. They only lash out at Rome's interference with their robbery."

Joshua pulled at his mantle to tighten the hood over his head, as the rain pounded harder. "You defend the Romans? They house their legion in that God-forsaken fortress next to the Temple. They allow a criminal like Herod to ignore Torah."

"The Romans don't need an old woman to defend them. Their swords speak for them."

"Exactly. And that's why the language of the Sicarii is the only tongue they understand. Besides, some of the Sicarii believe we live in Messiah's time. They say that all He awaits is a little boldness on our part before descending in power."

"Joshua, the Almighty does not wait on us to tell him when Messiah's time has come. The Lord, blessed be his name, knows the time."

"Maybe so. But I say the Lord sides with those willing to stand for righteousness. If I didn't have the responsibilities of the inn and Naomi and these three children, I just might have to take a dagger in hand myself and use it against these Gentiles."

A burst of laughter from Deborah took Joshua aback. "Forgive me, but the life of an innkeeper hasn't prepared you for murder, unless you intend to poison them with your cooking."

"Don't mock me, woman. The days are coming when the Romans, and Herod, will pay. Hanukkah remembered the Maccabees' rebellion against the Syrians. Maybe our children's children will celebrate our generation's loosing of Israel from Rome's grip."

Deborah's hand seized the elbow of Joshua. "Such talk doesn't suit you. You have a wife and children to consider instead of this foolishness."

"Foolishness? More and more, these thoughts are whispered in Bethlehem, often across the table in my inn. I sense some look to me for leadership in this." Joshua tugged his arm free. "Someday, you'll see how you've misjudged me!"

Deborah knew any further talk useless with Joshua. Her son-in-law's verbal ambitions never failed to far outstrip his achievements. An innkeeper he was and an innkeeper he would stay. The only time he'd ever wield a knife in the presence of a Roman soldier would be to slice his bread. She figured at this very moment Joshua would be imagining himself leading a band of ruthless Sicarii – in Deborah's imagination, he did so with the inn's butter knife in his hand!

* * *

An hour after the families left, Nathaniel's servant brought news of a visitor. "Sir, a messenger sent by Saripheus." Nathaniel left his study, where a fire burned to break the damp chill of this morning. He met the courier under the shelter of the porch.

"My lord Saripheus sends his greetings, Nathaniel. He needs to speak with you in the Sopher's chambers. I'm to accompany you there."

Nathaniel hurriedly donned his winter cloak and set out. An unscheduled meeting on the day after Hanukkah's end signaled something unusual. Perhaps Herod's health worsened. Curiosity as much as the weather sped their pace to the Temple. When they arrived, Saripheus waved Nathaniel into his room and dismissed the messenger.

"My apologies, Nathaniel, for such short notice."

"I was merely reviewing some matters for the Sanhedrin's next meeting. They can wait."

"Good. By the way, how did the week go with your houseguests?"

"Tolerable. Infants squealing at all hours provided ample reason to wish them a speedy journey home."

"My sympathies, though when the squeal is of one's own child, it's not nearly as shrill." Saripheus pushed his chair away from the writing table, stood, and faced away from Nathaniel. "That's partly why I called you here today."

Nathaniel's head tilted slightly. "I don't follow your meaning."

Saripheus turned, his eyes reddened. He motioned Nathaniel to sit.

"I had dinner last night with my son. Afterwards, I spoke to him about the danger he risks in criticizing the Herodians. All to no avail. Judas remains adamant."

Nathaniel didn't know what to say. From their previous audience with Julius and Alexas, Nathaniel understood the risk involved. "I am truly sorry, my lord. Is there anything I can do to help? Perhaps some way I might intercede with your son."

"Thank you, Nathaniel, but last night convinced me it's too late for Judas. He will not LISTEN!" Saripheus slammed his first on the table with his final word. An awkward silence followed, broken only when the Sopher resumed. "That's why I needed to talk with you today. We must hasten your apprenticeship. My son's actions will compromise me, sooner than later."

"But Saripheus, you're loyal to the High Priest. Even more importantly you've rendered faithful service to Herod and the Romans. They'll see that."

Saripheus leaned forward in his chair. "Scribe, don't

disappoint me with naiveté. Logic might judge me innocent, but we're talking here about the whims of a dying king. That's why Julius spoke so forcefully about having me confront Judas. If Judas falls, I follow."

"Then why not denounce him yourself to Herod? Surely that would prove your loyalty."

Saripheus stroked his beard, studying the face that had just suggested betraying his own son. His words came out in a slow measured cant, the arteries of his neck throbbing. "I once told you I considered your lack of family an asset. You'll not be compromised as I have been. But never again suggest I betray my son. You've no idea what you ask!"

Nathaniel considered asking who's being naive now, but decided against it. Besides, if Saripheus was right, it insured Nathaniel's own ascent. The apprentice felt it best to placate his mentor. "You're an honorable man, Sopher. I ask your forgiveness if I offended you."

"You have my forgiveness, Nathaniel." The two men stood and shook hands. Nathaniel looked upon the Sopher Kohen Gadol with an air of superiority. The one held in such regard by Julius and Alexas had shown a fatal weakness in his unwillingness to deny Judas. Nathaniel swore to never let any other, including family, render him impotent.

* * *

Julius led two soldiers past the Hippodrome to the Temple's southern entrance. There they'd wait for Judas, who was teaching inside the Temple. Julius didn't plan an arrest, but a private conversation with the Sopher's son. After meeting with Nathaniel, Saripheus had informed Julius of his failure to dissuade his son the previous night. When the Sopher left, Julius decided on an intervention of his own. If a father's pleas left him unfazed, perhaps interrogation in one of the Antonia's cells would convince Judas of his teachings' hazards. Julius had fathered no sons himself, but he felt the pain in the voice of Saripheus. How could a son be so callous? How could one who calls himself a teacher of Torah break its command to honor one's father? Saripheus deserved better. Julius planned to impress that on the mind, and body, of Judas.

Late afternoon brought no warmth to the day, and its rain and wind made the Romans' task easier. On comfortable days, a cluster of students might have followed Judas out, asking questions and continuing the dialogue. Today, however, everyone's hurry to get home would make any notice of the approach of two legionnaires and a centurion less likely.

Julius recognized Judas as he descended the steps. No crowd joined him, but another person did walk with him. As they neared, Julius recognized the face to be that of Matthias, another scribe of the Pharisees. Like Judas, Matthias' teaching flirted with sedition. Unlike Judas, Matthias didn't have the benefit of a father in high places. Julius quickly calculated Matthias's presence as an opportune coincidence. "Lucius, Demetrius: We'll take both of the men walking toward us. Wait for me to step in front of them, then come from behind."

As the pair walked up, Julius stepped into their path. "Judas, son of Saripheus, you will accompany me." As he spoke, Lucius and Demetrius emerged to flank the two scribes.

"Why? Am I being charged with something?"

"No charge, scribe. But you will come with me. And no questions."

"He will not go alone." Matthias's voice boomed strong and clear. "And certainly a man can ask questions."

At that remark, Lucius drove a fist into Matthias's side, dropping him to his knees. "No questions means no questions," Lucius snarled, pulling Matthias to his feet. "Move!"

Julius led the group around the southern and then up the Temple's western edge. Few people stood outside, and none were watching the scene, raising the scribes' anxiety.

Once inside the Antonia, the soldiers muscled the

scribes into the basement. Lucius and Demetrius pushed Matthias into one cell, while Julius summoned a third guard, Antioch, to stand outside an adjoining cell where the centurion would interrogate Judas. The Sopher's son saw Julius murmur instructions to Lucius, then the centurion entered the cell and shut the door.

"So, you are the renowned Judas, son of Saripheus." Julius spoke Hebrew, causing the scribe's eyebrows to raise. "Tell me, Jew, since this fortress borders the Temple, do you feel the protection of your sanctuary here?"

"It is not the Temple that protects me, but the God who dwells within it."

"Good answer," Julius replied as he circled the chair on which Judas sat. "They say you always have answers for those who wait on your words. So another question. Why do you suppose we drag such a wise fellow as yourself to such an unpleasant place?"

"I wouldn't know. I tried to ask, but you didn't say. Remember?"

"That is simply how we do things here, scribe. I ask the questions. You give the answers. Again: why do we bother ourselves with such a trove of wisdom like yourself?"

"Perhaps Jewish wisdom may help Rome's ignorance."

Julius slammed the back of his right hand into Judas' face with such force it knocked him off the chair. "Not a good answer, scribe. In the Antonia, unlike the Temple, we don't play word games. Let's try this again. Why are you here today!"

Judas used the chair to pull himself off the floor. "I don't know your mind. Perhaps you took offense at something I said."

"I'm disappointed in you, Judas. For a scribe of such wisdom, you show great slowness in getting to the simplest of points. So let me help you." Julius paused, and in the silence Judas could hear the sounds of Matthias being beaten.

Julius allowed the noise of the beating to go on before

continuing. "Apparently, your friend is even slower than you are. I hope for your sake that your answers come swifter than his."

Judas realized he could do nothing for Matthias, beyond hastening the pace of his own interrogation.

"What do you want to know of me?"

"You still miss the point. I know all that I care to know of you. My concern is that you lack self-understanding. You don't know what you are."

"And just what would that be, centurion?"

"A scribe of the Torah, who doesn't know the Torah. Such a pity."

Judas' hands gripped the chair. His effort at self-control, weakened when he heard the beating of Matthias, now unraveled as this Roman mocked the Torah. "Don't speak to me of Torah, Gentile. You're the one who seizes innocent citizens to beat them. You're the one – "

A punch from Julius sent Judas tumbling back over the chair onto the floor. "And you, scribe, are the one who commits suicide. Isn't that prohibited by your Torah? Are you too stupid to see that all you accomplish by opposing Herod is your own death?"

Judas looked up from the floor at Julius with bewilderment. "Why is the death of one Jew defending his faith of any consequence to Rome?"

Julius had wondered earlier whether to speak openly on this issue, but he felt the severity of the situation required it. "Because your suicide, insignificant as it would be, would become an act of patricide. Another breach of your commandments."

Struggling to stand, Judas realized this had to do with his father. "My father put you up to this? First a traitor to his people, and now to his son!"

At those words, Julius seized Judas by the robe and drove him backwards into the wall. "You miserable son of a bitch! Saripheus spends his life for your people, and now he tries to save you. You really don't understand what's happening, do you?" The centurion rammed his knee into Judas's groin, then tossed the scribe onto the stone floor. "You'll end up dead, your wife widowed, your father disgraced – but that doesn't bother you, the great Judas!"

Judas crawled onto his hands and knees, barely managing to lift his head enough to see the face of Julius. The centurion continued. "You have your warning, Jew! This doesn't have to do with ideas about some god high in the heavens. This is about who's in charge here." Picking the scribe up by the armpits, Julius dragged him to the cell door and knocked. "Don't preach Torah to me, Jew! You're the one who'd let your father die. Is that how you keep the Law?"

When Antioch opened the door, Julius hurled Judas against the wall opposite it. The scribe crumpled to the floor alongside a battered Matthias. Julius squatted down, thrusting his face into Judas's. "Your father knows nothing of my talk with you today. And if I ever hear he finds out, I swear I will personally cut out your tongue and give it to your wife. Understood?"

A labored nod of Judas' head satisfied Julius. After ordering Lucius and Demetrius to release the pair once it was dark, Julius walked to his own chambers. Five years of dealing with religious fanatics in this land gave him no great optimism for deterring Judas. Bludgeoning bodies was far easier work than changing minds. At times, pain could induce silence. But Julius couldn't be sure in this case. If Judas possessed his father's fortitude, it would only be a matter of time until more serious measures might be required. The centurion allowed himself a moment of pity for Saripheus should this afternoon's beating go unheeded. Then, washing his hands and feet of the blood splattered upon him during the beating, Julius calmly resolved to keep a closer eye on Nathaniel. Thanks to Judas, his time as Sopher hastened.

CHAPTER VIII

As Elias and Joseph planed a bench for the synagogue in their work shed, their attention shifted to the approach of two small boys. Saul carried a wooden mallet in one hand, and with the other led his younger brother Levi into the shop. The boys went to the corner where their father and Joseph tossed shavings and discard pieces. Here, the youngsters often erected lofty towers, wrestled in olive and cedar chips, and sometimes just watched their father and his friend work. Joseph smiled at the oversized lunch bag slung over Levi's shoulder, as if there were miles rather than steps between him and his mother's table.

Joseph walked over to the boys and lifted the flap on the bag. "Elias, your sons have brought us a feast today! Raisins, a bit of cheese, bread – but Saul, have you no dried meat of the mountain lion you killed last week?"

Levi's eyes widened at the mention of such an animal. Had his brother slain such a beast?

"That was only a pretend story. The day Levi and I played shepherd and sheep."

"Oh, no! I shall have to go to the marketplace today. I told everyone there about how you slew a lion last week with a stone from your sling."

"No you didn't. You're just teasing!" Saul leapt upon Joseph's leg, as if to wrestle him to the ground. Levi, imitating his brother, waddled over and wrapped Joseph's other leg in his sixteen-month old arms.

"Elias! Please, help! Your sons are about to bring me down, as Saul brought down the mighty lion last week."

Elias noted that, for a man who waited so late in life to marry, Joseph had a gift with children. Saul and Levi played with him in the shop whenever time permitted. Evenings would often find Joseph's lap filled by Yeshua and the twins of Naomi and Joshua, as the carpenter spun tales. Yeshua loved to snuggle under his father's chin, using his beard for a pillow.

"Saul, Levi: Joseph and I have work to do. After lunch, there may be time for a story."

The boys released their holds and returned to the corner. A pile of odd-shaped blocks became the bricks of a fortress wall stretching from table leg to awning post.

"Your boys play well together. I hope the time will come, God willing, when Yeshua has a brother or sister to enjoy life with."

Elias nodded. "The children bless not only Rebekah and me, but one another."

"Indeed. But, you're also right about the work." Joseph slapped his partner on the back. "This bench will not smooth itself." The two men resumed their careful stroking with planes, transforming rough boards into suitable seats for Bethlehem's worshippers.

* * *

"Can I walk the donkey today, mother?" Simeon's voice echoed off the sides of the small cave. Mary and Naomi had taken their children to the stable this morning, where feeding and watering the stock was a daily chore.

"Yes, go ahead. But don't be gone long." Naomi knew Simeon didn't like to spend all his time with the younger children. Besides, he'd just finished cleaning the stalls, and a bit of fresh air would be a welcome change. Mary and Naomi, having finished with their work, took two milking stools from the stable and sat outside. They savored the fresh scents of wet clover pushed down the hillsides by the breeze. Sounds of the toddlers playing inside rose and fell. The women relished such moments.

"I think our little ones would spend all of their days in that stable, if they could."

Mary nodded her head, her eyes studying the pattern of broken clouds left from last night's rain. "Yeshua always wants his father to tell stories of the animals."

"And I see that your son still looks with wonder at the trough you laid him in."

"Sometimes, when Yeshua and I come here alone, he places one of his wooden animals in the manger and covers it with hay."

"I still marvel at you and Joseph, delivering your child in there. Did you know Rachel now encourages anxious mothers-to-be by telling them about you? `You remember Mary,' she says. `A healthy baby boy born in a stable. You'll do just fine with a birthing in your home.'"

"Well, but for the kindness of you and Joshua, my birthing stool might have been a rock out on the hillside. And Yeshua's first cradle a hollow in the ground. Who knows what might have happened? But as it was, the Almighty watched over us."

"When Rachel first told me I carried twins, all I could think of was my stillborn son, and his delivery that nearly killed me." Naomi seldom spoke of this tragedy, and its words still caught in her throat. Mary's hand clasped that of her friend. Several tears loosed from Naomi's eyes fell lightly upon the interlocked fingers. "I sit here now, listening to Hannah and David laugh and play. It's as if the earlier pain makes today's joy greater."

"Perhaps that is how the Almighty balances our lives. Without pain, the joy goes unappreciated. Without joy, who could live?"

Naomi studied Mary's youthful face. "You've unusual wisdom for one who's not yet seen her eighteenth winter. A gift for the word, or touch, needed at the moment."

Mary lowered her eyes. "I am the one who daily learns of life. From you and Rebekah. And Joseph."

"We may have the advantage of added years, but you perceive matters that sometimes escape the rest of us. Yeshua is blessed to be raised by one with your spirit."

Just then, the dull thud of a pitchfork toppling, followed by the wail of a child, signaled an end to the women's leisure.

* * *

"All rise! Bow before the King of Judea, friend and ally of Rome and Emperor Augustus, architect and builder of the Temple: Herod, our beloved Ruler!" The palace steward announced the king's entrance with great solemnity, even though the audience consisted only of his three closest advisors. With larger gatherings, and those of lesser rank, the presentation would be even more florid in its attributions of praise. Increasingly, the flourishes of Herod's introductions stood in stark contrast to the sight – and smell – of the ailing monarch.

His doctors feared to reveal the extent of his tumors and syphilis, lest they be punished. They settled for encouraging Herod's travel when possible to the sulphur baths of Callirrhoe or the hot springs at his palace in Jericho. Soaking brought brief comforts, but no cure.

Slaves carried Herod into the courtyard on a pallet. The disease slowly rotting the lower half of his abdomen prevented Herod from walking. Flowers and perfumed robes decked the royal pallet, an effort to disguise both the appearance and stench of putrefying flesh. Alexas and Gaius and Julius bowed in Herod's direction. All received their summons to this audience an hour before. Herod's pallet was set next to a cart that held the statue of an immense golden eagle. Herod dismissed the slaves, then motioned the three to come near.

"I have a matter of great urgency to discuss with you. Before that, what words do you bring to the king?" This last sentence reflected a peculiar custom Herod developed since the onset of his illness. It was not an invitation to communication, but homage. Alexas approached, then dropped to his knees and bowed his head to Herod.

"Majesty, I am unworthy to come before you. Your courage in conquering this affliction moves me and your sister to tears. Your example inspires us and all Jerusalem." As Alexas continued with his display, Julius briefly glanced at Gaius, rolling his eyes at this effusion of adoration. Alexas did this so well, it became an amusement of sorts. When he finished, the time came for Julius and Gaius. The tribune addressed the king.

"Excellency, I offer not only my personal wishes but those of Emperor Augustus. He daily offers sacrifices for your recovery, as do we in the Antonia."

"And may the god of your people be merciful to the king who holds David's scepter." The perfectly accented Hebrew of Julius caused the corners of Herod's lips to edge upwards. Herod considered himself a keeper of Israel's covenant. Had he not rebuilt the Temple? Did the Psalms not sing of Israel's king as God's chosen?

"Thank you, centurion, for a blessing in my tongue. Sometimes I find more praise among Gentiles than among my own. But enough pleasantries. THIS is why I called for you today." Herod pulled himself up, pointing to the eagle. "I directed my craftsmen to fashion this magnificent creation. It will soon be displayed in the city."

"A splendid piece of work," Alexas offered. "It will remind the people of Jerusalem and its visitors of your desire to bring beauty to the eyes of all."

"Quite true. Its display must be in a fitting place, one suited to contemplation. I've decided to erect it over the portal that between the Temple porch and the Sanctuary."

Even Alexas was speechless. Any image in the Temple area would raise concerns over the Torah's commands against idolatry. But since eagles adorned Roman shrines, placing this particular symbol above the building which housed the Holy of Holies defied belief.

"Do any of you see why I should not do this? Especially you, centurion Julius, who speaks the language of my people?"

Julius rarely addressed Herod in such an audience, as Gaius preferred to speak on behalf of the Roman cohort in Jerusalem. This, however, came as a direct question – and Gaius made no effort to respond for him. Julius had to answer as delicately as he could.

"Excellency, were your only concern for those of rational minds, the issue would be settled. Works of art deserve exhibit. Fanatics abound, however, who would not appreciate such a piece. Their closed minds would be blind to its elegance, twisting such an exquisite reflection of nature into an imagined rival of your god. And with such a perverse imagining of this work's noble purpose, they might bring false accusations against you, its glorious creator."

"Such as Judas, the son of Saripheus."

Herod's linking of those names left a hollow feeling in the stomach of Julius. His interrogation of the scribe well over a year ago initially produced greater discretion on the part of Judas. Over the past two months, however, his attacks on the Herodians grew.

"Yes, Excellency, Judas is a radical, as is his colleague Matthias. They could seize upon the placement of this eagle over the Sanctuary portal to incite unrest."

"And that, centurion, explains why I have summoned your tribune here. If trouble results, the cohort in the Antonia must be prepared to respond. Even if it means taking your troops inside the wall within the Temple's outer plaza."

This last word stunned Gauis and Julius. All along that wall, separating the court of the Gentiles from the Temple's inner confines, hung signs that all warned: "*No foreigner is allowed within the balustrade surrounding the sanctuary and the court encompassed. Whoever is caught will be personally responsible for his ensuing death.*" The signs were written in Greek, Latin, and Hebrew, to insure no one misunderstood.

For Herod to waive that prohibition, and to do so for armed Roman troops no less – to Julius, it was madness that would have no good end.

"The eagle will be set up in time for the Festival of Purim next week. My workers will hoist it in place the night before so there is no opportunity for a crowd to interfere."

"A wise precaution," was all Gaius could manage.

"Gaius, I want your spies to listen for any grumblings. Judas and Matthias have reached the limits of my tolerance. As your centurion accurately notes, they are fanatics. Their words have become too dangerous to tolerate any further."

"They will be monitored, Excellency."

"One more matter. You may have noted the absence of Saripheus among us today. I want nothing said to him of this. His son encourages sedition, so the father is no longer to be trusted." Herod lifted a hand as if in blessing. "As of today, I decree that the apprentice Nathaniel assumes the office of Sopher. Should any action be required against Judas, I want Saripheus taken into custody. He carries too much knowledge to remain free. Alexas, see that Nathaniel is informed. You all have your orders. See that my will is carried out."

Herod rang a small bell hidden in the bedding of his pallet. Four servants hurried in to bear him away. The two Romans and Alexas bowed as Herod left the room, then stared at one another in utter bewilderment.

"Of all the places to put that damned eagle," Julius began. "He wants a riot. I talked to him of scribal fanatics, while letting the real fanatic go unchallenged in his stupidity."

"You had no choice," Gaius replied. "To speak the truth would have cut your own throat. And mine as well. Anything even bordering on questioning him, and we'd need food-tasters the rest of our lives."

"Listen to Gaius, Julius. Herod's mind was made up. Consider yourself fortunate not to be Saripheus. A career stamped by loyalty, to be rewarded with arrest for his son's folly. What a pitiable excuse for a world we live in."

"Pitiable or not, it's the world Herod controls at the moment, Alexas. Julius and I must be on our way. We have spies to loose and plans to be develop. . . all for Herod's art show."

Walking with Gaius back to the Antonia, Julius thought of Saripheus. At this juncture, he couldn't even speak to his friend, lest Herod's informants report it as an act of treason. The centurion's mind returned to the interrogation of Judas. Unconsciously, he mouthed his final thought out loud: "I should have killed him."

"What did you say?" replied Gaius.

"Nothing. Nothing to be done about now."

The two men strode on in silence. Both calculated Herod's soaring eagle might be destined for a short flight – and bloody fall.

CHAPTER IX

Preparations for the afternoon Purim service brought Judas and Matthias to the Temple shortly after daybreak. Entering the Court of the Gentiles, Matthias looked up and was astounded: "Judas! Something's been hung above the portal." The pair sprinted across the plaza. Initially, the sun's gleam off the gold shape prevented its identification. Only when they stopped at the base of the steps leading to the Temple porch did the outline of an eagle become clear.

"An eagle, Matthias. A Roman eagle in the Temple!" Though nearly out of breath, Judas raced up the steps to gain a closer view. The statue was affixed to the lintel above the portal, twenty feet off the ground. The eagle's sight would be unavoidable to worshippers.

The two men gazed at the Temple's newest adornment. At this early hour, they were alone. Judas shook his head. "Herod wasn't content to desecrate the city. Now he blasphemes the very Temple. The Romans worship their standards, and eagles top those standards."

Matthias stared at the idol high above. "Something must be done. We let ourselves be silenced by that beating in the Antonia. But look at this!" Picking up a small rock from the pavement, Matthias flung it toward the eagle. It caromed off the wall, short of its target. "Herod continued his crimes in our silence, and the Temple goes profaned. It cannot stand!"

Judas surveyed the eagle. "It will not stand. No matter the cost."

Matthias knew his friend did not exaggerate. Herod

staked out a public challenge with this eagle. To speak in opposition would be an assault on the king's authority. To act in defiance insured a charge of treason, if one survived to trial. "I'm prepared, Judas. But what will we do?"

Judas felt a sudden urge to rush home and spend what few remaining hours he might have with Miriam. But he and Matthias needed time to prepare: for the Purim observance, and for a response to this abomination. Time for loved ones had run out. "Let us make ready for Purim."

* * *

Worshipers in Bethlehem started to arrive at the synagogue. As the Purim ritual involved children, the services took place in the early afternoon. Older children collected stones that would be used during the reading from the scroll of Esther. Slightly rounded rocks, the size of a hand, were preferred. That lessened the possibility of smashed fingers when the rocks cracked together each time the rabbi read the name of the villain, Haman.

Simeon and Saul had gone together to find their Purim stones. This was the first year Saul had the privilege of bringing stones. Younger children and most adults simply stamped their feet. To bring his own stones was a source of pride for five-year-old Saul.

"Elias, can you see if Saul is on his way back yet?" Rebekah knelt near Levi's mat to pick him up. "We need to be leaving for the inn."

Elias looked out the doorway. "Yes, the boys are playing in the alley."

"Come hold Levi for me. You'll need to carry him while I ready the cheeses." The three families would celebrate the Purim banquet together after worship. Rebekah had earlier taken an assortment of fruits to the inn, while Joseph and Mary prepared a lamb stew. Breads and wines would be stocked by Naomi and Joshua. The Purim wine celebrated a tyrant's fall.

Elias and Rebekah met the two boys in the alley, and

from there they went to the inn. Deborah offered to stay at the inn while the others went to synagogue. It seemed unlikely any traveler would need lodging on Purim, as this was a day to be with families and friends. But if any came, Deborah could take care of them until Joshua returned. As everyone prepared to leave, Deborah hugged Simeon. "Since I won't be at synagogue today, I want you to cheer extra loud at the sound of Mordecai's name."

"I will, grandma. And when the rabbi says `Haman,' I'll strike these rocks together just the way you taught me, so they spark."

"Well, Deborah," Elias solemnly pronounced, "Now I know who to blame if his sparks set afire the bench Joseph and I made for the rabbi."

"Blame Haman," Joseph interjected. "Sparks wouldn't fly if it weren't for his deeds."

"Thank you for defending this old woman," Deborah gave Joseph a quick hug. Then, turning to Simeon again, "Don't you worry about making sparks."

Joshua picked up David. "Time to go, or we'll miss the reading of the scroll!"

* * *

Judas and Matthias stood in a storage room located at the north end of the porch called the Ulam. Outside, from the top of the Ulam steps and facing the Court of Israel, the High Priest Mattaiah read the scroll of Esther. A large crowd, many of them students of Matthias and Judas, listened intently to the familiar story. The two scribes spoke in hushed tones.

"Have all the preparations been made?"

Matthias nodded. "Jacob and Abraham guard several lengths of rope and a dozen axes on the porch roof. The others stand ready."

"You know, Matthias, this is our last opportunity to change our course. Once the High Priest finishes the scroll and I speak, our end is assured."

"If our deaths are needed to cleanse the temple, so be it."

"We won't have much time once the Romans see the unrest."

"Don't worry. Before you begin to speak, I'll make my way to the stairway. Once on the roof, I can direct the men there when it comes time to act."

"Good." Judas peered through the barely opened door toward the crowd in the Court of Israel, now jeering and stomping at the sound of Haman's name. Glancing back at Matthias, he put a hand to his shoulder. "I may not see you again in this life. You are a true son of Israel."

"As are you, Judas. And the Almighty will raise the just. To the holiness of God!"

As the two embraced, the door suddenly swung wide open. Startled, the two scribes turned as a familiar figure stepped into the room: Nathaniel.

* * *

"So, having been told who Mordecai's people were, Haman plotted to destroy all the Jews, the people of Mordecai, throughout the whole kingdom of Ahasuerus."

As the rabbi spoke, the crowded synagogue of Bethlehem erupted in a cacophony of hisses and whistles, foot stomping and rocks striking together. Though Rabbi Hananiah had voiced these particular words for thirty-five festivals of Purim in Bethlehem, they always rolled off his tongue like the fresh but sickening revelation of a fatal disease.

In his early years, Hananiah read this sentence with a dramatic flair. In Purims of late, he became convinced the words themselves possessed all the requisite power. This year, the rabbi intoned them almost matter-of-factly, to test the congregants' ability to discern evil in the midst of the ordinary. Their loud response to his understated reading pleased him.

* * *

"Nathaniel!" Matthias hoped his voice cloaked a rush

of anxiety inside him.

"Judas, you look pale. Will you be able to speak when Mattaiah finishes with the scroll?"

"Yes, yes. I did feel a bit lightheaded, which is why we came back here."

"I see. And Matthias was holding you up as I entered?"

Judas looked at Matthias, suspicious of Nathaniel's queries. But he could allow nothing to stop their plans. "If you must know, Nathaniel, my father invited Miriam and me to his Purim banquet. When I refused, my wife and I had bitter words. Matthias simply consoled my anger."

Nathaniel knew Judas and Saripheus to be estranged. As plausible as the story sounded, however, Nathaniel sensed something more – something neither scribe appeared ready to share.

"Forgive me for prying. My only concern is your Purim address. Mattaiah nears the end of the scroll, and I thought it best to seek you out."

Matthias put a hand on Judas' shoulder. "Don't worry about what happened earlier. Such things have a way of working themselves out. If you'll excuse me, I'll try to find Miriam to give her your message." After bowing in Nathaniel's direction, Matthias left.

"A large gathering today, Judas. Matthias will be fortunate to find your wife."

"I have faith in Matthias. He'll find his way."

"Which is what we should do, if you wish to offer the sermon for Purim."

"That I do, Nathaniel, that I do."

* * *

The worshipers and Rabbi Hananiah greeted one another at the conclusion of the Purim service. "Another fine Purim reading, Rabbi," Joshua offered as he and his family exited. "If only those who currently whittle away at us Jews understood this story, there might be more fear of the Almighty in Jerusalem's palaces and barracks."

Joshua's words took the rabbi and others aback. It was one thing to whisper such opinions in secret. It was quite another to broadcast them at the synagogue door.

"Joshua, we're not at the inn!" Naomi's voice firmly but quietly expressed her irritation, though all it evoked from Joshua was a self-satisfied grin. His talks with those who contemplated ways to resist the Herodians and Romans grew more frequent. Recently, his inn hosted a Galilean teacher named Judas, whose father had been executed by Herod as a common bandit. Judas of Galilee preached a kingdom ruled by God and God alone. Some said he traveled south of Jerusalem and Bethlehem to meet with leaders of the Sicarii to strike alliances.

"Mordecai did not overcome Haman by engaging in palace intrigues," interjected the rabbi, "but by making appeals through the queen, a Jewess herself by God's mercy. Lawlessness does not bring an end to lawlessness." Hananiah knew of Joshua's dabbling with those on the edges of rebellion. The rabbi believed revolution's most likely outcome to be greater repression.

Elias interrupted any further discourse on the matter, just now coming through the crowd and unaware of the previous exchange. "Blessings upon your house today, Rabbi. By the way, did your sharp ears detect the boulders struck together by our young Saul?"

Hananiah laid his hand upon Saul's head. "You made mighty sounds in there, young man. Were Haman here today, you'd have given him quite a fright." Then, seeing Simeon behind his friend, the rabbi added: "And you, too, son of Joshua. When Haman's name crossed my lips, I thought I saw sparks fly. Did your father teach you that trick?"

"No, rabbi, my grandmother." Everyone burst into laughter.

"Your grandmother? Tell her I expect her to come with you next year. Between the two of you, we could add a new tradition: a Purim fire, whose flames dance at the name of Haman!"

***

"Men of Israel, each Purim we hear the scroll of Esther read. The scroll begins with treachery, the threatened extinction of our people by one whose hatred is as ugly as his deeds. Yet the scroll ends with courage, the deliverance of our people by the heroism of Mordecai and Esther. These two Jews, who held positions that could have guaranteed safety if they remained silent, risked all by condemning Haman's evil scheme."

Judas paused to scan the crowd, then glanced briefly at the eagle above and the roof overhead it. "Treachery and courage, extinction and deliverance. Purim's story is familiar to us, heard year in and year out. We may believe we know this story so well, that it will never dare raise its murderous head again. If that is so, we give the Hamans of this world a free hand to plot their destructions. And they do! Even now. Even in this city. Even upon this Temple!"

At these words, a dozen or so of Judas' students stepped from the front of the crowd and ascended the steps of the Ulam. Young men, in their late teens and early twenties, Judas had trained them as Pharisees. But they didn't come forward as students. Half formed a semicircle behind Judas, to prevent anyone from the entourage of the High Priest from interfering. The rest stood in a phalanx immediately in front of Judas.

Nathaniel, sitting alongside the High Priest and other temple officials, thought back to his encounter with Judas and Matthias. Did whatever was happening now relate to that meeting? Nathaniel quickly weighed his options. The Sopher gauged the students would stop anyone attempting a move toward Judas. Nathaniel settled on his goal: cross the Court of Israel to the Chamber of the Hearth, and its adjacent tower: the tower Saripheus had brought him to, the tower that would enable him to reach the Antonia unseen and alert the cohort. As Nathaniel calmly strode in that direction, the sermon of Judas continued.

"How many of you, with righteous indignation, howled in anger and crashed your stones together at the sound of Haman's name today?" A huge roar rose from the multitude. Judas savored the noise, then lashed out in the ensuing calm. "And how many of you, in righteous indignation, did the same when you beheld this brazen idol at the Sanctuary of the Almighty?" Half-question, half-accusation, the words muted the worshipers. There had been words and questions about the eagle, but no outcry. Till now.

"What can we do, Judas?" someone shouted.

Yet another cried, "This is Herod's work!"

Judas lifted his arms for quiet. "Because there's risk involved, are we to remain silent? Silent to an idol at God's own Temple! Silent to polluting these holy courts by an image worshiped by Rome! Is that Purim's lesson? Is that why we cheer Mordecai and Esther, because they exercised caution and whimpered: *'What can we do, it's Haman's work?'* No! They raised their voice! They defied a king's order that threatened death to the people of the Lord Adonai!"

Judas detected a rumbling among the crowd by his stirring of anger and shame. The time had come to incite action. "Purim recalls the day our people were delivered by acts of courage. Does God give us these stories that we should wallow in fear? Does God speak of his holiness, that we should allow the Temple's desecration to go unchallenged?"

Many of those gathered shouted back: "NO!"

"Then the time has come to set our hands as well as our voices to the keeping of God's Torah. A new Haman fouls these courts by the hanging of this idol. Herod commits idolatry against the God of our fathers – it cannot stand! IT CANNOT STAND!"

At the sound of Herod's name, the students surrounding Judas raised their stones and began cracking them together. Within seconds, the action spread through the crowd. A sound like a flood washing down a rock-strewn valley swept through the inner courts. At the same time, movement broke out on the roof. Men stood close to the edge, waving to those below. The bodyguards surrounding Judas hoisted him on their shoulders, hailing the scribe as Judah's new Mordecai. Herod's eagle had spawned a riot.

* * *

"What is the meaning of this, Nathaniel?" Julius had hurried to the small room in the Antonia above the temple passageway. Word reached him that Nathaniel insisted on speaking to the centurion. "We had no meeting today. Are you sure no one saw your use of the Tower?"

"I can't be sure, centurion, I – "

"You can't be sure? If you want the office of Sopher beyond today, you'd best be sure. What possessed you to disregard the use of this passage?"

"I had no choice but to come here. The temple borders on riot."

"The eagle?"

"What else? After the scroll's reading, the son of Saripheus rose to deliver the Purim message. From the outset, it took on political overtones. I left, trying not to draw attention to myself. Judas's words became more volatile as I walked away. He was goading the crowd into action, Julius. By now, who can say what's happened."

This satisfied the centurion's misgivings. "Nathaniel, stay here in the Antonia until I send word you can return. Lucius, alert Gaius to the situation. Tell him additional troops will be needed here for security. Demetrius, order the century to assemble. NOW!"

Another sound snatched Julius's attention away from the room. Several pairs of footsteps ran down the hallway. "Centurion Julius, where is he?"

Julius swung the door open. Two legionnaires, nearly

breathless, saluted the centurion. "Sir, the lookout on the Tower says the Jews in the Temple's inner court are in an uproar. Some have moved onto the roof, and it appears they prepare to rope down to the eagle."

"To your duties," Julius commanded. To himself, he muttered, "An old man's artwork will be washed in young men's blood. Damn you, Herod! Damn you for taking so long to die!"

CHAPTER X

"A toast to Purim's feast!" Joshua stood, as did his and Naomi's guests. "Mordecai and Esther delivered our people from the evil of Haman, and today we honor that deliverance. Mordecai in his wisdom, Esther in her courage. To Mordecai and Esther!"

"TO MORDECAI AND ESTHER!" responded the others, lifting chalices and drinking the sweet red wine from Galilee. As they started to be seated, Joshua interrupted.

"There's more to the toast." He looked at Naomi, remembering the exchange with her at the synagogue. "A toast to God's raising a new Mordecai and Esther against those who press their feet against our necks: Jews who not only remember they're Jews, but who don't forget their enemies. May the gallows, upon which Herod and the Romans kill us a little every day, become the scaffolding from which we hang them high as Haman!"

Though embarrassed, Naomi could not contradict her husband in the presence of guests. Deborah shook her head in disgust at her son-in-law's growing obsession with revolutionary babble. An awkward silence followed, broken at last by Joseph. Slowly lifting his chalice toward Joshua, the carpenter intoned: "Whether gallows be needed, I wouldn't know. I prefer to fashion wood into furnishings used in living, not instruments employed in killing. But if your toast is for God's deliverance, then I join you in it."

"To God's deliverance," added Elias, then the others.

"To God's deliverance," concluded Joshua, convinced deliverance required a blade.

* * *

"Make sure they're secure before you lower the ropes!" Matthias shouted to be heard above the crowd's din beneath them. Three young men clambered down the facade of the Ulam's wall, axes in hand, toward the large statue below them. Once they reached the eagle and began hacking away at the posts holding it in place, Judas waved for Matthias to come down. But Judas couldn't be sure whether Matthias even saw his gesture, much less understood.

A fourth rope lowered a basket containing the remaining axes. The crowd at the porch snatched them, eagerly awaiting the toppling of the golden idol. Judas no longer controlled the mob whose creation he provoked. Several temple guards and priests managed to escort the High Priest Mattaiah into the Sanctuary, closing and barring the door behind them. Herod appointed Mattaiah to this office less than a year ago after Simon's death. A few in the rabble might have enjoyed bludgeoning one they counted as little more than the king's religious mouthpiece.

The crowd fanned away from the porch as the idol teetered precariously on its damaged supports. The three men suspended by ropes swung wildly with their axes as the eagle wavered more. One of them managed to wedge himself between the statue and the wall. He kicked and pushed at the eagle's head, while his colleagues hammered at the lower supports. A series of loud cracks echoed over the Temple complex, the eagle twisted sideways, then crashed to the ground.

Those on the roof lowered the three to the ground before racing down the stairs leading to the porch. The mob surged around the statue. Individuals shared the axes passed down from on high to allow as many as possible the chance to batter the scorned idol. The crowd took up the chant of "JUDAS" as they passed him overhead until he'd been set on the shattered remains of the eagle. Judas motioned in vain for them to be still. When that failed, he resorted to shouting.

"Friends, friends! Please! I am not the one to receive your praise. The Almighty gives us the power to do this. Think of it! The abomination which Herod slung upon this wall lies beneath our feet. God has given us victory! Who knows, God may bring down the one who committed this blasphemy. If Herod's idol falls, will not Herod be soon to follow?!"

"YES!" roared the crowd, intoxicated by the sight of the broken eagle.

"Perhaps Herod is already dead!" cried someone from the midst of the crowd.

"Herod IS dead, or his troops would be here by now," voiced another. People sang and danced. Soon the cry of Herod's death became a chant, accompanied by the cracking of Purim stones together. Neither Judas nor Matthias, who rejoined his friend atop the eagle, could regain the mob's attention – not even when the two scribes paled at a new sight coming into view. Two columns of Roman soldiers advanced through the gates to the north and south of the porch. Judas looked at the broken eagle beneath him. Its cost would now be exacted.

* * *

Before leaving the Antonia, Gaius had briefed Julius and his century. The tribune's orders called for minimizing casualties. A bloodbath on a Jewish festival would have repercussions for years, especially one in the Temple. On the other hand, physical resistance to dispersal or arrest was to be met with deadly force. Gaius charged them to arrest Judas and Matthias, and others directly responsible for the toppling of Herod's eagle. Gaius himself would lead another century, in addition to a detachment of archers, to secure the walkways atop the Temple's outer wall.

Those objectives in mind, Julius massed his troops before the assault, crouching outside the wall surrounding the Temple's inner courts near the gate leading into the Court of Women. While he would lead the eighty soldiers of his century, Julius presumed there would likely be close to a thousand worshippers crowded into the Court of the Israelites where the riot was centered. Still, he was confident that the element of surprise and battle-ready legionnaires far outweighed numbers. Julius gave a final review of how their mission would be carried out.

"Cassius, take forty men west along this wall, and from there follow the north wall till you reach the Water Gate. I'll lead the rest to the gate on the eastern wall into the Court of Israelites. When you hear the trumpet signal, move inside the gate and angle a skirmish line alongside the steps to isolate the leaders on the porch from the main crowd in the court. We'll execute the same maneuver from the east and meet you at the center of the steps. Remember: as little fighting as possible. The only prisoners we want are the leaders. Let the others escape through the Nicanor Gate, unless they attack. If they do, put them down. At once."

"Herald, you come with me. When we've reached our gate and the archers under Gaius are ready to fan out along the upper wall, I'll give you the order to sound the attack call."

Julius surveyed the century now in readiness. "You have your orders!" The company snapped their right fists to their chests in allegiance to the centurion's commands. "For Rome!"

* * *

In a matter of minutes, the crowd celebrating the fall of Herod's eagle stood dumbfounded as two columns of Roman solders entered the sacred Court from each side. Most expected Temple police, Jewish guards under the High Priest's authority, to make some effort to quell the disturbance. But the spectacle of Rome's legions invading this space shocked everyone. When archers could be seen taking position on the high outer walls, fear took hold.

Some fifty students of Matthias and Julius encircled

the two scribes. The Roman columns cut them off from the wider crowd, who now surmised the advancing soldiers wouldn't topple as easily as the eagle. In moments, a human stream flowed out the Nicanor gate into the Women's Court, and from there through the Court of the Gentiles and off of the Temple mount itself.

The legionnaires converged just below the twelve steps leading to the porch. Behind the Jews who surrounded Matthias and Judas, the sealed door blocked any retreat. In front of them, a Roman century arrayed themselves for battle. A line of thirty legionnaires formed at the base of the stairs, shields up and spears lowered. The remaining members in Julius' century stood behind them to insure the crowd dared not to attack them from the rear.

Twenty or so students rushed down the steps. Throwing rocks and wielding axes, they tried to wedge an opening for their colleagues to reach the gate. The attempt ended in seconds. Without shields, the students proved easy targets for Roman spears. As another group of students prepared a similar assault, Judas raised his voiced. "Hold your place!"

The centurion stepped forward through the skirmish line and eyed Judas. "Tell your people to empty their hands of stones and weapons, and raise their arms. No more need die!"

Judas recognized the face and voice from his interrogation in the Antonia. "We have no choice," Judas shouted to the phalanx of students around him, sensing the futility of further attempts to escape. "Too much blood has already been shed."

The few remaining axes and Purim stones dropped to the ground. The troops surrounded Judas and Matthias and bound their wrists behind their back. Julius made his way to Judas.

"Congratulations, Jew. Does it make you proud to see the guts of your followers spilled out on these steps?"

"You don't understand, Roman. Herod blasphemed

this Temple. He left us no choice."

"No, scribe, YOU don't understand. The blood of these children stains this Temple and writes your death warrant. All for a lifeless statue. Was it worth the cost?"

"You serve your emperor, centurion. I serve my God. You led your men to risk their deaths for what you call a lifeless statue. I'd say we're more alike than you care to admit."

"Get him out of my sight, Cassius!" Julius would hear no more.

* * *

"Down on your knees before your King!" The palace steward's instruction was accompanied by Herod's guards shoving Julius and Matthias, still bound, onto the floor.

Julius watched from the rear of the hall into which Herod's pallet bearers carried the king. To the centurion's eyes, his flesh seemed more pallid than in the previous week. Perhaps today's events took their toll, or the disease had worsened each day. Julius wished both to be true.

"What wretches dare destroy my statue, dedicated to the Holy One of Israel? Why have you sinned against the Chosen King of the Almighty? Look what you have done!" At these words of Herod, servants towed in a cart holding the broken hulk of the eagle.

"I ordered this work in gratitude for the years God has allowed me to reign. I arranged its display to celebrate Purim, a gesture of my devotion to the Temple which I, I myself, rebuilt so that sacrifices to Elohim Adonai could be offered in a place of beauty. But you have defiled the Temple by the destruction of this offering. You have broken the ways of our fathers by plotting the downfall of God's anointed King. What have you to say?"

Judas staggered to his feet. "If Herod wishes an answer, I would offer one."

"And I as well," added Matthias.

Herod's eyes opened wide, bloodshot from nights made sleepless by pain, a wild mess of hair entangling the crown nestled on his head. "I'll abide the voice of only one criminal in these halls!" Herod shrieked. "Let it be yours, Judas son of Saripheus. And do not think your father's former service will be of any avail to you. He, too, will suffer my judgment."

"I cannot speak for my father, nor do I make appeal to him. You should be congratulating, not punishing, his subservience to your breaches of Torah in this city."

"Lies, all lies, criminal! I've devoted my life to keeping Torah."

Knowing his sentence assured, Judas spoke freely. "You have devoted your life to twisting the Law, ignoring its accusing finger when you transgress it. You wed your niece, debauching the marriage bed with incest each time you slithered between her legs."

"You try my patience, scribe."

"You rebuild the Temple out of bloodguilt from murdering your own kin."

"You will die for your transgressions, Judas. I will see you die!"

"And now your own body rebels against you. It rots from the inside, because even it cannot tolerate the filth and stench you have become."

"GUARDS!"

The hilt of a sword smashed into the back of Judas' head, sending him reeling to the floor. Watching his blood pool on the stone, Julius allowed the condemned Judas a measure of respect. Truth was rarely spoken these days in Herod's palace.

"Enough! Take the traitors to the Antonia. Inform Gaius they are to be marched to Jericho in chains! And send Saripheus with them! He shall witness his son's treachery rewarded."

* * *

After its uneasy beginning, the Purim banquet at Bethlehem's inn went well. At meal's end, the adults told stories while Simeon demonstrated the fine art of making sparks with Purim stones to Saul. The youngest children squealed with delight when Joseph agreed to tell them a story about David, the shepherd boy of Bethlehem. Half the story remained when a furious pounding on the inn's door startled everyone.

"A minute, please!" yelled Joshua, as he stumbled toward the door, his feet tangled by the meal's several toasts of wine. "Don't you know this is Purim?"

As Joshua unlatched the door, someone pushed hard from the other side. It swung open, slamming Joshua's chest and sending him tumbling backward. A young man, perhaps twenty, rushed in. Although sweat poured down the stranger's forehead, a reddish mud caked his face.

"Husband, he's bleeding!" Naomi rose to tend the cuts on his face, only to see his right arm and both hands torn and bloodied. "Mary, Rebekah, I'll need water. And some linen."

Elias and Joseph helped the man to a bench near one of the oil lamps, where wounds could be better seen and tended.

"The robbers are active again," said Deborah, wetting a cloth to wash his brow.

"No, no, not robbers – Romans!" The young man's final word silenced the room.

"That is a serious charge." Joseph offered, looking deeply into the stranger's eyes.

"At the temple today. Herod erected an eagle. Hung it over the gate to the Sanctuary."

"What?" blurted Rebekah. "An idol, there?"

"Made of gold, or so it appeared," continued the stranger. "At Purim service, the scribe Judas denounced the desecration, challenging us to act."

"At least someone in that city knows what needs to be done," Joshua slurred. "I hope all Jerusalem has raised arms against Herod by now!"

"Would I be fleeing if they had?" retorted the young

man, taking a deep gulp of wine before resuming his story. "Judas rallied the worshipers to attack the idol, which we did. Brought it to the ground. Destroyed it. But then..." The young man's eyes filled with tears, and he turned away from those attending him.

Mary rubbed an ointment made from aloe on the wound on his arm. "You don't have to say anything more, not until you're ready. Do you have a name?"

"Abraham. My name is Abraham." A moment of silence passed before he spoke again. "I was on the roof, helping lower those who hacked the eagle down. By the time I descended the stairs, soldiers came. One, maybe two, Roman centuries. On the walls, inside the courtyard. I tried to reach Judas, but the crowd broke into a run. They spilled around me like sheep startled by lightning. There was no way to reach the porch. I tried – as God is my witness, I tried!"

Naomi tended a deep gash above his eye. Abraham's last words seemed a plea. "We believe you. You have the proof of your wounds." Her words, spoken to soothe, only scorched.

"Wounds! I gained these when I fell. Running away."

"Abraham, it sounds as if everyone took flight when the Romans came. You had no choice." Elias was no coward, but he understood the young man's predicament.

"Not all ran. When the crowd surged toward me, I leapt behind the bronze laver used by the priests. From there, I saw the Romans close on the group surrounding the scribe. Two dozen or so rushed at the troops to defend Judas. The soldiers butchered them. They had no chance."

Everyone in the room felt their throats tighten at this news. All save Joshua.

"Do you see now? Why men like Judas of Galilee and the Sicarii hold our best hope? Herod and his Roman mercenaries will NEVER heed mere words. The only thing they'll understand will be our swords!"

When the women finished caring for his injuries, Abraham drew Joshua aside. "You're right. As is Judas. I'd heard, after his lectures in Jerusalem, he planned to come to Bethlehem, David's city. That's why I ran here. I sought not only sanctuary – but those who understand the time for redemption draws near. A time to raise more than voices."

"You've come to the right place, Abraham, and to the right person. God's deliverance dwells in the hands of those with the zeal to seize it."

The pair clasped hands. Only afterwards did Joshua notice the stain on his right hand, made by the blood of Abraham.

***

"What is this?!" The bedding sheets about Herod flew, as the king raged at this disturbance. Sleep provided the only escape Herod knew from the pain and discomfort of his disease. "Haven't I endured enough this day?"

The palace steward, Archelaus, quaked at the reproof. He advised against the interruption of the monarch's sleep, but Alexas overruled him.

"Brother-in-law, forgive me, forgive me! But as the Almighty gave the righteous Job one test after another, it seems He does with you."

"Is that you, Alexas?" The lamp held by the steward made Herod's eyes squint at the approaching pair, still blurred in his sight. "What are you prattling on about?"

"As I said, Highness, I beg your forgiveness. Nothing but an extraordinary act could drive me to demand that your steward rouse you."

"Get on with it, Alexas, so I can get back to sleep."

"This is difficult to say, my king." Alexas felt his throat tensing with the news. "A group of astrologers, from those of the Magi caste in Persia, came to the palace an hour ago."

"Well, give them shelter. I'll see them in the morning if they desire an audience."

"Excellency, you may wish to talk with them tonight. They've journeyed for some months to see – well, to see the child their star charts claim has been born this past year or so."

"A child?" Herod began. "What of it?"

"Not so much _a_ child," Alexas replied, drawing a deep breath and summoning what courage he possessed, "_the_ child, they say. The child to be the Jews' king and Messiah."

CHAPTER XI

Shortly after midnight, a chariot raced toward Herod's palace. Its passenger, Nathaniel, considered if this might be some bad dream that would soon end. The previous day's events left him restless on his bed. But it seemed his sleep had been only minutes when an officer of Herod's palace guard roused him, announcing Herod's summons to the palace. Now, the cold night air pummeled his face as the chariot's swaying made him nauseous. Once at the palace, another guard whisked Nathaniel from the chariot and hastened him through torchlit corridors until they reached a door flanked by two sentries, who stood aside to allow Nathaniel passage.

"Welcome, Sopher. I trust your ride went well." Alexas' words sounded artificial.

"Alexas, bring him over here." The voice came from the room's center, a room Nathaniel found to be uncomfortably humid. Lampstands provided dim illumination. Only as he neared the lamps did Nathaniel fully grasp the setting: a bathing room. The king of Judea soaked in a marble-tiled pool filled with hot water.

"This is our first meeting, is it not, Sopher?"

"Yes, your Highness."

Alexas noticed puzzlement on Nathaniel's face as he stared at the water. "The baths bring his Excellency relief in his affliction. Heat and moisture restore his strength."

Nathaniel bowed in Herod's direction. "I pray for my king's recovery."

"Pray then also for our meeting tonight, scribe. I've

need of your services."

"Whatever I can do, I will."

"What do the scriptures say of Messiah's birth? More specifically, the place of birth?"

The Sopher's mouth gaped open. Messiah? Gossip occasionally spread of Herod's fancying himself to be the Promised One. Nathaniel pondered a reply that would not offend.

"Forgive me, Highness. But you are the king, and you hold David's scepter. God would not raise up Messiah when one already chosen to rule sits on the throne."

"My thoughts exactly. Why would Messiah come, when I still rule? But perhaps a false claimant might arise. And if that were to happen, or if others sought to make such claims about someone, where would the birth need to occur to fulfill prophecy?"

Nathaniel once more weighed his response. The king piqued his curiosity with these questions. "Forgive me, Excellency, but has someone made claim to be Messiah?"

Herod took a cloth from the bath's edge and wiped the perspiration from his face. "After my meeting with you, I have an audience with a group of Persian Magi. They are, if you don't know, persons who believe the stars reveal the future. These Magi spoke to me earlier, saying they journeyed here to see a recently born Jewish king, an event revealed to them in the sky."

"And your Highness believes them?"

"My belief, Sopher, is beside the point. THEY believe, and that concerns me. And it strikes me more than curious their arrival coincides with the Purim riot. What if some of today's schemers heard of the Magi's arrival and its reason? What if rebels sought to undermine my rule in order to enthrone, for example, a child, who could be easily manipulated? Before I meet again with these astrologers, I need to know where the pretender would arise."

"In the scroll of the Twelve, the prophet Micah praises

the Judean village of Bethlehem. `*For from you shall come a ruler who is to shepherd my people Israel.*'

"Bethlehem is the consensus of the rabbis for this?"

"Yes, Excellency." Nathaniel paused. He would say more, but his choice of words needed care in the choosing. "May I be permitted to add what only amounts to rumor, but which tends to follow your majesty's line of thought about conspiracy?"

Now Herod was the one whose curiosity had been touched. "Go ahead."

"I have distant relatives in Bethlehem, whom I hosted for Hanukkah a year and a half ago. I vaguely recall hearsay that someone from David's line had resettled in Bethlehem. The words seemed innocent at the time, so I gave them no further thought."

"Was anything said of a new son in that family?"

Nathaniel stroked his beard, as if to extract some obscure bit of information that, in truth, rested on the tip of his tongue. "It's been some time since then, Highness. But, yes, I recall mention made of a recently born infant – and yes, I believe they indicated a boy." Nathaniel chose to be evasive. Revealing his far more extensive knowledge might bring him into suspicion.

"This all falls into place, Alexas," Herod began, his eyes widening as he continued. "The riot, some distant kin of David in Bethlehem, these stargazers: someone has gone to great lengths to lay the groundwork for rebellion. But it shall not go unpunished."

While noting gaps in Herod's logic, Alexas knew that raising them could be taken as sympathy with the imagined plotters. "Your wisdom sees what remains hidden to ordinary eyes."

The king sat slightly forward, the top of his reddened shoulders breaking the water's surface. "Here is what must be done. As planned, I'll travel tomorrow to Jericho in preparation for the trial of the rioters. Alexas, see that the leaders of the Sanhedrin and some of Jerusalem's other notables join me there the following day. That way, if any of them are involved in this plot, they'll be unable to hatch plans in my absence. As for the Magi, Sopher, I'll instruct them to bring you word of this child's identity after they return from Bethlehem. Alexas, have one of my guards follow the Persians to Bethlehem. That way, we'll know where to find this false king. Once the foreigners leave, we dispose of the problem. Agreed?"

Alexas forced a smile, as if to indicate approval in a child's murder. "Yes, Excellency."

"Do you wish my presence when you greet these Magi?" asked Nathaniel.

"Yes, that might be helpful. In case they have further questions about the prophet's words. But give them the impression that this Messiah's identity is a revelation we gladly await – which it is!" Herod laughed, reveling in the thought of another rival's elimination. "Now leave, so the servants may dress me. Wait outside the door."

Alexas thought back to similar plots devised by Herod. Advisors, friends, even wives and sons brought to the grave. . . and now, some unknowing child in Bethlehem about to die.

As for Nathaniel, his mind turned to that child in Bethlehem. Unlike the speculations running through Alexas' head, this was not a faceless infant in the Sopher's mind. The victim would be Joseph's son, Yeshua: once a guest in his home, whom he had held in his arms. Naomi needed Mary's help one morning to bathe the twins, and Nathaniel received the sleeping Yeshua from her. The light had cast a soft glow on the infant's face. The remembrance passed quickly, not to be considered again. The boy was as good as dead. Better not to think of it, of him.

* * *

"Yeshua! Time to go to the stable!" The toddler ran into his mother's arms. Mary swept him up, kissed him, then set him back down on the ground. Holding hands, they left the inn and walked toward the cave that Joshua had used for the inn's stable. Naomi had taken her children to visit Rachel. Joseph worked with Elias to fashion a new lifting arm for the town's well. So Mary decided to take her son this afternoon to his favorite spot in the village.

"What shall we do at the stable, Yeshua?"

"Manger, mama."

"You want to hear the manger story? Again?" Mary laughed. No trip to the stable with Yeshua could be made without telling him the story of his birth there in the feeding trough. "Your father tells that story much better, but I'll try. First, let's feed the lambs and calves!"

The little boy ran ahead of his mother into the stable, reaching into a burlap bag to get a handful of oats. He giggled as the lambs nuzzled into his palm, their tongues licking up the oats. Mary helped with the calves, who sometimes bumped his head after they'd cleaned his hands of food. Yeshua thought this great play, especially when they pushed him over and nudged at him to get up. He liked to pet the animals after feeding, as they'd crowd around in hopes of more oats. The lambs' fleece felt soft and warm. Sometimes he rubbed his cheeks and chin against them.

"Time for the story, Yeshua." Mary stood by the manger. Yeshua came running.

"Yes mama. Manger."

The two sat at the foot of the trough, their backs to the cave's opening so Yeshua could look in at the animals. Three lambs and one calf wandered over and settled down in the straw next to the mother and child. Running her fingers through Yeshua's fine dark hair, Mary told of that night: the village overflowing with visitors, obtaining the stable through the kindness of Naomi and Joshua, Yeshua's first cry, the manger, the visits of shepherds and midwife.

The story's telling so engrossed Mary that she didn't notice her audience had suddenly increased. At the cave's entrance, four men listened intently to the young woman's words. They took special interest in her recollection of shepherds and a vision seen in the sky.

When Mary finished the story, two of the men stepped inside. Mary and Yeshua still had no idea of their approach until several lambs bleated. Mary turned to see what caught their attention. "Aaah!" Her gasp at the sight of two strangers was quickly followed by her gathering Yeshua up in her arms. She stepped back and to the side, keeping the manger between her and the intruders. The sunlight streaming in from the cave's entrance prevented her from discerning the looks on their faces. "What do you want here?"

In broken Aramaic, the taller one spoke. "Forgive us, good woman, we did not mean to startle you. We are travelers, seeking a place to rest and feed our camels."

"The owner runs an inn nearby." Mary's voice wavered. "You need to speak with him."

The men looked to each other, then the tall one continued. "We've found what we seek."

Mary retreated, eyeing a pitchfork hanging from a rough beam. Setting Yeshua down behind her, Mary took the pitchfork in hand. Yeshua peeked around his mother's skirt while she spoke in a steady voice. "Be assured, my screams will be heard. And in the meantime, I'll put these tines to good use, mind you."

"Please, you misunderstand!" The voice of the stranger sounded sincere. The second man said something to his companion in a tongue Mary did not recognize. The pair then dropped to their knees, bowing low in Mary's direction. Again, the taller man spoke.

"We came to this stable to feed and water our animals. But as we drew near the entry, we heard your story. We listened as you told your son about shepherds who visited here, and their words about lights and voices in the night."

Her grip on the pitchfork remained firm. "What is any of that to you?"

Now the second man spoke, in flawless Aramaic. "We are Magi, astrologers from Persia. More than a year and a half ago, strange conjunctions occurred in the sky. After much study, my friend Balthasar and I concluded it was the natal star of the Jewish Messiah. Our attempts to convince others failed, so we decided to journey here and see for ourselves. But arrangements had to be made, and the distance was great. That's why it has been so long."

Mary set down the pitchfork. "You believe my son is this One you seek?"

"Didn't you say the shepherds spoke of Messiah when they came to see your son? And is it accidental that you named him *Yeshua,* `savior' in your tongue?"

Mary eyed the men closely. Balthasar, the first to speak, wore a robe of white linen, its hood pulled over his head. He had remained bowed as the other spoke, but now he lifted his eyes to Mary. She could see no sign of deceit in them. The second man's face bore the color of ebony, a rare and exotic wood Joseph once showed her. Over his white robe hung a tapestried cloak, golden threads racing through purple velvet in wild designs of stars and moons and suns.

"My husband named our son, that name given to him in a dream. Do you believe the Almighty speaks in such ways?"

"If knowledge can be read in the stars," answered Balthasar, "it is not difficult to conceive of inspiration coming in dreams."

Mary reached down and pulled Yeshua tighter against her. "My husband and I both received visions prior to Yeshua's birth. The shepherds repeated words we'd each heard long before. And now, you say you've discerned the same in stars."

"It IS the King", cried Balthasar, lowering his face to the ground.

Utan joined his companion in prostrating before child and mother. "Woman, we bring gifts for the child. May we set them before you?"

Mary nodded. Balthasar rose and went to the two men who remained outside.

"The others, are they Magi as well?"

"No, they are our servants. Would you permit them to enter? To see the child?"

"Of course. And my name is Mary." She stepped toward the Magus named Utan, who remained kneeling. "Please stand. Neither I nor my son are accustomed to this."

Yeshua could see boxes being drawn out of a saddle bag by Balthasar. The child pointed to the trough: "Manger."

Utan gently enclosed the boy's tiny hand in his own. "Yes, little one, manger. Where your God placed you as a gift, my friend will set these gifts – for you."

Yeshua started to squirm, pointing to the manger, so Mary lifted Yeshua to set him into the manger as Balthasar entered and placed three boxes beside him.

One by one, Yeshua opened them. The first held a gold ring, sized to fit an adult finger. The second contained a pouch of frankincense, whose sweet balsam aroma contrasted with the stable's pungent odors. In the third was a small glass vial, which Mary gently took from Yeshua.

"Myrrh", announced Utan, "a gift of my ancestor Sheba to the great king Solomon. And now, a gift for another of Solomon's line."

"These are wonderful gifts," Mary said, "and your coming so far to bring them."

"To see this child is the journey of a lifetime!" He turned to Balthasar. "We must travel on. Tell the servants they may come in to see the child before we depart."

When Balthasar returned with the servants, an animated conversation ensued in their native tongue. Mary judged from the pitch of their voices that they discussed something of importance. Utan listened, then spoke at some length. Finally, all four nodded. Balthasar and the servants returned to the camels with feed and jugs of water.

"Mary, our servants spotted a man who watched as we came in here. He has been following us from Jerusalem, though we thought initially he was simply taking the same road. To be safe, stay in the stable, out of sight, when we leave. We'll wander from street to street, as if we continue to search after tending to our animals. If he continues to follow us, we will lead him away from here. If he maintains his watch on this place, well, we will tend to that as well."

"Is there danger?"

"I hope not, but be cautious. Wait for half an hour to pass before returning to your home."

"Who would want to follow you?"

"We made inquiry in Jerusalem last night of the new king's birth. Naturally, we assumed the palace to be the place to start. Only there did we learn of Bethlehem."

"You don't think Herod has his hand in this man who follows you?"

Utan thought for a moment, then glanced at the child and back to Mary. "Perhaps you'd best tell your husband about today. Even in our land, we've heard stories of the king. Herod asked us to return with news of the child, but this spying convinces us not to do so. If you have any misgivings, or need refuge, our order maintains a home in the city of Pelusium, east of the Nile's delta. We'll go there straight from here to alert its steward that you may need sanctuary."

"We have home and friends in Bethlehem, Utan. It would be difficult to leave."

"It would also be difficult for a young woman to ward off four intruders with only a pitchfork," bringing a smile to them both. "Yet you prepared to do just that. If your dreams, and our journey, aren't to be in vain, other choices may be demanded of you to protect this child."

"They will not be in vain. My son will be protected."

"Then may your God keep you – and you, Yeshua." Utan brushed the child's forehead with his fingers before rejoining his companions. The four resumed their meandering through Bethlehem. Mary rocked Yeshua in her lap as he played with the ring. She prayed he'd live to see it fit his finger, as she prayed the Magi be kept safe – and the secret they now protected with her.

CHAPTER XII

Evening brought little relief from the warm damp air in Jericho and the valley of the Jordan. Even now in early spring, the modestly warm temperature combined with the evaporating waters of the Jordan River and Salt Sea to produce a stifling sultriness. Sweat poured down Herod's forehead as he lounged in the courtyard of his winter palace. Earlier today, the king condemned Judas and Matthias to be executed in ten days.

The heat and humidity may have oppressed others, but it soothed Herod. As his disease found comfort in the hot springs nearby, so too did Jericho's sweltering air bring some relief. Still, it left unaffected two frustrations weighing on him. Herod had intended to punish Saripheus by forcing him to view his son's execution. But whether from the stress of the trial or the heat of his cell, Saripheus collapsed this afternoon. By the time a physician reached him, the former Sopher lie dead. A punishment from God, thought Herod, for a father unable to control his son.

And there were the Magi. Four days had passed, and no word reached him yet about Bethlehem's pretender to Herod's throne. Not knowing a potential enemy gnawed inside Herod. Which of Bethlehem's children might be his new rival – and needed to be his next victim?

"Excellency!" The king's steward emerged from a row of palm trees lining the courtyard. "A rider has arrived, one of your Syrian guards from Jerusalem. He comes from Bethlehem!"

Herod wiped his brow on the sleeve of his robe. "Bring

him to me." A smile creased Herod's face. His fear of not find-ing the child could now be set aside. A few minutes later, the Syrian sent to spy on the astrologers appeared, bowing low before daring to speak.

"Majesty, Alexas and Nathaniel dispatched me to you."

"Ah, they wished me to hear the good news as soon as possible."

The guard called Antiochus stared down at his feet. Had it been good news, he thought, the king's brother-in-law and the Jew advisor would have brought it themselves to bask in its honors. Instead, they sent him alone when truth needed telling.

"Majesty, I did exactly as you commanded, following the Magi to Bethlehem. After feeding their animals, they wandered the streets, speaking with various individuals. But they did not enter a single house. And never did they spend any time with a child."

A new sweat began to dampen Herod's skin and spirit. "What are you saying?"

"I watched carefully for any sign of interest in a family or particular residence: there was none. Except for a stable where they fed and watered their camels, they never lin-gered anywhere. Just to be sure no one else was inside, I kept the stable in sight as long as I could before having to set out to keep track of the Magi. But no one emerged."

"What did you do after that?" Curiosity was quickly becoming impatience.

"I tracked them through Bethlehem. But as I said, they never once entered a home. They didn't even dismount their camels. It appeared they simply asked questions, then moved on."

"Did you trail them back to Jerusalem?"

Antiochus cleared his throat. "They didn't return to Jerusalem, my king. Once they left Bethlehem, they headed south. Midway between Bethlehem and Gaza, they encamped – so I did the same. During the night, two men seized me. All they said was, `Our masters bid you farewell.' Then I felt a blow to my head, and everything went black. When I came to, the morning light revealed they'd driven off my mount and slit my water skin. I had no choice but to walk back to Bethlehem. Once there, I commandeered a horse to return to Jerusalem as quickly as possible to report to Alexas. He conferred with Nathaniel, and they dispatched me to you."

Herod sat for some time without speaking. If there was a child in Bethlehem threatening his throne, his identity remained cloaked. The Magi tricked him, a fact guaranteed by their dealing with this guard. Or had they bribed the man kneeling before him?

"Steward, send in my personal guards!" Antiochus looked around in panic as four soldiers appeared. Herod glared at the messenger. "Tell me: how much did the Magi pay you? Who is the child they visited?"

"Excellency, everything I said is true. There was no child. They gave me nothing. I serve only you!"

"One of you, fetch a rope!" Herod's order to the guards was followed by the king peering at one of the balconies overhanging the courtyard's edge. "We'll hang the traitor from there."

"No, my king, I did nothing. Nothing!" The guards surrounding Antiochus stuffed a rag in his mouth. The prisoner struggled wildly, but to no avail. A noose looped around his neck. Two guards held him while the others tightened the knot and tossed the rope's other end over the balcony's stone railing.

"Wait!" The king ordered his pallet carried to where the execution was about to occur. "One more time, Antiochus. Did the Magi bribe you? Did they visit a child? You'll have no further chance to tell the truth!"

One guard pulled the rag from his mouth. "My king, I swear on my father's honor I didn't betray you. I took no bribe. There was no child. Please! Believe me!"

"Very well, I believe you." Herod smiled at Antiochus, who gasped in relief. The king continued. "But you did allow yourself to be overcome." Herod waved his hand. One sharp pull and the head of Antiochus snapped up. His legs kicked wildly for awhile, then swung limp.

"Steward, send a messenger to Jerusalem. Inform Alexas to bring Nathaniel here, along with Gauis and Julius. Immediately." As the steward turned to carry out the orders, Herod called out. "Before you go, have this corpse removed. It's such a pleasant evening, I don't wish to be disturbed by the sight."

* * *

In the hallway outside the king's bedroom, two pairs of men waited for permission to enter. Gaius and Nathaniel stood silently by the door. Alexas and Julius paced further down the hall, engaged in a subdued yet intense conversation.

"Alexas, calm yourself! If Herod wanted you dead because of these Magi, why would he have summoned the tribune and me?" Julius tried to reassure Alexas their journey to Jericho was not merely a ruse to arrest the king's brother-in-law. "From what you say, Nathaniel's the one who stands in greater danger. The spy was to have reported to him. He was the one who suggested Bethlehem in the first place."

"You forget the guard's fate, Julius – hanged for being ambushed! The king grows more unpredictable each day."

"Lower your voice, Alexas. You've survived all these years with Herod and his intrigues. I can' believe his purpose was to murder you. Or even Nathaniel. There must be something else."

The door to Herod's room swung open and the steward ushered the four men in, then left. The late afternoon sunlight illuminated the king's bed. Numerous soakings in the hot springs left Herod's flesh swollen. The king motioned them closer.

"My voice does not have the strength it once did, you'll have to draw near."

Alexas moved to the bed, taking Herod's hand in his own. "Your dear sister sends her love, my king. We pray your recovery will be swift and complete."

"My physicians babble the same sentiments, Alexas, though I'm the one who suffers their ignorance. If I ruled as they medicate, Judea would have died two decades ago."

"Excellency," interjected Gaius, "know that Augustus conveys his good wishes. And if you desire, the cohort's physician can be summoned to assist."

"Thank you, tribune. Perhaps I shall accept that offer another day. But for now, more pressing matters. Nathaniel! Did the spy we sent after the Magi give you any report?"

The sudden shift in topic concerned Nathaniel. "Nothing. Nothing of substance. He indicated they stopped at no house. Just a few minor conversations with passersby, then they left. Nothing to speak of."

"You're not withholding something from me, Sopher?"

Herod's tone unsettled Nathaniel. "Absolutely not, your Highness. The spy told me no more than what I tell you."

"I see." Herod studied the face of the Sopher, looking for some hint of guile. "I thought perhaps you and the Syrian decided some matter might be best left unsaid to me. Unhappily, for the spy, that cost him his life. Alexas, what was that man's name?"

"Antiochus, your Majesty."

Herod leaned back upon his pillow, pain shooting up his spine like fire racing up a dry branch. "If he was married, see that his wife receives a pension. If not, give his parents some payment, perhaps a year's wage. That should assuage any grief."

No one knew what to make of this. Was it a bizarre pang of conscience, or the ramblings of one whose mind slowly disintegrated with his body?

"You still insist, Nathaniel, that Messiah is to be born in Bethlehem?"

Nathaniel nodded his head. "Yes, Majesty, that is how the rabbis read Micah to mean."

"There is our problem. These Magi claim a King has been born, sometime within the past year or so. Yet, I am king. My son Archelaus, who will one day succeed me, was born in Jerusalem. These Magi must conspire with other liars to proclaim a false King."

"If that is so," reasoned Alexas, hoping to defuse the king's fears and his own, "there can be nothing to what these Persian Gentiles claim."

"There you are wrong, brother-in-law. The Persians came seeking a new king: whether from the stars, as they say, or from darker motives. Either way, it doesn't matter. Traitors could use the claim of a Messiah's birth to stir revolt, much like the Purim outburst. Think on this: that riot occurred the very day these Magi arrived! There IS a conspiracy! And all is based on these claims of a king born in Bethlehem. These wretches twist scripture into treason!"

"Perhaps," Nathaniel interjected, "we should publicly discredit any remaining conspirators. I can arrange for the Sanhedrin to insure those involved are thoroughly shamed."

Herod shook his head. "We can't do that. Any public attempt to deal with this matter will only give it notoriety. Besides, we still don't know those who conspire beyond the Purim rioters. No, another tact is required. Which, Gaius, is why I have summoned you here, along with Julius. I've a plan to solve our problem. And it is Rome's problem, too, if unrest festers."

The tribune folded his hands. "What would you have the Jerusalem cohort do?"

"This entire plot hinges on the birth of an alleged king in Bethlehem. Eliminate that birth and the scheme unravels."

Gaius began to feel uneasy. "What do you mean by 'eliminating the birth?'"

"Come now, tribune, you're a man of action. The death of whoever is claimed to be Messiah ruins the schemers' plan."

"Forgive me, Excellency." The voice belonged to Julius. "But the spy's failure to link the Magi to one house or family prevents us from knowing that individual, if indeed there is one."

"Quite right, centurion." A raspy cough interrupted Herod's rejoinder. He wiped the phlegm on a cloth already yellowed and slightly bloodied from before. "Beyond that, if we questioned the villagers to root out the pretender, the news of whom we seek and why would circulate, allowing time for our enemies to spirit the child away."

Julius decided to press the matter further. "But if I understand your peoples' writings, this Messiah must be from David's family, not just his birthplace."

"Very good, Julius," Herod admitted. "But thanks to the knowledge of this village by our new Sopher, we know there is indeed a family there who claims Davidic ancestry."

The public disclosure of this information, and more importantly its source, gave Nathaniel a measure of pride. Julius, however, grew more wary of where this was leading.

"Excellency, if, we can't make further inquiries about this child or his family to single them out, and if we still don't know who they are: how is the threat to be eliminated?"

"Simple. We know where the child is, we know about how old, so we act. Gaius, a detail from the cohort will execute all male children in Bethlehem under the age of two."

Even for Alexas, who'd seen Herod scheme to kill members of his own family, the idea sounded outrageous. Nathaniel's thoughts raced not just to Yeshua, whose life he earlier signed away, but to his nephew David. Julius felt rage building inside. Gaius offered a mild protest.

"Excellency, what is the need for Rome to do this? We are soldiers, trained for war. Your personal guard from Syria could easily perform this task."

"Yes, tribune, they could. But troops under my command would bring blame for the act against me. The people hate you Romans already. There'd be no need for elaborate explanation, only a Roman troop gone out of control. And this is not a request I make, tribune. I command you in the name of Augustus to carry this out! Sedition is abroad. I expect you to quell it."

"Sedition?" Julius exclaimed. "You call the murder of infants quelling sedition? My men fight those who bear swords, not rattles!"

"Enough, Centurion!" Gaius stepped between Julius and Herod, glaring into Julius' eyes. "I speak for the cohort, not you." Gaius hoped his upbraiding of Julius would satisfy Herod.

"Make sure my orders are obeyed, tribune Gaius!" Herod's screamed in anger, resulting in a fit of coughing and wheezing. Once it subsided, the king supported himself by his forearm at the edge of his pallet and stared hard at Julius. "Centurion, since your heart seems to have softened over the years, you shall be the officer in charge of the Bethlehem detail."

Julius ached to respond, but realized anything further would possibly result in his being the second soldier hung on Herod's balcony this week. "As you command."

"I'm glad we have this settled," Herod spoke as he settled back on the pallet. "I look forward to receiving your report, centurion. This action, by the way, will take place nine days from today: the same day as Judas' and Matthias' executions, the first day of Nisan. On the calendar of the Jews, that day observes the `New Year of Kings', when anniversaries of reigns are reckoned." Turning to the tribune, the king's lips twisted into a leering smile. "A fitting anniversary present for my rule, wouldn't you say, Gaius? The deaths of this pretender and the rebels who spawned him. But there must be absolute secrecy about this. Inform your soldiers only the night before, so the imposter has no chance of forewarning."

"Your word will be carried out, Herod." The tribune's monotone response failed to stifle the revulsion churning his stomach.

"Nathaniel, this word of secrecy applies to you. Your family cannot be told."

An image of the twins in Naomi's arms lingered for a moment, then departed. "You have my word, my King. I will not inform my family."

"Well, you all have duties to prepare for. See they're carried out."

Julius offered a stiff bow in Herod's direction, then he and the others left the room. Never in his service of the empire had Julius ever questioned an order. But then, never had his service required the murder of children.

* * *

Eight nights later, the Antonia's courtyard bustled with activity. Two dozen foot soldiers, along with an equal contingent of cavalry, awaited orders from Gaius. The men had been told that afternoon they would take part in an operation outside the city. Most presumed a raid on a Sicarii stronghold in the eastern wilderness. The usual murmurings before battle, however, diminished at the sight unfolding in the sky. Though there were no clouds, the moon's light began to fail. As they watched to see why, the moon itself began to disappear: an eclipse!

A bugle's shrill blast pierced the yard as Gaius stepped onto the balcony above them. Men and animals shifted into array, cavalry to the rear and flanks of the infantry. Most eyes remained fixed on the sky. Soldiers going into combat tended toward superstition. The moon's disappearance might be a bad omen.

"Legionnaires! Your orders are these. Stage in the hills outside of Bethlehem tonight, and remain hidden through morning. In mid-afternoon, you will sweep down into the village and put to the sword all boys there two years of age and younger. No exceptions."

An audible gasp arose. Some thought the tribune misspoke. Others considered the moon's disappearance might have cast a spell to result in such a command.

"Silence!" Julius' shout brought his detachment to order. In normal circumstances, such a display would incur swift punishment. As Julius recalled his own reaction to Herod's plan more than a week ago, the men's response seemed natural and even admirable.

Gaius continued. "Herod has ordered this operation. Every one of you swore a vow of obedience to the Emperor, whose will it is for Herod to rule. Which of you opposes the will of Augustus?" No one spoke. Their oath as legionnaires bound them to absolute loyalty on pain of death. "Very well. See to it you obey your orders. Julius! I give the troops to your charge!"

Gaius watched the detachment leave the courtyard and exit the Antonia through the western portal. Returning to his command room, the tribune glanced at the maps used to plan this raid. Gaius fingered the purple stripe on his toga, the sign of his office. It had always been an emblem of honor to him. Tonight, its soft texture reminded him of the fleecy bedding with which his wife lined their son's crib years ago. Children, he thought. I've just sent my men to butcher children! Gauis swung his arm across the table, scattering maps and charts across the floor. He dropped into his chair, hands pressed to his forehead. Children, he thought, just children.

* * *

"Mary!" Joseph bolted upright in bed, his body shaking and drenched with sweat.

"Joseph, what is it?" Mary held her husband's hand and felt a cold clamminess.

"Yeshua! Yeshua, is he here?"

"Of course. He's asleep in the corner. What is wrong?"

Joseph sat very still. "Pack what's needed for a journey, a long one. Yeshua is in danger."

"Danger? Joseph, you frighten me. What has you so disturbed?"

"Do you remember my telling of the dream that convinced me to remain with you? Like the dream that told me what name to give. But now..." His words trailed off.

"You've had another dream?"

"First the Magi came, the ones you told me of. They tried to warn us of something. Then a man wearing a bloody crown broke into our room, demanding we give him Yeshua. When we refused, he grabbed him. I lunged, but could only lay hold on Yeshua's blanket. We struggled, and he pulled Yeshua away. He wanted Yeshua, Mary: Herod wants him now! We have to go!"

Dreams directed their lives at critical times before. While the idea of leaving Bethlehem bewildered her, Mary knew her husband to be serious. "In the morning, we – "

"No, you don't understand. We must leave now, tonight!"

"Joseph, there must be more time. There's the packing. And friends to tell."

"There IS no time. The dream wasn't exact, but the danger is near."

"Very well." Tears in her eyes, Mary tossed off the blanket and began to dress. "I'll put clothes together, if you pack food. Then we can waken Naomi and Joshua to say goodbye."

Mary was not prepared for Joseph's reply. "It's best we tell no one."

The young woman spun to face her husband. "These people took us in, gave us a home! And you'd have us walk out, without even a word?"

"I know, I know. It hurts me to think of such flight. But it's for their own good."

"You think avoiding them will make the pain less?"

"No, it probably worsens it. But if this threat to Yeshua

does indeed come from Herod, our friends are better off not speaking to us. If it's discovered they did, Herod would question them. Even if we told them nothing, they might not be believed."

"Shouldn't we at least warn them of the danger?"

"Herod seeks Yeshua. The best way to protect Naomi and Joshua, and Rebekah and Elias, is to give no hint of our leaving. That way, they have nothing to hide."

Mary buried her face in her hands. Too much to think of, too little time. The dreams had not failed them before. Joseph's reasoning made sense. Yet leaving without a goodbye? She felt suddenly cold, and afraid, and alone. Joseph held her close. "For Yeshua's sake, we have to go. And for our friends' sake, we must not tell them. Not now."

Within an hour, the family stole in silence to the stable. The donkey twitched its ears as Joseph bridled her and gave her a long drink of water before setting out. An extended and difficult journey to the southern city spoken of by the Magi loomed before them. Neither Joseph nor Mary dwelt on the exceptional darkness of this night. The dream's threat cloaked all.

Without the moon's light, none observed the family's departure – not even a lone Roman scout, posted northeast of town. Only a few hours now separated Joseph's dream and Bethlehem's nightmare.

CHAPTER XIII

The morning outside Bethlehem proved far more taxing for Julius and his command than expected. They had arrived close to midnight after the five-mile march from Jerusalem. Even for soldiers used to bivouacking in the field, the stony fields on the ridge above Bethlehem made for uncomfortable sleeping. Making matters worse was the wind that arose shortly after dawn. It was not a cooling breeze that might invigorate after a restless night's sleep. The wind blew hot, wafting scents of sulphur and bitumen up from the direction of the Salt Sea. Within a few hours, the wind increased in speed, lofting up dirt and fine sand into the air.

Julius spent the morning making sure that men and horses were sheltered from the wind's effects and hidden from sight. He hoped the water they brought would be enough, since it now had to be used to slake thirst as well as soak kerchiefs shielding noses and mouths. Closer to noon, Julius scrambled across to the sentry's position for a report on any activity.

"Town was quiet all night, centurion. What movement started with daybreak died down quickly with this damned wind."

"Very good, Marcus. It'll just be a couple of hours until we strike. Until then, keep watch as best this weather allows."

Before Julius started back, Marcus asked: "Sir, do you think this wind has anything to do with last night's eclipse? On the march, there was a lot of talk about it being some omen, especially with what we've been tasked to do."

The thought had crossed Julius' mind as well, but superstitions were not something to be encouraged on the eve of missions. "Moon and wind are beyond our control. What we do in spite of such things are what serving Rome requires. Carry on." Julius headed back to rejoin the rest. He knew he'd not fully spoken the truth. It was not just moon and win beyond our control. It was the ravings of Herod. Ravings that poised Julius and his men in service that would soon have them killing children.

* * *

"Steward, have my orders been carried out?"

Antigonus bowed low as he stopped at Herod's bedside. "Yes, my King. Two piles of wood have been prepared, soaked with oil. And the guards report that Judas and Matthias have been bound in preparation."

"Fine. Fetch the house servants to dress me, and the pallet for carrying me into the courtyard. It will bring joy to see these two tossed into the flames, a fitting sacrifice for their unthinkable destruction of my eagle. I only regret Saripheus didn't survive to see this day. That would have pleased the righteous anger of Adonai Elohim, don't you agree?"

Once again, Antigonus bowed. This time not in deference, but in hopes of hiding his recoil at this last bluster. "My Lord, your wisdom is unapproachable."

Antigonus left Herod's sleeping quarters to summon the servants. Herod's mind drifted from disappointment at the untimely death of Saripheus to a timeliness the king considered delicious. The hour of the scribes' immolation would coincide with the time, as Gaius had sent word, that the troop led by Julius would swoop into Bethlehem and eliminate his rival there.

* * *

"Praise be to Adonai for this newborn son of the covenant!" Rabbi Hananiah spoke the blessing even before the midwife had completed her cleaning and swaddling of Bethlehem's most recent arrival. Normally, the rabbi would have waited a few more hours to visit the family after birth. But what with the wind seeming to grow each hour, he decided to come once he heard Rachel had been summoned. And Hananiah was pleased he had: to be present for this child's birth, to hear the mother's wailing in birth pangs replaced with joyful cries at the sight of her firstborn, to attend to a father's words of love as he held onto his wife in wonder and relief. It seemed to the rabbi such moments as this only magnified why the Torah so celebrated the love and power of God for life.

Perhaps it was such focus of this moment's joy that caused Hananiah and the others to disregard another sound that had nothing to do with the wind's howling. What could not be ignored, however, was a pounding on the door. The parents looked up in their embrace, bewildered at who would dare venture out into today's storm? Rachel held the newborn in her arms, the swaddling still not done. Hananiah moved to the door and asked, "Who do you seek?"

The answer came in the door being flung open and two legionnaires striding into the room, gladius' drawn. Their first sight was Rachel with the child.

"Boy or girl?" came the shout in broken Aramaic.

Rachel clutched the child more tightly and glared at the intruders. "How dare you? This child has just been born, what business is that of yours?"

"Boy or girl?"

The demand infuriated Hananiah, who now stepped between Rachel and the soldiers. "You have no place here. In the name of Adonai, I – "

One of the Romans slammed the hilt of his sword into the rabbi's face, sending him sprawling back onto the floor. "For the last time, boy or girl?"

Rachel's eyes widened in anger and fear. "Get out of this house!"

The other Roman, called Demetrius, had enough.

Drawing his arm back, he swung and slashed his gladius across the neck of the child and then struck deep into the chest of Rachel.

"No! No!" The mother's scream at the sight was joined by her husband flinging himself in the direction of the executioner. Before any revenge could be taken, the gladius of Demetrius' partner struck him down, dropping the father's body on top of his lifeless son and Rachel, whose gasps for breath were choked by blood before ceasing altogether.

"Let's go, Marcus, nothing more to do here." On his way out, Demetrius kicked the rabbi as he struggled to pull himself up. "Stay down, old man, or you won't see another day." As the pair walked out the door, all that could be heard were the rabbi's groans and the guttural soundings of a mother's inconsolable grief. This was the first of Bethlehem's homes and families to be violated – but not the last.

* * *

"Your Majesty, please reconsider. The winds of the *khamsin* fill the air with sand. Venturing into the courtyard for the executions could make your breathing more labored and – "

"Silence!" Herod's patience with his two court physicians had long since been taxed by their failure to improve his health to date. "Seeing those two burn for their crimes will be far better medicine than the toothless potions you've concocted."

The pair bowed before Herod, who was already placed on the pallet and waiting to be carried out for the spectacle. The senior of the two offered before they exited, "May this day bring you, O King, the satisfaction you seek and the healing you deserve."

Once they had left, Herod turned to Antigonus. "Are all things ready in the courtyard?"

"They are, Majesty. The guards have bound Judas and Matthias hand and foot, and they are stationed by each of the pyres, waiting for your order to set torches to the piles."

"And they have not gagged them, have they? I want to hear their screams!"

"It is as you directed, my king."

"Very well. Let us be going."

"One more thing, my king." The steward held up a long linen scarf in Herod's direction. "To filter the dust from the air, as the wind has not let up as yet."

Herod grabbed the scarf, then threw it back to Antigonus. "No doubt, those damned physicians gave you this, as if I never knew life in the desert. Fools! We go, now!"

The steward signaled the servants on each side of the pallet, who now took hold of its handles and lifted, then made their way to the door leading to the courtyard. Earlier in the morning, Antigonus had summoned the house servants to seal the windows and doors as best they could to prevent the wind from howling into the king's room. But now, once the door opened, a blast of hot air burst through, carrying a cloud of fine particulate that immediately evoked a surge of coughs from the pallet bearers as they made their way forward.

"Antigonus! The scarf!" The steward rushed to cover the king's face as he gasped for breath. "Why didn't you tell me it was this bad?!"

The steward's apology could barely be heard above the wind as the cortege entered the courtyard bearing the king. Herod could make out the figures of Judas and Matthias in the hands of his guards. "Take me to the prisoners!"

Once the pallet was borne next to the two, Herod ordered the pyres to be lit, then looked at the condemned. "A fitting day for your deaths! No one follows you now, no one will remember you. Especially you, Judas, now that your father is dead – and your wife, whom I will soon see to it that she becomes camp whore at some Roman outpost on the frontier. Die in that knowledge, die in – " Whatever Herod intended to say was lost in a fit of raspy coughs triggered by the dust choking his throat in spite of the scarf.

In that halt to Herod's invective, Judas shouted: "Your death is not that far away, pig. Your putrid flesh is a judgment of the Holy One on the abomination you have become!"

Herod's eyes widened in anger, but his choking prevented voicing anything other than a high-pitched, "Into the fire!!"

In the moments since being lit, the wind fanned the oil-soaked wood into a rage of flames. Two guards grasped each prisoner, one under the arms and one at the ankles. Swinging the captives back and forth to gain enough force to pitch them high, the guards let the prisoners fly. Both landed in the midst of the flames, their weight crushing down the top level of branches so that they sunk into the heart of the conflagrations. Herod's wish to hear their screams came to fruition but was short-lived, as the heat sucked the oxygen from their lungs and silenced them.

Whatever expected satisfaction the king received by hearing their death throes was interrupted by a sudden shift in the wind's direction that flung embers from the fire straight onto the pallet and Herod. "Help! Damn you fools! Help!"

The servants rushed to move the pallet out of the wind's path. "Water, get water!" Antigonus' screams bolted the guards toward the courtyard's fountain, where pots and helmets were used to douse water at the outbreaks of fire on the pallet and Herod himself. As they did, Herod bellowed curses and pleas to God.

Once the final bits of smoldering on the pallet had been extinguished, Antigonus ordered that the king be returned to his chamber and placed in the bath. Herod soon immersed in cooling waters poured over him. As he took away the scarf from his face, Herod thought he could smell in it the scent of the scribes' burning flesh. Or was it the smell, as Judas' dying curse invoked, of Herod's own putrid flesh? Herod shuddered in the answer now forming, as the water began to sting the open sores and ulcerations that betrayed Herod's living decomposition.

* * *

By late afternoon, the column of Roman cavalry and foot soldiers led by Julius was less than a mile away from Jerusalem. Unlike many returns after action, there was not the usual undercurrent of bravado regarding who had demonstrated the greatest valor, or whose sword had achieved the most kills. Part of the quiet owed to the continuing wind and dust that plagued them as they marched. Part of the quiet owed to the lifeless bodies of Demetrius and Marcus, strapped across the backs of a horse, cut down by the blade of the village's now-dead carpenter.

But even more, the quiet owed to the orders they'd followed that day. Every manchild under the age of two had been put to death – and where there was uncertainty as to age, no chance was taken. Blood flowed. Not every member of the detachment had used their gladius, but those who didn't had witnessed the killing blows to toddlers and infants, and those adults who paid the price for interference with the detachment's purpose this day. In the aftermath of ordinary combat, to have an enemy's blood splattered on one's uniform or arm was something of a badge of honor. As these men rode or marched toward the Antonia, the first wish of more than a few so marked was not a jug of wine – but a hot bath to wash away all traces of today. The wine would help later, to forget, if you could forget.

So it was for Julius. While he never used his own weapon, he'd seen his fill of carnage against children. Beyond that, the killing of the two men in his detachment had taken place right in front of him. On the ride back, he had run the scene over and over again in his mind, wondering if any of the fault for their deaths owed to him. The only mistake, it seemed, was that they didn't take into account the possibility of resistance.

Julius thought back to the time when Demetrius

asked him when they would see any action, a typical attitude of newly assigned legionnaires. Julius recalled he only cautioned that such encounters would come soon enough. Maybe he should have upbraided the young man even more, or doubled-down on his training. But even had he done so, would that have been preparation for a knife pulled from beneath a robe? As for Marcus: Marcus had seen action. Julius selected him as sentry on this command, for he knew and trusted him. Marcus loved the legion – yet that very love, Julius considered, became his blinder. His thought of taking vengeance against the slayer of Demetrius caused him to act rashly, thinking only of how he might take down this man and not how to defend himself if needed. More training should have been done, Julius thought – more training WILL be done in the wake of today.

Today. *What have we done today?* Julius thought back to what preceded the deaths of his soldiers, how he had spurred his horse to cut off the retreat of families rushing for safety? *What if I had just let them go? What if, in just this one instance, Herod's orders had been set aside, and I'd told the men to just move on? Two children would have lived. A father would have lived. Demetrius and Marcus would have lived. Was it worth it? Was Herod worth it? Was the oath I once took to serve Rome worth the blood needlessly shed in that alleyway, in the whole town?*

"Enough!!" Julius' outburst caused Lucius, his second in command riding behind him, to come up beside Julius and ask what the centurion had meant, as the wind made hearing difficult.

"Nothing really, Lucius. This day has done enough. Pass the word back to have the troop pick up the pace, so we can end this god-forsaken day and spend whatever's left in the Antonia."

Julius listened to Lucius' shouts as he rode back to pass on the command. But even the quickened pace could not quiet the question filling his mind and sickening his stomach:

What have we done today?

CHAPTER XIV

A single lamp flickered in a desolate room. Deborah, Naomi, and Rebekah huddled around it, as if nearness to light could dispel the darkness that had engulfed Bethlehem.

"David. DAVID!" Hannah sobbed her dead twin's name in sleep, as Naomi rocked her daughter in her arms until she slumbered once more. Naomi was grateful for Hannah's clinging tonight. David was dead. Joshua, disgraced before all, had fled into the hills. Simeon had refused to allow his mother's or anyone else's touch after witnessing his father's cowardice. Naomi had only Hannah to clutch. She held on as though Hannah anchored her to a life never to be again.

"What evil has Bethlehem done to you, O Lord, that you bring this upon us?" Deborah swayed back and forth as she raised her lament. "You slew the Egyptian firstborn to break Pharaoh's stubbornness of heart. Why have you slain our lastborn, and broken our hearts?" Deborah's wail resembled the sound of a mother moaning in birth – but no life came tonight.

Rebekah sat still much of the evening. Staring into the lamp's flame, she conjured images of the hurried burials that afternoon. Tradition called for interment before nightfall on the day of death. So many victims – seventeen children and five adults – meant little time spent upon each individual. A cursory washing of wounds preceded anointing the bodies with the few spices and ointments at hand. Mourners then wound long cloths round each corpse.

A problem arose: where to bury the dead? A trench

large enough to fit the victims would have required enormous effort to dig in the rocky soil. No one in Bethlehem possessed the physical or emotional strength needed for such a task that day. Caves large enough to hold that many bodies were located too far away. All, that is, save one.

Two of Joshua's acquaintances, men with whom he frequently aired his talk of revolution, suggested the cavern chamber located at the back of the inn's stable. "It's not far to carry the bodies. Besides, Joshua has no life here anymore. He let his son be killed by his own blade."

Word of Joshua's act spread. Few had risked their lives by daring to prevent the slaughter. Some, like Rabbi Hananiah, were beaten. Others were killed, including the village's midwife Rachel. But of all who stood by and did nothing, Joshua's performance reeked as that day's most blatant cowardice. Naomi did not object to using the stable for the burials. She wanted nothing more to do with Joshua, no reminder of him or the stable whose safety escaped them.

Rebekah pondered how Naomi must feel. But the widow of Elias also wondered if anyone could understand her emotions. Joshua was a coward – but Joshua was alive. Elias was dead. Did he have to attack the Romans with his knife? Did he have to leave her a widow? Rebekah swallowed her pain, not wanting to reveal the anger toward her husband.

At the same time, a new role faced Rebekah. She was the widow of one already being exalted as a hero, a martyr. She looked at Saul, sleeping in the corner. In one hand, he held the bloodstained carving of a wolf. In the other, he grasped pieces of a wooden lamb, broken when his brother Levi fell to the ground in death. All afternoon, Saul tried to put those pieces back together. He fell asleep this evening, the shattered fragments of the lamb still in his hand.

* * *

"Julius! I expected to see you much sooner after your return from Bethlehem."

The centurion saluted Gaius. "I've been soaking in the baths of the Antonia, Tribune. It turns out the blood of children does not scrub off so easily."

Gaius discerned a slurring in Julius's speech, and suspected no small amount of wine had accompanied his washing. "This has not been the best of our days, my friend."

"To the contrary!" Julius flopped down on the couch of Gauis. Not usual behavior for a centurion in the quarters of his superior, but Gaius allowed that this was no typical day. Julius rambled on. "Actually, this was an easy day – killing infants is simple, you know. With a man, you've got to take care to aim your sword thrust, lest you only wound him. But with a child, there's no worry, Gaius. The blade's broad enough to kill, no matter where you strike!"

Gaius recognized the bravado. He'd heard it before, typically from men who killed for the first time. The bluster attempted to mask that initial revulsion at taking another's life. "Julius, listen to me. Herod ordered this. You had no choice. Don't carry his guilt on your shoulders."

"Guilt? Did I speak of guilt?" Julius rolled onto his back, staring at the ceiling's mosaic tiles. "We do not give Herod enough credit. Rome wastes so much by fighting armies. Why not seize the initiative, kill our adversaries while they suckle their mothers' teats? It's all so simple!"

Julius' attitude began to irritate Gaius. Drunkenness did not excuse lack of control or judgment, especially for a centurion. The tribune took a different tack. "I see. All we have to do is convince Augustus and the Senators of the Legions' new role: slayers of children!"

"Precisely."

"And what better spokesman than you? Tell me, since the Senate will no doubt ask: what's it like to kill a child?"

Julius sat up. The day's events surged back through the wine's blur. "What's it like ripping a child out of a mother's arms, and skewering the body on a sword or spear?!" The centurion's head spun, but he continued. "What's it like trying to take a child from an old woman who refuses, then slashing them both with a gladius?" Julius felt the same cold sweat that had driven him to the baths and the wine. "What's it like to kill children, tribune? It's to butcher whatever it is that separates us from animals." Julius paused, then spoke in an even-toned voice. "We crossed that line today, Gaius. We've become Herod's animals. We murdered children!"

The head of Julius slumped and he began wringing his hands. He couldn't see any blood, but he felt its stain. Silence held between the two men for a long time. The tribune finally grasped the shoulders of his centurion. "The murders are Herod's, Julius. Not yours, not your men's – but Herod's. The guilt belongs to him."

Julius lifted his head. His eyes met those of Gaius. "Then why wasn't Herod the one staring into the faces of the mothers we ruined? Why weren't his the hands splattered red? Tell me that, Gaius. We'll have the nightmares, not him!"

"Listen to me, Julius. The wine not only makes you melancholy – it dulls your reasoning. Herod commanded us instead of his own troops to commit this outrage for one purpose: he doesn't want the blame. But it is his! The only way guilt escapes Herod is if you take it on yourself. Don't give him that victory!"

The words sobered Julius. "You may be right. But you weren't there today."

Gaius released the centurion's shoulders and walked to a window overlooking the courtyard. Unlike the night before, the moon shone bright and full. "Killing is not new to us, Julius. You and I have spilled the lifeblood of many with whom we've had no personal quarrel. In that sense, they differ little from Bethlehem's children. You didn't raise your sword today in anger or passion, but obedience. Guilt belongs to pigs like Herod, who abuse obedience. They're the murderers. We're only soldiers."

Only soldiers, thought Julius. Did the people of Bethlehem make such distinctions this afternoon? Did the boy sprawled across his dead father, holding some carving against his neck, view Cassius and Lucius as pawns of Herod? Julius looked down at his own hands, still wrinkled and moist from bathing. In truth, he'd not wielded his sword against anyone today, child or adult. He, like Herod, simply ordered others to do the work. The centurion found himself brooding as he drifted into sleep: just how different was he from Herod?

* * *

"Who's there?" The doors creaking startled Naomi and the other women. In grief, they expected no one at this hour. What if the Romans came back to finish today's grisly work?

"Naomi," came a whisper, "it's me. Joshua." Naomi, along with Rebekah and Deborah, stood up and stared at the haggard figure stepping into the room. Dirt covered his face and clothes. Bruises and scratches marked his feet and lower legs. He moved toward Naomi.

"Don't come any closer!" Naomi stood. "What do you want?"

"Naomi, this is my home. I've come to – "

"Home? You dare speak of home?" Deborah glared at Joshua. "What did home mean to you this afternoon, when you stood by and let your son be killed!"

"Woman, I'll not be spoken to like that in my own house!"

Deborah thrust her face inches away from his. "Don't speak of manners to me, coward! You blathered for years about fighting Rome. Your chance comes, and what do you do? You hand your knife to a Roman, who kills your son with it. Then he taunts you to use it on him when he tosses it back to you! And all the while, you stay on your knees. You disgust me!"

Deborah punctuated her closing insult with a slap across Joshua's cheek. He raised his hand, only to feel his wrist seized. "Don't dishonor yourself any further, Joshua.

Or is striking a woman your brand of courage?" The voice belonged to Rebekah.

Her rebuke stung Joshua far more than Deborah's. This was the widow of his best friend. The sight of Elias knifing the two Romans, only to be killed, haunted Joshua.

Rebekah released his wrist. "You disappoint me, Joshua. Had you joined Elias, he might have survived. Our children might have survived. But you didn't – and they didn't. You are as a dead man to me, as one never born." Rebekah turned her back to him.

Joshua looked at those in the room. To Rebekah, he no longer existed. Deborah defied him by her very presence. His oldest son, Simeon, rolled over and half sat up, wakened by the noise, rubbing the sleep from his eyes. And there was Naomi.

"Naomi, please, can we talk?"

"There's nothing to say, Joshua." Naomi's voice cracked "Nothing."

"You're my wife. We've a son and daughter to think of."

"We had two sons, Joshua. TWO sons!" Naomi felt her voice break, but she pressed on. "You had two sons to think of today, but you only thought of yourself."

"Then you would have preferred my death?"

"Don't twist my words. I didn't want you dead. Rebekah didn't want Elias dead. But you might have saved David's life, or at least avenged him. He was your son, for God's sake!"

"So I'm to be blamed for the Romans killing David, and Levi, and Elias, and the others."

Naomi shook her head, tears streaming down her face. "Joshua, you never will understand! I don't blame you for the Romans' atrocities. I blame you for not treasuring your son's life enough to risk your own. Would you have done anything if Hannah had been threatened, or Simeon – or me? Or not even then?"

Joshua stood silent. Similar questions nagged him

since he left. But he wanted to hide from their answers. All he could manage now was, "Am I not allowed in my own house?"

Naomi's two fists slammed into Joshua's chest. "Get out of my sight! All you see is yourself! I hate what you've become, Joshua. Leave us alone, as you left David to die!"

Sobs engulfed whatever other words Naomi intended to say. Deborah and Rebekah supported Naomi as her body tremored uncontrollably. Simeon walked to her side. When Joshua reached his hand toward him, the boy recoiled. "Now you've hurt mother, too. I hate you!"

Eyes out of focus, head ringing as though a clap of thunder exploded inside his ears, Joshua stepped out the door and into the night. Never again could he walk through that threshold. Joshua's life in Bethlehem was ended. Dazed, he plodded to the east. To the wilderness of the Salt Sea. To the hideouts of bandits called the Sicarii.

* * *

"Julius. Wake up!" Gaius shook the arms of the centurion. More than an hour had passed since Julius dozed off on the tribune's couch.

The centurion started to stand and stretch, then abruptly dropped back to the couch, his hands pressed against his temples. It did nothing to relieve the ache in his skull, but his mind cleared. Parts of his earlier conversation with Gaius flashed before him.

"Gaius, forgive my behavior when I came. And my words. I had no right."

"No apologies needed. Had I your assignment, I would probably have said worse."

"Thank you for hearing me out. But I should leave so we both can get some sleep."

"Before you go, Julius, one matter needs discussion. Do you feel up to it?"

Though his temples still throbbed, Julius nodded in affirmation.

Gaius pulled a chair in front of the couch and sat in front of the centurion. "Tomorrow, I send a messenger to Herod, bearing a report on Bethlehem."

"I'm sure he'll be pleased."

"Pleased, yes. Satisfied – I don't know. You spoke your mind when he gave this assignment, and Herod does not tolerate honesty very well."

"After witnessing the slaughter, my words then were too mild."

"You'll get no quarrel from me on that. But Herod is apt to hold that against you. Even though you carried out his command, he's still liable to seek revenge and send out his killers."

The back of Julius stiffened, a smirk crossing his face. "Trust me, Gaius, I'd receive Herod's envoys with the same welcome given those toddlers in Bethlehem. Except I would thoroughly enjoy my work."

"Julius, you know such men don't give opportunity for defense. They wait for sleep, or some unguarded moment. You're too valuable to the legion, and too good a friend, to risk losing. Here." Gaius handed Julius two rolled parchments, both bearing the tribune's seal. "Take these to Varus, the Roman governor in Antioch. One document orders your assignment to the Legion headquarters there. Even Herod doesn't dare send his murderers into the provincial capital."

Julius took the two papers. "You're the only tribune under whom I've served, Gaius. I stand ready to remain with you here."

"I know, Julius. But I will not allow Herod to rob Rome of one of its finest."

Julius stood straight, raising his right arm to his chest in salute. "No centurion has ever had a better tribune, Gaius."

Gaius returned the salute, his face opening into a large smile. "The second document I've given you requests my immediate transfer to Antioch. If Varus agrees, and he does owe me a favor or two, I'll soon be there to make sure you tell others what an outstanding leader I am!"

Both men burst into laughter.

"The next time we meet," Julius offered, a more serious tone entering his voice, "we'll drink Syrian wine. And if the Fates are just, Herod will be dead by then. If so, I say we toast his dear memory by pissing in the wind that carries his rotting body and spirit to hell."

CHAPTER XV

The wrinkled hands of Rabbi Hananiah ben Johannan unwound the Psalm scroll, his face still bearing bruises from the beating he endured the day of the massacre. In all his years in Bethlehem, the rabbi had never presided over such a service. Seven days had passed since the slaughter and hasty burial. These days of *shivah* required the bereaved to stay in their homes. The rabbi had declared a special service of prayer on this eighth day, when families and townspeople could gather to remember the slain. The synagogue over-flowed with worshippers, spilling into the courtyard and around the building. Hananiah's fingers traced over lines he slowly pronounced: *"Out of the depths, I cry to you, O Lord. Lord, hear my voice!"*

Other sounds accompanied the words of the rabbi. Some mourners whispered prayers, others moaned or wept. An eerie harmony blended this outpouring of grief with the readings. In the midst of this, two women shrouded in black spoke in low tones.

"Naomi, I must speak to you." Rebekah leaned toward her friend so no other could hear. "It's about Mary."

Naomi cast reddened eyes to the widow of Elias. "Have you heard from her?"

"No. But I've been thinking about her, and Joseph – and Yeshua."

"As have I, with thanks. Whatever reason they left, at least they were spared our loss."

Rebekah's throat tightened. "That reason is what interests me, especially today. While we grieve our sons' and my husband's death, Mary rocks Yeshua in her arms."

"Rebekah!" Naomi's voice raised, then lowered again. "Mary had no hand in our grief!"

"That's what I first thought. Their departure seemed only a fortunate coincidence. But over these past seven days, I've had much time to think."

"Think of what?"

"Did you hear what the soldier said to Joshua after David's murder?"

Naomi bowed forward, pressing fingers into her forehead. "Isn't it enough for this service to remind us of that day?"

Rebekah wrapped her arm around Naomi's shoulders and whispered more urgently, "I only do this because I feel there's more to Mary's absence than we think."

"I heard nothing. I collapsed at David's murder."

"Naomi, the guard that ridiculed Joshua said something about Herod being wrong – a king never would come from such a town."

Naomi shifted on the bench to face Rebekah. "What are you saying?"

"Remember our first meal with Joseph and Mary? When we learned his family actually came from Bethlehem, and descended from David's line? Joseph mentioned then he didn't want anything said of his ancestry because of Herod."

"Yes, but – "

"Everyone knows Herod's behind these murders! Rumors of his illness abound. What would he most fear, but someone stealing the throne in his weakness!"

"But what has all this to do with us, Rebekah – or with Mary?"

"With Mary, perhaps little. But with Joseph, everything! No family left in this town has ancestry that could make claims to the throne. None has Davidic lineage, save Joseph! His son was the only one in the entire village Herod might perceive as a threat!"

"Why? Why would a king fear a child?"

"Who knows? Many say he's mad. But I swear I heard the Roman say `Herod' and `a king from this town' and `your sons' when he humiliated Joshua. Think of it. Only one son here possessed royal blood and a father who feared Herod – Yeshua!"

"But Yeshua wasn't killed, he was gone. Why our children instead?"

"Maybe the Romans weren't sure which young boy he was, so they took no chances."

"And Mary and Joseph?"

"They had to have learned about the raid somehow. It's no coincidence, their leaving that very night. They knew, and they didn't tell us! They gave us no warning!"

"No – "

"They allowed all the sons of this village to die!"

"No more, Rebekah, please!"

"They stripped us of our children, and their boy lives!"

"DAVID!!!" Naomi tore away from Rebekah's arm, jostled through the crowd of startled worshippers, and ran out the door. "They've killed my David! Murderers!"

Rebekah followed after Naomi, finally catching up with her in the stable. Ax in hand, Naomi swung wildly at the manger. "Your son should have died, not mine! Your son!" The mother of David collapsed into the trough's broken fragments, weeping.

Rebekah embraced Naomi, joining in her tears before intoning a curse. "Blood calls for blood! Like our sons, may Yeshua die in another's place – condemned by his father's silence!"

* * *

"Come closer, Cassius." The guard's report of the assault on Bethlehem pleased Herod, who received the legionnaire in the Jericho palace. Gaius had already dispatched a messenger with news that the king's orders had been obeyed. But Herod was not satisfied with a sketchy sum-mary of the operation. He demanded testimony from an eyewitness to the operation. Gaius obliged, sending Cassius some days later. The king wanted to be sure the plotters had been foiled. He needed assurance the right child had been killed.

Cassius did not disappoint him. With embellishment of his own role, the legionnaire assured Herod that no boy under the age of two survived.

"You've served me well, Cassius, as have your fellows. As token of my gratitude, take this. I'm sure the century will find use for its contents." A steward handed Cassius a square wooden box and opened the lid, revealing a cache of silver shekels.

"Excellency, you are more than generous, though no reward is needed."

"You rendered me a great service. And I repay my friends. That reminds me, I ask that you take a message with you to the Antonia."

"With pleasure, your Majesty."

"Tell Julius I desire an audience with him. I wish to personally reward him."

"Excellency, Julius was transferred to Antioch. He already serves there."

The news disappointed Herod. The centurion's insolence at their last meeting gnawed at him. But perhaps, it was revenge enough that Julius commanded the death of Herod's rival.

"Tell Gaius, then, to send my thanks to Julius. By the way, did you find your quarters comfortable last night?"

"Far more than I'm accustomed to, Excellency. These baths rival those of Rome."

"Yes, they do. A safe return to Jerusalem for you, legionnaire."

Cassius saluted the king, then bowed. The steward Antigonus escorted him out the door and led him to the stable. Anxious to be within the Antonia's walls by nightfall, Cassius urged his horse up the road that ascended from the Jordan valley.

Several miles into the canyon rising from Jericho's plain to Jerusalem's ridge, Cassius thought back to his visit with Herod. In spite of all the rumors of his noxious spirit, he'd spoken pleasantly enough. And didn't the king give him the box of shekels?

Cassius reflected on the resentment he faced as a soldier of Rome, resentment arising from jealousy of his and Rome's power. It must be the same with Herod. People hate him simply because they envy him. The weight of the shekels encouraged the thought that people didn't see the good qualities of this generous monarch – even as Cassius didn't see movement in the rocks ahead where the road made a sharp bend.

* * *

"My name is Kharman, steward of this sanctuary of the Magi." The man towered above Joseph and Mary, but his smile relaxed the pair. The grey-white hair topping his head and fluffing his beard contrasted sharply with dark bronze skin. "May I help you?"

"I hope so," Joseph replied. "We need lodging."

"Pelusium has several fine inns for pilgrims. I can escort you to several close by."

"A magus named Utan directed us to come here. He spoke with me in Bethlehem."

Kharman turned to the woman who addressed him, then to the child carried in Joseph's arms. His eyes closed as he inhaled a deep breath. "May God be praised for your safe arrival." Opening his eyes, he continued. "Utan and Balthasar said you might come, though I had no idea when. Please, consider this your home for as long as you need. Come inside and rest."

His emphasis on their safe arrival puzzled Joseph and Mary, but the invitation to rest took precedence for the moment. For eight days, the family journeyed on foot to this distant destination. They traveled mainly at night to avoid contact with Roman or Herodian patrols. Once south of Gaza, they relaxed, feeling safe distance separated them from Herod. Utan's suggestion of using Pelusium as a refuge brought them here.

Kharman escorted the travelers to an inner courtyard. At the center stood a fountain flanked by marble benches, where pomegranate and sweet-smelling laurel trees provided shade. He pointed to a door west of the fountain. "You enter your rooms there. One for sleeping, one for cooking, another for cleaning. I will arrange for hot water to bathe." Mary looked down to her arms and feet, caked with dust, as were Joseph's. The offer came as a welcomed luxury.

"And if you please," the steward concluded. "I would be honored to host you at my table for the evening meal. Meet me here when the sun is just above the outer wall."

"Thank you, Kharman. We will join you." Though his host was Egyptian, Joseph understood the gift of hospitality. If God brought the Magi to them, surely the Almighty would abide their breaking bread with a Gentile.

As Kharman turned to leave, Mary called to him. "When we came, you offered a prayer of thanks for our safe arrival. Had there been some question of that?"

"Your journey was a long one, Mary. Bandits often ply that route. But now, if you'll excuse me – "

"Wait." Mary stepped close to her host. He sought to avert her eyes, but she saw in his signs of moistness. "What do you hold from us, Kharman? Please."

The steward sat on one of the benches, motioning his guests to do the same. Joseph set Yeshua between himself and Mary. The fountain's bubbling provided the only sound for some time. Finally, Kharman spoke. "You've not encountered other travelers on the way?"

"No," said Joseph. "We avoided contact with anyone."

"And how long has it been since you left?"

"This is the eighth day. Why?"

"Ships sail from nearby ports on the Nile to Caesarea. Yesterday, a trader from Alexandria visited our market. He'd heard news of an atrocity ordered by Herod."

The sound of Herod's name caused the couple to tighten their grip on one another's hands. Mary stroked Yeshua's head with her free hand as Kharman continued. "I'm not sure of the day, but it must have been soon after your departure. The king dispatched troops to Bethlehem. All boys under a certain age, the trader wasn't clear whether two or three years, were executed."

Mary gasped. "Not all the children! Surely, not them all?"

Kharman nodded. "That is what he said. Every single boy of that age. Dead. And others, too, seeking to defend the children. The trader specifically mentioned a carpenter and midwife."

Joseph felt nauseous. Hadn't he resisted Mary's advice to tell the others? Hadn't he decided to avoid giving them warning? The lives of innocent children, his friend Elias, even Rachel, paid for his miscalculation. Joseph seized his robe at the neck with both hands, then ripped it down the center seam as he fell to his knees. "My God, what have I done!"

Yeshua looked at his sobbing mother, and his father now pounding himself on the chest. Even the stranger in the white robe wept. It frightened Yeshua – he wanted to be safe. "Manger," he whimpered. "Manger." Then Yeshua cried too.

* * *

As Cassius rounded the road's sharp corner, his eyes fell on an overturned cart in the center of the path with a man trying to right it. To proceed meant riding close to either of the rockfaces that defined both sides of this narrow pass. Daydreaming of his audience with Herod made Cassius careless. He didn't study the craggy outcroppings above nor draw his sword as a precaution. Just as the Roman passed by the cart, the trap sprung shut. Two men leapt from the rocks above, pulling the legionnaire down from his horse. Two more sicarii scrambled down to help subdue Cassius. The cart driver produced a set of ropes used to bind the Roman.

"Get him into the cave before anyone else comes!" The men dragged Cassius to a grotto partway up the hill, obscured from any who might pass on the road below. Another sicarii tethered the Roman's horse behind a large boulder.

Inside the small cavern, thick fumes from an oil-soaked torch clogged the nostrils of Cassius when he woke. His head ached. Blood trickled down his forehead into his eyes, blurring vision. He tried to scream, but a cloth drawn across his mouth prevented it. His arms and legs were bound tight. He struggled. The men in the cave laughed.

"So, this is Cassius, the hero of Bethlehem?" Cassius groaned as someone kicked him in the stomach. "How many children died by your hand, pig?"

Several sets of hands lifted up Cassius into a sitting position, then dragged him so that his back pressed against the cave's wall. The cart driver knelt by him. "Herod's not the only one with spies. We know of your audience with Herod, concerning Bethlehem. Shall I go on?"

Cassius labored to shake his head from side to side.

"You weren't so modest at the palace, when you boasted of killing children."

Cassius again attempted to move his head, but a slap to the face stilled him.

"You disappoint me, taken so easily. You didn't disappoint Herod, or he wouldn't have given you all these shekels!" Another set the box on the soldier's lap.

"What is it you planned to buy with this reward, Cassius? A Phoenician woman's favor? Oh, I know, your BURIAL!" Cassius bolted upright, shocked by the burning of a dagger thrust in his side at this last word. His eyes wide open, Cassius saw the rest of his captors unsheath their daggers and advance. Cassius felt more burning – then he saw, and felt, no more.

* * *

At dusk, a Roman patrol spurred their horses through the gates of the Antonia. "Summon Gaius!" The tribune soon appeared. One man dismounted and ran to Gaius. "We found the horse wandering at the head of the canyon leading to Jericho. It carries Cassius."

Gaius went over to examine. The legionnaire had been strapped by ankles and hands around the horse's torso and neck. Stab wounds covered his body. A saddle bag held a wooden box, filled with a single bloodstained shekel. Wedged into the armor protecting his back was a dagger, the favored weapon of the Sicarii. A single word had been cut into one of the leather bands used to cinch his breastplate: *BETHLEHEM*.

CHAPTER XVI

The sandals of Alexas slapped the tile floors of the Jericho palace. His clopping footfalls on the marble hallway mingled with groans resonating from a room at the corridor's end. Moments before, one of Herod's physicians sent a messenger to waken Alexas with news of another setback that convinced the doctors of Herod's imminent death. The family must be summoned. Alexas now hunted for words to explain his wife's absence. A mixture of grief and relief at her brother's worsening condition had caused Salome to drink herself into a stupor.

At the door to Herod's room, Alexas paused. Two physicians engaged in muffled conversation stepped toward Alexas and bowed. "The king has little breath left," one whispered. "Go to him now. We can't say how long he will remain conscious."

Forewarned, Alexas moved inside toward the bed. Herod, who married ten wives and sired even more children, faced death without a single blood relative at his side. The king's habit of victimizing his own family succeeded in emptying his deathbed of mourners. Five days ago, a premature rumor of Herod's death motivated his son Antipater to claim the throne. Hearing the report, Herod ordered his bodyguard to kill Antipater, barely ten days after Bethlehem's carnage.

A low moan rumbled from Herod's chest, followed by a gurgling in his throat. In spite of the sour odor spewing from Herod's mouth, Alexas leaned close to the king's face and spoke. "It is Alexas." No response. Alexas strengthened his voice. "Herod, can you hear me?"

Herod's eyes rolled, then his head shifted to the side on which Alexas stood.

"My king, it is Alexas."

A raspy voice replied: "Alexas, thank you." Herod's breathing remained rapid and shallow, causing some time to pass between his phrases. "Salome... I don't see her."

Alexas grasped Herod's hand, only to let go when the king winced at the pressure. During his last trip to the hot springs at Callirrhoe, Herod remained in the waters longer than his physicians advised. His mind, dulled from drugs and disease, reasoned that doubling his immersion would likewise multiply its good. On being drawn out of the water, Herod's flesh became even more tender and swollen.

"Forgive me. I didn't realize the touch of my hand would hurt."

"Salome." Herod spit out a mass of phlegm to clear his throat. "My sister... Where?"

"Her love for you, her dear brother, only magnifies the pain she feels for your suffering. Grief overwhelms her."

"Damn her. . . damn them – all!" The rise in emotion clogged his windpipe. Coughing followed, then more gurgling. Alexas turned his head as a thick yellowish liquid dribbled out the side of Herod's mouth. "Why does none of my family attend me?"

"I am here, my king."

"My sons, I must get –" Herod's attempt to push himself up ended in a shriek at the fire racing through his arms. His eyes widened in terror, as if catching sight of some evil in the room. "Alexas... the pretender from Bethlehem... didn't we kill him? No! Get him out of here! Go!"

Alexas started to answer, but hesitated as Herod's face stiffened. One short gasp, then a sound like water swirling down a drain came from his throat. Herod breathed no more, a look of terror etched on his motionless face.

* * *

Sabbath brought a day of rest, if not peace, to the family of Joseph. Mary and Yeshua had yet to venture beyond the walls of the refuge. Only by insisting that he earn his keep had Joseph persuaded Kharman to allow him to practice his carpentry. The magus arranged small jobs in the city this past week, in addition to some overdue projects on these grounds.

Today, however, there would be no wielding of axe or saw. Instead, the carpenter began the morning by lighting a candle and reciting prayers. Mary held Yeshua on her lap while her husband intoned the *Shema: "Hear, O Israel, the Lord our God is one Lord. You shall love the Lord your God with all your heart, and with all your soul, and with all your might."* Mary repeated the words, words beginning to sound familiar to Yeshua.

The child felt his mother's body sway in rhythm with his father's chants. Finally, Joseph fell silent and Mary stopped rocking. Yeshua tugged at the scarf draped over her head and flowing onto her shoulders. "Manger now?"

Mary brushed her boy's forehead with her fingers. "Not now, Yeshua. It's a long way away." She pressed her lips to the top of his head, and a tear tumbled from the bridge of her nose onto his hair. Bethlehem remained a raw wound for her and Joseph. Yeshua only wanted to play in the stable with his friends.

Joseph took Yeshua from Mary and lifted him in the air. "What say we sail that boat of yours by the fountain?" Yeshua nodded. The boy wriggled out of his father's grasp and ran to retrieve the boat Joseph had carved for him.

Mary rested her head against Joseph's shoulder. "When will it get any easier?"

"Maybe the question is if, not when. Only Adonai can say."

In a moment, Yeshua raced back, boat in hand. Hollowed out from a twisted branch of willow the thickness of a man's arm, Joseph added a twig's mast with a triangle of cloth to imitate the boats that sailed the Nile. Together, the three walked to the garden fountain. Yeshua busied himself launching the boat, blowing the sail to speed it across the fountain, racing around to send it back again. If it touched an edge, he made sounds of some great shipwreck.

Joseph and Mary watched his play so intently that they didn't notice the approach of Kharman. "A good Sabbath to you," he offered. "I see Yeshua has an early morning at sea."

"A blessed Sabbath to you, Kharman," Joseph replied, stretching out his hand to shake that of his host, as Mary bowed slightly in the Egyptian's direction.

Kharman watched as Yeshua went around the far side of the fountain, then sat on a bench to see how long it would take his craft to run aground. "I have news you should find of interest," Kharman said. "While you were at your prayers earlier, I accompanied the servant to market. A seller of figs said his supplier told him that Herod has died."

Mary squeezed Joseph's hand. "Do you believe him?"

"If it had been only the one man, I might have doubted. But others in the market spoke of the death also. When I made inquiry at our city's garrison, they said the same. Died in Jericho."

"Then we can go home to Bethlehem!" For the first time since arriving in Pelusium, Mary's voice rose in excitement.

"Maybe home," Joseph replied, "but not Bethlehem. I don't believe I could face those we left – I left."

"Joseph, you can't keep blaming yourself." Mary stroked her husband's chin, but he showed no response. The guilt of giving no warning to the others still gnawed at him.

Kharman laid a hand on Joseph's shoulder. "Mary's right. But as for going home, stay here for the time being. Herod's death may actually result in more strife, at least in the short run. Those he's kept under thumb could stir trouble, and there's no need placing yourselves – and Yeshua

– in jeopardy. Let a few months pass and see. Then you can decide. In the meantime, Pelusium and I remain in need of a good carpenter."

Joseph knew Kharman to be right in his reasons for staying, even as he had come to appreciate the Egyptian's friendship in the time spent there already. "Thank you."

Kharman glanced over to Yeshua, still at play. "I am the one to be thanking both of you.
You give me the privilege of offering sanctuary to your son."

Yeshua blew on the sail until the boat and he came round the pool to rejoin his parents and Kharman. Kharman knelt down beside Yeshua, who now had the boat in hand. "Someday, my young sailor, you shall set forth on a great voyage."

* * *

Julius reined his horse to a stop. The news of Herod's death had taken several days for messengers to make the long journey from the Antonia to Antioch. Several more days had passed before Julius could prevail upon Varus, Rome's governor at Antioch, to grant him leave for this journey. By the time Julius had reached the fortress of Herodium, after a brief but necessary stop in Bethlehem, it had been more than two weeks since Herod had been entombed here. Scanning the royal resting place, Julius thought how in death Herod remained as obscene as he was in life. Before constructing the fortress, Herod commanded an unusual feat of engineering. The hill on which it would be set was raised and shaped to resemble an immense breast. Perhaps the king felt, in specifying Herodium for his burial, he might slumber within its earthen bosom. Julius spurred his horse up the hill to trouble Herod's sleep.

A guard posted at the gate stepped alongside the centurion's horse. Julius handed a scroll to him. "I am the centurion Julius, sent by his excellency Governor Varus, from Antioch. I bear special oblations for Herod's tomb."

The Syrian eyed the seal on the parchment. "Inside.

And ask for Onias."

The centurion followed the instructions, glad that Gaius insisted on providing official documents. Once inside the fortress, another guard directed Julius to Onias, a scribe charged with the care of Herod's resting place. "Let me have a look at your scroll." Onias scanned it, then looked at Julius. "You bring an imperial gift for Herod's tomb, approved by tribune Gaius?"

"Yes. Gaius and I served Herod in Jerusalem for a number of years. It's Rome's tradition to offer a gesture of regard to a fallen leader."

"Very well. I'll take you there. Tether your horse to one of these posts."

Securing his mount, Julius followed Onias through several passageways, descending stairways at the end of each. Julius estimated they'd gone down some forty feet below the fortress' entry before reaching a door manned by two guards. Onias waved them aside, pulled a key lashed on a long string to his belt, and opened the door. A mound of dirt still somewhat fresh stood heaped in the middle of the room. "The body was set in a marble sarcophagus, then lowered into the ground. It wouldn't do to have pilgrims watch nature's work on the body."

"No," answered Julius, "I suppose it wouldn't." Julius approached the mound. As he knelt at what he presumed to be the head, he noted Onias remained in the room.

"Onias, I intend no disrespect, but might I have this moment to myself?"

"I'm directed to remain in the room, to prevent profaning of the grave." Onias clasped his hands behind his back, glanced through the door, then shuffled to the side of Julius. In a lowered voice, the scribe intoned: "But, you being a centurion, perhaps an exception could be made."

Julius jingled some coins inside a small pouch beside his sword. Onias bowed. "I see no reason to interfere with your ritual." On the way out, he counted the coins Julius handed to him.

Once Onias closed the door, Julius ran his fingers through the dirt covering Herod's grave and whispered. "I've heard the Pharisees speak of some doctrine called resurrection, where the dead are raised from the ground." Julius lifted another pouch hidden underneath his breastplate. Opening the drawstring, he poured coarse soil from it into one hand and said loudly. "I bring you a gift, Herod son of Antipater." Julius tilted his hand, allowing the dirt he'd gathered on the outskirts of Bethlehem to spill upon the grave. The Roman kneaded this dirt deep into the burial mound, then intoned his final words in Latin, in case Onias or the guards were listening:

"Sentimus humum Bethleem Herode inebriabitur sanguine filiorum interfectae. Illic dies puli valeant vicus testimonio tuo damno et requiem dabo tibi."

("Feel the weight of Bethlehem's soil, Herod, soaked with the blood of its murdered children. Should there be a day of raising: may the witness of this village damn your soul, and give you no rest.")

CHAPTER XVII

Dawn's mist hugged the land, a thick white cloak hovering a few feet above the ground, shrouding landmarks, making travel impossible save for those acquainted with the terrain. Abraham risked the journey to Bethlehem, as he had done every month or two for the past ten years to bring a stipend to the widow of the martyr Elias. No one, not even the Rabbi Hannaniah, questioned the source of Rebekah's income. It was enough to know the widow received support, no matter the hand that offered the gift.

The community from which Abraham bore these gifts burrowed deep in the Salt Sea wilderness. Known as *New Damascus*, its residents long ago fled Jerusalem's corrupted environs for a purer outpost in which to keep God's Law. A peculiar mingling of the Sicarii's tactics with an extreme devotion to Torah mingled visionaries together with men-of-arms.

Two such men accompanied Abraham on this trip. The first was a Pharisee called Saddok, the second a Galilean named Judas. "Before we go to the house of Elias' widow, we must see the cave." Abraham reined his horse to a stop and dismounted. His fellows did the same. Tying their animals to a post, the three men entered a grotto in the hillside. "Oil lamps burn as a memorial," Abraham added, taking one from its holder at the entrance to light the way.

Wooden stalls and troughs showed no signs of recent use. A few seasoned implements hung from rafters wearied with the weight of years: a long-handled sickle, several rakes and hoes, an old pitchfork. At the cave's rear, a passage jagged sharply to the left, only to be blocked by rows of rocks reaching from floor to ceiling. At the base of the rows stood a clay jar, which Abraham opened. Saddok reached in, retrieving a dusty leather scroll. As he unwound it, Abraham held the light to illumine the scroll's script.

Saddok's eyes reddened as he turned to face Judas. "The names of the innocents, and those who died with them." Saddok pronounced each name silently in his mind, before speaking: "And here, at the end, is the name of Elias. The only one who shed Roman blood that day."

"May his name be praised," offered Judas. "This is a solemn place you bring us to, Abraham. Even after ten years, the blood of these martyrs cries out. Anyone who tolerates Rome's violation of our land should make pilgrimage here. Maybe then, vengeance would flow."

Kneeling before the wall of rocks, Judas stared at the beams overhead. They brought to mind timbers used in another Roman atrocity. Shortly after Herod's death, this same Judas led an uprising in Galilee. He and his followers raided the royal armory at Sepphoris near Nazareth. For a week, the newly-armed rebels held the upper hand. Then, two Roman legions from Syria arrived and squelched the rebellion. Judas escaped, but many of his men were captured. To discourage further uprisings, the Romans crucified all of the captives. Their deaths inflamed even greater hatred in Judas. God claimed the right of revenge in the scroll of Deuteronomy. Judas simply longed to be Adonai's right hand in exacting that retribution against the crucifiers of his men – and, looking to the scroll in Saddok's hand, the murderers of these children.

* * *

"Joshua! More wood for the fire!" The voice of Kohath spurred Joshua's foraging for sticks and branches, not an easy job in these hills. Few bushes, and fewer trees, survived the arid climate. Still, he'd managed to find an armload of tinder, enough to warm waking comrades until the sun's heat made them yearn for evening's coolness.

"Damned cook, you still don't know to get enough wood the night before for morning!" Kohath, leader of this small group of bandits, enjoyed bullying Joshua. He didn't like the man nor did the others, as the former innkeeper lacked the stomach for violence and the cunning to plan robberies. However, they'd never had a cook as good as Joshua. Keeping him for those chores enabled them to focus their skills in thievery. Merchants, caravans, an occasional Roman supply column: Kohath and his men took every opportunity for ambush that came their way.

In his early years with Kohath, Joshua sought to advance in the band's ranks. Such challenges always involved fighting. The few times he brought himself to blows, Joshua received dreadful beatings. In time he gave up, and accepted the abuse heaped on him.

"Be grateful I keep you to fix our meals," Kohath blurted, as Joshua dropped the wood next to the fire. Then, grabbing hold of Joshua's tunic, Kohath pulled the hapless cook down to him and announced: "Maybe if you cook well, we'll find silk garments for you in the next caravan. Then you can dress like the woman you are!"

Harsh laughter from the others followed Kohath's insult. But Joshua thought to himself: what could he do? Better ridicule than fists.

This day, Kohath had more pressing business than the usual mocking of Joshua. "Lamech and Benjamin and I go to Tekoa," he announced. "Judas the Galilean has called a meeting."

"Watch yourself!" cautioned Tobias, second to Kohath in authority, "Judas and his kind are fanatics."

"What's wrong, afraid they'll make a rabbi out of me?"

Tobias scowled. "The last sons of bitches to follow Judas ended up on crosses."

"Don't take me for a fool, Tobias. Judas and his Torah have no hold on me."

"So why meet with him at all?"

"Because I say so!" Kohath did not like his decisions questioned, even by his most able lieutenant. "I don't go there to be preached to. I go to see if a profit's to be made. And if Judas steals Rome's attention, that'll mean fewer patrols to worry us."

Kohath's words brought nods of agreement from the circle of men warming themselves at the fire. "Kohath, I could help you at that meeting." The voice belonged to Joshua, busy passing out brought bread and honey to the group. "For years I saw to the comfort of strangers staying at my inn. Once, I even met Judas when he lodged with us."

Kohath sneered. "Tekoa's not far from Bethlehem. Aren't you afraid your mother-in-law might see you? I hear she'd carve your hide to clean herself with when her blood flows!"

After more laughter, the others returned to tonight's plans. Joshua resumed his search for firewood, resigned to the only role these sicarii would allow him.

* * *

"Rebekah, this is Judas, from the town of Gamala in Galilee; and his companion, rabbi Saddok. Brothers, meet Rebekah, widow of Elias." As Abraham spoke, the visitors bowed low.

"Please, come inside. I'm sure your journey has you chilled."

As they entered the main room, a young man feeding sticks into the fire stood. Rebekah spoke again. "Judas, Saddok, this is my son Saul."

Though just fifteen years of age, Saul's height reached nearly six feet. Dark curly hair covered his head. Saul extended a hand to the visitors and his friend Abraham.

Judas admired the firmness of the youth's grip. "I am pleased to meet you, Saul. You remind me of my boys at your age. Except you already are as tall as they now stand!"

"You're Judas the Galilean?"

"I am."

"Would you tell me of the time you stole Herod's weapons? And your war with Rome?"

"We'll see. Although it's important to remember, it wasn't my war with Rome – it was our people's war. Your war."

"And the war of Elohim Adonai," Saddok added. "One of many battles that will be needed to rid us of these sons of darkness."

Saul's eagerness to hear more was interrupted by Rebekah's hospitality. "You would honor our home by breaking bread with us."

The five sat on cushions arranged around a low table. Platters crafted by Elias were laden with dried figs and goat's cheese and wheat bread. A pitcher filled with goat's milk passed from hand to hand as each filled their cup. Saddok offered a blessing, and breakfast commenced. The three men, hungry after their ride through the night, downed several helpings. Saul listened in awe to Judas' stories of the ill-fated uprising after Herod's death. Abraham recalled his first encounter with Rebekah and the martyr Elias on the night of the Purim riot, when he escaped to Bethlehem and found refuge at its inn. "Whatever happened to the innkeeper, the one who disgraced his family and village?" Judas asked.

Rebekah glanced at Abraham, then answered. "Joshua fled to the Salt Sea wilderness the night of the massacre. Some say he joined the Sicarii, though I can't imagine him as one. Others say he perished, punished for his sins."

"From what Abraham told us, Joshua deserved the Almighty's judgment." Saddok spoke without emotion. "You can't worship Elohim when you're on your knees before a Roman."

"And what of the coward's widow and children?" Judas continued.

"This past year," Rebekah began, "they moved to Jerusalem. Life was hard for them here. Many shunned Naomi for her husband's act. And her children, especially the boy, suffered greatly. The teasing he endured drove him to a temperament opposite his father. Simeon would fight anyone who insulted him."

"I never liked it when they made fun of him." Saul spoke the truth. More than once he waded into fights to rescue his friend.

"Such a tragedy," muttered Judas. "One son killed by a father's cowardice, while the other dies a little each day."

"It is as Moses taught in the Torah. `*I the Lord your God am a jealous God, visiting the iniquity of the fathers upon the children to the third and fourth generation.*'"

"You mean Simeon's going to be punished for what his father did?"

"Saul," said his mother, "don't question the rabbi."

"Actually, Rebekah, Saul's question relates to why I asked Abraham to arrange our meeting. It has to do with Elias – and Saul."

Rebekah puzzled at Judas' meaning. "Go on."

"Your husband – your father, Saul – is honored throughout the land. Even in Galilee, we hold the name of Elias in esteem. His martyrdom inspires those who seek to break the yoke Rome imposes on our people. Because of your father, the two of you will never lack for friends."

"We're grateful for that support. And my son and I share that same hope of deliverance."

"Then hear my request." Judas leaned across the table toward Rebekah. "Elias is a martyr: think of the excitement if the son of Elias joined with us. Abraham tells me your son is bright as well as strong. Allow him to study with those who've supported you, who believe Israel must be free to serve a God who tolerates no rival. Those who believe the death of Elias, and Bethlehem's innocents, require blood-vengeance."

"Eye for eye, life for life," Saddok punctuated.

Rebekah reflected on the offer, and the cost: a widow

of ten years, both parents dead, only Saul remained in her life. The possibility of losing her son stirred bitter memories of losing Elias. But the desire to avenge her husband's death had grown over the years. She looked at Saul. A leather thong encircled his neck, and a worn wooden figure hung from a knot in the leather: a wolf, with faint red stains marking the grain. "May I visit Saul?"

The face of Judas beamed. "Saul's education would be in Abraham's community, New Damascus. You can visit, or you can live there. Whatever you choose, Rebekah."

"And how soon would this take place?"

"I meet tonight in Tekoa with men interested in our movement. We'd pass through here again tomorrow, then journey on to New Damascus. You could join us, if you will."

Rebekah refilled the five chalices with wine. Taking hers in hand, she lifted it toward Judas. Rebekah's other arm clasped the shoulder of her son. "Saul, we have much to do. Tomorrow, you and I leave with these men for New Damascus."

"YES!" shouted Saul. Any regrets at leaving this village were, for the moment, lost in the excitement of traveling with the likes of Judas the Galilean.

Judas raised his chalice and struck it against Rebekah's. "You won't regret this decision, Rebekah. You bring honor to Elias' memory, and your own sacrifice. And you, young man," Judas continued, turning to face a grinning Saul, "what dangles around your neck?"

Saul fingered the wolf, then scooted his cushion next to Judas. The youth's smile disappeared as he told the story of the carving, and how it came to be stained with blood.

CHAPTER XVIII

"Simeon!"

Simeon slowed his pace, unsure whose voice called his name as he neared the home of his great-uncle Nathaniel.

Another yelled: "What's wrong, Simeon of Bethlehem? Afraid to stop?"

Recognizing the second voice to be Malachi's, Simeon spun around. Simeon and Malachi had apprenticed under a Jerusalem stonecutter for several months, a position arranged by Nathaniel when the family first arrived from Bethlehem. Somehow, Malachi learned of the shame of Simeon's father. One day at work, Malachi's needling of Simeon about his father ended in a fight. The stonecutter released both young men. The pair had not seen each other since.

"You cost me my job, coward."

"You should've thought of that when you wagged your tongue."

"Better to wag a tongue than turn a tail, as your father did."

"Watch your mouth, pig, or I'll bloody your face again."

"I don't think so. My friend Menelaus and I are going beat my lost wages out of you!"

"SIMEON! NO!" The cry startled all three. It came from Hannah, racing down toward the street from Nathaniel's porch. She'd been waiting there for her brother to return for lunch.

Malachi laughed. "Isn't that touching, Menelaus? Simeon has a woman to shield him."

"Leave my sister out of this, Malachi."

"Your sister? This is even better. After we've had a turn thrashing you, we can have a turn entertaining her! Having cowards for a father and brother hasn't spoiled her looks."

Hannah, not quite twelve years of age, matured early. Young men often presumed her to be three or more years older than she was. Hannah found her beauty and the attention it garnered a hiding place from being Joshua's daughter, much as Simeon sought escape in aggression.

"Hannah, go back home!"

Hannah stopped short of the trio but continued to plead her case. "Please Simeon, you know how your fighting hurts mother!"

Malachi howled as he goaded his intended victim. "Yes, Simeon, PLEASE! Mama doesn't want her little boy to fight. She wants him to grow up and be like his daddy – and run!"

Malachi barely finished speaking when Simeon's fist crashed into the taunter's mouth. The blow sent him tumbling back. In an instant, Menelaus leapt toward Simeon. Pivoting to one side, Simeon grasped the airborne attacker and slammed his back down against the cobblestoned alley. The impact emptied his lungs and left Menelaus gasping for air.

"Simeon, look out!" Hannah's scream caused her brother to raise his arms. His left forearm absorbed the blow of a brick aimed for his head. Malachi groped for another object to hurl, but it was too late. Simeon ran headlong into Malachi, driving him into a rock wall. Hannah covered her mouth as Malachi's head snapped back against the stone. The shock of the collision stunned both young men, their bodies crumpling to the ground. Simeon stirred, but Malachi remained motionless. Blood oozed from the back of his head.

Attracted by the initial shouting, Nathaniel and several servants had come out of the house and now reached the scene. "They picked the fight with Simeon," cried Hannah. "Then the one at the wall threw a brick at Simeon, and, and…" Hannah's sobs stopped her words.

A servant examined Malachi, then waved at Nathaniel. "The young man breathes, sir. He's unconscious, but his face winces when I pinch him. He should be alright."

"Simeon," Nathaniel shouted, "what is wrong with you?"

"They started it. If Hannah hadn't screamed, I'd be the one on the ground."

Nathaniel looked at Menelaus. "What do you say about this?"

"Malachi said we'd just scare him. Rough him up a bit, but that's all. When the girl shouted, I saw Malachi throwing a brick at Simeon." The young man had heard enough about Nathaniel's reputation to know he didn't want to risk becoming the Sopher's foe.

Nathaniel started giving orders. First, to his servant: "Take this Malachi home. Warn his family I'll not tolerate Simeon being attacked." Turning to Hannah: "You, go in and tell your mother no harm's been done. And Simeon, a word with you!" Nathaniel grasped Simeon by the shoulder: "What am I to do with you? Do you realize how close you came to killing someone?"

"I didn't look for this fight."

"The fact remains: you put us all in an awkward position – and today, of all days. The new Roman procurator receives me at the palace! Simeon, you and your temper disgrace us."

"I see no disgrace in standing up for one's family."

"You don't understand. Your fighting drove your mother to come here. This time you'll escape judgment. But what of the next time? Your next victim may not be so fortunate! What will it look like for one living under my roof to be found a murderer?"

"I see, this isn't about me, but you! Fine! I'll leave."

"And go where? Do what? You've failed every apprenticeship I've arranged."

"Then let me take up the one trade I have a knack for: enroll me in the Legion's auxiliary." Simeon had been considering this for some time, but feared to say anything until now.

Nathaniel leaned back, caught by surprise. "Serve in Rome's army?"

"Why not?"

"I don't know." Nathaniel paused to stroke his beard. "A member of the Sopher's family in the Legion? It may not be suitable."

Simeon's jaw tightened with anger. In one sense, his great-uncle and father were cut from the same cloth of preoccupation with self. "Then enroll me under a different name. That way, no one need know a kinsman of yours serves Rome. As for me, a new name offers a chance to get out from under the cloud of being Simeon, son of Joshua."

"That just might be a wise choice," Nathaniel mulled. "A new identity would suit you, as it would the family." More silence passed before the Sopher spoke again. "At my meeting this afternoon, I'll see if an arrangement can be made. But hold off on speaking to your mother or grandmother about this until we know more." Nathaniel and Simeon parted, both pleased at the possible release from burdens each tired of.

* * *

Several hours later, Nathaniel made his way toward the palace built by the late King Herod at Jerusalem's western wall. As troublesome as the episode with Simeon was, its consequence paled in comparison to the changes sweeping Jerusalem and Judea.

At Herod's death ten years earlier, a dispute over which of his sons would rule resulted in an agreement imposed by Rome. Three sons received portions of their father's lands. The elder, Archelaus, gained control of Judea and Samaria. His reign proved disastrous from the outset.

Rebels burned the royal palace at Jericho. The Temple's own treasury was looted. Archelaus lacked his father's survival instinct. Complaints against his rule mounted from Jew and Samaritan alike, until even the Romans wearied of his brutish incompetence. Less than a week ago, Nathaniel watched a procession exit the city gates. A Roman escort flanked Archelaus and family, their eventual destination rumored to be exile in the city of Vienne in Gaul. Archelaus' territory, including Jerusalem, passed into the direct control of the new Roman procurator Coponius. He, in turn, was under the jurisdiction of the provincial governor of Syria, Quirinius.

Nathaniel reasoned these larger matters did not bode well for his own position as Sopher. With Herodian rule in Judea eliminated, what if the procurator saw fit to govern without the Temple's input? What if today's summons to meet Coponius became a dismissal? Nathaniel had grown attached to the power he wielded. Its loss held no appeal.

"Nathaniel, the procurator has been expecting you." The steward Antigonus stood beside the eastern gate to the palace complex. "Please follow me, sir."

"Thank you, steward." A brief smile crossed Nathaniel's face as he walked behind the aged and stooped Antigonus. For years this steward served Herod and then Archelaus. No one knew the palace and its management as did Antigonus. Nathaniel admired the Romans for their wisdom in retaining his services to smooth the transition.

"Here we are, Sopher." Antigonus opened the door, and then added in a whisper, "I'm sure you'll remember the room."

Nathaniel remembered. His first meeting with Herod occurred here, as the king reclined in the large bath at the room's center. Today, servants scrubbed the tile of the emptied pool. An imposing man in a toga directed the uncrating of marble statuary.

"My lord Coponius, this is the Sopher Kohen Gadol, Nathaniel." Antigonus bowed and exited. Coponius turned to the visitor.

"Come in, come in. And watch out for the workers."

Nathaniel approached the procurator, bowing his head ever so slightly. "Welcome to Jerusalem, lord Coponius. The High Priest Joazar sends greetings and blessings."

"Give him my regards when you – say there, you two carrying that crate! Take care how you set it down!" Coponius shook his head. "Such servants they give these days. Unless you stay close to Rome, you never can be sure of quality. But what do the Senators care how their emissaries are treated, as long as they lounge comfortably in Rome?"

"If there is anything we can do to help, sir –"

"No, no, these are the burdens of public service on foreign soil. Being a procurator is a great sacrifice for a citizen of Rome, you know. Away from home and family, a barely livable wage. Why, a younger man would find a better career fighting the Gauls! I serve out of pure devotion to Augustus, and to lend my expertise to – look out, watch what you're doing with that pedestal! Just a moment, Nathaniel."

Nathaniel observed Coponius guide the servant's positioning of a cherublike figure near the bath. Sacrifice? Burdens? This Coponius might be shrewder than his meddlesome appearance revealed. It was known that only proven businessmen from Rome's equestrian class filled the ranks of procurators, along with an occasional Legion officer. The right placement by the emperor, proper attention paid to the position, and a procurator could harvest a windfall of profit, especially from tax assessments. The empire depended on provincial goods to fill its coffers, and procurators who generated such wealth shared in the bounty.

"Now, Nathaniel, where were we?"

"You spoke of the price of service as a procurator."

"Yes, that's right. A dear price it is." Coponius stepped close and put an arm around the shoulder of the Sopher, unaware of the traditions that called for Jews to avoid contact with Gentiles. "Nathaniel, you and I live in difficult times.

I hold no illusions that the people of Jerusalem desire a Roman to govern them. The only advantage I have in their eyes is the remembrance of Archelaus. Still, I can't ignore this province's severe fiscal needs."

Nathaniel nodded, judging that Coponius would now broach the real topic of the meeting.

"Nathaniel, even a procurator has those he must listen to. For me, it's Quirinius, the province's governor. Before leaving for Jerusalem, I spent some time with him in Antioch, reviewing his plans. One of those goals brings you into the picture. I'm told you are a man of influence in this city. With the Herodians gone, the people look to the Temple for leadership. As the Sopher to the High Priest, you have the ear of Joazar. And Joazar has the crowd's attention."

"I do advise the High Priest on some matters," replied Nathaniel, intrigued at the sudden insight shown in Jerusalem's workings.

"Don't be so modest, Nathaniel." Coponius led the two of them toward a small side room once used as a dressing chamber. "You understand how things are done, and how to get them done. In not too many days, your help will be needed."

"And what assistance could I provide the procurator?"

Coponius ushered Nathaniel into the side room, closing its door behind them and lowering his voice. "Quirinius has ordered a provincial census. I'm told there are Jews – some of them thieving Sicarii, some fanatic religionists – who might resist such a move with violence. We need responsible men to sway the populace from such an unfortunate response. Which, as we both know, Rome would be forced to suppress. We need Joazar to speak for reason and calm."

"Might the census be delayed, or an exemption granted for Judea or Jerusalem?"

"No. Accurate numbers are needed to assess taxes at a fair level. All provinces take census at regular intervals, and

Judea's is long overdue: twelve years, according to our records. This census is the first priority of Quirinius."

"How soon will this take place?"

"Shortly after your Harvest Festival – what do they call it?"

"Pentecost," came an answer from behind a table in the corner, "coming as it does fifty days after their Passover Feast."

Nathaniel peered at the man now advancing toward them out of the shadows. Grey streaks marked hair once raven black, but there was no mistake. "Julius!"

"Nathaniel. I'm honored that you recognize me."

"Quite a surprise, eh, Nathaniel?" The words of Coponius, along with an enthusiastic slap on his back, magnified Nathaniel's genuine shock. "I told Quirinius I needed someone with experience. He said he had a legion officer who'd formerly served in Jerusalem. Knew the people and the system here. Julius has been briefing me ever since. Even on you!"

Julius smiled as he noticed Nathaniel's eyes rise. "It speaks well that you still hold the office of Sopher, Nathaniel. The lessons of Saripheus must have taken root."

Nathaniel's thoughts flashed to this day's difficulties with Simeon. "I hope so, Julius. My predecessor was an insightful man."

"And a man of honor and family," added Julius." It seems his unjust end produced no good, save your rise to the rank of Sopher."

"An ascent I'd gladly have exchanged for his safety," countered Nathaniel, unsure if Julius intended his words as a mere comment or a critique. Nathaniel had known Julius and Saripheus enjoyed a mutual respect and friendship, something that had never developed between him and the centurion. Nathaniel had been pleased at the abrupt transfer of Julius years back. His reappearance now proved unsettling.

"Gentlemen, in spite of the pleasantries of reunion, we've a census to organize. I hope your past workings lay the foundation for a profitable venture in the days ahead."

* * *

Twilight's final tints of pink and blue splashed thin wisps of clouds to the east. By a grove of sycamore trees, nearly fifty men huddled round a burning pile of branches. What gathered this mix of rebels and thieves and pious fanatics was a meeting with Judas. Evening's chill drew them close to the blaze, as Judas' words enticed them to a far different conflagration.

"Long years ago, God raised up a prophet from this very village. Amos, the shepherd of Tekoa, a commoner like every one of us. But Amos heard the call of God, and announced God's judgment upon the house of Israel. Why? Because she mingled her religion with idolatry, and polluted God's commandments with injustice. The rich knew ease, the poor knew oppression, but Amos – Amos spoke truth to those grown fat on lies!"

The fire's flames made the face of Judas glow orange. Pitch-filled wood crackled in accompaniment to his voice. Essenes robed in white, Pharisees with hoods drawn tight against the night air, Sicarii clothed in coarse leather garments: all listened to the Galilean.

"And still in our day, idolatry and injustice foul this land and Mount Zion itself. In the Antonia, Roman soldiers bow down to their battle standards. In Herod's palace, a new procurator rules by Rome's law rather than the Torah given by Adonai Elohim on Sinai. God waits for us to act. Messiah will not come until we make the land fit for the Almighty's holy habitation."

Murmurs erupted. Pharisees and Essenes differed on the nearness of Messiah's coming. Most Sicarii had no interest in such conjectures. Kohath rose to speak on their behalf.

"Judas, my men want action, not talk. We'll stick our daggers in Roman backs when the time's right. But don't look for us to hang on crosses, like others you've led!"

Judas eyed Kohath, knowing the issue of timing to be on the mind of all those seated about the fire. "Do you know, Kohath, as you plunge down a canyon wall upon a Roman supply train, whether you will come away with a load of treasure straining your back or a legionnaires' sword burning your gut? Devotion to a cause needs no guarantees, only trust of the Most High."

Kohath pressed on. "We already wear warriors' clothes, teacher. What'll make these Pharisees and Essenes set aside prayer shawls for breastplates?"

"These times, Kohath, and their opportunities. Pharisees see Coponius as no friend of Torah. Essenes fled the Temple's corruption long ago, awaiting the day when sacrifices may be offered by pure hands. Our chance is finally at hand. No Herodian traitors remain in Jerusalem to deceive the people by false claims to royal authority. As soon as Coponius gives us cause to rise up, the crowds will follow. They've no other choice."

"But there still are some in Jerusalem," one of the Pharisees interjected, "among the traders and Temple authorities, who stand with the Romans."

"Indeed there are," answered Judas. "And they shall suffer judgment. The people grow sick with Jerusalem's pollution by these deceivers. Cutting them off will cleanse Zion. When our fathers first took this land, God commanded its unclean inhabitants to be put to the sword. Today, we need to reclaim this land, and purge it of its offenders. You, Kohath, and others of the Sicarii: you've wielded daggers for yourselves in days past. The Holy One calls for men zealous for his Torah, prepared to strike down the unrighteous. Do you add your arm to Israel's host?"

Kohath stood, stepping to the edge of the blaze. Drawing his dagger, Kohath ran its blade across his forearm until blood trickled down into the fire below. "Tonight, my blood feeds this fire. In nights to come, we will feed it with the blood of our enemies'!"

The fire hissed from drops of blood boiling on its embers. Moving alongside Kohath, Judas took the bloodied dagger and thrust its blade into the flames before drawing it across his own arm. "Let God's righteous fire purify this land through blood! We fight as those zealous for our King, Elohim Adonai. That is who we are, and how our enemies will know us: *ZEALOTS!*"

CHAPTER XIX

The hinges of the great oak door groaned as Nathaniel swung it open to enter the High Priest's chamber. Joazar awaited the Sopher, seated at a table bare but for two burning candles. As Nathaniel approached, Joazar motioned to a second chair alongside the wall. "Tell me of your meeting with Coponius yesterday."

Nathaniel drew the chair to the table. "Troubling matters loom ahead."

"Why?" The high priest's fingers drummed nervously against one another. Ever since he saw Archelaus paraded out of Jerusalem, Joazar feared he might be the next one removed. As Herod's last major appointee still in office, he speculated the Romans might make him their final victim of political housekeeping. Beyond that, reports came to Joazar of radicals among the Pharisees and Essenes contemplating action against him, even whispers of assassination.

"The procurator announced a census will be carried out in Judea."

"A census?" Joazar shook his head at the lack of judgment. "Doesn't he know our people's disgust at such countings? Grumblings still remain from the registration under Herod."

"Coponius doesn't ask our advice on the matter." Nathaniel leaned forward. His elbows and folded hands rested upon the table, forming a V-shape whose point aimed at the High Priest. "I have served you ten years, Joazar. May I speak frankly?"

"Go on."

"For now, the Romans value you as a spokesman, whose word still sways opinion in Jerusalem and beyond."

Joazar's tightened brow relaxed somewhat. "Perhaps I can use that influence to enlighten them, urging them to hold off on this counting."

"No." Nathaniel's blunt reply caused Joazar to shift back in his chair. "Your value to them only remains if you follow their purposes. Contradict them – well, you know the fate of Archelaus. I've no doubt Coponius would not hesitate to remove you."

"But what of the fanatics? You know the rumors, how the likes of Judas the Galilean plot to destroy any seen co-operating with Rome."

"Judas may be dangerous, but he doesn't have a cohort of armed legionnaires in the Antonia! Cast your lot with Co-ponius, Joazar. If the people raise an outcry against the census, tell them it's only a routine matter of bookkeeping. No freedom is lost."

"But Nathaniel, the Torah teaches how God punished Israel for the census in David's time. How would it appear for the High Priest to go against Torah?"

"Joazar, no penalty resulted when Moses conducted a census after the Exodus from Egypt. Torah tells us, God *commanded* that counting. Can God command the doing of evil?"

Joazar's appointment as High Priest by Herod stemmed less from sophistication in scholarship and more from being a brother-in-law to one of Herod's wives. Over the years, Joazar learned to rely on Nathaniel's insight when it came to the scrolls. "Well put. God could not command evil to be done, and still be God."

Nathaniel leaned back in his chair. "A census in and of itself doesn't transgress the Law. You can speak for its going forward in good faith."

"But there is still the matter of these fanatics."

"Joazar, if you support this counting, do you think the Romans would allow thieves to silence their chief ally? It would signal weakness on their part. Rome is, if anything, not weak."

The lips of Joazar parted in a smile. "Quite true."

Nathaniel dropped his voice to just above a whisper. "Although the needs of the Temple and our people remain paramount in your decision, this would demonstrate to Coponius your readiness to serve the new regime. Such recognition would certainly have its rewards."

"You understand, Nathaniel," Joazar cleared his throat before continuing, "this decision is not about me. Tell Coponius that, for the sake of Jerusalem's peace and in spite of great personal risk to me, I will speak for the census."

"A wise decision, Joazar, as is your custom. I'll bear your message at once to the procurator." Nathaniel clasped Joazar's hand, then left the room, striding toward the palace with steps hastened by self-satisfaction. Nathaniel had succeeded in his first assignment from the new procurator, forging the initial bond of alliance with Jerusalem's new leader. An alliance, hoped Nathaniel, that might also bring him greater opportunities – and rewards.

* * *

"You are Simeon, grandnephew of the Sopher Kohen Gadol?" Julius didn't lift his gaze from the scrolls sprawled across his desk. The visitor to his chamber, announced by one of the guards, stood rigid. "I am told you seek to join the legion."

"I wish to enter one of the auxiliary units, sir."

Julius pushed his chair away from the desk and walked around to where Simeon stood. Clearing a space at the table's edge, Julius leaned against it, arms folded, facing the potential recruit. "And what makes a Jew eager to take a vow of fidelity to Rome and Augustus? Why serve alongside troops who occupy the land your god supposedly promised to you?"

"It's personal, sir."

"'Personal' is a word of little consequence in the legion, boy. A legionnaire is a member of a unit. Personal matters interfere with obligations to your fellows and superiors. So unless you want this to go no farther, tell me these reasons."

Simeon didn't enjoy being pressed in this manner, but he judged that Julius would not be satisfied without an answer. "I have a knack for getting into fights. I decided I should put my skills to work where they won't land me in trouble."

Julius studied the features of the young man. Several facial scars spoke of truth in the youth's explanation. Still, Julius had commanded many men who possessed the cold stare of one not bothered by bludgeoning or even killing. Simeon didn't have that look – at least, not now. "And what drives you to fight?"

"The cowardice of a father."

"I thought your religion commanded the honor of parents?"

"Honor can be lost, sir."

"And what must a father do to so embitter his son?"

Simeon wavered, then reconsidered the words of Julius about the absence of "personal" in the Legion's service. The lure of enlistment and a fresh identity moved Simeon to speak what he'd been trying to flee since childhood. "Ten years ago, troops came to our village, seeking some child of a family once known to us. The soldiers slaughtered the town's youngest boys."

Julius wanted to stop the story then and there, as it was the same one he'd also tried to escape for those same years. To interrupt, however, might make Simeon suspicious.

"My family sought escape in a nearby cave, but a patrol cut us off. One of my father's friends died trying to protect us. My father – " For a moment, Simeon's voice failed. He forced himself to continue. "My father, seeing my brother seized, tried to resist. But he gave up his knife, then watched it used to kill his son. . . my brother. . ." Simeon's eyes moistened as his speech trembled. "The Roman threw the knife to my father, daring him to take vengeance. He did nothing." A silence followed, borne of Simeon's embarrassment and Julius' shame.

Simeon looked straight into Julius' eyes: "That, sir, is how a father embitters his son."

Julius shifted from his perch on the desk and returned to his chair. Julius had rehashed this very episode on countless nights when sleep would not come: the deaths of two of his men, the killing of their slayer and two children, a father dishonored by Lucius. Until now, Julius viewed this in his mind's eye from atop his mount, removed from the carnage below. But Simeon's tale forced Julius to witness the act from the eyes of a young boy losing a brother and a father, the same child now seated before the one who presided over his family's destruction.

Julius coughed before speaking. "You've cause to fight, Simeon. But why on the side of those who rode into your village? Why not their enemies, why not the Sicarii?"

"Because I've seen Rome's power. Ever since my father cringed, I vowed I'd never be like him, never be powerless. In this land, no force rivals Rome. So, I cast my lot with Rome."

"Nathaniel also mentioned something about using an assumed name."

"He fears for his reputation if word got out one of his family served in the auxiliary. And me, I've no desire to be known as Simeon, son of Joshua. A new name gives me a chance to start over. And the name I choose is Antony: after one of your generals who once ruled this region, the one whom Herod named this fortress after."

Julius felt drawn to the young man. The attachment had nothing to do with his being Nathaniel's kinsman. The bond had to do with the shared experience in an alley of Bethlehem ten years ago. Julius resolved to do what he could to assist in transforming Simeon into Antony.

"Report back to me one week from today, ready to

leave Jerusalem. I'll arrange your assignment to the auxiliary training post in Caesarea. My scribe will draw up the enlistment papers for a new recruit called Antony."

Julius stood and Simeon extended his hand. "Thank you, sir."

After shaking hands, Julius watched Simeon-soon-to-be-Antony exit the room. Before summoning the scribe, Julius drifted back to other memories. The day he clashed with Herod over the orders regarding Bethlehem – an encounter, Julius now recalled, attended by none other than Nathaniel. More disturbing thoughts surfaced. Hadn't Herod told Nathaniel that day about the need for silence? And Nathaniel, what was it he disclosed? *There's no reason to inform my family.* No reason? Julius never realized Nathaniel's family in Bethlehem included a child condemned by Herod's plan. Yet Nathaniel never warned them. "That son of a bitch," Julius muttered. One boy dead, another's heart wounded, a father disowned – a whole family disfigured, all to maintain Nathaniel's standing. Such ambition sickened Julius. Then again, it sickened him to remember he had followed orders requiring the murder of children.

* * *

In the wilderness between the Judean plateau and the Salt Sea, the midday sun transformed tortuous canyons into twisting ovens. Kohath's band retreated into the cool depths of a limestone cave. All listened to their chieftain report on the gathering two nights ago in Tekoa.

"It won't be long before we can leave this God-forsaken hellhole. With wealth enough to live wherever we please."

"What's the Galilean promised?" The ever-cautious Tobias still had second thoughts about this alliance. "Does Judas think God will slit Roman throats for us?"

"Judas can rot in Gehenna, for all I care," replied Kohath. "But there's going to be trouble for the Romans. Too many at Tekoa were ready to spill blood!"

Tobias remained skeptical. "Judas got plenty of Galileans ready to kill Romans, only to have their bodies splayed out on crosses. Is that your idea of escaping this desert?"

Kohath sprung to his feet and charged Tobias. Others jumped between them.

"Let me go!" ordered Kohath. The two men glared at each other. "Tobias, I'll finish what I've got to say. If you don't like it, leave – or put your dagger against mine!"

Tobias sat down, not taking his eyes off Kohath, who resumed speaking. "The Torah mumblers around Judas will be our road out of this damned desert. They may not like us, but they're stuck with us! They've never calloused their fists in fights. None of them have driven a dagger into somebody's gut. They can't succeed without us and our services."

"And what's to be our pay?" asked Tobias.

"What it's always been – the goods of others. Part of what Judas aims to do is kill Jews who side with Rome. Traders, tax officials, even some of the temple higher-ups: any who worm a living by licking Roman boots. Judas wants the traitors murdered, and us to do it. And I say to you as I said to him: if we get to strip their treasure in the process, then we do it!"

"A few slit throats are all that Judas wants of us, and he'll turn a blind eye to what becomes of their purses?"

"That's the agreement. He'll give us a list of those in Jerusalem that we choose our targets from. And since the choices are ours, we only take down those with plenty of gold and silver."

Heads nodded in agreement. Kohath knew he'd won. "And as much as I enjoy all of you," the bandit added, "I'd prefer to live out my days in a Philistine villa by the sea, resting my head between the two soft pillows of some whore's bosom."

Even the face of Tobias broke out in a grin, and he stood and embraced Kohath.

"Joshua!" cried Kohath, "Bring us the wineskin we got

from that Persian caravan!"

Joshua listened to their shouts echo off the walls while he retreated into the corner where supplies were stored. Maybe at last I'll be given a chance, he thought. Every hand will be needed when fighting breaks out. Joshua hurried back with the wineskin, eager to celebrate not only the band's good fortune – but possibly his own vindication.

* * *

The evening meal drew to a close. As Naomi and Hannah started to gather the platters, Simeon decided it was time to share his news. "Mother, I have something I need to tell you."

Naomi looked into her son's eyes. Had there been another fight? "What is it?"

Simeon looked at Nathaniel before speaking. "I wanted all of you to hear this. I've not been a source of much joy to this family for a long time."

"Simeon!" Naomi's brow creased. "That's not so!"

"Mother, let me finish. I've found no more peace here than in Bethlehem."

"That was Malachi's fault." Hannah's interruption did not silence her brother.

"Maybe so. But next week, or next month, someone will take Malachi's place. Someone who's heard I'm Joshua's son, someone who'll just goad me into another fight."

"Simeon," pleaded his mother, "time will bring an end to this."

"Maybe for others, but not for me. Even if no one else ever reminds me of my past, it remains mine to bear."

Deborah leaned forward, fearful of what her only grandson contemplated. "You cannot change what has been, and what was your father's fault. Not yours."

"Like it or not, as long as I am Simeon, I carry his sin."

"As long as you are Simeon?" Naomi began to feel it hard to breathe.

"In a week, I shall join the Legion's auxiliary troops.

With the name of Antony."

"What?" Naomi's face paled.

"No, Simeon! NO!" Hannah threw her arms around her brother's neck.

Deborah's folded hands supported her fallen forehead. "You still curse this family, Joshua," she said to herself.

For some time, only sobs arose from the table. But then Nathaniel spoke up. "My grandnephew makes a difficult – but wise – decision."

The three women stared incredulously at Nathaniel.

"I know this hurts now," he continued, "but Simeon chooses with the best interest of the family at heart. And that is of greatest consequence here."

"What are you saying, uncle? This is my son's life!"

"His life is in no more jeopardy there than here. He and I already spoke of this."

"You have?" sneered Deborah. "You've become mother as well as father to the boy? How thoughtful of you to withhold this from Naomi!"

Nathaniel stiffened. "Simeon needed a man's advice."

"But I'm his mother," protested Naomi. Then, looking to Simeon, "Why couldn't you have come to me with this? Are you that eager to set aside your family?"

Simeon loosened Hannah's grip from around his neck. "I didn't want you to worry, or try to talk me out of it. I wish it could be another way – but it can't. I can't go on as Simeon. Why can't you just let me go?!" Simeon sprung to his feet and ran from the house.

"You *made* Simeon want to leave. All of you, all of you!" Hannah burst into tears again. "You blamed him for the fights. NOW look what you've done. I hate you! I hate you ALL!" Naomi reached for Hannah, but the girl fled the table and closed herself in her room.

"The boy will be alright. Trust me." Nathaniel's reassurance sounded hollow in Naomi's ears. All she knew was a son's decision to rid himself of the name she breathed as he suckled her breast. A name she comforted when a brother's death broke his heart.

"Simeon," Naomi whispered. "Simeon." A name, and a son, now lost.

CHAPTER XX

A slowly-descending line of purple colored the chalk cliffs thrusting up from the sea's western shore, the early morning sun painting a momentary palate on the hills' otherwise grey habit. Below, the Salt Sea lingered in shadow as Rebekah and Saul strolled the shoreline.

The place possessed an eerie beauty. Brine-encrusted rocks resembling huge crystalline mushrooms sprouted across the shallows. Occasionally, the twisted trunk of a long dead tree rose up, doomed by a rise in the sea's level. While the wood rotted, a thick saline girdle crept up the victim from its base. And then there was the silence. No fish ever broke the surface of these waters, salty enough to float a body like a cork. The countless migratory birds following the Great Rift Valley, of which this sea marked the deepest depression, soared far above its lifeless confines. Only the wind, howling through canyons or piling up waves, orchestrated the sounds one could depend on hearing in this place.

"When you were at Torah class yesterday, Saul, Abraham brought bad news."

"What is it?" Saul stopped walking. "We aren't going to leave?"

A low-lying boulder caught Rebekah's eye. "Let's sit over there." The wind had weathered the surface of their bench to a tolerable smoothness. They sat, looking out over the sea's morning calm. The sun had yet to clear the eastern ridge. "We've been together in this place for nearly a month. You've made new friends here, and have teachers wise in the ways of God." She took her son's hand in hers, though she kept her eyes focused on the sea. "Sometimes we must do things, even when it would be easier not to. Abraham says I should return home. Judas believes the Romans intend some new act of oppression. He needs a reliable ear to listen for him in Bethlehem."

"If it's for Judas, then I suppose we can go."

Her hand gripped his more tightly. "You must stay here, Saul. Your lessons are important. And Abraham says the other students already hold you in high regard."

At fifteen years of age, a yearning for independence tugged hard at Saul. Yet, that desire's counterweight came in ten years shared alone with his mother. The death of father and brother still haunted Saul. The thought of separation from Rebekah upset him.

"But if there's trouble with the Romans, it may not be safe for you to be alone."

"Saul, don't make this more difficult." Rebekah let go of her son and tucked her hands underneath crossed arms. "Times of sacrifice come to us all. I'd prefer remaining with you. But I'm needed in Bethlehem. And your place is here, to prepare yourself. To be a leader as Judas is, you must learn to set aside personal needs." Rebekah shifted her position to face Saul. "This is how it must be. It's time you learn the pain of sacrifice if you'd honor your father's memory."

How those words marked Saul's life! Ever since the massacre in Bethlehem, the memory of his father had been regularly invoked to mold Saul's life. At first, Saul linked remembrance of his father to days of play in the woodshop, stories spun in the evening, and carvings so real they seemed to breathe. But over the years, such appeals narrowed his memory to a single act in a bloodied alleyway. For Saul, in this salt-sculpted landscape, carvings and stories and games played in sawdust all evaporated into martyrdom's brittle crust.

"I will honor his memory!" Saul almost shouted the words, as if volume could disguise doubt. The walk back home felt to Saul like the longest of his life.

* * *

"A visitor, my lord Coponius!" The guard stepped aside, allowing the fellow to enter the room. He wore an off-white woolen tunic hanging loose at the forearms. A cloak, whose scarlet color had long ago faded to a dirty brownish-red, draped one shoulder before tucking inside his belt in the back. Sandals of coarse camel hide padded his feet, while a strip of cloth covered nose and mouth from the summer sun and dust.

Coponius glanced up from his desk, where stacks of census scrolls from twelve years past awaited review. The procurator returned to Jerusalem only last night after spending two weeks in Caesarea, the new center for Rome's administration of Judea. Today's public announcement of the census ordered by Quirinius weighed upon him.

"I've no one listed for appointments at this time." The eyes of Coponius quickly fell back to the scrolls. "Your name and business, and be quick about it."

The stranger loosened his headband, removing the cloth that concealed his face below the eyes. "My name is Julius, and you'd be dead if I wielded a sicarii's dagger."

A startled Coponius jerked his head upward. "Julius! What are you doing?"

"I thought I should try my disguise on you, before taking to Jerusalem's streets."

"What are you talking about?"

Julius straddled a bench beside the procurator's desk. "My assignment here is to keep you informed on the city's gossip. That's what I intend to do."

"By going out as a spy? We have money to pay informants!"

"The days of relying on informants are waning. Our most dangerous threats come from those who can't be bought. In the Galileans Judas and Saddok, we have new enemies. Men who believe they do the work of their deity by spilling Roman blood."

The brow of Coponius wrinkled. "But the Jews have always had fanatics. Didn't you tell me of two scribes you arrested for destroying some statuary of Herod?"

"True. But then, the Jews focused their hatred on Herod. He's gone, and we alone hold power. Those two scribes you mention organized but a single event, and a suicidal one at that. Rumors abound of more ambitious plans. Some whisper about a figure they call Anointed One, *Mashiah* in their tongue. They say he will come down from heaven and lead them."

"Julius, these are but superstitions."

"Superstitions that bind conspirators far more tightly than greed ever could. You can't buy information from a fanatic who's certain his god requires rebellion."

Coponius shook his head in disbelief. A shrewd businessman, he knew firsthand how persuasive Roman silver could be. His own ascendance had been secured by well-placed gifts. As to gods, Roman or Jewish, Coponius paid no mind.

"Even if you're right, there's too much danger for you. You could be recognized."

"I appreciate your concern, Coponius. But my years of service in the Legion have accustomed me to risk. As for the danger of recognition – I've already tested it."

"Just because I didn't catch on when you walked in, you think you'll be safe out there?"

"That, and the fact that during your stay in Caesarea, I spent many hours in Jerusalem's bazaars and inns. I had grown puzzled at the lack of news our informants provided of late. Much of what I've told you comes from my own ears. I'm keeping an apartment in the Tyropean valley, for times when returning to the palace would be awkward."

Coponius studied Julius. A grizzled beard covered cheeks and chin. Hair grew to a length longer than the style favored by a Roman. "I suppose you're bound to do this."

"It's in Rome's best interest to have reliable knowledge with the census coming. And I know the Jews' customs, and converse in their tongue."

"Shall I inform Nathaniel of your plan? He might be of some assistance."

Julius thought to his interview of Simeon, and its revealing of Nathaniel's betrayal of his own family. "No, let's keep this to ourselves. The Sanhedrin has its share of conspirators. A word from Nathaniel to one he misjudges jeopardize us both."

"Agreed. But I hope you know what you're doing."

"The point is to know what they're doing. And from what I've found out already, ignorance runs the greater risk."

The two stood and shook hands, then Julius headed toward the door.

"By the way," Coponius called out, "what sort of Jew will you pass yourself off as, to gain the confidence of such men?"

Pulling his headband and cloth back into place, Julius smiled. "I hear there's need for men handy with a dagger, willing to slit throats of Roman oppressors and Jewish collaborators." He drew a knife from the folds of his cloak. "Perhaps I'll hear who draws your lot. And if not," Julius paused at the door, "be more careful whom you receive without a guard in the room!"

"Good luck, Julius." Coponius waited several minutes after Julius left, then summoned the guard in the hall. "From now on, search all visitors. No exceptions."

As the soldier exited, Coponius moved to the window. Julius made his way across the palace grounds. In a moment, he was out of sight. Jerusalem's maze had been entered.

* * *

"When will we hear from Simeon, mother?"

Naomi's fingers sifted through wheat displayed on a seller's table. "I don't know. It's only been a month." She bit one of the kernels for its taste. "Give us two measures of this grain, sir."

As the seller scooped grain onto his balance, Hannah resumed. "Lots of things can happen in a month. He could be sick, or hurt."

Naomi handed coins to the merchant after he poured the grain into a clay jar carried by a servant. Naomi next sought out a table bearing dried figs and olive oil, her servant walking a discreet distance behind the two. "Nathaniel assures us he's fine."

"I don't like Nathaniel. If it wasn't for him, Simeon would still be with us."

"Don't speak so loudly, Hannah. What if the servant were to hear?" Naomi spotted a fruit trader with whom she'd bargained before. The two engaged in the usual haggling over cost.

"Four denarii!?" he exclaimed. "I'd be taking food out of the mouth of my wife and children to sell at such a cost! I couldn't possibly accept less than ten denarii."

"Keziah, you know I lived in Bethlehem. Two denarii would easily buy such figs and olive oil. And a sight fresher, I might add."

The merchant flung his arms into the air. "Oh, but I have to pay for transport. And the taxes! The taxes alone leave me on the verge of debtor's prison! Nine denarii, and no less!"

"I'm sorry, Keziah." Naomi started to look around at nearby tables. "Surely another seller is accustomed to these expenses, and could sell at four denarii."

"Very well," he moaned. "eight denarii. And I'll not eat tonight."

"Five denarii," Naomi countered.

"Seven denarii, but your servant will have to fill the flask with olive oil himself!"

"Six denarii, Keziah, or I visit Eli's table."

"So be it!" Buyer and seller shook hands. "Tell others what a fair man I am."

A bundle of figs soon draped the servant's shoulder, who now also carried a large flask of olive oil in one hand and a jar of wheat in the other.

"You may return home," Naomi instructed the servant. "My daughter and I will bring the breads from the baker's bazaar." Once the servant left, Naomi turned to Hannah. "One of the servants spoke of a large caravan arriving from Babylon yesterday, with lots of linens. How would you like to look at material for new garments?"

"If you want to."

"Don't you?"

"I don't care."

"You don't care? I seem to remember an excited young lady on her first day in Jerusalem, seeing all the fineries. She said then she wanted a tunic of fine linen."

"That was then."

The terseness of Hannah's replies grated Naomi's nerves. The two strolled in silence into the bazaar of wool merchants. Some sold thread freshly spun from thick bundles of wool hanging from stalls. Others wove carpets, or stitched robes. Nearby, fullers washed and bleached raw wool and flax. "Do you want to talk about Simeon?"

"Why should I?"

Naomi stopped. "Enough, Hannah. I'll put up with anger, but not disrespect!"

Hannah gave Naomi a sidelong glance. Anger flashed in the girl's narrowed eyes, but sadness reddened them as well.

Naomi spoke with a softer tone. "Hannah, please, let's talk." The girl gave no reply as Naomi led her to a bench outside a weaver's workshop. Inside, the shuttle clipped steadily as separate threads meshed into a tapestry. Outside, threads of family unraveled.

"Hannah, I miss Simeon terribly, the same as you. But he made his choice."

Hannah trembled from stifled sobs. "I thought he loved us, but he left. Like abba."

"Simeon does love us. Believe me. He's just confused."

"Was *abba* confused when he let David die?"

Hannah's question struck a raw nerve. "What your father did then and what Simeon does now are entirely different things."

"Are they? You and grandmother always talk about *abba* deserting the family. Isn't that what Simeon's done?"

"Simeon's pain makes him thinks he needs to be away from us. But he'll change."

"You gave up on *abba*. You'll probably give up on Simeon!"

"Hannah – "

"I can't wait till I can leave this family! All anybody does is hurt each other. No wonder Simeon left. Maybe you drove *abba* away, too, and told lies to make the fault his and not yours!"

The palm of Naomi's right hand cracked against Hannah's cheek. Surprise, and tears, marked both faces. Hannah's crying drowned out the sound of the loom.

"I'm sorry, Hannah, I didn't mean to." Naomi tried to comfort her daughter, as she once did to for a little girl crying for a brother struck down in Bethlehem. But where the toddler snuggled into her arms, the adolescent recoiled from her touch. "Hannah, you're all I have left at home. We need each other, especially now."

As she sobbed, Hannah considered how love had rewarded her. One brother murdered before her eyes and another who deserted her; a mother who publicly humiliated her; a father who abandoned her, never to see his daughter grow up or say how proud he was of her. Hannah wanted the pain to stop. If that meant shielding herself from this day forward, so be it. Hannah vowed to never let love for another victimize her again. From inside the weaver's workshop, a shuttle kept up its relentless pace. Threads, and lives, were cinching tight into a pattern.

CHAPTER XXI

Three miles north of Nazareth, Sepphoris was rising as a Gentile phoenix from Jewish ashes. The Romans had leveled the city ten years ago to punish its inhabitants for assisting the rebel Judas. Within a year of the destruction, however, Antipas, one of Herod's surviving sons and the new ruler of Galilee, decided to rebuild it as his new capital. Since then, the population burgeoned. Demand for housing and public buildings created a profitable market for artisans. Architects and stone masons, sawyers and carpenters, all found plentiful work.

Joseph had been part of this boom from the start. His return with Mary and Yeshua from Egypt to their former home in Nazareth coincided with the reviving fortunes of Sepphoris. With the reconstruction, Joseph had as much work as he cared to accept. Mary devoted herself to raising Yeshua and his younger brothers and sister.

On this particular day, Yeshua accompanied his father to work. Though Yeshua still studied with the rabbi several days a week, Joseph had begun to teach his son the carpentry trade. Sometimes, Joseph and Yeshua worked side by side in his Nazareth shop. On other days, Yeshua travelled with his father to Sepphoris. The hour-long walk passed swiftly. Joseph and Yeshua talked about the cranes used to lift immense rafters, or the scaffolding they'd erect for stonemasons who busied themselves laying rows of white limestone blocks.

Most exciting for Yeshua, though, were chances to wander through the city during the afternoon break. On days when the sun burned hot, that respite could last two or three hours. Father and son would walk to the eastern edge of town. There, a series of waterwheels powered by the pacing of slaves drew water from the aqueduct on the valley floor up to this city set on a hill. Fountains and gardens provided a pleasant place to rest and cool.

The great forum in the center of the acropolis provided another of Yeshua's favored destinations. In Nazareth, Yeshua watched artisans and farmers and an occasional trader in the bazaar; but in the forum of Sepphoris, the boy might see a patrol of Roman soldiers or Arab caravanners or Greek bankers. The ever-changing mix of people intrigued him.

"Yeshua, hand me the mallet." Joseph and Yeshua stood on the scaffolding fronting the theater. A wood pin needed pounding into the holes of two timbers held gingerly in line. The mallet passed from hand to hand, the dowel was driven – and a new level of scaffolding took shape above them. Planks handed up from below provided footing for the stoneworkers. "That's it for now, boy. Time to climb down."

Yeshua enjoyed the climbing for carpentry work here. Shinnying up the oaks outside of Nazareth didn't compare with the scaffolding's handholds and footholds. Leaves encumbered the view from trees. Not so on the timbers of Sepphoris. From the higher platforms, he could look down into the Bet Netofa valley, trailing eastward toward the Sea of Galilee sixteen miles away.

For Joseph, the climbing posed a difficult but necessary nuisance. Knees that had seen fifty-one winters cracked with each deep flex. "Wait for me at the bottom." Joseph smiled as he spoke. He remembered hearing those same words from his father many times.

Once on the ground, Joseph consulted the foreman. Bricklayers still worked atop the adjacent scaffolding. Noontime neared. "You and your son might as well leave.

These masons take forever, and I've nothing for you in the meantime. Make it up later this afternoon."

Joseph and Yeshua headed toward the waterwheels and the shade of trees planted by the fountains. Chunks of bread and cheese packed by Mary, washed down by the town's sweet water, combined with the heat to induce drowsiness. Joseph and Yeshua reclined under an olive tree's thick foliage. Hushed conversations around them and the stirrings of crickets formed a soft blanket of sound as they dozed.

Joseph's reverie was broken by the noise of an assembling crowd. Another speaker, he thought, stretching muscles that reminded him of the morning's labor. Since many came to the fountains to wile away the afternoon rest, the location served as a favored spot for aspiring orators. Jews might cluster around Pharisee or Essene teachers. Gentiles gravitated toward those who preached the Stoic or Epicurean ways. Three or four such groups were apt to form at any one time. Today, however, Joseph noted one large crowd assembling around a single figure, who was accompanied by two legionnaires.

Yeshua yawned and tapped his father on the shoulder. "Can you hear what he's saying?"

"I don't think he's started yet. But with so many people, maybe we'd better go to listen." The pair strode to the edge of the crowd and worked their way closer.

"Excuse me," Joseph said to someone in the row in front of him, "do you know what this is about?"

"Not altogether," he replied. "I've a shop in the marketplace. Everyone gossiped about the Romans making some announcement by the fountains this afternoon."

Joseph turned to Yeshua. "Let's stay and find out."

"I hope it's not too long. It's hot with all these people."

"We'll see. If it –"

"Attention! In the name of Augustus Caesar, First Citizen of Rome and Lord of her Empire!" The official raised his hand, signaling for quiet. "From Quirinius, governor of Syria, legate appointed by Caesar; to the people of Sepphoris and Galilee, and all the region of Syria. There will be an imperial census conducted in the province of Syria."

Murmurs and then a few shouts rose up from the crowd. The legionnaires struck their shields with swords to restore silence. "Everyone must register throughout the province. If you own land, register in the town or city it is located. If not, register where your family arose, based upon your father's residence. Registration for Sepphoris will be at the Acropolis. Avoidance of registration will result in fines or seizure of property. Opposition to the census is a crime against Augustus, punishable by death. Hail Caesar!"

* * *

The caravansaries of Jerusalem hosted a variety of drivers and traders from caravans supplying the city. Their tables fed Arabs and Greeks, Egyptians and Persians. The noise and smell of camels stabled nearby, not to mention that of the caravanners themselves after long desert treks, led to locating such inns on Jerusalem's fringe. On this day, an entourage filed into the caravansary of Ishmael, commandeering a large table in a windowless corner.

"Afternoon. What'll you have?" Ishmael used no names, though he knew two of the men. "I've got a lamb stew that'd be soon done."

"Bread's all we need. And wine." The voice belonged to Judas of Galilee.

The men said nothing while the innkeeper fetched a freshly baked loaf and a pitcher of wine, along with five goblets. After setting them on the table, he bowed and added: "If the stew's aroma changes your mind, just call old Ishmael."

Ishmael returned to his cooking shed. He'd learned in his years at the caravansary to recognize which customers sought privacy more than food. Of late, such men came to his place with greater frequency, including this Judas and Saddok. Ishmael stirred the stew with a long wooden spoon, and kept his good ear cocked to the doorway.

Judas poured the goblets full, then lifted his own. "May Elohim Adonai be praised! Today, the Romans give us the excuse we've awaited. A toast to this census!"

The men struck their goblets together, then drank. Ishmael's wine stock ran strong to the point of bitterness. The remaining wine would be sopped with bread. Judas considered the others: Abraham from New Damascus, Saddok, the Essene Bartholomew, a Pharisee from the Sanhedrin called Lot. All had heard the rumors of an imminent proclamation by Rome to be made at the steps leading up to the Temple square. After listening to the herald announce the coming census, they made plans to gather at the caravansary.

"The hour is upon us. There can be no doubt."

Saddok concurred. "This census is an abomination. When David numbered Israel, the Samuel scroll tells how the Lord struck down seventy-thousand Israelites. How much more when the Lord rebukes Rome? Their blood, and our freedom, will flow."

"The Sanhedrin will have to convene about this," Judas noted. "What do you say, Lot? Will they oppose the census?"

The Pharisee nodded his head. "I've already had a number of private conversations. Many believe the rule of God over Israel must be established once and for all, with no more delay. Announcing the census will push those who waver to choose resistance or collaboration. No middle ground. The argument will be ours, and the Lord Elohim's!"

"Judas, I'm still troubled by including men like Kohath and others of the Sicarii." Bartholomew spoke softly, knowing this to be a subject of disagreement. "The Almighty cannot be pleased with thieves and murderers. By involving them, we risk alienating those who cannot tolerate using the unrighteous to oust the Romans."

"My friend," began Judas, "how often must we revisit

this debate? We need every man available for this struggle."

Saddok cleared his throat. "Bartholomew, you continue to overlook the precedents in the Scripture. Does the Lord God condone prostitution? Yet God used the harlot Rahab to save Joshua's spies in Jericho! Does the Lord God condone false witness and murder? Yet the scroll of Judges praises Jael. She enticed Sisera into her tent with a promise of sanctuary, then waited till he was asleep before driving a tent peg through his temple! God used such as these to secure this land. And if God can use such men as Kohath to reclaim the land, then the Scriptures say through Rahab and Jael: so be it!"

Bartholomew mulled the words, though his heart remained divided.

"Are we are agreed, then?" Judas looked square in the Essene's eyes. "We accept any and all willing to take up arms against Rome and its traitors among our people."

"Agreed," said the others.

"Then here is –" Judas stopped midsentence. When they'd first entered the caravansary, it appeared all the tables had been empty. But now, a chair's scraping against the floor silenced them. It came from another corner, shielded from their sight by a plank set with goblets and platters. That section of the room, like theirs, had no windows to break its darkness. Sandals clapped against the planked floor, coming in their direction. Abraham put his hand to a knife concealed in his robe. Judas did the same.

The stranger stopped. "I don't come to rob or threaten. My hands hold no weapon."

Judas stood, a firm grip on the dagger now held in the open. "A man who sits in the dark to listen to the words of others plays a fool's game."

"A preference for shadows is a habit of my work," replied the stranger. "It's amazing what one learns of unguarded caravans and the like when wine loosens tongues."

"We don't trade in caravans." Judas took a step toward

the intruder, raising his dagger to the fellow's chest. "And listening in on our table's conversation could have grave results."

The stranger looked down to the dagger, then to the one who wielded it. "You could kill me where I stand, no doubt. But you wouldn't hear what I would say. Or offer."

"Be quick about it."

"There's five of you here, so no chance I'd overwhelm you. Let me sit and speak. After that, I'm at your mercy."

Judas admired the fellow's brazenness. While keeping the dagger in hand, the Galilean pulled a chair and shoved it over to him. "What do they call you?"

Without pause, Julius continued, "Nabal of Tyre. My father was a Syrian trader, and also what you Jews call a Godfearer, worshiping in your synagogues. But his trust of this city's richer merchants brought him grief when they demanded bribes. His attempt to expose their thievery resulted in a Herodian knife plunged in his back. And Rome's refusal to investigate."

"A touching story," mocked Abraham. "Why do you think this allows you to spy on us?"

"It's joining, not spying, that's brought me to your table! When my father died, I swore vengeance. Learning about the caravans lets me make a living by stripping profits from those who saw to my father's death. But it hasn't stopped them. They remain hypocrites who parade their piety at the Temple, but cheat and lie whenever they can. I heard you say you'd accept anyone willing to strike against Rome and the traitors who support it –we share the same cause!"

"How do we know you are to be trusted?" Saddok demanded. "Did your father instruct you with the proverb told by Solomon: `Like the glaze covering an earthen vessel are smooth lips with an evil heart`?"

Julius leaned across to Saddok. "Take me at my word alone, and you'd be the fool. Trust comes in the earning. All I ask is an opportunity to act alongside you."

"*The enemy of my enemy is my friend.* Isn't that how the nomads put it?" Abraham's comment sparked knowing glances among the conspirators.

"Maybe we can provide you a chance to prove yourself, Nabal." Judas put away his dagger, then resumed talking. "And sooner than you think. Meet us here one week from tonight. For now, that's all you need to know. But for now, leave us!"

Julius stood and bowed, then left the caravansary for his apartment. He wished to stay, but knew he mustn't rush their confidence. The information about Judas frequenting Ishmael's inn had proved correct. An extra five denarii would have to be paid to the informant, who at the moment savored a taste of his own thick lamb stew.

* * *

"Mary, are the children asleep?"

"Anna is. Yeshua is telling James and Joseph one of the rabbi's stories."

"Not so loud as to wake our daughter, I hope."

"No, not at all."

Mary reclined beside her husband, eyes fixed on the stars beginning to show in dusk's final light. Another warm evening had brought Joseph to the rooftop. Mary joined him once she tucked in the little ones. Mary rested her head on Joseph's chest. Calloused hands, accustomed to handling rough-edged timbers, gently stroked the face of Mary. Though she'd borne four children, and now carried a fifth within her, Mary's skin retained the smoothness of her youth.

Joseph would have preferred simply drifting off to sleep, but thoughts that had nagged him through the day need airing. "I'm afraid we must talk about this enrollment."

"Isn't there a way for you to declare your family's land in Bethlehem when you register your residence here in Nazareth? Won't they have the records from the last census available?"

"Not here. And since Judea's under a procurator at the moment, they'll insist on registering on site. Rome's interest is their tax rolls, not our convenience."

Mary drew herself up, kissing Joseph's cheek above his beard. "Then we'll figure a way for us to make a trip to Bethlehem, husband, as we did when Yeshua was born."

Joseph shook his head. "I've puzzled on that ever since hearing the news. Much as I dislike the idea, I'll have to go alone."

"Alone? No, Joseph, there must be another way."

"We risked this journey once with you carrying a child. I don't want to do that again. Besides, Anna still suckles. The trip would be difficult for you both."

"Then at least take Yeshua with you. If you were injured, or fell ill, you ought to have someone with you." Mary's concern was spurred by a couple of incidents in the past year, when Joseph complained of having brief pains in his chest at work.

"Now, Mary, I've got the constitution of a twenty-year-old."

"And sometimes the judgment of one half that age!" Mary playfully, but firmly, grasped Joseph's earlobe between her thumb and index finger. "You are not going alone." A smile crossed her face as she edged her lips toward his. "You're going to take Yeshua with you."

Grasping her arms, Joseph shifted onto his back and gently brought her on top of him. "I must be your captive. Do I not do everything you say?"

Mary lowered her head to his, kissing his brow and then his lips. "Then, for me, take Yeshua to Bethlehem with you."

"I will. For you." Joseph eased her next to his side. No words passed between them as the sky darkened into night. Only at the moon's rising did Mary break the quiet.

"Will you seek out Rebekah, or Joshua and Naomi,

when you go?"

A deep sigh heaved Joseph's chest. "Maybe I've run from this long enough. To avoid them when I'm in Bethlehem would be wrong."

Mary brushed the hair from Joseph's forehead. "Forgive me for not going with you, making you bear this alone."

"You've no need of forgiveness. I was the one who insisted we leave without a word."

"Joseph, we've been through –"

"I know. I thought this would protect them along with us. But I was wrong. Maybe this trip to Bethlehem will help somehow. If nothing else, Yeshua will see his birthplace."

"And the stable," added Mary. "Do you think the manger might still be there?"

"I don't know why not. Elias built it for Joshua just a few years before we came."

"Promise me, Joseph. If it is, tell him the manger story. He used to hear it almost every day there. He may think he's too old for it, but I'd like to think it still has a place in his heart."

Joseph ran a finger beneath Mary's eye, wiping a tear loosened by the remembrance of Bethlehem. "Yeshua will see the stable. And if the manger's there, I'll tell him the story."

CHAPTER XXII

Nathaniel struck the brass *magrefa* to signal the High Priest's entrance into the Chamber of Hewn Stone. Its clanging tones reverberated against the limestone blocks. All talk ceased as the Sanhedrin members stood. Joazar raised his arms and intoned: "*Hear, O Israel, the Lord is our God, the Lord alone. Blessed be the name of the Lord.*"

"*BLESSED BE THE NAME OF THE LORD!*" echoed Jerusalem's elders.

Joazar lowered his arms, and those assembled took their seats. The Sanhedrin's seventy members sat on benches curved into a semicircle, the High Priest's chair at the center front. Three more rows facing the semicircle's open end provided seating for guests. Bitter wrangling between Nathaniel and Lot had determined who sat there today. Guards stood at the chamber's portal. Crowds packed the Temple's outer courts, waiting to hear the Sanhedrin's word.

"My brothers," began Joazar, "we meet this day for one purpose only: the census called by Quirinius and Coponius for Judea. Unless there is a question I would like – "

"A question, Joazar!" Lot sprang to his feet.

Joazar glowered at the interruption. "What would you ask, Lot?"

Lot strode to the far end of his bench, adjacent to a cluster of students. "These youths study under our supervision. Each day they strive to understand Torah's obligation. They do so because of one principle: there is no person, no authority, with the right to stand between us and the demands of Elohim Adonai. You called us to order with the words of the Shema: `*Hear, O Israel, the Lord is our God, the Lord – ALONE.*'"

"Forgive me, Lot." Joazar leaned forward in his chair. "I know my ears grow older each day: have I missed the question you pose?"

Whispers of agreement with Joazar's chastening clashed with the clicking of tongues by those who took offense at the ridicule.

"My question is this: if we who recite the Shema submit to Rome by agreeing to this census, have we not set the law of Caesar above the word of God's Torah? Have we not renounced the kingship of Adonai for servitude to Augustus?!"

Raucous cheers broke out among some. Others hissed and whistled in disapproval.

Nathaniel repeatedly struck the *magrefa* until the room grew silent again.

Joazar strode into the center of the room, facing the rows for student guests. "Your presence here is a privilege, not a necessity. You sit in the Sanhedrin, not an academy for adolescents! Disrupt these deliberations again, and you'll be removed. Is that clear?"

No one moved, much less spoke.

After returning to his chair, Joazar scanned the robed figures before singling out his adversary. "Lot, let me offer my response. No one in this room holds the decrees of Rome as equal to the Torah. No one renounces the Lordship of Elohim."

"Then why – "

"I will finish!" Joazar raised his right hand to silence Lot. "The census involves no worship, but bookkeeping. Those who clamored for the removal of Archelaus – and I believe you urged that action, Lot – had to know the Romans would not leave Judea to fend for itself. You brought this procurator, and with him now this census, upon us."

The High Priest surprised Lot. Joazar usually contented himself to moderate the council, allowing Nathaniel to fight his battles. "Joazar, don't twist our opposition to Archelaus into support for Rome. This census is an abomination to God, like the one enforced in the last years of Herod. The people know that. They wait to see if their leaders have the courage to say so."

"You speak of courage quite easily in the safety of this chamber." Joazar moved into the heart of the room again, fixing his stare on Lot. "But will you speak so easily when Roman swords let Jewish blood? Will your words still flow when those who cling to them hang on Roman crosses? You're right, Lot: we ARE leaders – and we must protect our people from the foolishness of misplaced zeal."

Lot noted the nodding heads of those he reckoned as uncommitted, those needed to condemn the census. Alarm pitched his voice higher. "You call adherence to the Torah misplaced zeal? You call remaining steadfast to the rule of Adonai misplaced zeal?"

"No. I call rabble-rousing misplaced zeal. Or have your forgotten that the Torah itself tells of God commanding Moses to conduct a census not once but twice in the wilderness? How can what you call an abomination be attributed to the Holy One?"

"Joazar's right." Nathaniel unwound the scroll held just for this moment in the debate. "In the scroll of Numbers, it is written: `The Lord spoke to Moses in the wilderness of Sinai, saying: Take a census of the whole congregation of Israelites.'" Setting down the scroll, Nathaniel asked, "Does Lot accuse God of abomination?"

Lot stood silent. Nathaniel's question left him with the choice of either blasphemy or contradicting his own argument.

"Listen to me." Joazar's eyes scanned every member of the Sanhedrin. "The Romans don't tell us to suspend our sacrifices at the temple. They don't demand we end our prayers and alms. They don't require we cease to observe Sabbath. They only require a census for taxes we already pay. Our people and God's Torah have survived before under foreign rule. Do we want Jewish blood to be spilled for such a trifling matter?"

As the vote proceeded, Lot shook his head in disgust. Only twenty-seven members stood against the census. Oddly, as the Sanhedrin disbanded, few congratulated Joazar. His strongest appeal had been to fear of Roman reprisal, and such men as sat on the Sanhedrin didn't like admitting to fear. Nathaniel stood by Joazar and smiled as he watched the room empty.

On his way out, Lot stopped before Joazar's chair. "It's a sad day when the High Priest disgraces the Torah and persuades the Sanhedrin to duplicate his folly."

"And a sadder day still when a Pharisee plasters over his own defeat with an insult to the leader of our people!"

Nathaniel's retort induced an angry glare from Lot. "Your advice always has swayed Joazar, Nathaniel. May the Almighty soon reward your faithfulness."

* * *

Saul hurried toward Abraham's house in New Damascus, puzzled at what awaited him there. A messenger had interrupted Saul's class on the campaigns of Joshua, whispering something in the ear of the rabbi who had been speaking. The rabbi then called Saul forward and said only that he was needed at home. Curiosity and then worry sped Saul's steps. Had Abraham not told him he would be gone a week or more in Jerusalem – and it had only been two days since he left! The midday heat shimmered off the cliffs and the Salt Sea's surface, causing the youth to space his sprints with walking. Sweat flowed freely by the time he reached the mudbrick structure at the community's edge. He drew in a deep breath, then called: "Hello?"

"Out here, in the courtyard."

The voice was Abraham's. Saul hastened toward the courtyard, wondering what this was about.

"Abraham! I didn't think I'd see –"

Saul's words and steps came to an abrupt halt when he stepped into the courtyard. Standing with Abraham was Rebekah!

"Surprised?"

"Mother!" Saul ran to embrace Rebekah. He'd assumed it would be months before he'd see her again.

Abraham patted the youth's back. "Sit down. There's water in the pitcher." Abraham pulled a chair over for Rebekah, then sat on a bench, his back against the wall.

"What happened?" Saul asked after downing some water.

Abraham and Rebekah glanced at one another before Abraham spoke. "Events have moved far swifter than anyone expected. Can you keep a secret?"

"Yes!"

"I'll be speaking at a meeting of the elders of New Damascus tonight. The Romans have called a census – and Judas has called for revolt."

For the last month, another of his classes studied the scrolls of the Maccabees, Jewish rebels of four generations past who rid Jerusalem and Judea of other tyrants. The idea of taking part in such an uprising thrilled Saul. "When do we join Judas?"

Abraham placed his arm around the young man. "Saul, your time of preparation here is not over. Not long ago, Judas branded those who follow our ways as *Zealots*. We have zeal for the Torah, zeal for Adonai Elohim. But it is not a zeal borne of ignorance. We study, that we may rightly follow. When we raise the sword, it must be the sword of the Almighty."

"I know, Abraham – I'm ready to fight!"

"Readiness to fight is one thing," said Abraham, his voice slowing and deepening, "but readiness to lead is another. We brought you here as one who will someday be a leader of our people. To do that, your learning must continue."

"But it's not fair," protested Saul, pulling away from Abraham's arm. "How can I help unless I take up the sword?"

"Let me tell you a story, Saul. Once, a young man in Jerusalem witnessed the Romans slaughter students, not much older than you, on the steps of the Sanctuary. Caught in a fleeing crowd, he wasn't able to lift a hand to help. He could only run – and he didn't stop running until he came to Bethlehem. From there, he journeyed into this wilderness, and eventually found Judas. And now, when the time to avenge those students' deaths comes: Judas asks that same man to guard others who study. Now: does that man help Judas by doing what is requested and staying here, though he'd rather be in the middle of the fighting?"

"Well, yes, I guess so."

"Saul, I am that man. As much as I want to exact vengeance, Judas orders me to watch over this community. And for you to remain here."

Rebekah held her son's shoulder firmly. "Abraham is right. These events change things for all of us. Even me. Judas felt Bethlehem too close to Jerusalem's dangers. Which is why he had Abraham bring me back to New Damascus."

"Then you'll be here, instead of in Bethlehem?"

"Until it's more certain what follows, yes."

Conflicting emotions churned inside Saul: relief that his mother was safe and with him, frustration at not being able to fight, fear for what could happen. The scrolls of the Maccabees narrated the deaths of the just as well as the unjust. And the massacre of Judas' followers in Galilee after the last uprising was a painfully familiar one. "Is Judas going to win this time?"

Abraham picked at the fringes of his robe. "As to Judas, I can't say. But will Elohim Adonai triumph over Rome and all His enemies? On that, I stake my life!"

* * *

"KOHATH! KOHATH!"

The cry sounded from the canyon floor, far below the

cave where Kohath's band took refuge from the heat. Two lookouts spied a lone figure on horseback, waving a white cloth. Kohath moved next to the cave's entrance, careful not to allow some hidden assassin clear shot. He cupped his hands to his mouth and shouted: "Who seeks Kohath?" Kohath eyed the cliffside below for any hostile movement.

"I'm sent by the Galilean, who spoke to him at Tekoa. Kohath will know who I mean. He told the Galilean of this cavern's location."

Kohath thought back to the meeting. He had given Judas a description of where he could be found. "Tie the horse and come up. If you've any weapons, leave them there."

The rider secured his mount, tossed aside a dagger, and scrambled up the rocks. While Tobias and Lamech searched him, the lookouts maintained their vigil. "Nobody else is out there," one shouted.

"My name is Matthias," the stranger began. "I need to speak with Kohath."

"Your speaking to him now," Kohath growled, "but crying out my name like that could've gotten you killed!"

"The news merits the risk. Maybe we should speak in private."

"What you've got to say to me, you say in front of my men."

"So be it." Matthias wiped the sweat off his brow. A young man, perhaps twenty, his features made him look like a boy compared to the weathered faces of those who called this wilderness home. "The Romans announced a census. Judas and Saddok have agreed the time's come to raise Israel's fist in the name of the Almighty!"

Inside, Kohath sneered at this boy who likely knew nothing of fists. Still, he brought the word Kohath had been expecting, a word that might bring eventual deliverance from this desert. "Joshua! Bring wine and bread for our new friend."

The traveler held up the wineskin, squeezing its contents into his parched mouth. The skin and bread passed among the men now gathering beside Kohath and Matthias.

"There's more," added Matthias, easing his backside onto a smooth stone ledge, "the Sanhedrin met yesterday. Instead of condemning the census and calling for resistance, they coddled up to their Roman friends and voted to comply with it."

"No surprise to me," said Kohath. "They're all alike, once you get up that high. Priest, lawyer, no difference. They spout off about God till their own skin's on the line."

His cynicism rankled Matthias. "Judas and Saddok are men of God. They don't run from confrontation with Rome."

Kohath ignored him. "Anything else from Judas?"

"He wants you and your men in Jerusalem in three days. He said to travel at night, by two's or three's so you don't draw attention. Go to the caravansary of Ishmael."

"Know it well," grinned Kohath. "We've met some of our best clients there!" Laughter erupted among the men circled. The clients Kohath mentioned were caravan traders, carelessly revealing too much of goods that soon changed hands in this canyon.

"Once there, Judas will contact you." Matthias walked to the cave's entrance. "The sun's low, and I told Judas I'd return tonight. Do you have water for my horse?"

"Joshua! Show Matthias where we keep the stock. Let him use the cistern."

The two men made their way down the slope. Joshua led Matthias and the horse into another cave set up as a stable. A hollowed rock served as a watering trough. As the horse stuck his muzzle in the water, Matthias turned to Joshua.

"Judas respects your chieftain greatly. He's glad to have warriors for this fight."

Joshua nodded. "The desert hardens us all."

"Tell me," asked Matthias, "I'm sure you've robbed. But, have you ever killed a man?"

"Why do you want to know?"

"I just wonder, about myself. What it'll be like."

Joshua thought back to Bethlehem. "You'll find out soon enough." A moment of silence passed between the men, broken when Joshua exited the cave's mouth to rejoin Kohath. "And when you do, you'll never be the same."

Before Matthias could ask what he meant, Joshua scrambled back up the hill to rejoin the others. Water dripped from the horse's whiskers and plopped in the trough. The ripples could barely be seen in the cave's darkness. Matthias, squinting to make out those lines on the water, realized he still looked for an answer to what it would be like for him. To end another's life – or to have his own ended. The ripples disappeared. The answer would have to come another day.

CHAPTER XXIII

"There, Yeshua. You can just see Bethlehem!" Joseph pointed toward a small ridge to the south. The late afternoon sun sparkled off its limestone buildings.

The boy squinted his eyes. "It looks like bits of snow."

"That's from whitewashing the houses."

Joseph and Yeshua walked on. Today marked their sixth day of travel. Two miles remained of the ninety or more separating Nazareth from Bethlehem. What Yeshua first considered an adventure had settled into a plodding course. Rugged switchbacks and summer's dusty heat combined to weary legs and lungs. The burden of carrying a mantle during the day found reward when its woolen fibers warded off the night's chill. By sleeping in the countryside, Joseph and Yeshua avoided the expense of inns.

"Do you think we might find a cave tonight?" Yeshua remembered waking to heavy dew coating his mantle this morning, and the added weight until the sun dried it.

"I'm hoping we can stay with Bethlehem's innkeeper."

"The one we stayed with when we lived here?"

"That's right. Once I'm done with the enrollment, we'll go to Joshua's inn."

"I wonder if his children are still there, the ones I played with?"

The question evoked memories of what kept Joseph away from this town. "That you did. And in the stable."

"The stable's what I remember! From the stories you and mother told. Can we go there?"

"We will, Yeshua."

Within an hour, Joseph and Yeshua ascended Bethlehem's ridge. Signs directed them to the census officer, a Syrian seated in a shaded stall. Joseph stepped up to the table. "I've come to register, sir."

The Syrian, looking uninterested and tired, didn't bother lifting his eyes from the scrolls stretched out in front of him. "Name, family, present residence."

"Joseph, son of Jacob. My family and I live in Nazareth now."

Taking a pen made from a split reed, the Syrian dipped the point in a thick black liquid and recorded Joseph's responses on a clean sheet of papyrus. "Occupation?"

"Carpenter."

"Ownership of land?"

"A small home in Nazareth. And here, a field to the west, five *semedhs* in size."

The Syrian raised his head, aggravated he'd actually have to look something up. "The name of your last ancestor in Bethlehem who registered this land?"

"Matthan, my grandfather."

The Syrian poured over several scrolls. "Ah!" Placing a weight to hold it open, he copied an entry from the scroll as he spoke it aloud. "Matthan, son of Eleazar; last registered under the census of Herod by Joseph." The Syrian took a small papyrus, wrote a brief line, then sealed it with wax and stamped his ring's impression upon it. "Your enrollment is complete." He handed Joseph the sealed document. "This is proof you've registered. Information for assessments will be dispatched to the Galilean tax officials."

"Thank you. Is that all?"

The Syrian heaved a sigh, exasperated at the thought of a man of his talents wasting time with such fools. "Is that all? Would you like me to buy your evening meal?"

Joseph bowed and left. After reaching a safe distance from the Syrian, Yeshua asked: "What's wrong with him? Why did he insult you?"

"Yeshua, that's what a man acts like when he hates his work. But since he must do it, or thinks he must, his hatred spills onto others."

"That's not fair."

Joseph smiled. "No, it isn't." Then, slapping his son on the back, "But now that the enrollment's done, it's time to get to the inn – and the stable!"

Though ten years had passed, the streets and shops still looked familiar to Joseph. "Wait a minute." Joseph paused by a merchant's table. "Let's get some fruit for Joshua and his family."

The trader finished a transaction with another customer, then turned to Joseph. "Can I help you?"

"I'll take a look at some of these figs."

"A good choice. You'll find no sweeter figs this side of Jerusalem. How many will you and the boy need?"

"Actually," Joseph began, "it's not just for ourselves. We've come for the census, and hope to visit an old friend and his family here."

The shopkeeper smiled. "Perhaps I know him."

"You probably do. He's the innkeeper, Joshua. The last time – "

"Joshua?" The merchant's face tightened as he folded his arms across his chest.

"Yes. It's been some years since we've seen him and Naomi."

"Listen," snarled the merchant. "That coward left long ago, and his family afterwards."

The bitterness in the trader's voice shocked Joseph. "Coward? But what – "

"If you must talk about him, go to the old rabbi, Hananiah ben Johannan. He lives in a hut beside the inn's former stable."

"Here," Joseph offered, drawing a coin from his purse, "I'll take a couple of figs."

"Not from me you won't. I'll do no business with a

friend of that snake!"

A somber Joseph took Yeshua by the hand. "We go to the rabbi."

* * *

Julius pounded on the door of the caravansary. Though it neared supper time, the door was barred. Soon, Ishmael's raspy voice sounded from within.

"We're filled for the night. Try another inn!"

"Ishmael!" countered Julius. "Nabal comes to meet a Pharisee and a Galilean."

Julius heard a small timber being pulled through iron brackets, then a key turning in the lock. The door creaked open. "The others wait for you."

Julius saw, and smelled, Ishmael's seasoned cooking apron. Camel drivers joked of knowing Ishmael's current menu by the most recent layer of drippings to cake the leather smock. Others made mock bargains for the privilege of carrying the apron on the next journey, saying that if food ran out, a man could live off what clung to the apron for a week. Ishmael smiled at their ridicule – and more than once, went to the kitchen and scraped off a rancid bit from the apron into their stews.

"Join us, Nabal." Judas and Saddok waited at the same table where Julius first met the pair almost a week ago. But today, a stranger sat with them. Julius reckoned him a formidable man from the hard look of his face and muscular arms.

"Judas, Saddok." Julius shook hands with these two. Then, holding out his hand to the third man: "I don't think I know you."

"You don't." When their two hands locked, their grips tested each other's strength.

"This is Kohath, Nabal," Judas began, "it seems you two share the same trade."

"Perhaps we'll work together," offered Julius.

"I choose who works with me," sputtered Kohath.

215

"Let's get on with it, Judas."

The four sat down. Judas spoke first. "You've no doubt heard the rumors. Several Roman patrols ambushed, reports of nearly a dozen legionnaires killed, merchants who trade with the Romans beaten, fires set alongside the Antonia and Herod's palace – the skirmishes have begun. But it's time to do even more. Kohath, we need your skills."

"Who do you need dead?"

Saddok looked to Judas, then spoke. "Last week, the Sanhedrin betrayed us. The High Priest Joazar, an appointee of Herod, argued against opposing the census."

Kohath's eyebrows raised. "You want the High Priest killed?"

"No," countered Saddok. "That would turn too many against us. But we need to send a signal to Joazar to convince him to change his view and reconvene the Sanhedrin. He still could be a powerful ally."

"So, how is that done, and what has it to do with me?" asked Kohath.

Judas poured wine for Kohath and Nabal. "Silence the man closest to Joazar: the Sopher of the High Priest, Nathaniel."

Julius avoided reacting to that name, sipping his wine as he mulled the choice of Kohath's target. He thought of Simeon, and the death of his brother. What a fitting irony if he, Julius, now condemned Nathaniel by silence!

"Just one man, eh?" asked Kohath. "They guard him heavy?"

"He's watched by the Temple police. But," added Judas, "that watch is reduced every Sabbath night. That gives you two days to survey his house and grounds. He has only two servants at night, while three women of his family stay with him."

"You're not saying we have to leave them alone and just kill Nathaniel? They could see us and cause problems."

"The house of the unrighteous deserves to perish," declared Saddok. "Nathaniel's judgment falls on them as well."

Kohath laughed. "Though with the women, judgment might take a little longer!"

"That's not what I meant," objected Saddok, "they are still – "

"You want Nathaniel dead?" Kohath slammed his fist on the table, spilling some of his wine. "If we do it, it's done our way!"

Judas folded his hands, and spoke in a soft but firm voice. "Nathaniel's household dies, Kohath. That is your charge. If you do more, the choice is yours. Understood?"

"Always have, Galilean." Kohath poured more wine. "Always have."

"There's another matter. I want you to use Nabal in your Sabbath venture."

"No!" Kohath leered at the stranger. "I don't risk my life with a stranger!"

Judas persisted. "He wants to fight, and this will give me a test of his loyalty."

"Test him yourself."

Julius decided to force the issue. "Maybe Kohath fears I'd show up his men, or himself!"

Kohath lunged at Julius, and the two sprawled on the floor. Julius blocked Kohath's attempt to draw his dagger, but both men found themselves unable to gain advantage. Ishmael ran into the room, wailing about the damage to furniture and dishes – while keeping a discrete eye to insure Julius' safety. Judas and Saddok pried the two apart.

"Stop it!" Judas stood between the two men. "We fight Romans, not each other!"

Ishmael and Saddok righted the overturned table and chairs, gathering the shards of the broken dishes. As they did, Judas faced Kohath. "Very well, Nabal doesn't go with you."

"Good." Then, in a begrudging tone, rubbing a sore jaw, "You fight well, Nabal."

Julius ignored the remark and faced Judas, "So what's

left for me to do?"

"Patience. There'll be other intrigues in need of your dagger. Wait for word from Matthias. He'll come to you soon."

Julius left the inn. A steady breeze chilled and freshened the air. The city's daytime sounds of market and commerce passed into evening's quieter tones. Julius found the cool stillness invigorating as he considered the options. While leaving Nathaniel to Kohath's knives tempted Julius, its intent of intimidating the Joazar might succeed. Besides, Nathaniel's servants and family had no guilt in this. Julius reasoned that without his intervention, the family would again suffer death because of Nathaniel. He could not let that be.

* * *

"Rabbi? Rabbi Hananiah?"

The old man napping in the chair twitched at the sound of Joseph's call. His head rolled back and forth as his eyelids lifted.

"My son and I need to speak with you, Rabbi."

Hananiah turned toward the voice, his eyes oddly unfocused. "Who is it?"

"I am Joseph, Rabbi. The boy is my son, Yeshua. We once lived here in Bethlehem. I've come to ask about the innkeeper Joshua."

The old man held out a trembling hand. "Forgive me, my eyes closed to the light more than five years ago. You say, Joseph? And Yeshua?"

"Yes, Rabbi. It's been over ten years since we left."

Hananiah brought his hand slowly to his mouth. "How old is your son?"

"I'll be twelve years this fall, Rabbi."

"Come closer to me, boy." Yeshua stepped directly in front of Hananiah, who studied Yeshua's face with his fingers. As he did, tears formed in the darkened hollows below his brow, furrowed by the years and the sun. "You alone live,

Yeshua. You alone," he whispered.

Yeshua felt a chill. "Rabbi – father – "

Joseph knelt beside the rabbi. "You know of these things? Forgive me, Rabbi!"

Hananiah's right hand searched for Joseph. "What happened has always remained a mystery to me. I believed your exodus traced to the hand of God. But why that hand did not shelter the others, I've never understood." The rabbi paused to wipe his cheek. "There were some who cursed you, Joseph, and this son of yours, as the cause."

"The cause of what?! What's wrong, father – what have I done?"

"Yeshua, it's nothing you've done."

"But what are you and the Rabbi talking about?!"

Before Joseph could answer, Hananiah spoke again: "Joseph, your son's questions are best answered in the place where your wife gave him birth. Take him to the stable. It will help you say what must be said."

"As you wish, Rabbi," replied Joseph, though he had no idea what was meant. "Yeshua?"

"I'm coming." The boy lifted Hananiah's hand from his forehead and held it for a moment before letting go.

As the two left the hut, Hananiah called out, "You are a child precious to God, Yeshua ben Joseph. But learn now just how dear your life is!"

Joseph and Yeshua walked the few steps to the cave's opening in silence. Joseph took an oil lamp from a small ledge inside the entrance, one of several left burning there. The stable must still be used, he thought, for lamps to be provided. But what use? The stalls and furnishings were in disarray. They walked in further. Joseph vaguely remembered a large room in the back corner. Upon making the turn and proceeding forward, however, a wall of rocks blocked the way.

"What's this been put here for?" Joseph muttered.

"Father, there's a jar below."

Joseph handed the lamp to Yeshua, then drew out a scroll he saw within the jar. Leaning with his back to the wall, Joseph read in silence.

"My God, my God!" Joseph slid down the wall, his fingers trembling as they traced the characters etched into leather.

Yeshua's fear grew as the lamp's flickering light showed his father's face grow pale. The boy longed to be back home in Nazareth, or scrambling on the scaffoldings of Sepphoris: anywhere but here.

"Yeshua." Joseph motioned his son to sit down beside him, then wrapped an arm around the boy. "Do you remember your mother and me telling of when we left Bethlehem, because we felt there was danger?"

"Yes."

"And how we fled without telling anyone, even our friends, because we feared people might harm them if they knew anything about us going?"

"I think so."

"We did what we thought was right. But later, we found out we'd been wrong. I'd been wrong. The people who came to hurt you ended up hurting other people. Neighbors. Friends."

Yeshua recalled Hananiah's words. "To hurt me? And what others? *Abba*, why did the rabbi keep saying, `I alone.' Do I have some fault in this?"

"No, Yeshua! The evil one person does is NEVER another's fault." Joseph looked down into his son's face, then to the cave's ceiling. "Adonai, how can I say this?" Turning back to Yeshua, Joseph pushed on. "Soldiers came to this town. You were just a child." Joseph's voice cracked. "Yeshua, they came here looking to kill you. But instead, they killed the children of Bethlehem! And this stable is where they're buried. Behind this wall."

Yeshua's eyes filled with tears. "Is this what the scroll says?"

"It lists the names of the children killed. And Elias. And Rachel. God, why didn't I warn them. GOD, WHY DIDN'T YOU WARN THEM!?" Joseph's body shuddered as words gave way to moans. To Yeshua, it was as if those groans shook the ground. The son threw his arms round his father's heaving chest. He clung tight, afraid that if he let go both Joseph and he might be lost in this room's gloom. He wouldn't let go, couldn't let go . . .

Time ceased to be in the stable's darkness, how long neither knew. When Joseph kissed his son's brow, it was evening. "Yeshua, we must leave this place."

Yeshua picked a small stone off the wall and slipped it into his pouch. It clanged against a gold ring given to him a long time ago in this same stable. The ring, one king's gift; the stone, one king's curse: Yeshua now carried them both. To remember kings, and children, who were no more. . .

CHAPTER XXIV

Broken clouds from a spent Mediterranean storm swirled over Jerusalem. The moon slipped in and out of opaque billows, the way a hunter slides from shadow to tree to boulder when stalking prey. Darkness provided welcome shelter to a column of Roman troops entering Herod's palace per the instructions of Coponius.

Several ambushes had plagued their three-day march from Caesarea. Rocks and arrows rained from the heights of the Shephelah foothills when they ascended the Aijalon valley. The urgent dispatch from Coponius and Julius, requesting another century in Jerusalem, ruled out any prolonged skirmishes along the way. The seasoned troops accepted the necessity for speed. But Lucius, the centurion in command, found himself stifling an impatience for action among several new men – including one called Antony. While his training was not yet complete, Antony's progress far exceeded his fellow drillmates. Lucius would have added the young man to his century even if Julius had not requested it in the dispatch's orders. Lucius and Julius went back many years, even before the night they'd been dispatched on Herod's orders to Bethlehem.

No fanfare greeted the contingent when they arrived at in Jerusalem. The troops barracked in quarters there once reserved there for Herod's elite guard. Antony stowed his gear in a tiny cell and peered out its narrow slit to the outside world. A sky that once seemed so vast when it stretched above Bethlehem's hills was now framed in a space the size of a brick. This was his new freedom. Antony stretched out on his sleeping mat. Muscles throbbed in protest, reminding him of the seventy-five-mile trek. Through the window, nothing could be seen, only the alternate glowing and dimming from moonlight's dance within the clouds.

As Antony passed into sleep, a figure emerged from the night's shadows to approach the palace wall's east gate.

"What do you want?" demanded a youthful guard named Arius.

"I've a note for your procurator."

"Let me see it."

The stranger drew up his hunched shoulders a bit straighter. "Julius sent me. `Only Coponius sees the note' is what Julius says."

"Listen, old man!" Arius seized the man, pinning his arms tight to his side so no weapon could be used. "I know many men called Julius. Give me the note!"

"But there's only one Julius that reports to Coponius!"

At those words, Arius relaxed his grip. "What proof do you have?"

The stranger drew an *armillae* from his purse. Arius held the bracelet up to the torchlight: it bore the insignia of the Roman eagle, and the inscription *Julius, Primus Pilus*. Arius knew the new advisor to Coponius, whose name was Julius, had held this title prior to his new rank.

"Diogenes! Stand watch while I escort this fellow." Arius accompanied the stranger through the gate and into the palace compound. A filthy apron, brought into view when the stranger removed his mantle, hung round his neck.

"I doubt the procurator will receive you in that."

The stranger grinned, revealing black gaps between a scattering of yellowed teeth. "Why, this is just my uniform, same as that helmet and chestplate you wear." The old man scraped a fingerful of splatterings from the apron and slipped it into his mouth. When Arius winced, the stranger chuckled. "Providing folks with food is just how Ishmael ekes out a living, boy. 'Course, passing information to you

Romans sweetens the pot, too!"

* * *

Long after the caravansary's other guests headed to their rooms, Kohath's men sat at several tables pulled together in the eating hall. Less than an hour earlier, Ishmael had stacked the serving table with enough bread and stew and wine to keep them satisfied.

"You'll have to fend for yourselves," Ishmael had announced, pulling a mantle over his apron, "but I just got me a new heifer in harness, and she's ready to be plowed."

"Then you'd better wear blinders tonight, Ishmael!" Tobias yelled as the innkeeper left. "Any cow who'd let you furrow her field must be ugly enough to stop the sun!"

Ishmael turned, feigning laughter with those who howled at him. Once the door swung shut, Ishmael felt in his purse for the scroll and bracelet slipped to him earlier that night. Their carrier had whispered the paper came from Julius and must be given to the procurator immediately. Ishmael also fingered the cool round shapes of silver shekels, passed to him for this night's work. "Laugh while you can," he muttered under his breath, "it's your graves I'll be plowing." Ishmael began the long walk to the palace.

Meanwhile, Kohath's men downed the food left for them. They knew Kohath had met with Judas and Saddok that afternoon, and waited now for their leader to tell them what he'd learned. Once the food was gone, Joshua started clearing the tables, leaving only the wine. Kohath stood and motioned for silence.

"Listen up! Two days, and we draw first blood."

Some nodded heads, while others grunted their assent. Though relaxing at the caravansary provided a respite from the desert, no profit came in leisure.

"It's a wealthy house," Kohath continued, "and its size means we all have work to do. Three or four stand watch outside. The rest go in."

"Won't they have guards?" asked Lamech.

Kohath swilled a mouthful of wine, some splashing out the goblet's side and running down his chin. "It'll be Sabbath. All but two of the guards won't be working." He wiped his face on the sleeve of his robe. "But poor men like us work whenever we can!"

"A toast to Judas," offered Tobias, raising his goblet, "for a Sabbath gift to our purses!"

Kohath hoisted his goblet. "It's not just our purses that'll be grateful. Judas says there's three women in the household. I figure we can have a go with them before sealing their eyes!"

All goblets rose at these last words, and a few shouts rang out. Even Joshua joined in the celebration, stopping for a gulp of wine before loading a trayful of dishes.

Tobias yelled for attention. "Another drink to our Sabbath host. Whose house does Judas send us to, Kohath?"

"The Sopher to the High Priest – Nathaniel!"

Platters crashed to the floor, interrupting the revelry. All eyes glared at Joshua, who knelt beside the strewn pieces. "Thank God we've Ishmael to get our meals," bellowed Tobias, "our cook grows clumsier each day!" A kick from Tobias sent Joshua sprawling. Laughter, and more talk and wine, flowed.

Joshua was grateful their attention shifted back to the tables. None saw his hands trembling as he cleaned the mess. Nathaniel! Of all people in Jerusalem, why Nathaniel? Joshua considered what sort of fate, or God, conspired for their paths to cross his path in such a manner.

On his way to the kitchen to find a broom, Joshua brooded over his options. He could try to warn Nathaniel. But would he be believed, and what could he say? *I've just spent the last ten years with a band of Sicarii, and now they plan to kill you.* What prevented Nathaniel from having him arrested then and there, even executed as a criminal? Worse, if his attempt to alert Nathaniel failed and Kohath found out about it: Joshua shuddered to think of those results. But what if he didn't warn Nathaniel? Joshua thought back to Bethlehem and David's death. Then, too, inaction resulted in death. Then there was the fate of these women Kohath mentioned.

As Joshua searched the kitchen for a broom, his eyes fell upon a slotted wooden block where Ishmael stored his knives. A new possibility emerged: one quick draw across his wrists, and there'd be no more confusion. No more decisions to make. No more risks to consider. The pain would be over. Forever.

With a dazed deliberateness, Joshua reached for one of the knives. Its smooth wooden handle reminded him of those once fashioned by his long-dead friend Elias, another of his victims. Laying the knife across his left wrist, he felt the coolness of the blade. Hands quaking, he turned his eyes away and started to press down.

"More wine, Joshua!" Nearly a minute passed, and no response.

"MORE WINE, JOSHUA!" Kohath was not accustomed to waiting for commands to be answered. "Damn him anyway!" he sputtered, pushing his chair from the table and striding toward the kitchen.

"Joshua, we –" Kohath stopped at the kitchen's portal. He saw Joshua seated on the floor, draining the contents of a large wineskin down his throat. What Kohath didn't note was the knife resting set between Joshua's legs. "Go ahead, drink yourself into a stupor! We'll both be happier with you out of my sight." Kohath grabbed a large jug of wine and returned to the main room.

With Kohath gone, Joshua lowered the wineskin. He'd relearned an awful truth. His fear to live was surpassed only by his fear to die. Joshua lifted the wineskin again and leaned back, mouth wide open. Maybe the wine would dull his pain, if only for a night.

***

An hour had passed since Coponius dismissed Ishmael.

How Julius trusted such a character with this scroll eluded the procurator's reasoning. But that was of little importance now. Forty-eight hours remained before Kohath's raid on the home of Nathaniel, and much needed to be done: the more under the darkness of night, the better. Coponius reread the scroll several times as he waited, to insure he understood exactly what Julius wanted him to do and say.

At the sound of footsteps, Coponius rewound the scroll. A knock at his door was followed by the voice of the steward Antigonus: "Coponius, Nathaniel is here."

Coponius motioned at the guard to unbar the door. The procurator stifled a yawn when Nathaniel entered. "Be seated, Nathaniel." Coponius waited until his guard shut and barred the door. "No one knows of your coming here?"

"Only the servant who wakened me. Your messenger ordered him to tell no one."

"Good." Coponius folded his hands. "Nathaniel, I've come into information about a plot to murder you."

Nathaniel snapped forward in his chair. "What?!"

"Apparently part of this protest to the census. But rest assured, no harm will come to you. We know the details of the conspiracy. And a plan for your safety is already developed."

"Then tell me. I'll need to have my servants arrange the household for extra guards, or should we –"

"Calm yourself, Nathaniel! We don't want to tip off the plotters. There'll be no change in routine or guards at your home – at least what meets the eye."

Nathaniel's head tilted back. "What meets the eye?"

"All you need to know is this. The attack is planned for the night of your Sabbath. Tomorrow night, when we're certain no one is watching your house, a detachment of soldiers will sneak into your home and remain hidden throughout the next day. Sabbath eve they'll take up position to receive those who intend to slit your throat."

"I don't know that I like sitting inside a trap," protested Nathaniel. "What if something goes wrong? What if your information is faulty and the attack comes sooner?"

"Trust me," offered Coponius, summoning his most reassuring tone, "our knowledge comes from a source I consider absolutely reliable."

"But what shall I tell my family, and the servants?"

Coponius grinned. "Nothing, at least now. Your household mustn't act any differently than on a normal Sabbath. Don't reveal anything until the soldiers are in place. Even then, just tell them some special precaution is being taken, which they must swear to hold in silence. For their own sake, Nathaniel, and yours."

"Wouldn't it be safer to hide me until the danger passes?"

"You'll be safe, Nathaniel. To remove you would risk our informant, and allow these murderers to plan another venture. This way: they go to your home, are ambushed and killed. When word of their fate spreads, this infatuation with rebellion dies out."

Nathaniel looked hard at Coponius. "Your best men will be assigned to this?"

"The best, I assure you." Coponius joined Nathaniel by the brazier. "Another century has arrived from Caesarea. We'll have no problem protecting you. Now, go home and say nothing."

Nathaniel stood to leave, but on his way out turned back to the procurator. "My life and the lives of my family are in your hands, Coponius."

"I'll not disappoint you. Trust me, Rome will watch over you."

* **

Ishmael traversed the alleyways of the Tyropean district. He passed the street that led to his caravansary, choosing to descend into a thicket of crowded stone dwellings. Ishmael congratulated himself for having cajoled an oil lamp from Coponius. Didn't want a light coming to the palace, he'd said, someone might follow. But as for going back: it's a dangerous thing to be traveling so late, especially with a purse freshly weighted with Roman silver. And the *armillae* of Julius: what if some robber fell upon him, then took the bracelet to Kohath? Coponius relented to the waves of Ishmael's pleadings, less in agreement as to get him out of the room. The lamp in Ishmael's hand finally cast its faint light on the house he decided to visit at the last minute. He pounded three dull thuds, waited, then struck twice more. He heard movement inside. "Nabal?"

"Who wants to know?"

"Ishmael. I've got something of yours."

The door opened. Ishmael took a step and a half in, then felt his head snap to the side as a hand covered his mouth. The door slammed, and as he was wrestled down to the floor the lamp fell out of his hand and broke A foot across his neck prevented Ishmael from crying out. Had he been mistaken about the house, or worse yet, had Kohath –

The figure above him reached for another lamp, and knelt down to examine the face of his victim in the light. "So it is you, Ishmael," he whispered. "I didn't expect you tonight." He lifted his foot, allowing the innkeeper to catch his breath.

"You bastard!" exclaimed Ishmael, "You've a fine way to repay your couriers."

"I needed to make sure someone wasn't using your name."

Ishmael looked at the broken shards of pottery and oil spilled on the dirt floor. "Look what you've done to my lamp! Coponius gave it to me. Carried it with him from Rome, he said. At least HE was grateful to see me. You'll need to pay me extra for the loss of that."

Julius picked a piece of it up and laughed. "You old thief, I can take you to the pottery house in the Hinnom valley where they make these by the hundreds. See that mark?"

"Why, here I took the procurator at his word."

"Ishmael, this is Julius you're talking to." Dropping the shard, he reached for a goatskin filled with wine, then handed it to Ishmael.

The innkeeper hoisted it, squirting a purple stream into his mouth. He swirled it around, then swallowed. "Julius, if you ever want to earn an honest living, spying on rich traders instead of poor thieves and rabbis, I'd be honored to have you as partner. We'd make hell of a pair!"

"We do already," laughed Julius. Then his voice took a more serious edge, "But why did you come here tonight?"

Ishmael dug into his purse, removed the bracelet and handed it to Julius. "I didn't want this with me any longer than needed. What with Kohath's thieves around, someone's hands might get too curious."

Julius took the bracelet. "You do well to be cautious."

Ishmael handed his host the goatskin and wiped his lips on his apron. "Well, speaking of caution: there's no holes in this Sabbath plan, is there? I'll not want those cutthroats coming after me when the dust settles."

Julius helped him to his feet. "If Judas and Saddok are at the inn on Sabbath eve, as you overheard, just do as we agreed. My men have their instructions."

"You're sure you can't be there yourself, to see it goes right?"

"Don't worry, Ishmael, it will. But like I said before, I'll be spending Sabbath with an old acquaintance."

* * *

A narrow shaft of light beaming in and the thick aroma of porridge woke Antony. The night passed swiftly, even with the extra hour of sleep given to the century. Antony stood, then bent over to touch his fingers to his feet several times. He stretched, twisting his torso to one side and then the other. There'd be exercise after breakfast, but he wanted to work out the stiffness left from the trek. As Antony donned his leather cuirass, a sharp rap sounded on his door.

"Legionnaire Antony!"

"Yes sir!" Leaving the buckling of his breastplate, Antony walked to the door and opened it. "Centurion!" He snapped to attention.

Lucius walked into the room and sat on its one chair. "We need to speak."

"Yes, sir." Antony closed the door, then resumed a rigid posture.

"You can relax, Antony. Sleep well?"

Antony spread his feet apart and clasped his hands behind his back. "Very well."

"Breakfast'll be soon, so go ahead and fix that cuirass while we talk." Antony began buckling the straps together as Lucius continued. "Several from our century will go with me on an assignment tomorrow night. I've been told you speak Hebrew. We've need of someone who can do that. You've been chosen."

Antony's fingers stopped threading the last of the buckles at this news. "Thank you, sir."

Lucius leaned his chair back, balancing it on its rear legs. "Don't thank me. I'd probably not choose a fresh recruit for such a task as we'll have. Back in Caesarea, I told you your training record made the difference for being added to the century. Truth is, as good as that record was, someone requested you be added. Someone named Julius."

Antony didn't know how to read Lucius. Was he angry, or just testing him? "I ask no favors, centurion. Of you or Julius. Only to do my job."

"And that you'll do, legionnaire." Lucius rocked the chair back onto its four legs and stood. "Julius was once my centurion, and a damned good one. He's not one to play favorites. He's got a good reason for this, whatever it is."

Lucius walked up to Antony until their faces were but inches apart. "So don't disappoint him by disappointing me. Understood?"

"Understood, centurion!"

"Good. I meet with the men in this detail later today. You'll get word when. Now finish gearing up!"

"Yes, sir!"

Lucius strode out the door. Julius had a good eye for men, he thought. This Antony didn't flinch when they stood toe to toe. But how was he at killing? Tomorrow night would be the test.

Back in the room, Antony considered this turn of events: Julius had a hand in his return to Jerusalem! But why? To keep a protective eye on him? To test his loyalty to Rome? Antony decided to rest his imagination and wait for Sabbath night to provide an answer.

CHAPTER XXV

Jerusalem's streets swarmed in the final hour before sunset on Sabbath eve. Sellers hawked perishables in one last frenzy. Buyers haggled, hoping to snare bargains. Timing comprised the art in this weekly melee. Sabbath laws dictated the stalls be closed and cleaned before sunset. Since not every merchant lived near his shop, closing time varied with the distance to be traveled before dusk. Carts laden with animals and pungent foods and silken goods added to the congestion clogging Jerusalem's alleyways in the rush home to keep Sabbath.

In the midst of this furor, two men jostled through the crowds in the Tyropean quarter. No one hurrying past noticed how the robes of these two bulged at the shoulders and again at the waist and thighs. The pair entered a caravansary's courtyard and pounded on the door.

"Go away," scowled a voice inside. "Sabbath's got us clean full!"

The men looked around the courtyard. Normally crowded with beasts of burden resting from the day's journey, no animals could be seen. The taller spoke, not in the common tongue of Aramaic but Hebrew: "The zeal of Adonai consumes the house of the wicked."

The door cracked open. The innkeeper peered out, then waved in the supplicants. "I feared you'd been delayed. Or worse."

Judas and Saddok stepped inside, then pushed back their hoods and shed their robes. Both wore metal chestplates, a type newly introduced to Roman troops. Each had a *gladius* hanging from one side of their belts, a dagger scabbarded on the other.

Ishmael ran his fingers across Judas' chestplate and sword, then raised his head and grinned. "Kind of the Romans to lend you their gear."

Judas drew the sword, giving Ishmael a closer look. "Until two days ago, its use came at our expense. Now, we will chip the blade on the bone of Israel's enemies."

"The Lord confounds our enemies with his might," declared Saddok. "Rome's own weapons will slay her sons."

Kohath stood at a corner table flanked by Lamech and Benjamin. "So, Judas, good hunting?"

Judas and Kohath shook hands. "Very good. A Roman patrol guarding tax officials from Jericho – all dead. Besides weapons and armor, we got three horses. And," throwing a weighted purse toward Ishmael, "some land levies. Put that toward the expenses for Kohath's stay."

Ishmael passed the purse from hand to hand, back and forth, eyes gleaming. "They'll be as well cared for as my own dear kin."

Judas pulled a chair alongside Kohath's. "Everything ready for tonight?"

"Scouted the house yesterday evening, then twice more today." Kohath spit on the floor, grinding it into the rough plank with his sandal. "Nathaniel's as good as dead."

"So be it," pronounced Saddok.

"Kohath, Saddok and I must prepare for Sabbath. We'll await your return."

"Do what you will," he replied. "We'll be back after midnight."

"Right," added Lamech, "once all our chores are done!"

Kohath slapped his companions' backs. "Up to the room. Last time to rest before we do business with Nathaniel – and his women!"

When they'd left, Saddok turned to Judas. "How the Lord stoops to use the unrighteous in his cause remains a mystery to me."

"Mysteries have a way of resolving themselves, rabbi. After we've cleansed this land from the corruption of those above us, we can deal with the scum beneath us."

* * *

Nathaniel sat anxiously at table with Deborah and Naomi and Hannah while his servants remained in the kitchen. As instructed, those two rooms were the only ones in the house with a lamp burning. Once stars appeared in the night's descending darkness, sounds stirred from the cellar storeroom. Feet shuffled. Men whispered. Hands groped along walls seeking doors and stairs. In ten minutes, all grew quiet again.

Edging closer to the table, Nathaniel spoke in a hushed tone. "The guards are in position. There'll be at least one in each of your rooms at all times, others scattered around the house. Remember, we're being watched. You must act as though nothing is different."

"I'm afraid," Hannah said. "I don't know if I can do this."

Naomi took her daughter's hand. "We're all afraid. But it will be alright, trust me."

"Listen to your mother," added Nathaniel. "Rome's finest guards watch over us."

"And the hand of Almighty," Deborah added as she glanced from Hannah to Nathaniel.

Nathaniel stood. "It's best we go to our beds. Don't forget: act as if this were any other Sabbath."

The women left the table, each receiving Nathaniel's kiss on their forehead. The servants cleared away the food. Naomi walked with Hannah, holding her hand and assuring her all would be well. When they reached Hannah's room, Naomi left her lamp in the hall and opened the door. She could barely see the outline of a legionnaire by the wall. "You there," she whispered. "I need a word with you."

The guard moved in the shadows by an unshuttered

window, avoiding the light cast inside by the lamps. "My name is Arius. What is it?"

"I am Naomi, niece of the Sopher. This is my daughter's room that you guard."

"Those are my orders."

"Remember, she's still a child. I want nothing improper between you. My uncle wields great power in this city, and if there IS any problem –"

"There will be no problem. My commander issued the same orders to me already."

Arius' comment surprised Naomi. All her life she'd heard nothing but evil of Romans. "You'll do well to follow them."

"I will do as commanded."

Naomi kissed Hannah on the cheek. "Goodnight, dear."

"Goodnight, mother." Though Hannah heard herself say the words, her thoughts drifted. Hannah had studied the features of Arius while her mother talked with him. He couldn't be more than twenty. Light brown curls lay matted on his head. His face didn't show as yet the stubble requiring a razor's edge. A sleeveless red woolen tunic extended to his knees, baring muscled calves. A rush of excitement overtook her, a feeling she'd occasionally experienced gazing at other young men in the last year. Hannah wondered: would Arius look at her in the same way?

"Go in your room, Hannah." Naomi's voice roused Hannah from her reverie. "It's late."

Hannah took her lamp and stepped into the room while Arius hid in the shadows again.

* * *

Nathaniel made his way up the stairs. Never had the steps seemed so high or many in number. The thought of serving as bait for this snare still distressed him. His breath quickened as he neared the door. One hand pushed it open, while the other held a tight grip on his lamp. All looked normal, until he noticed his bed. Someone reclined under the fleece cover! "What?"

"Ssshhhh!" The shush came from behind the door. "Leave the lamp outside."

Nathaniel set the lamp down in the hall and entered the room. The door shut behind him. He turned to see who closed it, though his eyes needed time to adjust to the dark. At first, all he could make out was a bearded man who wore no uniform, only common street clothes. Could the sounds heard at the table have been the assassins, not the guards?! Nathaniel stumbled back.

"Nathaniel," said the stranger, whose eyes had long since grown accustomed to the dark, and now saw the look of horror on the Sopher's face. "You look as if a ghost stands before you."

While he still could not see, Nathaniel suddenly recognized the voice: "Julius!?"

"Lower your voice."

Nathaniel shuffled in the blackness to a cedar chest in which he kept his clothes, then sat on its rounded lid. "Coponius said nothing about you being involved."

Julius stepped alongside the chest. "I'm sure that was just an oversight," Julius replied, knowing full well he'd asked the procurator not to tell Nathaniel he would guard him.

A movement under the bed's fleece cover reminded Nathaniel what had first startled him.

"And forgive me, Sopher. This will be your other protector tonight, a Greek named Diogenes. A good fighter."

Nathaniel felt sweat beading on his forehead. "Shall I switch places with him?"

"Let me ask you a question first," answered Julius. "It's summer. Don't you usually sleep with the drapes and balcony door open?"

"Why, yes; but I thought –"

"Nothing can be out of place. Go back and get your

lamp; we'll stay out of sight. When you come back in, open the balcony door and pull the drapes aside. Then crawl in bed and put your lamp out. Then either stay there, or slip out and let Diogenes back in your place."

"I think I'd prefer sleeping in bed to sitting and worrying."

"That's your choice," stated Julius, "although we're not sure what weapons they plan to use. If they come with daggers and swords, we'll make short work of them once they're in the room. But if they've someone outside with a bow, they might fire a few arrows into your side before we can get to them."

Nathaniel hoped to hear a laugh from Julius, as if this were some macabre attempt at humor. No laughter came. And Nathaniel's eyes, adapting now to the dark, could see it was a sober face that concluded: "Whatever you prefer, Sopher. You choose."

"What of the danger to Diogenes, if he remains in bed?"

"He wears armor. But if you'd like, you can take his place."

"No, let Diogenes have the bed. But perhaps, if I had a sword?"

Julius laughed. "Weapons in untrained hands cause strange things to happen. Remember some years back, when you sat in on the meeting where Herod assigned me to a detail in Bethlehem? That day, I watched a Jew pull a knife on one of my men. Probably could've killed him if he hadn't froze. Then this same Jew watched his son be slain with his own knife."

Julius drew a dagger from within his cloak, holding its tip inches from Nathaniel's chin. "I could give you this. But then, I might think you'd be ready to use it, and assume you'd take care of yourself in the fight. But what if you panicked like that Jew in Bethlehem? You'd be dead before I had a chance to help!" Julius punctuated this last statement by lightly pressing the dagger's point into Nathaniel's flesh before returning the weapon to its sheath. "No, better you stay out of the way. Let somebody else do the killing. No sense you risking yourself, is there?"

The Sopher pondered the dagger's barb along with the reference to Bethlehem. Did he imagine hearing an accusatory tone in Julius' voice? What else might he know of that day? In another time, Nathaniel might have pursued such questions. But not now. His life depended on Julius, and this wasn't a time to challenge his bodyguard. "No, Julius, I suppose not."

*　*　*

Hannah lingered at the small table next to her bed. A polished circle of bronze mirrored her reflection as she unwound her braids and brushed her hair in long slow strokes. At times, she tilted her mirror as if to examine some tangle, but in truth to see if Arius watched. Once or twice, she thought his eyes caught hers. Each time, a demure smile crossed her face, then she'd quickly toss her head in another direction.

Arius crouched by the door. He reasoned an entry through the window, narrow and on the second story, would be easily repelled. The door presented the main danger. He wedged a small chest against the wall beside it, so that even if the intruders swung the door open to charge in, it wouldn't strike him – and he'd have his sword through the first man's side before being seen.

"Arius?" Hannah said as she passed the ivory-handled brush through her dark tresses, "Have you a wife in Rome?"

"Keep your voice down, Hannah!"

"Very well," she murmured, "but do you?"

Arius shook his head. "No, I don't. I'm not even from Rome."

Hannah set down the brush and scooted across the bedding to the side closer to where Arius knelt. "I'm not from Jerusalem, either. We come from a town called Bethlehem."

"Oh."

"Arius, do you find me pleasing to look at?"

"Hannah, both your mother and my officer made it clear that –"

"Either answer my question," Hannah interrupted, her voice becoming louder, "or I shall scream and say you were rude with me!"

Arius put a finger to his mouth. "Alright, if it'll keep you still. Yes, you're attractive, for a girl your age. But please, you have to be quiet. This is a serious night."

A girl my age, she thought. Hannah knew at least three girls her age already betrothed. Arius' other words, about the gravity of this evening, reminded her of the fear she felt earlier. Perhaps this was a good time to revisit that fear. Extinguishing the lamp's flame, she whispered softly, "I'm afraid, Arius."

"Don't be afraid. We've plenty of guards in the house. No harm will come to you."

"But it scares me, Arius." Hannah slid off the bed and knelt next to Arius, wrapping her arms around his neck. "It scares me."

"Hannah." Arius started to pull her arms away, but she clung tighter.

"Please, Arius. I'm afraid." She turned her face toward his. "I'll be quiet if you hold me. I promise not to tell."

"Just for a minute." Arius used one arm to hold her while keeping a firm grip with the other on his gladius. He realized it had been a long time since he felt such warmth by his side. Unlike other Roman posts, the Antonia had no campwomen to serve the soldier's needs. The Jews hated prostitution, death being the common penalty. Only a return to Caesarea or some other distant post brought ready access to a female. But interrupting this moment's ease came remembrance of his commander's orders and the girl's mother.

"Hannah, you must get to bed. Now."

Lifting her arms away, she brushed her lips against his cheek and moved toward her bed. She paused to remove her outer tunic, leaving only a linen slip against her. Arius watched as moonlight flooding in from the window silhouetted her body's soft contours. She looked at him once more, smiled, and slipped under the sheets.

Minutes passed without a sound. Arius sought to return his focus from her flirtation. Julius would have his hide if he failed. Vigilance was everything.

Hannah, on the other hand, let her thoughts drift. Arius would protect her this night. And hadn't he held her when they sat next to one another? Didn't he stare at her when she removed the tunic? Hannah clutched her pillow tight. "Arius," she sighed, just loud enough to be heard by her guardian, "I will see you again after tonight. I promise."

CHAPTER XXVI

Three men crouched beside a low rock wall lining the alley, less than fifty yards from Nathaniel's home. One of the men cupped his hands to his mouth and mocked a turtle-dove's cooing. From a distance, what sounded like another dove returned the call. Within a minute, two others crept alongside the first three. The action periodically repeated over the next few minutes, until all of Kohath's men knelt beside the wall.

The last trio to arrive included Joshua. He studied the darkened house, thinking back to when he'd been its guest. His kinsman, who'd bought the purification sacrifices for Naomi, would soon be executed. Even wine from the skin smuggled from the inn couldn't blot out his betrayal. The memory of Nathaniel holding David flashed through his mind, shattered by the image of a dagger slashing them both. Joshua's growing panic was interrupted by Kohath waving the group together.

"Listen!" came Kohath's hushed voice. "Lamech, take charge of the outside guard. One man at each corner of the house, and you stay be the gate. Anything goes wrong, get inside!"

Lamech clasped Kohath's hand, then tapped his men, one of them being Joshua. They left to take their positions.

"Benjamin, you and your men cover the first floor. Take care of the two guards if they happen to still be awake. Once we're upstairs, go to the stairway and whistle. That'll be the signal to break into the rooms. Make sure to gag the women to keep things quiet."

Benjamin took his men and headed toward the house.

Five men remained, huddled around Kohath. "Tobias, you'll climb Nathaniel's balcony. If he tries to escape by it when I come through the door, kill him. Once he's dead, you and I search the house for valuables. You others guard the hall. Afterwards we'll have our turn at the women."

Instructions complete, Kohath led the five along the rock wall. With the moonlight, extra care was taken to stay in the shadows. Upon reaching the gate, the sicarii dashed across the open courtyard and into the house. Moving quickly, they headed down the hallway, past the kitchen, and up the stairs. Outside, Tobias climbed a tree that grew next to Nathaniel's balcony. Once on the balcony itself, he situated himself next to its door to the inside.

At the southeast corner of the house, Joshua quaffed the last of his pirated wine. It did nothing to help. His hands shook. Sweat soaked his robe. How many minutes did Nathaniel's have left? Would Kohath kill him in his sleep, or wake him to see the kill stroke coming? A sound he thought came from inside the house snatched Joshua attention, then silence. It wouldn't be much longer now. Even if he wanted to warn Nathaniel, it was too late. Joshua's temples throbbed from wine and guilt. Joshua looked around. A twisting alley took off directly across from him. Another glance revealed that the two outside sentries who might be in a position to see him had focused their concentration on Nathaniel's house, waiting to storm in. Another chance might not come again. Joshua bolted for the alley.

On a nearby rooftop, two of the legion's archers drew back bowstrings. "Wait," whispered the lead bowman. "The others hold fast, and the runner hasn't yelled alarm."

They paused, until the alley's shadows swallowed the fleeing figure. "Too bad," murmured the other, easing the gutstring's tension and letting the bow flex back into position. "He'd have been easy game."

* * *

Nathaniel's chin dropped to his chest, bobbed up, then slid down again in fitful sleep. At least he wasn't snoring, Julius thought. That sound coming from somewhere other than the bed might raise suspicion if the assailants exercised caution. Nathaniel's head slumped to one side, cheek pressed against shoulder, arms folded –

Suddenly, Julius flinched at the sound of a stone jar scraping across the balcony floor. Under his blanket, Diogenes twitched. Earlier, the Romans settled on their strategy: Julius would take anyone coming through the door, leaving Diogenes responsible for the balcony. Julius heard Diogenes breathe heavily, as a man fast asleep might do.

Kohath crept to Nathaniel's door. He watched the others take their positions in the hall, waiting for Benjamin's signal. Kohath thought of desert raids he'd led for years. Swooping down in a scorching sun on caravans; sneaking through freezing nights to ambush supply columns: those were hard times. Better times would soon begin, thanks to Judas – and, tonight, Nathaniel!

At the stairway, Benjamin judged the time to be right and all at the ready. He pursed his lips and whistled. The sound of six doors flung open came with a rush of footsteps.

Hannah sat up when the door opened, then shrieked as a stranger rushed at her. Arius leapt behind him and thrust in his gladius. Hannah fainted as she saw a spray of blood gushing from the assailant's stomach as Arius' blade passed clean through.

Kohath flung his door open and headed in, only to stop a few feet inside. The figure in the bed had thrown off the cover and jumped toward the balcony. Tobias came through the balcony door, dagger drawn, seeing too late that the figure coming from the bed wore armor. The last thing Tobias saw was a sword flash by his left ear, then a hot burning in his neck.

"NO!" Kohath shouted, recognizing the trap. He spun round to the door, only to have it slammed shut by a man blocking the way.

"Lay down your dagger, Kohath, or die!"

The familiar voice stunned the intruder. "Nabal! You miserable bastard!"

Sword drawn, Julius advanced. "My name is Julius. Put down your dagger!"

Kohath glanced back at Diogenes, then to a man in the corner stumbling to his feet.

"Nabal – Julius – whatever your name! I'll see you in hell!" Kohath sprung toward the waking man, figuring him to be Nathaniel. Just as quickly, Julius leapt between Kohath and Nathaniel. Kohath's knife slashed out. Julius countered by slashing the hand wielding the dagger. Dropping to his knees in pain, Kohath fumbled inside his robe with his left hand. As he went to pull out another blade, Diogenes drove his gladius under the bandit's shoulder blade, twisted, then withdrew it. Kohath's upper body shuddered. With his remaining energy, Kohath snapped his left wrist, sending the dagger flying toward Nathaniel. The Sopher's scream in Kohath's ear disappeared as Diogenes slashed the back of the bandit's neck, sending him sprawling headlong onto the floor. His gurgling attempts to draw breath ended quickly.

"I'm bleeding!" Nathaniel's cried out. "Julius!"

Julius leaned over to examine Nathaniel's wound. "Your shoulder's scratched at the surface. Nothing serious. Diogenes, tend to him while I check the rest of the house."

Julius' first concern was Hannah's room. He'd heard a scream, the only one Julius recalled. Peering through her door, he saw the girl being comforted by her mother and Arius standing beside them. "What happened, Arius?"

"The girl lay awake when the assailant burst through the door." Arius wiped the blood from his sword. "She screamed as soon as she saw him."

"Was she hurt?"

"No, sir. She fainted when I ran him through."

Julius looked at the corpse. "Have one of the servants

help you drag him away."

In each room, Julius found one or two sicarii on the floor. A few still labored to breath. Julius ordered their throats slit.

Outside the front entrance, the body of Benjamin lay crumpled on the ground. Three arrows impaled his chest and legs, bringing an end to his attempted escape.

Stepping into the front yard, Julius saw archers dragging four bodies to the front. All had been brought down by arrows. "Claudius," Julius called to the archer's officer, "any problems?"

Claudius saluted. "No sir. Although just before the assault, one of their sentries sprinted away. We didn't shoot because no one else moved, and we didn't want to tip them off."

"That's odd," said Julius. "If he saw us, I didn't hear any shouts of warning."

"Neither did we, which is why we held back. Otherwise, we struck down all the sicarii who remained outside."

"Well done, Claudius. And one other thing. Once the bodies are removed from the house, take them to the garbage dump of Gehenna."

"Very good, sir. Is there anything else tonight?"

"Yes, there is," a pensive Julius replied. "But that task belongs to others." Julius strode to a legionnaire holding the reins of an ebony stallion. Julius mounted, took one last look at the bodies being heaped together, then set off toward Ishmael's.

* * *

Judas peered out a window of the caravansary's eating hall, staring at the night sky. No clouds marred the view. "I wonder if father Abraham saw such a sky when Adonai promised descendants as numerous as the stars?"

Saddok joined him by the window. "If all goes well, perhaps it won't be long before Abraham's descendants move as freely in Judea as these stars course the sky." And may the Lord Elohim send him who was promised in the scroll of Numbers," Saddok replied, his gaze fixed on a particularly bright star in the southern horizon. "`A star shall come out of Jacob, and a scepter shall rise out of Israel; it shall crush Moab's borderlands.`"

Judas nodded. "Who knows? We may yet be blessed to see that star arise."

Ishmael broke the night's stillness with a clattering of cups and platters as he set the tables. "How about some wine mixed with hot water? Helps a body sleep."

"We'll wait for Kohath," answered Judas. "His news will give us sleep enough."

"Suit yourself," the innkeeper replied with a shrug. "I've hosted these men before. Once they're back, it'll get loud and stay that way till morning. Sleep won't be easy."

"We'll take our chances. Saddok and I wouldn't want to miss their return."

Ishmael wiped his knife on a clean section of his apron before slicing a loaf of bread. "No, I suppose not."

Judas reached for one of the slices – then stopped, cocking his head toward the door. Footsteps: first in the street, then by the gate, finally through the courtyard and on to the door. A hand pounded the wood. Saddok closed his eyes and murmured a short prayer. Judas looked to Ishmael and nodded his head. Ishmael set his knife on the table and walked to the door. "Go away! Sabbath's filled our rooms!"

A voice called out in Hebrew: "The zeal of Adonai consumes the house of the wicked!"

"Adonai be praised!" shouted Saddok.

"Go on, Ishmael. Let them in!" Judas' command came with joy: the password had been given, the plan had succeeded!

But as Ishmael drew back the lock bar, the door crashed in against him. A dozen armed men rushed into the room. Judas and Saddok had no opportunity to draw weapons before being overpowered. Two men dragged a sputtering Ishmael away from the door.

"You'll be disappointed robbing this poor innkeep," Ishmael protested. "Can't you see I've only two guests?"

"We're not thieves, rebel!" said one of the men. He pulled his hooded robe off, revealing a Roman uniform. "I am Lucius, centurion to Caesar's legion. And I declare you all enemies of Augustus, condemned to death!"

"By damn, there's a mistake!" yelled Ishmael. "I just run this caravansary. You can ask anyone! And these two are traders from Jericho, been friends for years. We're no –"

"ENOUGH!" The fist of Lucius smashed into Ishmael's mouth. "Oron, you and Shobal take this fat oaf to the kitchen." Lucius turned to the pair held captive. "Judas of Galilee and Rabbi Saddok, you stand guilty of sedition and murder."

"It's not murder to strike down God's enemies," muttered Judas. "You may kill us, but others will take our place. And Adonai will give your bodies to the worms."

"You don't frighten me, Jew, nor your god. And after others see what becomes of you, I doubt there'll be a rush to follow your path."

From the kitchen came the dull thuds of kicks and punches, along with groans from Ishmael. "No, PLEASE!" After the innkeeper's shout came a scream, then something falling against a table to the floor. The two legionnaires, wiping their swords, returned to the hall.

Judas fathomed his and Saddok's fate. "Centurion, if we're to die, allow me one question. Whose Hebrew tongue betrayed his people?"

Lucius thought: if Antony would ever be tested, this was the opportunity. "Legionnaire Antony, come next to me."

"Yes sir," he responded, walking from the door he'd been guarding.

Lucius handed the young man his sword. "These are condemned criminals. I give you the privilege of execution."

Taking the sword, Antony stepped before Judas, held fast by two guards. Antony looked to the weapon, then into the face of Judas.

"Hear, O Israel, the Lord is One!" Judas prayed in Hebrew.

Antony's head twitched at the familiar words, then his hand drove the sword upward through Judas' gut toward his heart.

"You betray your own people and Elohim Adonai!" cried Saddok, seeing Antony's reaction to Judas' final words. "May your family live in filth and –"

Saddok's epithet ended abruptly as Antony ran his gladius into the Pharisee's side. Saddoks's eyes widened as the blade burned inside him. He wanted to speak, but a knife drawn across his neck from another guard behind him severed his windpipe. Antony stepped back as Saddok collapsed. The rabbi's hands grasped at his throat, his body jerking in spasms. The movements reminded Antony of a lamb he once helped slaughter. Soon the thrashing ended.

Lucius took his sword. "Well done, Antony. You other men, bundle these two bodies for transport. Julius wants them spiked to crosses atop the rest of Gehenna's garbage."

Antony stepped outside. The stars seemed to focus their light his way, allowing no shadow to engulf him. Warming his fingers with his breath, Antony was surprised at the steadiness of his hands. His lack of emotion surprised him even more. Killing had been easy.

"Antony!" cried Lucius, "we leave!" Antony joined the column marching to Gehenna. He no longer felt cold. He no longer felt anything.

* * *

Julius eased his horse into the caravansary courtyard, then dismounted. No other animal stirred. The main door stood ajar. Julius drew his sword and stepped inside. Tables and chairs lay strewn across the floor. At a corner table, the one where he'd first met Judas and Saddok, pools of congealed blood mottled the floor. Smeared streaks led from them to the door.

But where was Ishmael? Julius scanned the other corners of the room. The innkeeper was nowhere to be seen. "Ishmael!" No response came. "ISHMAEL!"

"In the kitchen." Julius recognized Ishmael's voice, though it sounded shaky. Entering the kitchen, Julius found the innkeep on the floor, his back leaning against a cutting table.

Julius knelt beside him. "What happened to your face?"

Ishmael spit his words through swollen lips. "Your bull of a centurion! Knocked out a tooth, of which I've not too many to spare these days!"

"I told him to give the appearance of roughing you up, in case anyone heard the scuffle and spied." Julius took a cloth from the table and went to clean Ishmael's mouth, only to have Ishmael raise a bloodied hand from within his apron.

"You'd best tend my side first."

Julius pulled away the innkeeper's apron. Blood seeped from a puncture wound. "Those fools!" spewed Julius. "Which of the guards did this?"

Ishmael's hand fumbled for a nearby wineskin. "By damn, it wasn't one of your men."

Julius paused at the news, then tore a cloth to put a dressing on the wound.

"Maybe ten minutes, after they hauled Judas and Saddok out. I heard a sound in the hall, then someone calls for Judas. So I began to groan, thinking you'd sent someone."

"I didn't."

Ishmael took a long drink from a wineskin Julius handed over, then belched. "So I found out. One of Judas' men. He'd been here before. Name of Matthias. He asks me what happened. I said Romans busted in, that they killed Judas and Saddok, left me for dead. But the son of a bitch didn't believe it! Leastwise, about me. He starts shouting about why'd they leave me when they took the two of them. Then he tells me to get up, and when I tell him I can't, he goes for his dagger. He got me in the side." Another drink followed, then Ishmael drew out his own dagger. "'Course, I cut his arm good."

Julius sat back, the bandaging done. "That was it?"

"Must've been his first knifing," said Ishmael. "Didn't know a killing wound from any other. And I wasn't about to set him right."

"I've a horse outside. If you think you can ride, we'll leave."

Ishmael grinned. "I've had women scratch me deeper than this."

Julius lifted Ishmael to his feet. "Your work here's over, friend. After you're patched up at the Antonia, we'll get you to Caesarea, and from there on a boat to Rome."

"I'll miss this place," Ishmael laughed, "maybe for an hourglass of time. I hear Italy's got warm weather and good women, or maybe the other way around! Either way suits me."

Once outside, Julius helped Ishmael onto the horse, then got on himself. "I assume everything went as planned with Judas and Saddok."

"Well, my ears were still ringing from that centurion's punch. But from what I heard, they'd no problems. Somebody called Antony killed the two Jews. Know him?"

Julius spurred the horse on. "I do now."

CHAPTER XXVII

Seven days had passed since Matthias brought word from Jerusalem to New Damascus. Wails of mourning for Judas and Saddok still echoed within the houses and off the surrounding canyon walls. Tonight would be a special Sabbath service in remembrance of the martyrs. The elders of New Damascus entrusted Abraham with the memorial's leadership. Rebekah had asked to speak to the assembly, a privilege rarely granted to any woman. Her status as a martyr's widow swayed the decision in her favor. But in deference to tradition, the elders decreed she would speak only after the men had done so.

Abraham had provided Matthias with lodging through the past week. In that time, Rebekah tended to Matthias' stab wound while Saul listened in dismay to the stories brought from Jerusalem. The gruesome report of Matthias spurred a recurring nightmare for the youth. Running from unknown pursuers in the dark, Saul would stumble and fall into smoldering garbage. He would pull himself up, only to see Judas crucified above him, the dead man's eyes wide open. Saul screamed himself awake to escape.

After supper on Sabbath's eve, Rebekah carefully rewrapped the arm of Matthias in fresh bandaging, having rubbed the scabbed-over puncture with oil pressed from aloe leaves. "Are you sure you feel strong enough to speak tonight at the *yizkor*?"

Matthias looked at her, then to Abraham and Saul. "I feel fine. Nothing will keep me from the memorial." Lowering his gaze to the ground, Matthias added, "It's all that's left to do for Judas and Saddok. I failed them last week."

Abraham walked to the young man's side. "Matthias, stop blaming yourself. Judas ordered you to watch the Antonia. You did what you were told."

"I know, I know," answered Matthias, dropping his chin, "but if I'd only gotten back to the caravansary sooner. Maybe, well, maybe –"

"Maybe you'd be dead!" Rebekah cinched down tight on the last knot of the sling. "Sometimes the difference between living and dying has nothing to do with courage."

Matthias moved his arm to test the sling. "I don't know that I understand you."

"I lost my husband and a son ten years ago, for no other reason than we happened to be in Bethlehem at the wrong moment. Whatever his purposes, God spared us for another day. That is what sustains Saul and me – to avenge Elias and Levi. For you: what's done is done. But now, live to avenge Judas and Saddok!"

"And vengeance I will have." Matthias focused on the scene haunting his mind's eye. "The sight of Judas and Saddok spiked to timbers jutting up from Gehenna's refuse, with Kohath's men strewn below like so much trash, will never leave me!"

Abraham poured a cup of wine. "Many such sights fill the eyes of our people. You, Matthias, have Gehenna's atrocity. Rebekah bears the sight of Bethlehem's massacre. I carry the image of students slaughtered on the Temple steps. But never forget: it will be the vision given us by God that leads to our freedom."

Matthias ascended the steps of the courtyard wall. He looked across the community and down to the Salt Sea. Fog formed on the water's surface. By nightfall, vaporous fingers would snake up the draws and wadis surrounding the lake. Matthias considered it a sign from heaven: God's cloaking the martyrs' memorial with a pall.

* * *

"Three more slices of lamb, Joshua! And two bowls of the pottage."

Joshua carved the pieces from a roasted quarter of lamb on the spit. A strong smell of mint arose from a sauce coating the meat. Taking a ladle, he dipped into a blackened iron pot and filled a pair of bowls. Lentils and bits of onion thickened the ruddy-colored stew.

Bildead, who ran this inn at the outskirts of Emmaus, set the lamb and bowls on a tray and headed back to the eating hall. Joshua sat down, wiping the sweat from his brow. Customers had filled the inn's tables for the past three hours. Still, this work felt good. Clean, he thought. Just then Bildead returned to the kitchen area.

"Another order?" Joshua asked.

"No, we've served everyone." Bildead deposited a handful of copper mites and one silver shekel into his money box, tucked within a small alcove carved into the wall. "It's been a good night, too. You know, we're fortunate you came when you did, Joshua. What with Martha injuring her back, I don't know what we'd have done. I'm not the cook she is, but you are. Though if you tell her that, she'll slap my ears but good!"

Joshua laughed at the wiry man's remark. Martha was a barrel-chested woman whose upper arms rivaled the girth of Bildead's legs. When Joshua entered the Emmaus inn the day after fleeing Jerusalem, he heard the innkeeper telling a townsman of Martha's misfortune. "Why, she's lifted those wine jars all her life. Never a problem. Now she can't even stand long enough to cook." Having money for only a day's lodging and food, Joshua excused himself for overhearing Bildead's lament and offered to hire on as a cook in return for room and board. A desperate Bildead agreed. "Got no choice but to try you out," he said, "before I drive away any more guests with my swill."

The following days proved successful. Joshua's kitchen skills pleased not only Bildead but Martha, who was grateful to have meals prepared by someone besides her husband. Joshua found the time there healing, with neither Kohath nor Tobias constantly ridiculing him. Bildead treated Joshua with respect and a measure of generosity.

"By the way," Bildead continued, "several travelers at the tables come from Jerusalem. Didn't you say you'd been there recently?"

Joshua's throat tightened. "Yes."

"Then you already know what happened there last week."

"Not really," he began. "I just passed through, kept to myself."

Bildead motioned Joshua closer as he lowered his voice. "The rebel Judas and his Pharisee friend Saddok. The Romans crucified them, and on Gehenna to make it worse."

"On Gehenna? Crucified?"

"And more. Below the crosses, they piled the bodies of thieves caught breaking into some official's house. I think I heard him say the leader's name to be Kohath."

At the sound of that name, Joshua choked on the water he'd started to swallow. Bildead slapped Joshua between his shoulder blades. "You've heard of this brigand?"

"Well, yes," Joshua sputtered, catching his breath, "he'd quite a reputation where I used to work." Joshua paused. "I suppose they got him for murdering this official."

"That's the strange thing. From what the travelers said, the only ones killed were the bandits. But to get a dozen men like that, there must've been a trap." Bildead scratched his head, squinting one eye tight. "Makes you wonder, doesn't it?"

Joshua considered what sort of fox could have tricked Kohath; and Nathaniel's survival, despite Joshua's flight without giving warning; and to his own escape, and the fate he would have shared with Kohath and the others. "Yes, I guess it does, Bildead."

* * *

Antony followed Arius through the halls of Herod's palace. He'd seen little of it in the ten days of his posting here, save the cramped barracks and the grounds used for drilling. But now, summoned to meet with Julius, Antony marveled at the marbled floors and statuary lining the way, only to remember such beauty had been provided by the very one who had ordered the death of Bethlehem's children, among them Antony's brother. How could a king who commanded such wealth fear the children of peasants? Antony's thoughts came to a halt when Arius stopped. He knocked on a door flanked by two potted palms.

"What is it?" came a voice from inside.

"Centurion Julius, I have Antony."

"Enter." The door swung open, and the pair walked in. "That will be all, Arius."

Antony saluted Julius by snapping his right fist to the left side of his chestplate.

"Take your ease, Antony. In fact, why don't you sit down?"

Antony relaxed as he sank into the cushioned chair, a luxury for a foot soldier in the legion. "Thank you, sir."

Julius briefly stared into the young man's eyes. "Lucius gave me an accounting of your actions at the caravansary last week."

"I trust he found no problems."

"If Lucius hadn't been pleased," Julius replied, "you'd have caught fire from him. And Lucius is not the sort of man you want stoking coals beneath your feet."

Antony's face hinted a smile. "I take your meaning."

The creases in Julius' brow crinkled as he continued. "I wasn't aware Lucius planned to have you carry out the executions. Such killing can be far harder than what's required in battle."

"My centurion gave me an order. That's all I let myself think of."

"Then you've learned the first duty of a soldier." Julius

rose and walked to a stand supporting a bust of the emperor Augustus. "Orders and obedience are what hold the ranks together. They alone can mold a collection of individuals into a fighting unit. Following orders is our lot. You do well to grasp that lesson early."

"Yes sir."

Julius looked at the fog enveloping the city as the day's heat mingled with the night's cooling. "Tell me this. Lucius said one of the fellows, the Pharisee I believe, called you a traitor because you knew Hebrew." Julius turned and stared at Antony. "Do you have any second thoughts about your desire to enter Rome's service."

Antony shifted in his seat. "May I speak freely, sir?"

"Go ahead."

Leaving his seat, Antony strode to the pedestal. He stopped when the bust stood between him and Julius. "A traitor must first have a people to call his own. My father saw to it I had no people – at least, none who would claim the likes of me. So how can I be a traitor to those who judged me an outcast?"

As at his first meeting with Antony, Julius thought about how that day in Bethlehem continued to claim its victims. In spite of all the brutality he had seen and even meted out, Julius was always proud in knowing himself to be a Roman. Standing before him was a youth who took no such pride in home or *patris*. Julius could not restore what Antony lost in Bethlehem's alley years ago. So he offered what he could.

"By rights, Antony, several more months of training stand between you and a full commission to the legion. But you have proved yourself to Lucius, and to me. I have seen to it that those requirements have been waived in your case." Julius clasped the shoulders of Antony. "Report to the palace courtyard at ten o'clock tonight to take the legion's oath of allegiance. Serve Rome well, and you'll be her citizen when your enlistment is over."

The two men embraced in silence: Antony, speechless at finding a patron for his future; Julius, wondering if he'd found atonement for his past.

* * *

"Hannah, there will be no more talk of such nonsense. Especially on Sabbath!"

Hannah flung the hairbrush down, though she was more careful with the polished bronze mirror. "Mother, he saved my life! I don't see what harm there is in seeing him."

Ever since Simeon left, Hannah frequently tested her mother's patience. The current argument swirled around Arius, Hannah's guard the night of the ambush.

"You will not see him." Naomi insisted. "He is a Gentile. It would be a disgrace."

"A disgrace! As you and uncle consider Simeon a disgrace?"

"Enough, daughter! That you would even consider meeting this, this ROMAN, is foolish! Have you forgotten what Romans did to this family? To your brother David?"

Naomi's last remark stoked Hannah's fire. The memory of her dead twin remained an open wound that time did nothing to mend. Her mother's invoking of David only rubbed salt in that wound. "You just want me to be as lonely as you are, ever since you drove father away."

"No more, Hannah!" Naomi pointed to her daughter's bed. "You will go to bed now and not MOVE from this room until you care called in the morning! Am I understood?"

Naomi stepped into the hall and slammed the door shut.

Hannah lay on the bed, looking out its open window. A thick mist diffused the remaining oranges and yellows of dusk. In a few minutes, Naomi and Nathaniel and Deborah would leave for synagogue. Why did they all have to be so unfair? It wasn't like she asked to marry Arius. Just to see him. Just to thank him. Just to sit next to him, as they had that night. When he held her, when he looked at her, when he saved her...

Listening to the door close downstairs as her family left for Sabbath service, an idea came to Hannah. Why not see him? The Antonia, where her friends said all the soldiers lived, was not far. In the dark of night and this fog, no one would notice a girl making her way to its gates. A thick-trunked vine that climbed the wall beside her window offered her a path of escape. No one would look for her tonight. And if they did, she could place a few pillows under her bed's covering, with a tunic showing where her shoulders should be. No one would notice her gone!

Moving quietly so the servants wouldn't hear, Hannah arranged the bed. Next, she slipped on the white linen tunic bought only weeks ago at the bazaar. The trader said its Egyptian weave rivaled the texture of silk. Feeling its cool material against her skin, Hannah understood his claim. She wrapped a dark wool cloak about her, drawing up its hood. Carefully, she got a handhold on the vine trunk, then swung her legs outside the window until her sandaled feet gained a foothold. Descent proved awkward at best. The cloak tangled in the branches several times. Halfway down, the tunic snagged on a limb and tore a portion of the hem. Hannah examined the tear when she finally reached the ground. What would she tell her mother? Hannah set aside those thoughts as she took one last look at the house. No one watched. She was free.

Gliding through fogbound streets, Hannah imagined her meeting with Arius. At first, he'd be upset. But then, seeing how she risked her mother's anger to see him, and seeing how the linen dress clung to her, Arius would relent. They'd talk of their lives before this: the village he grew up in, her years in Bethlehem. Such thoughts made the journey a swift one. Before all her hopes for their meeting could be anticipated, Hannah saw the Antonia in front of her, its towers disappearing into the night's mist. For a moment, the stone blocks of the fortress frightened her. But the anticipation of

Arius' greeting gave courage.

Two guards at the entrance watched the lone figure approaching. It was unusual for Jews to wander so near to the gate, especially at night. Their stance relaxed when a girl's voice spoke from within the hood. "I've come to see Arius. A member of your legion."

"Arius? Isn't he posted at the palace until –"

The guard's words were interrupted when his partner, Varix, jabbed him in the side with an elbow. The two whispered, then Varix spoke.

"Beg my friend's ignorance, lady. He's just been assigned here, and doesn't yet know everyone. Artemis, not Arius, has duty at the palace. Follow me, and I'll take you to Arius."

"Thank you."

The gate opened and Hannah walked into the compound, following Varix down a flight of steps in the nearest tower. "Watch your step now," offered her guide, "we wouldn't want you to go and hurt yourself. Not tonight."

Hannah didn't understand why the guard laughed after he spoke.

* * *

Joseph lay still on his sleeping mat while Mary knelt beside him. A physician, an old Greek who served Sepphoris and Nazareth, finished examining the stricken carpenter. Joseph's once-robust voice strained to answer the physician's last question. "I'd not been feeling well all afternoon. . . the foreman told me to go home and rest. . . Mary set down the food, and then, I'd never felt such pain. . . around into my arms. . . I couldn't breathe."

Mary cooled her husband's brow with a cloth dipped in water and oil. "Rest now." Closing his eyelids, she kissed them each. As she raised her head, the physician pointed to the opposite side of the room. She joined him there. The two conversed in whispers.

"Your husband's quite ill. Besides rest, there's nothing

much to be done for him."

Her body trembled at his words as she struggled to keep emotions under control. "He will heal, though?"

The Greek placed his hand on her shoulder. "It's an ailment of the heart. Many never live past the first terrible pain. That your husband has speaks well for his strength." The physician rubbed the bridge of his nose and sighed. "I've learned not to give false hope. Even if he overcomes this, it's my experience the pain will eventually return: a month, a year, five years, who's to say. But one day it will take him."

Mary's tears streaked her face. "But what can I do? What can I say?"

"Mary, we can do only one thing at a time, any of us." The Greek pointed to a chair for her to use. "The most important thing for you to do is to care for yourself, and your children. Only then will you have the strength to help Joseph."

"But how will we live while he cannot work?"

"That oldest son of yours, Yeshua. I know your husband's foreman in Sepphoris. He speaks highly of the boy's work. Well, the man owes me several favors. I'm sure I can convince him to take on Yeshua as an apprentice. Maybe even earn close to Joseph's wage."

Mary looked up to the physician. "Why would you do this for us?"

The old man smiled. "I've been to your synagogue from time to time. The rabbi and I sometimes talk. He, too, is most impressed with Yeshua. Let's just say I do it for the boy."

Mary clasped the physician's hands and kissed them, a rare gesture for a Jew to make toward a Gentile, even if he was a God-fearer. "All I can offer is my thanks."

"That's all I require." Reaching into a pouch slung over his shoulder, he drew out a small glass vial containing a clear liquid. "I'll leave this with you. The vial contains oil made from the yellow poppy. Give Joseph a drop at night to aid his sleep, two more should the pain return. But no more than needed."

Joseph's low groaning interrupted their conversation. They returned to his side.

"Joseph? Do you hear me?"

He answered the physician with eyes opening and a labored nod of the head.

"Listen to me. You need to rest. I've given Mary something to help you sleep."

"Physician," Joseph began, his voice slightly stronger, though still pausing for breath. "I watched my father die... with such pain in his chest... is that my lot?"

The old man studied Joseph's face. Even in his condition, the carpenter's eyes shone clear. "You've done well to survive the illness this far. There's no balm I can give to insure your healing. But if you rest, if you allow strength to return, I can tell you that recovery is possible."

Joseph's head nodded.

"Now," concluded the physician, "I must go. Tomorrow, Mary can talk to you of our conversation. The important thing, Joseph, is that you rest and not set your mind to worry. Mary, I'll let you give him the medicine for his sleep."

"Please... let me talk with my wife... and my oldest son."

The Greek stroked his beard. "Just a few minutes, that's all."

The physician left the room with Mary. As she called for Yeshua, Joseph's mind focused on what he wanted to say, in case another time to speak never came.

CHAPTER XXVIII

"Yeshua, come close." The boy sat down beside his father's sleeping mat. Joseph lifted his right hand and placed it on Yeshua's forehead.

"My son, you must be strong. . . until I am better."

"And you will be better," added Mary, "but to do that, you need to rest."

Joseph's hand dropped back to the fleece that covered him. "And I will rest, once I've talked. . . Yeshua, your mother and brothers and sister. . . look after them."

His son nodded. "I will, father."

"It may be possible. . . for you to work under my foreman. . . tell him what happened. . ."

Reaching around her son, Mary held Joseph's hand. "Joseph, don't trouble yourself with these things. The physician has already promised to speak with him about hiring Yeshua."

"The Greek is a good man, a Godfearer." Joseph's chest ached as he coughed.

"It's time you sleep." Mary opened the vial left by the physician. The glass top had an inner stem for a seal. As she drew the top out, a drop of the oil clung to the stem's tip. "Open your mouth." Joseph obliged, and Mary placed the drop on her husband's tongue.

In a few moments, Joseph's eyelids felt as if heavy weights pulled them down. A soft buzzing, like bees hovering over a hillside meadow in bloom, echoed within his ears. He couldn't remember feeling so tired.

"Yeshua," Mary said, while resealing the vial, "kiss

your father goodnight."

Yeshua leaned over, his lips pressing into Joseph's beard. Once Yeshua started to pull back, Joseph reached both hands to the boy's face. "I need your promise."

Yeshua looked across to his mother, then to his father. "What about?"

"The children in Bethlehem. . . behind the rock wall in the stable. . . never let them be forgotten. . . the children." If there were more words Joseph wanted to say, this night would not hear them.

Mary glanced at her son's reddened eyes.

"The promise will be kept," Yeshua whispered to his now sleeping father. Then, turning to Mary, he added, "I will keep it with my life."

His vow stung Mary's heart. How could such words come from one who just turned twelve years old? But looking at Yeshua, remembering other words spoken of him before his birth – perhaps they could. Perhaps they must. She wrapped Yeshua in her arms. The tighter she hugged, the more resolute his promise echoed inside her: *with my life.* Mary feared if its keeping might involve another wall of stone.

* * *

"How far to the room of Arius?" Hannah had accompanied Varix through yet another lengthy hallway followed by a second flight down circular stairs lit by torches in iron brackets.

"We've just about reached the place where you can meet your legionnaire," he answered. "And to keep things proper, I'm taking you to a meeting room. Wouldn't be fit for a young girl to be alone with some soldier in his own room, now would it?"

"No, I suppose not." The guard's tone made her uncomfortable, as did laughter and boisterous talk sounding from a room at the hall's end.

"Follow me in, and I'll explain your business here."

When Varix opened the door, one of the men inside yelled "What do you – "

All noise ceased when Hannah stepped into the room behind Varix. A dozen or so legionnaires stared at the young woman, an unprecedented sight in the barracks. Hannah studied the faces, hoping to see Arius. Varix slipped behind her and closed the door.

"Arius isn't here," Hannah announced, then turning to Varix. "Take me to Arius."

"Why don't you let me take your cloak instead," Varix replied.

Hannah heard the sound of benches being pushed together. Varix reached toward the clasp that fastened her cloak at the neck.

"NO!" Hannah's attempt to slap his hands away failed when someone seized her arms from behind and pinned them to her side. "ARIUS!"

A towel jammed into her mouth. Varix loosened the cloak, letting it fall to the floor.

"Throw it with some other robes on the benches," came a shout from the corner. Hannah kicked at the soldier grabbing the cloak, but other arms took hold of her ankles.

"You've worn fine linen for us." Varix smiled as he ran his hands against the material, first across her breasts and then down to the joining of her thighs. "Fine, indeed."

Gagged, Hannah's screams sounded only within her mind. She wanted the men to stop, she wanted Arius to burst into the room and save her. But instead, she found herself splayed across the robe-covered benches.

"Give her some wine, Varix, so she can bear your ugly face!" The laughter sounded demonic in Hannah's ears. A skin of wine passed above.

"Quiet!" Varix shouted. "Let me talk to her!" Her escort into this hell knelt beside her. "Listen to me. I'm going to take the gag from your mouth, but no screaming! Understand?"

Hannah thought maybe he'd listen to reason, maybe if she'd just be able to say who she was, and who her great-uncle was, they'd let her go. Hannah nodded. Varix removed the gag.

"Please," Hannah began, "I must – "

"Silence!" The back of Varix's hand cracked across her face.

The guard now spoke so close to her ear she felt the heat of his breath. "You just relax. The men here want only to enjoy themselves. If you want, you can enjoy it, too."

"My name is Hannah, and my great-uncle is – "

Varix's hand clamped her mouth. "I'll tell you who you are! You're a Jewess, who came at night to the Antonia seeking a Roman's company. That'd make you a whore in your people's eyes, fit for stoning. No one would trust any protest you'd make. Besides," concluded Varix, moving his hand to take her by the neck and squeezing, "a throat that talked too much might meet with an accident. And such a lovely throat!"

Hannah screamed. "Please, I've done you no harm. I'm just a child!"

Varix stood. "We'll see for ourselves."

One soldier yanked the dress down from her shoulders below her breasts, while another hoisted the dress's lower half above her hips. Everyone leered at what no man had ever seen of her. "You're woman enough for our needs," Varix intoned as he began to straddle her.

"STOP IT!"

A stream of wine poured down her throat, drowning out Hannah's last words. When she tried spitting it out, someone's hands seized her jaw and mouth, so that she had to swallow in order to breathe. When the hands loosened, Hannah tried to scream again. A fist slammed into her cheekbone, snapping her head against the bench.

The room spun out of focus. Hands groped, a body's weight pressed down – and then, feeling herself split apart and impaled, she lost consciousness. For the next two hours, Hannah knew no distinction between nightmare and reality.

* * *

The detail assigned to the induction ceremony, where Antony would take his oath of allegiance, was led by Lucius into the center of the palace courtyard where the rest of the century waited. Two rows of date palms flanked the assembled soldiers. The sweet smell of ripening fruit clashed with the thick odor of burning tar. Bitumen smeared on the end of bundled green sticks produced an effective but pungent source of light. The night's fog trapped the acrid smoke rising up from the torches.

"Come to order!" Lucius' command brought them all to attention.

Julius emerged from a side colonnade and walked next to Lucius. Lucius saluted his former commander, then faced his men. "The recruit Antony, forward!"

Antony stepped from the rear row and marched along the troop's side to the front. Between the smoke and his nervousness, Antony found breathing a chore. His steps quickened as he passed the last row of men and approached Lucius.

"Kneel before the standard, and remove your helmet."

Antony fumbled at the chin strap as he bent his knees, then pulled off the helmet. Lucius took the helmet from Antony and moved aside. Julius stepped before his charge.

"Hold the standard with your right hand."

Antony grasped the iron shaft slickened by the damp air.

"Swear your allegiance to this standard, Antony. Follow it into battle. Sleep only where it is pitched. Never allow an enemy's hand to seize it, even if it means your death." Julius drew his gladius, placing one edge upon Antony's shoulder. "Do you swear to serve Rome's emperor and legions with your full obedience and life's blood?"

Antony lifted his head and looked at Julius. "I swear."

"Do you make this sacred oath of your own free will, promising your service until Rome releases you?"

"I do."

Julius switched the sword to his left hand, extending his right arm to Antony and pulling him to his feet. "You are now a legionnaire in Rome's auxiliary, Antony!" The gathered soldiers shouted approval. Julius hugged the young man, slapping him on the back. Antony felt awkward. Nathaniel had never been one to show affection. It had been long years since Joshua held his son. But now, a Roman embraced him. Awkwardness gave way to relief. A new family replaced the one lost years ago in Bethlehem.

Julius drew out the sword from Antony's sheath, and handed him the one that had rested on his shoulder during the ceremony. "A gift, Antony. Use it with skill and honor."

Antony ran his hand along its edges. Newly forged, never used. A sign, Antony hoped, of his own life this night. "I will do my best, Centurion Julius."

"Then you will do well," he answered. After Lucius dismissed the assembly, Julius watched Antony disappear into the ranks of his fellows. A sense of pride filled Julius. But just as a sweet hint of dates in the air quickly gave way to the stench of smoldering black pitch, remembrance overwhelmed pride. What had been accomplished here by Julius was birthed, and stained, by Bethlehem's massacre. Julius looked once more on Nathaniel's nephew. Maybe Antony would succeed in escaping his past. . . something he, Julius, had found impossible.

* * *

At the synagogue of New Damascus, speaker after speaker eulogized the fallen martyrs, Judas and Saddok. More than once, Abraham had to assist someone from the lectern when voice succumbed to emotion. The men frequently bowed back and forth like reeds swaying in the wind, as a mix of prayers and laments curled from their lips to the ceiling. Grief wailed from women crowding the outer gallery, separated from husbands and fathers and sons by a screen formed of wood and tradition.

Abraham approached the lectern. The *hazzan* had just led the worshippers in singing one of David's songs of lament:

> *My God, my God, why have you forsaken me?*
> *Why are you so far from helping me,*
> *From the words of my groaning?*
> *O my God, I cry by day, but you do not answer;*
> *And by night, but find no rest.*

"My brothers," Abraham began, "one more voice remains to mourn the martyrs. The widow Rebekah: whose husband Elias and son Levi were struck down by Rome, who first came to us with her son Saul at the bidding of Judas. It is right for us to attend her words tonight."

Everyone quieted as Rebekah walked from the gallery into the hall, through the crowd of mourners, and on to the lectern. Even with the elders' approval, a woman addressing the synagogue still concerned many. How could Rebekah speak on a night when so many men found their words overwhelmed by grief?

A black tunic and robe draped her. Stepping up to the platform, she removed the veil from her face so her words would be heard. Abraham remained by her side.

"The Lord God gives, and the Lord God takes away," she intoned. "Yet blessed be the name of the Lord. The God of our fathers, the God of the martyrs Judas and Saddok."

"Blessed be the name of the Lord," responded the worshippers.

"When Matthias came to us last week, bearing the terrible news, an old wound reopened within me. A wound of betrayal, a wound of undeserved death. As Matthias declared at this lectern, there can be no doubt Judas and Saddok were betrayed. Handed over to Roman executioners by some traitor to Adonai Elohim!"

The power in Rebekah's voice surprised the listeners. Emotion that caused other tongues to fail seemed to feed and strengthen the widow.

"Ten years ago, my martyred husband and son lost their lives for the very same reason. We, too, were betrayed. A family fled our village the night before the slaughter. Fled without warning us, leaving the town's sons to Roman swords, while their son lived. My Elias and Levi then, as Judas and Saddok now – delivered by traitors to their deaths!" Rebekah drove her fist into the lectern's wooden top as she pronounced *deaths*.

"Saul, come forward!" His mother's summons surprised him. She'd said nothing to Saul about taking part in the service. But now, those around Saul urged him forward.

"Rebekah," Abraham whispered, "the elders had no notice of your son speaking."

"I do not bring him forward to speak, Abraham," she replied.

Before Abraham could ask her purpose, Rebekah resumed.

"Tonight, our hearts break at the loss of Judas and Saddok, martyrs to Israel. It is a time for sadness, but not just sadness. It is a time for grief, but not just grief. It is a time for commitment. A time for dedication. A time to ensure the work of Judas and Saddok presses on, until God reigns in this land from both Temple and Throne!"

Admiring murmurs swept through the gathering. Men resumed rocking back and forth. Prayers changed from grief-stricken laments to pleas for justice and vengeance.

Saul reached the platform, wondering what his mother intended. He stepped up beside her. Rebekah lifted her right arm, her fingers but inches above Saul's head.

"When Elias and Levi were taken from me, I swore vengeance on the betrayer of their lives. Now Judas and Saddok lay in the grave, crucified by the same Roman hands that stripped my family of life! So in your presence, I make this sacred vow. I dedicate my son to avenge the murders of Elias and Levi, Judas and Saddok; and to exact blood vengeance on their betrayers!"

"Blessed be the widow of Elias!" shouted one of the chief elders, palms raised heavenward, "who gives the fruit of her womb to God's righteous judgment!"

"With you as my witnesses," Rebekah concluded, "I give my son new names to seal this vow. To remember with infamy the one who brought death to our family, I call him *Yeshua*. And to remember with honor the father who sired him, I call him "son of the father" – *Bar Abbas*. Saul no more, my son shall be called: YESHUA BARABBAS!"

"YESHUA BARABBAS," cried the crowd, until it became a chant growing louder with each call. "YESHUA BARABBAS! YESHUA BARABBAS!" The chant became a prayer for retribution, invoking God's judgment on his foes. "YESHUA BARABBAS!" In the din, no one, not even Rebekah, noticed the perplexed look on the face of the young man known till this moment as Saul.

* * *

In the hour after midnight, four of Bethlehem's children labored to see through this night's thickening fog.

Yeshua couldn't sleep. Rolling onto his side, the boy looked outside. All he could make out in the dark mist was the outline of his father's carpentry shop. Yeshua's thoughts drifted to the rabbi's frequent encouragement to become a teacher of God's Torah. Mary and Joseph spoke vaguely of how they knew this from long ago. Yeshua found it difficult to explain why the calling seemed unsurprising to him. But now, his father's illness threatened that dream. As the oldest son, it fell to Yeshua to support the family until Joseph recovered – if he recovered. Peering at his father's shop, Yeshua wondered how long it might be before he could trade the carpenter's adz for the Torah's scrolls.

Antony stared out the window in his room. His first night in Jerusalem, moon and stars shot beams through the narrow opening. Tonight, a mere hint of light seeped through the mist. Round clear jewels of water dripped from the slit's upper edge. The earlier elation from his induction into Rome's legion had left him. He'd achieved his goal of a new identity, proven by not fearing to strike a foe as his father Joshua once failed to do. But at what price? Tonight's ceremony owed to Antony's execution of two Jews held fast by Roman arms. For a moment, he longed for things to be different: to be with his mother, to tease his sister Hannah. Maybe... "No!" he spoke aloud. "I am Antony!" He reclined on the cot, grateful for this haze that swallowed light and left him alone in darkness.

Even with the fog rising off the Salt Sea, the night remained warm in New Damascus. Rebekah's son made his bed in the courtyard. Saul, now Yeshua Barabbas, tossed on his mat in that time between wakefulness and sleep. He imagined hearing a voice cry "Saul:" he turned, but no one was there. Then another spoke "Yeshua Barabbas" but no one came into view. At last, the face of his father, Elias, floated in the air, calling for his son. Yet, when Saul ran to him and cried out, Elias said, "I seek Saul. What's become of Saul?" The young man awoke in a sweat.

By one of Jerusalem's fountains, a young girl pulled herself to the stone rim of the pool. Hannah splashed a handful of water in her face, the cold water stinging the cut on her lip. Gathering up cloak and tunic, she stepped into the water. It came only to her knees. Hannah slid down until the water lapped her waist. She began to rub the inside of her thighs, trying to wash away the congealed residue of blood and semen and fluids that had spilled from within her during her tortured hours in the Antonia. Hannah cried as she bathed. Hers tears were not of sadness, but rage: rage at men who abused her, rage at a mother who misunderstood her, rage at a father and brother who deserted her, rage at herself for being foolish. No one escaped her rage, especially not the one her mother blamed for the family's grief long years ago:

Yeshua.

Yeshua. Were it not for Yeshua: David would still be alive, the family would still live in Bethlehem. And she would not have been raped. "Someday, Yeshua, I swear I'll do to you what you've done to us – and what's been done to me. Do you hear, Yeshua? DO YOU HEAR!"

Hannah's shouts passed into sobs, her sobs into the mist. . . and the mist, into long and difficult years for four innocents so rudely come of age.

BOOK TWO

"RECKONINGS"

CHAPTER XXIX

Standing atop the seawall overlooking Caesarea's ship basin, Hannah watched an endless succession of waves rolling and breaking on the jetty sheltering the harbor. In her years here, she never tired of this vista. The waters of the Great Sea, what her Roman customers called *Mare Nostrum*, "our sea," provided a palette daubed with ever-changing shades of blue.

Cloudy nights conjured a black sea, a realm of demons set on plundering ships and stealing souls. Stormy days spewed a slate-blue cauldron, whose waves foamed and crashed in an effort to devour mariners foolish enough to venture out. When sunset splashed the horizon in the colors of fire, the waters mingled blues with reds and oranges, purples and pinks, until the Great Sea swallowed the sun whole. But Hannah loved best of all the clear azure blue fashioned by a high sun on a cloudless sky, when little wind stirred the water's surface. On such days, the water's clarity allowed the white sands in the shallows and the dark green strips of seaweed to streak the seascape stretching out to the horizon.

The sea's beauty concealed a more practical value to those who lived on its edge. The architects of Caesarea designed its sewers so that the Great Sea's tides daily flushed out the city's effluence. Hannah wished the waters could cleanse her as they did the city.

"Are you the woman called Hannah?"

Hannah turned to see a man walking towards her.

"Draco, captain of one of those ships you see below."

She studied him. Unlike common sailors dressed only

in loincloths, Draco wore a short wool tunic. Its red dye had faded from labor in the salty marine air. The closely-trimmed beard on his face suggested a man of Greek or Cretan heritage. "Who told you to seek me here?"

"The harbormaster." The captain stepped next to her and placed a hand on her hip. "I'd asked about someone to keep me company this night. I sail on tomorrow's tide."

Hannah took his hand, gently but firmly moving it off her waist. "Sorry, captain, but I already have an engagement this evening."

"Can't you break it?"

"It's not wise in my business to disappoint a Roman. Perhaps another time."

"I'll make it worth your while." Draco hoisted a small purse, letting the coins inside drop into his other hand. They amounted to almost a week of Hannah's usual wage.

Hannah wrapped her fingers over the hand holding the coins. "I can't neglect the Roman. But," she added, moving closer to him, "I could spare two hours now, if you like." The pair strode toward the city. Draco put aside thoughts of tomorrow's departure to enjoy his purchase. Hannah put aside thoughts of the sea's cleansing in order to ply her trade.

* * *

"No! That'll never do!" Lucius descended the balcony above the Antonia's training ground. Two soldiers stood in the middle, ringed by the men of Lucius' century. Coming through the circle, Lucius faced the larger of the pair. "When you grab a man from behind, you can't just take his neck in your hands, leaving him free to flail around!"

The big man, a Syrian recently transferred to Jerusalem, scowled at the upbraiding. Lucius read the man's face. "You have something to say, legionnaire?"

"In Antioch, no one escaped when I hold them by the neck. And none can here."

"Not only that," called out one of the men in the ranks fresh from Antioch, "but one day, he broke the neck of a thief with that hold. Snapped it like a dry twig."

Looking at the hulking Syrian, Lucius could believe it. The man stood a head above the tallest of the others. Still, he'd been careless in his neck hold, a mistake that others without his size couldn't afford. As much as the Syrian, they needed a correction.

"Well, champion of Antioch, I want you to repeat your hold." As Lucius peered at the men, more than one set of eyes avoided his in fear of being chosen. "Antony."

The Syrian sneered. He was twenty years old, and it appeared the man walking toward him had been in the legion nearly that long.

Lucius glared at the Syrian, then gave Antony instructions: "The boy needs a lesson in combat – and respect. Make sure he learns it in pain so he'll remember."

Antony nodded.

"Everyone, pay close attention!" shouted Lucius. "Someday it may save your life." Turning to the two men now facing each other, Lucius gave them their orders with one hand raised. "Take your hold, Syrian. When I lower my hand, do what you need to control him."

"Don't worry, old man," the Syrian mocked as he moved behind Antony and put his hands around the neck of Antony, "I won't squeeze too hard!"

As the Syrian's hold tightened, Antony replied. "Squeeze as hard as you like, whelp. It'll remind me of your mother squeezing me when she was camp's whore."

Lucius had no chance to signal. The Syrian bellowed, clamping his grip around Antony's neck. The older man arched his back and drove his buttocks hard into the Syrian's abdomen, then kicked a foot straight up into the Syrian's groin. The hands clenching Antony's neck loosened. Antony spun with one elbow extended, smashing into his opponent's temple. As the Syrian staggered at the blow, Antony pivoted behind him and locked his forearms around his opponent's neck. The younger man tried to repeat Antony's initial move, but was blocked at each attempt. Unable to breathe breath, the Syrian's motions weakened and slowed. Antony waited until there was almost no resistance before throwing him face down on the ground.

When the Syrian managed to roll over, Lucius reached down and lifted his head by the hair. "Next time I instruct you, pay heed! NEVER take a foe for granted." Lucius let the Syrian's head drop to the ground and turned to face his troop. That goes for the rest of you! Dismissed!"

Lucius ascended the balcony. The newer troops who knew the Syrian looked befuddled. The veterans laughed as they huddled around Antony to congratulate him.

"Antony!" Lucius called out. "Come up here! I need to speak with you." Antony left the group still recounting his humiliation of the Syrian. The afternoon sun already edged lower in the sky as a breeze dispersed the day's heat. When Antony reached the overhang above the training grounds, Lucius offered him a chalice filled with Galilean wine. "Well done!"

Antony gulped a mouthful. "Lucky for me he didn't know that move. You could've had a broken-necked cripple on your hands!"

"Luck's got little to do with it," Lucius countered. "Besides, I wanted the whole century to see you work."

Lowering the chalice from his mouth, Antony eyed Lucius. "Why?"

"Because in another two weeks, you'll be their centurion."

"What? You've got a transfer?"

Lucius beamed, slapping Antony on the shoulder. "Better than that. I've got my discharge! Plus a donative that'll let me live in ease. But you, it's your turn to command. That's what today was about. Leading men doesn't come by just a rank. It's about them looking up to you. And it doesn't hurt for fear to enter their minds, either. Everyone who watched you take down that fool now knows what you're capable of. Make sure they never forget."

"I'll try not to."

"Good." Lucius sat down on a bench, propping his feet on the stone balustrade encircling the balcony. "Take tomorrow off. You're to see the tribune the following day so he can give you the details of what your promotion brings. After that, we'll work together with the troop so the change in command goes smoothly. If you've got no questions, you're free to go."

"No sir – and thank you." Antony saluted, and started down the staircase. At the first landing, he paused and turned: "Centurion, what if that Syrian had defeated me?"

Lucius laughed. "The only way that oaf could've beat you was to break your neck. If you'd have let that happen: you wouldn't deserve to be centurion, and I'd be stuck here without a successor. Let's be grateful your neck's still straight!"

Antony shook his head and resumed his descent of the stairs. It wasn't the humor of Lucius' reply that struck him. It was the truth.

* * *

The white cotton awning appeared to be a landlocked sail billowing in the wind. Most of the courtyards in New Damascus had such shelters from the sun. This far below sea level, situated in the deep trench that formed the Salt Sea's valley, avoiding the sun's onslaught was as much a matter of survival as comfort.

Late afternoon brought the first hint of relief in a breeze lofting the cloth overheard. Wakened by the awning's flapping, Yeshua Barabbas stretched out his arms and yawned, then watched Abraham stir from sleep. The older man's hair flowed silvery white, worn long in the custom of the Essenes. It contrasted with the short black curls matting Barabbas' head and the stubble sprouting unevenly from his face. But far greater differences wedged these men apart.

For ten years after leaving Bethlehem, Barabbas had

lived with Abraham, studying Torah and preparing himself as a leader among the Zealots. But rivalries arose. The sons of the martyr Judas also vied for primacy. With Rebekah's urging, Barabbas decided that he needed to grow as a man of battle as well as one versed in Torah. For the last ten years, Barabbas led a small band of Zealots who harassed the Romans whenever possible. They lived in the Judean wilderness, though their raids sometimes took them into Jericho and even Jerusalem.

Yet, as Barabbas and most of the New Damascus community had accepted the need for violence to usher in God's kingdom, Abraham found himself pulled in another direction. Four years ago, the appearance of the Baptizer unsettled the community. His preaching of God's reign and Messiah depended not on upheavals of government, but turnings of hearts and wills. Repentance, he called it.

Herod Antipas had the Baptizer beheaded this past year for denouncing his marriage to his sister-in-law. The Zealots took the execution as validation that nothing short of revolution would transform Israel into a land ruled by God. For Abraham and a few others, the Baptizer's end sealed the verdict that violence only spawned more of the same. Besides, hadn't the murder failed to stifle his message? Rumors now spread of a Galilean rabbi whose preaching carried on the spirit of the Baptizer's. Some whispered he might even be the One promised, whose way the Baptizer spoke of preparing.

"I see you're awake, Barabbas. Some water?" Abraham filled two cups from a pitcher. The men sipped, letting the water moisten their lips and cool their mouths before drinking. "I'm glad you've returned," said Abraham.

"I had to speak with the elders. You've heard the news from Jerusalem?"

"That the procurator Valerius Gratus returns to Rome? Yes, two days ago."

Barabbas leaned forward on the bench. "No one knows

his successor. But the change
could serve us well."

Abraham felt uneasy about the conversation's direction, but knew Barabbas meant to press it. "With Sejanus holding the ear of the emperor, I doubt it. One of our Essene brothers in Jerusalem told of a traveler from Rome who reported persecution of the synagogue there. Sejanus despises our people and sways Tiberias to do the same."

"That's just it," countered Barabbas. "We can count on Sejanus to appoint one who shares his hatred, one who will inflame this land and hasten its rising against Rome."

"Barabbas, you know my thoughts on that. I've no wish to argue more than we have."

"Well, what would you have me talk to you about? This sultry weather?" Barabbas set his cup down hard, splashing out some of its water. "What's become of you, Abraham? You witnessed Rome's barbarism when I was a child! You received Matthias into this very home when he came with the news of Judas and Saddok!"

"And," an irritated Abraham broke in, "I was the one who buried Matthias, killed during some fool raid of no consequence. Taking up arms leads only to death, Barabbas."

Barabbas pushed his bench back and stood. "I think it best if I leave now."

Abraham looked up into an angry face, an anger he'd felt in his own life for many years. As Barabbas started toward the courtyard's gate, Abraham rose and called out, "Wait." Walking to Barabbas, he clasped the younger man's shoulders. "You're the closest I've come to a son, Barabbas. Let's not turn our backs to each other. Come back when you're finished talking with the elders. We can sup together, and speak of Rebekah – and this sultry weather."

The faintest hint of a smile came to Barabbas' face. "Agreed."

* * *

Less than an hour remained before sunset as Hannah

neared the end of her preparations for the evening. A warm soaking bath followed Draco's departure. Oils added to the water softened her skin. When Hannah first left Jerusalem, youth alone provided such smoothness to the touch. Since then, age and use – and abuse – took their toll. Over time, she poured ever-increasing amounts of oil into her bath to maintain the softness desired by clients.

Sitting at the small dressing table by her bed, Hannah held a circle of polished bronze and rubbed a bright red cream colored by mulberry juice on her cheeks. She disliked its look. What difference such decoration made when it came time for bodies to intertwine in darkness escaped her. The Romans favored this rouging, though, and Hannah knew that such attention to details could result in an extra coin or two.

The cream applied, Hannah struck a flint to light a thin stick of incense. As its smoke began to curl toward the ceiling, she held a cloth overhead and leaned over, trapping the aromas against her shoulders and hair and face. Hannah allowed the smell and taste of citron to soak into her before extinguishing the incense. Tossing her head back, she drew the bristles of her hairbrush through dark brown tresses falling to her shoulders. She'd not quite finished brushing when the clopping of hoofbeats on cobblestones came down the street, then stopped. Footsteps approached. A fist rapped on her door. "Yes?"

"I've come with a carriage for Hannah."

Hannah recognized the voice. It belonged to the servant who spoke to her yesterday, the same one who procured her services for other evenings. "I'm on my way." Hannah wrapped a cloak about her, covering a sheer silk tunic. She wore this tunic only to palace affairs. It was too expensive to waste on everyday clients.

Without a word, the servant helped Hannah into the carriage. Equipped with curtains and a canvas top, a fleece-covered cushion padded the inside bench. She heard the driver click his tongue at the horses, and the carriage rocked forward. Within ten minutes, they reached the palace built by Herod the Great that rose from a rocky promontory jutting into the sea.

A steward emerged from within the palace to escort her along the flag-stoned walk. "Welcome, Hannah. The fates smile on you tonight. Your summons is for a banquet given in honor of the retiring procurator, Valerius Gratus, who sails tomorrow for Rome."

"Am I to be the procurator's companion?"

"You?" The steward laughed as he led her through the single land entrance to the complex, the noise of music and applause drifting in their direction. "I said the fates smiled on you, not adopted you. What I meant is, the room fills with people of wealth and power. A woman of your, ah, talents could make some profitable contacts, I would think."

Hannah bit her tongue. Antagonizing this steward could jeopardize any future work there. Besides, boorish as he was, the steward spoke the truth. "Who am I to be with this evening?"

As she asked the question, Hannah and the steward stepped into the open-air center of the palace. A huge freshwater pool dominated the quadrangle. Boxes filled with hyacinth and anemone blooms had been set between the surrounding colonnades, while musicians performed at the pool's far end. The entrance to the dining hall stood at the near end of the pool, marked by two columns cut from a rare blue marble.

Hannah followed the steward into the hall. Several rows of tables ran lengthwise toward the room's rear wall, where a semicircular fountain formed the backdrop for the host's table. Her eyes studied the men without companions, attempting to see which one awaited her arrival. To her surprise, the steward led her to the procurator's table. One place was unoccupied. A man beside the vacant spot noticed their approach and stood.

The steward stopped and bowed in the man's direction. "My lord, this is Hannah."

The Roman dismissed the steward. "May I take your cloak, Hannah?"

"Yes, my lord." As he loosened the clasp that held the cloak about her shoulders, Hannah took note of his silver hair and seamless white toga. Perhaps he was a diplomat, although the weathered look of his forearms and face suggested a more active career.

The Roman handed the cloak to a servant, who'd brought a cushion for the new arrival. "Please," said the Roman, motioning for her to sit.

The servant returned to fill her chalice with wine. The Roman knelt down on his cushion beside her. Raising his chalice, he tapped it against hers. "To our evening, Hannah."

Hannah lifted her chalice. Instead of drinking, she leaned in his direction. "Forgive me for not toasting you in return, my lord, but I've not been told your name."

The Roman smiled. "An oversight easily corrected. My name is Julius."

CHAPTER XXX

A driftwood fire volleyed sparks into the evening air. Lighter embers spiraled up, swirls of bright orange stars growing dim in their ascent. Heavier cinders arced in random directions. Some thudded into the sand, others sizzled in the shallows of Galilee's sea. Green branches skewered with fish ringed the blaze, their tips bent flameward under the weight of thick-bodied *tilapia* caught that day. Nearby, a boat teetered to one side on the shore, its nets draped from poles to dry. They belonged to Peter, a disciple of Yeshua.

Peter had just returned to the fire from his home less than one hundred yards away. Yeshua and his disciples lodged with Peter's family so frequently that Yeshua considered this house and Capernaum to be his second home. The group customarily ate their meals in Peter's courtyard, but not tonight. Jacob, son of the martyred Judas, had come with a delegation of Galilean Zealots to meet with Yeshua. The two groups were not strangers to one another. Two of Jesus' disciples, Simon and Judas Iscariot, had once followed Jacob. Five others of Yeshua's inner circle grew up along this northwest coast of the Galilean Sea, a seedbed of hatred toward Rome. Few missed the irony of Yeshua's teaching one day on a nearby hillside. He uttered a blessing on peacemakers within earshot of a cave regularly used by rebel arms makers. Yeshua's praise of those who strove to fashion shalom mingled with the sounds of a bellows' hiss and a blade's hammering that drifted out from the cave's mouth.

"Rabbi Yeshua," asked Jacob, "might we have a few moments before supper?"

Yeshua agreed, stopping to inform Peter. "Call us when the fish are ready. Jacob and I will be down the beach."

"Don't worry about these fish. We can move the sticks back so they cook slower."

"That's not necessary. We have all evening to talk after dinner."

Yeshua and Jacob headed south until the last of the houses had been passed, then walked out on a rock-strewn point extending into the lake. To the north, the lime-plastered homes of Capernaum dotted the hillside. To the south, Galilee's waters stretched miles before funneling into the Jordan. Ripples swayed the reeds growing in the shallows before lapping against the pebbled shore. The aroma of cooking fish scented the breeze. The lake had been generous today.

"The rabbis in Jerusalem can prattle all they want about where Eden lies hidden," offered Jacob. "This sea and Galilee's hills settle the question for me."

Yeshua skimmed a flat stone across the lake's surface. "A place's beauty can be measured in the sights it brings, or the bounties it yields. Galilee has the rare gift of bestowing both."

"Well spoken, rabbi. Some of our teachers lose touch with the land's blessing. Which makes them prone to forget the importance of the land's freedom."

Yeshua smiled. It hadn't taken Jacob long to broach the issue of their meeting. "In some ways, Jacob, the land stands indifferent to freedom. No Roman edict has changed where the tilapia feed at dusk in these waters. No earthly power commands when Galilee's grapes ripen. The land's true freedom comes in its harmony with God's decrees."

"As does our own," Jacob interrupted, eager for the argument. "God set our people apart as a holy nation. Our very existence turns on heeding the rule of God in this world. Yet how can we be free to follow God as King when we allow Roman rule in our land?"

"A question for you, Jacob. How was Daniel free to serve God under Nebuchadnezzar? How was Elijah free to prophesy under Ahab? But they did! The kingdom of God proceeds from the heart, not a throne. Rome has no power to penetrate those workings."

"They have the sword's power, Yeshua ben Joseph. Can a man's heart survive once he is struck down? Like the Baptizer? Like my father?"

Yeshua searched Jacob's eyes before speaking in an even voice. "I've been told your father lived in strict accordance with his beliefs. For such integrity, Judas is to be commended. And I, too, share your grief of losing a father too soon in life. But Judas chose, as have you, the way of the sword. Its end will always be the same."

"Whose end is EVER different than the grave?" Jacob's face flushed. "Until we throw off Rome, we'll have no freedom to truly serve God in this life!"

"If we raise the sword to remove the rule of violence, we become as those we deem enemy. Or do you argue that we serve God by replacing Rome's aggression with our own?"

Jacob looked out over the Sea of Galilee. "Every time I am away from here, I thirst for these waters." The Zealot knelt down, dug under the pebbles lying at the surface, and raised a handful of the damp earth as he stood to face Yeshua. "This land, Yeshua, thirsts for freedom. Some say you are the One promised to ease that thirst by breaking Rome's yoke. Are you?"

"Many yokes enslave, Jacob, and many freedoms disappoint. I know what you and the Zealots seek. All I can tell you is: judge me for what I do, not for what others expect."

"And what of these hopes that you are God's Messiah?"

"The hopes of others," Yeshua spoke with measured deliberation, "I cannot control."

Jacob let the dirt fall to the ground. Yeshua turned and headed back toward the cookfire. He stopped when he heard Jacob call out.

"If you are Messiah, will you make that known in Jerusalem on your next pilgrimage? The crowds grow impatient, and we stand ready to act!"

Yeshua waited for Jacob to rejoin him. "It is for God to reveal Messiah, at the place and time God chooses. And blessed are those who yield to God's purposes, instead of demanding God conform to their own!"

The two men stood in silence, weighing one another's words. From a distance came the faint sound of Peter's voice announcing supper. Yeshua and Jacob each wondered if they'd been understood by the other. Neither expected they had.

* * *

Inside the dining hall, a troupe of Ethiopian dancers pantomimed a lion hunt. Tall drums, carved from hollowed logs and covered at both ends with zebra hide, pounded ever faster rhythms. Circles of men and women, caked in wildly colored powders, tightened around one performer wrapped in a lion's skin. A shout arose from the dancers when they seized the lion, lifting it into the air and passing it overhead to the table of honor. The banqueters cheered when the captured prey, set before Valerius, unwrapped her naked body from within and handed the skin as a trophy to the departing procurator.

As the dancers exited the room, Julius studied Hannah. She was speaking with a woman next to her, the consort of an Egyptian official. From what the steward told Julius beforehand, he knew Hannah to be experienced in her work. But something was different about her from women whose company had been arranged for him on previous occasions. Perhaps it stemmed from her presence at the table. Hannah conversed with Julius and the other guests with intelligence and ease. Most of his previous escorts to such affairs looked equally stunning, but never shared in the discourse as Hannah did. Or maybe the difference resided in the fact she was a Jewess, another detail shared with him by the steward.

"Julius, is something wrong?"

Hannah's words startled him. He wondered how long she'd been watching him stare. "Forgive me. Between the wine and the noise, my mind must have wandered."

Hannah laid a hand on his shoulder. "Would you like to leave the room for awhile?"

"Yes," he answered, taking her hand. Others had already excused themselves, including Herod Antipas, so the departure would not be seen as a breach of protocol.

Julius helped Hannah to her feet, asking a servant to fetch her cloak. He stepped over cushions strewn on the tile floor to stand before Valerius. The procurator's drunken attempt to fit himself into the lion skin had his companions guffawing. Fortunately, Julius and Valerius had already exchanged their parting words on the trip from Jerusalem. When Julius asked to take leave, Valerius tried to stand and roar his approval – only to tangle his feet in the skin and stumble onto the table. Julius assisted him to his cushion and rejoined Hannah.

Once outside the hall, the pair walked along the pool, then out to the palace dock. "All my years in the legion, the thing I missed most was this sea. I grew up by it."

"Is Rome on the sea?"

"Rome's not, but my village of Ostia is. When I was a boy, I wanted to be a sailor. My grandfather was always telling me stories of the voyages of Jason and Ulysses."

"Are they heroes of Rome?"

Julius laughed. "No, they're legends from the Greeks. Similar to your people's stories of Joshua and Samson."

Hannah sat down on a marble bench. "You know I'm a Jewess?"

"Does my knowing bother you?"

"Why should it?"

Julius stood behind her and massaged her neck and shoulders while he spoke. "I've lived long enough in this land to know your people look on us both as outcasts. Me as a

Gentile, especially as an advisor to Rome's procurator, and you – well, as one whom pious men condemn with words while yearning to have you under their bellies."

"So, now you're a philosopher in addition to a procurator's advisor." Hannah shifted to one side of the bench, motioning Julius to sit beside her.

"FORMER advisor," added Julius, sliding next to Hannah. "When the new procurator arrives this week, I'll help in the transition. But then I finally begin my retirement."

"Let me guess. A villa by the sea outside of Ostia."

Julius scanned the Mare Nostrum, jogging memories of childhood when he thought the steady rising and falling of these waters was simply the earth breathing in and out. "Actually, no. My brother's family lives on our parents' estate. Most of my friends have gone, or died, or grown fat and lazy from too much ease. There's nothing there for me to return to."

"Then where will you go?" she asked, twirling several strands of his hair in her fingers.

"I hear Tiberias, on Galilee's Sea, is quite agreeable. Before you arrived tonight, Antipas boasted of all his new constructions there. He even offered me an apartment."

His response caught Hannah off-guard. Not that a man in Julius' position wouldn't receive such an offer from Galilee's ruler, but that he should speak of it so routinely. "Then I suppose you'll leave here and become a wealthy Galilean vineyard owner."

Julius laughed. "I doubt that. Any grapes depending on my care would never survive to the press. My time of late as advisor would make me prone to talk them to death."

The last comment provoked a burst of laughter from Hannah. Her trade provided personal experience with more than a few administrative types. Invariably, words exceeded performance.

Julius straddled the bench, facing Hannah and taking her hand. "My enjoyment lately has depended largely on some winegrower's efforts. But not tonight. For that, I have you to thank."

Other clients complimented Hannah with such words, although they tended to be spoken after services had been rendered. But always, in a day or two, they'd been forgotten. Life returned to normal. A normalcy that reminded Hannah of her role tonight. "There are more ways I can make you grateful, Julius. I'm arranged to be in your service till morning."

Julius admired her frankness. In an odd way, her words recalled his own devotion to duty. But something more than concluding a dutiful albeit enjoyable transaction encouraged Julius to speak words that he'd not spoken to any other. "Hannah, what would you say to staying on with me past the morning? You'll not want for anything, as long as you remain in my house."

While his words surprised her, the proposal was not a new one. Hannah had twice entered such arrangements with men of substance. Both times it proved profitable, until the patrons found a new mistress to intrigue them. "And if I decide to leave?"

"You're free to go at any time. No conditions."

The offer tempted. The hazards of Hannah's profession weighed in favor of mistress over prostitute, if only for a time. Any way she could take advantage of a Roman brought some redress, however fleeting, to her memory of the Antonia. But still, she wondered. "Why offer this, Julius? We've not even shared a bed to judge your liking of me."

Julius lifted Hannah by her hand and led her onto the dock. A small sailing boat tied to a pier bumped the wooden platform with each swell of the harbored sea. "I've been too long without someone to lie beside at night. The truth is, I don't want to live out my days alone."

"But you don't know me, beyond my being a Jewess and a whore."

Julius stopped and spoke to Hannah while peering out

to sea. "I've known Jews I respected and Romans I hated; I've seen my share of respectable families, even in Jerusalem, whose members do far worse than you. Except, they try to hide it behind piety."

Hannah felt a chill when Julius spoke of Jerusalem's families. After a moment, she touched the shoulder of Julius. "I'm not to be your housekeeper or servant, to be clear."

Julius stepped closer to Hannah, removing the cloak and letting it slide to her feet. His hands reached around her back, pressing into the silk tunic as he pulled her against him. "I don't seek a servant or housekeeper, Hannah. Only a companion. And a lover."

Hannah placed her arms around his neck. "Then that is how I come. Nothing more, nothing less." The two kissed and stepped onto the boat. Its sails, folded on the deck, cushioned and covered while the sea rocked them – first in love, then in sleep.

* * *

"ANTONY!" The voice seemed part of a dream. Only a coarse hand pushing on his shoulder and a lamp's glow made Antony realize it did not belong to a dream. "Wake up." Eyes squinted, still unfocused but discerning the outline of a man standing by his sleeping mat.

"What is it?"

"I'm sorry, but an old Jew says he must speak to you."

Antony yawned. "Have the guards tell him to come back in the morning."

"The man didn't come by the gate, but through the Temple passage."

This news roused Antony in an instant. Only a select number knew of that tunnel, and fewer still were allowed its passage. Lucius had only recently disclosed its existence to him.

Hastily donning his uniform, Antony followed the guard. In a matter of minutes, they'd reached the room harboring the passage's entry. Two guards inside came to attention, while a cloaked figure with a hood drawn over his head sat at the small table.

"Guards, wait in the hallway. I'll speak alone with the Jew."

"Very good, sir." The guards saluted, then closed the door behind them.

Antony walked to the table and sat on a chair directly opposite the stranger, who now drew back his hood. The lamp glowing in the table's center cast enough light for his face to be clearly seen. The head was bald, except for a ring of hair above both ears and around the back. A thin grey beard followed his jaw line, accenting the chin's sharp contour. The man's profile suggested the likeness of a vulture to Antony. A likeness, he realized, that even after so many years could not be mistaken.

"Nathaniel?"

The man nodded. "You remember me, Antony. Or should I say, Simeon?"

"You've no need to speak of Simeon anymore."

"No, I suppose not." Nathaniel observed how easily the curaiss hung from the young man's shoulders. "This Antony seems to be a man well-respected in the ranks."

"I'm to be made a centurion."

"Congratulations. You've come far in this new life. I'm proud to have helped out."

"Nathaniel, it's been twenty years or more since we last talked. Now you come in the middle of the night, demanding to see me. Let's not waste our time. What do you want?"

"I see the years have not moderated your father's impatience."

"Nathaniel – "

"Very well," the Sopher interrupted, raising his hand the way a teacher might silence a child. "My coming tonight is because your mother insisted I get word to you."

"Word about what?"

"Your grandmother Deborah died. She's to be buried tomorrow in Bethlehem."

Antony sat back, clasping his hands behind his head and taking a deep breath. He thought separation from his family all these years might make such a moment pass more easily. But Nathaniel's message left Antony's stomach feeling hollow. "I'm sorry."

"As am I. But nothing's to be done about it now." For a moment, Nathaniel's throat tightened. Ashes of long-dead emotions for Deborah had been stirred by her sudden illness and death. As quickly as they kindled, however, they fled. Nathaniel sought no consolation nor did he offer any. "Naomi wishes you by her side at the burial tomorrow."

"I'm afraid I'd just upset matters." Antony had not seen his mother since joining the legion. "Hannah would give better comfort."

"Maybe, but Hannah's been gone for years," Nathaniel briskly countered, "and we've no idea where she is." Nathaniel stood and shuffled toward the trapdoor leading to the passageway. "If you don't come, your mother will be disappointed – though probably not surprised."

"Wait!" Antony stepped over to pull the trapdoor open. "Tell her I'll be there."

"The funeral is at the ninth hour. Would you travel with us?"

"No, I'll go by horseback, so I can return by evening."

"So be it." Nathaniel descended the ladder into the passage. "By the way," he called out, "I wouldn't wear that uniform."

Antony closed the trapdoor above the passage and slid the locking bolt back into place. For twenty years, he thought he'd left the life of Simeon for good. How ironic, Antony thought: death, and Nathaniel, and Bethlehem, once again conspired to grieve his life.

CHAPTER XXXI

Rabbi Joachin picked at his beard. Word reached Bethlehem's rabbi late last night that he would be needed for Deborah's burial. The messenger came from Jerusalem, sent by no less than the Sopher Kohen Gadol himself. That alone disturbed Joachin. When he then remembered the deceased was related to the disgraced innkeep from the massacre, the rabbi grew anxious. Might there be trouble at the funeral? The only others in the synagogue this afternoon besides him were two local widows hired as mourners. The rabbi knew from past performances they excelled at lament, even for a stranger. The extra money the Sopher provided to pay mourners at least meant that none of the synagogue's welfare fund would need be spent for their wails. Joachin's rambling thoughts were broken when the front door opened and a solitary figure entered.

"Rebekah?" The rabbi's surprise triggered widening eyes and a slight pallor to his face. "Is there something I can do for you?"

"I've come for Deborah's service."

Words escaped the rabbi. Of all the people who might have cause to disrupt the funeral, Rebekah loomed foremost. Since coming to Bethlehem one year ago, he'd heard the story of the massacre and Elias' martyrdom any number of times. Blame always fell not only upon Herod and the Romans, but on Joshua, Deborah's son-in-law. Joachin had also been made aware of Rebekah's respected place among the Zealots, her home often serving as a waystation for its adherents. For all Joachin knew, Rebekah might have arranged for some of them to carry out an act of vengeance against the family of Joshua today.

"May I have a word with you, in private?" Joachin didn't want this conversation in the hearing of the two mourners. Their voices had a bent for gossip as well as lament.

"As you wish." She followed him back into the room used by the rabbi for study.

Once the door closed, Joachin spoke. "I'm not sure how to say this, but why have you come for Deborah's service?"

"What sort of question is that, Rabbi?" Irritation sharpened Rebekah's tone. When the synagogue needed a new leader last year, the elders chose this student of Gamaliel, Jerusalem's noted Pharisee. Like his teacher, Joachin proved gifted in his knowledge of the Torah and its traditions. Unlike Gamaliel, he proved extraordinarily ill at ease when dealing with people.

"Forgive me Rebekah, but I understood your family and the family of Deborah to be, well, estranged. Because of Joshua, and –"

"How dare you! Deborah's daughter and I are friends. We both lost sons in the slaughter."

"Oh. But I thought –"

"No, you didn't think," snapped Rebekah. Few women dared talk to a man in this way, fewer still to a rabbi. But Rebekah had the standing and temperament – and now cause – to do so. "You DIDN'T think, you just assumed! You live too much in your scrolls, Rabbi, instead of out among the people you're supposed to guide!"

Joachin remained silent for fear of creating further offense. To his relief, he heard his name called out by the hired mourners. The funeral procession from Jerusalem had arrived. "We'd better go," he mumbled, opening the door for Rebekah.

"Speak well of Deborah," Rebekah warned. "She and

Naomi deserve better than what life's given them."

Through the doorway, Rebekah saw Nathaniel escorting Naomi. The two women approached one another and embraced. The paid mourners from Bethlehem and two other women hired and brought from Jerusalem by Nathaniel began to moan and strike their chests.

"I was so sorry to hear about Deborah," intoned Rebekah, hugging her friend tight against her. "She was a good woman."

"She was, she was." Short breaths, almost gasps, interspersed her words. "And thank you for coming, Rebekah."

"When the burial is done, I want you and Nathaniel to come to my house. I've prepared the *seudat havraah*."

Naomi managed a smile. "The messenger told us you'd offered to host the meal. You've always been a friend."

They stood, wrapped in one another's arms, while Nathaniel and Joachin discussed the details of the service. Joachin would lead the cart bearing Deborah's body to the burial ground.

Just then, the synagogue's front door swung open again. When Naomi looked back, her arms let loose of Rebekah. "Simeon. SIMEON!"

* * *

A cloudy afternoon brought respite from the sun's heat for the four men who had set out from New Damascus to Jericho. Abraham and Yeshua Barabbas led, while two of Barabbas' men followed. Ruins of an ancient settlement lay strewn beside them. Steps leading to an empty cistern, and broken remnants of walls from structures fallen long ago, were all that remained. After a futile attempt to farm the nearby hills, the would-be settlers abandoned the site centuries ago. Abraham often visited this place for times of extended prayer. "These people must have known how hard this would be. Yet they still tried to make a life."

"Look what it got them," replied Barabbas, "a heap of stones with no name. And no life."

"At least the stones survive." Abraham glanced over at Barabbas, catching his eye. "Do you ever wonder what we'll leave behind?"

Barabbas shook his head. "We've no control over what's to be remembered of us."

"I'm not so sure," replied Abraham. "Take the reasons for our journey to Galilee. You go to meet your Zealot friends and plot trouble for the new procurator. I go to find Rabbi Yeshua."

"I don't follow you, Abraham."

"We take the same road, but for entirely different purposes. You, to scheme unrest and worse. Me, to learn if this rabbi is the One the Baptizer spoke of. Tell me, Barabbas: if something happened to us on this road, which reason would you rather be remembered for?"

Barabbas laughed. "Abraham, your arguments twist more than those canyons to the west. But since you offer your understanding of our journey, let me give mine. I go to Galilee to plan our people's deliverance, while you chase after another fool's dream. Now, which would YOU want to be remembered for?"

"You dismiss this Yeshua without ever having heard or seen him?"

"When Messiah comes, ALL will know it. And you can be sure God's Holy One will not be spawned of Galileans, nor waste his time among publicans and fishermen."

The trail crested, and from their vantage point the Jordan valley stretched north far beyond the Salt Sea. Where the river meandered on the valley floor, thickets of brambles and tamarisks lined the banks. Away from the river, too far for roots to tap into the stream, the land stretched desolate. In some places, only a few feet separated lush undergrowth from barren soil.

The four traveled some distance before Abraham spoke again. "The Baptizer ministered in this wilderness, and many rejected him because he didn't come from Jerusalem. So maybe a Galilean-born Messiah who labors amidst fish nets is not so farfetched."

"You're a dreamer. Until your rabbi storms the Antonia, he's of no interest to me."

* * *

Deborah's body lay in a shallow grave. At the eulogy's end, mourners tossed handfuls of dirt on the linen-wrapped corpse. Antony completed the work by shoveling more earth on top, until a small heap mounded over the grave's site. Naomi stood by her son's side while Joachin led the group in the prayer of *kaddish*.

Arms accustomed to wielding a gladius now awkwardly clutched his mother. Antony couldn't remember when he'd held her for so long. Was it when a nightmare of David's death left him shaking and sobbing in the night? Or when he'd come home, bloodied and bruised, from fighting one of many who taunted him with his father's cowardice?

"Simeon, you don't know how much it means, having you with me."

Naomi's words unsettled her son, even more than the jeers of the Syrian he'd recently fought. He didn't like hearing the name Simeon used, and he knew he wouldn't stay long. He'd given up his family and preferred to leave it that way. It was easier. But for now, he felt he couldn't say anything to his mother. In silent memory, he abided her clinging.

Nathaniel touched them both on the back. "Before we leave for the meal at Rebekah's, we should thank Rabbi Joachin for his words."

Mother and son released one another, but only Naomi joined Nathaniel. "The two of you can speak to him," Antony said, "I should thank Rebekah for opening her table."

Antony walked toward Rebekah as she stood at the grave. He marveled at how little she'd changed. Her hair had some gray streaks run through it. A few more lines and folds creased her brow. But overall, Rebekah was as he remembered her twenty years past.

"Rebekah," bowing slightly, "my mother and Nathaniel and I are grateful for the invitation to break bread in your home."

Rebekah glared at Antony, whom she'd not seen since his family left Bethlehem. "Come with me. I have things to say I do not wish your mother to hear."

The others took no special note of Rebekah and Antony walking by themselves to an ancient olive tree that stood nearby. Once an entire grove grew here, but this tree alone remained. Ripened fruit hung among gnarled branches in need of pruning.

"You honor your grandmother's memory by coming, Simeon." She spoke the words as if by rote, with the exception of the emphasis put on his name.

"It was the least I could do."

"I suppose it was, Simeon." Once again, her accent fell hard on "Simeon."

While he might be willing today for his mother to call him by that name, Antony saw no need to extend the privilege. "Did my mother tell you I go by another name now: Antony?"

Rebekah looked back at Deborah's grave. "She has, along with the reason why. Naomi's mourned twenty years for her lost Simeon."

Antony cleared his throat. "What I did was best for everyone."

"Don't mask self-indulgence behind concern for others." Rebekah peered hard into Antony's eyes, as words followed more spewed than spoken. "You and your sister both! You deserted your mother because neither of you had the spine to stand by her. And now, you serve with the filth who murdered your brother – while Hannah whores with them."

"That's enough, Rebekah!!" A rush of anger and embarrassment and disbelief flushed Antony's face. "Say what you will of me, but Hannah would never do such a thing!"

"What would you know, Simeon, or Antony, or whoever you think you've become! You've not shown your face to family for twenty years. But I speak the truth."

Antony's thoughts jumbled with various images of Hannah: a toddler trying to waken a fallen brother, a young girl clinging to another brother about to leave home. But a prostitute? What if Rebekah was right? "I had no idea," he said in a voice hollow and far away. "Perhaps it would be best if I return to Jerusalem now."

"You'll do no such thing!" countered Rebekah. "Naomi's waited too long to have you walk out on her so soon. She expects you at the meal."

"You'd have me sup in your home?"

Rebekah's attention so riveted on Antony, she didn't notice the approach of Nathaniel. "For the sake of Naomi, I do. But this day only. Otherwise, I count you a traitor to Israel. One for whom I would not grieve if my son struck you down."

"Saul's always been a friend. Why would he do that?"

"Because he is a Zealot!"

Antony's mouth dropped. "Saul?"

"Saul no more. Like you, my son goes by a different name: Yeshua Barabbas. Except for him, the change had nothing to do with disgrace. Yeshua recalls the one who brought the massacre upon our families and town, and Barabbas—"

"Forgive me for interrupting." Nathaniel's words startled both Antony and Rebekah. "I thought you should know that Naomi's ready to leave."

Antony strode briskly toward his mother. Nathaniel, leaning his left arm on a cane, offered his right hand to Rebekah. "I didn't hear what you were saying to Antony, but your voices sounded strained. Was there trouble?"

"No trouble. Just a few remembrances in need of sharing." Rebekah recalled Deborah's innate distrust of Nathaniel, and disclosed nothing further.

Nathaniel bantered on as they walked back toward the others. "That boy has brought this family nothing but grief. Serving in the Legion, abandoning his name, staying away all these years. But look at Naomi now. You'd think she'd understand he's no better than his father. Maybe worse, since Antony deliberately chose his life."

Rebekah made no reply. As a mother, she understood Naomi's need to have her son by her side in such a time. But Rebekah found herself agreeing with Nathaniel's assessment of Antony – and Naomi. In Rebekah's mind, Naomi showed weakness by allowing Antony back. Rebekah offered an inaudible prayer of thanks for the strength Elias' death implanted in her, and for a son who was a patriot – not a traitor – to Israel.

Nathaniel's thoughts also gravitated to Rebekah's son, whom he'd just overheard to be Yeshua Barabbas. There'd always been rumors of Saul's ties with rebels. But Yeshua Barabbas? Only the sons of the martyred Judas had names more revered among the Zealots – and more feared by the Jerusalem authorities, Jewish and Roman. Certain men on the Sanhedrin might find this knowledge useful. Even more so, Nathaniel welcoming the new procurator with information on a Zealot captain's identity might prove a valuable asset. For the first time in years, the Sopher thought kindly of Antony, who unwittingly had given him this next chip for bargaining.

* * *

Construction of Tiberias was still ongoing. Only six years past, Herod Antipas announced the relocation of Galilee's capital from Sepphoris to this site, named to honor emperor Tiberias. Besides being closer to the other district Antipas ruled, Tiberias possessed a warmer climate and sulfur springs only 20 minutes south at Hammath. Antipas shared his late father's fondness for such waters. The only hurdle to these plans for a great city rising on the shore of Galilee's sea came in the first winter of construction. While sinking a foundation for its fortress, workmen unearthed an ancient cemetery. Most Jewish workers left immediately, citing the Torah's warning that contact with a corpse left one ritually unclean. Some rabbis argued the cemetery made the entire site unfit for habitation. Their stance infuriated Herod, who then offered land and housing in the city to any who would settle there. Not many Jews took advantage. But on the city's southern edge, one such individual came to open and tend an inn: his name was Joshua.

"Innkeep, my friends and I need more bread." Three men sat at table, the only customers this early in the afternoon.

Joshua brought in a loaf of wheat bread, baked this morning in the clay oven outside the kitchen. "I've got your room ready, whenever you need it."

"Fine," announced the one who'd called for the bread. "By the way, you said your name was Joshua?"

"That's right."

"An Israelite name," said another. "Tiberias has precious few of your people."

"The old cemetery kept many away."

The first man spoke again. "Joshua, would you join us?"

Joshua looked outside. Another hour remained before the first workers would come for dinner. A fish stew simmered above the fire, ready to be served. "For a bit."

Joshua sat. The first man continued. "Why didn't the cemetery keep you away?"

"I've been a man who's worked for others longer than I care to remember. When I heard of Herod's offer, it seemed an opportunity to get out on my own."

"And your family?"

The faces of Naomi and Hannah and Simeon came to Joshua's mind, wife and children not seen in thirty years. "I have no family."

"You speak with a Judean accent." The third man's voice sounded accusatory.

"And you, as a Galilean," countered Joshua.

"A Judean Jew who lives among Gentiles in Galilee." The first man spoke once more. "It seems to me you might be able to use some friends."

"One always needs friends. But why would Galilean Jews befriend a Judean?"

"What makes you think we're Jews?"

Joshua leaned back in his chair. "A good host heeds his customers. Before, you asked if I made my fish stew with *clarias*. Gentiles just care that the stew tastes good. Only Jews worry if it contains fish the rabbis pronounce unclean."

The first man smiled and nodded at the others. "Now that, Joshua, speaks directly to our interest in you. We need someone who's observant at these tables. Especially, say, if talk turned to things Roman. Tiberias already attracts Herod's associates, and rumors of a legion detachment to be assigned here circulate."

Old feelings stirred in Joshua. His failure as a sicarii under Kohath never totally erased his longings to throw in his lot against Rome. Maybe Tiberias presented a second chance. "Then you have a friend at this inn. Will you come here often?"

"From time to time. We occasionally meet with other friends from Judea. Plus, we follow closely the progress of the Rabbi Yeshua."

"I've heard of him, though he's never come to Tiberias." Joshua paused. "Some say it's because there's too many Gentiles here, others because of Herod's spies."

The three strangers laughed, then the first man answered. "This Yeshua is no fool when it comes to Herod. The rabbi calls him a fox, and for good reason." Leaning closer to Joshua, he continued. "Keep your eyes and ears open. Pass on what you learn to me, or others who will come in my name."

"And what is your name?"

"Jacob, a dresser of vines. Speak only to those who tell you my name and work in just those words."

Joshua offered his hand to Jacob. "You have my word."

As Jacob clasped Joshua's hand, he placed five silver shekels in the innkeeper's palm. "Consider this a seal of our friendship."

Joshua filled four goblets with wine, and the men drank to their new relationship. A breeze from the south carried a rank odor from the springs. When Joshua first came to Tiberias, he thought the smell might drive him away. Now, he hardly noticed it.

CHAPTER XXXII

An honor guard of legionnaires lined the palace dock while musicians rehearsed in the courtyard. Shortly after daybreak, a sentry had spotted a sail on the horizon bearing the imperial insignia. Julius spent his time since then making final arrangements for welcoming the new procurator. Within the past hour, one of the two skiffs he sent out raced back under full sail. The procurator did not wish to arrive at a common wharf used for cargo. Instead, his galley would sail as close to the palace dock as possible. Only then would he transfer onto the second boat to disembark in surroundings more suitable for one of his rank.

As Julius waited on the dock, he couldn't help but laugh. A hundred yards offshore, a tiny figure clambered down the side of the Roman galley into the second sailboat he dispatched. Julius knew it to be the same boat he and Hannah had lain within eight nights ago.

"My lord, most honorable Julius."

Julius wrinkled his brow at the familiar voice and turned. It belonged to the chief steward of Caesarea's palace, whose bulbous round face enveloped a fawning smile.

"Forgive me, Excellency, but I wanted to tell you myself, we stand ready in the dining hall. And let me say, the cooks have outdone themselves. I've never seen peacock roasted so tender. And the shellfish, oh, the shellfish—"

"Thank you, steward. I'll see the procurator is duly informed of your work."

"Thank you, Julius, sir. May the gods reward you for looking after your servant. I always told Valerius he was fortunate to have such a man as you at his side. Our new procurator could do no better than to have your wisdom and insight to guide him."

"Hadn't you best return to the hall? Once the procurator arrives, we'll go directly there."

"Oh yes, yes, quite right." The portly steward half-bowed, unable to bend too far down because of the rippled folds of flesh under his robe. Shuffling backwards in deference to Julius, he stumbled and fell when his heels struck the first of the steps leading from the dock up to the palace. Several guards hooted as he struggled to his feet and hastily ascended the steps.

Julius rolled his eyes. Leaving such sycophants behind provided one of the most appealing aspects of retirement, but even more so did his relationship with Hannah. This past week reinforced how much he had yearned for the company of a woman with whom to spend more than a few hours only to never see again. It was far too late to consider marriage, but Hannah's companionship already seemed a given in his life. Last night, they talked of the apartment Herod Antipas offered him in Tiberias, and her decision to go there with him.

Such pleasant thoughts might have continued, had the approaching vessel not regained Julius' attention. The boat dropped sail as it coasted to the dock. Julius signaled a servant at the top of the steps. Horns blared a fanfare as the boat slid against the dock, the impact cushioned by sacks of hay set along the sides.

A robust man clad in a white toga edged with purple stripes stepped off the vessel. The legionnaires at Julius' side snapped right arms to chestplates in salute: "HAIL CAESAR!"

The procurator raised a hand in acknowledgement. Julius marched forward, bearing the legion's standards. "The Augustan cohort salutes you. These are yours, as our commander."

"In the name of emperor Tiberias, I receive them. Give

them to one of the men to hold."

Slightly bowing, Julius continued: "I am Julius, advisor to the former procurator."

"I've read the dispatches from Valerius. He greatly valued your service."

"Thank you, sir."

The procurator started up the steps with Julius at his side, then lowered his voice so as not to be heard by the escorting guards. "Rest assured that Valerius also indicated your years of service, and hopes of retiring. I carry the papers of your discharge and imperial donative. Once the transition is accomplished, you will be free."

Julius wanted to shout, but settled for an enthusiastic "Yes sir!" After ascending several more steps, Julius attended to the demands of protocol. "A reception in your honor awaits in the palace hall. How shall I introduce you?"

Arriving at the top of the steps, they looked across the palace courtyard and its pool. Players of lyres and flutes stood between the columns. At the courtyard's far end, a crowd of officials and servants flanked the entryway to the royal dining hall. After surveying the scene, his answer came: "Procurator of Judea, Pontius Pilate."

* * *

Across the Valley of Jezreel, rows of bare grapevines lined the land's gentle contours. Spent from summer's harvest and not yet showing next year's growth, the vines resembled wooden weavings. Elsewhere, fields normally plowed by now for the planting of wheat still sprouted the last crop's stubble. The season of early rains had not yet arrived. A scattering of clouds borne by a southwest breeze buoyed hopes of its coming.

"You should come to Galilee when these vines sag to the ground under the weight of grapes," Jacob bragged.

"And you, to the hills outside Bethlehem, when sheep thick with winter's wool resemble moving fields of snow." Yeshua Barabbas was not about to let a Galilean boast go unchallenged.

Coming to a stone fence marking the border between two vineyards, Jacob sat and hoisted a skin filled with wine to his mouth. After swilling a mouthful, he offered the skin to Barabbas. The Judean leaned back and squeezed off a mouthful. Drinking it down, Barabbas continued. "You've heard the new procurator arrives soon in Caesarea."

"Yes," replied Jacob, "though nothing about him."

"According to an Essene at New Damascus, there's been persecution of late at the synagogue in Rome. Sejanus, Tiberias' advisor, is blamed. And assuming his influence on this appointment, that might well bring us a procurator who'll not be so tolerant as Valerius."

Jacob's hand reached through one of the vines, snapping several twigs. As a youth, he'd spent many hours pruning vineyards. Sometimes he wished that was all he had to do now. But Jacob remained his father's son, determined to carry on the fight against Rome. "All the better. People saw little need to cause trouble under Valerius."

"My thoughts run the same, Jacob. It's hard to convince others to take up the sword when you forget there's one stuck in your back."

"We may have to remind the people. Force the procurator to a show of strength."

Barabbas nodded. He'd long considered what might be done: a raid on the procurator's palace, an assassination of an officer in the cohort, even a murder made to look like the act of Romans. He kept these thoughts to himself, except for one. "Or, we could let the new procurator do the work for us."

"What do you mean by that?"

"Jacob, suppose we're right, that he's a Jew-hater like Sejanus. He'll WANT to come in with a heavy hand."

"Go on."

"If we stir up trouble which Rome reacts to, we run the risk of losing favor. Especially if others judge their suffering to be on our account. But let the procurator wield the sword first: we intervene on behalf of the people, who then naturally turn to us."

Jacob considered the argument, and its flaw. "But what if he behaves as Valerius?"

"If he does, then we act. But why not give him opportunity to strike first?"

"You know, Yeshua Barabbas, for a Judean you think well."

Barabbas gave Jacob a shove. "I have to, given that thick Galilean head of yours."

"That's because the Almighty gave us brains worth protecting."

"Is that so? That must mean you'll have the good sense not to wrestle with me."

The Galilean hopped off the wall. "Not at all, my dim friend. It just means I'll enjoy putting you on your back all the more."

The contest was more a friendly ritual than a test between rivals. Each stepped forward with his right leg, then locked knees together. Right hands clasped the other's wrist. "Ready?"

Barabbas nodded his head and shouted, "NOW!"

For nearly a minute, arms pushed and pulled, while legs strained to drive the opponent off-balance. The end came when Jacob feigned a slip backward. Barabbas pushed forward as hard as he could, only to have Jacob jerk him hard that same direction. His balance lost, Barabbas fell forward. Only Jacob's grip on his wrist prevented Barabbas's nose from being planted in the ground with the grape vines.

"The shame of being beaten by a thickheaded Galilean," Jacob mocked. "Will you ever recover your honor?"

"Next time, Jacob." Barabbas dusted himself off, then reached for the wineskin placed on the stone wall for safekeeping. After taking a drink, Barabbas sat down again. "By the way, what's become of your Galilean Messiah? Will he be of any use to us?"

"Rabbi Yeshua? He's a puzzle, that one. If he gave the word, a sizable mob would march on Jerusalem. But whenever some press for such action, he backs away. I've been told he once fled into the hills when a crowd wanted to proclaim him king."

"Then he's just afraid."

"Fear's the wrong word, Barabbas. I've seen fear in men before, but I don't find it in him. Reluctance. Stubbornness. I don't know what to call it. He doesn't betray his thoughts easily. Not even when I ask him directly about this idea of his being Messiah. Not that I think so, but many wonder about it." Jacob looked out across the vineyards, to the fields awaiting rain and plow. "But if he were the Chosen One of Adonai God, Barabbas, you and I would be on the verge of Israel's greatest victory. Many have always thought we could hasten Adonai's intervention by acting on his behalf. Maybe it's that way with Yeshua. We may need to push him."

"I wouldn't put my hopes in him." Barabbas drew a sword from underneath his robe. "THIS is what Messiah will use when he frees us. Your rabbi doesn't sound like a fighter to me."

"No, I suppose not. But give him a little longer. We've a man who follows the rabbi as a disciple. He assures us there's hope our time of waiting is over."

The clouds above remained scattered, though a darker band billowed over the Menashe Heights. "Maybe for the rain," noted Barabbas, "but I venture that's all."

* * *

"Quick! To the viewpoint!" Taking Hannah's hand, Julius half-ran with her in tow to one of the shelters scattered along the seawall's walkway. During hot summer days, the roofs provided shelter from the sun. On this autumn evening, they shielded Hannah and Julius from large cold raindrops flung down by a sudden squall.

Hannah shook her head as she ran her fingers through

her hair. "The procurator had best count himself fortunate he landed today. I'd not want to be at sea in such weather."

"This spoken by the woman who wanted to walk the seawall tonight?" Julius dried her hair with the inside of his mantle. "Who told me she didn't care if those clouds opened on us? Here I thought you'd want to go out for a sail this evening."

"Watching a storm is one thing," Hannah replied. "Riding it out, with only a few planks of wood between you and the sea, would be quite another."

Julius looked at the sky. Overhead, a green-black bank of clouds drenched the harbor as it moved inland. Out to sea, a distant line of yellow light edged the squall line. "As fast as the clouds move, we'll soon be watching sunset with a clear sky above."

Taking off his mantle, Julius turned it on its side to wrap it around his and Hannah's shoulders. As he did, Hannah put her arm around his waist. "I've heard it said that Galilee's Sea has such sudden storms. Is Tiberias within view of its waters?"

"Antipas built his palace on a plateau above the lake, while the city lies between the plateau and the water. He told me the apartment offered us faces the lake."

Hannah and Julius listened to the rain pounding on the roof tiles. Julius drew her closer. There was one matter he'd not yet broached, and this seemed as good a time as any. "Hannah, you've never spoken of your family. Do you ever miss them?"

"What makes you talk of them now?"

Julius felt Hannah's body grow rigid as she answered. "I've been thinking. Before we go to Tiberias, we could arrange to visit them."

"Don't be foolish." Hannah pulled away, stepping close to the seaside window. The rain blew against her face and dampened her cloak. "Do you think they'd want to see a daughter who's whored twenty years?"

"But you could tell them that life's over and done."

Hannah looked at Julius. She marveled at how one whose advice steered Rome's course in Judea could be so naïve about this. "Really! And how do I explain that? By telling them I've given up the life of a prostitute for that of a Roman concubine?"

"I just didn't want you to feel I held you back from your family."

His attitude puzzled her. For years, those she bedded had their needs met, but never inquired of hers beyond the price of her services. Now this Roman comes along, seeming to care for her as something more than a commodity ripe for the picking. Julius' thoughtfulness mingled with remembrances of her rape by Roman soldiers, and back to her brother's murder in Bethlehem by other Roman hands. She almost wished Julius were more like those men. Hannah had learned over the years how to protect herself from the dangers such ones could pose. But with Julius, she felt vulnerable: unsure of how to protect herself from his care. "My family is largely what drove me to this life, Julius. Seeing them would only open unhealed wounds."

"Maybe they've not healed because you keep them inside. I could listen."

Damn him anyway, she thought. But if it's honesty he wants – "A Roman who listens? I didn't know that was a trait of your people!"

Julius took Hannah's hand. "Try me."

"Fine!?" Hannah snatched her hand from his and stepped into the rain. "Then listen, advisor to the procurator. When a dozen legionnaires stripped the dress off a girl barely 12 years old in the Antonia, none of them seemed to listen very well. When she pleaded for release, when she screamed in pain as one after another took his turn skewering her while she lay on her back, and then her stomach – no Roman listened! To ME!"

Julius' face blanched. "You?"

Hannah's eyes glared. "Does that surprise you, Julius? Why did you think I chose this life? For the money? For the joy of feeling a different stranger thrust between my thighs every night to earn enough money for one more day's food?"

"Hannah, I had no idea." Julius' tone shifted from compassion to anger. "Those bastards, doing that to a child!"

"Oh, Julius, don't get ahead of yourself. That was only the beginning." Tears and rain streaked the makeup under her eyes into black lines tracing down her cheek. "Three years I kept my rape a secret, not wanting to disgrace my family. When my mother then spoke of arranging my betrothal, I finally got up the nerve and told her. I had to."

"You had to?" Julius leaned on the viewpoint's ledge. "Why did you have to tell?"

"The marriage contract calls for an examination, to insure the woman is a virgin." Hannah's voice trailed off. Julius sought to embrace her, but Hannah cringed from his touch.

"I'm not finished." Drawing a deep breath, Hannah spoke on. "My mother convinced me to tell her uncle, with whom we lived. A member of the Sanhedrin, he'd see justice done, she said. Well, his reaction was touching. Embarrassed at having to break off the marital negotiations, he blamed me. Called me a harlot for going to the Antonia in the first place. When I tried to explain I'd been hurt, he growled about waiting so long to say anything. Maybe it wasn't as I said, he complained. And bringing Roman soldiers to trial for an act more than three years old, who'd believe it? My own mother agreed. But when he suggested that maybe I made this up to hide fornication. . ." Hannah attempted to wipe the tears from her face, but she managed only to smear what little cosmetics hadn't washed away already. "My own family didn't listen to me, Julius, didn't believe me. My great-uncle wanted me gone so badly he paid me. So I left."

"And you came to Caesarea."

"After a few years in Samaria. I heard there of women

living comfortably here, servicing the cohort at Caesarea, along with the sailors."

Julius studied Hannah's face. "You must hate anything, and anyone, Roman." His voice quieted, barely audible above wind and surf. "Why did you ever stay with me?"

Having revealed so much, Hannah saw no need to stop being honest, no matter the cost. "You offered an opportunity to get something back from those who took from me."

"And now, you stay with me now, you would come to Tiberias, for the same reason?"

"A lifetime of hatred can't be changed in a week." Hannah reached out to brush the rain from Julius' forehead. "But I tell you this, Julius, from my heart: no one, no one, has shown care and respect for me as have you."

"What my countrymen did to you, I can never undo." Julius pressed his lips to Hannah's hand. "But if you can, stay with me. I promise: I will not let anyone hurt you. Never again."

Hannah let him wrap his arms around her. Another burst of rain fell hard on the shelter. For the first time since Bethlehem, Hannah felt safe. And loved.

CHAPTER XXXIII

The previous night's storm dumped more than an inch of rain on Jerusalem. Tiny canals crisscrossed the Antonia's courtyard as water filled the mortar lines between stones. In the courtyard's center, a detail of legionnaires packed a cart. With a heavy mist soaking anything unprotected, they took care to keep the contents tarped. Besides routine supplies for the Jericho outpost, the cart carried the belongings of Lucius. A cedar chest, a chair given him by his century, some boxes: no cargo had ever been handled with greater attention.

"Now there's the respect you must demand, Antony." Lucius nudged Antony's side. "They reckon if they drop even one piece, I'll have their hide." "And I would."

"You'll be missed here, Lucius."

"Aah. More than one'll toast my leaving. But I kept them alive in our skirmishes with the sicarii, and taught the discipline required of a legionnaire. Just as you'll do."

Antony peered from under the balcony at the small cart. It held the sum total of this man's possessions. "Why did you choose not to return to Italy?"

Lucius adjusted the cloak around his shoulders. "If I went back, I'd just be one more veteran, unknown to anyone. Rome's a stranger to me, what I know of life is here."

A half dozen horses clopped into the courtyard. A large white mare with oversized hooves had the cart harness slipped onto its shoulders while a second draft horse was hitched to the back of the cart. Riders sat atop three mounts. A black Arabian stallion awaited Lucius.

Antony stiffened in one final salute to his now-former centurion. "A good future, Lucius. And if the boredom of too much leisure overtakes you, remember us here."

"I'll remember." Lucius walked into the courtyard, pulling the mantle tight around his neck and then calling back: "I'll remember you drilling the men in this God-forsaken rain, while I soak in one of Herod's baths tonight. Good luck to you, Centurion!"

The Antonia's gates swung open, and the patrol began its journey. Antony watched them enter Jerusalem's streets, still empty at dawn's first light. With Lucius gone, one of Bethlehem's children now commanded one of Rome's centuries.

* * *

"The advisor Julius to see his Excellency, Pilate, procurator of Judea and Samaria, honored servant of Tiberias!" The steward bellowed the introduction. Julius thought it out of proportion in volume and formality, but in keeping with the chief steward's fawning nature.

"Come in, Julius. Steward, take your leave."

"Whatever your Excellency wishes. If you want anything, I await your summons. Anything, any way to be of service."

"Yes, yes, I understand. Now go."

At the steward's exit, Julius walked to the procurator and saluted.

"Be seated. There's much to be discussed."

Julius sat across from Pilate. "You must forgive the steward his excessive flattery. Even though he does his job well, he imagines pandering keeps him in good stead."

"Actually, I find his manner fitting," replied Pilate. "A servant does well to remember who is master. Don't you agree?"

"Yes, when you put it that way."

"I'm glad, because that's how I view my commission to this office. These Judeans and Samaritans are Rome's servants. Our task is to remind them of their master."

"Understood. Do you have plans for that reminding, beyond what we already do?"

Pilate leaned forward, resting folded hands on the desk between the men. "I've come here from Tiberias and Sejanus with two actions in mind. Of course, I would hear your opinion."

Julius detected a perfunctory tone in Pilate's last phrase. "What would the actions be?"

"First, to commemorate my posting, I'm authorizing the minting of new coins, bronze and copper. Take a look at this." Pilate handed Julius a sheet of papyrus. "During the voyage, I directed a servant to sketch my ideas."

Julius studied two circular drawings. The first portrayed a *simpulum*, the ladle used to pour sacrificial libations in the worship of Rome's gods. The second depicted the staff used by an augur when prophesying the future.

"So, what do you think?"

"The drawings? Your servant has a gift for fine work."

"Don't evade the question, Julius. What advice do you give on their minting?"

Julius laid the sketches on Pilate's desk. "The images will likely stir trouble, sir. Jews have an unusual intolerance for religious practices beyond their own."

"But these are only pictures on coins!"

"These people have a peculiar tradition against the use of any image. They don't even allow their own god to be represented."

"That's absurd! Our laws govern this province, not theirs. The coins will be minted!"

Julius eased back in his chair. "Forgive me, procurator. I meant no disrespect."

"Valerius indicated your familiarity with the Jews and their foolish customs in his dispatches." Pilate's voice seemed less strained, but still adamant. "I'd hoped that knowledge wouldn't weaken your counsel on Rome's behalf."

"The sake of Rome has always been foremost in my counsel." Julius did not appreciate his allegiance being questioned, even indirectly. "I studied their ways for the sole purpose of securing Rome's position here."

"Knowledge of enemies can be a valuable thing. But reminding them of their place under our rule is even more paramount. Which leads to my second decision. We will rotate the cohort stationed in Caesarea with the one in Jerusalem."

"Will you accompany them to Jerusalem?"

"No. I'll winter here, acquainting myself with the posting. Valerius mentioned a religious festival of the Jews in the spring that I should plan on spending in Jerusalem."

"That would be what they call Passover. More pilgrims are in the city than at any other time. In the past, we've garrisoned extra troops in the Antonia for it, as the more rebellious faction known as the Zealots make a habit of agitating the city when the crowds grow."

"Well, let them. In any event, I'll go to Jerusalem for this Passover."

"Is there anything else, Pilate?"

The procurator stood, taking a fig from a bowl and biting off a piece. "I've sent a rider to the Jerusalem commander, notifying him of the rotation. I've issued orders for the new cohort to enter Jerusalem by day. That way, the standards with the effigies of Tiberias will be seen by all."

Julius found it hard to believe his ears. Standards had always been brought into Jerusalem by night to avoid the very sort of display that Pilate desired. "Sir, forgive me, but parading the emperor's likeness through Jerusalem in daylight will almost certainly trigger unrest."

"Julius, haven't you been listening?" Pilate sucked the remainder of the fig into his mouth, chewed it several times, spit out the pit, and swallowed. "These people need respect for their masters instilled in them. They are subjects of Tiberias, so let them see Tiberias. Once the cohort is in Jerusalem, I've commanded the votive shields to be hung from the Antonia's walls. We, too, have gods to watch over us."

Remembrances of an encounter years ago came to Julius' mind, when the dying Herod decided to set up a Roman eagle atop the Sanctuary entrance. "Since the orders have been given, procurator, my advice on this is beside the point. But such actions could drive many Jews to the side of those who preach revolution."

"Then they'll learn the folly of such action. This land belongs to Rome, and these Jews will be taught that! Even if the lesson comes at the point of a spear. Are you with me, Julius?"

Pushing away his chair as he stood, Julius bowed ever so slightly to Pilate. "I am, as always, with Rome."

"I see," sputtered Pilate, offended by Julius failing to offer allegiance to him. "By the way, take these scrolls. They release you from service, and authorize you to collect your donative from the treasury. I do expect you to remain in Caesarea until the troop rotation is complete." Pilate turned his back on Julius, selecting another piece of fruit. "If I require your counsel, I'll call for you. Otherwise, your presence here is no longer needed. That will be all, citizen Julius."

Julius took the scrolls without a word and left the room. Julius wondered not if, but when, Pilate would reap the confrontation his chosen course sowed.

* * *

Nathaniel stared at Naomi, seated across the table from him. Though nine years younger, she could easily pass for his elder. The drab clothes of mourning accentuated the pallor of her skin. Hair once prized hung in unkempt bunches of strands not touched by a brush in days. Gaunt fingers fidgeted at the food on her plate, but ate none. Her eyes clouded with a dull film.

"Naomi."

She neither moved nor responded.

"Naomi!"

Her head lifted slightly. "Yes, Nathaniel?"

"Isn't it time you ate something?"

"I have no appetite."

Nathaniel took a slice of bread and spread jam on it. "Here, try some of this."

"Maybe later."

The Sopher shook his head. The last time she'd eaten more than a few bits at a meal had been at Rebekah's, the day of the funeral. "A body can't live on what you give yourself."

"I've no need to live," she replied in a voice as listless as her appearance."

"No need to live?" Nathaniel's patience with her diminished each day. While this fasting concerned him, her despondency aggravated Nathaniel even more. Why she let herself wallow in despair escaped him. "Naomi, do you hear what you're saying?"

For a moment, she allowed her eyes to meet his. Then, her head dropped.

Nathaniel suppressed his irritation in an effort to reach her. "I know you miss Deborah, as do I. But Adonai blessed her with the sight of seventy-one springs."

"It's not just Deborah." Her voice barely rose above a whisper. "It's Simeon, and Hannah, and David. . . even Joshua. Everyone I've loved. All left. Left me."

"Well, I've not gone."

For the first time in over a week, Naomi showed a flash of life. "You were not drawn by a midwife from my womb. Nor did you offer me the vows of betrothal and marriage."

Nathaniel grabbed his walking stick and leaned on it to stand. "I will never understand you, niece. You plague yourself with these memories! Joshua's been gone thirty years. Simeon and Hannah divorced themselves from us. Why bother with them?"

"Maybe for the same reason you never gave up the hope of marrying my mother."

Her response touched a still-raw nerve in Nathaniel. He was not a man accustomed to failure, and his inability to convince Deborah to marry him continued to gnaw at his heart. "This is how you show your gratitude to me? For taking you in when Bethlehem treated your family like garbage, giving you a home as if you were my own daughter all these years?!"

Nathaniel swung his cane across the table, smashing plates and pitchers, sending fruit and cheese flying, splashing water and milk on Naomi's face and dress. Had she been Deborah, Nathaniel would have suffered a barrage of words, and probably worse. But Naomi, like a draught animal resigned to a beating, sagged her shoulders and bowed her head. She didn't bother wiping the food spilled on her.

Embarrassed as much by his outburst as her passivity, Nathaniel leaned over, trying to look into her face. "Naomi, I'm sorry. Naomi?"

She sat. Silent. Still.

The house servants, having heard the commotion, bustled into the room.

"See that she's cleaned, and after that take care of this mess on the table and floor." The maidservant bowed, helping Naomi to her feet and out of the room. Once they were gone, Nathaniel took his most trusted servant aside. "Send a messenger to Rebekah of Bethlehem, the woman with whom we lodged for Deborah's funeral. Tell her I'm sending Naomi to her. Naomi grieves too deeply for me to help."

"Very good, sir."

"And tell Rebekah I'll pay whatever is needed to keep Naomi." Reaching inside his robe, he took out a dozen silver shekels. "Have the messenger give her these as an advance on expenses."

Once the servant left, Nathaniel sat down. He thought of Naomi, driven to such a pitiful state by husband and children. Perhaps it was best he never succeeded in courting Deborah. Families, as Saripheus showed him long ago, only brought pain.

*　*　*

Abraham stopped to catch his breath. Leaning on a large basalt boulder at the side of the road, he looked back down the Valley of the Doves toward the Sea of Galilee. In less than three miles, the path had ascended nearly one thousand feet before leveling off, forming the plateau on whose edge Arbela sat. The trip from Magdala, at the valley's mouth, proved uneventful. Abraham offered silent thanks for a safe journey through the canyon whose other name was "Valley of the Robbers."

"We must be on our way. It's a long way to Sepphoris."

Abraham looked at his companion, a trader from Magdala. He and his son held tethers to three donkeys laden with baskets of salted fish. "Thank you again for letting me travel with you."

The trader cinched one of the donkey's cargo saddles tighter. "And thanks to you, friend. It's always better to journey this way with others. I'm just glad you told the innkeep in Magdala of your intent to visit Arbela, since he knew I'd be traveling past it today."

"Actually, he was the one who directed me here. I'd asked where I might find the rabbi called Yeshua."

"You know of Yeshua?" The trader handed one of the tethers to the boy and stepped next to Abraham. "I thought you said this was your first trip to Galilee?"

"It is. But the rabbi's reputation has spread far. I've known several men who heard him teach during last year's Passover in Jerusalem."

"Why do you come all this way to see him?"

Abraham sensed genuine interest behind the trader's question. "I am a disciple of the Baptizer. Before his execution, he spoke of preparing the Way of one come from God. From the stories I've heard of Yeshua, I decided to see whether the Promised One is with us."

"I've dealt with some Judeans in my commerce. Most

consider us Galileans only a step above Samaritans. You don't say a Judean like yourself awaits a Galilean Messiah?"

"Many in New Damascus chide me for the same reason. And such prejudice holds sway in Jerusalem." Abraham's voice lowered. "But the Baptizer once warned those who trusted in ancestry for righteousness, *God is able to raise up children to Abraham from the stones*. My belief is that Messiah belongs to God, not Judea or Galilee."

"Then may Almighty's shalom bless your search. My family and I have heard the Nazarene speak many times. We've even witnessed events for which I have no explanation."

"Then you think he is Messiah?"

The trader waved at his son to bring the donkeys. "I'm a fish seller, not a Torah scholar. And besides, what I think of Yeshua doesn't matter for your journey's outcome. It's what you think that'll say whether you've made this trek in vain."

Abraham watched the two men and their animals head southwest. "May Adonai watch over you," he called out to them. After adjusting his sandals, Abraham set out for the village of Arbela, only a few hundred yards west. If Magdala's innkeeper was right about Yeshua being here, Abraham might have his wonderings about Yeshua and Messiah put to rest.

CHAPTER XXXIV

Atop the Antonia's southwest tower, Antony scanned the Temple courts below. Priests and supplicants flowed across the sacred precincts. The hawking of vendors and moneychangers mixed with chants and the wailing prayers of pilgrims. Bleating lambs and cooing doves, soon to be sacrificed on the Altar of Holocaust, blended their sounds into the cacophony. Turning his attention to Jerusalem's streets, the same air of normalcy reigned. Markets settled into their midday lull. None outside the Antonia suspected the outrage planned for this afternoon.

In a briefing two days ago, tribune Glaucus informed his centurions of a message received from the new procurator. The cohort from Caesarea would arrive in Jerusalem two days hence. It would be a daylight entry, Glaucus added, with standards leading the way. That detail evoked a mix of smiles and grimaces among the six centurions. Two decades had passed since Roman standards had been openly paraded through Jerusalem. Glaucas said his orders called for the resident centuries to stand on alert during the entry. Afterwards, the current Jerusalem cohort would be rotated to Caesarea.

The officers devised a plan to guard the incoming cohort's route through the city, a plan now set in motion. Antony's century was one of two held in reserve at the Antonia. Two centuries deployed their men atop the walls surrounding the Temple. Glaucas posted the remaining troops in the towers overlooking the Joppa Gate. All stood in position.

Though the rains finally ceased, thick clouds hung low

over the city. From the citadel's height, it seemed to Antony he could almost touch this net cast over Jew and Roman alike. The feeling of being snared nagged him. Not only was this his first test of command, it seemed unnecessary. Neither his men nor Jerusalem's populace needed an act of provocation to initiate Pilate's rule. No military advantage would be gained, just an insult to peoples' sensibilities. It reminded Antony of his long-ago tormentors in Bethlehem, seeing how far he could be pushed before fighting. Was that Pilate's unspoken intent?

"Sir, there's activity near the western gate."

Antony peered in that direction. Barely half a mile away, wherever buildings didn't block his sight, he caught glimpses of people darting down alleys or streets. The figures converged near the gate between the palace and the three towers. While his view remained broken, a clear though distant sound could be heard. He first thought his imagination might be deceiving him, but there was no mistake. The low rumble of pounding drums accompanied the peal of trumpets. In tight formation, six hundred men in battledress now marched in formation down the Street of David. Each blow on the drums' taut skins mimicked and multiplied the soldiers' footfalls.

For a moment, Antony forgot Pilate's foolhardiness. The march stirred memories of why he joined the legion in the first place. The arrogance, the power: no Jew dared block the way, even though Gentiles carried idols upon Mount Zion. All other sounds disappeared from Antony's ears: only the drums, and Roman sandals tramping on Jerusalem's street, remained.

* * *

"I must speak to the High Priest. Now! Please!"

A frantic voice down the hall startled Nathaniel and Caiaphas, who had been discussing next month's Hanukkah observance. The noise of a scuffle brought both men to their feet. "See what the problem is, Sopher." While Nathaniel ambled to the door, cane in hand, Caiaphas took hold of a small knife used at lunch. Eight years in this office had taught Caiaphas to be cautious. Appointed to the High Priesthood by Valerius, Caiaphas always acted to favor his benefactor, much to the dismay of the Zealots and many Pharisees. Rumors of their desire to oust him made Caiaphas nervous at any sign of unrest. The recent exit of Valerius only increased his anxiety. Would the new procurator work with him, or appoint another as High Priest?

"Guards!" Nathaniel struck the door with his walking stick. "What's wrong?"

"Some merchant," came a reply from the other side. "He came racing down the hall, demanding to see Caiaphas."

"Do you have him under control?" asked the Sopher.

"Bound and gagged. What do you want us to do with him?"

Nathaniel looked to Caiaphas. The High Priest set down the knife and returned to his chair. "Bring him to me."

"The High Priest will see him." Sliding the lockbar from the door, Nathaniel swung it open. Two guards gripped a man between them, the fellow's arms tied behind his back. A small gash on his forehead dripped bright red blood down his nose and onto the cloth tightened across his mouth. The guards forced the captive to his knees.

"You are fortunate the High Priest Caiaphas is a gracious man," Nathaniel began. "You could be on your way to a cell. If you want this gag removed, there'll be no shouting. And speak only when given permission. Understood?"

The man nodded his head.

"Remove the gag." The guards obeyed, while maintaining their hold on him,

"Tell me," Caiaphas began, "what brings you in such a turmoil to my door?"

"My lord High Priest, it's the Romans. They're entering the city."

Caiaphas glanced at Nathaniel, then back at the merchant. "This is not a matter of concern. The Romans exchange their troops in Caesarea with those here, as expected."

"But that's not all, sir. They –"

"Silence!" interrupted Nathaniel. "You were told to speak only when allowed."

The man lowered his face.

"If you have more to say," Caiaphas said with what sounded like a yawn, "make it brief."

"It's not just troops," replied the man through clenched teeth. "They're marching through the city with standards unfurled." Summoning courage, he raised his head and glared at Nathaniel. "As we speak, their medallions of Tiberias parade past the Temple."

Nathaniel's cane started tapping a slow, methodical beat on the floor. The shoulders of Caiaphas slumped, fingers rubbing the bridge of his nose. Even the guards relaxed their grip.

"You're sure of this?" asked Caiaphas.

"I've seen with my own eyes, as have hundreds of others who rushed into the streets. I felt you should be told, so I came here directly."

"You've done right in bringing me this news. Excuse the guards for their handling of you, but there are those among us who disrespect the High Priesthood."

"I understand, my Lord. That wasn't my intent."

"Guards, escort our guest out. Leave the Sopher and I in privacy."

The guards lifted the man from his knees and cut the cord binding his wrists. Reaching inside his robe, Nathaniel drew out a purse and placed a few coins in the merchant's hands before he was escorted out by the guards.

"This does not bode well, Nathaniel. The Zealots will seize on this to inflame the crowds. And if we don't protest, we'll be judged conspirators with Rome."

"But if we act too rashly," countered Nathaniel, "we

earn the new procurator's wrath. And it's him, not the Zealots, who can appoint another High Priest."

Caiaphas clasped his hands atop his head. "Tell me something I don't already know." Nearly a minute of silence passed before Caiaphas spoke again. "We must do something."

The tip of Nathaniel's cane scraped against the floor, back and forth, then in loops and curved lines, as if writing on the stone. "Summon the Sanhedrin for a meeting. Tonight. Let it be known you feel the Romans have gone too far. In the meantime, I'll go to Tribune Glaucus. He can tell us whether the procurator has come with these troops, or if he's still in Caesarea."

Leaning forward in his chair, Caiaphas' fingers ran through his beard. "And then what?"

Nathaniel continued. "At the Sanhedrin, press for a meeting with the procurator. A delegation from the Sanhedrin, maybe a few of the city's other leaders. Let me serve as your emissary. We'll let the delegates vent the anger in public, while in private audience I'll assure the procurator that the High Priest seeks a beneficial relationship with the new representative of Tiberias. That way, any Roman repercussions to the protest won't fall on you. And the Sanhedrin and, shall we say, your zealous detractors will see you involved in organizing the opposition."

"I've always admired your ability to think in a crisis, Nathaniel." Caiaphas began writing on a sheet of parchment. "Have messengers assemble in the Chamber of Hewn Stone. I'll read them this summons for the Sanhedrin's convening in four hours, then send them to announce it."

"And I'll be on my way to Glaucus," asserted Nathaniel, rising to his feet. "Once I learn the procurator's whereabouts, I'll return to you before the Sanhedrin gathers."

The two men shook hands, then Nathaniel left the chamber. He crossed the Court of Israel to the small guarded tower at the northeast. As he had done so many times over the past thirty years, Nathaniel coursed the tunnel leading to the Antonia.

* * *

"Rabbi, a word with you!"

The disciples of Yeshua encircled their teacher as he left Arbela's synagogue. The afternoon's teaching had ended a week's stay in this village for the rabbi. From here, they would travel to Magdala. A crowd of well-wishers followed to where the road began its descent through the Valley of the Doves. But while most all who were not his disciples turned back, one did not.

"Yeshua of Nazareth, may I speak with you."

Yeshua stopped to see whose voice cried out with such insistence. A man clad in the white garments of an Essene waved to the rabbi

"What is it you want of me?"

"The chance to speak with you, rabbi."

Yeshua studied his face. "You already heard me in the synagogue, if I'm right."

"You are, rabbi. I've attended your teachings for several days now."

"Then you must be a man of great patience." Yeshua smiled, patting the stranger's shoulder. "But my disciples and I go to Magdala."

"Perhaps I could travel with you, and we could talk on the way?"

"Let's be off," Yeshua replied, resuming his way down the road with the stranger at his side. "By what name are you called?"

"Abraham. I come from a village near the Salt Sea."

"The Salt Sea. I've only been there once," Yeshua laughed. "Like most who are used to Galilee's Sea, I had to see for myself whether the rumors of floating without effort were true."

"Nearly everyone does that, rabbi."

"And do they all itch for hours afterward?"

Abraham smiled at the thought of Galilee's renowned rabbi bobbing in the lake, feet and arms out of water, then scratching the rest of the day because no one told him to scrub off the minerals. "That's one reason we've so many *mikvehs* in our villages, to bathe away the salts."

The two men continued to walk side by side. The other followers of the rabbi spread themselves two or three abreast ahead and behind as the road narrowed in a deepening canyon. Although daylight remained in the sky, the steep cliffs cast shadows on the way ahead.

"What would you speak to me about, Abraham?"

"These past days, rabbi, you've made Torah live as no other teacher I've heard."

"Torah's life comes from God. A teacher merely harvests the crop already there."

"But are you only a teacher?" Abraham became somber in face and voice. "I followed the Baptizer until his death. He spoke of One who was to come. One who was God's Messiah."

"I see. Tell me, what do you suppose this Messiah would do if he were to come?"

"The Zealots say he'd rid the land of Roman soldiers, and reign as Zion's king."

Yeshua nodded. "I know what the Zealots say. Several of my followers share their hopes. But what do you say, Abraham, about Messiah?"

"I've seen violence firsthand, Rabbi. I don't believe the Chosen of God will brandish a sword, relishing the blood of enemies. I've wondered whether Messiah will resemble more the servant of whom Isaiah speaks, one whose sufferings bring deliverance for Israel. But I don't know. That's why I came to hear to you."

"And after listening, what have you decided?"

"That you make Torah live. That you give people truth and hope." Abraham paused, took a deep breath, and said, "That I would be honored if you'd allow me to tarry awhile among those who follow you."

Yeshua looked around at the others. Nearly thirty people now, the number varied from town to town and season to season. "You'll be with those who once cast nets or collected taxes, Abraham. There are women among us, unlike the schools of other rabbis and your Essene communities. We have to watch out as closely for the spies of Herod Antipas as we do for the thieves in these hills. Is that the sort of life you want for yourself?"

"I seek a life blessed by God, Rabbi. And I believe you can help me in my search."

"So be it," pronounced Yeshua. "Journey with us as a friend."

A handshake sealed the agreement. Abraham followed Yeshua.

* * *

Murmurings filled the Chamber of Hewn Stone. Men stood in small clusters, arms and hands gesturing excitedly in conversation. The members of the Sanhedrin awaited the arrival of Caiaphas with vigorous debates over what course should be taken.

Starting with those closest to the door, a wave of silence rippled through the room as the entourage of the High Priest strode into view. Two temple guards led the way, followed by a young scribe ringing the *magrefa*. Then came Caiaphas, palms raised in blessing. Three paces behind Caiaphas, Nathaniel shuffled in, carrying several scrolls. Two more guards followed. The Sanhedrin remained standing until Caiaphas reached his chair and sat. The High Priest studied the faces of those seated in the room. After some moments of silence, Caiaphas removed his blue headdress that ordinarily would be worn throughout any such gathering and set it on the floor at his feet. Murmurs swept through the hall in response to this unexpected act.

"Today," Caiaphas began, "Rome has bared all our heads in shame. Idols have been marched through the holy city. Shields used in Rome's pagan worship hang from the walls of the Antonia in clear view of all. And they have done this, when the light of day reveals the shame of Gentile blasphemies for all to see and grieve."

"We share your indignation, lord Caiaphas." Rising to speak was the Pharisee Lot, Nathaniel's nemesis going back to the days of Joazar. "All Jerusalem mourns this abomination. But what would you have us do?" In those previous times, Lot would have favored a response like that of the martyred Judas, willing to take up the sword. Judas' fate and an accumulation of years made Lot more cautious. He respected the Zealots, but felt their cause naive. Lot no longer sought revolution, but renewal from a strict keeping of Torah.

"My brother Lot would agree that we cannot expel the Romans by force." Caiaphas leaned over, picking up the head-dress and placing it back on his head. "But what if we raised our own cohort, a host of righteous men armed with the Almighty's decrees? What if we sent such a legion to this new procurator, Pilate, to boldly protest this desecration?"

Many in the Chamber nodded their heads in agreement. A few Zealot sympathizers whispered to one another. Their spokesman, Lamech, stood. "Would you have us believe Rome will be moved by words? The new procurator, we have all heard, comes appointed by Sejanus: a man who hates our people and persecutes our synagogue in Rome. Do we really think a man like that, or his newly appointed lackey to be procurator, will heed our words?"

"Not our words, Lamech," interjected Nathaniel, "but God's words. Did Isaiah not write that God's word *shall not return to me empty, but it shall accomplish its purpose, and succeed in the thing for which I sent it*"?

"And I suppose you, Nathaniel, shall be the one to carry these words to the procurator, accustomed as you are to speaking with Romans."

Lamech's words stung Nathaniel. But the rebuke gave

Nathaniel opportunity to spring his and Caiaphas' plan into effect.

"Lamech, I do not presume to seize such an honor. Caiaphas and I believe a large delegation representing Jerusalem and all of Judea should be sent to the procurator. And the head of that delegation must be a man trusted by everyone in this assembly for integrity to the Torah. That way, there'll be no cause for questions or recriminations."

Nathaniel paused, allowing Caiaphas to make the pronouncement. "The duties of the high priesthood bind me to Jerusalem. So I ask the Sanhedrin to empower Lot as our spokesman."

Words of assent rose from the assembly, even as Lot's jaw dropped open. Nothing had been said to him beforehand. But now, it was too late to raise objections. To refuse the offer could be yaken as an insult to the office of the high priest or an act of cowardice.

Lamech weighed the proposed scenario. Such a delegation could raise hopes among the people. And if Rome turned a deaf ear to the pleas, which he judged inevitable, more radical responses would be demanded. "My lord High Priest," Lamech called out. The assembly quieted. "Some of us believe even stronger measures are in order. But we will not stand in the way of the action you propose. If a delegation led by Lot is your response to this Roman sacrilege, so be it."

As Lamech sat, first one, then several Sanhedrin members began to clop their sandals upon the stone floor as a sign of approval. Others joined in until the chamber echoed with the sound. Nathaniel leaned over to Caiaphas, offering congratulations. No one noticed the only feet remaining still belonged to Lot.

* * *

Different sounds echoed off the walls of a room in Jericho. Water splashing, a woman's laughter, a chalice being knocked onto the floor. The woman, a Nabatean slave assigned to the Roman outpost in Jericho, slipped out of the water to dry herself. Lucius stayed in the pool formed by hot springs, leering at the curves of her smooth damp skin he had so enjoyed in the waters. The girl pulled on a robe as he reeled under the intoxication of desire and wine.

"Come back here," he slurred, "we've not finished."

The young woman, Aricea, knelt by the edge of the pool, massaging his shoulders. "You're such a wicked man, Lucius. I suppose you'd kill me if I refused."

The effects of the wine let down his guard. "I've killed younger than you."

Aricea kneaded her fingers into his neck. "But I'm not even seventeen. When has the legion ever warred against children?"

"Too many years ago for you to remember," Lucius blurted out.

"Remember what?" she whispered in his ear with a kiss.

He'd never spoken to anyone of Bethlehem, but the wine and heat and Aricea's touch clouded Lucius' judgment. "Herod," he grumbled. "Killed his own sons, then had us kill others."

Aricea's hands stroked down his back and across to his chest. "What others?"

"Bethlehem. Something about a king, a Jew boy. Told us to kill them all."

"All of who?"

"The boys. Under two. Or three? Who knows, who cares."

"You killed children yourself?"

"Easy enough work." Lucius stood and attempted to feign a sword thrust, but managed only to lose his balance. His grasp at the side of the pool missed, and he fell underwater before bobbing up and sputtering, "Help me out of here!"

"Lucius, don't scold at me." Taking his wrist, Aricea

steadied his balance, then helped him out of the pool and onto a table. She wrapped him in a towel and threw his robe over his chest. "Wait for me," she said, kissing him on the forehead. "I'll be back." Stopping at the door, she saw Lucius already dozed.

Once out of the room, she hurried down a hallway past several unoccupied baths. A large door opened to a kitchen where a turbaned man sorted through figs. "What is it?" he asked.

"You told me to keep my ears open to the Romans when you bought me."

"I did," replied the steward called Isaac. "Have you heard anything?"

"The one you said was a centurion, Lucius? He got himself good and drunk, and just now he just spoke of murdering children. Said it happened years ago. On orders from Herod."

Isaac's face, flecked by a silver beard, grew ashen. "Bethlehem?"

"Well, yes," Aricea's voice quaked, "how did you know?"

"Never mind. You've done well, Aricea. Tell no one."

"Yes, lord. But what of Lucius? He sleeps unattended."

"Leave him alone for now," he muttered. "I'll see he's paid a proper visit in time."

CHAPTER XXXV

Antony's century had arrived in Caesarea and rejoined the cohort stationed there only two days before the Jews from Judea and Galilee converged on the city. Those protesting the standards brought into Jerusalem numbered over five hundred. Each morning, they gathered outside the palace where the new procurator stayed. No one entering or leaving could avoid their shouted prayers and endless Torah recitations. The Sanhedrin delegation led the public protests, their request for a private audience with Pilate denied. Only Nathaniel abstained from the demonstrations, maintaining his legs couldn't handle the stress of standing outside for hours.

"What is wrong with these Jews!" Pilate paced the floor. "You're supposed to be the expert in their ways. Don't they understand what they risk by defying me?"

Julius stood rigid. When news of such a delegation being gathered had reached Pilate, he reversed his decision to see no more of Julius and summoned him to the palace. Now that he stood before the procurator, Julius' first instinct leaned toward having warned this would happen, but tactfulness prevailed. "These people have a fanatical devotion to their law. Obedience to it is akin to the legion's oath. Many would die before dishonoring their Torah."

"Damn it, Julius! You talk as if these Jews are our equals."

"In truth, I only say they are different in what they stake their lives upon."

"I suppose your counsel would accede to their demands."

"Giving in would be seen as weakness. But not negotiation. In return for removing the standards from Jerusalem, you could exact some price from them."

"Rome doesn't bargain with her subjects! They've nothing of value that we can't take for ourselves anytime we choose."

"True," countered Julius, "but the question comes in the cost paid for the taking. The Zealots long to set the price in Roman blood."

Pilate's eyes widened and he shot back: "It seems the years here have made you soft, Julius. We can't be afraid to confront our enemies – which is what I've already ordered."

Julius' heart pounded as his fingers squeezed into a fist. Another pompous civilian risking the lives of soldiers for no good reason! And now, for the procurator to accuse him – "Let me tell you about those enemies, Procurator. Your choice to aggravate the Jews has filled Caesarea's streets with men who'd otherwise prefer going about their work and prayers, leaving the likes of you and me alone! But you paraded the standards – and now, scribes talk like men of arms. Every day you let pass without resolving this only sparks the tinder that the Zealots hope to ignite." Pilate's face flushed, but Julius was not done yet. "These people and their cause will not go away, Procurator, just because you choose to play the strong man!"

Pilate sneered. "And you, Julius, play the fool. An old and tired fool. These are new days for Rome's provinces. An example must be set! Report to the amphitheater tomorrow for one final duty. Then you'll see how these Jews cower when Rome speaks with authority. Guards!" Two legionnaires opened the door. "Escort the advisor home. See that he and his consort are at the amphitheater tomorrow by 3 o'clock."

Julius saluted and turned to leave.

"And Julius," Pilate called out, "give my warmest regards to your Jewish whore."

Knowing the guards would prevent any reprisal for this parting insult, Julius walked out in silence, disgusted that Rome had come to be represented by the likes of Pilate. Exiting the palace, Julius was surprised to see the protestors gone. "Guard, what happened to the Jews?"

"Pilate's to meet with them tomorrow at the amphitheater. But he demanded these demonstrations cease as condition."

The other guard, who had once served under Julius, added: "I'd say tomorrow's meeting will not be a pleasant one. At least, that was the general tone of things from the briefing we got from our new centurion. Maybe your paths crossed at some point. His name is Antony."

* * *

In Bethlehem, a chilling rain fell on the roof of Rebekah's home. A small cookfire simmered a kettle of lentil pottage and offered a measure of warmth to the room. But it also sent up wisps of smoke, collecting in a thin haze along the ceiling. Rebekah took one of the ladles carved by her husband and stirred the pottage. Barabbas sat cross-legged by her side. Behind a drawn curtain, Naomi spun flax into yarn.

"I've been here three days," Barabbas whispered, "and Naomi's hardly said a word."

"I told you." Rebekah sipped from the ladle, then crumbled a bit of coriander into the pot. "It's been like this ever since she arrived from Nathaniel's."

Barabbas picked at his fingernails. "You'd think after everything else she suffered, Naomi could've handled Deborah's death."

"She let the other things wear her down. I warned her, but she wouldn't listen. Then Deborah dies, and Naomi had no strength left. Only the blame she carries against herself."

"Blame for what? She did nothing."

Rebekah took a threaded needle from a basket woven of reeds, and resumed her mending of a tear in Barabbas' cloak. "Blame for marrying a coward like Joshua. Blame for letting David be taken from her arms that day and murdered. Blame for how Simeon and Hannah turned out."

"That's taking a lot on her shoulders that belongs on others."

"That may be," Rebekah replied, without lifting her eyes from the sewing. "But Naomi chose to squander her life in regret and guilt."

Barabbas' head cocked to the side. "Harsh words for a friend to say."

Her fingers paused in mid-course, a stitch's loop half-pulled. "Friend or not, they're the truth. Naomi let herself grow weak, and that weakness sapped her life."

"So why keep her under your roof?"

"Because she is my friend. Nathaniel gave up on her once Deborah died. And what with a traitor for a son and a whore for a daughter, she'd no one left." Rebekah drew the stitch too tight, breaking the thread.

As she reached into the basket for a new line of thread, someone pounded on the door. "Is this the house of Rebekah? I bring a message for Barabbas!"

Barabbas whirled into a crouch, creeping low until he knelt alongside the door's hinged side. Only then did he wave Rebekah toward the door.

"Yes, yes, I'm coming. Who is it?"

"Caleb. I've been sent by Isaac of Jericho."

Barabbas rose to his feet and opened the door. "Get in – and no more shouts!"

The stranger hurried in from the rain.

"Here, sit by the fire," directed Rebekah, "I'll hang your mantle to dry."

Barabbas eyed the young man. "What proof do you have that Isaac sent you?"

"Am I speaking to Barabbas?"

Barabbas seized Caleb's robe. "Give me proof of your sender, or you'll regret ever coming here!"

The young man showed no fear in his eyes. "Isaac said the man I seek wears the carving of a wolf, stained by his father's blood."

Barabbas released his grip. "Go on."

"I believe it best we speak alone."

"My mother, Caleb, is the widow of the martyr Elias. She stays."

"Very well. I'd been dispatched to Jericho by our Zealot brothers in Bethsaida on a mission. Isaac told me to contact you on my return."

"And why is that?"

"Isaac said he's found a Roman who took part in a massacre here years ago."

The chest of Barabbas tightened, while the sewing basket tumbled off Rebekah's lap as she abruptly stood, spilling needles and threads. "What else did this Isaac say?" she asked.

"The Roman came to Jericho recently, retired from the legion. He drank too much one night, and blurted out his story to a whore, who passed it on to Isaac. His name was Lucius."

Barabbas stared vacantly at the cookfire, hands now fumbling with the carving around his neck. "Lucius," he mumbled.

Rebekah started to reach a hand to her son, then drew back. "You remember, too." Her voice grew raspy. "The guard who killed your father and kicked you away, that was what he called himself. Lucius. After all these years, he lives."

Barabbas began rocking back and forth. Drawing out a knife from inside his robe, he quietly uttered, "I will kill you, Lucius. The son of Elias will watch you die!"

Rebekah leaned across, took the knife from her son's hand, and spat on the blade. Before she could return it, another hand reached from behind her to take hold of the *sicar*. Using the knife's tip, Naomi pricked her finger, then let the blood drip on its edge. Handing it back to Barabbas, she spoke only three words: "For my David."

* * *

Lot raised his hands to quiet the crowd. "Hear, O Israel, the Lord our God is One."

"BLESSED BE THE NAME OF THE LORD GOD OF ISRAEL!" shouted the crowd of Jews who gathered on the grounds inside Caesarea's amphitheater.

When Lot received news late yesterday that Pilate agreed to see them, hope swept through the pilgrims: the protests had their desired effect, their case could be stated. Some in the Sanhedrin delegation expressed uneasiness over Pilate's summons. What if he meant to arrest them? With everyone in one place, they'd only be doing the procurator a favor. Lot disagreed, arguing a public site was far safer. Plus, having hundreds of supporters together guaranteed no divide and conquer tactics would succeed. The Sanhedrin delegation stood at the crowd's front, directly below the procurator's box. Only three guards stood at the wall's base, a token show of the legion's presence. As three o'clock neared, the amphitheater's benches began to fill with local officials and ambassadors to Pilate's court, along with curious onlookers. The Jews continued to offer prayers and recite Torah. As for Nathaniel, fear dominated. Pilate had refused a private audience with him, so his message from Caiaphas had gone unheard. Nathaniel could rely on no protection from his rank as Sopher should Pilate decide on a more aggressive display of power.

A trumpet fanfare drew the spectators filling the stadium's seats to their feet. After a dozen legionnaires entered the procurator's box and took position along its edges, Pilate descended the steps as the crowd cheered. On a signal from Lot, the Jews bowed. Among other officials seated behind Pilate were Julius and Hannah. Pilate, now standing in front of his chair, lifted his palms in the air. The fanfare ceased as did the shouts of acclamation. Walking to an elaborately carved podium set by the wall, he addressed the protestors below. "I am Pilate, procurator of Judea, legate of Tiberias to the Jews. Who is your spokesman?"

"Lot, a Pharisee of Jerusalem," Lot declared in return, stepping forward from the others. "I bring you greetings from the Sanhedrin and our High Priest, Caiaphas."

"You bring me more than greetings, Lot of Jerusalem." Pilate leaned forward, resting his arms on the top of the podium. "You bring strife and discord to the capital of this province. What have you to say for yourself and this rabble?!"

Pilate's vehemence surprised Lot. He expected an audience, not an accusation. "We found no other way, Procurator, to express our concern over the standards brought into Jerusalem."

"Rome's standards go with Rome's legions. They are our concern, not yours."

"Since the days of Coponius, Rome's procurators have respected our God's injunction against images."

"I've been informed of those traditions," answered Pilate, glancing back at Julius, "but Rome has new ways. The provinces must obey them. Your master, Tiberias Caesar, has authorized me to carry out his will in his stead. Disobey me, and you disobey Caesar."

"We do not seek to disobey Caesar. Only to obey our God." Lot's jaws clenched. "The Almighty, blessed be His name, commanded us against the use of images."

"Well, then, obey your law and don't use images. But don't presume to command Rome on what her legions may or may not do."

Lot turned to look at the crowd gathered behind him, then fixed his gaze back on Pilate. "The images of Tiberias paraded through Jerusalem and hung on the Antonia's walls represent an abomination to our God. We come, asking they be removed."

"Then go home without receiving what you ask! And

tell your kin in Jerusalem to get accustomed to the standards in full view. Tiberias rules Jerusalem as well as Rome. His image is worthy of display wherever he reigns as emperor."

Angry murmurs swept through the protestors. Lot raised his arms. "Procurator! We will not leave here until this matter is settled."

Pilate lifted his right arm high and clenched his fist above his head. At this signal, legionnaires poured from every gated opening into the amphitheater's grounds. A stunned Julius watched as another two dozen soldiers ran down the aisle of the imperial box and swung over the wall's side to the ground. Julius caught sight of the face of one of those men: Antony!

Julius rose to his feet and watched as Antony took his place directly before Lot. Another figure who'd been at the crowd's front attempted to squirmed his way deeper inside the ranks of the Jews. An old man, he used a cane in an attempt to wedge his way through. But the troops had crowded the people too close together for Nathaniel to make any headway. Julius estimated the entire cohort, nearly five hundred legionnaires in all, had encircled the Jews, weapons drawn.

Pilate glared at Lot. "You have your choice, Pharisee. Abide by Tiberias' images on the Jerusalem standards and forego this protest, or lose your lives here and now!"

Even among the onlookers in the seats, gasps and muffled cries arose. Julius slipped next to Pilate. "Think what you will of me, Pilate, but this is madness! Most of these people form a bulwark against the Zealots. Eliminate them, and you give a free hand to the rebels."

"Step back before I have you arrested!" Pilate muttered.

Julius returned to Hannah's side and whispered, "The bloody damned fool!"

"Does he really mean to kill them?" Hannah folded her

hands across the bridge of her nose, ready to cover her eyes if need be.

Julius thought to answer, but noticed a stirring in the crowd. Lot and several others from the Sanhedrin huddled together. At the end of their talk, all nodded their heads. Save one. Nathaniel, a wild look on his face, appeared to implore Lot and the Zealot called Lamech. Heads shook back and forth. Soon, whispers threaded back through the crowd. It was easy to trace the progress of whatever message was being relayed. As soon as one finished speaking to another, he faced Pilate's direction and knelt. Eventually, the entire crowd was on its knees. Only Lot and Lamech remained standing.

"You see!" Pilate turned, taunting Julius. "Their will's been broken. They yield!"

"Pilate," shouted Lot. "We have our answer."

The procurator, almost gleeful, faced his humbled subjects. "You accept the standards with your emperor's image in Jerusalem?"

"Not at all, Roman. We will die first!" Having spoken, Lot dropped to his knees before Antony, as did Lamech. "The blood be on your head!"

Pilate's eyes widened at the defiance. He felt his legs grow unsteady, his stomach queasy. "Raise your swords!"

Antony lifted his gladius and poised to strike, revulsed at what was about to happen. Pilate watched for a sign of weakness among the crowd, some individual or group who would break off and cry for mercy. None stirred. The only response belonged to Lot. Glancing at Lamech, then up to Pilate, Lot pulled away his mantle and robe from his shoulder, baring his neck. Lamech followed him. Soon, every Jew kneeling on the ground did the same.

"You will die – all of you!" Pilate's shout echoed throughout the circular stadium. By now, no other sound could be heard. Most of the spectators had covered their faces or turned away, unwilling or ashamed to watch. More than a few legionnaires silently cursed the procurator. Antony looked back toward Pilate, awaiting the final signal. Only then did he see Julius. He noticed a woman next to him, though her hands covered her face.

Julius held Hannah in his arms, as memories of another slaughter came to mind.

And then – Pilate slumped back into his chair, motioning toward one of his personal guards. Pilate spoke something in the man's ear, then stood. Scowling at Julius, he departed from the box, flanked by several guards. When they'd left sight, the soldier to whom Pilate spoke stepped to the wall and announced: "On order of the Procurator, the Jews will leave the stadium at once. His Excellency declares that, to protect the images of Tiberias from the thieves who terrorize Jerusalem's streets, they shall be returned to Caesarea for safekeeping."

A shout rang out from the Jews, who jumped to their feet and hugged one another. Even Lot and Lamech, bitter opponents for years, embraced. Antony and the other centurions signaled their troops to lower their swords and exit the stadium. For his part, Antony was relieved he'd not been forced to execute old men – and sickened that he and his century lost face.

Julius shook his head in amazement and disgust. Pilate proved himself a swaggerer who backed down once his bluff was called. Such a man signaled danger: not only for Jews, but for those charged to carry out his orders. "Time to leave, Hannah. Nothing keeps us here anymore."

Meanwhile, Antony had heard of Julius' retirement and wanted to wish him well. But by the time he reached the imperial box, Julius was nowhere to be seen.

"Probably on his way to Tiberias already," said one of the guards when Antony asked of Julius' whereabouts. "He and his mistress. Do you want me to try and find them?"

"No. I'll find a way to meet up with him later. Carry on."

* * *

A weary Lucius stretched on his stomach across the dressing table. The news of the legion's humiliation in Caesarea several days before had been washed away in too much wine, too much time in the hot springs – and too much of an old man's energy spent between this young woman's obliging thighs. He mumbled something to his mistress about sleep.

Aricea finished rubbing his back. "Let me get a warm towel for you."

Lucius didn't bother lifting his head. He'd known other campwomen before, but none like her. So skilled, so young. He dozed with the thoughts of her caresses...

"Cccchhhh – " Lucius awoke to the sound of his own throat's gurgling, his head snapped back by a cord drawn tight around his neck. He attempted to grab it, only to find his arms held fast to his side as other hands gripped his ankles. Eyes wide open in panic, he struggled to focus on the figure standing before him. Another stuffed a cloth in his mouth to muffle further sounds.

"How does it feel to know you're about to die, Lucius?"

Lucius didn't recognize the man whose face was now only inches from his. He began to feel faint for lack of air.

"Remember Bethlehem, Lucius? Remember a father murdered, a boy not important enough to kill?"

Lucius' head spun. A memory flashed. Two families, a child.

"Meet that boy, you bastard!"

The Roman saw a dagger go past his eyes, then felt an ice-hot sensation along his throat.

"Blood for blood, Lucius," Barabbas said, wiping his blade on Lucius' eyebrows.

For Lucius, the room dissolved from a blood-red haze into sheer darkness.

Barabbas ordered his men to dump the body in the pool. Only then did Isaac bring Aricea back into the room.

"You've done well," Barabbas began. "You remember the plan?"

Shaken at the sight of blood pooled by the table and Lucius' lifeless body floating, the girl stammered her reply. "I'm to wait ten minutes, then, then, I'm to start screaming. When others come, I tell them a Zealot named, uh, Barabbas, Yeshua Barabbas, burst in with his men, swearing vengeance on Lucius."

"Stick to the story, and you'll be fine," added Isaac.

Barabbas stepped next to the girl. "Forgive us, but to be believed, you'll have to look the part." The girl cringed as Barabbas swung the back of his hand across her face, splitting her lip. Another man punched her face several times more, so her cheeks and eyes swelled from the beating. "We don't want to risk the Romans thinking you had anything to do with this." Barabbas pressed one cheek to hers, then the other. "We've left your payment with Isaac."

"You should be off before someone stumbles in here, Barabbas."

The son of Elias clasped Isaac's hand. "Until God joins our ways again!"

Barabbas and his men crept out a window into the courtyard, then over a low wall to an alley. Isaac returned to his room, counting the time before the girl screamed for help. Aricea slid down to the floor, leaning against the marble dressing table for support.

And Lucius: Lucius sank in the water of Jericho's springs, his eyes frozen open – as if still fixed on a young boy's eyes peering through an executioner's glare.

CHAPTER XXXVI

A frigid wind knifed down the slopes of Mount Hermon, slicing into the basin enclosing Galilee's Sea. Though clouds barred any view of the snow-topped peak, lakeside travelers could feel its icy heights in the squall's biting gusts. Those who earned their livelihood harvesting the lake's fish would not venture onto the water today.

For Joshua, however, the storm brought a boon in business. Though there was still light left in the sky, all of the inn's beds were let. Many of the guests sat down to an early supper, eager to fill hungry bellies before returning to their rooms. There, they would wrap themselves in fleece blankets and hope that dreams might carry them to warmer environs.

Joshua rushed from kitchen to dining hall, taking orders and carrying platters. His young Gadarene assistant, Demas, tended the cookfire and washed dishes when he wasn't setting out the customers' food. While others in Tiberias shivered at the unseasonable temperature, sweat dripped from the brow and armpits of the Gadarene.

The door to the inn swung open, a blast of cold air accompanying the entrance of two men. Once inside, they loosened tightly wrapped mantles and drew aside the bands of cloth that protected their faces from the wind. Joshua wiped his hands on his apron. He recognized the taller of the two as Jacob, but had not seen the other man.

"There's a place in the corner. You'll find the fire's heat collects there."

"Thanks, innkeep." Jacob looked around. Several legionnaires sat at one table.

"I'll bring bread and wine in a moment," Joshua said, excusing himself. A quickened pace brought him into the kitchen and to the side of his helper. "Demas! Put on a fresh apron. I need you to serve tables for a time."

The Gadarene pulled his hands from the washing pot, drying them on a cloth. "Not all the dishes are done. And the stew, it needs – "

"Just do as I say! You can stir when you come back to fill orders. I won't be long." Joshua rushed out with a platter bearing bread, a pitcher of wine, and two goblets.

Demas shook his head as he donned the apron. "Dishes, fire – now the tables, too! This should be the inn of Demas, not Joshua, for all the work I do."

Upon reaching Jacob's table, Joshua set down the bread and wine and scooted a third chair over to sit beside the Zealot. Jacob tore off a chunk of bread, dipping it in the wine before stuffing it in his mouth. His companion did the same.

"It's been a hard day's journey, Joshua." The bread Jacob chewed muffled his words. He then drank long and deep from his goblet. "This is Judas the Iscariot, a friend of mine."

Joshua nodded his head, then spoke in a low tone so as not to be overheard. "There've been rumors of late among my Roman guests about a murder near Jericho."

Glancing at his companion, Jacob nodded. After another sop of bread, he spoke. "More than rumors." Jacob leaned over, keeping his own voice down in spite of his pleasure in the words to come. "A Judean zealot, Barabbas, executed a centurion in Jericho last week, right in the Roman's own bath. I hear they're still scrubbing blood off the tiles!"

"No wonder there's been such tension on their faces."

"As well there should be, what with Pilate playing the fool in Caesarea. It seems these Roman gods have clay feet after all."

Joshua glanced around again to make sure no one, especially the soldiers, paid attention to this table. "The only word I heard of it, besides yours, mentioned vengeance of some sort."

"Vengeance, indeed. It'll give the Romans pause, if they die for deeds thirty years past."

"Thirty years?"

Jacob decided there was no harm in letting Joshua know the truth, since the innkeeper had thus far served him well. "The assassination goes back to Herod's time. This centurion had been part of the massacre at Bethlehem, one of those who slaughtered the children..."

Jacob went on to tell of Lucius' execution, but Joshua heard little after Bethlehem and children. One detail in Jacob's narrative, the knife used on the centurion, brought back Joshua's remembrance of a knife held in his hand. A knife handed over, a knife ripping into his son...

". . . Barabbas sent a message to every Roman in this land who spills our people's blood. No matter how long it takes, life for life will be the toll exacted." Jacob paused, noting Joshua grew ashen and sweaty. "Something wrong, innkeep?"

A long-forgotten panic seized Joshua as he fought to hold back the memories. "Your remark about Bethlehem. I had friends there."

"I thought you came from Emmaus?"

"I did. It's just that the slaughter affected everyone in Judea."

"Yes, I can imagine." Jacob sensed more to Joshua's reaction, but couldn't be sure. Anyway, other business remained. "I need you to listen for any word of Roman reprisal."

"Won't they focus their efforts on this Barabbas?"

"Barabbas has escaped them before. If he continues to elude their traps, the Romans might counter in some other way." Jacob finished his wine, then turned to a commotion at a nearby table. "Maybe you'd best return to your duties here. Your helper appears a bit harried."

Joshua looked to see Demas fumbling over the details of the dinner charge to a table of aggravated Syrian traders. The innkeep stood and bowed. "Good evening to you."

Jacob tossed several coins on the table and walked with Judas to the door. As Jacob reached for the handle, the door opened from the outside. The Zealots waited as a man and woman entered. He appeared to be a Roman of some years, though still strong in features; she, a Jewess considerably younger. The sight of such a pairing caused Jacob to grimace, though this was not the place or time to cause trouble. Joshua saw the couple, and made his way to them.

"I've no rooms left, though I can give you a meal."

"That's all we seek."

Joshua walked them to the same table where he'd sat with Jacob. When he pulled a chair back for the woman to sit, she pushed back the hood of her cloak from her hair. Something of its texture and color reminded him of a woman from so many years past it seemed like another life. The thought quickly departed when one of the legionnaires called out: not for him, as Joshua initially supposed, but for the Roman.

"By the gods! Is that you, Julius?"

* * *

The two guards in the tiny room grew still. Beneath the trapdoor, down the passageway leading to the Temple, came a distant rhythmic clicking sound. Its beat slowly grew louder, until the tapping ascended the stairs below the entrance.

"The old Jew again," muttered one of the guards.

His partner slid the bolt from the trapdoor. Normally, procedures called for identification of anyone using the passage before unbarring the way, but the sound of the cane had become a familiar sign. The guard swung the door open.

"Good day, Sopher!"

Nathaniel had his cane raised, prepared to rap on the portal. "You should be more careful, unlocking before you see who's there."

"Nathaniel," said the first guard, as he offered a hand to the elderly Jew, "the cane proclaims your arrival as sure as any herald."

"Remember that when some Zealot comes tapping a stick to fool you."

The second guard laughed as he knocked on the hallway door, signaling the guards outside to unbar and open it. "And if he knows to tap each step of the stairs twice as you always do, he may actually catch a glimpse of this room before we cut him down."

"That kind of cockiness probably rewarded your Lucius with a slit throat!" Nathaniel didn't like to be ridiculed, and his reply had the desired effect of silencing impudent tongues. The Sopher shuffled his way down the hall to the chamber of Pilate.

The procurator had arrived in Jerusalem only yesterday, intent on taking personal charge of the investigation into Lucius' murder. After the debacle at the amphitheater, Pilate knew he must reassert his authority in Judea. Nathaniel understood that too, even as he viewed Pilate's dilemma, and invitation to meet, as an opportunity to ingratiate himself to the new procurator.

"The Sopher of the High Priest, Nathaniel!" Pilate looked up from the table where he worked. Beside the legionnaire stood an old man, leaning on a gnarled wooden cane. The sight confounded Pilate: this was the mediator between the Temple and Rome?

"Guard, help him into the chair."

Nathaniel strained to hide his offense at the procurator's patronizing welcome. But as he thought on it, Pilate's attitude might prove helpful. An old man posed no threat to such a one.

Once the guard seated him and left, Nathaniel spoke. "I bring you greetings from our High Priest, Caiaphas. And my own gratitude, for allowing me this time to meet with you."

"Valerius left word of your importance to his administration."

Nathaniel lowered his head. "I was pleased to serve the former procurator, as I am to serve you now. Not all in Jerusalem are rabble-rousers, like the demonstrators in Caesarea."

Pilate cleared his throat, not welcoming a reminder of the amphitheater. "Those people risked great harm. They were fortunate I saw fit to show mercy."

"Indeed they were." Nathaniel sat forward, resting his elbows on Pilate's table. "And I regret we weren't able to arrange a meeting while I was there. As I hoped to do then, I come here now on behalf of Caiaphas to strike a more harmonious relationship than Caesarea afforded."

"Go on," Pilate replied.

"We believe it's in our mutual interest for the affairs of Judea, and Jerusalem in particular, to flow calmly and peacefully. You, for the safety of your legion and the coffers of Rome; us, for stability in the ritual and leadership of the Temple."

Pilate studied Nathaniel. Perhaps the Sopher's frail appearance misled him. "And how would you propose these mutual interests could be advanced?"

"In Caesarea, you made a gesture of goodwill, sparing those who defied you. Today, I humbly want to repay your benevolence."

"By doing what?"

"By offering information that could lead you to the murderer of Lucius."

Pilate's briefings thus far informed him the search for this Barabbas would be difficult. The legion had known of him for some time, though all previous attempts to capture him had failed. The Salt Sea wilderness with its remote hideouts always managed to conceal him. But now, this aged Jew sat before him, offering the elusive prize. The procurator stood and walked beside the chair of Nathaniel. He took the cane from the old man's side, running his hands up and down the polished grain. "Why would one Jew betray another Jew to a Roman, Nathaniel?"

"The more time you spend here, Procurator, the more you'll see there are as many differences among Jews as among Romans. This Barabbas is a Zealot, a faction unhappy and impatient with those of us who manage the Temple. The Zealots pose as much a threat to Caiaphas as they do to you. Weaken them, and both our positions strengthen."

"Why didn't you offer up this Barabbas earlier?"

"The knowledge came from a conversation overheard, and brought to our attention, that disclosed Barabbas to be the killer of Lucius. Caiaphas and I felt it our duty to bring this information to you as soon as possible. For both of our sakes."

Pilate handed the cane back to Nathaniel and sat on the table's edge, arms folded. "Tell me, Nathaniel: if this information leads to his capture, what might you want in return?"

Bracing himself on the cane, Nathaniel got to his feet. "You made a gesture of goodwill in Caesarea. This I freely make in return on behalf of Caiaphas. We seek to work with you, Procurator. It's an arrangement Valerius profited from, and we hope it will do the same for you."

"Will your Temple police arrest the bandit?"

"No. The place where Barabbas can be caught is not Jerusalem. It will take time, but I can arrange the setting of a snare. Then, there'll be need of a dozen or so of your troops."

"I will see to it." Pilate stood and walked the Sopher to the door. "Let me know when your plan can be set. Once we hold Barabbas, you and I shall talk of Rome's gratitude."

After Nathaniel bowed and exited, Pilate returned to

the table. The old man had surprised him. Time would tell if the Jew was to be trusted, but Pilate felt the risk acceptable. The capture of Barabbas would go a long way toward erasing the indignity of Caesarea.

* * *

Their dinner finished, Julius filled the wine goblets one final time from the earthen jar. "A toast, legionnaire Diogenes" Julius offered, "to the only Greek who fights like a Roman!"

"But not legionnaire for long, centurion."

"Just Julius, please. If you've not heard, our illustrious new procurator chose to make me a man of leisure."

Diogenes heard the bitterness in Julius' words. "It's well the procurator doesn't visit Tiberias too soon. After news of the amphitheater reached us, there've been plenty of murmurings against him. It's bad enough we've got to watch our backs against the Zealots, without having a commander who has no grasp of consequences to his blunderings."

"You're close to your own discharge, Diogenes. You don't want to speak such thoughts where others might hear," Julius cautioned. "Take my word for it, I speak from experience."

The two men nodded. Over dinner, Julius had explained what Pilate did to him in Caesarea. In his words to Diogenes now, Julius spoke out of concern for one once under his command. Hannah observed the depressing turn the conversation took, and decided to change it.

"Tell me, Diogenes: what is there for Julius and me to do in this place, now that we're to take up residence here?"

Diogenes looked at Hannah sitting beside Julius, thinking it was about time the centurion afforded himself the luxury of a woman. And such a fine-featured one at that. "Well, unlike today, much of the year you can soak in the sun's heat. Cool off in the lake when you want. Better yet, hire a boat with sail to catch the winds."

"But what can be done during these winter winds?"

she replied.

"Two things. One is to visit the hot springs south of here, at Hammath. Some say they're the real reason Herod Antipas built Tiberias in this spot. So he could soak in the springs whenever he pleased."

"Like father, like son," muttered Julius.

Hannah gave a puzzled look at Julius. She'd not heard him speak much of Herod the Great, though from other comments she understood Julius had known him. Hannah considered asking what he meant. But then she realized Diogenes had mentioned two things to do – but described only one. "And what of the second thing?"

Diogenes drew his chair closer to the table, lowering his voice. "See the teacher of Nazareth, a rabbi called Yeshua."

Hannah and Julius looked at one another in surprise. A Roman advising a former centurion and his consort to see a rabbi? "Why on earth do you say that?" asked Julius.

"I remember your insights into the Jews, Julius. How you learned all you could of their ways. Let's just say, I've followed your lead in my career."

"And what does this have to do with going to a Nazarene rabbi?"

"He's an unusual man, Julius. I've gone in disguise to hear him several times."

Hannah's mouth opened at the admission. Not many of the legionnaires who'd hired her services seemed interested in spiritual quests. "What made you do that?"

"He's a teacher, unlike any I've ever known. Not even in Greece. And more than that."

Julius waited for him to go on. When he didn't, Julius prodded, "More than what?"

Diogenes rubbed his chin, looking at Julius and then Hannah before confessing, "Besides his teaching, I've seen him heal. Not like the charlatans in the bazaars, mind you. Leprosy, blindness. I've seen with my own eyes. I can't explain it. You have to see for yourself. He's often in Capernaum, or Magdala, if you're at all interested."

Julius slapped Diogenes on the shoulder. "You sound like one of his, oh, what do they call such people who cling to a rabbi, Hannah?"

"Disciples."

"That's it! From legionnaire to disciple," Julius laughed, "is that your plan?"

Diogenes laughed. Hannah noticed, though, that Diogenes' laughter didn't seem the sort that carried on a joke. It was the kind she remembered from clients when they wanted to shut the door on things too personal. Without understanding where the words came from, Hannah found herself saying, "Maybe we should see this rabbi, Julius."

* * *

Abraham huddled close to the remnants of the cookfire, stirring its embers now and then to loose what heat remained. All the others had found places to sleep in the home of Peter. But even though tomorrow would bring Abraham the first of a number of days' journey to New Damascus, he felt restless. With sleep evading him, he found himself trying to recall every detail of his time with rabbi Yeshua. Every parable, every sermon, every conversation they had: all weighed on Abraham's heart to remember, so he could tell those willing to listen in his community. As hard as he pressed himself to remember, though, fear overwhelmed Abraham: fear that he'd forget, that he'd not do justice to the words. Maybe he should stay longer. . .

"Only Adonai Elohim goes without slumber or sleep."

A startled Abraham turned to see Yeshua standing behind him. As he started to get up, the rabbi placed a hand on his shoulder. "Stay there. I'll join you by the fire."

"I hope I didn't wake you, rabbi."

Yeshua sat down and fixed his eyes on the glowing coals. "Not unless you've discovered how to waken others with your thoughts." The rabbi let some moments of silence pass before continuing. "And what thoughts trouble you enough to tend the fire so late?"

"My leaving tomorrow." Abraham took a small branch and rustled the coals until their soft orange light grew bright again. He laid the branch on top. "I don't know if I'll be able to put this all in the right words. So others will listen. And hear. Really hear."

"I see." Yeshua watched the branch smolder, its orange glow beginning to dim again. Leaning over, he blew gently on the embers. More smoke arose. He blew again, slightly harder, and the orange intensified. Pursing his lips, Yeshua blew harder still – and the branch erupted into flame. Both men's eyes winced at the burst of light in the dark room. "Now, you see."

Abraham's eyebrows raised. "Excuse me, rabbi?"

"This branch already possessed the ability to give heat and light, even before it lay on the coals. Once on the embers, it needed only wind to stir the flame within."

"I'm still not understanding you."

The eyes of Yeshua penetrated Abraham's. "The word of Adonai, once in a person's heart, needs only the breath of Spirit to kindle its flame. The words will come to you, Abraham, because they are already there. You needn't worry. God's breath will kindle."

The words struck home to Abraham. Yeshua had that gift when speaking to others. Abraham observed it many times. "I will miss your wisdom, rabbi. Perhaps on your next visit to Jerusalem, you can come to New Damascus. Or, if you'd rather be closer to the city, I have friends with whom we could stay in Bethlehem."

"Bethlehem? Bethlehem Ephrathah?"

"Yes, the village of David. It's but five miles from Jerusalem."

"I know. It's the village of my birth."

"What?" The loudness of Abraham's response surprised even him. He quickly lowered his voice so as not to wake the sleepers. "But you are a Nazarene, a Galilean."

Perhaps it was the lateness of the hour, or the burden of carrying this truth inside for so long, but Yeshua confided in Abraham what only his closest disciples knew. "While Nazareth is where I spent my youth, Bethlehem was my birthplace. My parents moved from there some thirty years ago, when I was only a toddler."

Abraham stared at Yeshua. "Why?"

"Abraham, you and I both have journeys to undertake tomorrow. Perhaps it's best if we use what remains of this night for sleep."

Yeshua rose and walked back toward his sleeping mat. After warming his hands by the fire one final time, Abraham returned to his bed and curled beneath a blanket provided by Peter's mother-in-law. This revelation of Yeshua's birthplace played on his mind, but so did the sudden onset of drowsiness. Abraham wanted to puzzle through a maze of thoughts spurred by Yeshua's mention of Bethlehem. The prophet Micah's words about Bethlehem. . . the time of Yeshua's leaving the village. . . how close in age Yeshua might be to the slaughtered innocents. . . Rebekah. . . Barabbas. . . Before they could come into focus, sleep won out.

Not so in the corner of the room where Yeshua reclined. Even with eyes shut tight, the images came clear. An aged blind rabbi, a wall of stones in a cave, his father weeping, children muted in death. What Yeshua anticipated in Jerusalem already haunted him from Bethlehem.

CHAPTER XXXVII

Antony cupped his hands and dipped them into the wash basin beside his bed. Lowering his head, he splashed water around his eyes and mouth, loosening sweat-caked dirt. The night air made the water feel warm on his skin. Antony dunked his entire face into the basin, rubbing hard to break loose the remnants of the past day and night's foray into the canyons surrounding Jericho. A Zealot raid on a supply column intended for Jericho's outpost sent Antony and a column of cavalry troops out in a pursuit from which he had just returned.

But now, instead of settling into sleep, Antony readied for an audience with Pilate. Word of the meeting greeted him on his return at the stable. Looking at arms and legs streaked with dust, Antony wished he had time to soak in the Antonia's baths. He hadn't felt truly warm since leaving Caesarea several days ago to escort Pilate to Jerusalem. Antony pulled on a fresh woolen tunic before donning his leather cuirass. The leather still smelled of sweat and horse.

The stairs of the Antonia's tower seemed steeper than usual this morning. Legs and back, stiffened from being jostled all night on rocky paths, protested each new flight. Antony strode two steps at a time to put the task behind him quicker. The last stairway ascended, he entered the corridor which led to Pilate's chamber.

The guard outside Pilate's door saluted, then called out: "Centurion Antony has arrived."

"Send him in," replied a voice from within.

The guard stepped aside to allow Antony entrance,

then left the two men alone.

"Hail, procurator!" The centurion's eyes drifted to the food laid out on Pilate's table. A roast hen, some fruit and vegetables, fresh baked bread –

"Did you find the column's attackers?"

Pilate's words refocused Antony's attention back from the food. "No, excellency. We rode the canyons between here and Jericho all of yesterday, but found no sign. We even kept up our patrol through the night, in hopes of spotting a camp-fire."

Pilate reached for the hen, tearing off a leg and taking a bite. The meat's juices dribbled down his fingers. "But you found no one?"

"No sir. This cold must have them deep in the caves, where their fires can't be seen."

"You're right about the cold, centurion," replied Pilate, chewing off more of the hen's leg.

"Maybe that's what makes these Jews such a boorish lot. Just like the Germanics, foul weather breeds foul people."

Though it had been more than twenty years since he admitted himself a Jew, Antony stiffened at Pilate's assess-ment. To contradict the procurator, however, would not be a wise choice. News of the abrupt dismissal of Julius had spread quickly. "Will you have us return to the canyons to continue the search?"

"I've assigned others that responsibility."

Antony swallowed hard. Removal from this detail so soon suggested punishment.

"A more important mission awaits you. Didn't you serve under centurion Lucius?"

"Yes sir, for many years."

"I recently received information that should eventu-ally lead us to his murderer. Choose a dozen of your best men. Men who might have the misfortune of passing as Jews. Like yourself."

Antony had heard that Sejanus had arranged Pilate's

appointment because of their shared hatred of Jews. "Will the tribune develop the plan for capturing the killer?"

"No. You're to work that out with the Jew who brought us this knowledge." Pilate sopped a piece of bread in his wine. "His name is Nathaniel, advisor to their priest."

Antony had no surprise at hearing his uncle's name attached to intrigues.

"He's a strange one. He's got the look of an impotent old man, but he has cunning.

Antony nodded his head. I hear others share that same opinion."

Pilate chortled. "Let's hope they're right. From the reports I've seen, cunning is exactly what'll be required to catch Barabbas."

"Barabbas?" Antony's thoughts rushed back to Bethlehem, to Deborah's funeral, to Rebekah's tongue-lashing of him at the cemetery and her disclosure: *He is a Zealot. . . Like you, my son goes by a different name – Barabbas.* "Barabbas murdered Lucius?"

"While you were on patrol yesterday, officers from Jericho briefed me. A whore who'd been with Lucius at the time of the assault said the leader was called Barabbas."

Antony's mind fogged, not wanting to believe this. "Maybe she lies to save herself."

Pilate nodded. "I considered that. But the officers conveyed she'd been badly beaten, and what had been done to Lucius wouldn't be possible for a woman her size. We already had reports this Barabbas is a leader among the Judean Zealots." Pilate broke off a wing from the hen and bit into it. "And that's reason enough to strap him to a cross for the birds to pick at."

More to convince himself than Pilate, Antony replied: "Perhaps Barabbas will be like those we sought in the canyons last night, knowing every cave where they can stay out of sight."

"That's where the Jew Nathaniel fits in. He came to me

yesterday, promising information on exactly where Barabbas may be found." Pilate stood and came around the table to face Antony. "Given that information, your job is to accomplish Barabbas' capture. Valerius may have put up with excuses for why this criminal eluded us in the past, but I won't. Understood?"

"Yes, Procurator."

"Good. I'll arrange a meeting for you with Nathaniel. Dismissed."

Antony saluted and left. Memories of Saul now Barabbas mixed with imaginings of Lucius' murder. How could Nathaniel possibly know where Barabbas – damn him, anyway! Antony recalled that when Rebekah spoke to him after his grandmother's burial, Nathaniel suddenly appeared. He must have overheard Rebekah near Deborah's grave. He KNOWS!

* * *

"The lake truly is beautiful, Julius."

The Roman smiled at Hannah, pleased to see her happy. In Caesarea, reminders of her former life seemed to always arise and depress her: former customers encountered by chance, staring or asking the price of her services these days; the sight of marketplaces and harbor taverns, where Hannah once solicited her trade. Julius hoped the move to Tiberias would help release her from all of that. "You handle yourself well on that horse. Did you own one before?"

"No, but when I was a child, I loved to ride. Only then, it was a donkey!"

The pair rode further to the north and west. The winds had died down shortly after dawn, and cloud breaks allowed the sun to warm Galilee's shores. After breakfast, Hannah talked Julius into riding to Magdala, a journey of a little more than three miles. There, they could inquire into the whereabouts of this rabbi whom Julius' friend Diogenes had mentioned at the inn.

The horses' gait remained steady along the shore road

that headed north from Tiberias to Magdala. Near the intersection of their route with that which headed up the Valley of the Doves toward the interior, Julius pointed to a tower in the distance. "See that? The tower that gives Magdala its name. Diogenes said we could ask about the rabbi at the custom house there."

Hannah looked across the valley to the village as they drew nearer. Nets and boats lining the lakeshore revealed its major industry. Several large outbuildings used for smoking fish scattered along the shoreline. Two of them had smoke curling from openings in the roof, whose scent presently wafted in their faces. "Heavens, Julius, what a smell!"

"Wait till we go to the Hammath springs. This stench will seem like Egyptian perfume."

Hannah twisted on her reins to move alongside Julius. "The night I met you, I wore Egyptian perfume." Careful not to lean too far, Hannah put one arm on Julius' shoulder and angled her chin toward his shoulder. "Are you saying I smelled like aging fish?"

"I'd never say such a thing. Although," he added, moving his horse away, "if you remember, I did end up taking you on a boat that night."

Hannah attempted to give Julius a playful slap, only to lose her balance. A timely grab of her elbow by Julius prevented Hannah from tumbling to the ground. "Let's be going," Julius laughed, "before this rabbi has to heal your injuries from a fall and my bruises from a beating."

* * *

Antony sat in the room alone, listening for a sound from the underground passageway. Pilate sent word of Nathaniel's coming after lunch. Antony decided to meet his uncle in this isolated space. He dismissed the guards, telling them Pilate desired this to be a private audience.

"Thanks for the favor," one joked. "That old Jew never fails to bring a foul mood."

"So I've been told," replied Antony, closing the door.

What had played in his memory since meeting with Pilate had been the scene at Deborah's burial, when Nathaniel interrupted Rebekah's rebuke. His uncle gave no indication, then or later, he'd overheard the disclosure of Barabbas's identity. But now, there could be no doubt. Antony mulled over his predicament. Barabbas – Saul – had been his closest friend in Bethlehem, the one who took his side and fought to protect him when other boys taunted the coward Joshua's son. That was why Antony had done nothing with his knowledge of Barabbas when Rebekah blurted out the truth over a month ago. But now, Pilate's orders demanded obedience. And obedience meant everything, as Julius once imparted to him. From deep below, Antony heard a steady tapping. The noise echoed, growing louder, until footsteps ascended the stairs, with two tappings on each stair.

When they stopped, a voice called out. "You on duty in there. Wake up! It's the Sopher!"

Antony unbolted the trapdoor and lifted, moving behind it so Nathaniel wouldn't see him.

"Come on. Give me a hand." Nathaniel reached one arm up, using the other to steady himself on the cane. "Give me a hand, fool, or Pilate will hear of your insolence!"

Antony stepped from behind the door and grasped Nathaniel.

"What did you think – " Nathaniel paused, peering at the familiar face. "Antony?"

"Surprised, uncle?"

"Yes, I am. I'd understood you to be in Caesarea."

"My century escorted Pilate here."

Nathaniel considered telling Antony about his mother's condition, and her staying with Rebekah. But the day's agenda pressed on him. "I've a meeting your procurator has arranged. Maybe we can talk later."

"Oh, I think we'll talk now, uncle." Antony straddled a chair and pushed a second one in Nathaniel's direction. "I'm the one Pilate arranged to meet with you."

"You?" Nathaniel's eyes widened momentarily as he sat down. "I had no idea."

"Really?" Antony's words spewed disdain. "Tell me, Sopher Kohen Gadol: how does it feel for so righteous a Jew as yourself to betray the son of Elias and Rebekah?"

Nathaniel clenched his teeth and said nothing.

"Uncle, this is no time for modesty. What did informing on Barabbas gain you? More silver in your purse? Or just the satisfaction of gaining Pilate's ear for some future patronage?"

The tip of Nathaniel's cane struck hard against the stone floor. "Enough!" The older man pointed a bony finger at Antony. "I will not have the likes of you take that tone with me on betrayal. You gave up the family who bore and named you. You're the one who enlisted in the same legion that murdered your brother and Barabbas' father. Don't presume to lecture me!"

"I did what I had to do."

"As I do now," hissed Nathaniel. "What Barabbas has done threatens rebellion and reprisal. He must be stopped, and the Zealots with him."

"And it just happens your betrayal of him will set you in good stead with Pilate."

Nathaniel shook his head. "I see Antony remains Simeon, his father's son, destined to failure. Yes, giving the information to Pilate advances me. Where is it commanded we must never do what brings gain to us? You apparently didn't balk at promotion to centurion."

"You twist the truth to suit you, uncle."

"No, you refuse to face reality. And this is reality, Antony. You chose the legion long ago. And now, Pilate orders you to seize Barabbas. Do you imagine the Romans care a whit about some childhood friend of yours?" Nathaniel leaned back in his chair, resting both hands on the top of his cane. "Don't blame me for the road that led you here – you took it on yourself. Choose Barabbas, or choose the legion.

You can't have both."

In spite of the loathing he felt for Nathaniel, Antony knew him to be right. The only way to avoid taking part in Barabbas's capture would be to disobey the orders of Pilate, to turn his back on the legion – and with it, the last twenty years of his life.

Nathaniel glared at Antony, waiting for him to speak. A tired voice uttered:

"How do you propose Barabbas be taken?"

* * *

Julius and Hannah never made Magdala's customs house. A gathering of thirty or so persons near the village well caught their eyes. Tying their horses' reins to a post, they walked to the crowd's outer circle. Everyone listened to a speaker in the center.

"Excuse me," Julius asked one of the bystanders, "who is the teacher?"

The stranger turned to Julius. The Magdalene saw the man was no Jew, yet he spoke the Judean dialect of Aramaic. "The rabbi Yeshua, of Nazareth."

Julius nodded to Hannah. "It's him. Yeshua."

Another woman turned to face Julius. "Ssssh! Be quiet so we can hear the rabbi."

Julius bowed his head to her, then he and Hannah pressed closer within the circle.

". . . a man can love his friends with ease. But it takes the working of God to love those who show no love in return."

"Like the Romans!" shouted one fisherman.

"Now Elijah, the Almighty must greatly love the Romans," cried another, "since Adonai created no people on earth who can stomach them!"

Many roared in ridicule. Others, including a few standing close to the rabbi, allowed a smile to cross their faces. Julius noted one of them to be vaguely familiar. He'd just seen him, but where? Perhaps the inn of Tiberias –

"Then you've not yet understood the promise given to Abraham." The strength in Yeshua's voice commanded the crowd's attention, including Hannah's and Julius'. "Is it not written in the Torah's first scroll: `By your offspring shall ALL the nations of the earth gain blessings for themselves.'* Does anyone declare God's promise to Abraham void?"

"You misunderstand us, rabbi." The voice belonged to the fisherman Elijah. "Love of enemy is fine and well, until his foot crushes the breath from your throat. How can I love those I can't even forgive?"

Murmurs of assent swept through the gathering, now numbering close to fifty. Yeshua looked at Elijah, then stepped over to him and placed a hand on his shoulder. Julius and Hannah wondered what sort of confrontation would unfold.

"You could ask no question more important," the rabbi began, "for where there is no forgiveness, there can be no love."

Hannah felt her eyes moisten at the rabbi's words.

"If you would learn of love, then first learn of forgiveness. It is like a man," Yeshua continued, now turning and raising his voice to address the whole gathering, "with an impossible debt accumulated over a lifetime. When the debt came due, he pleaded with his creditor for more time. And what did this creditor do? Not the JUST thing, by insisting on the agreed-upon terms. Not even the KIND thing, by extending the time of repayment. No, this creditor did the GRACIOUS thing: he FORGAVE the debt. Set it aside. Declared it over and past."

The fisherman's face hardened. "And you expect us uo be so forgiving of the Romans?"

"Listen to the story's end," replied Yeshua, "then decide for yourself. The individual who'd been forgiven encountered a neighbor who owed him a mere pittance. It amounted to a hundredth, no, make that a thousandth, of the debt forgiven him. Payment was demanded, but when it wasn't forthcoming, the forgiven man had his own debtor tossed into prison. Tell me, then, how do you suppose the first creditor felt when he heard this?"

"Angry, I'd think," answered Elijah. "Disappointed."

"And why would that be?" asked Yeshua.

"He probably thought the man should have acted as he had been treated himself."

Yeshua placed both hands again on Elijah's shoulders. "God forgives our sins. Even the worst. So what might Adonai Elohim want from us, from you – especially when it comes to our enemies? As you rightly said: to act as God has treated us."

All stood silent, focused on Yeshua's words and his firm hold on the fisherman's shoulders. It was if the rabbi clung to one in danger of slipping under the waves.

"You ask too much," Elijah mumbled. He swept Yeshua's arms off with his own, then stepped back. Yeshua moved toward him, only to be met with a shouted, "You ask too much!"

When Elijah left, the crowd dispersed. Only a small group remained by the rabbi.

"You did ask much of the man," Hannah heard one of those close to the rabbi say. Like Julius, she thought she'd seen him at the inn.

"No more than I ask of myself, and all who follow me, Judas. God asks much of us all, but only because God offers so much more." Yeshua looked at those around him – and, Hannah and Julius each thought to themselves, at them. "God offers each of you so much more."

To Hannah, his eyes evoked longings she once sensed when gazing on the waters of the Great Sea at Caesarea. She'd thought Julius erased these longings for healing and cleansing. But what if they were still there? What if the rabbi could see the wounds and hatreds in her? What if this Nazarene came up and spoke to her as he did to that fisherman?

Almost in a panic, Hannah squeezed Julius' hand.

"Take me back to Tiberias."

Julius considered asking if she wanted to meet the rabbi. But he also felt a strong urge to leave. The two spoke little on the ride to Tiberias. Neither shared with the other what troubled them both: words of forgiveness that sounded as if aimed in their direction. Words that risked revealing scars best left hidden. Words best left behind.

CHAPTER XXXVIII

Caiaphas sank into the upholstered chair and groaned. The responsibilities attending the first day of the month's New Moon observance exhausted him. While lesser priests handled the details of the slaughters, tradition demanded the High Priest's presence in the Court of Priests all day. The only exception came when he officiated at the service of prayers for the pilgrims gathered in the Court of Israel.

The High Priest's breastplate, with its metal strappings and inlays of gems, slumped his shoulders. As he worked to undo its clasps, Caiaphas considered an even more wearying burden. Nearly two weeks had passed since Pilate's arrival. Barabbas still roamed free. The Zealots and their allies used the time to stir unrest in Jerusalem. Ordinary folk now questioned the allegiance of the Sanhedrin and the Jerusalem priesthood. With minor incidents of defiance in the city, and hit-and-run tactics in the countryside, the Zealots pressured the Romans. They hoped to trigger some overreaction from the troops that might sway the crowds into even greater resentment.

All of this troubled Caiaphas. As oppressive as Rome seemed now, conditions could worsen. Other peoples under Roman rule had far less religious freedom than the Jews. A man like Pilate would not hesitate to impose more severe restrictions to bear on Jerusalem and Judea. Caiaphas deemed it his duty to keep both Zealot extremism and Roman suppression at bay. If either got out of hand, the people of Israel would suffer – and the Temple could be put at risk.

Just then, a voice called out beyond the door. "Caiaphas, it's Nathaniel."

"Come in, Sopher."

Nathaniel entered the room. Caiaphas stared at him, trying to decide what made Nathaniel look so different. Only when the Sopher sat across from him did Caiaphas recognize the cause. Totally out of character, a broad smile decked his advisor's face.

"Why Nathaniel, you look as though the Almighty has blessed you with some great gift."

"He has, Caiaphas, he has. And the blessing also falls on you."

Caiaphas stroked his beard and wondered at his Sopher's claim. "What is this blessing?"

"The blessing of Solomon. When God offered him any gift, he chose knowledge."

"I don't follow you."

"Some time ago, the Lord delivered a piece of long-hidden information into my hands. And ten days ago, I gave that knowledge to Pilate in exchange for his favor toward you and me."

The news pleased Caiaphas, though he remained puzzled about what exactly Nathaniel meant. "Just what knowledge buys us the friendship of Pilate?"

Nathaniel set the cane across his lap and folded his hands. "The knowledge which leads his troops to the murderer of Lucius. Tonight."

"Tonight? How do you know this? And how did you come into – "

"It would be better if I don't trouble you with the details, Caiaphas. Should some opponent ask, you may truthfully deny knowing anything beforehand. Which is why I withheld telling you until now, in case the Romans' trap of the killer, the Zealot called Barabbas, was compromised. But now, the plan is for him to be seized when darkness falls."

"What can I say, Nathaniel? This will be a serious blow

to the Zealots, just when their fortunes were ascending. And to have Pilate indebted to us as well."

"Plus, by having the Romans seize Barabbas," Nathaniel interjected, "our hand is nowhere to be seen. A fact we need not share with others."

Caiaphas stood and walked to Nathaniel. "Once more, you've served the Temple and your people well. May the Lord bless you, Nathaniel, for the peace that will come of this."

Nathaniel's chin dipped to his chest as he felt the High Priest's hand placed on his head in benediction. Nathaniel thought back to Antony's accusation of betrayal against the very same act which none other than the High Priest now blessed: the same Antony poised at this very moment outside Bethlehem, commanding the detachment to seize Rebekah's son. If there was treachery in this night, Nathaniel reasoned, Antony's share loomed far larger than his own.

* * *

Light faded quickly from the sky over Bethlehem. A gathering of clouds swept up and over the far western hills. In the home of Rebekah, a lamb stew neared completion. Her son's arrival that morning called for a special meal. This was their first time together since Barabbas executed Lucius. That act filled Rebekah's heart with pride for his act of carrying out God's retribution. Her hopes for him were coming to fruition.

"Is anyone home in the house of Rebekah?" came a man's voice from outside the house.

Rebekah puzzled over who might visit so close to the evening meal. Barabbas expected no one and proceeded to hide himself, not wanting to reveal his presence in town to some stranger. Rebekah unlatched the door and cracked it open. A failing twilight only outlined the man's figure, but the glow from the cookfire within the house illumined his face. "Abraham!" Rebekah threw open the door and embraced him. "I had no word you were coming!"

"It's good to see you, Rebekah. Too much time has passed since my last visit."

Rebekah stepped back to look at her friend. Dirt covered his outer mantle. "Come in. I'll hang your cloak outside and beat it, to remove this dust you've carried with you."

"Don't bother. I came to visit, not watch you do chores. Besides," he added, stepping inside and removing his mantle, "this dirt has been my one companion since Galilee."

"Galilee!" shouted another voice from the bedroom. "Then you've come back from your search." Barabbas stepped out of the shadows and gave Abraham a hug.

"I had no idea you'd be here, Barabbas. You look well."

"As do you, for an old man!" Barabbas slapped Abraham's back, causing a puff of dust to rise from the robe. "Galilee must have no soil left since you've carried so much with you."

Rebekah filled a chalice with wine. "Don't listen to that son of mine, Abraham. When he comes from the wilderness, his face is so caked with dirt I have to use one of Elias' chisels before kissing him." Taking Abraham's arm, Rebekah offered: "We'll be eating soon. Please, sit down down, and break bread with us."

As Abraham started to kneel beside the table, another person emerged from the bedroom. Dressed in black, ashes etched in her brow, the woman's face showed the wear of more than age. Rebekah stepped by her. "Abraham, this is Naomi. Do you remember?"

"Naomi? Why yes, the wife of – "

A quick shake of Rebekah's head cut off his words.

"Naomi's been staying with my mother," added Barabbas.

Abraham walked to Naomi. "It's good to see you after so many years." He clasped her hand. She offered no response to his touch and, without a word, retreated to the bedroom.

The others returned to table and resumed their conversation in quieter tones.

"What happened to her?" asked Abraham.

"Do you remember her mother, Deborah? She died little more than a month ago, and Naomi's not recovered. Mother took her in when Nathaniel gave up on her."

"If I recall, that would be her uncle?"

"Yes," replied Rebekah, "he lives in Jerusalem, the Sopher to the High Priest."

Barabbas grunted. "He cares for Torah so much, yet abandons his own family."

"So, Abraham," continued Rebekah, shifting the subject to more pleasant things, "tell us of your trip to Galilee. Barabbas only said you'd hopes of seeing some rabbi."

"And not any ordinary rabbi," laughed Barabbas, "but one from Nazareth, whom some of our slow-witted Galilean brethren tout as Messiah! Isn't that right, Abraham?"

Abraham slowly set down his chalice and looked at the younger man. "The last time we spoke, you said my journey to Galilee was a fool's dream. But I'm here to tell you, Yeshua Barabbas, that this rabbi Yeshua speaks and acts as God's Anointed One."

The smile left the face of Barabbas. "You can't be serious."

"I've never been more serious in my life." Noticing a look of dismay coming to Rebekah as well, Abraham reached a hand to hers. "You of all people know I don't judge hastily. I followed this rabbi for weeks. Not only did I hear his wisdom, I saw his deeds. He healed people, Rebekah. Lepers. The blind. Maimed. He gave people hope."

"How can this be?" Rebekah asked.

"I'll tell you," interrupted Barabbas. "People will believe anything, so long as it takes the burden off their backs. I've seen these so-called healers at work, performing their magic on men they've bribed to stand up and leap after feigning paralysis, to free more shekels for their act."

"Others use such tricks, Barabbas, but not this rabbi. Besides, there are his words, his teachings. No one I've ever heard speaks with such wisdom and compassion."

"And justice?" Barabbas shot back. "Does he speak of justice, Abraham?"

Abraham's shoulders rolled back as he stiffened his posture. "He does. The justice demanded by God's kingdom."

"Then let's see him DO justice. Rome's not threatened by a few cripples who imagine limbs to be suddenly young again. Let the rabbi of Nazareth, if he is Israel's Messiah, do something useful. Like execute one of the Rome's butchers."

"As I heard one of your comrades did in Jericho not so long ago?"

"Not one of my comrades, Abraham." Barabbas drew out his knife and tossed it in front of his mentor from long ago. "I did!"

"You?"

"The man I murdered had hands stained by my father's and brother's blood. Ask your rabbi to think of a better vengeance on one of those who executed Bethlehem's children."

Abraham handed Barabbas' knife back to him. "The rabbi Yeshua, whom I believe to be Messiah, IS one of this town's children!"

Rebekah's face paled. "This rabbi, Yeshua, is not a Nazarene, but from Bethlehem?"

Abraham understood the answer to Rebekah's question would not be easily said or heard. During the long journey from Galilee, Abraham deciphered the puzzle of who the rabbi truly was. That deciphering led Abraham to delay his return to New Damascus for the sake of visiting Bethlehem, in hopes of freeing two old friends from the burden of vengeance.

"Yeshua was born in Bethlehem. To parents with the names of Joseph and Mary."

* * *

With men and horses secured within a large cave near

Solomon's Pools, Antony walked outside to a vantage point where he could see Bethlehem, barely two miles away. The new moon and an approaching bank of clouds provided ideal conditions for cloaking their raid and then the return to Jerusalem. Antony silently assured himself, again, it was best that he led this detail, to prevent his onetime friend – and Lucius' murderer – from the troops' understandable thirst for revenge. Those he'd chosen for this task had openly voiced their desire to do to Barabbas what he had done to Lucius. But the centurion firmly stood by the orders to take him alive.

Five days ago, Antony had led the detail chosen to capture Barabbas to Herodium. There, they would train while awaiting news of the Zealot's arrival in Bethlehem at his mother's home. Late this morning, a messenger brought information that he was now there. Antony dispatched the man to the Antonia, to prepare for receiving the prisoner tonight. That done, Antony and his men rode northwest, staging at this cave in preparation for nightfall. If successful, Antony knew that Pilate would pass on news of the capture to Nathaniel. How grateful Pilate would be to the Sopher, how delighted Nathaniel would feel with pleasing his new ally. Damn it all anyway.

Antony returned to the cave's entrance and spoke to its sentry. "Assemble the men at the cave's mouth. And bring my horse out with theirs."

"Very good, sir."

As he waited, Antony drew out the sword given him by Julius. What had he said then: *use it in honor*? Antony felt no honor at the moment. But he also didn't have time to linger in such thoughts. Ten legionnaires emerged from the cave with their mounts, ready for final orders. It was time to act.

"Remember your assignments. The four of you designated as sentries stay on the street to guard the horses and our exit. There should only be the zealot and his mother inside. Maybe one other woman, according to the informer.

Those six who enter with me: do no violence to the women. We only want Barabbas, and him alive for trial. In and out, quickly and quietly. Once outside, we strap the prisoner to a horse and return to the Antonia. Understood?"

"A question, sir." The voice belonged to Tigranes of Cilicia, the only one besides Antony who'd served with Lucius. "If Barabbas resists, are we free to do what's needed to subdue him?"

Antony stepped up to Tigranes. "I know what you ask, and why. I also counted Lucius a friend." Antony now turned and eyed the other men. "But if anyone here strikes a killing blow to Barabbas, he'll answer to me, and after me the procurator. Pilate would take it as a personal affront for anyone to deny him the privilege of dealing with this Zealot himself."

Antony had no knowledge of any such concern of Pilate's. He just hoped the invocation of the procurator offered another way to protect Barabbas from retribution, if only for this day. It wasn't much, but Antony could do little more than bring Barabbas safe to Jerusalem.

No one in the circle raised further questions.

"Mount up." Antony ordered.

Before the column advanced, Antony gave one final command. None of the soldiers understood why, but they complied: each man donned a cloth mask provided before they left Jerusalem. Antony alone held the secret of why he wanted their faces, primarily his own, to remain unseen in the house that sheltered Barabbas.

* * *

"Is anyone home?" Julius heard no sound save that of his own voice. He looked at Hannah and shrugged his shoulders.

"We haven't ridden all this way for nothing, have we?" Hannah asked as she slid off her mount to the ground. "Or is it the wrong house?"

"No, the directions that fisherman gave were quite

specific. And look here, on the lintel above the door. *Peter* is carved into the wood. This is the right place."

Hannah sat on a large flat rock. Maybe they shouldn't have come here after all. Maybe they should have left it with hearing the Rabbi Yeshua in Magdala. But for days afterward, his words tumbled within her. About forgiveness. And enemies. And love. Only yesterday, she confided in Julius how much those words affected her – and to her surprise, and his as well, he confessed to the same unrest. Someday, they'd have to search the rabbi out and hear him again.

Today, after lunch, they finally decided to seek him out. A ride to the customs house in Magdala brought information he might be found in the town of Gennesaret, four miles to the north. Arriving there, Hannah and Julius found not so much a village as a scattering of houses on a large plain stretching from the sea into the hills. Neither the fishermen nor the farmers there knew much of the rabbi's whereabouts, though several of them spoke of when he'd fed a great crowd of Galileans nearby. They suggested the pair check at the home of one of his disciples, Peter, in Capernaum. The rabbi stayed there often. And now, Hannah and Julius stood at that house, only to find it deserted. Hannah took note of the sun disappearing behind the western hills. "What are we going to do? It's too late to ride back to Tiberias."

Julius shook his head. "I'm sorry. I lost my sense of time searching for the rabbi. There should be somewhere here where we can stay. Maybe there is a caravansary, or –"

"You there! Did you call at my door?"

Julius and Hannah turned to see the door to Peter's house now opened, and an older woman standing with an oil lamp.

"Yes, we did," answered Julius. "We were told the Rabbi Yeshua often stays at the home of one of his disciples."

"That would be my son-in-law, Peter. They won't be back from the synagogue for another hour or so. What do you want with the rabbi?"

"We heard him speak," Hannah answered, "and hoped to hear him again."

"But why come so late?"

Julius sensed distrust in the woman's voice. "We rode from Tiberias – "

"Tiberias?" The woman's voice rose in volume and pitch. "No decent Jew lives over the remains of the dead." She stepped forward and thrust the lamp into his face. "You're no Jew! Your features are Roman. Go away, you've no business here, Gentile!"

"We heard Rabbi Yeshua teach love of enemies," Hannah protested. "Do you shelter a teacher whose words you ignore?"

"Someone should school you in respect of elders." The woman now turned the oil lamp toward Hannah. "Hah, a Jewess, who gives company to this Roman. And who knows what else!"

"That is enough." Julius stepped between Hannah and the woman. "We came seeking Yeshua of Nazareth. It's clear we're unwelcome."

"Don't lecture me, Gentile. You Romans sought Yeshua before. To kill him."

"Woman, that's nonsense. Why would Romans harm some scholar from Nazareth?"

"He's not from Nazareth, not to begin with. Years ago, your murdering kind and Herod plotted his death, when he was a suckling at his mother Mary's breast in Bethlehem!"

Hannah threw one hand to her mouth, a wave of nausea rushing over her.

The woman's words chilled Julius. "Bethlehem?" he asked, eyes blurring.

"You Roman killers would have butchered him with the other children," the old woman exclaimed, "had the Almighty not warned his father to flee the night before. Get out of here!"

The door slammed shut.

Never had a sound pierced Julius' ears so deeply, followed shortly by the noise of Hannah retching. Still dazed, Julius rubbed Hannah's back as she bent over. All his thoughts converged on that day triggered by the old woman's revelation. This Yeshua escaped the death that others suffered in his stead – at the hands of those Julius commanded. In Bethlehem!

Julius felt a sudden craving to escape this place and, even better, this knowledge. "Hannah, let me help you to the lake," he offered, "I'll wet a cloth for your forehead."

Hannah stumbled, still nauseous, as Julius led her toward the shore. Images of her twin brother David playing, then his little body bloodied and lifeless in Bethlehem's alley, flooded her consciousness. Those images gave way to that of a child barely remembered, a child her mother cursed as the cause for all her family's suffering and estrangement – the missing accomplice in David's death, whose name was Yeshua. A child with a father named Joseph and a mother Mary. A child grown to manhood, daring to present himself a teacher of God! Yeshua!

"I found you, Yeshua!" she screamed, his name spitting from her lips as some obscene epithet. "I found you!"

CHAPTER XXXIX

Julius dipped his handcloth into laps of water swishing against the shore. After wringing it out, he brushed the damp cloth across Hannah's brow, then her lips and chin. As he did, Hannah glared back in the direction of Peter's house, rocking back and forth at the waist, arms pressing knees tight to her chest.

"Are you still feeling sick?"

"No." Her rocking continued.

Julius waited, hoping she'd say something, hoping her words might free him if just for a moment him from thinking of his unholy connection to rabbi Yeshua. But Hannah kept silent, leaving Julius mired in his thoughts. Did Yeshua feel anything for those who died that day instead of him? Was he even aware of their sacrifice, or their families' loss? Such speculation about Yeshua failed to deliver Julius from his own guilt. If only Hannah would speak.

"Hannah, what did you mean before, about finding Yeshua?"

"You don't want to know."

"Please, tell me." Anything, Julius thought, anything.

Hannah stopped rocking, though she kept her knees drawn close and her arms tight around them. "I told you before of my hatred for your people."

"Yes, because of the Antonia."

Hannah's head dropped. "Before the Antonia, there was Bethlehem."

"What of Bethlehem?"

Hannah resumed rocking back and forth again in silence.

"What is it?"

Slowly, Hannah lifted her head and looked out toward the sea. "David. Born of the same womb as I, only minutes later."

"A twin brother? You never mentioned him before."

Hannah's released the grip on her knees and lifted a hand to press against his lips. "David and I seemed like one. Our play, our laughter, our resting. I remember him, a beautiful child." Her words trailed off.

Julius' desire for her to speak, lest he have to, began to take on a sense of dread.

"I remember David." Her eyes incised those of Julius. Each phrase grew in volume and bitterness. "I remember when a legionnaire murdered him in Bethlehem. . . David, when it should have been Yeshua. . . Twenty or more others, when it should have been Yeshua."

The hand she had pressed to his lips now moved to his throat. Teeth clenched, eyes welling with tears, voice trembling, she continued: "All killed by Romans. All but the one called Yeshua, who left my brother and the others to die. Without a warning."

Julius didn't move when Hannah told of David's execution. He didn't flinch when she took his throat and laid the children's deaths to Roman hands. Deep inside, he wished Hannah's nails might dig in under the flesh, into the artery coursing just underneath, delivering him from the revulsion growing within him. Not only had he been part of the killings, no matter how he rationalized his actions: the murderer Julius had bedded one of his victim's sisters.

"Yeshua will suffer for David and the others," Hannah swore, loosing her hand from Julius' neck. "But you," she whispered, "I can't hate you for what others of your people did."

She leaned over to hold Julius, but he brought both palms up. "Don't, Hannah."

"Why? You've done me no wrong."

"STOP IT!"

The words, and eyes, of Julius startled her. "Julius, what's come over you?"

"Bethlehem," he breathed. Silence could no longer be justified. "Bethlehem. I was there."

"You?"

"I raised no sword myself. But the detail required a centurion. I. . ." Julius paused to look into her eyes, thinking she might plead for him to stop. But she did not, and he must not. "I stood by," he resumed, "and watched the children die."

"No, no, No, NO!" Hannah reached down, seized a small piece of driftwood and swung it wildly at his head as she screamed. Julius blocked her attempt and grabbed her arm.

"I swore when you came with me, I'd never let anyone hurt you." Julius released her arm, though it still held the driftwood club. "But my life's made me a liar to that promise." Throat choking, his next words came less spoken than pushed. "If I'd known, any of this, I'd never. . ."

He reached to touch her, but Hannah squeezed her eyes shut and drew back from him. "Leave me. NOW!"

Julius got up and walked away. A few feet from his horse, his back to Hannah, he paused and spoke. "If it's any comfort, know that I will go to my grave hating myself. For what I did to those children, and your David. For what I've done to you." He waited for a moment: whether to see if she might race to strike him, or cling to him, he wasn't sure. When neither happened, Julius mounted his horse. Riding to the south, he dared not look back, lest he see her pain again.

Once Julius disappeared from sight, Hannah flung the stick into Galilee's night-blackened waters. "You've taken everything from me, Yeshua. Everything!" Hannah rose to feet. But instead of tears came a rush of ideas. Killing the rabbi was her first thought. Hannah doubted, though,

385

whether she possessed strength enough to insure a killing blow. With his disciples always around, she risked being seized before she could even thrust in a knife, the only weapon she might manage. Besides, even if she did, his suffering would be only moments or hours. How many lifetimes of grief had Bethlehem's families suffered? Lifetimes he should be made to bear.

A new focus – and weapon – came to Hannah's mind. Why not disgrace him, make it appear Yeshua whored with her: THAT would be fitting justice! Hannah knew from her previous work how fearful of discovery were customers whose public reputations trumpeted virtue. Hannah also knew from experience how vicious a community could become when those reputations were stripped of their veneer. That would be her plan. She'd ruin Yeshua from the inside, leaving him to die a day at a time: as he had done to her, as he had done to an entire village's mothers and sisters and fathers and brothers. In the distance, Hannah saw lamps still burning in the synagogue, where the rabbi no doubt reveled in the Torah's light. Hannah plotted how she'd pull Yeshua into the darkness that had swallowed her and David whole.

* * *

A line of riders galloped from the southwest toward of Bethlehem. Sparks flew where hooves struck flinted rocks together. The night air stung Antony's lungs. After all these years, from this distance, in the dark: Bethlehem still looked the same. He wondered if Barabbas would look the same. He wondered if Barabbas would notice the eyes above his mask, and see in them a friend become an enemy. He spurred his horse faster, wanting to be done with this night.

In Bethlehem, Rebekah's stew neared a boil, as did the emotions around her table.

"Abraham, are you certain about the names of Yeshua's parents?"

Abraham understood what Rebekah asked, and why. If ever he hoped to dissuade them from the course their lives had followed for thirty years, Abraham knew he must speak the truth.

"I am. Mary still lives in Nazareth, though I didn't see her."

To hear her name linked to Yeshua chilled Rebekah. "And Joseph, what of him?"

"He died some time ago, the way the rabbi spoke." Abraham breathed deep. "But Yeshua did say he was a carpenter. The same carpenter, I believe, whom Elias befriended."

Barabbas and Rebekah looked to one another. There now could be no question. Abraham interrupted their glares with one final confirmation. "The same Joseph and Mary who, with you, took me under care when I stumbled into Bethlehem after the Jerusalem riot."

Barabbas grasped his knife and jammed it into the wooden table fashioned by his father. "Then this rabbi, this viper, is the one who left my father and brother to die!"

Abraham hoped Yeshua spoke the truth when he said words would come. "Herod and Rome brought death to this village, not Yeshua. God delivered the child for some high purpose."

"Do not blaspheme in my house, Abraham!" A wildness pitched through Rebekah's voice. "The Almighty would not spare a coward, leaving brave men like Elias and innocent children like Levi to die."

"Of Elias' and Levi's death, I can offer no reason. But think at least on this. When Pharaoh played the part of Herod and slew innocent children in Egypt, God gave sanctuary to an infant hidden by his mother among bulrushes. Moses lived to deliver the children of Israel. As I believe God spared Yeshua to do for us. For you."

Barabbas jostled the table as he leapt up, knocking over the chalices and spilling their wine, glaring down at Abraham. "You twist Torah to support your false Messiah! I once valued your wisdom, Abraham, but now it reeks of folly and deceit."

Abraham stood up and faced Barabbas. "Say what you will of me, Barabbas, but Yeshua is not your foe. He seeks more fervently than any Zealot the coming of God's kingdom."

Rebekah arose and stood by her son. "God's kingdom is not built on innocent blood."

"Yeshua had no fault in what happened here," Abraham pleaded. "You know his age. He couldn't have done anything."

"His parents gave us no warning. His mother said nothing to spare the life of my husband or son, nor did his father." Rebekah tilted her head to face the ceiling. "May the Almighty avenge the sins of the parents upon their wretched offspring."

"Don't say that." Abraham started to move toward Rebekah, but Barabbas stopped him.

"You were once as father to me. But if you side with Yeshua, you are my enemy."

Abraham looked to Rebekah. "Do you share that judgment?"

She took hold of Barabbas' arm. "I swore my son to avenge this village's shame. I keep my oath, Abraham, and swear its curse on any who defend the traitor Yeshua. You included."

Mustering his strength, Abraham raised his right palm to the pair, as a rabbi giving benediction. "He is Messiah, you will see."

Barabbas reached down, pulling his knife from the table and lifting it in the air. "He is condemned, *you* will see." Barabbas pressed it into Abraham's hand. "Feel the dagger that will kill your false Messiah, just as it cut down Lucius."

Just as Abraham grasped the dagger, the door burst open. Abraham whirled, knife still in hand. The first legionnaire through the door mistook the movement for an attack and struck Abraham's hand with his gladius. Abraham dropped to his knees, grasping at the spurting stumps of fingers that once held the blade. Before he could cry out, a second soldier slammed the butt end of his gladius against Abraham's temple, knocking him down in a daze.

Barabbas and Rebekah, frozen in shock, were slammed to the floor by the onrushing troops. Hands knotted ropes round his wrists and ankles. A gag bound his mouth. Barabbas watched as one soldier left the house and came back in with another. "This one swung at me with a knife, sir. It's not him, is it?"

The centurion looked at the man on the floor, then moved to the man trussed with rope. Barabbas saw only a centurion's helmet and breastplate. The centurion saw a youth grown older. "Leave the wounded one here. This one is Barabbas. Take him!"

"Barabbas!" Rebekah screamed, scrambling toward her son. Before she reached him, one of the guards kicked her in the face to stop her. The guard's sneer at her ended when Antony's fist slammed into his cheek, buckling his knees.

"I commanded the women be unharmed. Forget my orders again, and you'll be rowing some Egyptian galley! All of you, get Barabbas outside. Now!"

The soldiers dragged Barabbas out to the horses. Thinking himself alone with the wounded man and Rebekah, Antony bent over to see if her injury was serious. A moving shadow caused him to jump and spin, gladius drawn. Holding an oil lamp, a gaunt woman stood and looked at the intruder. She saw the breastplate, then the helmet. . . and then she saw the eyes. When she did, her own filled with tears. A child's eyes are not forgotten – nor a mother's.

"Centurion, we must go!" came a shout from outside.

Antony felt Naomi's hand take his, which she pressed to her lips and brow, then released. Without a word, she stepped past him and knelt beside Rebekah, still unconscious.

"Centurion!"

Antony raced out the door to his horse, then led his detail on a gallop to Jerusalem. He felt little of the air's cold bite on the journey. His eyes burned too much.

* * *

"Rabbi! Rabbi! You must return. These are important men, and important issues!" Yeshua paused outside the synagogue's door. Some of his disciples forged a way through the crowd for him to exit. Others pleaded with Yeshua to stay. Judas Iscariot counted himself among that latter group, voicing his concern as he sidled up to Yeshua.

"Please, Rabbi, don't walk away from Jacob. His word holds sway among the Zealots. He can do much for you. For us all"

Yeshua ignored the jostling and focused on the speaker. "Judas, you weigh the opinion of men too much. It's not God's kingdom that needs Zealots, but the other way around."

Judas drew his arm around the rabbi to pull him closer. He loved Yeshua for his wisdom, his innocence – but thought him at times grossly naïve in the ways of the world. "It's not necessary to wholly agree with these men, especially when it comes to violence. But they'd give Herod Antipas second thought about seizing you, as he did the Baptizer."

"It's said that those who swim in Hammath's waters begin to reek of sulphur themselves," Yeshua declared. "Immerse yourself with the Zealots, Judas, and it's not long before the stench of violence springs from you. You walked with them long enough to know that."

"That's why I left them to follow you! I only mean to say –"

"I know you intend well, and seek my protection. But Elohim is my guardian."

"Yeshua!" Jacob's voice cried out from inside the synagogue toward the rabbi. "When might we meet again to shed light on the obligations of God's kingdom?"

The crowd hushed. For over two hours inside the synagogue, Yeshua and Jacob debated matters ranging from Sabbath to the Baptizer to the assassination in Jericho. But all words inevitably returned to what the kingdom of God required in these days.

"You want to know more of God's kingdom, Jacob?" At Yeshua's words, those jammed between the two men moved aside until a path opened. Those standing by each man stepped back, so all might hear. But at that moment, murmurs arose in the crowd behind Yeshua.

"No, get back," some said.

"He's not to be bothered," another scolded.

The disciples closest to Jesus began to wag their fingers at whoever approached.

"Wait. Who seeks me?" asked Yeshua.

"It's only women," Peter growled, "Along with some youngsters, who should be on their sleeping mats by now."

"Go on with Jacob," Judas urged.

Yeshua looked at Jacob: arms folded, waiting a reply on the kingdom's demands. The rabbi smiled. "Bring the children to me," he announced.

Peter and Judas, among others, protested. "Rabbi, no! They're of no consequence and – "

"Let the children COME to me!" Yeshua did not speak in request but command.

Peter bit his lip and waved them forward. Thank God his wife and daughter were not among them, he thought, or they'd catch fire at home.

Yeshua gathered the children around him. Some neared the age when they'd take the commandments as their own responsibility. Others toddled. Yeshua took one infant from its mother and cradled it in his arms. The mothers stood close by. At the far edge of the crowd, another woman approached, just now able to hear the rabbi's words.

"You ask of the kingdom, Jacob?"

"I did, before you surrounded yourself with them."

Jacob's disdain at being made to wait for children shot through his reply.

"But these provide your answer."

"You speak in riddles, Rabbi."

"Perhaps," Yeshua replied. "But no more than Isaiah, whose vision of God's kingdom came in a little child's leading."

Jacob grew impatient. "I asked you seriously of your thoughts on God's kingdom. What have you to say?"

Yeshua looked down to the children at his side and the one nestled in his arms. He took no note of a woman who began pushing her way through the crowd in his direction. "What I say is this: God's kingdom belongs to little ones like these."

"He's no right to say that," Hannah murmured, moving closer to the inner circle.

"Whoever does not receive the kingdom of God like a child, Jacob," the rabbi continued, "will never enter it."

"He sins by even touching those children," Hannah spewed under her breath, now closing in on the rabbi through the human wall surrounding him.

Yeshua lifted up the child in his arms. "Whoever becomes humble like this child is the greatest in God's kingdom."

Hannah forced herself through the innermost row surrounding Yeshua, into the open.

"Whoever welcomes such a child in my name welcomes me."

"STOP!" she screamed, rushing at Yeshua. "He's no right to hold a child!"

Peter's rough hands, calloused from the nets, caught her before she reached the rabbi. Frightened mothers gathered their children, afraid of what this disturbed woman might do.

Hannah's screams kept up. "Yeshua's no teacher, but a hypocrite!"

"She's possessed," shouted several men close by. Others began to pick up stones, thinking to drive her off.

"He slept with me last night. He paid me for his pleasures!"

Her last shout silenced the crowd. Eyes not fixed on her shifted to the rabbi.

Yeshua stepped toward Hannah. "Why do you say these things, daughter?"

"You wanted me last night," she cooed, "why don't you want me now? Or would you have me come to you later, without all these eyes to see your lusts?"

Peter squeezed her arms tighter. "The rabbi spent last night in the boats with us, fishing till dawn. You break the commandments with lies."

"There've been other nights," she protested, hoping to mark Yeshua with some scandal in the ears and eyes of the crowd. "I whored for years in Caesarea before bringing my trade to Galilee. He's purchased me many times. And others, too."

"Lies!" shouted Peter, spinning her so that he glared at her face as he shook her. "Lies!" He raised one hand to slap her, only to have Yeshua catch his wrist.

"Let her go." The words came quiet but firm.

The fisherman scowled, but obeyed.

"I've never seen you before tonight." Yeshua paused, while he looked closely at her face. "Or have I? At Magdala. You, and another man. You listened to my teaching."

That Yeshua remembered her face from among so many, from only one encounter, unnerved her. Hannah wanted to level more accusations. But his recognition caught her off-guard. "Peter," Yeshua began, not taking his eyes from Hannah, "return home with the others. I will speak with this woman to see what troubles her so."

"It is unseemly, Rabbi. To be with such a woman, and alone, at night."

"She herself said she was a whore," added Judas.

"This is the company your rabbi keeps?" scoffed Jacob.

"A teacher doesn't school those already wise," Yeshua rebutted, "and those who would help the unrighteous cannot always be at prayer. Leave us, unless you think me too weak to defend myself from her."

Judas looked to Jacob, who rolled his eyes and walked away. The disciples followed an angry Peter to his home. The onlookers dispersed, more than a few tongues wagging in disgust. At last, only Yeshua and Hannah remained in the synagogue's courtyard.

"You and I need not waste time in falsehoods. Why do you slander me?"

If she could not ruin him with perjuries, Hannah decided to impale Yeshua with truth. "My dead brother David. With whom you and I once played in Bethlehem's stable. You are the reason he is dead!"

CHAPTER XL

Tiberias took shape in lamps flickering through windows and nearly-spent torches on the docks. Julius had no awareness of time since bolting from Capernaum. Early on, he abandoned the road for the beach. At times he spurred his horse through the shallows, soaking rider and mount. Wind from the gallop buffeted wet clothing and numbed skin, but Julius didn't care. He sought the deadening of flesh and mind to Hannah. Or was it to himself? Julius had vividly recalled David's murder when she described it. He hated himself for enabling that murder, and others with it. And he hated himself for breaking his promise to Hannah of never lettering anyone hurt her. Tonight, he'd hurt her deeply, as surely as he had wounded the little girl he could now visualize in his mind's eye, kneeling beside her dead brother in Bethlehem.

His mind continued to ramble. Long ago, Julius gave up any belief in Rome's gods. Too many stories mimicked human lusts and infirmities. The god of the Jews, though admirable, proved impotent: unable to save innocent children from Herod's barbarism, or Hannah from rape. With no gods left to blaspheme, Julius cursed himself. The idea of returning to his villa repulsed him. Its memories of Hannah's sight and smell and touch would only plague him. Julius needed refuge. Better yet, amnesia. Once in Tiberias, he reined his horse down a street into the courtyard of an inn. Leaving his horse in its stable, Julius half-ran across the courtyard to a door. The latch proved unyielding. "You in there," he yelled, "I need food and drink!"

Footsteps sounded inside. "We're done for the night,"

replied a youthful voice.

"I'll make it worth your while." Julius slid a silver denarius under the door. "Let me in, and you'll have another."

Julius heard another voice call out, then more footsteps. "Be warned," came an older man's growl, "if you've come for thieving, legionnaires barrack here tonight."

"I seek your board, not your coins."

A bar slid through iron brackets, and the door opened. "Well, come in then, and be quick about it." The innkeep led Julius to a table. "There's only bread and cold stew left."

"That'll do. And have your young helper there tend my horse. He's lathered and needs grooming for the night." Julius handed another denarius to the innkeep.

"I've work to do in the kitchen," protested Demas. "And I'm no stable boy."

Joshua pocketed the coin, worth far more than the job's value. "This gentleman's money says you are a stable boy. Get to it."

Demas headed to the stable while Joshua went into the kitchen. The innkeeper returned with a chunk of bread and a bowl of stew, then fetched a pitcher of wine and goblet. After filling the goblet, Joshua started to return to the kitchen with the pitcher.

"Don't bother taking that away," Julius said.

"There's much inside, sir," the innkeeper warned, "from Galilee's best vineyards."

Julius threw another denarius on the table. "Here's for your trouble." Julius downed the goblet's sweet red juice in one drink, then refilled it. "How about you? If you're through for the night, you can keep me company."

Joshua bowed stiffly and went to get a goblet for himself. As free as this Roman had been with his silver, Joshua surmised a friendly ear could prove profitable, not to mention gaining information for Jacob. When Joshua returned, Julius was well into the goblet's third filling. Joshua vaguely remembered the man having come here the week or so before. But wasn't there a woman then? "A lathered horse, and the way you drink, makes me think you have pursuers."

"You judge yourself a diviner?"

Joshua sipped his wine. "Meeting others' needs is my business, sir. If I can gauge what brings a man to seek table or bed, or company at either, then I can better serve him."

"I see." The wine and a fire in the hearth warmed Julius. "Tell me, oracle, other than having a wraith at his heels, what makes a man ride hard on a moonless night?"

"A debt's accounting. Some news to bear." Joshua paused, thinking back to the first time he'd seen this stranger. "Maybe a woman."

Julius tipped his goblet to the innkeep. "And what do you charge for your insights?"

Joshua's lips parted in a smile. "The service comes free with the wine. Though some say the wine drunk by others sharpens my intuition."

"Here's to intuition." Julius quaffed the last of the goblet's wine, then poured it full a fourth time. The grapes were providing his consciousness with a welcomed dulling. "I'd say you've spotted my pursuers well. So you're right, innkeep, or oracle, or whatever you are."

"Thank you." Joshua tipped his goblet to the Roman. "What is it you're called?"

"Julius. And yourself?"

"Joshua."

"Joshua?" Julius dipped his bread in the wine, softening the hard crust before chewing off a piece. "A Jew's name."

"By birth, though it's been some time since a synagogue heard my prayers."

Julius nodded. "Seems we've each given up part of our births, to get where we are now." The Roman wiped his lips and chin with his sleeve. "But I'd venture this, Joshua of Tiberias, it's not just wine sloshing between my ears that allows you to read my life."

Joshua laughed. "Then you think me gifted with prophecy by some god?" At least this drunk proved more entertaining than most at his tables.

"No." Julius' tone grew somber to the point of accusatory. "I say you can read me, because your own ledger looks the same. Like knows like, they say. Tell me, what chased this Jew to land in a city built over a cemetery? A debt, some news – a woman?"

The sudden twist in conversation caught Joshua off-guard. Without thought of consequences, he blurted, "A family, who count me dead."

Julius finished swilling his wine. His attempt to pour again left only a little more in the goblet than on the table. "Then we've both cause to mourn, Joshua. You, for a life you had. Me, for one I thought in hand. Only to have some rabbi snatch it away."

"Rabbi? I didn't think you to be a Jew?"

Julius eyes' lost focus. The room's heat became a thick blanket. Words slowed. "I'm not, but she is. Same as Yeshua."

Yeshua. Joshua knew of Jacob's interest in him. Maybe the Roman learned something that might be of value for Jacob. "Yeshua? The Nazarene rabbi?"

"Nazarene? Wish that he were." Julius laid his head on the table, thoughts rambling into dreamlike images. Horses. Children. Swords. "Same as she," he slurred, "Bethlehem."

Though Julius' first words were inaudible, the final one rung clear. "Bethlehem? What of Bethlehem?" Joshua spoke right into the Roman's ear, only inches away.

To Julius, the innkeeper's voice sounded as though it came from the top of some deep well into which he'd fallen. "Bethlehem, not Nazareth. Yeshua's from Bethlehem." With his remaining strength, Julius strained to lift his head. Tears filled his eyes. "Herod wanted him dead. But the others died. Children. All but Yeshua."

Julius' head slumped to the table, asleep. Joshua pressed his fingertips against his forehead, kneading its folds. Those ridges had been etched by a past long set aside. But the Roman's words made the furrows ache, as if all the pain that ploughed them returned. And, in truth, at this linking of Yeshua and Bethlehem and Herod and children – it had.

* * *

Yeshua's face froze. The image of a cave's rock wall flashed in his mind. "David?"

"Don't you dare deny it!" Hannah seethed with anger. "Don't you dare deny HIM!"

"I don't," he said quietly, words catching in his throat. "I remember him. My parents kept his name before me for years, so I'd not forget." Yeshua lifted his eyes to Hannah's. "And they spoke of a twin sister to David – I remember her, too."

"You mean me!"

"Hannah?"

Hannah drew her right hand back, then swung it full force into his cheek. The crack sounded as sharp as a whip's snap. "Murderer!"

Yeshua stood still. His next words came as almost a whisper. "I've been there."

Hannah caught no connection between the slap and his response. "Been where?"

"I was almost twelve when my father took me there. To Bethlehem's cave, with the rock wall inside. Where I was born. Now a burial pit."

"You want my sympathy?" she sneered in outrage at his words. "Let me tell you of my childhood, rabbi. Because of your family's sneaking away without warning, David died. My family divided. At the same age when you shed false tears in Bethlehem's cave, I provided a troop of Romans with a full night's sport in the Antonia's basement as they made a whore of me! That cave and that basement is what you do to children, Yeshua! And tonight, you dared hold a child in your arms to speak of God's kingdom? You, whose hands are stained bone-deep with the blood of Bethlehem's children? How I hate you, Yeshua! I hate you!"

Hannah punctuated her cries by pounding her fists against his chest. Yeshua received the blows, until her striking finally subsided in wails of anguish and tears. When her whole body shook, Yeshua put his hands on her shoulders and gently held on to her.

Hannah lost track of how long her trembling continued. It was only when she became aware of catching her breath between sobs that she felt his hands. At first, Hannah wanted to wrench away from him, or pummel Yeshua again. But somehow, his holding seemed an anchor against the raging inside of her. Hannah thought it a dream when she felt the sensation of fury ebbing from her body – surging out of her shoulders into his hands. She stole a glance at the rabbi, almost afraid of what she might see.

Yeshua looked skyward, where clouds concealed any hint of star or moon. Tears streamed down his face. His neck muscles tightened while his jaw clenched as if in pain. She felt no evidence of pain in his hands, though. They neither clenched her shoulders, nor pulled back from them. They rested, steady. His lips moved in words unspoken.

Hannah closed her eyes. She saw breakers of the Great Sea crashing into Caesarea's seawall, churned by wind and tides. In her mind's sight, the breakers slowly became waves, softly rolling, gently massaging the once-pounded shore. In time, the waves quieted to a calm sea, whose only movement seemed more like breathing. The waters rose and fell in rhythm with the filling and emptying of her lungs. She watched herself dive into that sea's deep waters. The currents buoyed her up. Her movement no longer came in struggle, but in rest.

"Hannah."

A liquid voice spilled over her, lifting her from the water.

"Hannah."

When she opened her eyes, Hannah saw Yeshua draw back his hands from her. Although she feared to touch them, something in their appearance made her think those hands had been seared with heat. And she'd not imagined Yeshua's tears before. While they flowed no longer, their streaking persisted on his face.

"I spoke of my hatred," she began unsteadily, seeking words for what escaped words, "and now I feel, I feel, light. Not empty, but light. I don't understand."

"Nor do I understand Bethlehem. So many innocents killed. And I lived."

Hannah looked at Yeshua. She saw no deceit. At first she hesitated, but then brought a hand to his. It felt warm to the touch. "You were only a child." Hannah knew neither why nor from where those words came, but come they did. "You merit no blame."

Yeshua's look embraced her. "For what you held against me all these years, you show great forgiveness, daughter."

"Rabbi, forgive me. Forgive me." Hannah's head lowered.

His hand lifted her chin until her eyes faced his. "God's forgiveness is already yours. That is what you experienced."

"I thought it to be, I don't know, maybe some type of healing."

"Many find it hard to distinguish between the two." Yeshua offered. "Perhaps because they're often the same."

Hannah looked at Galilee's waters. "I've been told the Baptizer preached sin's loosing required washing by water. I would be grateful, Rabbi, if I might receive such baptism by you."

Yeshua nodded, and they walked toward Galilee's shore. "I am the grateful one, Hannah. My father went to his grave regretting he didn't warn your family and the others. He thought ignorance of our flight would protect them, protect you. But Herod chose slaughter over reason." The sound of water lapping on the beach accompanied Yeshua's confession. "For that, innocents like David died instead of me." Yeshua stopped at the water's edge, as did Hannah. "When my work becomes exacting, or an easier life beckons, I bring their deaths to mind. My father told me never to forget those children in Bethlehem, Hannah. And you are the first of their families whom I've had opportunity to tell this. As I said: tonight, I am the one to be grateful."

Hannah waded with Yeshua into the shallows of the lake. The water's cold stung at first. She knelt down, hands clasped before her face and head bowed. Yeshua prayed.

"Behold the daughter of your fashioning, Abba, Hannah of Bethlehem, sister of David." Yeshua dipped his cupped hands into the lake and lifted them above her. *"Bless these waters as they wash over your child."* His fingers spread open over Hannah's head, the water running down in small streams upon her. *"Put sin behind her, and new life before her. Help her walk as a daughter borne of your holy name and spirit."*

Yeshua lifted Hannah by the arm, so that they stood together. He pressed one cheek to her face, then repeated the gesture on the other side. "God's forgiveness lays this discipline upon you, Hannah. To forgive others."

As they walked to shore, Hannah thought back to the other man with whom she'd gone to this lake tonight. "Yeshua, may I follow you? To learn how to forgive?"

Yeshua stopped, not far from where Hannah watched Julius ride into the night. "Learning comes in practice."

Hannah winced.

"But yes," he continued, noting her reaction, "follow me. You'll be in the company of others who strive every day to learn that same lesson."

"Rabbi, there is one whom I must speak to first. A man, the one with me in Magdala? He is, well, a Roman. And – "

Yeshua nodded. "Stay with the other women who follow me tonight. In the morning, you can set out."

"I came on horseback, so I won't be gone more than a

day or so. Where shall I find you?"

"Rejoin us here in Capernaum. We can talk of your family – and Rebekah's."

Hannah barely heard these last words. She had so many questions about what to say to Julius, other concerns paled. Besides, not since leaving Jerusalem had she heard of the widow Rebekah. And whatever became of her surviving son? With the honor given to the martyred Elias, Hannah felt sure their lives must have taken a far more peaceful and secure path than hers.

* * *

The courtyard of the Antonia was ringed by torches to illuminate the interrogation about to take place. Often used for ceremonies of the legion or banquets of the procurator, the courtyard tonight had a far different purpose. Legionnaires with spears lined its perimeter. Pilate sat in the judgment chair. To the right of Pilate was a more modest chair for Pilate's guest, Nathaniel. Glaucas, tribune of the Jerusalem cohort, stood at Pilate's left. An empty chair sat in the courtyard's center. A centurion's helmet and cloak hung on its back.

The sound of approaching footsteps drifted into the courtyard. Pilate rose. The cohort snapped to attention. A squadron of soldiers entered, led by the centurion Antony. Behind him, a pair of soldiers toward an unconscious man by the arms, his feet sliding on the flagstone. On reaching Pilate's judgment chair, the patrol stopped. Antony saluted his commanders.

"Procurator, Tribune!" He clapped his fist unusually hard against his breastplate, the metal stinging his hand. "The prisoner Barabbas."

The soldiers dragging the prisoner stepped forward from the column and threw Barabbas to the ground. Antony saw Nathaniel next to Pilate and felt a sour taste in his mouth.

"Well done, centurion." Pilate stepped down from the

small platform used to elevate his chair, grasping the centurion's forearms. "Well done."

"Thank you," came a stiff reply.

"Glaucas, see that this centurion and his troop are given *armillae* bearing the name of Lucius. And an extra week's pay."

"As you wish, procurator." The tribune spoke earlier with Pilate about rewarding the detail once they came back with Barabbas. Such a gesture, he advised, might help Pilate restore his stature in the legion's eyes after Caesarea's embarrassment.

"You are dismissed." Pilate saluted the men who brought in Barabbas. "But you, centurion, join me by my judgment seat. You've earned a share in this night's proceedings."

Antony bowed his head. "Your invitation honors me, but my place is with my men."

"I insist, centurion. Rejoin your troop after we're finished here." Pilate paused, then drew his leg back and kicked the unconscious Barabbas in the side.

The thud sickened Antony. He hoped punishment would be swift. Following Pilate onto the platform, Antony stood beside Glaucas. He wanted nothing to do with Nathaniel.

Pilate motioned to two burly Egyptian guards, who came forward and placed a bucket of water in front of the prisoner. "Take off his gag and wake our guest."

The two men plunged Barabbas' head into the water. As he came to, they continued holding his head under until his legs, tied at the ankles, flailed and his head banged into the bucket. Antony turned away, only to see Nathaniel look at him and nod.

When Barabbas' submerged screams and gasps weakened, Pilate ordered his head drawn up. The procurator stepped off the platform.

Barabbas choked for air as he spit out water still bearing suds from the kitchen's scrubbing. "What!" he cried out, then looking at Pilate, "Who are –"

The procurator struck Barabbas across the mouth with his *flagrum's* leather thongs. Typically used to scourge a prisoner's back, the small lead balls and sharpened bits of bone at the thongs' ends split open the prisoner's lips and cheek.

"Show respect to Rome!" shouted Pilate. "What have you to say for yourself, murderer?"

Barabbas spit out blood and bits of teeth cracked off by the flagrum's impact. In spite of the pain, he glared at Pilate. "I say the Lord Almighty will spill Roman blood to free our land."

Pilate cracked the flagrum across the brow of Barabbas, narrowly missing his eyes. Blood streaming down his eyebrows dimmed Barabbas' sight. "That's odd, Zealot. I see no blood being spilled but yours. Perhaps your god has taken Rome's side."

"I think not, Gentile." Barabbas answered, before swishing his face in the bucket's water in hopes of clearing the blood away.

Pilate looked down on Barabbas and clicked his tongue in mock pity. "Rome is merciful." Taking a centurion's cloak that draped the arm of his judgment seat, Pilate wiped the blood from Barabbas' eyes and forehead. "Do you know this cloak, Barabbas?"

The prisoner said no word.

"Then let me tell you. It belonged to an honored soldier of our legion named Lucius. But some spineless bastard murdered him in his bath, a coward who feared to face him in battle."

"Let's be done with games!" Barabbas grimaced at his captor. "But if you'd speak of cowards, count this dead centurion above them all. His sword drew children's blood years ago, my brother among them. Lucius deserved the death he got, and far worse!"

"Let me tell you of death!" Pilate seized Barabbas by the hair, jerking his head back. "Your tongue wags bravely now. But you'll soon beg for death's mercies. And when it's time to die, I may still keep you alive, to feel even more pain. Do you understand me?"

"Oh, I understand. I understand the Lord God of Hosts will bare his arm and fling your kind onto Gehenna's heap with the rest of Jerusalem's stinking shit! May the God of–"

Pilate's flagrum whipped into Barabbas' face once more. "Silence! SILENCE!" Pilate ordered Barabbas draped chest-first across the chair in the center of the courtyard, then had him scourged across the back until the prisoner lost consciousness.

In the spectacle of Barabbas beaten and bloodied, Antony saw the truth of his own life. Try as he might to renounce it, he remained the son of Joshua: once by birth, now by deed. He had handed over to die one who once was as kin. Long-forgotten words from Jeremiah's scroll pounded inside Antony's head: *The fathers have eaten sour grapes, and the children's teeth are set on edge.* The harvest had come full circle.

CHAPTER XLI

Rebekah's body convulsed in sleep beneath the thick naps of a fleece blanket. Soldiers seizing her son, Abraham's mutilated hand – she screamed to wake herself. As she woke, she felt Naomi stroke beads of sweat from her face.

"My son," Rebekah whispered. "I have to see my son."

Rebekah caught sight of another figure leaning over her, whose hands restrained her when she tried to sit up. They belonged to Rabbi, Joachin.

"Lie back down, Rebekah. You need to rest."

"I must see Barabbas." Her voice grew louder. "Let me see my son!"

Joachin looked to Naomi's pallid face, then back to Rebekah. "He's not here, Rebekah. Do you remember last night?"

Rebekah tried to remember. An argument with Abraham, the door crashing in, a knife, a fist . . . "But that was just a dream," she protested. As she spoke, a sharp pain shot through her jaw. In the dream, she'd been kicked there. "No! Naomi, it's not true!"

Naomi nodded her head. "It is. They came."

"Abraham!" Rebekah's shout caused her jaw's pain to shoot behind her ear.

The rabbi firmed his grip. "Abraham is in my home. He lost several fingers and much blood, but I'm told he'll recover. We've sent riders to the New Damascus elders with the news."

Rebekah lie still. "And my son? What do you know?"

Joachin tugged at his beard. "Only what Naomi told

me. A Roman patrol took him."

"I remember nothing being said. Naomi, did they speak after I was struck down?"

Naomi closed her eyes and shook her head. "No."

"Several men from the village followed their tracks this morning," the rabbi offered. "They lead north, on the Jerusalem road."

Rebekah braced herself with her arms, then sat up. "The Antonia."

Joachin bent close to Rebekah's ear. "Those who went to New Damascus promised to speak with your friends among the Zealots. For help."

"If my son lies in the Antonia, he is beyond help."

"You mustn't give up hope," the rabbi offered. "The Almighty delivered the three from the furnace, and Daniel from the lions, and Elijah from Ahab and Jezebel. Trust in Elohim, Rebekah."

Rebekah stared hard at the young rabbi. "These are not the former times, Rabbi. The Romans don't take prisoners to the Antonia so that they may be set free. I can only hope Barabbas honors us with a martyr's death, like his father before him."

"Don't give up on your son's life," Naomi said. "Deliverance may yet come to Barabbas."

"Did deliverance come to our youngest sons, Naomi? Or to my Elias?" Rebekah resented these false hopes. "My son and I chose this path. It's his lot now to die well, and mine to accept it." Rebekah stood and went to a basin filled with water. She began to wash her hands and face.

The rabbi grimaced at her outburst and muttered to Naomi, "May Elohim Adonai have mercy upon her. Life has hardened Rebekah to the Lord's saving hand."

Naomi glared at Joachin. "Her hardness comes not from life, Rabbi, but death. Pray you never hold a murdered spouse and child in your arms, or carry such memories every waking hour." Naomi rose, her own face flushing. "Until you do, take care how easily you judge."

* * *

"I don't trust her," mumbled Peter, tearing off a piece from the loaf before passing it on. "Not only for the evil she accused you of, but doing it in front of everyone."

"And Jacob, especially. He's so close to allying with us."

Yeshua stared at Judas. "We've spoken of this before. Much still divides us from Jacob."

"More than what's between us and that madwoman?" Judas had made uniting Jacob and Yeshua his personal quest. Having been a disciple of Jacob's before choosing to follow Yeshua, Judas envisioned how powerful the two could be together. Last night's incident, first with the children and then with the Jewess, agitated him.

"Her name is Hannah, and she is no madwoman," Yeshua replied in a calm voice. "As I said, I baptized her in Galilee's waters and welcomed her to stay with us."

"Then why did she leave so early?" Peter's mother-in-law asked while placing a bowl of grain mixed with warm goat's milk before Yeshua. "She came to my door earlier last night asking of you. And with a Roman at her side."

"A Roman!" Judas exclaimed, throwing his arms in the air. "Rabbi, she could be a spy for all we know. Sent from Herod, or even Pilate."

Peter folded his arms on his chest. "We must learn more before she's given a place."

The loaf came round to Yeshua. He tore off a piece. "Levi," he sighed, turning to the former tax collector among his disciples, "when I called you to follow me, did I first insist on looking at your account books? To see who you had cheated and by how much?"

A thin man with a close-trimmed beard laughed. "No, rabbi. And if you had, I might have warned you there were too many such entries to take up your time!" Others in the courtyard joined in Levi's laughter, including some who formerly had their taxes exacted by him.

"Tell me this," Yeshua continued, "Have you cheated anyone since?"

Levi's face clouded, his mind struggling to recall some detail he might have overlooked. "Not to my knowledge."

"Nor to mine," the rabbi reassured Levi. "When God works forgiveness in a person's life, the old is put aside to give the new a chance to grow. That's how it's been with each of you. So don't require me to treat Hannah any different than I've treated every single one of you at this table. She sought forgiveness from God, and a new life, and I baptized her. So be it."

"But she still may turn on you," protested Peter.

"As may any one of you." Yeshua's retort hushed the circle. "What we do with the grace God bestows is left to us. To you, Peter, Levi. And Judas: all of you. And now to Hannah."

"We only seek to protect you from harm's reach, at the hands of a stranger."

"I understand, Judas." Yeshua looked him, and then the others. "But harm draws closest, and cuts deepest, when it comes in familiar guise. Be on guard, that you don't look so hard for sin in others that you fail to see its grip upon your own life."

Yeshua passed the loaf into Judas' hands.

* * *

Julius staggered up the front steps of the whitewashed stone villa. The residue from last night's wine pounded each step inside his head. His back also protested the climb, having slept through the morning and into the early afternoon bent over a table at Joshua's inn. But Julius had to return to make the arrangements filling his mind after he woke. He would instruct the servants to give Hannah use of the villa as long as she desired. After gathering a few clothes and necessities, Julius would set out for Hammath. A long soak in the springs, then he'd be gone. Maybe Caesarea. Maybe Jericho. He didn't know where. Just away from here.

"You in there!" he called out, expecting a maidservant's response. "It's Julius."

The door opened, but Julius froze when he saw the one inside. "Hannah?"

Her hand motioned him inside. "Please. We must talk."

Julius restrained his urge to embrace her. Hannah walked to several cushions strewn on the floor and sat. He followed her lead.

"Hannah, before you speak: the villa is yours. I came back only to get my things."

She shook her head. "Stay here, Julius. It's what you planned for yourself."

"No. I've done enough without forcing you to go back to Caesarea."

"I'm not returning to Caesarea." What she had to say next still amazed her, but Hannah wanted Julius to know. "I ride back to Capernaum. To follow the rabbi Yeshua."

"You what?!" The words shot from Julius' mouth. "Follow as in track down, or as in – "

"Disciple."

Astonishment overwhelmed shame. "Last night, you wanted to kill him for what he did to you, to your family! Now you want to follow him?"

"It's difficult to explain. I found him last night after you left. I confronted him in front of his followers, and many others. I charged that he whored with me."

"To disgrace him," Julius interjected. He understood her strategy, as well as its risks. "You know, they might have stoned you on the spot for such an accusation."

"I didn't care, so long as I took Yeshua down, after all he'd taken from me. And after you left –" Words failed Hannah for a moment, then she continued. "I only wanted to hurt him."

"And did you?"

"No one believed. One of his followers seized me, and

was about to strike me when Yeshua forbade him. Then the rabbi told the others to go, that he wanted to talk with me." A tear rolled down her cheek. As she brushed it aside, another followed. Then another.

"Hannah, I've put you through enough pain. You needn't go on."

"I have to. I told him of Bethlehem, and David, and my hatred." Hannah looked down at her hands. "I went into a rage, beating his chest, as if I could drive the breath from him. But after letting me pound at him till my strength left, he took hold of me."

Julius felt a surge, whether of jealousy or gratitude he couldn't be sure. "The rabbi didn't hurt you, did he?"

"Hurt me?" Hannah's voice softened, sounding in Julius's ears as that of a young girl. "Julius, he healed me. Healed me of the pain I've carried all these years. Of my hatred for him. Of the way I've hated myself. He assures my forgiveness by God. And I trust him."

"It seems to me his god should be the one asking your forgiveness for what's been done."

"That's how I thought all these years. But it gained me nothing but resentment. And today, I have peace."

Julius reached for her hand. To his surprise, she didn't pull away. "Then I'm grateful to this Yeshua. You deserve a new life, Hannah. I only wish," Julius paused, then drew away his hand, "well, it does no good now, knowing what's passed between us."

Hannah looked at the hand Julius touched. "I told Yeshua I wanted to follow him, so I could learn to forgive." Lifting her face to his, she struggled to express what knotted deep inside of her. "I want to learn how to forgive you, Julius. Because of what Yeshua said that night in Magdala: there can be no love without forgiveness."

The pair sat in silence.

Finally, Hannah broke the quiet. "I must return to Capernaum."

Julius nodded. Hannah leaned over and pressed her lips to his forehead, then stood. Once she started down the stairs, Julius called out, "I'll understand if you can't forgive for me, Hannah. I've never been able to forgive myself for Bethlehem."

Hannah looked back one final time. "Then maybe you should come with me, to seek Yeshua's healing for yourself."

"Go to him, Hannah. No god who could untangle what I've done. Much less some child-become-healer I once sought out to kill."

Hannah got on her horse and headed to the north. Julius pulled the door shut and leaned back against it, shoulders sagging, suddenly feeling very old. And very alone.

* * *

Fleeting sunbreaks teased warmth this winter afternoon. The ravine that passed as a road between Capernaum and Chorazin strained Judas' legs. He paused to relax on a ledge jutting out from the basalt. Some say Adonai carved this bench to give Father Abraham a resting place on his sojourn from Haran. A few hundred feet below Judas, the lake waters glistened, then dulled, in a shifting game played with sun and clouds. Above him, the gully twisted out of sight.

"Judas!"

Looking up and to the left, he saw Jacob waving. "Yes, Jacob." A short ridge jutted between Judas and the Zealot. "I'll be up in a few minutes."

"No, wait there. It's easier for me to come down."

Judas offered no protest. He watched the Zealot leader pick his way with ease across the rocks. Jacob's father Judas and grandfather Hezekiah once warred against foreign troops from these heights. As long as they kept within range of its caves and cliffs, they prospered. Only when Hezekiah ventured out against Antipater, and Judas against Herod, did both fall victim. Judas wondered if this generation of Galileans rebels would cling more closely to these hills, forcing the Romans to fight on its ambush-laden paths.

Jacob skidded down the ridge's lower face, scattering a dry shower of pebbles and dust.

"You get around these boulders better than the goats."

Jacob grinned and brushed off the bottom hem of his robe. "If we'd had rain last night, my backside would still be sliding."

"About last night." Judas knew he'd have to deal with that disappointment, and just as well now than later. "You have to forgive Yeshua for being distracted by that woman. The rabbi's compassion outstrips his judgment at times."

"Compassion, eh? For a moment, I thought she'd caught him with the truth. And for that, I wouldn't have blamed him either. She was finely cut."

Judas furrowed his brow. "Jacob, how can you even think that? Yeshua keeps the law more closely than any Pharisee."

"He's a man, Judas. Men can't help but look at such a woman and wonder."

"You don't believe –"

"No, no, I can't see your Yeshua jeopardizing himself even for her favors." Jacob leaned over, running his finger between foot and sandal to dislodge bits of rock. "But you have to admit, he does allow questionable sorts into his company."

"They stay on the fringes, not the inner circle."

Jacob tugged on the beard of Judas. "Judas, this is Jacob you're talking to. Levi is of the twelve, the tax collector who gouged the people of Capernaum for years; the one whom more than a few still think his discipleship to be little more than a convenient escape from his just rewards. It wasn't long ago there was talk of using him as anchor for the fish nets some night."

Judas sank onto the ledge. "Are you saying you've given up on Yeshua?"

"Not yet." Jacob sat beside Judas on the ledge. "You and I have been friends for years. When you told me of your call to pursue this Yeshua, the one thing that lessened my sadness came in what I, too, had heard of him. This wise teacher of Torah, this healer, the whispers even of Messiah among us. But it's been almost three years!"

Jacob cast a hand-sized stone down the slope. They watched it tumble and bounce, picking up speed before disappearing into a deep hole between boulders. "It's hard to stand on tiptoe this long, if you see nothing more on the horizon than before. And when he wallows in love of enemies, instead of freedom for our people – you tell me, Judas, is this the Messiah who will deliver us? The Messiah my father and grandfather died in hope of welcoming? Is he?"

"He must be waiting for the right time, the right place." Judas' inflection left it unclear whether he offered statement or question.

"Did he say anything new of Jerusalem?"

The sun broke through the clouds. Judas lifted his face to catch its warming rays. "After breakfast, he said he would keep Hanukkah with his family in Nazareth this month. But come spring, we'd make pilgrimage to Jerusalem. For the Passover."

"Good," declared Jacob. "A number of us will soon be meeting with Barabbas and our Judean brothers, to plan a fit reception for the procurator's first Passover in the city."

"This could work well," Judas enthused. "Perhaps Passover will finally unite us all."

Jacob stood. Already, the sun lowered in the sky as it approached the western rim of hills whose roots reached under Galilee's sea. "Yeshua's time to join us runs short. We will see what comes of his Passover in Jerusalem."

CHAPTER XLII

Julius awoke to the sound of a flapping sail. The rope used to wrap the canvas around the mast swung loose. An uncorked wine jug rolled free between the boat's wale and his shoulders. Whatever wine left before Julius dozed had long since soaked into the planks. The Roman's eyes squinted as he rolled onto his back. When he'd set out this morning, a light breeze descended from a cobalt sky. The wind's dying led him to pull up sail and partake of bread and a jug of sweet Galilean vintage. But as he slept, clouds gathered. The latter rains could still be expected into the month of Nisan, of which this day was the first. Julius breathed in deep to rouse himself. The smell of fish drifted into his nostrils, as did the sweet aroma of approaching rain.

Julius grabbed hold of the rope waving from the triangular sail's free corner and secured it to the boom. At once, the wind billowed out the cloth. Holding the boom-rope in one hand and a crude rudder in the other, he steered toward the beach below Tiberias. Julius muttered a word of thanks about the rope coming free, as the sail's fluttering had roused him. Storms rose quickly on these waters. Another half hour of sleep would have brought serious trouble. Even then, the landing was rough. Not wanting to risk lowering sail early, which would have meant dragging the boat through waves already piling up near shore, Julius left the sail in place till the last moment. The coarse scraping of wood on gravel and an abrupt stop disclosed he waited too long. With the help of several nearby fishermen who'd been mending nets, Julius dragged the boat onshore. After tying a rope from the bow to an anchor ring sunk in an outcrop of rock, Julius stepped back in and busied himself lashing sail to mast. So busy he took no notice of a figure who approached the boat's side.

"Julius?"

"What is it?" he grumbled. The mounting wind muffled the stranger's voice, and the Roman never bothered to look as he hastened to finish his work.

"It's me. Hannah."

Weathered hands stopped in the middle of a knot. He turned, fearing his ears betrayed him. It had been months since they last spoke. But his eyes did not deceive. "Hannah."

"Please, finish what you're doing."

Julius looked back at an unraveling knot. "Just a few seconds," he said, retightening the knot, then doubling it over for safety. He began to step over the boat's side, pausing only to kick the wine jug underneath the plank seat.

"Your servant told me you were sailing today."

"I was till this storm started up." Julius looked north, where a veil of rain quickly advanced in their direction. "We might make the villa before the clouds open up."

Several times on the brisk walk up the hillside, Julius caught himself glancing at Hannah. He wanted to speak, but could think of no fit words. They reached the villa as the first drops fell: a splattering of heavy loud plops, pocking dust here and there; then, a hard pounding of windborne sheets, blocking sight and cascading off the roof; and finally, a gentler but steady shower that would soak the ground rather than wash it away. From the villa's sheltered porch, they watched the rain's changing dance on rooftops and lake.

When the shower's sound became almost imperceptible, Hannah turned to Julius, both unsure of what was to follow. "Julius, I come to ask a favor of you."

"A favor? Anything, Hannah. Anything at all."

Hannah lowered her eyes for a moment, then took his right hand in hers. When she lifted her face, tears flowed down and streaked her cheeks.

Julius softly squeezed her hand. "How can I help you?"

"It's not me in need of help, Julius," she began. "The favor I ask is for Yeshua."

* * *

Joshua stared out the door. The storm turned the inn's courtyard into a thick stew of mud. White flagstones leading to the outer gate disappeared under slick brown clay spattered up by the cloudburst. Closing the door, Joshua walked back into the eating hall. The sole patron was working on a meal of goat cheese and barley bread. Joshua pulled up a chair and spoke.

"I've not seen your master Jacob for three weeks. I've no news to share, beyond rumors of whether Barabbas is still imprisoned or perhaps has already been put to death."

The young man sopped a piece of bread in his wine, a sour look curling his lips downward. "He's not here. Gone without taking me, just when things grow interesting."

Joshua glanced to check the whereabouts of Demas. He could see his helper in the kitchen, stirring the evening's stew of lamb and leeks. "What things grow interesting, Caleb?"

"Jerusalem." Caleb chewed off the wine-soaked crust, a small purple trickle dripping down his chin. "And Yeshua."

"The rabbi?"

Caleb's eyes narrowed. "I don't know if Jacob would have me say more, Joshua."

"You know Jacob trusts me, Caleb. We three have sat at this very table when I've passed on information to him. And he to me. Didn't he confide the details of Jericho's murder, even the name of Barabbas who carried it out, and then his capture?"

"That may be true, Joshua. But Jacob left me behind."

A hint of complaint in Caleb's last words provided Joshua with an idea. "No doubt, he needed to leave one of his best men of arms in charge, to ensure Jacob's will be kept in his absence. And that's all the more reason to tell me of Jerusalem and Yeshua. I can serve as your informer, as I have for Jacob, if I know what to listen for at these tables."

Caleb took a drink from the chalice of wine before him. "You may be right, Joshua." The young man leaned forward. "Your cook's not within earshot, is he?"

"Demas? No, he fusses back in the kitchen. He can't hear us."

"Very well." Caleb lowered his voice further, just to be safe. "Yeshua and his followers travel to Jerusalem in the coming week, to observe the Passover there."

Joshua shrugged his shoulders. "I understand he's done that before."

"Maybe. But not with the reception planned for him by Jacob."

"Reception?"

"Jacob and the inner council have decided to force Yeshua's hand. Either he declares himself Messiah once and for all, or he rejects the title – and any hope of our support."

Joshua pondered the young man's news. Rumors of Yeshua as Messiah had floated through Galilee and over this inn's tables for nearly three years. Beyond that, there were the words of that drunken Roman who came to the inn months before, slurring out some connection of Yeshua to Bethlehem – words that, if accurate, tied Yeshua to Joshua's fate. Joshua wondered if the Roman spoke the truth, or just rambled in wine-sotted imagination. Words he dared not share even with Jacob, lest the Zealot dig into Joshua's connection to Bethlehem.

"Joshua!" Caleb had waited long enough for a reaction. "Have you been listening?"

"Yes, Caleb, of course. I was just thinking, though. Jacob knows how strongly Rabbi Yeshua has resisted that claim. Why should this Passover in Jerusalem be any different?"

Caleb soaked the remaining bread in his wine. Perhaps he'd told the innkeeper too much already. But, as Joshua just assured him, Jacob had left him in charge. Caleb folded his arms and leaned closer to Joshua. "A demonstration is planned when he reaches the city, to greet him as king. If that fails to bring the rabbi's affirmation, he'll be turned over to the temple authorities. Charged with blasphemy, or sedition – whatever can be arranged."

"Those offenses call for death!"

Caleb ate the sop, then wiped his fingers and the corners of his mouth with the sleeve of his mantle. "That's the point. If he is Messiah, he'd have no choice but to say so."

"But if he's not?"

"Then we've the Sanhedrin or Pilate to remove him. There's no time to waste ourselves on pretenders. And Yeshua's taken too much of our time and the people's attention already."

"You'd let Yeshua die, even though he may be innocent of such charges?"

"That's why you wait tables, and I fight Rome." Caleb stood and tossed several copper mites in front of Joshua. "No one's innocent in life, innkeep. And if the rabbi's death hastens Israel's freedom, it's a small price to pay!"

Caleb sauntered out the door and plodded through the courtyard's mire. Joshua thought he should feel elation, or at least relief, with the news of what awaited Yeshua in Jerusalem. If the Roman had been right, the fate avoided in Bethlehem at the cost of so many others in his place loomed ahead for the rabbi. But instead of relief, Joshua found himself shaking. His lungs felt heavy as breathing grew more rapid. He remembered struggling for breath like this once before. When he knelt in one of Bethlehem's alleys. When other innocents died... including his own.

* * *

"Naomi," Rebekah called out again, "the men from New Damascus are waiting."

Inside the sleeping room, Naomi finished packing her belongings in a worn leather sack, and wrapped herself with a heavy winter mantle. Even though it was spring, a cold breeze blew hard from the north, as if directly from the snow still topping Mount Hermon.

"We must be going if we're to reach Jerusalem before nightfall. Can I help?"

"No, Rebekah, thank you." Naomi emerged from the room. Coals from the fire that earlier heated soup for lunch glowed a faint orange. Naomi walked to Rebekah, who warmed her hands by the coals. "I wish you'd let me talk to Nathaniel about your son. Maybe he could help."

Rebekah rubbed her hands together while she spoke. "No one can stop the execution. Public notice of the date has already been made."

Naomi's mind flashed to the night of his arrest, to eyes that flashed at her from above the centurion's mask, the eyes of her own son. "Perhaps The Lord will grant Saul deliverance – "

"My son's name is Barabbas, Yeshua Barabbas! And Elohim Adonai has seen fit to give him a martyr's death." Rebekah gazed into the eyes of her friend. "I've been a martyr's wife for thirty years, Naomi. The Everlasting One chooses me now to be a martyr's mother."

Naomi embraced Rebekah. "Are you sure you'll not stay with me at Nathaniel's?"

"I must be with my son's friends. We've much to discuss. And I," Rebekah continued in sharp tones, "have much to say to them about the traitor Yeshua."

Naomi thought to Abraham's visit on that terrible night, when he pleaded on Yeshua's behalf to Rebekah and Barabbas. A visit that cost him the better part of his hand by a Roman gladius in this very room. It seemed Yeshua still pained the families of Bethlehem.

"The men, Naomi. We must be leaving."

Rebekah and Naomi walked out to the wagon that would carry them to Jerusalem and the execution of Barabbas, decreed for the week of Passover.

* * *

"Yeshua? You ask a favor for your Rabbi?"

Hannah let go of Julius' hand and walked to the edge of the porch. A cool wet breeze blew into her face. "He doesn't know I ask. I only told him I needed to speak to you."

Julius stepped beside her. "I'm not sure what a Roman could do for your teacher."

"Protect him." Hannah answered. "He's in danger."

"What makes you say that?"

"There's been talk overheard by some of his disciples in the marketplaces. The Zealots grow tired of Yeshua's not rallying to their cause."

"But I hear even in Tiberias of his popularity with the crowds? The Zealots take a huge risk if they oppose someone with such a following."

Hannah nodded. "If that alone were the problem, I'd agree. But there's more."

"Go on."

"Yeshua himself. Several weeks ago, he decided to keep the Passover in Jerusalem, as has been his custom. But since then, he's spoken several times of Jerusalem as his place of suffering, even dying." Hannah drew close to Julius. "I'm scared of what's to come, Julius."

Julius put his arms around her, barely touching his hands to her back, the memory of the pain he brought to her still fresh in his mind. But she pulled him tight to her and held on. For several minutes, the two remained in each other's arms, listening to the sound of the rain and their own breathing. Julius broke the silence. "Tell me what would you have me do."

"Come with me to Jerusalem." Hannah backed slightly away, though their hands stayed on each other's backs. "I told Yeshua I would rejoin him there."

Julius could not stifle the smile that crossed his face. "I'm not sure Jerusalem would be ready for a Roman disciple clinging to the robe of a Galilean rabbi."

"Nor would Peter and the others welcome you at his side." Hannah's face brightened for a moment, then grew serious. "But you could remain on the fringes, ears and eyes open. You might know of places and persons where information could be gained. And if it came to a threat to on his life," Hannah's throat tightened, "you know the use of a sword. To protect him."

Julius recalled any number of times when he had put a blade to use – and Bethlehem, where other blades flashed in an attempt to silence the one for whom Hannah now pleaded. Julius took one of her hands and placed it upon his chest. "I do this for you."

"Bless you, Julius." Hannah leaned over and pressed her lips to his cheek.

* * *

With the inn closing for the night, Joshua secured the lockbar and headed to the kitchen. Ever since Caleb left, Joshua's mind had drifted. His confusion with orders this evening made Demas wonder if his master had drunk too much of the day's profits. But memories, not wine, accounted for Joshua's disarray. Memories of a child he let die, and a family forfeited. Memories of fleeing the house of Nathaniel on the night Kohath planned the Sopher's murder, and then hearing Kohath died in an ambush that should have ended his own life. And premonitions. Though he'd never seen the rabbi – at least, not since Yeshua was a child playing with David and Hannah – Joshua imagined Yeshua entering the holy city. Jacob and others hail him as Messiah. The rabbi balks at their words, denies them. A knife flashes, then another. Joshua sees Yeshua sprawled on the Temple steps. Only now, the face becomes that of a boy who played in the stable. Then, Yeshua becomes David, lifeless, lying before a cowering father...

"Joshua. Joshua? What is it?" The innkeeper looked up.

Demas was washing the last of the platters and chalices, now wondering whether Joshua's condition might not be the wine after all. Perhaps Joshua's mind took leave of him, the way those possessed of demons lost all sense. The stories from his home village of such a one who, until of late, wandered naked among the tombs gave him pause. "Can I get you something?"

"No, I'm alright." Joshua studied the portly young man. Adequate with cooking, sharper with money, the Gadarene served him well these past years. "Actually, yes. Sit with me."

Demas pulled a stool to sit down, taking care to stay within reach of the block which stored the knives. If Joshua were possessed, some protection might be needed.

"How long is it you've worked with me now, Demas?"

"Two years." The Gadarene's fingers drummed on the table's surface.

Joshua cleared his throat. "I've need to make pilgrimage to Jerusalem for the Passover. What would you say to running this inn in my stead for several weeks?"

The eyes of Demas widened. Joshua rarely offered words of praise, certainly nothing that hinted such confidence as entrusting the inn. By instinct, Demas muffled his reaction with a practical concern. "That would be a great responsibility for one paid an apprentice's wage."

Joshua smiled. He would lose no money with Demas in charge. "Fairly spoken, Gadarene. While you do my work, you'll get my pay. When I return, we'll talk of a new wage."

"Agreed." Demas stood, offering his hand to Joshua. "And when do you leave?"

"Tomorrow," the innkeeper replied, clasping the hand of a greatly surprised Demas. "I've much to do in Jerusalem. It's been too long."

Face gleaming, Demas left the kitchen for his room. Thoughts of opportunity raced through his mind. He'd send word in the morning to his family in Gadara of his success. For at least a few weeks, this would be the inn of Demas.

Joshua remained in the kitchen, filling a small chalice

of wine. He still didn't completely understand, but Joshua's resolve was set. Unlike David, for whom he failed to raise a hand; unlike Nathaniel, from whom he'd crept away without warning: Yeshua would find an ally in Joshua of Bethlehem. The rabbi would be told of the Zealot's plot. Joshua downed the wine in one long drink. "If the Roman's words be true, the father of David shall meet Joseph's son!" His oath sworn, Joshua hurled the chalice against the brick hearth. Shards littered the floor. The road to Jerusalem had been joined.

CHAPTER XLIII

Only stars illumined the streets of Bethphage, a settlement of Galileans on the Mount of Olive's eastern slope. It had taken Judas ten minutes to reach this village from Bethany, where Yeshua and the rest of his followers lodged. All the disciples slept hard, and even Yeshua didn't rouse when Judas unlatched the door to walk into the night.

Past the village well in Bethphage, the light of a single lamp shone through the narrow slit of a window in the agreed-upon place of meeting. Judas walked to the home's door and knocked twice. Jacob opened it and motioned him inside. Someone took the lamp from the window and set it in the middle of the room where Judas took his place in a circle of men. Some he recognized from Galilee as followers of Jacob. Others he presumed to be Judean Zealots.

"Welcome, Judas." Jacob sat next to Judas. "Any trouble leaving your rabbi tonight?"

"Not at all. The week's journey from Nazareth exhausted everyone." Judas sipped from the cup. "And your directions proved easy."

"We were pleased to get your message of Yeshua's lodging in Bethany tonight. It's best he not see us until tomorrow. And with all the other Galileans in this village, no one here paid attention to a few more when we arrived."

Judas looked around the circle again. In the lamp's dim flickering, he sensed a mix of tension and anticipation present. "I take it everything's set?"

Jacob nodded. "Yeshua will find a welcome neither he nor the Sanhedrin can ignore. I assume, coming from Bethany, that he enters through the Golden Gate?"

"That's what he told us at the evening meal."

"Good. That brings everything directly into the temple precincts. For all to see."

The man to Jacob's right leaned over and whispered into his ear. Jacob nodded. "Our Jerusalem friend wants to know when you'll leave Bethany. To be sure we are ready."

Judas looked at the Jerusalemite who spoke to Jacob. A jagged scar ran from the corner of one eyebrow to below his ear. Jacob once told Judas of this man, grazed by a Roman spear while ambushing a patrol near Jericho. The legionnaire missed his chance, but Reuben made no such mistake. Searchers later found the soldier impaled to a tree by his own spear. "Our hosts in Bethany insisted Rabbi Yeshua break the morning bread at their table and visit, since we arrived late in the evening. So it will be mid-morning."

Jacob nodded at Reuben. "All will be set. And now," Jacob added, tapping Judas on the knee, "you'd best return to his side. We need no suspicions."

The two men stood and hugged. Judas whispered, "I must speak with you, alone."

They walked outside and sat by the well.

"I know this is the time when Yeshua must declare himself, Jacob." The face and reputation of Reuben returned to Judas' mind. "But if he doesn't, I want no harm to come to Yeshua. Let him go back to Galilee. He'll pose no further problem."

The Galilean Zealot eyed his longtime colleague. He still trusted Judas. Hadn't he provided information on Yeshua all along? Hadn't he made it possible for tomorrow's plans to proceed by supplying the rabbi's itinerary? Yet, the years Judas spent with Yeshua softened him. Not all of the Zealots' designs for the coming days could be shared.

"You needn't be anxious, Judas. No one seeks the Rabbi's harm. Now, go to your rabbi. Let's hope for a glorious day before us."

"Thank you!" Buoyed by Jacob's assurance, Judas strode into the darkness.

Jacob watched him leave, then returned inside and rejoined the circle. "Reuben, your people understand what's expected of them?"

"This rabbi of yours will think all Jerusalem acclaims him."

Another voice sounded from a corner opposite the door. "The Sanhedrin's fear of Roman crackdowns on unrest will make some members eager to muzzle Rabbi Yeshua."

"You're sure you can arrange that?" asked Jacob.

"Oh, I won't have to arrange anything." The speaker stepped into the circle. The lamp's light shone on Lamech, member of the Sanhedrin and spokesman for the Zealots. "Caiaphas and Nathaniel will do it for me. One outdoes the other in appeasing Pilate and keeping order."

"Remember, Lamech, if Yeshua throws his lot with us, we need your defense of him before the Sanhedrin should they summon him."

"As long as I speak for him, he'll be safe." Lamech took the cup used by Judas and downed its contents. "But this Judas better see to it the rabbi declares himself on our side. Otherwise, Yeshua will have no one to speak for him when trouble falls."

* * *

By midmorning, broken clouds drifted above the crest of the Mount called Olives. Some of the pilgrims journeying to Jerusalem for Passover broke the walk's monotony by imagining shapes in the billows.

"A footstool!" a woman pointed. "The footstool of Adonai, blessed be the Name!"

Several small puffs of clouds alongside one long rounded cloudbank sparked a father's words to his son. "See those bits of white? They're like the rounded stones of David's sling. And that giant of a cloud must be Goliath himself." The young boy's eyes widened.

Nearby, Hannah and Julius smiled at the comment as they walked among the pilgrims. No one would have gauged him a Roman. Atop a plain white tunic, Julius wore a shawl with four fringed tassels at each corner, worn by Jews as a reminder of the commandments. Julius and Hannah kept a discrete distance from Yeshua and his followers. If the rabbi saw the two of them together, he might remember Julius from Magdala. Hadn't he recognized Hannah's from that one encounter? Besides, as Julius stressed to Hannah, the Zealots wouldn't dare strike against Yeshua in daylight, in sight of the crowds. If closer guard were needed, it would come later.

"SEE, IT IS THE SON OF DAVID. HOSANNA – SAVE US!"

"BLESSED BE THE KING WHO COMES IN THE HOLY NAME OF GOD!"

The shouts ahead caused Julius to look at the clouds, to see which formation had the appearance of a king, or at least a king's son. Hannah looked, not to the sky but toward the rabbi. "Julius, the cries come from near Yeshua!"

Julius instinctively reached for his well-concealed gladius as he strained to peer forward, trying to see the reason for the clamoring.

"BLESSINGS TO THE KINGDOM OF OUR FATHER DAVID – AND TO DAVID'S SON! SAVE US, PLEASE, SAVE US!"

The volume increased, as did the frequency of outcries. Julius and Hannah pressed on, but the crowd tightened. The shouting increased as they neared the crest of the ridge. With some pushing and maneuvering, the pair reached the summit. Jerusalem spread out before them. Smoke rose from the altars of the Temple. But immediately ahead of them, a mass of people sang and danced before Yeshua, acclaiming him with cheers.

"BLESSINGS TO THE KING WHO COMES!"

"SAVE US, SON OF DAVID! HOSANNA!"

Julius stopped in midstride when he noticed another detail of the celebration: palm branches. Pilgrims waved palms before and after the rabbi. Palms cushioned the rocky

path
switch-backing down into the Kidron valley before ascending the ridge called Zion to the Golden Gate. "Shit!" he muttered, loud enough for Hannah to hear.

"What is it?"

"Palms."

Hannah looked puzzled. "What's wrong with palms? These people simply honor the rabbi."

Julius took Hannah's arm and quickened their pace. "They do more than honor him. Palm branches are a symbol for the Zealots, serving for them as the legion's standards for us."

Hannah's thoughts began to race. "Do they mean to start a riot?"

"From what you've told me of his teachings, I don't see that succeeding." Julius studied those besieging the rabbi with cheers, then shifted his sight to the Temple walls and beyond to the Antonia. The barracks of Rome's Jerusalem cohort, the residence of Pilate, the tunnel connecting the fortress to the Temple...

"Maybe they don't need a riot," he reasoned aloud. "Maybe they just need Yeshua to be seen at the center of this uproar."

"By whom?"

"By any who would take the palms, and the chants of a new king, as a challenge."

Julius tightened his grip on Hannah's arm. In an instant, Hannah found herself almost running to keep up with Julius' strides as they skirted the crowd's edge and scurried down the slope. Near the bottom of the valley, they paused to catch their breath. Flower blossoms and the new leaves of olive trees sweetened the air. Hannah recalled this grove from her childhood in Jerusalem. She recalled it being named after the nearby oil presses: *Gesamani*.

* * *

"What is it, centurion?" This interruption of breakfast

irritated the procurator. "I told the steward I'd not be disturbed."

Antony maintained his salute. "Forgive me, but I thought you should be told."

"Told of what, man? Get to the point!"

"A disturbance outside the city walls, sir, to the Temple's east."

Pilate jammed the bread knife into the loaf. "These Jewish sons of bitches!" Wiping his mouth, Pilate recalled warnings about Passover here, and how the Zealots often used the cover of crowds to carry out some act of treachery. "Do we have a detachment from the cohort on scene?"

"Not as yet, Procurator. I thought it best you look for yourself first. They near the Golden Gate, the one that opens to the Temple's main courtyard."

Pilate grabbed his mantle and started on his way to the fortress' observation post atop the tower. "And just who are `they', centurion?"

Antony stepped to open the door for the procurator, then matched strides as they ascended a twisting stairway. "An informant says the turmoil concerns a Galilean rabbi."

"A rabbi? Centurion, I'm told this city fills with rabbis when Passover approaches. Will I be disturbed at the entry of each one?"

Before Antony could answer, Pilate reached the top of the stairway. He pushed open a weathered wooden gate opening onto one of the Antonia's parapets. The guard on duty came to attention. "There, sir," pointing at the tumult to the southeast, "they've just entered."

Pilate peered down. From this height, it looked like a swarm of bees buzzing and circling. In the center, he spotted one figure dismounting from a horse or donkey.

"Just what is the problem, centurion? I see no trouble."

"Can you see branches being waved, Procurator?"

"You'd summon the cohort to arrest those who litter the courtyard with leaves?"

"No sir." Antony's contempt for Pilate, first experienced in Caesarea's amphitheater, came rushing back. "The branches are palms, emblem of the Zealots."

"Zealots? In an open demonstration?"

"With so many branches, we can't be sure whether all are Zealots, or if they handed out palms among the crowd to hail this rabbi. But make no mistake, the Zealots have a hand in this."

"Why this rabbi?"

"According to the informant, some acclaim him as Messiah."

"Messiah?" Since ridding himself of Julius, Pilate sought no one to counsel him on Jewish customs. "Just what is a messiah?"

"In the Jews' tradition, one anointed by God as king."

"They already have Caesar as king."

Antony looked out again at the demonstration. "That's why the palms wave, Procurator. The Zealots and others believe Messiah will rid the land of Caesar's rule."

Pilate eyed Antony. "You seem to know a great deal about this people, centurion."

"I've served here many years, sir." Antony countered.

Pilate peered down at the tiny figure in the center of the mob. Nothing distinguished him from the others. In fact, in the crowd's pressing movement, he had the appearance of a stick caught in the swirling currents of a river eddy.

* * *

The cheering echoed off the walls separating the Temple from the rest of Jerusalem. Pilgrims and worshippers swelled the crowd who'd accompanied Yeshua from the Mount of Olives. Those who remained within the inner courts to offer sacrifice found their prayers engulfed by the noise radiating from the Golden Gate into the Court of the Gentiles.

One small group left the Chamber of Hewn Stone, the Sanhedrin's meeting place. Four temple guards marched in tight order, two in front and two to the rear. Three men walked between the guards. One babbled on, one wore the garb of the High Priest, and the third struggled to keep up with the others, his gait aided by a cane.

"I've never seen or heard anything like it. Palms everywhere. What do you think the Romans will do? For the life of me, I cannot –"

"Just be quiet!" Caiaphas grew irritated at the man, a minor official in the Temple treasury, who had brought the news of this disturbance. "We'll see for ourselves soon enough."

Nathaniel walked in silence, aggravated at reports of a mob waving palms inside the Court of the Gentiles. The cohort couldn't fail to overlook such an act of defiance. And after all the efforts to mend matters with Pilate! Whoever was responsible for this would pay, and pay dearly. Once they neared the Beautiful Gate, which led from the Court of Women into the Court of the Gentiles, the leading guards pushed aside onlookers to clear a path.

"Look!" someone shouted, "The High Priest goes to greet David's Son. *Hosanna!*"

Nathaniel shot an angry glance at the man. He knew he'd seen him before – with Lamech. "Zealots," he muttered under his breath.

As Caiaphas and the others strode by, a woman they passed cried out, "The Almighty blesses Jerusalem as Caiaphas blesses God's chosen!"

Caiaphas would have rebuked her, but the din of shouted acclamations and songs of praise accompanying the rabbi made any sustained dialogue impossible. Once they descended the steps leading down from the Beautiful Gate to the courtyard, the group stopped. The guards cleared a space so the High Priest could have an unobstructed view.

"There!" shouted the man who had told Caiaphas of the uproar. "That's him!"

In spite of the mass of folk, both Caiaphas and Nathaniel easily picked out the individual. No description was necessary. Everyone's attention focused on the bearded figure who held his arms up in a vain attempt for silence. Palms waved in his face, sometimes so close that his disciples brushed them back lest the rabbi's eyes be poked.

Caiaphas turned to the informant. "Did you hear the name of this rabbi?"

"Yeshua. Yeshua of Nazareth."

Caiaphas motioned to Nathaniel. "He says the rabbi's from Nazareth. Yeshua."

Nathaniel nodded. He'd heard of this teacher, even the rumors of his being Messiah. Such gossip circulated about others in the past, but none came to the Temple in the week of Passover while being acclaimed as David's Son with palms.

Some started to chant the 118th Psalm. Its words celebrated a king's gratitude for deliverance, used now to welcome a would-be king to the Temple with waving branches: *"BLESSED IS HE WHO COMES IN THE NAME OF ELOHIM ADONAI. WE BLESS YOU FROM THE HOUSE OF THE ALMIGHTY!"*

The implications of these words joined to palms chilled Nathaniel.

CHAPTER XLIV

"All Jerusalem is yours, Rabbi!" Peter shouted. "Elohim Adonai has opened the people's hearts to you."

"*HOSANNA, SON OF DAVID!*"

The crowd thrust palm fronds skyward in rhythm to the repeated chant, while many clapped and danced to celebrate the rabbi's entry. It seemed the only one not elated in this procession was Yeshua, whose smile on first seeing the city had long since disappeared.

Judas put his arm around Yeshua and raised his voice to be heard above the clamor. "Rabbi, why don't the cheers raise your heart? It's you they come for!"

"Do they, Judas? The palms tell me they come for other, more zealous, reasons."

Before the disciple could respond, Judas found his attention as well as Yeshua's shifting elsewhere. The crowd's chanting quieted to a hushed "ahhh" as a young child, passed overhead from one set of hands to another, neared the rabbi.

Peter received the girl, perhaps six years of age, then handed her into Yeshua's arms. The rabbi looked into the young child's face: her lower lip trembled while large tears formed.

"Can I tell you something, daughter of Jerusalem?" Yeshua's voice softened so only the child could hear, and his smile returned.

She barely nodded her head.

"I think these grownups play a game today. Do you like games?"

The beginnings of a grin tugged the corners of her

mouth.

"I like games, too. What's your name?"

"Ruth."

"A beautiful name! My mother used to tell me the story of Ruth from the writings."

"What kind of games do you like to play, rabbi?"

Yeshua smiled. "Oh, let me think. I know: shepherd and sheep. And dreidel."

"I like those, too!"

"I knew there was a reason we got along. By the way, Ruth, did some grownups ask you to play a game today?"

Ruth pursed her lips together and squinted her eyes.

"I mean, did they tell you to do something when you came to me?"

Ruth moved close to his face and whispered: "It's a secret."

Yeshua stroked his chin, then whispered back, "I can keep a secret."

From within the folds of her robe, the little girl drew out a small palm frond and kissed the rabbi on the cheek. "The man said to give you this palm."

"Was the man's name Jacob?"

Ruth leaned close to Yeshua's ear again. "How did you know the secret?"

Yeshua looked at Ruth. Anger surged against Jacob's use of such an innocent. No doubt, the Galilean zealot wished to remind him of their last encounter involving children outside Capernaum's synagogue months before. But Yeshua resolved not to let his resentment spill over on Ruth, who came bearing a child's gift. After kissing her on the cheek, Yeshua took the palm from her hand. The crowd roared its approval.

"Joanna," he called to one of his followers. "See that Ruth finds her family. And you, Ruth of Jerusalem," Yeshua continued, bending to set her down, "may God bless you."

"God bless you, rabbi," she replied, taking Joanna's

hand, looking back at Yeshua as they walked away.

Yeshua watched the pair disappear into the crowd. He would have searched the faces in the crowd for that of Jacob's, but a new commotion caught his eye. The surging of people to greet him had emptied the Temple's other gates and courtyards. For moneychangers and merchants near the Golden Gate, business boomed. But traders in other areas of the courtyard now took action to regain customers. Crossing the main plaza, they began haggling prices with their competitors' customers, trying to draw their share of pilgrims back.

"That man robs you. I can give you two doves for what he charges you for one."

"Exchange those Roman coins by the Hulda Gate instead of here, and you'll have money left for the evening meal."

The merchants of the Golden Gate countered. "Everyone knows the scales by the Hulda Gate use false weights."

"SILENCE!" Yeshua's voice thundered above the running squabbles.

"Tell them, rabbi," shouted one merchant, "these pigeons are without blemish."

"For you, rabbi, an exchange of money at face value, to show our respect for – "

"Respect? You reduce the dwelling of the Holy One to the haggling of coins, and dare speak of respect?" The anger initiated by Jacob's use of the little girl converged with outrage at the scene spilling out before him. "You will not conduct your thievery within these walls!"

Yeshua ripped open a nearby coop of pigeons, then another. The birds winged out and up until they soared over the Temple's walls.

"Rabbi, please!"

Yeshua swept an arm across the table of a moneylender, strewing piles of coins and balance weights across the stone pavement. Several merchants who'd come from

437

the other gates laughed at the sight. "See, even the rabbi agrees these are robbers at the Golden Gate. Now, if you would –"

"You think yourselves more righteous?" Yeshua interrupted. "You lie to those who come to worship by saying your scales are fairer and your animals purer than any other!"

"Rabbi, control yourself," offered a seller of lambs. "We only conduct business necessary to the Temple. If it weren't for us, these people couldn't worship."

"Couldn't worship! If it weren't for you, these people might understand worship resides in the heart, not in the fattening of your purses!" Yeshua seized an unused leash for lambs. "Leave this place!" he shouted, cracking the ends of the cord on the arms and backsides of several traders. "Take your fraud away from here!" Yeshua waded into the throng of shocked lenders and sellers. Those slow to leave felt the snap of rope sting their skin.

The crowd, who only moments before cheered his coming, watched Yeshua's outburst in stunned silence. Animals ran free in the courtyard. Overturned tables and benches, coins and emptied cages, littered the edges of the plaza. Some pilgrims shook heads in embarrassment, others in disgust at the sight of businessmen driven from their work.

As quickly as it erupted, the disturbance died down and the crowd dispersed: some to find a bargain from unnerved vendors, some to find solace by offering prayers within the Court of Israel. Yeshua led his disciples and followers out of the city and back to Bethany.

All that remained of the celebration for Yeshua's entrance were the palms. Palms strewn across the grounds. Palms betrayed by Yeshua. What kind of Messiah would drive out merchants while leaving Roman soldiers unchallenged in the Antonia? Yeshua's welcome to Jerusalem, and the hopes of many for his coming, lie scattered and soiled under palms trodden down.

* * *

A sullen mood steeped the Chamber of the High Priest. Caiaphas sat still, his chin resting on one hand. Nathaniel twisted his cane back and forth in a tight grip. Priest and scribe stared at one another, but all the two of them saw was Yeshua in the courtyard.

Caiaphas finally broke the silence. "I thought this Galilean had been in the Temple before. Surely he knew better than to cause a riot."

"He knew what he was doing. Those palms leave no doubt. Antagonize the Romans, bring them into the Temple courtyard to spark an even greater riot." Nathaniel let go of the cane and rubbed his eyes, a vain attempt to soothe the throbbing behind them. "We're fortunate the Zealots didn't better prepare the crowd. Had they joined Yeshua in attacking the merchants, the cohort would have been summoned. Lives would have been lost. Four days before the Passover lamb's slaughtering, our people's blood would have flowed in the Temple. That fool of a rabbi!"

"What else can you expect of a Galilean?" Caiaphas clasped his hands behind his head. "They're firebrands, all of them. And you can be sure Jacob's hand is in this."

"It's more than Jacob's hand. Lamech must be involved. They needed someone from Jerusalem, someone with influence and knowledge, to bring this about."

"Do you think this Yeshua could control men like Jacob and Lamech?"

Nathaniel sneered. "I'd say, more the other way around. The rabbi is likely just a convenient tool for the Zealots. So long as he holds the crowd's attention, he's useful for them."

"And so long as he holds the crowd's attention," added Caiaphas, "he's a problem for us. What if Yeshua takes his rabble to the Antonia tomorrow?"

"The best way to deal with this, Caiaphas, is to remove

Yeshua from the scene."

"But if you're right about the Zealots' using him, Jacob and Lamech wouldn't stand by if we seized the rabbi."

"If the pretense for our action were political, they'd protest." Nathaniel brought the cane to his side and stood. "But what if we brought in the Galilean for other reasons?"

"Such as?"

"Such as, religious causes. Rumors suggest he's broken Sabbath more than once. Perhaps we can catch him in a contradiction or lie in his explaining such actions. Besides," Nathaniel continued, "the gossip of his being Messiah could provide more incrimination."

"But on such talk, the Zealots would support him."

"Not necessarily. Maybe the rabbi would say something that disturbed Lamech and the Zealots, and bring their condemnation, if his idea of Messiah doesn't mesh with their plans."

The High Priest walked to a small window overlooking the Court of the Priests. Sacrifices burned. The blood of slain animals ran down the drains near the place of slaughtering. Nathaniel hobbled over to stand alongside the High Priest and spoke. "You saw what happened today. If the Romans don't see us exercise control, they might step in. Forcefully. Or, they could find others to take our place to bring order. As High Priest, you must act to save those who look to you for protection. The life of one Galilean can't compare with the well-being of our people."

Caiaphas weighed Nathaniel's words, then gave his answer. "Notify the members of the Sanhedrin. We meet first thing tomorrow morning, to discuss what is to be done with Yeshua."

Nathaniel bowed and departed. Caiaphas remained by the window, staring at the altar of holocausts. The smoke from its charred victims curled upward. Sacrifices had always been necessary, he thought. One life for the sake of many. Even the Galilean must understand that. Caiaphas donned his shawl and prayed for Jerusalem's safety.

* * *

Julius led Hannah through alleys he'd not traveled in almost twenty years. At length, a familiar weathered sign came into view, hanging precariously from a tilting wooden arm that jutted out over the alley. Carved into the sign were rough outlines of a bread loaf and cot. Camel dung splotched the ground underneath. "This will be our place to meet, away from where Yeshua's followers might see us together."

Hannah shuddered. The rundown caravansary reminded her of too many places she'd known, and plied her former trade, in Caesarea. "You're right, Julius. The disciples would never think of coming to such a place."

Even though the afternoon sun shone bright, most the caravansary's eating hall remained dimly lit save for a few lamps. Julius chose a table close to a ventilation slit in the wall.

"Nephew," cackled a voice from a corner opposite the pair, "quit fussing on that soup. You've got customers, likely near their death of thirst."

Julius heard movement in the kitchen, then a figure came their way. But something about the voice in the corner unsettled him.

"What'll it be? Some bread and wine? Or maybe," he offered, taking note of Hannah, "you'll be interested in a room for the afternoon?"

"Mind your tongue, innkeep, if you want to keep it."

"No offense intended, graybeard." The innkeep spoke plain and strong, not wanting to drive away a customer but not intimidated, either. "What do you want?"

"Wine and bread will do," Julius replied.

After the innkeep returned to the kitchen, the voice from the corner spoke again. "Forgive my nephew. He's not possessed of his uncle's delicate understanding of such things."

"Such things as what?" Hannah asked.

"Is that a woman's voice? Curse these blind eyes that won't let me see."

Julius couldn't believe what, or who, he heard. "Why don't you join us?"

"An invitation I'd keep, sir. But this old body can't move much out of my chair anymore, save to find my relief in a bed or a pot."

Julius stood and exclaimed. "By the gods! Is that you, Ishmael?"

"Depends on what rogue wants to know?"

Julius took Hannah's hand and they walked to the darkened corner. There, in a chair cushioned with fleece, sat an obese man of indeterminate years. A mess of uncombed white hair covered his head. A soiled apron spread across his chest and ponderous belly.

The Roman leaned over, grasped the old man's arms and whispered: "It's Julius."

Ishmael reached out a hand in Hannah's direction. His fingers traced across her hands and wrist. "How can you be Julius, with such a pleasant young woman at your side?"

Julius glanced at Ishmael's face. Supposedly blind eyes were busied in studying the rest of Hannah's figure. "I see old age hasn't broken you of lies or lechery."

Ishmael dropped his voice. "I speak of blindness as a convenience, Julius. It frees people to reveal what they hide from the sighted." Ishmael gazed again at Hannah. "But I spoke no lies of your wife. What gave your thick Roman head the sense to wed such a fine lady as this?"

Julius looked down to the floor.

"I'm not his wife," Hannah answered. Placing a hand on Julius' back, she spoke again. "My name is Hannah. Julius is a good friend."

Ishmael sensed the awkwardness. "Just as well," he sputtered, "better in love than in harness."

"Ishmael," Julius began, wanting to change the subject as well as satisfy his curiosity, "The last time I saw you, you waved farewell from a ship bound for Rome. I thought you planned to live out your days there."

"I did. And for a time, it was a good life for a wreck like me. Warm weather, sweet wine, ripe wenches – excuse me, lady, my tongue's wagged among caravan traders too long."

"You speak no different than most I've known."

Ishmael's eyebrows lifted slightly in Hannah's direction. "Anyway, too many years passed. Got too old to enjoy life there. And I started thinking, why not come back? Might as well be buried with family, seeing as how I spent so little time with them alive. So, three years ago, I came back. And still, Elohim Adonai keeps me from the grave."

"Elohim Adonai? I've known you for many things, Ishmael, but not a godly man."

"Well, you've not seen the greenings of eighty-three springs, friend, or the cold of that many winters. Time makes old men think of such things."

Hannah leaned over and held Ishmael's hand. "In some ways, thinking of such things goes to why Julius and I have come to Jerusalem. I follow the Rabbi Yeshua."

Ishmael let loose with a howl. "Hoo, hoo!! Now there's a teacher I could heed! I heard what he did to those holy cutthroats this morning."

"Already?" Hannah and Julius surprised one another with the identical response.

Ishmael nodded. "Travelers came in for lunch, whining about some Galilean rabbi who took a whip to the oversized backsides of those temple thieves! At least my years of shortchanging and overpricing never claimed the Almighty's approval."

This last disclosure induced Hannah to trust Ishmael. "I fear Yeshua is in some danger. That's why I asked Julius to come to Jerusalem, to watch over the rabbi."

Ishmael motioned Julius and Hannah closer. "I sit all day and evening in these shadows. Folks sometimes think my blindness affects my ears, which is fine with me. A man never listens nor learns too much in life."

"Then you've heard something about the rabbi?" Julius asked.

"Enough to say your woman has a feel for knowing trouble's about." Ishmael glanced to make sure his nephew hadn't returned to the room. "Zealots come to these tables now and again. What happened here long ago with Judas and Saddok makes them consider this a sort of shrine."

"Judas and Saddok?" Hannah's voice raised in surprise at names heard from childhood.

"All I can say about your rabbi is, watch his back these next days. I've heard some speak of how important this Passover is, how time runs short for the rabbi's declarations."

"What do they mean by declarations?" Hannah asked.

"And watching his back?" added Julius.

"Of the declarations, I don't know. But of watching his back, the Zealots said last night he'd stay in Bethany. And that they'd soon know which gate he'd come through, and when, for some welcome they'd planned. It seems to me, Julius, they've someone in his circle. For now, to give information. For later – well, who's to say. But between them and those pious kissers of Roman ass that run the Temple, I'd venture this rabbi had best be on guard."

CHAPTER XLV

"Have a chair, centurion." Antony bowed stiffly and sat before Pilate. The procurator stretched his arms high above his head, rolling his neck back and forth. Stifling a yawn, he said, "I've a special assignment for you this day."

"What is it, Procurator?"

"Beside you, on the floor," Pilate pointed to a large sack to the left of Antony. "My steward gathered these for your use."

Antony loosened the cord that cinched the bag's top. Inside were clothes.

"I've had outfits gathered for you and five others in your century, whom you're to choose. Take these men with you to the Temple."

Remembrances of the courtyard yesterday came to Antony's mind. "No disrespect, sir, but I'm not sure six of us could prevent another riot."

Pilate filled a chalice with water. "You couldn't. The centuries of Maximus and Claudius will be posted atop the Temple's walls. Extra guards will stand at all the Temple entrances."

Antony picked through the sack: inside were various robes, head scarves, and prayer shawls. "I take it we'll do more in the way of reconnaissance?"

"That's right. Shadow this Galilean rabbi. Listen to what he says." Pilate drank from his chalice. "I've been told you can converse in Aramaic, and even have a smattering of Hebrew. Make sure those you choose can be trusted to work in such disguise."

"Do you wish us to take any action, or simply listen?"

"Today you listen. See if the rumors of Yeshua being some sort of king come from his own lips. Take note of anything you think significant." Pilate stepped over to a window overlooking the Court of the Gentiles. Red-orange clouds accompanied the day's dawning. "Their high council meets this morning, to consider Yeshua's outburst at the Temple. Don't be surprised if you see others watching and listening."

"I've one concern, Procurator. A low wall fences off non-Jews from the Temple's inner courts. If the rabbi teaches within, we'd be unable to attend his words."

"Then cross that barrier!" Pilate shot back. "Pass as a Jew. With these clothes and your capacity at their language, none should suspect. Instruct your men to follow your lead."

"As you wish, sir."

Pilate sat down. "Return to me this evening with a report."

"Yes sir," Antony stood and saluted. *Pass for a Jew*, he thought. Antony wondered if he'd remember enough to play the part – or too much to keep his secret intact.

* * *

Worshipers crowded the Court of Israel through the ritual of morning sacrifices. Wine hissed into steam as priests poured it upon oblations being burnt on the altar. The resulting vapor stung the nostrils and steeped the clothes of pilgrims. The Levites' chanted psalms mingled with the priests' lifting of prayers. Smoke and smell and sound swirled around all.

Nathaniel and Caiaphas waited in the Chamber of Hewn Stone for the service to end, at which time the Sanhedrin would convene. As the High Priest had no part in this liturgy, he had taken counsel with his Sopher. Their conversation reviewed strategies for dealing with the Sanhedrin's three main parties on the matter of the Rabbi Yeshua.

The Sadducees had seen enough in the Temple courtyard yesterday. The disrespect shown by the Galilean rabbi for the holy shrine and its lucrative commerce sealed their view. The Pharisees remained open to a teacher some still considered one of their own. Too hasty a judgment might stir their opposition. And who knew how the Zealots would play their hand?

Nathaniel cracked the door of the chamber open and looked out upon the crowd. The deputy high priest intoned the benediction. More than a dozen members of the Sanhedrin stood in clear view, among them Lot the Pharisee and Lamech the Zealot. At the crowd's far end, another face came into view. It belonged to Yeshua.

Even from this distance Nathaniel stared hard, trying to study the features of this new adversary. Advice spoken years ago by his predecessor Saripheus cautioned him to always pay more attention to enemies than friends. The advice had served him well. Nathaniel saw the rabbi looking in his direction. Was he looking at him? The Sopher quickly swung the door shut.

"The service is over?"

"Yes, well, close to it." The words stumbled out of Nathaniel's mouth the way a sailor sets foot on land after too long at sea. Yeshua's eyes had, even if for only a moment, seemed fixed on him. The Sopher was unaccustomed to being the one assessed.

After a few minutes, he opened the door once again. The service had ended. Most of the worshipers filed out the Nicanor Gate, though some headed toward this chamber. Nathaniel scanned the crowd but saw no sign of the rabbi. Maybe he only imagined the stare. Besides, the Galilean would soon enough be the one examined. Nathaniel felt his breathing slow.

* * *

"Naomi, a woman at the door asks for you. She gives the name Rebekah of Bethlehem."

Naomi set down her sewing basket. "Show her in."

The servant bowed and exited. Naomi had not seen Rebekah since they arrived a few days past. She wondered if Rebekah had been able to see her son, imprisoned in the Antonia. Then again, Naomi wondered about her own son, if he might be barracked in the Antonia.

"Naomi!"

Rebekah's greeting startled Naomi from her thoughts. "Welcome, Rebekah." The two women hugged, after which Naomi took Rebekah's hand. "Your son, have you seen him?"

"Not yet. I've been told the day after tomorrow will be mine to visit Yeshua Barabbas." Rebekah patted Naomi's hand and walked to a small potted palm. "Two days after that, according to Pilate's decree, is to be the execution."

"On Passover?" Naomi joined her friend. "That seems cruel even for Rome."

"For Rome, that is typical. The Procurator will no doubt take great pride in smearing Jewish blood on a cross-bar for the festival."

"Rebekah, let me speak to Nathaniel. Perhaps he can persuade the Sanhedrin to exert some influence on Saul's behalf."

Rebekah looked in pity at her friend. She'd long given up correcting Naomi every time she called Yeshua Barabbas by his old name. Besides, Rebekah didn't possess the heart to tell Naomi that the Zealots judged her uncle a traitor. His dealings with the Antonia garrison were well-known to Lamech and Jacob. Only age and attachment to the High Priest prevented direct action against him. "Yeshua Barabbas is beyond anyone's help. Pilate assures his martyrdom, and his martyrdom assures his influence. Perhaps more in death than life. Like his father."

Naomi thought of Elias, full of life, working in the carpentry shop. The face of Joshua also passed through her mind, only to be covered over with the sight of David. "We need no more dying in our families," she uttered, as much to herself as Rebekah.

"Not all of my news is bad, Naomi. Did you hear of yesterday's riot?"

"Nathaniel only spoke of it in passing."

"Did he tell you who was at the center?"

"No. Why?"

Rebekah took hold of Naomi's shoulders. "I watched the scene in the courtyard myself. The one causing the riot came from Nazareth of Galilee. The rabbi Yeshua!"

Naomi's mind flashed to the evening of Abraham's visit to Bethlehem: an argument concerning a Nazarene rabbi named Yeshua, Abraham's stunning revelation this Yeshua had been born in Bethlehem, to Mary and Joseph. "Yeshua? Here?"

"Yes, Naomi, and in trouble! Did Nathaniel tell you he'd be gone this morning?"

"Yes, for a meeting of the Sanhedrin."

"They meet to discuss what to do with Yeshua because of yesterday. And there's more."

"What?"

Rebekah stood silent for a few moments before continuing. "I've not been told everything, but those with whom I stay –"

"Zealots?"

"Yes. They hint Yeshua faces severe testing, and not just from the Sanhedrin."

"What do they mean by severe?"

Rebekah smiled. "The week will show."

"Have you told them what we learned of Yeshua from Abraham? Of his guilt in Bethlehem's killings?"

"As long as the rabbi brings disaster upon himself, I'll hold my tongue. Perhaps another day will sharpen that information's bite. I trust you'll keep it to yourself."

Naomi nodded. "Whatever you say. I'll –"

The approach of footsteps stilled Naomi. The women waited to see who drew near before continuing. "Mistress Naomi," said the same servant who announced Rebekah, "another woman has come to the gate, inquiring of you."

"Did she give her name?"

"I did." The reply came from a woman now stepping through the doorway connecting the courtyard to the house.

"I instructed you to wait in the front hallway," the servant scolded. Then, in a pleading tone, "Forgive me, mistress Naomi. She must have followed me."

Naomi took no heed of the servant. She only saw a face: older, but still known. And still loved. "Hannah!"

Mother and daughter embraced in tears.

* * *

"You defend the actions of rabbi Yeshua in the Temple yesterday?" Some rapped their staffs on the floor in agreement with Nathaniel's question of Lot.

Lot waited for the room to quiet. "Defend? No. But understand? Tell me, Nathaniel, don't you ever find the haggling over prices so close to the Holy of Holies offensive? If the merchants don't wish to be charged with unseemly practices, maybe they shouldn't engage in them."

"So the Galilean has poisoned you with his lies of fraud in the Temple markets?" Nathaniel lifted his cane, pointing it in the direction of Lot. "I took you to be a wiser man than that. What Yeshua did yesterday was dangerous. To the Temple, to us all."

Until this point, Lamech remained silent. Nathaniel's argument, however, provided an opportune moment to move the discussion in the direction Jacob had urged. "What do you mean by `dangerous,' Nathaniel? Dangerous to profits gouged at the height of the pilgrimage season?"

Nathaniel took the bait. "I'd have thought you understood the greater danger best of all. How do you think a riot appears in the Antonia's vigilant sight? It's fortunate the rabbi left when he did. Innocent lives might have been lost if the Romans had moved in."

"Then you think the rabbi to be a revolutionary, Sopher?"

"The more pertinent question, Lamech, is what you and the Zealots consider him?"

Lamech grasped the inner edges of his mantle in his hands and stood, tilting his chin up slightly while he eyed Caiaphas and Nathaniel. "All in this room know the talk of Yeshua as prophet, or even Messiah. But as for me, and those with whom I stand, we say no more of Yeshua than what he says of himself. And to this day, to our ears, he says little more than rabbi and teacher. So, I say no more of him."

Heads nodded not only among other Zealots sympathizers but among the Pharisees.

"Does one who aspires only to be rabbi and teacher enter this city bedecked in palms?" Nathaniel's voice pitched higher. "Does one who aspires only to be rabbi and teacher commit violence against godly men on the Temple mount? Does one who aspires only to be rabbi and teacher risk the lives of pilgrims by such an outburst in plain view of the Antonia's garrison? NO!" Nathaniel struck his cane on the stone floor, its echo sounding through the room.

The intensity of Nathaniel's response stilled the Sanhedrin. Only in time did Lot stand to address the council. "Caiaphas, may I make a suggestion?"

The High Priest lifted a hand in acknowledgement of the Pharisee.

"Yesterday does call into question the motives of rabbi Yeshua, both by his actions in the courtyard and the risk taken of Roman response. On that much, I agree with the Sopher. So I suggest this. Let him be asked, in public, of those motives."

"And of Rome," interjected Lamech, eager to force Yeshua's hand regarding the issue of greatest concern to the Zealots. "If the Sanhedrin is to weigh this rabbi's risk, we must know what he teaches of our conduct toward the Romans."

Nathaniel leaned forward, surprised Lamech would

want a Zealot rabbi put on the spot. "I agree with my brother Lamech," the Sopher injected, wanting to seal this opportunity to expose Yeshua's connections, "and with Lot's suggestion. We need to find out what this Galilean plans, in order that we may be prepared to deal with him appropriately."

Caiaphas spoke next. "A delegation from the Sanhedrin will ask these things of the rabbi Yeshua this very day. On the morrow, we shall meet to consider his answers, whether they merit further examination by us. And let no one forget," Caiaphas stood and deepened his voice, "it is the will of God for Jerusalem's safety that moves us on this course. Let us pray the rabbi Yeshua understands, lest he be at odds with both God and man."

* * *

A solitary figure knelt under a crude shelter: sticks propped up the corners of his mantle, spread out and angled to provide the greatest shade from noonday's sun. The man piled rocks and stones around the bases of the sticks to insure the wind would not topple them. His covering secured, he took a drink of water and chewed on a date purchased in Jericho.

Since leaving Jericho at first light, Joshua traversed the steepest and most dangerous section of the road up to Jerusalem. Bands of red ocher streaking the cliff walls gave this valley its name of *Adummim*. Those same rocks figured in its other title, the *Ascent of Blood*. Generations of robbers used these rocks and blind corners for ambush.

Joshua had pressed to reach this broad opening in the valley before resting. He remembered enough from his time with Kohath to know how quickly a sleeping traveler could be separated from goods and even life. This level terrain made a stealthy approach far more difficult than in the canyon. Resting under his canopy, Joshua also recalled how Kohath never travelled through any wilderness without a supply of sticks. During the day, they helped to provide shade.

At night, they could be burned to warm the body.

Joshua closed his eyes. In an hour or two, the journey would be resumed. Jerusalem would be gained by nightfall. But what then? Since leaving Tiberias almost a week ago, that thought gnawed at him. How would he inform Yeshua of the Zealots' plottings? Indeed, how would he even find Yeshua in a city filled with Passover pilgrims? And even if he found him, why should Yeshua believe him? The rabbi may have heard of his cowardice years ago in Bethlehem. And a coward's word counted little more than a Samaritan's or a Gentile's.

Joshua considered the option of simply interceding for Yeshua with others. The Zealots had their enemies in Jerusalem. *Maybe if I went to the Temple authorities*, Joshua mused, *or even the Romans*. But again, credibility weighed against him. A Jew who lived in Tiberias, a city considered unclean by its construction over a cemetery, would not be welcomed by priests. Nor would a Zealot informant find sympathetic ears in the Antonia.

The innkeeper arched his back and wriggled to find a more comfortable position on the ground. *Maybe this was a fool's journey*, he thought. *Maybe it'd be better returning to Tiberias, and let the rabbi fend for himself.* Just then, a sharp rock turned on edge by his squirming jabbed into his side, causing him to sit upright. Joshua rubbed where the stone poked deep. Its discomfort reminded him of pains much deeper, and older. "Not again," Joshua said. "Not again." Joshua lay back down. He would rest, then resume the ascent to Jerusalem . . . and, God willing, to the rabbi.

CHAPTER XLVI

The late morning sun glared a harbinger of summer. Sweat beaded Antony's forehead as well as dampening his robe under the armpits and down his back. But not all perspiration owed to the heat. Antony glanced at one of several signs on the stone fence dividing the Court of the Gentiles from the inner Temple precincts. It warned Gentiles in Greek and Latin not to enter these courts under penalty of death. Antony and five other soldiers in disguise had just spent the morning ignoring that ban as they kept watch on Yeshua. Antony's men performed well: bowing when others bowed, raising hands when others praised. The only test came when a Jew from Alexandria asked one man his home.

"We all come from Emmaus," Antony replied in his best Aramaic. "My companions have taken a vow of silence until we celebrate the great meal of deliverance."

"The Almighty's blessings rest upon you," answered the Egyptian.

At the moment, Antony and his squad walked discretely behind the Galilean rabbi. After an impromptu discussion of Sabbath with several Pharisees, Yeshua and his disciples appeared headed toward the Golden Gate and the Kidron valley beyond it. Antony noted another group veering quickly toward the rabbi. An escort of Temple guards suggested it was an official visit, perhaps by the Sanhedrin. The rabbi had not reached the gate when the delegation stopped him.

"Rabbi, we would speak to you. Of your teachings."

From prior trips to Jerusalem, Yeshua recognized the

speaker: a Zealot sympathizer and Sanhedrin member called Lamech. "What of my teachings interest you?"

"We seek the authority you claim for your words," replied a priest named Eli, whom Caiaphas had designated to lead the questioning, "and for your assault on the merchants."

Peter and his brother Andrew stepped closer to Yeshua, fearing some reprisal. Judas scanned the gathering crowd for Jacob or the men he'd seen at Bethphage. Antony eyed the legionnaires stationed atop the Temple wall. He hoped the Galilean's followers and the Sanhedrin delegation would keep those guards in mind if this escalated beyond words.

"My authority?" Yeshua brushed Peter and Andrew aside and stepped toward Eli.

Eli moved forward so that the rabbi and priest stood face to face. "Yes. By what right do you disrupt the Temple?"

"I will answer your question if you answer mine. By what authority did John the Baptizer minister in the wilderness?"

Eli fumbled for a response. To admit the Baptizer acted on God's authority condemned the decision of Jerusalem's elite to steer clear of his teachings and any association with him. But to charge John acted on his own authority invited the people's condemnation. The Baptizer's beheading by Herod had made him a revered martyr.

"Of the Baptizer, we can't say for sure," admitted Eli.

The reply brought cackles from a number of bystanders. "Who cares about the Galilean's authority, so long as he can silence the priests' babbling," one loudly snickered.

Now it became Lamech's turn to interrogate the rabbi. "Yeshua, we admire your sincerity and wisdom. We've heard how you uphold the old teachings while bringing fresh life to them. But perhaps in Galilee, Rome's presence is not as pronounced as it is here, where the Antonia clings like a leech to these holy walls."

Antony shuffled closer. Pilate would likely find interest in this unfolding exchange.

"You speak boldly enough for us both," Yeshua offered.

"But do I speak for you, rabbi, on the matter of Rome?"

Yeshua smiled. "It's difficult to say, since I've not heard what matter concerns you."

"As I said, you have a reputation for truly teaching God's Torah. So please, tell us, what do you teach concerning the taxes Rome extracts from our purses to glut her already bloated treasuries? Is it lawful for us to pay them or not?" Lamech folded his arms across his chest. "A simple answer will do, Rabbi Yeshua. We're but simple men here, interested in simple truth."

Antony admitted a grim admiration for the way Lamech circled his prey. How could the rabbi avoid an answer that wouldn't either offend patriots or preach sedition?

"Lamech," Yeshua began, "what coin is used to pay this tax?"

The Zealot reached into his purse, pulled out a denarius, and tossed it to the rabbi.

Yeshua studied the coin for a moment. Without looking up, he asked Lamech, "Whose head is imprinted on this?"

"Caesar's."

"Well, there's your answer. Give Caesar what belongs to him," Yeshua said, flipping the coin back to Lamech, "and give God what belongs to God." The rabbi started to walk away, then paused to look back at his inquisitors. "I trust my answer is simple enough."

Antony watched as Yeshua left a befuddled crowd and exited the Golden Gate. Some argued whether he'd just supported or opposed the taxes. Others spoke words like "foolish" and "disrespectful." Antony heard several speak of further questioning, or even arrest. He found himself wondering how the procurator would interpret Yeshua's response on the taxes – and what his interpretation would mean for this Nazarene rabbi.

* * *

Naomi and Hannah clung tightly to one another, as if each feared the other might slip away if they let go. For Rebekah, the embrace offended her sense of decency. A daughter who'd whored among Romans would not be given such a reception by her. The scene brought back feelings experienced at Deborah's funeral. Then, Naomi wrapped her arms around a son who'd abandoned not only his family but his people to serve in Caesar's legions. Now, Naomi caressed a daughter whose body had been slickened with Roman sweat and more.

Naomi brushed tears from her eyes and looked toward Rebekah. "My daughter," she sobbed, "you remember, Hannah?"

Rebekah glared at the younger woman. "I do."

"This is Rebekah, Hannah. From Bethlehem."

Hannah let go of her mother and reached out a hand to her mother's friend.

Rebekah looked down at Hannah's hand, keeping her own rigidly by her side. "I've no inclination to touch a whore."

"Rebekah –"

"Please, mother," Hannah interrupted, "I deserve her greeting far more than yours." Hannah withdrew her hand. "You've every right to look on me with disgust. That's how I looked on myself until this past year."

"Really, Hannah. And what's changed? Don't the Romans like their harlots' hips to widen, or their breasts to sag? How timely to return when your features grow less marketable!"

Naomi stepped next to her daughter and took her arm. "We've all made mistakes, Rebekah. My whole life shouts that. But what matters is, my daughter's come home."

"But why?" Rebekah replied, "Why now, Hannah, after all these years?"

"Mother, can we sit? There's much I need to say."

Naomi nodded. The two older women sat on a bench, while Hannah moved a wooden chair across from them. She anticipated a hard-enough time speaking to her mother about Yeshua, and Julius, and all the ties that led back to Bethlehem. But now, Rebekah too? Hannah remembered Rebekah and her mother blaming Mary and Joseph for the disaster brought upon their families. Before she'd left, Hannah had heard the rumors of Rebekah's ties to the Sicarii, who now aligned with the Zealots.

"I'm not sure where to begin. Since I left, I spent most of my years in Caesarea, making a living from its garrison and seafarers."

Naomi closed her eyes. Rebekah winced and shook her head. She kept her words under her breath, but Hannah knew them to be cutting.

"In my own way, I sought vengeance on Romans for what they did to me at the Antonia."

"Hannah, Hannah," her mother interjected, leaning back on the bench and tilting her head up, "don't go back to that story now. You know how Nathaniel and I felt about it."

"You mean, how you let him convince you it didn't happen?" Hannah felt an old bitterness rise, but knew this wasn't the time to dredge it up. "For what I did when I left, the shame is mine. But I knew of nowhere else to turn. And no way to change. At least, not then."

"And now, you do." Rebekah could no stay silent. "Just what brought on this change?"

"At first, someone who cared for me, Rebekah."

"Let me guess. A mariner, whose time at sea confused lust for love. Or maybe a Roman."

"Yes, a Roman." Hannah spoke in a firm voice that took even her by surprise. "But more importantly, a good and decent man. He helped me leave my whoring."

Naomi's hand covered her mouth. "You married this Gentile?"

"No, though we considered it."

"Ah, a Gentile who redeems whores and gives them leave to visit their mothers."

Hannah ignored Rebekah's insult. "This Roman, Julius, is only part of why I found it possible to come back. More importantly is the Rabbi Yeshua, who – "

"Yeshua!" Rebekah spewed the name. "What have you to do with rabbi Yeshua?"

"He helped me. By him, I found forgiveness from God, and from myself, for what had come of my life."

Naomi leapt up and cried out, "No, not Yeshua, not him."

"Mother, what's wrong?" Hannah couldn't understand her mother's outburst, since she hadn't yet revealed the secret of Yeshua's identity.

"What's wrong," Rebekah retorted, "is you've traded a Roman bed for the coward responsible for the death of your brother, and my Elias and Levi! Yeshua is no Galilean: he's the son of Joseph and Mary, the one Herod sought to kill, only to kill our sons instead."

Without thinking, Hannah blurted, "You knew?"

Rebekah paused, letting the implications of Hannah's words swirl inside her head and heart for a moment, before continuing. "Yes, I knew. As did your mother." Rebekah stood and walked toward Hannah. "And you did, too! You came to this house, intending to praise the very one who let your brother's blood flow instead of his own? You filthy rag!" The palm of Rebekah's hand cracked across Hannah's face, leaving a wide red mark on her cheek.

"You can't condemn him for that," Hannah protested. "He was a child, without blame. He speaks of the innocents with great remorse. He told me he'd take their place even now if–"

Rebekah slapped Hannah's other cheek. "Enough of his lies! Enough!" She drew back her hand now curled into a fist for another blow, only to be restrained by Naomi.

"You'll not strike my daughter again, Rebekah. No

matter what she's done."

Rebekah relented, shocked by strength she'd not heard Naomi speak with in years. Hannah stood to embrace her mother, but Naomi stepped back. "You'd best leave, Hannah."

"There's more I need to tell you. About me, about Yeshua."

"I've heard enough for one day, daughter."

Hannah took her mother's hand. "I will come back. That is, if you want me to."

"I do. But for now, I need time to myself"

Letting go of Naomi's hand, Hannah left the courtyard.

* * *

Pilgrims drawn by Passover bolstered the usual mix of traders and merchants in the caravansary. Bowls of fruit and platters of bread flowed in a constant stream between kitchen and hall. A half dozen or more dialects muddled the room's noise. Bedouin traders spoke Syrian or Aramaic. Diaspora Jews and Gentile God-fearers stirred the tongues of Egypt and Babylon along with Galatia and Greece into the meld. The cacophony gave Jacob and Reuben no cause to muffle their conversation. More importantly, they took no notice that the inn's resident eccentric cocked an oft-avowed deaf ear in their direction.

"Is this your Galilean idea of Messiah!" Reuben laughed. "Someone who frees pigeons from cages and thrashes their owners, while telling us to pay Caesar his due?"

Jacob wrung his hands. "I know. I know. Three years he's gone on like this. Teasing the crowds with his talk of God's kingdom, then refusing to confront its chief enemy."

"You asked us to wait, and we waited. You wanted crowds to acclaim him, and we arranged them. What now, Jacob? How much longer will your miracle-worker hold us back? Until he welcomes Pilate into his circle of disciples?"

"You've made your point!" Jacob shot back. "His time is past. So be it."

Reuben watched Jacob pick at a plate of figs. Neither man spoke for some time. Reuben never expected much of the Galilean rabbi. Today simply confirmed his judgment.

Jacob, on the other hand, thought back to the early days when Yeshua first made a name for himself. He recalled the enthusiasm for the rabbi by his own followers, Judas and Simon. They told him this one was different, this one made people feel and believe and hope like no other teacher. Jacob recalled listening to Yeshua and being impressed. But how could Yeshua preach the kingdom of Adonai without condemning Rome's stranglehold on Judea?

"Then, we move ahead with the plan for the Sanhedrin?"

Reuben's words reminded Jacob there could be no turning back, Judas' plea at Bethphage notwithstanding. "We do. Send word to Lamech. Are your witnesses ready?"

Reuben's smile put a fold in his scar. "We've a pair rehearsed on Yeshua's blasphemies. Lamech knows them, so there'll be no problem getting them called to testify. After that, a few well-placed words of treason brought to Pilate, and Rome does our work for us." Reuben lifted his cup and tapped it against Jacob's. "And that will take care of the rabbi."

"Yes it will." Jacob hoped he would be relieved, but he wasn't. Handing over a Jew, and a Galilean at that, gnawed at him more than expected. But sacrifices had to be made.

* * *

An hour later, most customers had left the caravansary. An old man sat in one corner, the inn's stable boy sitting before him. "Tell me the directions I gave you again, so you understand."

The boy repeated the words a third time. "I'm to go to the well at Bethany, and ask for a Galilean who knows of Ishmael. The man will have a short beard."

"Go on."

"To make sure he's the right one, I'll ask the name of his friend from Tyre. He's to say *Nabal*, and I tell him to see you right away." The boy added, "But listen, wouldn't it be smarter for you to just tell me his name, so I could call it out and find him easier?"

Ishmael reached his hand out as if to pat the boy on his cheek, then grasped his earlobe and pinched down hard.

"Oww!"

"Don't question your elder, whelp! I'd have told you his name if I wanted you knowing it. And I don't!" Ishmael let go of the ear and drew a copper mite from his purse. "Remember, this'll be yours for getting him here by nightfall. And if you don't, I've a mind to tell my nephew that camel dung burns better if he'd have you press it by hand before it dries."

A wide-eyed "Yes, sir!" came as the boy raced out the door. Ishmael watched the boy run and smiled. Now came the wait.

CHAPTER XLVII

Hannah sat under an awning with the other women who followed Yeshua. The canvas above hung limp in a breezeless afternoon. Some rested. Others exchanged hushed words over the morning's encounter with Lamech and Eli. Yeshua's rebuttal of their attempts to trap him elicited new concern. Most understood Lamech and Eli to be powerful men in Jerusalem, not likely dismissed without repercussion. Hannah tried listening to the women recount the scene, but her mind drifted to her own encounter that morning. She tightened the veil across her face, not wanting others to see the marks left from Rebekah's slaps. She worried about how many others in Jerusalem knew Yeshua's identity besides Rebekah and her mother.

"Would anyone here be kind enough to draw a cup of water for a traveler?" The words came from a man who had stopped in the street just beyond the awning's shelter.

"A moment while I fetch a cup," Mary replied. "Please, take your rest in the shade."

"Bless you, woman."

Most of the women wondered why the man didn't pull away his hood once he stepped into the shade of the awning. But Hannah didn't. She knew Julius didn't want his face to be fully seen. "If you like," she said, "I could show you the village well, to fill your waterskin for later."

"I'd appreciate that," came his reply as he reached for the cup brought by Mary. After drinking, he returned it with thanks. "May Elohim Adonai bless your Passover in Jerusalem."

"I won't be long," Hannah told Mary.

Hannah and Julius walked wordlessly until they turned a corner. "We need to meet Ishmael. Can you come to the caravansary for supper?"

"I think so. Julius, the women talked of some clash at the temple today."

"I know, I watched it." Julius refrained from saying more, not wanting to disclose his growing sense of gloom. "And your family? How did it go with them?"

Hannah shook her head. "Maybe, in time, my mother will come round. But a friend of hers who was there made it clear that she'd receive no daughter who whored."

"That's behind you, Hannah." He touched his hand to hers, then quickly pulled back in case someone might see. "And what of your uncle? How did he react?"

"My mother's uncle. I don't know, he wasn't home. Apparently he still serves as Sopher to the High Priest."

Julius stopped mid-stride. "Sopher? You never mentioned that before."

"No, I suppose I didn't. I guess I wanted no more to do with Nathaniel."

The name left Julius breathless. Nathaniel! Again Nathaniel! Julius' mind spun. He'd need more time to sort through this revelation, and its implications. "Rather than have you walk through the city alone to the caravansary, I'll wait for you in the Gesamani garden, near the olive presses. You'd better get back before you're missed."

"What time shall I meet you?"

"Whenever you can get away. I'll go there now and wait."

The two parted: Hannah, to Yeshua's refuge in Bethany; Julius, to the garden, where he would ponder how to unpack for Hannah his own connections to Nathaniel.

* * *

Inside the house, most of the disciples reclined, wearied as much by the day's heat as the encounter at the temple.

The only noise came from one corner where Peter snored. Mary glanced around the room. Yeshua's half-opened eyes met hers. She stepped lightly to his side and knelt. "I'm sorry, but a man seeks you. He says you may remember him from Arbela."

Yeshua yawned. "Did he give his name?"

"Abraham of New Damascus. I recall his face, though not the wound to his hand."

"Abraham, wounded?" Yeshua rose quickly. Once out the door, Yeshua saw a

white-robed figure with his back to him. "Abraham?"

The man turned and smiled. "Rabbi Yeshua!"

The two embraced. As both let loose, Yeshua took Abraham's right arm and looked down at the hand. Three of the fingers had been cut off. A jagged scar marked where a fourth had roughly knit together. "What happened?"

"A Roman's gladius, though I suffered far less than another that night. Yeshua Barabbas."

"The one arrested for murdering the legionnaire in Jericho?"

"The same. We'd known each other years before – " Abraham stopped. He wanted to tell Yeshua of Bethlehem, of Elias and Rebekah, and their imprisoned son. But not yet. "Well, that is not why I'm here. I came to Jerusalem last week, to prepare for keeping Passover with friends from New Damascus."

"I remember our conversations in Galilee about your Essene brothers."

Abraham nodded his head. "I have talked to them much of you. And even though I count myself among those who follow you, they still keep an open ear to me."

"Open ears can lead to open hearts."

"They are good men, Rabbi, seekers of truth. And they, that is, we, want to extend hospitality to you. A room to keep the Passover tomorrow night."

Yeshua puzzled at the offer. "Passover is not for several more nights."

Abraham smiled. "For all the rest of Israel, that is true. But we Essenes use a different calendar."

"Ahhh," Yeshua stroked his chin, "Yes, I recall hearing this from some disciples of the Baptizer. Another means of separation, or should I say purification, from Jerusalem's cult?"

"It is. I know it would be unusual for you to keep the feast tomorrow, but others in Jerusalem follow our calendar. It would be our honor to provide a place for you and your disciples. The meal, the settings, all will be prepared as you wish. And if you chose, you could still observe the feast on its more traditional day later in the week."

The rabbi thought hard on Abraham's offer. It did provide one advantage: an earlier keeping of the Passover meal with his disciples. Between yesterday's confrontation and today's questioning, events long anticipated seemed to be accelerating. Waiting to celebrate until the end of the week might be too late, and Yeshua longed to eat the feast with his disciples one last time in Jerusalem. Yeshua took hold of Abraham's shoulders. "So be it. We'll keep the feast tomorrow night. And may Elohim Adonai bless you, Abraham, for hospitality to pilgrims."

"God's blessing be yours, rabbi, for hospitality shown this pilgrim long ago. Meet me at the Golden Gate tomorrow, near the eleventh hour. I will lead you to the room prepared."

The two men hugged, then Abraham left. Only after he was out of sight did Yeshua realize he'd not asked further about the injury, and its connection to Barabbas. Yeshua decided it could wait until tomorrow.

* * *

Even before Caiaphas entered, the Sanhedrin roiled in heated debate. The merchants had seared more than a few ears in vigorous complaint of yesterday's outrage. Today's encounter with Yeshua humiliated the Sanhedrin's delegation by its challenge to their authority. The words on paying to Caesar what is Caesar's irritated all who bore any resentment of Rome's rule. Yeshua's defenders dwindled to a handful of Pharisees who argued he spoke only as a reformer.

"Let the assembly come to order!" Nathaniel shouted from the door to the Chamber. After ringing the *magrefa*, he intoned: "The High Priest Caiaphas, and Annas." The father-in-law of Caiaphas, Annas had himself served as High Priest for the ten years prior to Caiaphas. Though holding no office presently, Annas possessed enormous informal power accrued over time. His presence in the Sanhedrin today signaled that serious matters awaited – a sign underscored by the entry of Caiaphas clothed in the full vestments of the High Priest.

One of Herod's legacies left the Roman procurators in control of the vestments until one week prior to festivals. A blue robe fringed at the bottom with gold bells and pomegranates, the embroidered vest known as the *ephod* with intertwining bands of gold and purple and scarlet, the square metallic frontispiece inlaid with 12 faceted gemstones. Ordinarily, Caiaphas wore these only when officiating at the altar. Perhaps another sacrifice was in the offing.

"Elohim Adonai, great is your name and holiness." Caiaphas uttered the words with head and eyes cast upward. When his gaze lowered, he spoke to the council. "Has anyone not heard of our delegation's meeting with Rabbi Yeshua, led by Eli?"

No one spoke. The news had spread rapidly.

Caiaphas looked briefly at Nathaniel and then Annas. "Even though he does not serve on the Sanhedrin, I would ask Annas to share his wisdom on these matters before us today. That is," Caiaphas continued, looking directly at Lot, leader of the Pharisees and one of Yeshua's few remaining sympathizers, "if no one objects to his speaking."

Lot dipped his head in deference.

Annas stood, holding on to his chair's arms to steady

himself. "The Council is generous to hear out an old man. But it is an old man who has seen much. Much suffering for our people, when enthusiasm runs unchecked. Much distress inside this Temple, when those who do not understand its workings try to force new ways. And new is not always right." Annas released the chair from his grip, and shuffled toward the center of the semi-circled benches. "I myself have not heard the Galilean Rabbi, so I do not pass judgment on him." Turning in the direction of Lot, he added: "Not yet. But what I have heard of him worries me. Worries all Jerusalem. And what worries us will worry the Gentiles in the Antonia. For that reason, we must act."

Lot took a deep breath and stood. "Is this action arrest, because he teaches new things?"

"Lot, do not interrupt before he is finished!" Caiaphas rose as he spoke.

"No, no," Annas offered, waving a hand in the direction of Caiaphas. "My Pharisee brother is right to air his concerns. Contrary to what you might assume," he resumed, "I do not seek Yeshua's arrest. If I did, it would only be for disruption, or sedition, or blasphemy."

"Blasphemy?" Lot blurted out, as much surprised by his own voicing of the word as its first hearing. "What blasphemy?"

Annas tilted his head to the side, catching a glimpse of Lamech. "There have been rumors," he enunciated slowly, allowing silence between each word for emphasis. "Now, I do not bide by rumors. But if such things are being said, for the rabbi's own protection we should find out from him their substance or falsehood. Would that not be the fair thing to do, Lot?"

"Not by arresting him?"

"Absolutely not! Arrest would be too strong an action. But summoned for a private interview, where conversation can be candid and without the crowds' fervor to confuse? I say to the Sanhedrin: bring Yeshua to my house. In the evening, perhaps tomorrow, where we can talk freely. If any have charges to bring, they can be dealt with then. A few guards can insure order."

"But there can be no trial of the Sanhedrin by night!" Lot looked around for support. The Arimathean, Joseph, nodded his head. But only one or two others.

"Lot, this will not be a trial. Merely an interview. We do this for his sake as well as our own. And the city's." Having spoken, Annas returned to his chair and sat back down.

"Do we have agreement on this?" asked Caiaphas.

Before Lot could muster thoughts for an alternative, most of the Sanhedrin members rose and uttered a resounding "Amen." The Pharisee slumped down onto the bench. Through the converging of members around Annas to thank him for his plan, Lot noticed Lamech, Nathaniel, and Caiaphas standing together. Smiling.

* * *

Having heard Antony's report on this day's spying on Yeshua, Pilate focused on the exchange between the rabbi and the Sanhedrin members. "The Galilean told the Temple Jews to pay Caesar what they owed Caesar?"

"And God what was due God."

Pilate looked hard at Antony, still in disguise. "You were there, what did he mean?"

"As I said, that is the puzzle. He didn't say. He left it for them to decide."

Pilate poured a small amount of wine into a goblet, sipped a mouthful, swirled it around, and swallowed. "His intent, no doubt. Leave room for denial, if any wanted to press him about the truth of what he said." Pilate raised the goblet once more, then stopped before it reached his lips. "But you also said something of his meeting with one of those, what did you call them?"

"Essenes. Most live in communities by the Salt Sea."

"Are they in league with the Zealots?"

"Not always. Though this one, who came to where the

rabbi stayed in Bethany, was the same man wounded the night we seized Barabbas."

"Really?" Pilate emptied the wine in the goblet. "Then our Yeshua may be more than a spinner of riddles. Did you did leave one of your men to keep an eye on him?"

"Yes sir, and I assigned another to watch the Essene. He stays in the upper city, in a small neighborhood where others of their sect also stay during the festival."

Pilate poured a small amount of the wine into the goblet and handed it to Antony. "You've done well, centurion. Unlike Julius, you use your knowledge of these Jews to good advantage. To Rome's advantage."

"Thank you, procurator." Antony's aversion to Pilate and this insult of Julius soured the mouthful of wine Antony swallowed. "Is there anything else, Procurator?"

"No. Just maintain contact with those who watch the rabbi and his Essene partner. Continue your assignment tomorrow in the streets. And keep me informed on what you find out." Pilate returned to scanning parchments containing reports from prior years of Passover in the city. He didn't know the handwriting belonged not to the cohort's tribunes, but Julius.

Antony saluted and left. Still clothed as a Jew, he thought of visiting a caravansary in the lower city known to be a haunt of the Zealots. He remembered when he'd been to that place more than twenty years ago. Then, Lucius had him execute two Zealots captured in a trap set by Julius. Word had it that Zealots still favored it as a meeting place. But Pilate was at the moment more concerned with the Galilean rabbi. The Zealots, and the caravansary, would have to wait.

* * *

Hannah lost track of time after leaving Julius, her mind returning again and again to her encounter with her mother. Hannah knew she must see her again. Perhaps if Rebekah were not there, words might be easier, for both. Complicating all was her growing concern for Yeshua's safety. And it would not be long before she must go to *Gesamani* to meet Julius...

"Hannah." Mary's hand touched her arm. "You walked past our house, as if in a daze. When I called out, you didn't answer. Is everything alright?"

Hannah looked at Yeshua's mother. The image of the woman remembered from childhood had changed. Mary's soft olive skin had creased and hardened. Flesh showed splotches caused from too much wind and sun. Hair once raven black now wove white and gray into the mix. "No, they're not. It's my mother. Our visit didn't go as I hoped."

"I remember your saying something to Salome to that effect, but I didn't want to interfere. Did Naomi refuse to speak with you?"

"No. We had words. Some good, some not. Rebekah proved harder."

"Elias' widow?" Mary thought back to times in the carpenter's home, and Rebekah's and Naomi's friendship. "Does Rebekah live with Naomi?"

"I hope not. Something was said about her staying elsewhere."

Mary saw two young women with infants walk by. "Hannah, would you mind if I went with you the next time you visit your mother? I haven't seen her since the night we fled."

Hannah's face revealed a slight grimace. "My mother still blames you and Joseph for leaving without warning. If she saw you, I don't know what she might say. Or do."

"I understand. But I might finally be able to tell her why we acted as we did. And if she listens, it might help persuade her of the changes in your life."

"Maybe you're right. Come with me, the next time we have free," Hannah suggested, "when Yeshua and the others are busy elsewhere. Perhaps tomorrow. I can't promise anything."

"Tomorrow," Mary affirmed. The two women hugged. Mary remembered holding Hannah in her arms years ago, before so much had changed for them both. "Tomorrow."

CHAPTER XLVIII

Sunlight angled through the spindly upper limbs of the olive trees. Though another hour of light remained in the sky, the ridge capped by the Temple already cast shadows across *Gesamani*. Julius sat alone among those shadows lacing the grove's floor. His backrest was a circular stone trough used at harvest to bruise olives for cooking oil. Directly across from him stood the pressing basin. Dismantled now, a wooden beam and stone weights leaned against the rounded basin. Julius stared at the weights, feeling his own shoulders sag under Hannah's disclosure of Nathaniel as her great-uncle. In the few hours since, Julius wove what had been isolated threads into a sordid tapestry knotting his life to Nathaniel's.

He thought back to the seawall in Caesarea, where Hannah had railed against a family that deserted her when she disclosed her rape. She remarked then of a relative, a member of the Sanhedrin, who paid her to leave home so as not to disgrace the family. Nathaniel's doing. Then there was Julius' meeting in the Antonia with a young Jew disgraced by a father's cowardice. To be done with him, his great-uncle had arranged for Julius to take the boy into the legion. Nathaniel's doing. There could be no doubt. Antony and Hannah were brother and sister, each fleeing in different directions from what had been done to them in Bethlehem.

In Bethlehem. Julius did more than imagine the pair as children there. He now clearly remembered them. He remembered them in the street, escape cut off. He remembered a cowering father, a dead brother. But most of all, he remembered an earlier meeting on the night when Herod commanded the massacre of Bethlehem's children be planned and carried out. Nathaniel was at that meeting. Nathaniel swore he'd remain silent about the plan, knowing full well he condemned his own flesh and blood to death. Nathaniel!

"Julius?"

Hannah came into view around the corner of the stone trough. For a moment, her face juxtaposed with that of a toddler, crying beside her lifeless brother. Behind her, Julius could envision Nathaniel mouthing his oath of silence to Herod.

"Julius, is something wrong?"

Julius pulled himself to his feet, took her hands into his, and pressed his lips against her forehead. "On the way to Ishmael's, we must talk." Julius wrapped his arm around her shoulder, no longer caring if anyone took notice. "It's about Nathaniel. There are things you must know."

* * *

Nathaniel wiped his mouth and beard with a square of cloth. Though he loved soups, his hands no longer possessed the steadiness of youth. The cloth swiped away bits of lentil from hair and chin.

Naomi saw his bowl was empty. "Can the servant ladle another serving for you?"

Nathaniel shook his head, blew his nose into the cloth, then wadded it and tossed it into his bowl. "No, this was plenty for me. But please, Rebekah, feel free to have more. No guest should leave my table hungry."

The mother of Barabbas sipped one more spoonful from a bowl still half full, then pushed it away. "Forgive me, Sopher, but I have little appetite these days."

Over dinner, conversation limited itself to pleasantries. Now, however, Nathaniel broached what he knew to be the reason for Naomi's inviting of Rebekah to supper. "A son imprisoned by the Romans, set to die. Who can blame you?"

Nathaniel eyed Rebekah closely as he spoke. "But he chose his fate, especially when he raised a knife to that Roman in Jericho."

Rebekah stirred her soup, stifling a desire to snatch at Nathaniel's baiting. But she still had need of him. "We all choose our fates. Though that Roman killed by my son had long ago robbed my husband and our youngest boy's ability to choose anything." Rebekah set her spoon on the table. "But these are things past, and cannot be undone. Today, I come to ask a favor."

"A visit to your son in the Antonia?"

"Did Naomi already tell you?"

Naomi reached her hand to Rebekah's. "I hope you don't mind."

Before Rebekah could speak, Nathaniel reached for his cane and, with effort, stood up. "It's well she did speak. What with Pilate planning the execution for the day of Passover, time runs short. Arrangements require time."

"But they can still be made?" Rebekah asked.

"Actually, have been made. Tomorrow, an hour before noon. Come to the High Priest's chambers. Temple guards will escort you from there. You'll have fifteen minutes."

Naomi gasped. "Fifteen minutes? Is that all a mother has?"

"That's all that can be done." Nathaniel shuffled to a cushioned chair and sat down. "For what he did, I'm surprised the Romans allowed that. And Rebekah," Nathaniel added, "prepare yourself. The guards at the Antonia treat their prisoners harshly."

Naomi lowered her head. Rebekah stared hard at Nathaniel. "My son is a strong man, Sopher. Without regrets. Elias died well. So will Barabbas."

Nathaniel clasped his fingers together on the cane and rested his chin on them. "I admire your courage, Rebekah. And your conviction. God willing, your son inherited both."

A long silence ensued. Naomi had hoped Nathaniel

might somehow still arrange to spare Rebekah's son. But that was not to be. Thinking of her friend's impending loss of a child suddenly reminded Naomi of a matter not yet shared with Nathaniel.

"Uncle, there is other news today. About Hannah."

"Hannah!?" Nathaniel exclaimed.

Naomi felt Rebekah's hand slide from her own. "Hannah came here today."

"She was in my house?"

"Hannah is still my daughter. She's given up her old ways for a new life."

"New life!" Rebekah's voice rose, "New life by taking up with a Roman, and following the Nazarene Yeshua."

"She says she's changed," Naomi insisted.

The two women engaged in a brief exchange, though Nathaniel barely heard their words. One of his own family taken up with Yeshua? Nathaniel's mind drifted to his apprenticeship with Saripheus. Foolish actions by the son of the former Sopher had condemned the father. If word about his connection to Hannah got out, he might suffer the same. On the other hand, knowing someone inside Yeshua's circle might provide helpful information. If he might convince Hannah he simply wanted to learn more . . .

". . . I told her I will see her again, uncle. If you don't wish her in this house, we will go elsewhere. What is your judgment?"

Nathaniel caught these last sentences and weighed his response. "If mistakes cannot be amended, who among us can ever hope to stand before Elohim? Mind you, I'm not condoning what she's done, Naomi. But yes, have Hannah return. And at a time when I might speak with her as well. Who knows what the Almighty will make of all this?"

Naomi went over and kissed her uncle's forehead. "Thank you."

Rebekah observed the scene. Naomi, ever the victim of emotion. But Nathaniel? From her own experience and the conversation of Zealot friends, Rebekah knew him to be a man of stealth. This sudden tolerance did not fit his character. Rebekah found herself wishing she knew what Nathaniel saw in this reunion for him.

* * *

Julius broke the last piece of bread in two, giving half to Hannah. No words passed between them, and hardly any words had been spoken during the meal. The discussion from Gesamani to the inn had been hard for Hannah to hear and Julius to say.

Hannah dipped the bread into wine to soften its texture. Julius chewed a dry hunk from the loaf, washing it down with a drink from the chalice. He thought of downing what remained in the whole pitcher, and perhaps ask for another. But wine would not let him forget. Not anymore.

"He knew." Hannah set the sopped bread onto the plate. "He knew what would come of David, and the rest of the children. All along."

Julius glanced around to make sure no one overhead them. "You must be careful if Nathaniel is around when you visit your mother. For your own sake, as well as Yeshua's."

"You think he knows Yeshua's true identity?"

"A man like Nathaniel makes it his business to know. But even if he hasn't made the connection with Bethlehem, he holds great sway in the Sanhedrin. And unless I'm mistaken, this morning's questioning of Yeshua is only the beginning."

"The beginning of what?"

"I can't be sure. It sounds from the questions asked that they were gathering evidence. But whether they plan to challenge him, or try him, or something else, I can't say."

Hannah slipped the wine-soaked bread into her mouth and ate. "You have no doubt that Nathaniel will stand with those who oppose Yeshua."

"After what your rabbi did to the merchants, then trapped the Sanhedrin's men in their own words? No doubt.

And as we both know, Nathaniel can be ruthless. Nothing, no one, stands in his way. Not you, not Antony." Julius paused, then uttered. "Not David."

Hannah's eyes closed. She blamed Yeshua for David's death for years on end. Now, the real betrayer came into view. "Do you remember the first day we heard Yeshua? He spoke of forgiveness for enemies." Hannah opened her eyes, searching those of Julius. "Yeshua, I forgave. And you. Do you think I can forgive Nathaniel?"

"Can you forgive Nathaniel? I'd say, why would you want to?"

"Because God has forgiven me of so much." Hannah's words came out half-statement, half-question.

Julius fingered the sides of his temple. "Hannah, I don't pretend to understand this new religion you find in Yeshua. I see you gain peace from it, so for that I've your rabbi to thank. But forgiving enemies: Ask your rabbi how he would forgive someone who doesn't even consider what he does to be sin! But no matter what, Hannah: even if you do somehow forgive Nathaniel his past, don't forget it! Don't forget what Nathaniel is capable of."

Julius might have continued, but Hannah's squeezing of his hand silenced him. He felt, and smelled, a grimy hand on his shoulder and a head leaning beside his own. "Excuse me for taking so long, Julius, but I didn't want to be seen coming to you right away. Other eyes beside mine pay attention to such things."

"Have a seat, Ishmael."

The old man straddled the bench next to Julius. A brief smile toward Hannah quickly dissolved into a frown. "Things don't go well for your Nazarene rabbi, lady. Two of the Zealot chieftains met at noon, which is why I sent for you two."

"What do they intend?"

"I didn't catch everything, but here's the core. The Sanhedrin will convene. A few witnesses testify to blasphemy. Others speak of treason."

"Blasphemy secures the council's judgment, and treason Pilate's," Julius reflected in grudging admiration. "But what did they say of the plan itself?"

"Nothing of when it happens, or how. Just it's going to be the Sanhedrin's doing."

Hannah leaned toward Ishmael. "And Nathaniel's?"

Ishmael winked at Hannah. "You've a quick mind for such things, lady. These days, the Sanhedrin does nothing without Nathaniel's hand in it. Been so ever since you and I first worked together, Julius. If I learn more, I'll send word to you again. But if I were you, tell the rabbi to watch out for himself – and don't get too close to him yourself. Who knows how they'll come after him? Especially if the plan unsheathes the Zealots' knives."

Ishmael lumbered to his feet, took a few steps, then turned and announced so all in the room could hear: "I'll tell my nephew you think his stew is the best in Jerusalem. Come back anytime for more." Ishmael picked his way back to his chair, feigning failed eyesight with a few bumps into chairs or tables.

Hannah and Julius left the caravansary. No words passed between them on their way to Bethany until they reached Gesamani. Julius broke the silence. "I have to speak with Yeshua."

Hannah stopped. "Now?"

"Tomorrow. Find a way to bring him to the garden, where you found me today. Without all the others."

"And if he'll not come?"

"Then find me, and I will come to him." Julius looked up. Stars canopied the grove of trees and a full moon hung above the Mount of Olives. "Let's hope we're not too late already."

* * *

Nathaniel pulled an outer cloak over his night robe, disturbed at being roused from an early bed. Rebekah had returned to her lodgings shortly after supper. When Naomi said she would bathe before sleeping, Nathaniel took the opportunity to retire for the night. The next day would be long, Caiaphas having told him he would be needed at first light to help arrange Yeshua's being taken into custody later that evening. But no sooner had he reclined on the sleeping mat than the steward brought news of a Temple guard escorting a visitor.

Carefully measuring his steps down the stairs so he stayed in the light of his servant's lamp, Nathaniel reasoned this must have something to do with plans regarding Yeshua. But who, and why at this hour? Another day remained. Once at the bottom of the stairs, Nathaniel dispatched the servant upstairs to stand by Naomi's room. If she did come out from her bath, he didn't want her stumbling into temple business.

Nathaniel could now see the outlines of two figures on the porch. The uniform of a Temple guard became clear as Nathaniel neared, but darkness still cloaked the other fellow's identity. Nathaniel walked to the opened door. "Who seeks the Sopher?"

The guard bowed low. "Excuse the hour, Sopher. But this pilgrim came to the temple, inquiring for you. I told him to wait until morning, but he insisted. Said he would come to your house, that he knew the way. I thought it best to accompany him, to be safe."

Nathaniel pulled his cloak tighter against the night air. "What makes this visit so pressing, traveler, to roust me from bed?"

The stranger stepped into the light cast from the inside. "I had to see you, Nathaniel."

The Sopher's eyes squinted, trying to connect the voice with the face. "Do I know you?"

The stranger took a deep breath, then spoke. "Yes, you do. I am Joshua, Naomi's –"

"Joshua? What are you doing here? After so many

years?"

"It's a long story, Nathaniel. I've been in Galilee, at Tiberias. I came to Jerusalem needing to talk to someone. And then I heard the Sopher to be named Nathaniel, but I didn't know if it might be another Nathaniel, though I couldn't be sure without coming." Joshua stopped, realizing all of the rehearsing of what he'd say, and to whom, was quickly failing him.

"Get on with it. But keep your voice down." Even in his shock, Nathaniel didn't want Naomi hearing his voice. At least not yet. "What do you want?"

Joshua clasped his hands and started again. "I come to speak for another, Nathaniel. A Nazarene rabbi named Yeshua."

Nathaniel stood rigid, stifling any response that might betray his hand. "Guard, give us a few moments to ourselves. But stand by."

The guard walked down to the street, still close enough to keep watch.

Nathaniel turned to Joshua. "What of him?"

"You've heard of Yeshua?"

"Only briefly."

"Well, this rabbi is in danger. The Zealots plan to have him killed unless he follows their lead in some demonstration against Rome."

So Lamech had planned this all along. Nathaniel wondered how much more Joshua might know. "Do they plan to murder the rabbi outright?"

"No." Nathaniel's openness eased Joshua. "They plan to bring charges through the Sanhedrin, which is why I hoped I'd find you to still be the Sopher. You could intervene."

"Yes, I could. And I very well may. But tell me this, Joshua: why do you come all the way from Tiberias to intervene for this man?"

There was no turning back. Joshua had carried this

inside, unspoken, too many years. "I had to, Nathaniel. For David. I let David die. I can't let Yeshua."

"David? And Yeshua? What could they possibly have in common?"

"A Roman confided to me that it was Yeshua they'd come to kill in Bethlehem."

"Really? You think this Yeshua from Nazareth and Yeshua of Bethlehem are the same?"

"I learned that, too."

Nathaniel pressed on. "Let me try and understand. You say David died, when it should have been Yeshua. And now you say, you want to save Yeshua? It seems, Joshua, you'd be better served seeing Yeshua dead. Or at least, you'd want to finally take vengeance on the Romans!"

"Maybe once. But Yeshua had no blame for what the Romans did, any more than David deserved to die. So, if I can save Yeshua, it doesn't bring David back, but it does spare one innocent. As for the Romans, I did seek revenge. I joined a band of Sicarii led by Kohath and – ." Joshua stopped abruptly. He hadn't intended to bring that up. "But that is all past."

Nathaniel glared at Joshua once the name Kohath had been pronounced. He watched closely when Joshua stopped mid-sentence, seeing sweat form on his brow in the evening chill. The past was not all past. "Kohath?"

"Yes." Joshua swallowed.

"How long were you with Kohath?"

"Not too long."

Nathaniel seized Joshua's mantle. As he did, the guard stepped briskly toward them. "Not too long? But long enough to know they plotted against me!"

"Nathaniel, I had not part in that!"

"In THAT? You did know!?" By this time, the guard pinned Joshua's arms against his body. "You did know, and you didn't warn me!"

"I wanted to, but I couldn't. They'd have killed me!"

"Shut your lying mouth," Nathaniel spewed. "They would have killed you, like that Roman would have killed you if you'd taken the knife after David's death. But you wanted to live. Even if I died!"

"Nathaniel, please! I snuck away before the attack started. And then, when I heard Kohath and the others were killed, and you lived, I thanked God – "

Nathaniel struck Joshua's leg as hard as he could manage with his cane. "Leave God out of your coward's act! Besides being murderers, Kohath and his men executed Romans. That makes you an insurrectionist, Joshua, for which the penalty is death." The Sopher looked past Joshua to the guard. "Take him to the Antonia. Tell the officer in command I'll send formal charges of murder and rebellion in the morning."

"But what of Yeshua, Nathaniel?" Joshua cried out. "At least save him!"

Nathaniel jutted his face directly into Joshua's. "You let your precious David die. And now, poor Joshua, poor hapless Joshua, go to your grave knowing that once again you are a miserable failure. I will personally see to it that Yeshua follows right behind you in death!"

CHAPTER XLIX

"This is simply not right!" Judas paced before Yeshua and the eleven, who stood in the center of the room. Other followers, including the women and Hannah, sat around the edges. "We have always observed Passover according to the custom of the Temple, not the calendar of these wilderness fanatics."

"The Baptizer favored the Essenes," Andrew interjected. "I heard him speak well of them."

"No one questions the Baptizer," Judas insisted. "But in all the time you followed him, did you ever keep the Essene Passover?"

"No, but that was because I returned home to celebrate with Peter and –"

"There is my argument! Passover is about our traditions, not those of strangers."

"Judas speaks the truth." Peter had been uncharacteristically quiet to this point. No longer. "Those of us who've made the trip to Jerusalem before, we've always kept the traditional feast. This is no time to start new ideas, especially with the Sanhedrin watching you, Rabbi. I say we turn down Abraham's offer. For your own good."

"Would anyone else speak?" Yeshua waited. All but two of the twelve had voiced an opinion since Yeshua announced Abraham's invitation and his intention to accept.

Judas returned to his place just to the left of Yeshua. "Peter's right. It's for your own good. Don't give your enemies any more reason to hold you over the fire."

Yeshua studied the now-cooling embers of the morning's cooking fire. "You have a point. Safety resides in keeping to what has always been." The rabbi took a long stick and stirred the embers apart. Wisps of smoke arose, then disappeared. The fire neared dying. "Life would have been much safer for you, Peter, had you kept to your nets. And you, Levi, to the tax tables. It's the same for everyone here." Yeshua looked beyond the inner circle, to those on the outside, to Hannah. "Not a single one of you is safer because you follow me. Least of all now, when Jerusalem brings the promise of suffering."

Peter stepped in front of Yeshua and pointed a finger in his face. "Rabbi, why do you insist on this talk? We need victory, not suffering. God slew the Egyptian firstborn, not those of Israel. He will do so again, and pray it be this Passover!"

"God will do what God will do when the Almighty chooses!" Yeshua spoke each word in ascending volume, until "chooses" rang off the walls. "Don't stand in the way of God, Peter. Or presume to know God's choices beforehand. You may miss God's workings."

Peter looked away. He'd come to recognize when the rabbi's will was set.

Judas, staring at the floor, spoke barely above a whisper. "And Passover?"

Yeshua rested a hand on the shoulder of Judas. "Tonight. At the place Abraham prepares. I long to keep it with you. With all of you." Yeshua squeezed Judas' shoulder at the word *all*. "We meet Abraham at the Golden Gate, at the eleventh hour."

"Rabbi, there is one matter." It was Andrew again. "From my time with the Baptizer, I recall the Essenes' keeping of Passover involves only men. What of the women?"

Yeshua looked at the women who came from Galilee, including his own mother. "Since we eat by his invitation, we keep to his customs."

"Could we also keep the traditional Passover later?"

Mary's request verged on plea.

"When the lamb is sacrificed, God's Passover will be kept." No one questioned the meaning of Yeshua's answer. The room slowly emptied, most for a morning walk. A few gathered under the awning or in the street to talk about what had just transpired.

Hannah waited until Yeshua was alone, then bowed slightly. "Rabbi, I seek a favor."

"Yes?"

"Before you go with the others to the Passover meal, a friend and I need to speak with you. Alone. At Gesamani."

"What friend would this be?"

"Someone who, well, someone you helped me to forgive."

"I see. And he has some need beyond your forgiveness?"

Hannah stepped closer. "We both have need. To help you. To protect you."

Yeshua smiled. "You've been help enough over these months. As for protection, what would you shield me from?"

"Hear us out. For my sake – for David's sake – if not your own."

Hannah had not mentioned David to Yeshua since Capernaum. For her to invoke his name now struck home to Yeshua. "For David," came his answer. The two left for Gesamani.

* * *

The guards flanking Rebekah uttered no word as they escorted her. Sandals clopped against the stone floors of the Antonia's corridors and stairways. This far down, where the foundations of the fortress burrowed deep into limestone, water constantly beaded on the walls. The guards' key unlocked another latch, and the men pushed open the thick slab of a door to another passageway. The smell inside reeked of urine and excrement. At the far end of the hall, the guards stopped. One took out an iron bar and ran it across the grated window of a cell door. Rebekah saw movement in the dark. "To your feet, Jew. You've company."

The other guard set a torch in a holder on the wall. "We'll be back when your time's up."

The pair walked away. Rebekah heard the door creak on its hinges and slam shut. Then nothing more, except a distant laugh from the direction of the guards.

"Barabbas. Can you hear me?"

A figure moved in the darkness, and then a face appeared behind the bars. "Mother? Thank God!" He reached a hand through the bars and Rebekah took hold of it. It felt as cold as the stone. "I thought I'd never see you." Rebekah peered at his face. Blood crusted over eyebrows and under lips. Dirt covered all. Tears began to form. "They told me I'd see no one, not until I carried my cross. . ." His voice trailed off in sobs.

"Don't let them break you, son. Don't give them the satisfaction. Be brave."

Barabbas reached his other hand through to embrace his mother as much as the bars allowed. She could feel several fingers in his hands to be broken, standing at strange angles. "I try my best. When they first brought me, I defied them at every step." Barabbas leaned his head to rest against the bars. "But I don't have the strength anymore. I haven't seen the sun since Bethlehem. If I speak to another prisoner, we're both beaten. Things have been done that – "

His teeth clenched to spare Rebekah, though the images tore through his mind. The opening of the cell door, followed by four and sometimes five soldiers pinning him down, feeling the guards' iron bar beat him until he almost passes out – but never quite. Then the same bludgeon thrusted inside him, slickened only by his blood. He'd lost count of the times but not the pain. His thoughts focused on Rebekah again. "I can't do this, mother, I can't."

Rebekah glanced quickly down the hall to make sure a guard had not stayed behind to listen. She could see nothing, but took no chances. "Keep your voice down. Would you have them hear you're defeated? Listen to me. You are held as a great man among the Zealots, and many others. That is how you lived – and that is how you must die."

Barabbas pulled back slightly. "You wish me dead?"

"Don't be foolish! I only wish you to make the best of what the Almighty can work through you. And right now, that is the martyr's path. Like your father before you."

"My father before me." The hands of Barabbas loosed from his mother. He used one to reach inside his torn robe and pull out a leather thong. On it hung a small carved wolf. "This is all I have left of my father."

The carving's sight surprised Rebekah. She turned her head aside, so her son would not see her own eyes tearing. The sounds of a key turning and hinges squeaking startled them both. "We've not much time." Rebekah reached through the bar to stroke her son's cheek. "Be brave, Barabbas." Rebekah felt her son's lips on her hand. Then his tears.

"You've had your time, Jewess. And you in there, back away from the door." The guard jammed an iron rod through the bars, catching Barabbas square in the shoulder. The guards led Rebekah away.

Only when he could no longer hear their footsteps did Barabbas make a sound. "I love you." Taking the carved wolf in hand, he slumped against the far wall of the cell. "I love you." No one in this darkness heard. Or cared.

* * *

Broken clouds provided passing shade on the walk down the Mount of Olives toward Gesamani. Hannah related how she once played in this grove as a child, pretending to be one of the workmen pressing oil along with her brother Simeon. Yeshua turned the conversation to Simeon, and asked what Bethlehem had done to him. He turned to the legion, she said, though her family spoke little of him after he left. Twenty years had passed without seeing him, or knowing where he was, or even if he was still alive. She recalled something of a new name taken to disguise his identity, a Roman name. Nothing more.

Once in Gesamani, the pair headed toward the presses. "I see your friend. Over there."

Hannah caught sight of Julius at the same moment as Yeshua. He stood at the gnarled base of one of the grove's patriarchs.

"This is rabbi Yeshua," Hannah offered, once they reached him. "and this is Julius."

Yeshua eyed the man before him. "A Gentile."

Julius, recalling his earlier days of mediating with the Sopher, offered no handshake that would bring uncleanness to a Jew. "A Roman," he bowed, "and a friend."

"Hannah calls you friend." Yeshua sat on one of the millstones while Hannah and Julius perched on a timber used for pressing. "But why would a Roman profess friendship to me?"

"When Hannah first saw you, I was with her. By the lakeside near Capernaum."

"And the night Hannah came to me through the crowd. You were there as well?"

Julius looked off to the side, the corners of his mouth tightening. "No. We had an argument that night. I'd left."

Silence passed. A dove cooed in the distance. "Hannah tells me she's forgiven you."

"Hannah finds forgiveness for many, rabbi." Julius looked back to Yeshua. "Certainly for more than I can."

"Yourself included."

The Roman tipped his head in grudging admiration. "Be that as it may, I didn't ask Hannah to bring you here to counsel me. To speak bluntly, you're in grave danger."

"Before I ask about the danger, what does a rabbi's fate count in Roman eyes?"

"Not much, truthfully – except for Hannah. I once made a vow never to hurt her, and you are someone she prizes for the peace you've brought her. Harm to you means harm to her. And I told her I would do what I could to protect you."

"And what can you do?"

"Stay close to you, if you'd allow. Though your Galilean friends might not look kindly on the likes of me clinging to your back."

"No, I suspect not." The smile that briefly came to Yeshua's face quickly passed as his brow furrowed. "And I wouldn't have you do that."

"Before you reject the idea, know that the Zealots have entered into some pact with the Sanhedrin. False accusations will be made: that you've broken your religion, acted against Rome. And I don't think they scheme to simply ruin your reputation." Julius leaned toward Yeshua. "It wouldn't take much for me to linger near you, in the background, to give some warning so you might flee. Or take some precaution. Or, if it came to that, help your Galileans stand for you."

The rabbi sat back, reflecting on Julius' words before speaking. "You put yourself at risk to find out such things. Both of you. And I have no doubt they're true. But – "

"Please, rabbi, let us help you." Hannah got up and moved to sit on the stone beside Yeshua. "We can leave Jerusalem before they act. Return to Galilee."

Yeshua sighed. "I cannot run, daughter. This is where I must be."

"Why not live to fight another day?" Julius stood and stepped next to Yeshua. Crouching before the rabbi, he added, "Why hurt Hannah, and those like her, who look up to you?"

"I do not intend to hurt Hannah. You and I share that much." Yeshua suddenly gripped the arm of Julius, surprising the Roman with his firmness. "But I must do what I know to be right, no matter the cost. You do understand that?"

The gesture and words caught Julius off-guard. He knew exactly what Yeshua meant. Julius understood what would've been the right thing to do years ago, and its likely cost to career and perhaps life. He also knew he failed to do that when he went ahead and led his troops into Bethlehem, a failure that had haunted Julius ever since.

"I do understand."

Yeshua loosened his grip and Julius stood. Yeshua did the same.

"One favor I ask of you, Julius. If this plot you warn of does take place, see that Hannah remains safe. She has great love for you. And, I can see, you for her."

Julius moved next to Hannah and slid his arm inside hers. "You don't condemn us?"

"I do not condemn love." The rabbi turned and started back on the path to Bethany.

Yeshua had gone a few paces when he heard Julius cry out: "Would you still say that, if you knew who I really was?"

Yeshua stopped. Pivoting to face the pair, he called out: "I do say that, and I do know who you are." Yeshua walked backwards several steps, then exclaimed: "Centurion Julius, head of Herod's detail to Bethlehem. Find your peace!" The rabbi departed, leaving the two in shock.

Once he was out of sight, Julius turned to Hannah. "You told him?"

Hannah's eyes widened and her face paled. "Of you and Bethlehem? I said nothing."

Julius and Hannah clung to one another, dumbfounded.

* * *

Out of breath, Judas finally arrived in Bethphage. He mostly ran the mile or so from Bethany, having his leave from the group when Yeshua departed with Hannah. He figured no one would care about his absence, absorbed as they were in hushed conversations about the rabbi's indiscretion for walking alone with a woman of her background.

The sight in front of the house he sought both relieved and unnerved Judas. Jacob, whom he hoped to see, squatted by the front entrance. Reuben, the Judean Zealot he didn't trust, knelt next to him. Another man exited the house and stood beside the pair. His robes suggested a man of wealth. Jacob stood when he saw Judas approach, as did Reuben.

"Judas! I thought we'd agreed to meet at night!" Jacob watched as Judas bent over at the waist, struggling to catch his breath, his cheeks flushed a bright red.

"Something must be wrong," Reuben muttered.

Judas straightened up, glancing at the fellow in rich robes. "We need to speak, Jacob," grabbing another quick breath, "in private."

Jacob patted Judas on the back. "Don't worry. This is Lamech, from the Sanhedrin. He speaks there for us. But let's go inside. You can sit and rest while we talk."

The four men entered the house. Reuben fetched a skin of water for Judas. Judas lifted the skin and opened his mouth. A stream splashed out, wetting beard and chin as much as throat.

"Your rabbi greatly disappointed the elders of the Sanhedrin," Lamech began. "First with his violence in the market, and then with riddles that make us appear as fools."

"He means no offense," Judas wiped his mouth dry, then drank again.

Reuben glared at Jacob. The Galilean nodded, then spoke. "Judas, you and I have given Yeshua every possible opportunity to align himself with us. But it will not be."

Judas set down the waterskin. "Maybe if he saw more of Rome's hand in this city. There might still be time to –"

"Your teacher's out of time. And we are out of patience." Reuben took the skin and squirted a small stream on the dirt floor. The soil soaked up the water, barely leaving a trace. "He brings the kingdom to Jerusalem as much as this water makes this dirt a garden."

"What has the Sanhedrin decided?" Judas looked at Reuben, then to Jacob. "There's to be no violence against him, we agreed to that."

"Of course not," Jacob assured. "They only want to

speak with him. In private."

"Absolutely" Lamech moved next to Judas and put a hand on his shoulder. "A private interview will simply give us opportunity to share our concerns. Once we've had our conversation, and matters are understood – we go our ways."

"Will you summon him for this interview when he teaches at the temple?"

"Actually, we hoped to arrange this for some evening, ideally tonight. Again, that way we avoid problems with the rabble misunderstanding. Or more extreme factions interfering."

Lamech paused, then softened his voice. "Judas, can you assist us on this? Let us know where we might find him tonight? It would be of great help to us. And to him."

"You'd be doing the rabbi a favor," Jacob added. "If all this can be handled out of the public's eye, out of Rome's eye, there's less possibility of trouble. Less danger for Yeshua."

Judas felt Lamech's hand massage his shoulder, even as Jacob's words soothed Judas' fears. It did make sense. Once the Sanhedrin had been satisfied Yeshua was no threat, the rabbi would at worst be sent on his way back to Galilee. Judas could still try to convince Yeshua to align with Jacob. "Tonight, we meet at an Essene home to observe the Passover by their calendar. Yeshua spoke of stopping afterwards at Gesamani for prayer. He has done so before."

Reuben smiled. "Gesamani would be an excellent place to seek the rabbi. But how will we know when you go there, so Lamech and the Sanhedrin can prepare a delegation?"

"I can leave early, once supper is done. While the others visit, I'll go to the Temple."

"To the meeting room of the Sanhedrin," Lamech specified. "We'll inform the guards at the Temple gates to expect your arrival, so you have no difficulty reaching the chamber."

Lamech moved in front of Judas, now placing both

hands on his shoulders. "You serve your people and your rabbi well, Judas. May God see that your deed goes remembered."

CHAPTER L

"My lord Caiaphas." Lamech bowed before the high priest. Caiaphas sat behind the table in his chamber with Nathaniel at his side.

The high priest nodded. "The steward said you bring news about rabbi Yeshua."

"Good news. He may be seized tonight after eating the Passover of the Essenes. Only a handful of his disciples will be with him."

"The Essenes?" The connection surprised Nathaniel. "Is he one of them?"

"No, but the rabbi apparently has some friend among them in the city. After the meal, on their way back to Bethany, they intend to stop at Gesamani for prayers."

"A well-suited place for his arrest," Nathaniel added. "Outside the city, cover of trees and night to hide the guards. But will they have to be there all night? Someone might notice."

"We can't risk a scene like the courtyard the other day," Caiaphas added.

Lamech rested his hands on the edge of the table. "The Galilean Zealots have an informant among Yeshua's followers. The plan is for this man to come to the Sanhedrin's chamber after the meal is done. Once time has been allowed for them to reach Gesamani, and let their prayers and the lateness of the hour lessen their vigilance – we go there and take him."

"It appears to be a good plan. What do you say, Nathaniel?"

The Sopher mulled the proposal in his head. In spite of his distrust of Lamech, it seemed sound – except for one detail. "What about the darkness?"

"Darkness? I thought the Sanhedrin preferred to seize him at night?"

"True. But unless you or I go along to point him out, the guards might not be able to pick out Yeshua from among the others. Any confusion or resistance, he might escape."

"And it would not be good," cautioned Caiaphas, "to have any member of the Sanhedrin present. We don't want to unnecessarily risk the reputation of this body."

Lamech straightened as he brought his hands up and behind his head. He knew they were right. The guards needed some way to insure they seized Yeshua, and not one of the other Galileans. And to do so in a way that did not raise suspicion of what was about to happen, so surprise could be maintained. A thought came to mind. "What of this? We have the informant accompany the delegation to Gesamani. Once the rabbi and his followers are spotted, the informant embraces the rabbi, even kisses him, to leave no doubt as to who is to be seized."

The high priest stood. "So be it. Once the informant arrives tonight, Nathaniel will explain this duty to him. And give a suitable reward. It's only fair that he be paid."

"Agreed."

"Just so we know: what is the name of the man I am to meet?"

"Judas. Judas Iscariot"

"Well then," Caiaphas concluded, "we will wait for our Judas."

* * *

Mary and Hannah walked the route taken by Yeshua and the twelve less than an hour before. The Essene villa offered by Abraham for Passover and Nathaniel's house were both in the Upper City. Mary had told Yeshua of their plans to visit Hannah's mother. His memories of Naomi were mostly recollections of both mothers watching him and Hannah and David play in the stable. Yeshua encouraged Mary to be patient: as with Hannah, years of anger and blame would likely spill out long before any hint of healing came. If it came at all.

Mary glanced at Hannah as they strolled through the same streets the three families had traversed more than thirty years ago. Then, she and Naomi cradled Yeshua and Hannah in their arms on the way to Nathaniel's hosting of them for the purification rites. Now, Naomi's daughter walked beside her. Mary could see the years had worn hard on Hannah. Little of the child remained in her face. She had her mother's profile, but the features seemed more chiseled, worn down, than what Mary remembered of Naomi. She wondered how Naomi would look now.

"Here we are." Mary stopped when Hannah spoke, looking at the house now before them. She'd noticed the dwellings on the last several streets becoming larger and more elegant. Mary saw the hint of a courtyard over a rock wall. But it was the porch and its colonnades that brought this place back into remembrance. This is where they had come and stayed for Hanukkah long ago. This is where she had first met Nathaniel, the one about whom Hannah and Yeshua had both warned her. Warnings, for reasons she could not clearly identify, that didn't surprise her.

The two ascended the steps to the porch and knocked on the door. As they waited, Mary and Hannah looked back toward the street. Some pilgrims, newly arrived to Jerusalem for the Passover, carried large packs on their way to family or friends. Others carried food for the meal: loaves of bread, vegetables to throw in a stew. A few carted sticks for a cookfire.

"Yes?" came a voice from inside.

They turned to the door being opened, expecting a servant. Instead, they saw Naomi.

"Mother." Hannah embraced Naomi, though the

mother's body stiffened as her arms wrapped around her. "I hope you don't mind my returning so soon."

"No, I said to come back." Naomi's words seemed distant as she stared at the woman standing behind her daughter.

Hannah stepped to the side. "I've brought a friend with me. You might not –"

"Mary." Naomi called out the name as one might cry out to rouse yourself from a nightmare. Mary stepped toward Naomi, arms outreached, but Naomi recoiled. "You! What are you doing here?" And then to Hannah, "Why did you bring this woman to my home?"

"As I said, she's a friend."

"A friend? Was she a friend of your dead brother David? Was she a friend of all those other poor children, whom she and Joseph deserted to save their child?"

"Mother!"

"No, Hannah, your mother has a right to say these things." Mary gazed into Naomi's eyes. They seemed full of fire. In her own, tears welled up. "Naomi, I can't tell you how many times Joseph and I regretted our decision. A dream of Joseph's warned that Herod's men sought Yeshua. We felt by taking him away, and not saying anything, the rest of you would be safe."

Naomi felt her whole body tremble. "Safe? No young boy, no family, left in the village was safe. Only yours. Only you."

"If we could go back to do this over, we would have warned you."

"But you can't, Mary. You left us. You left David. Nothing's to be done now."

Mary's head dropped, her chin pressing against the top hem of her cloak. "We, I, caused you pain we thought would only be levied on us. We just wanted Yeshua to live. We had no idea." Mary's voice trailed off in sobs. Regaining her voice, she lifted her face to look at Naomi. "You and Rebekah were my closest friends. When I most needed friendship. But when you needed me, I failed you both. I failed David, and the others. Forgive me, Naomi."

Naomi studied Mary, as if searching for something. Mary's tone reminded her of a fragile girl, for whose sake she scolded Joshua for leaving her in the stable. A girl who seemed more a daughter even as their children played together in the stable. As quickly as those images arose, others came. Of escape blocked, of David's lifeless body, of Joshua's cowardice.

"No, I can't." Naomi slowly pushed the door until it was halfway shut. "Come another day, Hannah." Naomi closed the door until it barely cracked open, enough to view Mary. Naomi looked at her. "No. Leave me, as you left David." The door shut. Hannah steadied Mary as she wept. Naomi leaned her back against the door, tears flowing. Only she had no one to hold her.

* * *

Yeshua and the twelve reclined on cushions around a low table. Remnants of the Passover meal remained on the table. A handful of grapes and dates, a mostly-eaten loaf of unleavened bread, the dish of bitter herbs, one leg of lamb with a few bits of meat clinging to the bone set next to the spit on which it had been roasted.

Multiple discussions took place simultaneously around the table. With tongues loosened by the feast's four ritual glasses of wine plus others downed afterwards, talk ranged from Essene hospitality to Yeshua's odd words that seemed to fuse bread and wine with body and blood. None dared ask their meaning, much less challenge their intent. There'd been more than enough talk about suffering and death on the trip to Jerusalem. Maybe it could be taken up tomorrow, but not tonight. Not the night that commemorated God's deliverance of Israel.

With all the conversations going on, no one noticed that the only one not engaged in conversation was Yeshua.

No one, except Judas. Judas' attention drifted in and out of the babbling to either side of him and across the table. Sometimes he'd laugh when others laughed, or feign attention to another's prattling. But all that concerned him was the meeting with Jacob and Lamech, and his decision. He knew it was right. For Yeshua's sake. Yet, each time he let his eyes drift in the direction of the rabbi – Yeshua stared back at him. Or so he thought.

The noise of table talk rose all around Judas. The meal finished, it would soon be time to leave for the Temple. To protect Yeshua. To do what was needed so the rabbi could return to Galilee: disciplined, maybe rebuked, but at least safe. The Zealots would find another on whom to pin their hopes. Shielded by the noise, Judas rose and walked around the outside of the cushions to where Yeshua sat. "Rabbi, may I sit with you a moment?" Yeshua looked up at the disciple. "May I?" Without a word, Yeshua moved to create space for Judas.

"I didn't think this right before, observing the Essene Passover. But Abraham proved a fine host. We've not had a better Passover in our three years together." Yeshua listened, eyes fixed forward. Judas leaned closer. "In all those years, I have always had your best interests at heart. Even when we've disagreed."

Yeshua dipped his head slightly, then shifted his shoulders to face Judas squarely. The rabbi's eyes appeared reddened. "And I had always hoped the best for you, Judas."

Judas squinted, as if to see something that remained out of focus. "What do you mean, rabbi? Do you no longer hope in me?"

"There is always hope, Judas. But you came here to speak. What did you wish to say?"

"Just what I said. I've always sought your best." Judas spoke faster, his breathing becoming more rapid. "Even now."

"Even now – even now, what? What is it you would do now?"

"I do what is best for you." Judas scooted closer, lowering his voice but maintaining its intensity. "To save you from those who would do you harm. Do you understand?"

"I understand, but do you?"

"Of course I understand!" Judas gripped the sleeve of Yeshua's robe. "You've let things go too far with the Sanhedrin, and the Zealots. Someone has to act to protect you. Someone has to deliver you – so you can return to Galilee, where you pose no threat."

"Do I threaten you, Judas?"

"No!"

"Do I ask you to do this?"

"Rabbi, the choice is mine. I HAVE to do this."

"Even if I tell you they only use you for their own purposes?"

The hand of Judas released Yeshua's robe. "No. that's not true. I have guarantees."

Yeshua placed his hand atop Judas'. "These men work treachery, Judas. They give such assurances only to gain your confidence... and to close your eyes to what they are about."

"No. I know them. They wouldn't. They promised." Judas pulled his hand away from Yeshua and stood. "I know what I'm doing, Rabbi."

"Then do it, Judas. And God have mercy on you."

Judas stared hard at Yeshua. How could the rabbi be so wrong? And what need of mercy did he have? He did this for Yeshua's sake, not his own. Why didn't Yeshua understand? "I do this for you," hc pleaded.

"No, Judas, you do this for you." The rabbi looked away. "Go. Be done with it."

Judas wanted to say more, but no words came to heart. Judas stumbled out the door and ran into the street. It was night.

* * *

A guard opened the door to the Chamber of Hewn Stone. A single bronze lampstand stood close to the seat usually held for the high priest. The light of its flame shone in the eyes of the guard and his companion. "Sopher Nathaniel, the man you told us to watch for is here."

"Send him in, and close the door. I'll call you when we are done."

"Very good." The guard stepped aside so the man beside him could enter.

As Judas stepped inside the chamber, the door swung shut behind him. He walked forward, past the rows of benches, until he stood before the high priest's chair. An old man sat there, clutching a walking stick. Judas bowed. "Lamech said to come here."

"By what name are you known?"

"Judas Iscariot. And you are the Sopher, Nathaniel?"

The tip of Nathaniel's cane clicked against the floor. "My name and position is of no importance. And you'd do well not to mention it to your rabbi or his followers. Understood?"

Nathaniel's forcefulness caused a slight stammer to Judas' "Yes."

"Very well. We've arranged an escort to go with you to Gesamani."

"What! I thought coming here was all I needed to do. Can't others bring him back?"

"We can't risk mistakes. The guards who go with you don't know the rabbi."

"I could describe him!"

"It will be dark. If there were confusion, the guards might not be sure who was the right one to seize. Or who to spare from violence, if they were opposed."

"There's to be no violence!" Judas raised his hand and pointed a finger toward the Sopher. "I do this to protect the rabbi, not bring him harm. I'll not be party to bloodshed."

Nathaniel thought of taking Judas to task for daring address him like that. But Lamech had let him know that this Judas truly felt he was acting to shield the rabbi. Nathaniel needed Judas for now, so there was no telling him the rabbi's fate was already beyond protection. As a result, a soothing voice from the Sopher answered the informant's demand. "We all act to protect the rabbi, Judas. Lamech, myself, Caiaphas. We may not approve of his actions of late, but we have his best interests in mind, and those of Jerusalem." The Sopher reached out to take hold of Judas at the elbow. "That is why we need you in the garden. To ensure no hurt comes to the rabbi, in case one of your fellow disciples misunderstands our presence."

"What am I to do there?"

"To make sure the guards understand who your rabbi is, embrace and kiss him. That will signal the escort to take only him in custody, to be brought to Caiaphas. Nothing more."

Judas considered Nathaniel's words. Adding the kiss as a signal was well thought out, since it avoided any confusion should one of the disciples come up to greet him. The kiss would clearly identify, and protect, Yeshua. "I will do as you say, Sopher. For Yeshua's sake."

"Fine." Nathaniel patted Judas on the back. "I'll have the guard take you to the Temple police, who will escort your rabbi." The two men walked to the door and opened it. The guard saluted. "Take Judas to Saul. He has instructions."

Judas turned to Nathaniel. "Please, see that Yeshua receives fair treatment." Judas held out his hand to shake that of Nathaniel.

"Have no fear of that, Judas. I will personally see that your Yeshua finds justice." Instead of clasping the hand of Judas, Nathaniel slipped a bag into it. "And this should take care of you for your trouble."

Judas felt the coins inside. "I am not doing this for myself," Judas protested, as he attempted to hand the bag back to Nathaniel.

Nathaniel refused to take it. "Then don't use it for your sake, but for that of others. You do the Sanhedrin a service deserving a reward. And the rabbi, too." Nathaniel closed the door.

"The captain, Saul, awaits you," the guard announced, leading Judas away. The weight of the coins surprised him for such a small deed. When this was over, Judas mulled, it would only be right that he would have Yeshua decide how to distribute them.

CHAPTER LI

Keeping his promise of vigilance to Hannah, Julius had followed the rabbi and his disciples from the city into Gesamani at a discreet distance to avoid being seen by them. Wrapping his cloak tight against the night air, he watched as clouds rolled in thick, blocking light from moon and stars. From his vantage point behind a low rock wall in Gesamani's olive grove, Julius could barely make out Yeshua offering words to a sky as dark as it was silent. The only other noises came from clusters of sleeping followers: an occasional snore, a rustling of garments when someone shifted from side to side, a voice mumbling inside a dream. Julius shook his head in disbelief. Such men were the rabbi's best after three years? Julius had heard Yeshua asking them to keep watch when he began his prayers not more than an hour ago. No one dared to sleep on watch in any century that Julius had commanded. But not a single disciple stayed awake. Only he, a Roman secluded from sight, maintained a vigil for Yeshua.

For Yeshua? For Hannah was more to the point. The rabbi told him in this very garden not to intercede for him. Instead, he said, take care of Hannah. Julius glanced again at Yeshua, still immersed in prayers. *And who will take care you, teacher?* Julius muttered the words aloud, though quietly as if someone might hear them. But who could hear? Disciples, dulled in sleep? Yeshua, deep in prayer? The one to whom Yeshua pleaded – if there was such a one?

Julius considered rousing the sleepers to chastise their lack of discipline. Better yet, why not take hold of

Yeshua's mantle and shake him into the truth that no god could possibly be concerned for him. Or anyone else. No god interceded for those children in Bethlehem who died for the delusion of a madman. Hannah flashed into his mind, and her trust of Yeshua. How could she, who had seen so much, be taken in by –

Julius snapped his head to the left as a light flashed outside the grove. He saw it again, then behind it another light. And another. Torches, guiding a group of fifteen, perhaps twenty. The lights drew closer. It became clear that all but one of the figures wore the uniforms of the temple police. Julius grabbed a dried olive pit off the ground, thinking to toss it near Yeshua as a warning, but he saw the rabbi was already standing. Julius decided to wait on Yeshua's response before stepping out from his hiding place. To be safe, he slid his gladius from its sheath and readied himself for a fight.

Disciples, also roused by the sounds of the approaching group, began to surround their rabbi. Yeshua motioned them to stop. One in the crowd walked ahead of the others and strode to Yeshua. Embracing the rabbi, he pressed his lips against Yeshua's cheek. In an instant, three guards moved quickly to the pair's side. Two seized the arms of Yeshua, while the third announced to the startled followers: "Yeshua shall be in custody of the temple for questioning."

"NO!" shouted one of the disciples as he drew out a short sword. Following his lead, other disciples brandished knives. In turn, the guards behind the torch-bearers unsheathed their blades, fanning out to encircle the rabbi's men. Julius gauged he could ambush their line from the rear, giving Yeshua at least a chance for escape if the others showed any mettle with their weapons. Gladius poised, Julius raised up from his crouch and prepared to slip over the wall.

"STOP IT! NOW!" Yeshua's shout froze everyone, including Julius. The guards gripping his arms loosed their hold. Yeshua seized Peter's wrist: "Put your sword away!" Yeshua slowly swung his head, glaring into the eyes of guards and disciples alike. "ALL OF YOU!"

For a moment, Julius thought Yeshua glared at him. "ALL of you. This shall not be."

"But rabbi –"

"Peter, do as I say."

The fisherman's shoulders drooped as he sheathed his sword. The other disciples put away their weapons. Julius slid down behind the wall, though he kept his gladius at the ready and his eyes on the scene. The Temple detachment encircled Yeshua. Judas reached his hand through those who held the rabbi, as if he wanted to say something to Yeshua, but the rabbi turned away. The guards started down into the Kidron valley toward Jerusalem with prisoner in tow. Peter and the other disciples scattered into the night, the way Julius had seen soldiers flee when their commander had fallen and the battle was lost. In truth, Julius thought, that was exactly the case. All that remained for him this night was breaking the news to Hannah.

* * *

Nathaniel fingered the marble bust of Tiberius. He wondered if Pilate displayed it on his desk for its beauty, or as reminder to anyone in the room that when they dealt with the procurator, they dealt with Rome. As the high priest's emissary for over thirty years, Nathaniel understood what it meant to speak with another's authority. And he knew tonight that Caiaphas and Tiberius would be well-served once he and Pilate came to an understanding about Yeshua.

"The Sopher of the Jews, excellency."

Nathaniel stood when the steward announced Pilate's presence. The procurator's disheveled hair indicated to Nathaniel he had likely roused Pilate from his bed.

"You may leave us." The Roman yawned the words as he waved his servant off. "What comes from the temple that can't wait until morning?"

"Forgive me, procurator, might I sit? The walk in night air, and these bones –"

"Yes, yes. Just get on with it!"

"Thank you." Nathaniel sat on the chair's edge, and pulled it close to the desk across from Pilate. "We have the Galilean rabbi, Yeshua, in custody."

"The one who caused the disturbance in the Temple two days past?"

Nathaniel smiled and nodded. The spies of Pilate had already been at work, it seems, if the rabbi's name and actions were known to the procurator. "The same one. His teachings threaten both the Temple and your authority, Pilate."

"Really?" Pilate rested his elbow on the table and scratched at the narrow line of beard that ran across his chin. "I've been told he teaches you Jews to pay Caesar's taxes."

Nathaniel saw how closely Pilate's men attended to Yeshua. "The rabbi loves to speak in riddles, procurator. In those same words, he also left the impression with others that Caesar is owed nothing, as everything comes from God."

"See here, Sopher, I've no interest in being roused from my bed to dabble in the obscurities of your peoples' superstitions. What do you want?"

"As I said before, the rabbi poses a threat to both of our positions. His teachings blaspheme our God, and his claims to kingship put him at odds with Caesar's throne."

"Oh yes," Pilate mused, recalling a much earlier conversation with Antony, "these claims of a messiah, or whatever you call it."

The Sopher straightened. He did not expect Pilate to have this much familiarity. But perhaps, it could make his case easier. "You are right, procurator. Our people, and the Zealots in particular, await one called Messiah to reign as king and war against any rival power."

Pilate laughed. "A rabbi who will kill legions with

scrolls. And palm leaves!"

Nathaniel allowed the procurator his moment before continuing. "Many who follow Yeshua have already set aside scrolls for swords. His claims of kingship embolden them. If he is allowed to continue, who knows what will happen?" The Sopher paused, then stood. "And if unrest becomes common in Jerusalem and Judea, who knows what Tiberius might implore the Senate to do with one who failed to squelch a rebellion when he had opportunity to do so."

Pilate glared at the old Jew. He did not appreciate being spoken to so bluntly. Then again, the Sopher spoke the truth. And Nathaniel had, after all, delivered up Barabbas. "When your council is done with the rabbi, bring him to me for trial. I shall judge what Caesar requires from your waver of palms."

Nathaniel bowed, and turned to leave. Before he reached the door, a knock came from the outside. "Procurator," the steward announced, "the centurion Antony."

"Send him in," Pilate answered.

The door opened. Antony entered for his audience with Pilate – only to face Nathaniel.

* * *

Julius had remained behind the wall until after the guards escorted Yeshua away and the rabbi's disciples fled, not wanting to risk being seen by either group. When no lights or sounds could be detected, Julius left the garden and ascended the hillside toward Bethany. He would tell Hannah what happened, and why he took no action. Julius replayed the scene in the garden time and again as he made his way up a path covered with palms only two days past. It was always the same. The rabbi's words, and then eyes, stopped him, stopped them all, long enough to insure no spilling of blood. For now. Julius recalled the first time he saw Yeshua's eyes in Magdala. Then, too, they stopped him short, making Julius want to flee before being found out for who or what he was. Those same eyes pierced him again tonight, as if the rabbi didn't want Julius to be found by guards or disciples. Julius quickened his pace. He could do little for the rabbi. He must do what he could for Hannah.

* * *

Antony, still dressed in the guise of a Jew, stepped around Nathaniel and saluted. "Procurator." After glancing at Nathaniel, he spoke again. "I come with news, for your ears."

"Does it regard the seizure of that Galilean rabbi, who dislikes moneychangers?"

"It does." He said no more. Not yet.

"You can speak in front of the Jew, centurion. He has already brought word of Yeshua's arrest by the temple authorities."

Antony did not like the thought of being upstaged by Nathaniel. "I would have come sooner, procurator, but I wanted to make sure I knew where he'd been taken. Two of us had been watching the rabbi in Gesamani when the temple guard arrived. We kept to the shadows, so no one observed us. After the arrest, we followed them to the house of Annas, one of their former high priests. I left my aide to keep track of matters there while I came here."

"Very good, centurion, you can withdraw your aide." Pilate looked at Nathaniel before resuming. "Since the Sanhedrin holds the rabbi for now, we've no further need to surveil him. Also, escort Nathaniel to the passage entry. On the way, make plans for the rabbi's transfer here when the Sanhedrin is through. You two worked well when it came to Barabbas."

Antony stiffly saluted the procurator. "As you wish."

Pilate yawned once more. "Go, both of you."

Nathaniel and Antony bowed, then walked out the door. The two men waited to speak until they had gone far down the hall, out of earshot from Pilate and his servant.

"So, nephew, we labor together again."

Antony stopped, mid-stride. "Not by my choice," he

sputtered in a low voice. "You betray another Jew to Rome? Barabbas wasn't enough?"

"Nephew – Antony – you disappoint me. I'd think you would be pleased to take vengeance on the one responsible for your brother's death, and your father's, well –"

"What do you mean?"

"I mean this." Nathaniel stepped into a darkened alcove in the wall that barely fit them both. "This Yeshua is no mere rabbi. He's the one Herod sought in Bethlehem years ago, the one in whose place your brother died, the one who left you an outcast to your people."

Antony felt as if his head spun round. "Don't lie to me!"

"This is no lie, boy. Herod stopped at nothing to eliminate this child. His parents, Joseph and Mary, left Bethlehem the night before, without warning anyone of the danger. Ask your mother Or even Rebekah. If you'll not trust me, they will both tell you this Yeshua is the one."

"He's the one who caused David's death, you are sure?"

"Without a doubt."

Antony threw his head back against the wall. Images of his dead brother, and cowering father, came to mind. He couldn't remember what Yeshua looked like as a child. He could only see him as an adult, in the temple courts yesterday and the garden tonight. Alive, while his only brother's bones lie cold and lifeless behind rocks piled in the back of a cave in Bethlehem. "Then, you and I have work to do."

Nathaniel took hold of Antony's arm. "And when our work is done, Yeshua will receive a death too long postponed."

* * *

While the rest of Bethany's streets and buildings remained dark, in the distance Julius saw one house filled with light. The closer he came, the greater his concern. This was the house in which Yeshua and his followers stayed, where Hannah and the women waited. But instead of it being crowded with his disciples, Julius could see and hear only women from his vantage point. Some wept in low tones, alone. Others swayed in embraces. Finally, Julius saw Hannah standing by an older woman. One of the women noticed Julius watching. He watched as she pointed at him, and suddenly the women knotted together, surrounding the older woman. It appeared Hannah said something to her, and then she stepped away from the group, out from under the porch, and into the street to stand beside Julius. "You could do nothing for him?"

Julius shook his head. "Is it safe to talk? I mean, will the women suspect you?"

"No, I've told them you are a friend."

"And the disciples –"

"The disciples? We've only seen two of them, who came to tell us what happened before they took off in fear of their own arrest. The rest never showed their faces, and no one knows where they are." Hannah gripped his hand. "What have they done with Yeshua?"

"Arrested. At least it was the temple guard, so it's likely he won't be in the Antonia. Not yet, anyway."

"And you could do nothing?"

Something in Hannah's voice reminded Julius of the night she spoke to him by the lake at Capernaum, when she learned of his role in David's death. This time, however, she did not swing at him with a piece of driftwood. This time, she held on to his hand.

"I could have. When they seized Yeshua, I positioned myself to strike down a pair of guards between me and him, to offer a path for escape. It even looked like the disciples planned to resist, as they'd drawn what weapons they brought. But then –" Julius felt his throat choking.

"Then what?" Hannah did not let go of his hand.

"He said no. `Put away the swords.' That's all I had, Hannah, that was all I could do for him. But he said `no' to it. He stared us all down – guards, disciples, he even looked my way. He wouldn't have it." Julius found himself touching the hilt of his gladius. "The one way I could have helped, he wouldn't have it. And now. . ." Julius' words trailed off and he looked away.

Another hand touched Julius. "My son would not have innocent blood spilled. Not others, not yours. Not again."

"Your son." Julius bit his lip. "Forgive me, my lady. I've not served him well this night."

"You have served him as he let you."

"Julius," Hannah offered, "this is Mary of Nazareth."

"And once of Bethlehem." Julius spoke the words almost unconsciously.

Mary studied the face of Julius, wondering where those words came from, before looking at Hannah. "We have much to consider," she said to the younger woman, whose fingers still laced with those of Julius.

Ashamed at having failed to help this woman's son, Julius pulled his hand away. "Hannah, perhaps it would be best if I left."

"Too many have already taken leave," Mary interrupted. "Please, stay with us."

Julius looked deep into her eyes, every bit as brown and engaging as her son's. What seemed a lifetime ago, this was the woman whose child he and his troops had sought to murder. "So be it. Perhaps I may yet be of service, Mary of Bethlehem. But first, there are things you must know. Of me."

The three sat on a bench under the portico. While the other women returned to bed, Hannah and Mary and Julius spoke the truths of their stories of Bethlehem, their long journeys since. . . and their connection to a once-fugitive child finally seized by the hands of his enemies.

* * *

Nathaniel arrived at the house of Annas after midnight, joining a circle of men seated around a small charcoal fire. Lamech the Zealot sat by himself, as did Lot the Pharisee. Caiaphas sat on a bench shared with his father-in-law

Annas. Nathaniel moved a stool alongside of Caiaphas. He saw guards standing by a room down the hall and presumed the rabbi to be inside.

"Caiaphas, your messenger said that Yeshua had been brought in for questioning." Lot leaned forward on his seat. "But we cannot conduct a meeting of the Sanhedrin at night."

"Do you see the whole body here?" countered Caiaphas. "We merely interview him. To understand what the council may have to eventually consider."

Lot remained uneasy. "This is very late for such a serious conversation."

Nathaniel breathed a deep sigh, glancing at Caiaphas and Lamech before speaking. "The Sanhedrin agreed to this interview, Lot. Besides, our tradition requires twenty-four days to pass from the first day of a person's detention before their trial – "

"Trial!" shouted Lot. "No trial has been decided!"

"That is why we are here," Annas offered in a soothing tone, "to discern whether or not a trial might be appropriate, even necessary, depending on the rabbi's words."

"If I may finish," continued Nathaniel, "the lateness of this hour is more than made up for by the fact that the Sanhedrin cannot convene or act on this matter until Thursday morning at the earliest. There will be no rush to judgment, Lot."

"If I may," added Lamech, "since Herod has arrived in Jerusalem to keep Passover here, I suggest when we've finished that Yeshua be taken to his palace for protective custody. That way, the Romans do not get their hands on the rabbi before the Sanhedrin meets, and we don't have to hold him at the Temple and risk protests there."

Caiaphas nodded. "Wise counsel, brother. It will be so. Now, if all is ready, let us speak with the rabbi. Lot, would you go to the room where he is held and bring him in?"

Once Lot had left the room, Nathaniel leaned over to

Caiaphas and whispered, "Pilate will be ready for him. And then, the matter will be out of our hands."

"Well done, Sopher. You have served your people well."

Nathaniel's smile triggered by the commendation of Caiaphas' curved downward as he saw Yeshua enter the room.

"Yeshua of Galilee, I am Annas. I served our people as high priest when –"

"I know of you," Yeshua interrupted. "And you, Caiaphas. And you," now looking at Nathaniel, "you would be the Sopher, Nathaniel?"

"I am of little import here, rabbi. But what right do you claim to break in when an elder such as Annas addresses you?"

Yeshua dipped his head slightly to Annas. "I spoke only to save us time. You all are known to me, and to the people, by your deeds."

Caiaphas brought his hands together beneath his chin. "I am afraid, rabbi, that our meeting tonight has to do not with our deeds, but yours. And words of yours that cause much confusion as to who you are, and what you claim."

"For what people make of my words, Caiaphas, I can't say. Especially those whose judgment is set before they even hear me."

At those words, a guard slapped Yeshua on the back of the head. "Take care how you speak to the high priest!"

Yeshua clenched his jaw. "If I have spoken wrongly, testify to the wrong."

Annas stood. "Testify? Those are words of a trial, rabbi. We had hoped a respectful conversation among this small circle might resolve matters of controversy. But since you insist on testimony, it is clear you seek a trial. And a trial you shall have!"

"Wait!" Lot sprung to his feet. "We've not even begun to talk."

"Annas is right," countered Lamech. "The rabbi himself set the terms. What can we do?"

Nathaniel and Caiaphas both nodded their heads. Yeshua said nothing further.

"Guard," announced the high priest, "keep the rabbi in custody for trial, to take place Thursday at noon. Until then, secure him in one of the cells at the palace of Herod."

Lot remained silent, realizing the matter to be settled. The guard tugged on the ropes that bound Yeshua's wrists, pulling him toward the door and past where Nathaniel stood. Yeshua paused for a moment in front of the Sopher. Nathaniel smirked, then turned his back to the captive. He held no respect for an enemy who let himself be so easily defeated. Too bad, he thought, that so many had to die for him years ago. Such a waste, for such weakness.

CHAPTER LII

Wednesday's dawn broke clear, a strong breeze having dispersed the clouds from the previous night. Mary and Hannah stepped out of the house and under the faded tan canvas sheltering the porch. Julius sat there, feet propped on a bench. The women had just wakened. If Julius had slept, he could not recall. "Julius," Hannah began, "Mary and I need your advice."

The words broke the Roman's gaze down the road that led toward Jerusalem, and brought him to his feet. "Please," he offered, motioning to the bench.

Mary shook her head. "Perhaps we could walk?"

"As you wish." Julius stepped next to Hannah, and the three walked toward the village well. Children of local families and Passover pilgrims filled the way, playing around the well where mothers and sisters drew water. Julius noted that Mary often brushed her hand across the head of a child who came close to her. Most smiled back. A few wondered this stranger's face on should look so sad on such a bright day. By the well, Mary sat on one of the limestone flagstones rimming its top. Hannah joined her, while Julius remained standing.

"Hannah has told me you know this city, and those in power here. Is there any way I could intervene for my son? Or, could you?"

Julius knelt on one knee before her. While Mary's face bore the weathering of nearly fifty years, her words seemed to him as child's – a child who had lost something of great value, and cannot find her way back to it. Julius would have embraced her as he prepared to say what needed to be said, but the sight of a woman touched by a man not of her own kin – much less a Gentile – in broad daylight would have been scandalous. Words alone would have to suffice. "I swear to you, Mary: if I thought anyone might be swayed by your word or mine at the palace or Temple or Antonia, I wouldn't hesitate." Julius cleared his throat before continuing. "But the truth is, this city has come to care little for justice. Whether the authority be Roman or Jew, the chief priority is saving one's own skin no matter how many others suffer."

"I feared as much." Mary placed a hand on his shoulder, much to his surprise. "But I thank you for your honesty. And for risking to be with my son last night."

Julius looked to see if anyone might see her touching him. "Mary, you don't need –"

She squeezed his shoulder and leaned closer. "I risk more defilement by speaking to Yeshua's enemies, who hide behind Torah to do evil, than a Gentile who seeks my son's good."

Julius gazed down to her feet, awed and shamed by her presence. Hannah had told him before of Mary's kindness. And last night, when he confessed to Mary the extent of his involvement years before in Bethlehem, and then his relationship with Hannah, Yeshua's mother uttered no condemnation. "Mistakes belong to all of our years," she had said. "The Almighty judges not so much deeds long past, but what we do about them now."

What we do about them now came to his mind again, as he felt the lightness of her hand on his shoulder. "I don't want to give you any false hope," he began, rising off his knee to sit beside her on the well's stone lip, "but let me see what I can learn at the Antonia, and elsewhere. Maybe there is some favor to be gained, or debt to be called in. I can't promise anything."

"Thank you, Julius. I see why Hannah loves you. You have goodness in your heart." Goodness? Regret he knew to be there, and bitterness. And hatred toward men like Nathaniel, who now manipulated Yeshua for their own ends. But goodness? Goodness he could not recall since before Bethlehem. Except perhaps when he had been with Hannah.

"Julius." Hannah's voice broke his thoughts. "Mary and I go to see my mother this afternoon, to tell her of Yeshua. After, we'll return to Bethany. Let us know what you learn."

"Better yet, meet me at the inn of Ishmael in the afternoon. The ninth hour. We can speak more freely, especially if the disciples have returned." Julius stood to leave, but another thought came to mind. "When you see your mother, be on guard if Nathaniel's about. Say nothing he might twist to use against Yeshua – or Mary." Julius bowed, and took his leave.

"God watch over you," Mary called out.

God's watch might have been more helpful in Gesamani, Julius thought. Then again, he himself had been unable to help for Mary's son last night. Julius walked faster, but the quickened steps could not escape Mary's blessing, nor her declaration of his goodness. Her words haunted.

* * *

On his way from the Antonia to Herod's palace, the strides of Antony resembled those of legionnaires on a quick march through hostile territory. Given the Zealots' past inclination to use the days before Passover for creating unrest, Antony's gait and those of the four soldiers who accompanied him seemed normal. Once they entered the palace, however, the pace slackened. Antony dismissed the four, ordering them to wait at the outer gate until his return. From there, Antony crossed the central courtyard. He carried a vague remembrance of this place: nearly twenty years ago, Julius had inducted him into the legion here. That had taken place at night, when the smell of bitumen from burning torches bittered the air. Now, in daylight, fragrances of spring flowers and the scent of dates just beginning to set on branches came to his nostrils. He breathed in deep, knowing the stench from the cells would come soon enough.

"Centurion Antony, to see the prisoner Yeshua." The Syrian guard at the door, one of Herod's retinue, called for his compatriot inside to open the door. This done, Antony stepped into the passageway. Once the door closed behind him, no sign of daylight betrayed itself.

A guard inside pulled down a torch from the wall and handed it to Antony. "Who's your business with, sir?"

"Yeshua, the Galilean rabbi, brought here this morning."

"Fourth cell on the left. Do you want me to go with you, centurion?"

"No, just give me the key for his cell."

"Private business, eh?" The guard sniggered as he reached into a pouch, pulled out a worn iron key, and handed it to Antony. "No other prisoners are in this section, sir, so do what you will with your holy man. No ears to hear, if you know what I mean."

"Why don't you join your partner for a break outside?"

"Whatever you say, centurion." The guard saluted. "We do have orders, though, to see this fellow gets to trial tomorrow. A dead prisoner wouldn't look so good for us."

"Don't worry, he'll be ready for trial." Antony closed the door after the guard left.

* * *

Nearly twelve hours had passed since Nathaniel talked in this same room with Pilate. The procurator looked fresh, having stayed in bed long past his usual time of rising to make up for the late-night interruption triggered by this rabbi's arrest. Dark circles surrounded Nathaniel's eyes, as the Sopher had barely slept before hurrying to meet with Caiaphas again and other members of the Sanhedrin, and now back to Pilate.

"Sit down, Sopher. You look like death itself."

"I feel as much, procurator." Nathaniel slumped into a chair and grunted. "But in a few days, when this business with rabbi Yeshua is over, there'll be time enough for rest."

"Centurion Antony gave me a report earlier about your meeting with him, and the plans for Friday's execution."

"Good. I hope they meet with your approval, procurator."

Pilate nodded. "But tell me more about this exchange of prisoners. Why not hoist Barabbas and the rabbi on crosses, and be done with them both?"

Nathaniel himself had wondered about the wisdom of Antony's suggestion last night before they parted, attributing it to his nephew's weakness toward an old friend. But Antony's arguments in time made sense. "The crowds will be moved by the release of Barabbas. Many will see it as a sign of Rome's strength, that she does not fear to release a man like him. And the Zealots, they'll likely have second thoughts about their one-time leader, wondering what he must have done or promised to be given such a reprieve."

"That I understand." Pilate tore off a piece of bread, dipped it in a wine goblet and began to eat. "But what makes you think Barabbas will go off into obscurity and not bother us again?"

"The night before his release, have one of your cohort visit him in his cell. Warn him that any more trouble on his part, and he'll be made a eunuch. And promise that his dismembered part will be handed to his mother, just before her own throat is slit."

Pilate coughed out a bit of bread being chewed. "For a man of religion, Nathaniel, you've a streak for intimidation. But how do we know he'll heed even this threat?"

"For the threat to himself, we don't. These Zealots can be an irrational lot. But to his mother," Nathaniel reached the loaf on Pilate's desk, broke off a piece of crust, dipped it in the wine, and ate. "The threat to her will move him. That I know, and of that you can be sure."

"Well enough. But how will Barabbas know that we

can carry out our threat against her?"

"Simple. Have your man ask about the carving of a wolf he wears around his neck. Maybe he should even snatch it away from Barabbas. Tell him that if the barest hint of rebellion on his part is ever heard, that Rebekah of Bethlehem will suffer as did his father."

Pilate smiled. "Rebekah of Bethlehem, is it? And why, knowing now who his mother is, should Rome not immediately take vengeance for rearing such a murderer?"

"As long as Rebekah lives, procurator, you control Barabbas. And Barabbas alive, judged a traitor and coward by those who once followed him, is worth far more than a dead martyr."

Pilate tipped a goblet of wine in Nathaniel's direction. "To a long life for this Barabbas."

As Pilate drank, Nathaniel spoke once more. "There's another matter, procurator. The temple police recently seized a thief named Joshua. He is now in your custody in the Antonia."

"I think I saw a report on the matter."

"This rogue served in a band of sicarii responsible for a number of Roman deaths. He even took part in an attempt on my life. I ask that he be put to death, the same day as Yeshua."

"That should be no problem."

"Thank you, procurator."

"But tell me, Nathaniel: why the interest in having this thief share Yeshua's day?"

Nathaniel leaned his weight to the cane and stood. "Let us just say, in my mind, they belong together."

Pilate had no idea what Nathaniel meant, nor did he really care. The old Jew had proved himself worthy of a favor. One more crucifixion would not matter.

* * *

Naomi interrupted her stitchery, a design of grape vines that ran along the hem of a dress being readied for Passover. The servant had announced her daughter and another visitor stood at the door. Naomi did want to see Hannah again. If the other person proved to be Mary, she decided she would simply ignore her. "Bring them in." She resumed her work, the stitches becoming quicker as the sound of sandals clopping on the tiled hallway neared.

"Mother."

"Ahhhh!" Naomi dropped the dress and grasped a finger poked by the needle.

"I didn't mean to startle you. Are you alright?"

"Yes, I just drew the stitch too tight." Naomi looked up at Hannah and smiled. Several steps behind she saw Mary. "I told you, Hannah, I would be happy to see you again. Not her."

"I know, mother." Hannah sat next to Naomi, while Mary did not move. "But we bring news. It concerns Mary's son, Yeshua."

"The one who lived while all the others died?"

Mary took one step toward the bench where the two women sat. "I know you blame me for that, Naomi. I can't change your feelings toward me. But Yeshua had no part in our decision to leave. And now –"

"Now he's arrested."

A few moments of silence passed before Hannah spoke. "Nathaniel told you?"

"He has. And of Yeshua's trial before the Sanhedrin, set for tomorrow. Tell me, Mary, how does it feel to have a son in jeopardy?"

"It feels like someone twists a knife inside my heart." Mary knelt before Naomi, placing her hands and then her forehead on Naomi's knee. "I'm so afraid of losing Yeshua. Please, don't hate him, too. Don't hate me, Naomi. I'm sorry, I'm sorry . . ." Her words dissolved into tears.

For years, Naomi yearned for Mary and Yeshua to feel the hurt and loss she knew. Now that it came, now that it seemed Yeshua's judgment had arrived: what Naomi felt surging inside was not satisfaction. More of regret. And sorrow. At another mother's loss of her child.

Slowly, awkwardly, Naomi raised her hand. Hannah thought at first her mother might push Mary away for all those seasons of pain. Instead, Naomi stroked Mary's hair, the same way she once stroked Hannah's and David's. "I am sorry this comes to you, Mary. I forgive you."

* * *

Yeshua heard a key turning inside the lock of his door, then the door opened. The torch held by the visitor stung eyes that had seen no light since being thrown into this cell.

"On your feet, prisoner. You are the rabbi Yeshua?"

"I am."

Eyes still adjusting to the light never saw Antony's punch coming. The impact sent the rabbi staggering backwards against the wall.

"Come now, rabbi. Let's see if you fight as well as you speak!"

Yeshua tasted blood streaming from a cut lip. "You'll have no sport here. I will not raise hands against you."

Antony swung the back of his left hand across Yeshua's cheek, snapping his head against the rough stone wall. "Maybe it's not sport I seek."

Yeshua could feel a knot beginning to swell on the back of his head. His eyes could now make out that his assailant wore a centurion's uniform. "What do you want with me?"

Antony seized the mantle of Yeshua just below his neck, and pressed him against the cool damp stones. "Answer me this, Jew. Was Bethlehem your birthplace, and Joseph your father?"

Yeshua looked hard into the soldier's face. He remembered Hannah's telling him how her brother sought refuge in the legion years ago. Even in this dim light, he bore some resemblance to her. "If I may ask: was Bethlehem your birthplace, and Joshua your father, and David –"

Antony screamed and flung Yeshua across the cell onto the floor. The rabbi doubled over, pain shooting through the shoulder he landed on. Moving next to him, Antony held the torch between his face and the rabbi's. "I'll take pleasure in watching you die, Yeshua ben Joseph. You stole my family: David in death, my father in cowardice, my sister in whoring–"

"Hannah has given up that life to follow me, centurion. Or should I say, Simeon?"

"Enough!" Antony drove his fist into Yeshua's stomach, doubling over the rabbi.

"Let's see who follows you when you're splayed to a cross!"

* * *

The sight of Julius standing at the door outside the caravansary relieved Hannah. Though she didn't share her fears with Mary, Hannah had not wanted to enter the inn if Julius was not there. The thought of being gaped at and scrutinized by its rougher guests would have been bad enough for the memories evoked. And to subject someone like Mary to that, especially with her son's imprisonment weighing down on her, would have been even worse.

Julius held the door open for the two. "Ishmael has a table near the kitchen for us."

The three made their way to a table lit by a small oil lamp, where an old man in a soiled apron sat. No other customers were to be seen. As the women reached the table, Ishmael made an effort to stand and bow. "Hannah. Julius. And you, you would be the rabbi's mother?"

"My name is Mary."

"Yes, Mary. Please, sit down. Can I have my nephew fetch some food for you?"

"Thank you, innkeeper," Mary replied, "but I've no appetite."

Ishmael and Julius shared a bench across from Mary and Hannah, facing the door in case anyone entered. Ishmael poured wine into four goblets. Ishmael and Julius took deep draughts. Hannah barely sipped from hers, while Mary only ran her fingers up and down the goblet's edge.

After a long silence, Julius spoke. "What I've learned is not good. They hold Yeshua at Herod's palace until his trial before the Sanhedrin tomorrow. Then, he's to be given to Pilate."

"But if the Sanhedrin judges him," Mary interjected, "there's at least a chance he'll be found innocent, or perhaps guilty of a lesser crime. He could return to Galilee after punishment."

Ishmael looked to Julius. Before the women arrived, the two discussed what each had learned. Ishmael agreed to be the one who'd tell the worst of it. "What my friend here means to say, Mary, this trial has nothing to do with finding out truth. It's just appearances, to keep the crowd happy." Ishmael paused, looking at the woman across from him. "Maybe I should stop."

"No." Mary looked into Ishmael's eyes. "Tell me what you know. So I can prepare."

Ishmael clasped her hand. "I don't say this to hurt you, but they have knives out for your son. Word is, the elders and the Romans have already made their decision. Lies bought and paid for, some of them over these tables. Damned pious backstabbers!"

Mary turned to Julius. "And you agree, this is how it shall be?"

"From what I gained from a few trusted friends at the Antonia – yes, Ishmael has it right. The Romans believe Yeshua faces crucifixion, as early as Friday."

Mary's hands began to tremble out of control, then her whole body. Hannah hugged her close as Ishmael clasped her hands even tighter. Mary thought she could hear Julius say, "I'm sorry," but everything spun out of focus. Only one word, one image, remained clear. Crucifixion. She remembered seeing its torture on a previous trip to Jerusalem, impaling the sons of other mothers. Now it would be her son. Mary imagined Yeshua on those timbers, bloodied and dying.

"Not my son, not my son, not my son." Mary's words became wails, wails that Julius
remembered from thirty years before, when they sounded from other of Bethlehem's mothers.

"Please, not my son... not my son."

CHAPTER LIII

Judas pulled up the collar of his robe and tightened it around his ears and mouth, hoping to obscure his face as he kept watch on the door leading to the Chamber of Hewn Stone. A few worshipers gathered early this Thursday morning inside the Court of Israel, along with others spurred by curiosity. The Sanhedrin was rumored to meet this morning to examine the rabbi Yeshua. Examine, Judas thought. That's what they said. But other stories spread quickly of a trial, and one whose verdict might already be settled.

All of yesterday, Judas sought to learn of Yeshua's whereabouts. He took care in that searching, not wanting to risk contact with the other disciples. The garden appeared to make him out a traitor, even though what he did there it was for the rabbi's safety, and the rest of theirs as well. Peter and the others would not understand, not yet. With a few well-placed bribes, using several of silver coins given him by Nathaniel, did Judas find out Yeshua had been taken to Herod's palace. Late Wednesday afternoon, Judas had finally gotten up the nerve to go to the palace, where he asked to see the rabbi and palmed a shekel into the hand of one of the guards. In return, the Syrian smiled, tucked the coin away, and told him to leave. Judas' protest led to a knee in his groin and laughter from the guard's compatriots.

But today would be different. Judas had brought the rest of the silver given him for his role. He would demand to see Nathaniel. The money would be returned in exchange for Yeshua's release. If not, Judas reasoned, he would appeal that Jacob address the Council to have Yeshua returned under his safekeeping to Galilee. In time, Yeshua would come to understand...

The sight of Nathaniel broke Judas from his thoughts. The Sopher made his way to the door of the chamber, accompanied by – "Lamech! Nathaniel!" Judas darted from behind the column he'd used to shield himself from observation. "We must speak."

The Sopher looked to the Zealot, whose eyebrows raised slightly before turning to Judas. "Yes, Judas." The Sopher stepped into the chamber and closed the door, leaving the pair outside.

"I must talk to you."

Lamech took hold of Judas' arm, and moved them away from the door and around the corner. "My friend, you've done well. Our interview with Yeshua will soon begin."

"Interview? You mean, trial. Something's gone wrong, Lamech. You need to protect the rabbi! It's your duty."

At the word "duty," the Zealot's eyes narrowed and he squeezed the arm of Judas. "Duty? My duty is to my people. Your rabbi endangers them by failing to call Rome to account."

"But you promised – "

"I promised what? Yeshua's safety? Every day he lives, he brings our people closer to ruin. Him, with his talk of turning cheeks and loving enemies. Your rabbi would have us love the Romans while they give us the lash and raid our treasury and blaspheme our God. He would make us slaves, and pitiful ones at that. No, the only good he can serve now is to stretch his arms on a cross and show how much he loves Rome, and let us get on with a future free of his kind."

Judas reached into the purse, drew out the remaining shekels given to him by Nathaniel on the eve of the garden, and held them out to Lamech. "I don't want your blood money."

Lamech looked at the coins, and then at Judas, and

laughed. "MY blood money? What a fool you are, Judas! The blood stains your hands – or should I say, your lips? Your kiss betrayed him. You, Judas, not me!" Lamech took hold of Judas' hand holding the coins, and clenched the fingers back on top of them. "The silver goes with you, as does the kiss. Now leave here, and do not return." Lamech released his hand, stepped toward the door – but not before adding. "No wonder Yeshua will go to his death, with the likes of you as friends. You sicken me."

Lamech left. Judas dropped to his knees. One by one, the coins fell from his hand as his whole body quaked. Lamech was right. Judas sickened himself.

* * *

The tone of the *magrefa* called the Sanhedrin to order. Caiaphas took his places in the high priest's chair, then motioned to guards standing at a side door. The door opened, and another two other guards entered the room, arms locked on a prisoner between them. Bruises marked Yeshua's face and he limped, remnants of Antony's visit. Some who'd seen Yeshua in the temple earlier in the week remarked how different, and weaker, the rabbi appeared to be.

"Silence!" The voice of Nathaniel cut through the room. "The Sanhedrin of Jerusalem will convene under summons from our High Priest, Caiaphas. May Elohim be praised, and may his truth be found here this day."

Caiaphas rose to his feet, and slowly walked to the bench where Yeshua had been seated. "Elders of Jerusalem, serious words have come to us about this Galilean rabbi called Yeshua."

Turning to the rabbi, Caiaphas continued. "We have brought you here in protective custody for your own safety. I fear that if the charges to be presented against you had reached the public's ear before this, we could not have saved you." Caiaphas paused, expecting some retort from the rabbi. None came. "You face grave accusations, rabbi. Witnesses will speak of sedition, and blasphemy. If I were in your position, I would ready myself."

Yeshua looked up to the high priest. "You are not in my position, nor does it appear I am in yours." Yeshua turned his head away from Caiaphas.

"Is that the deference you show the High Priest?" Nathaniel demanded.

Yeshua fixed his eyes on those of the Sopher, until Nathaniel found himself averting those eyes, as he had done just days before in the temple.

Caiaphas returned to his chair and summoned the witnesses that Lamech and others arranged. Several testified to Yeshua's outrage at the temple, disrupting the commerce of honest merchants whose work benefited the temple and served the pilgrims. Two spoke of the rabbi's allegation that he would destroy the temple and restore it in a matter of days, a temple that had taken Herod decades to erect. Others recounted rumors about claims of Yeshua being the Anointed One of God, the *mashiach*. After each witness, Caiaphas gave Yeshua opportunity to question or refute the witness. Each time, Yeshua refused. Even Lot and the few others sympathetic to the rabbi grew frustrated. If he would not speak, why should they?

When the last witness had testified, Caiaphas stood and walked once more to stand before Yeshua. Nathaniel hobbled to the side of the high priest.

"So, Rabbi Yeshua," Caiaphas began, "serious charges have been made. And you insult the Sanhedrin by giving no answer! What have you to hide from us?"

Yeshua began to stand, but one of the guards behind him shoved him back down on the bench. The rabbi lifted his head to look at Caiaphas. "Hide? I have spoken openly in the temple, and in the city, before the crowds. You are the one who seized me by night, out of sight of the people. And you charge me with trying to conceal?"

"Why do you not speak to contradict these witnesses if you've nothing to hide?"

"Witnesses bought and paid for have no need of contradiction. If you would know what I truly speak, you would have called in persons who actually heard what I said. Instead, you settle for those who have been paid to tell lies for the sake of their zealous purposes."

Yeshua barely finished his words when Nathaniel cracked his cane upon Yeshua's shoulder. The Sopher bent down to shout in the rabbi's ear, "How dare you speak to the High Priest in that tone, and with such accusations? We seek truth here!"

Yeshua leaned toward the Sopher, whispering in his ear so no one else could hear: "What truth would you like revealed, Nathaniel? Your betrayal of family to Herod? Your role in the death of Bethlehem's children, including David? Shall we speak such truth, Nathaniel? Shall we speak of your truth!"

The Sopher would have raised his cane to Yeshua again, but breath failed him. The room whirled and blurred. Nathaniel could recall nothing of the next few moments, except the puzzled look on the face of Caiaphas as several guards helped Nathaniel back to his chair.

"No, take him outside the room." The voice belonged to Jehu, an elder who had some acquaintance with medicines and herbs. "Let him breathe the outside air to return color to his face." As the guards half-carried Nathaniel through the door, the Sopher looked back at the prisoner. He could not be sure, but it seemed Yeshua mouthed the words "your truth" once more.

Caiaphas called the Sanhedrin back from hushed conversations about the Sopher. "We still have business to conduct. And you, Yeshua, still have reply to make to these charges."

The rabbi breathed deeply, and spoke no word.

"Have you no answer, Yeshua of Galilee? You have heard this testimony. We need no further witnesses. What have you to say to them?"

Again, Yeshua remained silent.

Caiaphas weighed the situation. Though damaging to his reputation, the witnesses had not proven a crime that required death. Should Lot and others wish to press the case for censure rather than condemnation, something stronger needed to be said, and admitted.

"Rabbi, some have said you are the Expected One, the *mashiach* of the Holy One, blessed be his name. But tell me, do you also say you are the Son of the Blessed?"

As Yeshua began to stand, Caiaphas waved off the guard who would have kept the rabbi in his chair.

"I am." The room erupted in shouts of "no", with some covering their ears. Caiaphas motioned them to be still. He wanted Yeshua to finish. "And you will see the Son of Man seated at the hand of power, coming on the clouds of heaven."

Now Caiaphas led the outcry. "Blasphemy! He blasphemes in the Temple itself!"

Some tore at their robes, others surrounded the rabbi and began to strike at him. The guards offered only a half-hearted shield, allowing more than a few fists to pummel Yeshua. Caiaphas rang the *magrefa* until the outburst ceased. The rabbi had walked into the trap.

"What more do you need to hear? He has testified against himself, he has blasphemed against Elohim Adonai, claiming to be a son of the Almighty, like one of the Gentile myths."

"He deserves to die!" shouted Lamech.

"Stone him!" replied others. "Silence his blasphemy!"

As the Council pressed around Yeshua, the guards finally tightened their circle around the rabbi so none could strike him, or worse. It would not do to shed blood in the Temple itself. Caiaphas sounded the *magrefa* again until the elders returned to their seats.

"The Sanhedrin has spoken," pronounced Caiaphas. "But lest those who still follow him seek vengeance on us for this decision, I propose we give rabbi Yeshua to Rome for execution. Crucifixion will end his following once and for all. Does the Torah not teach that to hang upon a tree means to be cursed by God? Let him be cursed by God, and put to death by those whose hands are bloodied already. Does the Council agree?"

"So be it." Lamech spoke the words first, then another took them up, and finally it became a chorus taken up by nearly all in the room.

"So be it – crucifixion!"

Caiaphas turned to Yeshua. "You go to Pilate for trial, and then you die on a Roman cross: cursed by the Holy One of Israel for your blasphemy!"

Yeshua offered no word. As if from a distance, the sight of a cave in Bethlehem came to his mind, and other innocents before him. Now he would join them.

* * *

Nathaniel slowly revived in the fresh air of the courtyard. Jehu promised to send herbs to be taken before sleep, and encouraged the Sopher to go home and rest. Nathaniel muttered agreement to the herbs, but would have nothing of returning to his house yet. There was business to be done. News of Yeshua's blasphemy and the Sanhedrin's decision had been relayed to him. He would need to accompany Lamech this afternoon to Yeshua's trial before Pilate.

"I've business to attend to, Jehu. I will take my rest, and your medication, tonight."

"Then let me come with you to –"

"That's not necessary. I feel my legs strong enough. And my business needs my attention alone. But thank you again."

As Jehu walked away, Nathaniel was glad the elder would no longer be hovering about. The Sopher now set out to find Lamech. Once the trial before Pilate was finished, this business with the rabbi would soon be passed. Those words about Bethlehem, and children: they could be dangerous if heard by the wrong ears. Nathaniel jostled through the crowd filling the courtyard on this eve of Passover. Obsessing on Yeshua's words, and the strangers moving and standing all about him, made progress difficult. More than that, they diverted Nathaniel's attention from the solitary figure who shadowed him since Jehu left, and who now stepped next to Nathaniel's side.

Nathaniel felt the arm holding his cane grasped by another's hand. "What do you mean by – " Nathaniel's words froze as he turned and recognized who held him: "Julius?"

"I've need to talk with you. Inside the tower."

"I don't think so." Nathaniel tugged his arm away, but Julius gripped tighter.

"You know me, Nathaniel. I will have my word with you, or the temple police will wonder what zealot put his knife between your ribs."

Nathaniel felt a sharp barb press into his side. "This is folly!"

"Perhaps. But I am willing to die a fool here and now. Are you?"

The tip of Julius' knife pressed harder. "Very well, what is it you want to say."

"Not here, Sopher. Tell the guards inside I've been assigned to accompany you. We'll speak in the passageway."

Nathaniel tried to hastily figure out some option or means of escape, but none came to mind. Once they arrived at the tower's door, he spoke to the guards as Julius directed. Once inside, the door closed. The pair moved to the inner door, which Nathaniel unlocked and opened. They stepped in, and Julius closed the door behind them. A single torch lit the staircase that descended to the passageway. "Move down the stairs, Nathaniel. And no shouting." Nathaniel's cane tapped each step, echoing down the long hallway. Once at the bottom, Julius and Nathaniel stood beneath another torch. Nathaniel rubbed his forearm where Julius had held him. "So, Julius, what does Rome's former prodigy in Jerusalem have to do with an old Jew?"

"A plea, Nathaniel. Don't let this plan against Yeshua unfold."

"Yeshua? I had heard this rabbi speaks of Samaritans with respect, but does Rome now find welcome and alliance with him? Maybe the Zealots were right after all!"

"Let's not waste one another's time, Nathaniel. You and I have killed innocents before. I only ask to let this one go free. Yeshua does no harm: not to Rome, not to the likes of you."

"Your compassion touches me, Julius. But your reasons for it interests me far more."

"My reasons are my reasons, that's all you need to know. The rabbi poses no threat and doesn't deserve death."

"Now that," Nathaniel answered, "rests in the hands of Pilate. You'd best speak to him."

"I speak to you, Nathaniel. I know you in such matters. If you would, you could turn Pilate's ear with the right words."

"You give me too much credit, Julius. But even if I could, I would not. You are mistaken about this Galilean. He is dangerous. His cross will benefit my people."

As in the courtyard, Julius seized the arm of Nathaniel. "Not all your people, Nathaniel. He is an innocent man!"

"Innocent!?" Nathaniel's voice pitched higher. "Don't talk to me of innocents, centurion. Bethlehem knows your respect of innocents!"

"Your hand in Bethlehem is no cleaner than mine."

"Really?" Nathaniel moved to free his arm from Julius, but failed as before. "Let's say, Bethlehem finally catches up with your innocent Yeshua, the one who escaped your detachment, who lived while others died. His time simply comes up now. And, centurion, you will be glad to know your successor will be given the privilege of watching him writhe on that cross tomorrow."

"Antony?"

"Yes, the one you promoted will be executioner of your innocent rabbi. And in a stroke of irony even you would appreciate, another to be crucified will be none other than your protege's father, the coward who gave Antony reason to deny his family."

"Hannah's father?" blurted Julius.

"Hannah?" Nathaniel's mind raced to the night he learned Hannah had left her whoring to follow the rabbi, and taken up with a Roman. And now, Julius reveals he knows Hannah to be Antony's sister? "Julius, you wouldn't be Hannah's consort, would you? Answer me!"

Julius said nothing.

Nathaniel stared hard at the Roman. "You are, or you'd deny it! You plead for the rabbi to favor Hannah. Oh, Julius, that makes you almost family to me. How touching!"

Julius let loose Nathaniel's arm and drew out his knife. "You cannot do this, Nathaniel. You can't have Antony stand by and watch his own father die. You can't do that to Hannah. And you cannot let the rabbi go condemned. He's no guilt in any of this!"

"And what will you do, Julius, if I refuse? Run me through with that blade, and put more blood of Hannah's family on your hands?" Nathaniel paused. For a moment, for all he knew, Julius might be willing to do just that. But Nathaniel watched as Julius slowly sheathed the knife.

"In the name of your God, Nathaniel, don't do these things."

The removal of the blade set loose Nathaniel's bravado. "Don't talk to me of my God, Roman. I can see the rabbi's weakness has infected you as well. So be it. Go your way, as I go mine." Nathaniel walked back toward the doorway they had entered. He listened for Julius to follow him, but when no sound came, Nathaniel cried out, "Prepare Hannah to be orphaned a second time! Watch the boy crucify the father! And know you have let Yeshua die, as surely as those others in Bethlehem. Goodbye, Julius!" The Sopher closed his final word with laughter.

    Julius slumped to the floor, head in hands. He took out his knife and tossed it aside. Useless, like him, to save innocents. In Bethlehem. And now in Jerusalem.

CHAPTER LIV

Pilate sat on his judgment chair in the Antonia's courtyard. Not many weeks ago, he had interrogated Yeshua Barabbas there. This morning, he awaited the arrival of the Sanhedrin's delegation bearing yet another Yeshua, whom some called their king. Today's agenda had been sealed by Nathaniel and Pilate in their previous meeting. A swift trial, and a swifter execution, would fall on the next day's festival of Passover.

But Pilate had been pondering this day's business ever since that meeting. Lest Nathaniel think he'd manipulated the procurator to do exactly what the Temple leaders wished, Pilate had come up with a twist to the plan. Drumming his fingers on the arm of the chair, he looked forward to the aggravation it would cause these Jews, reminding them of Rome's upper hand in all matters. At the same time, it would strengthen his relationship with Herod Antipas, ruler of Galilee and a favorite of Emperor Tiberias. Pilate knew that ingratiating himself to any friend of the Emperor could prove a boon to his own career.

The procurator's reverie was broken by the heralding of the delegation's arrival with its prisoner, as the cohort's scribe assigned to record the trial declared: "Pontius Pilate, procurator of Judea, now stands in judgment of the prisoner named Yeshua."

The Temple guards who escorted Yeshua positioned him to stand directly before Pilate. The Sanhedrin's delegation, led by Nathaniel and Lamech, took their place behind Yeshua. A group of onlookers stood further to the back.

Antony and a detachment from the cohort paid particular attention to the crowd to insure no disruption of the proceedings – and to carry out other orders Pilate had given to Antony. Pilate could see saw bruises and cuts on the rabbi's face, inflicted by Antony's beating the previous day. Those same injuries alarmed another, standing among the onlookers. To Julius, they signaled the execution had begun before the trial.

* * *

The walk to the house of Nathaniel seemed an eternity for the women. Mary shuffled her feet, thoughts of her son's condemnation absorbing her thoughts and energy. Hannah walked close beside her. It had been Mary's decision to see Naomi again. Naomi's word, and touch, had triggered conflicted memories in Mary. She remembered the joy of Naomi and Rebekah befriending her shortly after Yeshua's birth, when she had no one beside Joseph. She remembered the anguish when learning of the slaughter of Bethlehem's innocents, innocents that included Hannah's son and Rebekah's son and husband. Even with Naomi's forgiveness, Mary struggled in the wash of these memories with forgiving herself.

As she and Hannah approached the low wall that enclosed Nathaniel's home, a figure walked down from its colonnaded porch to the gate that opened to the street. Hannah abruptly stopped. "Mary, stop. I think –"   But it was too late. At the same moment, Rebekah had looked in their direction and cried out, "Wait!" and then walked briskly toward the two. Hannah drew Mary close to her side. Rebekah disregarded Hannah's attempt at sheltering, stepping directly in front of Mary and glaring into her face. "So, it is you. Naomi told me this morning when I came to visit that you'd been here yesterday. And here you are again. How fortunate I left when I did, so I can speak to your face what Naomi was too weak to say, what we have carried all these years. And to do so on the day before justice will finally be done to your son – and through his death, to you!"

Hannah tightened her embrace of Mary. "Rebekah, please. We've come to see Naomi."

"Rebekah?" Mary's already reddened eyes widened and moistened. "Rebekah?" She reached one hand up to touch the face of one she had seen for years only in dreams.

Rebekah gripped her hand before it touched her, then shoved it backwards. "How dare you! Do you think a gentle hand, and a tear or two, erases what you've done? The hands lifted against my husband and son, the tears I shed, while you fled into the night to save yourself and leave the rest of us to die? How dare you!"

Mary dropped her eyes to the ground. "You've every right, to condemn me, Rebekah. We, Joseph and I, made a mistake. We thought our leaving would protect you."

"Protect us? You left us to face Herod's killers without warning." Rebekah thrust her index finger into Mary's face. "You and your coward of a husband slinked into our midst. We showed you hospitality, took you into our homes. Elias even gave Joseph a job. But in doing so, we welcomed a viper into our nest!"

Rebekah now jammed that finger into Mary's chest. "And in that bosom, you suckled a viper's spawn. Who lived when others died. Well, Mary, it's high time for your Yeshua to die, and for the pain I've suffered all these years to finally eat away your blackened heart."

Hannah could remain silent no longer. "That's enough! Your suffering doesn't give you the right to inflict pain on others. Mary is innocent in this, as is Yeshua."

Rebekah sneered at Hannah's words, though she refused to look at her, keeping her gaze fixed on Mary. "I'll not be lectured on innocence by a whore to Romans. Though if the rumors of her dalliances with your son are correct, Mary, perhaps Hannah doesn't spread her legs only for Gentiles, an art she perfected in the Antonia. Isn't that right, Hannah?"

The memory of the Antonia, and Rebekah's use of it as

a weapon, stunned Hannah into silence. But not Mary.

"Say what you will of me, Rebekah. You have cause. But treat your friend's daughter like this? I would ask what has come of you. But I fear we both know the answer. It isn't grief, its hatred. Hatred has twisted you, Rebekah, from the woman I once knew."

Rebekah glared at Mary for a moment, then swung her right arm full force so that the palm of her hand cracked loud and hard across Mary's face, knocking her backwards. Mary could feel blood running down her chin. Without a word, she stepped forward and turned the cheek that had not been struck toward Rebekah. "Would you strike me again? Would that give peace to your soul? If it would, be done with it. But know this: no amount of violence will undo the violence done to you and to your family. Hold me guilty for that if you will, but not my son."

Rebekah did not lift her hand, but struck with her tongue. "Two sons will die tomorrow. At least mine will die for something, a martyr. Your Yeshua will die a failure."

"I can't say what will come of my son's death, Rebekah. But I can say this: my son has lived not to take life but give life." Mary drew a deep breath, her cheek and lip still stinging from the blow. "You spoke earlier about justice coming to my son. But isn't the giving of life, rather than its taking, what the Torah means by justice? Even if in the giving, one's own life goes forfeit? Isn't that the justice Elias lived by, and died for? To give life to save life?"

Mary's words caught Rebekah off-guard. They evoked Rebekah's initial feelings in the wake of Bethlehem's massacre, how Elias had left her alone. How his death seemed so senseless, how they might have escaped if he had not insisted on warning Joshua and Naomi. But such thoughts fled as quickly as she came. She scowled at Mary, and for a moment saw her as the young woman who'd given birth in Joshua's stable. Still a naïve child. Justice as giving life?

"Believe your fantasies, Mary. You, and your son, will

find out soon enough how the world practices justice. After you see Yeshua die on the cross, tell me of justice." Rebekah whirled round, her outer cloak billowing, and walked away.

Drained by their run-in with Rebekah, Mary and Hannah decided to postpone seeing Naomi. Hannah would come early tomorrow to visit her mother before heading to the execution. Perhaps another time would come for Mary to call on Naomi. But none of the women noticed, during the confrontation, a figure standing on Nathaniel's porch. Naomi had watched, and listened to, all.

* * *

Pilate struck a pose before the crowd gathered before him, grasping a pleat of his toga while lifting his chin. "What business does the Sanhedrin bring for my judgment this day?"

Nathaniel bowed. "Procurator, we come with a prisoner who has made blasphemous remarks regarding our religion, which our law deems punishable by stoning. But we do not wish to act apart from your sanction over all capital offenses."

So far, Pilate continued with the agreed upon script. "I am no judge of Jewish law, and Rome has little interest in religious viewpoints, apart from regard for the emperor."

Nathaniel smiled. "We understand that, procurator. But this man calls himself a king not subject to the emperor, and has already incited one riot in the city."

"I see. Sedition is, of course, a different matter. By the way, what is the name of your prisoner, and where is his residence?

"Yeshua, my lord. Yeshua of Nazareth."

Now it was Pilate's turn to smile. "Nazareth? Tell me, Sopher, is that not in Galilee?"

The question caught Nathaniel off-guard. "It is, procurator."

"Well then, you have come to me too hastily. If he is Galilean, he is subject first to Herod Antipas. And since

Herod stays in the palace for tomorrow's festival, I decree that this Yeshua should be interrogated by him first, to see if his case merits further review by me."

Nathaniel and Lamech exchanged looks of shock: Nathaniel's of surprise, Lamech's of anger. The Sopher had assured the Sanhedrin, and Lamech in particular, that all had been arranged. Gathering his thoughts, the Sopher made appeal. "Procurator, we would not burden your time with having to arrange a second hearing. It seems –"

"Enough! I've made my ruling. Yeshua is Galilean, so let him first appear before Herod. If there is no resolution, then bring him to me at tomorrow's first light." Pilate raised his hand and pointed at Antony, who led the detachment that took custody of Yeshua from the Temple Guard and brought him to the Antonia. "Deliver the prisoner to Herod, and direct him to the review the charges brought by the Sanhedrin." What Pilate left unsaid was that Herod had already been informed, and had agreed to return Yeshua to Pilate for judgment the next morning.

The detachment led by Antony set off for the palace. Nathaniel and Lamech engaged in an animated conversation among the other Sanhedrin members. What if Herod set Yeshua free? What would happen then – and who would take the blame?

As they discussed and argued, one of the onlookers set off after the soldiers and their prisoner. Julius followed at a discreet distance until the Antonia's courtyard had been left behind for the maze of Jerusalem's streets. Julius had gone to the Antonia, simply wanting to see what the next steps would be for Yeshua. But when he caught sight of Antony in the courtyard, Julius decided this might be his last opportunity to intercede: if not for Yeshua, then for Antony.

"Centurion Antony, a word with you." Julius cried out. Antony turned see who called out his name, while the soldiers he led abruptly stopped and drew their weapons in case of a trap. Julius held up both hands, palms open. "It's Julius, Antony."

"Julius!?" Antony half-ran to his sponsor into the legion. "I can't believe it!" The two men hugged. No one noticed the eyes of Yeshua widen at the sight of Julius.

"Centurion. The prisoner. This is not a good place to stop." The warning was spoken by Naaman, a Syrian second in command in the century assigned to Antony. Naaman knew of Julius from Antony, as well as from stories told by soldiers who had long-served in this region. But this was no time for reunions.

Antony turned to Naaman and the detachment. "Let us be on our way. And Julius," turning back to his mentor, "we can speak as we walk. How long has it been?"

As the detachment resumed its march, Julius drew Antony's arm to bring him closer, then spoke so that no other beside the centurion could hear him speak.

"Antony, we must talk. In private."

Antony's brow furrowed. "What is it – something wrong?"

"Will you be free after sunset tonight?"

"Yes. Come to the Antonia. I'll leave word you are expected."

"Good. And another will be with me. Hannah, your sister.

Antony stopped abruptly. "My sister?"

"We must speak in private. About Nathaniel. And about Yeshua."

"Yeshua? There is nothing to be said about him, nothing good anyway." Antony leaned toward Julius and dropped his voice. "Well, the one good thing about him is that I've been given the honor of heading the detail that will crucify him tomorrow. A death long overdue."

"Do you trust me, Antony?"

A look of surprise came over Antony. "You're the one who gave me a new life, when I couldn't abide the old one. I owe you everything."

"Then I call in that debt tonight." Julius glanced ahead to the detachment. Naaman glared at him, as he held up his right arm to bring the detail to another halt, having realized the pair had been left behind. But Julius also saw Yeshua's eyes focus upon him. Now, as at Magdala, Julius felt himself seen by the rabbi in some way that defied understanding. For an instant, he thought Yeshua nodded at him. Looking back to Antony, Julius added, "Trust me, and hear us out tonight." Having spoken, Julius turned and walked away.

"Centurion, we must be on our way." Naaman interrupted Antony's wonderings of what Julius could possibly have in mind. And why, and how, Hannah and Julius had come to be connected? The detail resumed its march toward the palace. Antony mused on what this evening might bring. As he did, Julius made his way toward to the caravansary of Ishmael.

* * *

Ishmael swilled a mouthful of wine. "So that's how it's to be done, then." He had patiently listened as Julius related what had happened since they last spoke. The failed attempt by Julius to dissuade Nathaniel from carrying out Yeshua's execution . . . the revelation that Nathaniel had set up Antony to unknowingly preside over the crucifixion of his own father. . . the abbreviated appearance of Yeshua before Pilate . . . Julius' meeting with Antony . . . "Pilate serves up the rabbi to Herod just to get another set of hands on the death warrant. And this Nathaniel – maybe you should have left him to Kohath's blade years ago."

Julius grimaced at the irony of it all struck hard. Years ago, he had not intervened to save the innocents in Bethlehem. Yet he had saved the life of Nathaniel, the very one who knowingly betrayed those innocents – and who now stood to accomplish what Herod had failed all to do: the execution of Yeshua. And in another twist, Nathaniel had arranged Antony to be in charge of the killing. Would the boy recognize his own father, or the father his son, after all these years?

Julius swirled the remaining wine in his cup. He thought of filling it again, and again, until thoughts no longer plagued him. Instead, Julius sent it flying against wall. Pottery shards flew everywhere in the dining hall of the caravansary, empty except for these two.

Ishmael had not only been listening to Julius. As his friend spoke, and in the ensuing silence, the old man had been formulating his own thoughts of what had come to be. And what needed to be said – and done. "Twenty and more years ago, you sought out my ears in exchange for Roman coins. Which was fine with me then. But over time, Julius, you've become a friend, and more. If I'd ever stayed with a woman fool enough to put up with the likes of me, I'd have been proud to have a son like you. Which is what you've come to be."

Julius studied Ishmael, still wearing the old soiled apron from when they first met. Julius thought he could see the old man's eyes redden a bit. "I left my family nearly forty years ago to join the legion. For a long time, the cohort was my family. And men like Gaius. But no one, no one, has been family to me longer than you, Ishmael. You, and Hannah, are all I have left."

"Then hear me out, Julius. Go to Hannah. I've seen the way she looks at you – and you at her. Hold on to her. Who knows, maybe you'll find a way to help her brother."

"Maybe. But the rabbi, Yeshua, I couldn't help."

The jaw of Ishmael clenched. "You did all he'd let you, if I rightly heard your account of Gesamani. Sometimes, people land beyond help. Especially when scum like Nathaniel have their way. As for Nathaniel – justice may not always be swift, but she finds her way. Like I said: see to it you care for Hannah, and let her care for you. As for me, I'll see to the caretaking of Nathaniel, so that pious old bastard never betrays again."

"Ishmael, what are you – "

"Don't worry yourself about that, Julius. And don't

worry about me. I do as I choose – always been that way for me, no sense changing things now. No regrets."

Ishmael grabbed his cane and stood, holding out a free hand to Julius. Instead of shaking Ishmael's hand, he walked around the table and embraced the innkeep. "No regrets, Ishmael."

Both men let go of each other without further word. Julius headed out the door toward the home in Bethany where Hannah was staying. Ishmael headed out to find the stable boy. On Monday, Ishmael had sent him with a message for Julius. This afternoon, he would send him with a message for the leader of the Galilean Zealots, Jacob: a message that the betrayer of his father in this very caravansary twenty years before could be had.

CHAPTER LV

Yeshua fell hard on the floor of his cell, pushed from behind by the guard called Naaman. Naaman had escorted him back to the Antonia after the rabbi's hearing before Herod ended. "Sleep well, Yeshua, king of the Jews!" Naaman laughed. "I'll be back to fetch you in the morning. Once Pilate's done with you, we'll have your throne waiting on Golgotha."

Once the guard left, Yeshua thought back on the farce of his interview by Herod. The same man who had executed Yeshua's cousin, John the Baptizer, was only interested in having Yeshua perform one of those tricks or miracles that Herod had heard so much about. Yeshua did not prove entertaining. The only word he spoke to Herod asked if the king still feared John in death as much as he had in life. Herod abruptly declared the trial to be over and Yeshua a fraud.

"Are you Yeshua, Yeshua of Nazareth?" The voice came from the cell next to Yeshua's.

"Yes. Who asks?"

"My name is Joshua. An innkeeper of Galilee of late, but long ago of Bethlehem."

* * *

Another prisoner in a cell at the far end of the dungeon heard the approach of a single pair of footsteps. No other prisoner was held at this end, a solitude meant to further punish the murderer of Lucius. Barabbas wondered what was to be, as the guards had never before come to him alone. The visitor set the torch into a holder by the cell. "Barabbas!"

The prisoner slowly moved to the barred window in the cell door. "What do you want?"

Naaman lifted the torch and held it up to the bars. "Come closer."

Barabbas stepped up to the cell bars.

Naaman studied the face of Barabbas in the light. "You are the killer of Lucius? You don't look so threatening now. More like a dog beaten into submission."

"Appearances can be deceiving." Barabbas attempted a defiant tone, though weeks of imprisonment and torture imposed a wavering quality to his voice.

"Quite right. Appearances can deceive." Naaman paused, recalling the instructions Antony had gone over carefully with him, assuring the orders came directly from Pilate. "Such as, for you, the appearance of betrayal if enemies suddenly treat you with mercy."

"Mercy?" Barabbas blurted out. "I don't know who you are, but no mercy's come to me these past weeks."

"Who I am doesn't matter. But who I speak for does. Pilate has decided to become your benefactor. Tomorrow, instead of crucifixion, you're to be released."

Barabbas' head spun. Was he dreaming? Was this some hoax foisted on him at the last moment as yet another act of cruelty? "Why should I believe you?" he finally uttered.

"I don't care if you believe me. But here is what you better believe. When you are freed tomorrow, you will cease any association with the Zealots."

"What makes you think I would agree to such a thing, even for my life?"

Naaman thrust one hand through the bar, seizing the robe of Barabbas to pull him close. With the other hand, he snatched the leather thong around his neck that held the carved wolf with such force that it snapped off.

"No!!" Barabbas reached to grab it back, but Naaman used his grip on the robe to snap the chest of Barabbas into the iron bars, then let go and glared into the prisoner's face.

"Listen, Jew. It's not just your life on the line. Rejoin your rebel friends, and we'll find you and use a dull stone blade for your castration. Then we'll take that miserable remnant to your mother Rebekah, so it's the last sight she sees before we kill her. Understood?"

"Why don't you just kill me, now, and be done with it?"

"Because we're not done with you, that's why. Warn her or your Zealot friends of any of this, and we'll see that her death is not a swift or pleasant one. So choose, Barabbas. Death or life, for you and your mother!"

Barabbas stared at the wolf, torn from his neck and held by this legionnaire. But it wasn't all that was torn from his life. His father long gone. His mother who urged him to embrace martyrdom. He felt dead already. All he could save was his mother. "Alright. Just leave her be."

Before returning to his post, Naaman tossed the carving back into the cell and laughed. "Here is your toy – never say that Rome is not merciful!"

Once Naaman was out of sight, Barabbas took the wolf in hand and pressed it against his chest. "I'm sorry, father. I'm sorry, *abba*. I'm sorry." The words spilled into the darkness. The darkness returned no comfort.

* * *

"Joshua, of Bethlehem?"

Joshua reached his arm through the bars in the cell door's window, extending his hand in the direction of Yeshua's cell. "You wouldn't remember me, you were too young. But your mother and father, they came to my inn for your birthing. In the stable."

"Yes, I do remember my parents speaking of you. And your wife."

"Naomi."

Yeshua stretched his arm out as well and clasped Joshua's hand. "And your children. Simeon, and the twins I played with in the stable."

"David and Hannah." Joshua's voice broke as he spoke the names of one who was dead and the other not seen by him since she was a toddler. "I'm sorry, rabbi."

"Sorry for what, Joshua?"

"I came to Jerusalem this week to warn you of a plot I learned of. I came to save you," Joshua's words caught in his throat, "but I failed, or you wouldn't be here. Nor would I. I failed you, rabbi, as I failed my David. And my whole family."

Joshua attempted to let go of Yeshua, but the rabbi kept a firm grip. "Joshua, listen to me. What's done is done. But it took courage for you to try to warn me. And at such risk."

"Rabbi, you don't know what I've done – and what I shirked from doing. My son died because of me, and my friend Elias. He fought. I cowered. And now, I've let you down."

Joshua again tried to pull his hand loose, but Yeshua would not let go. "You have not let me down. When I was arrested, most of those who followed me fled. But you came. And here you make yourself known to me, when you could have hidden in the darkness. Joshua, there is good in you. Find forgiveness in your heart – for yourself."

"You don't know how deeply I've hurt my family, rabbi. They would never forgive me."

"Of your wife, Naomi, I can't say." Yeshua gripped Joshua's hand. "But of your daughter, Hannah, she has forgiven you."

"My daughter – Hannah? What do you know of her?"

"She is among those who follow me. Beyond that, Hannah has spoken to me of you, and of her forgiving you. I swear to you, she has released what she once held against you. If she can do this, Joshua, you can forgive yourself. Don't let the past destroy you. You started on a new path by risking all to warn me. Continue on that way, Joshua. Continue on that way."

Joshua wept, while Yeshua held on to his hand. After

some time, Joshua leaned his head against the door. "If I am to die tomorrow, rabbi, know that you have given an old man peace."

"And you, Joshua of Bethlehem, know that I bless you for sheltering my parents all those years ago. And for fathering a daughter who would make you proud."

* * *

"Hannah, a moment." Julius and Hannah stopped just short of the gate that led into the Antonia. "Are you sure you want to do this – to enter this place?"

Hannah looked at Julius, and then at the massive tower. She recalled the last time she came here, and what happened to her inside. The memory caused her to shudder before she answered Julius. "I'm grateful you would have come here alone for my brother's sake. But I must do this, Julius. For Simeon – and for myself."

Julius nodded. Hannah had been adamant about coming when he told her he'd arranged to meet with Antony. Even when Julius disclosed the Antonia as the place of encounter, Hannah would not be deterred. With the ramparts of the fortress looming over them, Julius took hold of her hand. "If at any point you need to leave, let me know."

"I will, Julius, I will." Hannah took her free hand and brushed it against the face of Julius. "But we need to be going. Time is short."

The pair unclasped hands, and strode to the gate and its pair of guards. "I am the former centurion here, Julius. I come with a friend to meet with Centurion Antony."

After saluting, the older of the guards replied. "Antony sent word to expect you, sir." Looking now at Hannah, who had pulled the hood of her cloak over her head, the guard winked at Julius. "No mention of a friend – but maybe he wanted to be discrete, eh?"

An old guilt twisted inside Hannah for a moment, though it was quickly stilled by Julius stepping up square into the guard's face and speaking in a firm tone. "You would do well, legionnaire, not to insult a family member of the centurion, lest I report your words to Antony."

The guard snapped to attention." No offense intended, centurion!" Turning toward Hannah, he added. "My apologies, lady, for ill-spoken words." With that, he pounded on the gate. "Visitors for Antony." The guards inside opened the gate, and Julius and Hannah entered.

* * *

In the caravansary, Ishmael watched the door swing open. A group of five men entered. One stayed at the door while another took his place at the entry to the kitchen. Jacob, Reuben, and Lamech walked to Ishmael's table and sat across from him. Without a word, Ishmael filled three chalices with wine. His own cup already full, Ishmael lifted it, tipped it in their direction, and gulped a mouthful. The three took note that no one besides Ishmael was in the caravansary.

Reuben was the first to speak. "The night before Passover, and all Jerusalem is full of pilgrims – and your inn is empty?"

"I thought that the things I needed to say shouldn't be caught by ears other than your own. And especially Jacob's."

Jacob took a drink of the wine, then eyed Ishmael intently. "The boy you sent said you had some word about the betrayal and murder of my father. You have my ear."

"And mine as well, Ishmael." Lamech, the chief spokesman for the Zealots on the Sanhedrin, pushed aside the chalice set before him. "Tell us what you know."

Ishmael propped his cane between his legs, and rested his hands on its top. "What I know goes far beyond the murder of your father in this inn, Jacob. It goes back years ago, back to Bethlehem, and the murder of its children."

"The slaughter carried out by Herod and Rome?"

Ishmael smirked. "Herod and Rome? Do you think they acted without someone else providing information? One of our own people?"

Lamech interrupted. "What do you mean, `our own people?'"

"A Jew. A Jew who had Herod's confidence. And not only Herod, but someone who had the confidence of Bethlehem's families – and who could feed Herod's fear of a new king with knowledge that came to him of an heir to David."

"What about my father's betrayer?" Jacob demanded. "What has some imagined heir have to do with his murder?"

"Not so much what, Jacob, but who. Nathaniel. The Sopher told Herod such an heir had been born some months before – and Nathaniel was the same one who was conspired in your father's death, just as he's done these days to insure Yeshua's death."

"What has Yeshua to do with any of this?" Lamech interjected.

"Everything." Ishmael glared at the three before him. "He was the boy, the Davidic child, Herod sought in Bethlehem in the first place. Nathaniel informed Herod of Yeshua's family line, even though that put children of his own kin in the path of Herod's swords. And now, you three, and your ilk, are about to do what Herod failed at – killing Yeshua."

Ishmael could see not only shock etching the faces of his audience, but Reuben reaching beneath his robe, and the glimpse of a knife. All needed to come to light, and quickly.

"You asked about your father's betrayer, Jacob. Nathaniel knew a trap was to be sprung against him and said nothing. He'd learned his own life was in jeopardy, and received protection from the Romans. Those same Romans, who saved Nathaniel's skin, lured your father into this caravansary, along with rabbi Saddok, and executed them."

Jacob sprang to his feet and swept the cups and pitcher off the table. "How do you know these things, Ishmael? How do you know!?."

Ishmael leaned forward and stood, steadying himself on the cane. "Because I was here, Jacob. Because Rome paid me to hold my tongue about the plan to kill your father and Saddok, and to let its executioners into my doors. And my only regret," Ishmael managed to lift one hand from his cane and point it at the three before him, two of whom had already drawn their blades, "is that I did not insist that Nathaniel pay then for his bloodguilt. A man that you, especially you Lamech, continues to deal with, who splashes you all with the blood of Bethlehem's children. You think you use him to get Yeshua – fools! Nathaniel uses you. He's always used you!"

Reuben plunged his blade into Ishmael's side, followed by a thrust from Jacob's knife. The innkeep slumped down, his cane dropping to the floor. He touched the blood coursing out from the wounds, as if it were a dream. In his mind's eye, he saw Julius – and Hannah – before refocusing on the men in front of him.

"Great warriors, killing an old cripple." He coughed, tasting a mix of blood and phlegm in his mouth. "And you'd let the betrayer of children, and family, and nation, die a peaceful death? Cowards, bastards, every damned one of you!"

Reuben leaned over to put his mouth at Ishmael's ears. "Make a place for Nathaniel in Sheol, innkeep. Mark my words, he'll be with you soon enough."

Ishmael nodded, then felt Reuben's blade slice across his neck.

Reuben, who had relatives that lost children in the massacre, glared at Jacob and Lamech. "A dying man doesn't lie. I don't care what consequences there might be from the Sanhedrin or even Caiaphas: for Bethlehem, Nathaniel is a dead man!"

Jacob took his bloodied knife and touched the tip of Reuben's. "And for my father."

CHAPTER LVI

Julius and Hannah paused outside the door to Antony's room. When the guard inside the gate had described where the centurion's room was, Julius told him they had no need of an escort to guide them. It had been his room years ago. Hannah had held tightly onto his hand as they walked through the corridors. The smell from torches conjured painful remembrances of her only visit here. She was glad Julius walked beside her now.

"This is it," Julius announced as he came to a stop, then knocked on the door. When it swung open, Hannah looked at the man standing before her in a white tunic and leather cuirass. The years had hardened his features, but his deep brown eyes had not changed. "Simeon!"

Antony recognized in Hannah's face the traces of a sister not seen in over twenty years. His mind flashed to the day of his grandmother's funeral, when Rebekah not only rebuked him but spewed disgust at Hannah's having become a prostitute – and then to yesterday, when Yeshua asserted that Hannah had become one of his disciples. But all these faded into the background. Before him stood his sister, his chief defender in the family, the surviving twin of his dead brother David.

"Is it really you, Hannah?!"

Hannah threw her arms around her brother's neck and kissed him. "Simeon!"

As the two held one another in a tear-filled embrace, Julius viewed their reunion through a shroud of scenes: Bethlehem's streets, a young man's plea for a new identity, a boat rocking in Caesarea's harbor, a confession of his role in David's death, forgiveness extended to him that Julius could not extend to himself. When the two finally broke their hug, Antony stepped toward Julius and grasped his shoulders. "Julius, to have you both here – words escape me."

Julius wished he could provide Hannah and Antony hours to relish this moment. But time was short. "Antony, please. We must talk."

Antony pulled a chair out for Hannah at his table, then sat on the edge of his bed. Julius took a seat alongside the bed. "I asked earlier today for your trust in hearing me out."

"Say what you need to, Julius. But know this. When we spoke earlier, you mentioned Yeshua, and Nathaniel, as cause for meeting with me. I don't care a whit about what you say about my uncle. OUR uncle," he added, glancing at Hannah. "But Yeshua is a different story. He must pay for the death of my brother, and the deaths of too many children in Bethlehem."

Hannah reached a hand to her brother. "Simeon, you don't understand."

"I DO understand. I know his parents fled our village in the night, leaving others to die so that he might live. He might as well have plunged the knife himself into David."

Julius drew out a blade from under his robe and set it on the table. "Then let's be clear. If you would welcome Yeshua's death tomorrow for David's sake, you might as well to use this knife on me. Because unlike Yeshua, I was there. I was part of the killing squad dispatched by Herod. The blood of your brother is on my hands."

Antony's eyes widened. "You? No, that's not true. You're just trying to save Yeshua!?"

"It is true. If I could save Yeshua, I would. But that's not why I, why we, have come tonight. We come for you. To save you from being party to yet another of Nathaniel's schemes."

Antony's temples pounded. Julius had been in Bethlehem? He tried to push it out of his mind for now. "Of Nathaniel's schemings," Antony began, the memory of Barabbas's betrayal still fresh in his mind, "I am overly acquainted."

"I fear you don't know the whole of them," Julius continued. "Am I right to guess that Nathaniel was the one who informed you of Yeshua's identity?"

"You are. But so what?"

Hannah leaned closer toward her brother. "But did he tell you, Simeon, of his own role in the killing of the children, and David?"

"What are you talking about? Nathaniel was in Jerusalem! How could –"

"In Jerusalem, yes," Julius interrupted. "But when rumors swept Herod's palace of a Davidic heir born in Bethlehem, Nathaniel told Herod that Yeshua's father descended from David's house. Your uncle told the king he came into this knowledge through his own family in the village. Nathaniel betrayed Yeshua's family, and yours, to curry Herod's favor."

"But Julius, if Herod only wanted Yeshua to die, why were all the children, why was David, killed when Yeshua was not found?"

Julius sighed and swore a silent curse again the long-dead king. "Because Herod wanted no risk that the one child he sought might somehow escape. He ordered, he demanded, the execution of all the boys, two years and younger, to make sure the one he wanted perished."

"That makes no sense," Antony protested. "Nathaniel may be ruthless, but even he wouldn't allow his own family to suffer death."

"He would, Simeon. And he did. I was in the room with Herod and Nathaniel when the king ordered the massacre. Herod explicitly told your uncle not to warn his family. Nathaniel agreed without any hesitation. He'd no more regard for his family then than he has now."

"Now?"

Julius looked toward Hannah, who nodded. "Go on, Julius. He must be told."

"Told what?"

"I confronted your great-uncle this morning to intercede for Yeshua. I failed. But in the process, Nathaniel divulged that you will be in charge of tomorrow's crucifixion detail."

"True enough. I'll oversee Yeshua's execution, and with no regret."

"Simeon, there'll be two other prisoners executed tomorrow." Julius paused, gathering the nerve to tell Simeon what he'd just disclosed to Hannah on the way here. "One of them will be your and Hannah's father."

"My father?" Simeon's face grew ashen. "My father?"

"I've no idea how he came here, nor what charges rate crucifixion. Though my gut tells me it's Nathaniel's doing. In any case, Antony: he arranged for you to be in charge of your father's execution without warning you – just as he gave your family no warning years ago."

Antony's face flushed as he drew his hands into fists. Long ago, his father failed to draw a knife to save David. But now, Nathaniel had for all intents and purposes put a knife in the hand of the son to kill the father.

"Damn him!" Antony's fists slammed into the table, then he sprang to his feet. "I swear, I will kill him!"

Julius sprang to his feet and stepped in front of Antony. "Don't. That would be Nathaniel's way."

The centurion glared at Julius. "He deserves to die."

"You'll get no argument from me on that. But not by your hand, Simeon."

"Why do you now call me Simeon? You gave me the name of Antony!"

Julius saw a sheathed gladius hanging from a hook in the wall. He stepped over to it, drew out the gladius and ran his fingers over it, then faced Antony. "I gave this gladius to a young man named Simeon. I asked that you use this blade with honor, as Antony. You have. But what Pilate orders you to do tomorrow, through Nathaniel's intrigue, has no honor."

"But I swore obedience to the legion. As you once did, Julius."

"I did. And I obeyed. All my life I obeyed. Even in Bethlehem, when my horse prevented the flight of two families, so that my men could put a pair of their sons, and a father, to the sword." Julius ran his hand across the edge of the gladius, then let it drop to the floor with a loud clang of metal against stone. "And I have not wakened to a single day since that does not remind me of my shame and guilt. Obedience can be blind to greater matters, Simeon. I didn't recognize that in Bethlehem, and my sworn oath has damned my life with innocent blood."

Antony found the implication hard to believe. "You'd have me disobey what the procurator commands?! Do you know what you are asking me to risk, Julius?"

"I do know. But I've learned, after years of regret, that sometimes a higher obedience is demanded, one that can't be ignored without even greater risk. Call it honor, call it family, call it God, whatever. Just be clear on this, Simeon. Before you swore that oath to Rome, you were – and you remain – by blood, the brother of Hannah, the son of your father. Even the kin of Nathaniel. No matter how deserving he may be, you mustn't be the one to shed Nathaniel's blood. And above all, you can't be party to shedding the blood of your father, and Yeshua, tomorrow. Enough innocents have died in the name of obedience, Simeon. Enough!"

Antony walked to the small slit in the wall that served as his window. It overlooked the Antonia's courtyard. Moonlight cast its glow on the paving stones below, reminding him of the night of his induction into the legion two decades past. Then, he sought escape from family by shedding the name and life of Simeon, and taking up a new one. Antony. Then he sought escape from the memory of his brother's murder and his father's disgrace at the hands of Rome by pledging his fealty to Rome's power. As Antony, he would no longer be the victim. But now, tonight, the weight of bearing that oath, and its adopted name, felt unbearable.

"You were there, Julius?" Antony spoke into the night. "Why didn't you tell me before?"

Julius walked to his side but stared straight ahead. "At first, I thought it was to protect you. But I've come to see, it was to protect me. You held your father a coward for what he failed to do on that street in Bethlehem. But the real coward was me, for what I did on that street. And later, for not having the courage to tell you when it might have made a difference in your life." Julius now turned to look at his protégé. "Yeshua is not the one who should be dying, Simeon. I am the one. What happened to David, what happened with your father, rests on me, not Yeshua."

"Stop it!" Hannah's shout startled both men. Her hands grasped the cloak of Julius. "Will you never forgive yourself? Will you always cling to the guilt that belongs to Herod and my uncle? You've told me time and again how sorry you are that you didn't object, that you didn't find another way. I believe that, Julius. I forgive you. The sister of David forgives you. For the sake of the Almighty, for your own sake, let go of this! You're not the one who should be dying. You are the one who should be living – and you have been, seeking to make this right ever since. That's all you can do: turn your back on what is evil, take on what is good. You've done that, Julius. Let go of guilt that belongs to others!"

"Sister," Antony asked, "do you love this man?"

Hannah was taken aback as much by his words as by the quickness of her response.

"I do."

"You love the man who saw to our brother's killing – how?"

"Because of the man you would crucify tomorrow," she answered. "Because of Yeshua, who taught me the path of forgiveness, whose way I've chosen to follow."

Antony walked back to one of the chairs, grasping its back and leaning on it for support. "Rebekah once told me you whored with the Romans. Did your Yeshua forgive you of that?

Hannah looked to Julius, then back at her brother. "He did. Even as he helped me learn to forgive myself for what I'd done." Hannah laced her arm inside that of Julius. "But you should know, I'd already left that life, thanks to Julius. It was just that, before Yeshua, I hadn't let loose of the anger and bitterness over what drove me into it in the first place."

"Which was?"

When words choked in Hannah's throat, Julius blurted: "Which was her gang rape in these barracks, when she was a young girl."

"What!?" Antony clenched the back of the chair even tighter. "My God, Hannah! Here?" Wonderings about which men he might have served with had done this to his sister dissolved into a confession. "I'm sorry, Hannah, I'm sorry. You always stood up for me. And when you needed me then – Hannah . . . I'm sorry."

Hannah embraced Simeon, then stepped back. "Brother, you're here now. The past – I wish I'd never come to this place that night. I wish what was done to me had never been done. But I refuse to let it destroy my life any further. What's important for me, for you, for Julius – is this moment, and what lies ahead. Old choices can't be undone. But new ones can be made."

"And the first choice," Julius added, "is what's to be done about tomorrow's crucifixions."

Antony looked at Julius. "What choice do I have?"

"Hear me out. In the morning, after you've received the prisoners from Pilate, inform the detail that you hand over leadership of them to me. I'll be in charge of the executions."

Hannah lowered her head. Though they'd discussed

the plan, the idea of Julius being saddled with this still grieved her.

"But what if Pilate notices the change? Won't he ask questions?"

"The procurator is a coward who wouldn't dare set foot out of the Antonia. Once he's passed judgment, he'll retreat to his quarters. That's when you make the transfer."

"But, what do I do then?"

"Your sister will need someone beside her tomorrow."

"And our mother as well," Hannah added. "She doesn't yet know about *abba.*"

"And beyond tomorrow: a widowed mother will need of someone to care for her. By my recollection, you've got your twenty years of service in. Submit your resignation from the legion. The donative you'll receive could support the both of you."

A long silence passed between the three, finally broken by Simeon.

"Why are you doing this, Julius?"

"I owe a debt to a young man who once came to me. And I do this for his sister."

"Whom you love?"

"Whom I love. Hannah is the one and only good left in my life."

Simeon turned to Hannah. "Would you have a brother again in your life?"

"Would you have a sister again in yours?"

Brother and sister embraced. Julius hoped this reconciliation would sustain them, and him, tomorrow – when he oversaw the execution of the one who made it possible.

CHAPTER LVII

Pilate fussed to achieve the proper drape of his toga across his shoulders. Part of the difficulty owed to the early hour, barely six hours after midnight. The greater challenge came from an unexpected heat enveloping the city. A wind from the southeast had blown all night, transporting the Salt Sea's oppressive warmth up the ridge which anchored Jerusalem's foundations. Pilate found himself already damp from sweat when he awoke. As he dressed, his perspiration made tunic and toga cling to his flesh. Pilate cursed the day's beginning – and the restlessness of the night just past. The sultry air had made sleeping fitful at best – and even when sleep came, his dreams verged into nightmares. "Damn this place, and these Jews," he muttered, finishing his preparations for the trial of Yeshua.

A sharp knock on his door was followed by the steward's voice. "Procurator, the guards have arrived with the prisoner for trial."

"And the other three?"

"Two wait in cells for execution. The legionnaire Naaman has the third man in custody, as you directed, in the side vestibule. He awaits your signal."

Pilate fluffed the dampened toga sticking under his armpits. The procurator hoped to be done with this quickly so that he could refresh himself in a cooling bath. "Let's get, then."

The steward opened the door for Pilate, and the two walked the corridors that led to the Courtyard of Paved Stones. They paused at the courtyard gate so the steward could announce the procurator's entrance. That done, Pilate stroke into the early morning sun and sat on the judgment seat. The century led by Antony ringed the courtyard to guarantee security.

Standing immediately before Pilate was Yeshua, flanked by Antony and the chief officer of the Temple Guard. Behind them stood the Sanhedrin representatives, headed by Nathaniel and Lamech. The Pharisee Lot had come, though he remained in the middle of the delegation rather than at the front. Lot had been disappointed in the rabbi's failure to defend himself before the Sanhedrin, though he still objected to the punishment now sought. If Pilate left an opening for a lesser judgment, Lot figured, he could raise his voice to sway the procurator. But if no opening presented itself, Lot resigned himself to say nothing. Had silence not been Yeshua's course? And if the rabbi did not speak on his own behalf, Lot surmised, why should he?

The courtyard's remaining space filled with a crowd of onlookers, many of whom had been bought and paid for by Jacob and Reuben to insure an outcry for crucifixion. The pair also arranged a small contingent of Zealot sympathizers to accompany Rebekah there, whose late husband Elias was revered as a martyr – and whose son would shortly provide another. Rebekah's other motive for attending the proceedings was the satisfaction of seeing Yeshua condemned, an overdue vengeance against the one responsible for the deaths of Elias and Levi.

Off to one side, careful to keep a line of sight open to Antony, a man snugged the hood of his cloak over his head. After the trial, he would make his way to where the prisoners would be staged until the procession to Golgotha. Julius would then remove the cloak, hiding the uniform not worn for years, and receive command of the execution detail from Antony.

* * *

Hannah made the long walk from Bethany to the

house of Nathaniel alone. Mary would leave later for Golgotha with the other women to stand vigil at her son's cross. Hannah and Julius had tried to dissuade her from going, so that she might be spared the horror of crucifixion's tortuous death. But Mary told them she'd brought her son into this life, and would not let him pass out of it alone. Hannah assured Mary she would join in Yeshua's vigil as well as her father's. Walking up the steps to Nathaniel's house where her mother stayed, she wished this day might end otherwise for Yeshua and Joshua. But she knew that was not to be.

The chief servant of the house greeted her at the door and went to fetch Naomi. Hannah wondered if her mother might yet be in bed at this early hour, so the sight of Naomi approaching, fully dressed, took her slightly aback.

"Hannah, my child." Naomi embraced her daughter.

"Mother, you're up early."

Naomi ran her hand through her daughter's hair. "I know this will be a difficult day for you. And Mary. I've thought much about our last conversation with you both." Naomi sat down on a bench on the porch, and as did Hannah. "I can't deny bitterness remains over the flight of Mary and Joseph all those years ago. But seeing her distress over her son's execution, and then, overhearing the way Rebekah treated you both yesterday."

"She told you?"

Naomi shook her head. "No. But when I heard Rebekah cry out your name, I came out and stood on the porch, just behind one of the columns to stay out of sight. I couldn't hear everything, but I heard enough." Naomi took her daughter's hands into her own. "What I want to say, Hannah – what I want to do, actually, is be with you today. And Mary, if she would have me. To stand with you both. I know this won't be easy for the two of you."

Tears began to stream down Hannah's cheeks. "Mother, forgive me."

"For what? I know this will be hard, but I want to be

there for you. For her."

Hannah looked up to the sky, then back into her mother's eyes. "I came here today," Hannah's voice began to crack, "I came here today . . . O God!"

"Hannah, what is it?"

"I came here . . . to tell you . . . that it's not only Yeshua and Barabbas who will carry a cross today. . ." As many times as she had rehearsed this, Hannah struggled to speak.

A puzzled expression came to Naomi's face. "Who else, child?"

Hannah paused to offer a silent prayer, then answered. "My father. Your husband."

Naomi gasped. Images of Joshua careened through her mind: the day they wed; the moment Joshua froze while his son was murdered; the last sight of his face, when Naomi pounded on his chest and told him never to return. All these disappeared into a face, and body, impaled upon a cross. "Joshua?" Naomi buried her face in her hands. "Joshua?"

Hannah held Naomi close. "Mother, I'm sorry to be the one to tell you this. I'd hoped Nathaniel might have told you."

"Nathaniel, he knew?"

"Oh, yes, Nathaniel knew! There is so much that Nathaniel has known all along, and never told us. Even going back to that awful day in Bethlehem. And David's death."

"What? What things did he know?"

Before leaving for the trial, Julius had told Hannah it would be mid-morning before the crucifixions actually took place. Sitting now with her mother, Hannah figured she still had an hour or more before needing to leave for the rock outcropping known as the Place of the Skull, where the Romans staked their victims. Taking her mother's hand in hers, Hannah unveiled Nathaniel's role in all these things, from Bethlehem's massacre to today's executions.

When that long and tangled story had been told, the two sat in silence, tears streaming down both their faces.

Hannah finally spoke again. "I must go now, mother. I told Mary I would join her at Yeshua's cross. And I'll keep vigil at father's." Hannah stood. "And also, Simeon should be here shortly. He wanted to see you before he joins me at Golgotha as well."

"Simeon?"

"Yes."

Naomi stood, wiping at the tears still streaming down her face. "Then I must get ready. For my son." Embracing Hannah, she added, "I will join you both, to see my husband."

* * * * *

After hearing the Sanhedrin's final witness, Pilate motioned for quiet. Although he'd read its contents last night, Pilate opened a scroll as if to study it, then rolled it back up and pointed it at Yeshua.

"Herod's report of last night's interview has no good to say of you, Rabbi. He adds his voice to those in this courtyard who would have you crucified."

Yeshua turned his head toward the Sanhedrin delegation, then back to Pilate. "My accusers hold Herod in contempt for his killing of the Baptizer. They would gladly cry for his crucifixion as well, if they dared."

A smile briefly crossed Pilate's face. Whatever kind of religious fool he was, this man understood his enemies. "Tell me, Yeshua of Nazareth, are you this king some claim you to be?

Nathaniel grew uneasy. Why didn't Pilate just pronounce judgment, rather than allow Yeshua another opportunity to stir up trouble with his words?

"Is this something whose truth you seek for your benefit, Procurator, or is it only what others put in your mouth to ask?"

Pilate's back stiffened and his voice pitched higher. "No one puts words in my mouth, prisoner. I am Caesar's representative, and I determine what is true or not. Your own people have placed your fate in my hands and authority."

"Authority comes and goes with the wind. Those who bestow it can remove it just as quickly," Yeshua glanced toward Nathaniel, "particularly when authority goes abused."

"Are you daring to say I abuse the authority of Caesar?"

Yeshua fixed his gaze upon Nathaniel as he answered Pilate. "I would not hazard to speak for Caesar, if that is where you trace your authority. I speak only of authority entrusted by God to those who then use it to hand over innocents to death."

"Then you say you are innocent, rabbi?"

"Since I stand in trial before you, Procurator," Yeshua declared, now turning to face Pilate once more, "that would be yours to decide."

"It is mine to decide." Pilate rose and glanced toward the vestibule, where he saw Naaman bring the prisoner Barabbas into position. "And Rome can be merciful as well as just."

A gasp arose from the Sanhedrin delegation, suddenly uncertain if Pilate intended to go back on the plan to execute Yeshua. Lamech quickly signaled those who had been brought to insure Yeshua's death, resulting in several voices crying out "Crucify him!" Those voices were joined by others, and shortly their cry became a chant taken up by nearly the entire crowd: "Crucify him!" "Crucify him!" "**Crucify him**!"

Pilate raised his arms – "Silence!" As he did, Lamech signaled for his agents to be still. The chant ceased. Pilate addressed the crowd.

"As I said, Rome can temper justice with mercy. And so, I give you a choice today. I will release one of two prisoners. If you choose, I will release this misguided fool before you, whom I take to be little more than a man deluded by too much religion. Yeshua of Nazareth."

Shouts of "No!" and "Crucify him!" erupted from the crowd. Pilate once again raised his arms, and the crowd quieted. That accomplished, the procurator pointed at Naaman and waved him forward. The legionnaire stepped into the courtyard with his prisoner in tow.

As they moved to the front, Pilate intoned: "Or, if you choose, I will release an enemy of Rome. Not a harmless religious fanatic, but a murderer. I believe you call him: Barabbas!"

At the sound of that name, shouts of joy erupted. "Barabbas! Release Barabbas!"

Pilate allowed the outcry to continue. Lamech, along with the other Zealots and their sympathizers in the crowd, were ecstatic. Nathaniel feigned shock, though inside he was relieved that Pilate followed through on the plan he'd suggested. Eventually, the shouts died down. Pilate sat on the judgment seat.

"Hear then Rome's ruling. The rebel Barabbas will be spared. Yeshua, your king, will be crucified. Let the judgment be carried out." Pilate stood and left the courtyard. Antony took hold of Yeshua and headed toward the cell holding the two other prisoners to be executed.

At the courtyard's center, the crowd pressing in upon Barabbas with congratulations now parted to give Rebekah a path through. Everyone cheered when mother and son embraced. Those who saw tears streaming down the face of Barabbas took them as joyous. What they didn't hear were the words Barabbas whispered repeatedly into Rebekah's ears. "I'm sorry, I'm sorry. . . ."

* * * * *

Antony and Naaman escorted Yeshua at a brisk pace to the holding cell, where Joshua and another condemned prisoner waited. At the cell, Antony ordered the two prisoners be brought out. Joshua trembled as he was pulled from his cell. Yeshua grasped the older man's arm to give him support, but just as quickly had it wrenched away by Naaman. "No contact between prisoners." Naaman punctuated his order with a slap across the face of Yeshua.

He drew back to deliver another blow, but another

arm seized Naaman's. "These men will be hanging on crosses soon enough, legionnaire. That is punishment enough."

When Naaman whirled round to see who dared to rebuke him, he found himself staring into the face of Julius.

"What ?!"

"There's been a change in orders," Antony announced. "I entrust command of the execution detail to Centurion Julius. Obey him as you'd obey me – or you'll answer to me."

Naaman and the rest of the detail looked at each other, but none dared question the order. Antony had earned their loyalty and, as Lucius had urged him long ago, their fear. Besides, the reputation of Julius was still well-respected in the ranks. Naaman figured that Antony, or someone above him, must have good reason for the switch.

"Centurion Julius, the detail is under your command. The execution takes place on Golgotha." Antony saluted Julius, and then unsheathed the gladius Julius once gave to him and handed it over. "A symbol of my authority, to execute this command."

Julius took it in hand and saluted. "Thank you, Centurion. You honor me."

When Antony left, Julius ordered the detail to move the prisoners to a nearby stack of crossbeams. Each prisoner would bear their own instrument of death, one further insult imposed by Rome on its victims. Julius watched as the guards marched the prisoners by him. Yeshua stumbled over a loosened cobble as he passed. When Julius reached a hand to steady him, Yeshua whispered: "For Simeon's sake, and his father's, thank you for what you now do."

The procession began as they left the Antonia and stepped into the street. The jeers and wailings of the crowd lining the way were drowned out in Julius' head by the echoes of Yeshua's words. Even in death, the Roman thought, this man holds others in regard. Even his executioner.

* * *

Nathaniel left the courtyard and headed toward the

Temple. He would inform Caiaphas of the trial's end before heading way to Golgotha. The Sopher relished the thought of seeing his plans for Yeshua and Joshua and Antony come to fruition. He had not yet reached the High Priest's chamber, though, when a Temple guard came up behind him. "Sopher, please, a word."

Nathaniel didn't recognize the guard, but then he didn't mingle with those charged with the Temple's protection, save its top officers. "What is it?"

The guard lowered his voice. "The procurator sends word to have a private audience with you. Something about gratitude for your role in today's outcomes."

"Gratitude?" Nathaniel's lips cracked in a smile, as he calculated what benefit might soon come to him. "Do I return to the Antonia's courtyard?"

"No, the procurator doesn't want to raise suspicions of any who might see you return there, and wonder what business you have at the Antonia after the trial. He says to use the passageway from the tower in the temple courtyard. He'll wait for you in his chamber."

Pilate's concern for his safety pleased Nathaniel. "Very well then, I'll be on my way."

"Would you like me to escort you, sir?"

"No, no, that's not needed. Return to your post."

The guard waited until Nathaniel disappeared from sight, then entered a small storage room. Once inside, he stripped off the guard's uniform provided to him, dressed in his own clothes stashed there before daybreak, and counted the coins given him by Jacob and Reuben. It was the price agreed upon, apparently this week's going rate for betrayal: thirty silver shekels.

CHAPTER LVIII

It took the better part of an hour for the detail led by Julius and their prisoners to reach Golgotha. Once there, the first order of business involved establishing a perimeter around the execution site. The crowd who'd followed from the Antonia were moved back by the guards, so that the bystanders now stood in a circle a dozen or more yards away from the crosses.

That done, the task of affixing the condemned men to the crossbeams began. Julius wiped the sweat from his brow and ordered his men to proceed. The *patibula* were laid out on the ground, and each prisoner was forced down on their back with arms outstretched along his crossbeam. Once cords secured the wrists to the timber, a mallet pounded a nail through each hand, transforming the victim's pleas for mercy into screams of pain. Then, one at a time, each *patibulum* was lifted into place atop a tall wooden stake anchored permanently in the ground. Two guards on each side of the beam hoisted it up, while a fifth stood on a crude ladder to maneuver the crossbeam into place on top of the stake, then securely lash the two together with rope. That accomplished, the prisoners' feet would be tied and then nailed to the stake to prevent legs from thrashing. The first two prisoners passed out when these nails were driven, only to be revived by water splashed in their face by the soldiers.

Yeshua was the final one hoisted. When that job was completed, Julius ascended the ladder to affix a small wooden sign to the cross as ordered by Pilate. Scratched into its surface was the procurator's death taunt: "King of the Jews." Julius watched from above as the guards spread out to insure onlookers kept their distance. As they did, Julius leaned close to the rabbi, whose screams had subsided. "Yeshua, it's Julius. Don't fight against death. It's your one release now from suffering." Placing his hand on Yeshua's shoulder, he added. "For what's done to you today, for what I do now – and could not do for you before – forgive me." Julius climbed down the ladder and set it on the ground. Nothing more could be done. Or said.

"Father!" The strength of Yeshua's shout startled the guards, who pivoted to see if something had gone wrong. Julius looked up, his hand instinctively grasping the hilt of his gladius. "Forgive them. They don't know what they're doing."

Once the shock of hearing the victim's outburst wore off, many of the bystanders resumed their jeers that had accompanied Jesus' hoisting. The guards maintained their watch. Julius' hand slipped off the gladius, chastened at what Rome was doing to yet another of Bethlehem's innocents – and ashamed that, again, he served as its agent. Tempering that shame, however, were Yeshua's whispered words on the way, thanking Julius for taking Simeon's place.

* * *

Among those who followed the procession, and watched from a distance so as not to be seen by the Roman guards, were Rebekah and Barabbas. Initially, they had set out from the Antonia's courtyard in the company of several Judean Zealots. Barabbas, however, insisted he must go to the crucifixions with Rebekah alone. No one questioned his request, and mother and son made their way to Golgotha. Rebekah stepped briskly, talking all the way about how his return would breathe new life into the Zealots' fight against Rome. Barabbas remained silent. When Golgotha, and its three impaled victims came into view, Rebekah's joy spilled out.

"Finally, the deaths of your father and brother

avenged. Yeshua takes the place he deserved all those years ago."

Barabbas could take no more: "Mother, don't you see? He dies in my place now."

"All the better. His death frees you to send more Romans to the grave. It will be – "

"Enough! That life is over for me."

Rebekah stopped abruptly. "What do you mean? Your life is ahead of you! A life to honor the martyring of your father and brother by exacting vengeance on their murderers."

"Damn it, can't you let that go?" Barabbas turned his head away so that he would not have to look at Rebekah, only to see Yeshua on the cross that should have been his.

"Let it go?" Rebekah seized her son by the shoulder. "This is what I live for, my son, my *Bar-abbas*. To see Rome pay by your hands. Have you lost your heart, your love of family?"

Barabbas ached to tell Rebekah he did this for her, for family. But he remembered the warning from the prison guard to tell no one, including his mother. If word got out he had, even if he avoided death, she would not. "Think what you will. But I'm done with revenge."

Barabbas barely finished his words when Rebekah's palm cracked across his cheek, drawing blood from the corner of his lip. "Then I am done with you. I'll not have a coward in my family." Rebekah spit at his feet. "You are dead to me, as surely as the one who hangs on the cross. Don't let your shadow cross my path again!" Rebekah spun round and headed back toward Jerusalem, toward the Zealots whom she must now inform about her son's spinelessness.

As for Barabbas, he sat on a rock that afforded him a view of the one who'd taken his place. Those who walked by could only wonder which victim grieved this man who wept alone.

* * *

As Nathaniel traversed the passageway between the Temple courtyard and the Antonia, Saripheus came to mind. Saripheus, the Sopher who made Nathaniel his apprentice long years ago, who had first walked him through this tunnel. Nathaniel clearly remembered the words spoken by Saripheus after their final return together through this corridor. Jeopardized by a son's actions that would soon cost him both office and life, Saripheus had warned Nathaniel: "you must have no one so close you cannot set them aside, if need be."

Another memory, and face, flashed before Nathaniel: his grand-nephew David. "No," he spoke aloud, surprising himself and breaking the quiet in the passageway. "I had no choice."

"Do you always speak to yourself, Sopher?"

The voice behind him startled Nathaniel. "Who's there?"

"Why should you worry, Sopher, you have Rome's cohort but a few steps away."

Nathaniel trembled – this second voice came from in front of him. Before he could see its source, a foot kicked away his cane while an arm reached around his neck from behind and clamped against his throat. "Don't move, Sopher."

A figure now walked toward Nathaniel from ahead. At first the man was obscured in shadows, but as he drew closer the light shed by a lamp hanging on the wall next to Nathaniel disclosed his identity: it was Jacob, leader of the Galilean Zealots.

"This is an outrage!" Nathaniel would have said more, but Reuben's arm drew more tightly across his neck, causing the Sopher to gasp for breath.

Jacob took the lamp and held it up to Nathaniel's face. "An outrage, is it? Tell me, did you judge my father's execution, and your betrayal of Bethlehem's children, outrages as well? Or just part of a Sopher's duties to keep Rome's peace?"

Nathaniel attempted to respond, but couldn't draw

breath. Even the brightness of the lamp in the corridor's darkness began to blur before Nathaniel's eyes. Reuben moved his lips beside Nathaniel's right ear. "Have you ever been to the wall in Bethlehem's cave, Sopher? The wall that cloaks the massacre's victims in unending night? I have family there. And so do you."

Reuben relaxed his grip, and Nathaniel panted in an effort to fill his lungs. The gasps ended quickly, as the Zealot again constricted his arm around Nathaniel's neck.

Jacob pressed his face close to Nathaniel's. "My father was a warrior. Perhaps if you had not betrayed him, another would have. Or he may have fallen in battle. It is the life, and risks, we choose. But you, you gave up your own family. And not men of arms, but children in mothers' arms. Children, whose bones have been drying up in the dark of Bethlehem's cave ever since. Your debt's come due, Sopher."

Nathaniel felt a sharp point pierce his side, and then a series of shallow pricks and slices up and down his chest and arms, and across his face. Reuben continued to hold the Sopher so Jacob could execute his cuts – and so Nathaniel could not cry out in alarm. Or pain. Or plea. The searing found no relief, no matter how tightly Nathaniel shut his eyes. For a moment, Nathaniel imagined himself a boy again ranging Bethlehem's hills: except the boy's face shifted from his own to David's, streaked with blood, whose lips formed a single word: "why?"

And then, for Nathaniel, imagination itself disappeared.

Once death was certain, Reuben dragged Nathaniel's corpse toward the stairway that led up to the Antonia. Jacob took the Sopher's cane in hand and mimicked the tapping that tipped them off earlier of Nathaniel's approach. On reaching the stairway, Jacob loudly tapped on the first stair and shouted: "Guards, the Sopher comes with an urgent message for Pilate!" Jacob and Reuben then raced back toward the Temple, taking with them the lamp used to light the stairway.

The shout from below the trapdoor startled the guards above. No one had sent word of the Sopher's coming. And while the voice sounded odd, the tapping of the cane was a familiar signal. To be safe, before opening the trapdoor, Claudius directed his partner to warn the guards in the hallway to be on alert. That done, Claudius drew his gladius while Aram slowly unbolted and lifted up the trapdoor.

"Sopher, the door is open." Aram saw nothing in the dark below, only hearing some distant footfalls. He asked Claudius for a torch, as the lamp below had apparently gone out. Aram held it down the opening. At the foot of the stairs, the light revealed the crumpled and bloodied body of Nathaniel. "Claudius, summon more men. Now!"

* * *

Julius drew his cloak across his face, a vain attempt to block out the particles of sand whipped into the air by the growing *khamsin* blustering up from the southeast. It was all too much like that day in Bethlehem, he thought, when those innocents had been put to the sword. As conditions deteriorated now on Golgotha, most all of the onlookers withdrew. Having vented their taunts, they returned to the city to prepare for Sabbath. With the crowd rapidly dwindling, the guards huddled in a circle, taking turns so only one had to stand, exposed to the elements.

A pair of women along with one man approached Yeshua's cross, only to be blocked by the sentry. Julius got up and walked to the guard. "Go ahead and join the others. I'll take a turn here." The legionnaire saluted and rejoined the circle, glad for what refuge it provided from wind and dust. Julius turned to trio. The man he didn't know by name, though he'd seen him with the rabbi the day when Jerusalem was first entered. But even with veils drawn close around their faces, Julius easily recognized Hannah and Mary. With his back to the guards, and the rush of the wind, Julius knew he would not be overheard. "If you wish to stand closer to

Yeshua for a moment, you may." Then looking at the man with them, "and you as well."

"This is John," Hannah offered, wishing she could hold Julius. "He is the one disciple who has come, besides the women who follow behind." Julius saw another group of women down the hillside. Further still, Julius could make out another couple making their way up. It was an older woman, along with –

"Antony!"

Hannah nodded. "With our mother."

Julius felt Mary's hand touch his. "Hannah told me what you've done for her brother."

Julius shook his head. "I wish I could have done more. And for your son."

"You've done what you could, when others would have done nothing. Bless you."

No longer caring if he were seen by the detail, or anyone else, Julius took Mary by the arm, and escorted her to the foot of her son's cross, followed by Hannah and John. He stepped back to give them what privacy was possible. Julius could not make out what the three spoke to the rabbi. But whatever it had been, there was no mistaking the voice of Yeshua cry out:

"Woman, behold your son! And your mother."

Yeshua's words jostled the attention of the guards, and several began to stand. Julius signaled them to keep their place as he stepped in their direction: "Pay no attention to this Jew, or those who keep his vigil. This wind will have them gone soon enough." When Naaman pointed toward the pair who had just come up the path and now stood beneath the criminal called Joshua, Julius knelt down in the circle. "A word with you all. Centurion Antony arrested that thief. The woman he escorts is the fellow's soon-to-be widow, done as a favor granted the man in exchange for information about a Zealot hideout. Antony and I switched places today so he could honor the bargain and escort the widow here. But keep this to yourselves. Understood?"

The men looked at each other and tipped their heads in agreement.

"Your centurion will be grateful. And, given the foulness of this day's weather, I'm sure he wouldn't mind if you broke into that wine jug stashed under the prisoners' robes." Julius punctuated the invitation by slapping the back of the guard who thought he'd hidden it from Julius' sight earlier. The guards laughed, and the jug was quickly fetched and passed around. Julius resumed his watch, intentionally placing himself between the soldiers and the cross of Joshua, where Antony and Naomi stood – joined now by Hannah.

CHAPTER LIX

Beneath the cross of Joshua, his family was riveted as much by the sight of his crucifixion as by the flood of memories of long-severed connections. Feelings of anger and abandonment mingled with wonderings of "what if..."

Joshua himself could barely make out the outlines of three strangers below him, what with the sweat and sand burning his eyes, and a fog of pain blurring his mind. Why they stood there, he had no idea. That they were there, he didn't care. He only wished the pain to end.

"Joshua." Naomi's voice cracked, but didn't fail. "Joshua."

The name wafted to Joshua as in a dream. He looked again toward the figures, though his eyes couldn't clearly focus.

"Joshua, it's Naomi."

The voice in the dream sounded familiar, very much like one he'd struggled to hold in mind for years. But it couldn't be. Not after all he had done, and not done. "Who are you? Why mock me with that name?"

Naomi felt like running away, but she grasped the hands of her children and held her ground. "I *am* Naomi, Joshua. I don't mock you. Nor do your children, Simeon and Hannah. We are here. To be with you."

Joshua blinked and peered hard. For an instant, focus returned. The face of the woman had aged, but the outlines of her features, and most of all her eyes, revealed the truth of her words. "Naomi, my God, Naomi!" Sobs overwhelmed him, broken only by a burst of regret: "I'm sorry, Naomi, I'm sorry."

Naomi's hand trembled as it reached up to touch Joshua's feet, bleeding and broken by the spikes. "I love you, Joshua."

Naomi felt the hand of her daughter join hers: "Father, it's Hannah."

The pain in Joshua's chest made speaking difficult. "Naomi, Hannah. And Simeon." Joshua gasped for breath, then continued. "That the Almighty gives me sight of you again –" After a deep cough cut short his words, Joshua cleared his throat of the phlegm and blood building up. "I never loved well, but I never stopped." Another spell of coughing seized Joshua.

Simeon peered up at the man toward whom he carried so much hatred. But now, it was not anger and betrayal that washed over him, but pity. "Abba, don't speak if it hurts."

Joshua spit to clear a way for his words. "I've known greater hurts than this, my son. Of abandoning family. Of cowering. Of David."

"What's done is done, father," Hannah offered. "We all bear regrets for something. What matters is, we – you – are loved. And forgiven."

"The one called Yeshua, beside whom I now hang, spoke such words last night. He told me that you follow him, Hannah."

"I do."

"His words gave me peace. And now, to have the family I deserted stand by me, I – I –"

Another fit of coughing gagged Joshua. Only this time, coughs did not clear his throat. His gasps for air became frantic, then stopped altogether. His head slumped.

"Joshua! Joshua!!" Naomi dropped to the ground, wailing his name. Simeon and Hannah knelt down and embraced her. After some moments, Naomi felt another hand stroke the top of her head. Turning, she saw Mary, weeping. Naomi stood, and the two women embraced.

* * *

Pilate had just finished his second cooling bath of the day, attempting to counter this unrelenting heat. He'd drawn the drapes tight to block out the wind-driven sand. A knock on his office door raised his mood, assuming it would bring his noonday meal. "Come in, steward."

The door opened, but it was not the steward. Flavius, the century's second-in-command to Antony, saluted. "Forgive the interruption, procurator, but there's disturbing news."

Pilate immediately thought to today's executions, and their timing on the eve of Passover. "Have the Zealots stirred some trouble on Golgotha?"

"Not on Golgotha, sir. But the Sopher, Nathaniel, was assassinated in the corridor that leads here from the Temple."

"What? Did they breach the entryway?"

"No sir. The body was left by the stairway, beneath the entry door. For precaution, we summoned reserves to guard the entry and dispatched a squad into the corridor, but found no one. Apparently, whoever it was wanted only the Sopher."

"Was any message left as to why?"

"None at all, sir. We also dispatched another detail to Golgotha to stand by, in case of some connection. But they just sent a runner back, reporting all to be quiet. The messenger indicated the weather severely cut back on the numbers of those who usually watch."

"Send word to the High Priest about the Sopher, and the need for someone to take Nathaniel's place. Report back any response from him, or if more is learned about the attack." Flavius saluted and left. Pilate walked to a window and parted its curtain ever so slightly. The wind, if anything, had grown stronger and hotter. Oddly, it seemed to be getting darker. *Must be all the sand in the air*, Pilate thought, as his musings turned to the now-dead Sopher. *A man as ill-tem-*

pered as this damned wind. At least, Pilate reckoned, Nathaniel had served Rome's purpose. Yeshua would soon be dead, and Barabbas no longer a threat. Some consolation found in this miserable day. *Now, what is keeping the steward with my lunch . . .*

* * *

Julius took a long drink from his wineskin, shielding his mouth with one hand to prevent sand from blowing into the wine. It was not just this damnable duty he sought relief from, but the mix of news roiling in his mind. When he saw an extra set of guards from the cohort take position further down the hillside several hours ago, Julius sent Naaman to find out the reason.

"An incident near the Antonia, sir," Naaman reported to Julius on his return. "Some temple officer named Nathaniel was knifed to death."

Julius struggled to stifle a smirk. "Go on."

"The cohort felt an additional detail was needed here, in case this was part of some wider plot. The whole fortress stands at alert."

"A prudent move."

Naaman coughed, and spit out a bit of sand he'd inhaled on the way back up the hill. "Maybe it's unrelated, but the guard spoke of one more murder inside the city last night or early this morning. The innkeep of a caravansary."

Julius recalled Ishmael's last words with him, assuring that he would see to Nathaniel finally receiving justice. "Was any name given to this innkeep, or any tie to the temple official?"

"It wasn't clear if they meant suspects or victims, but when the patrol was briefed before coming here, they were told to listen for any mention in the crowd of Nathaniel or Ishmael."

For Julius, whatever come-uppance felt at the death of Nathaniel was swallowed up in the loss of Ishmael. "Very well, Naaman. Dismissed."

For a moment, the wind's howling yielded to the pounding in Julius' head. Nathaniel dead, after all these years – but Ishmael, too. And soon to join them, as Julius looked back at the crosses, the one whom Nathaniel long ago conspired to murder. Death raked in innocent and guilty alike this day. Even in the heat, Julius shuddered from a sudden chill. He'd lost men before in battle. But he'd never lost such a friend as Ishmael.

* * *

The sight of the additional patrol unsettled Barabbas. When they first approached, he thought perhaps they came for him. But when they didn't make any move in his direction, Barabbas kept his perch on the rock and resumed his fixation on Yeshua, the one whose escape years ago had set Barabbas's course in motion. Then, his father and brother died in Yeshua's place. But now, the Romans impaled Yeshua on the cross that should have been his own. *Is this justice*, Barabbas thought? *What kind of a god would stand aside so Rome could slaughter innocents, and now lets a murderer go free and a teacher goes crucified in his place? What kind of god gives free rein to killers, and then lets those who do the killing live? Like those executioners on the hill . . . like me!* "Damn them all!" Barabbas blurted out.

"Lower your voice, brother, or those Roman bastards might hear you."

Startled, Barabbas spun around to see – Reuben!

Reuben crouched next to Barabbas and smiled. "In days gone by, none could have snuck up on you as I just did. You need to be more careful."

Barabbas glanced back at the Romans, to make sure they weren't watching, then turned to Reuben. "Leave. Now. I can't be seen with you, or any of the others."

Reuben's jaw clenched. "Your mother told me you'd lost your nerve. I told her your time in prison must have just made it seem so. That deep down, you'd be the same. With time."

Barabbas looked to the crosses above. "Those men have no time, Reuben. And I, I should have been there, you know. My time runs out with theirs, with Yeshua."

"You speak in riddles, brother. Truth is, thanks to Yeshua, you've all your time ahead of you. To rejoin us. To avenge your family."

"You don't understand, Reuben. My time is as forfeit as theirs. I can't rejoin you."

Reuben gripped Barabbas' wrist. "Can't – or won't? One doesn't walk away from oaths. And brothers." Reuben reached inside his cloak, where Barabbas assumed would be a knife.

"Go ahead, Reuben. But even if you do slip your blade between my ribs, my cries will bring those pigs down on us both. I don't care if I die on this hill – but I doubt you're ready."

Reuben weighed the situation. The Romans were within earshot, and Barabbas might put up a fight. With Nathaniel's blood still fresh on his hands, Reuben thought it wise to await a better opportunity. Withdrawing his hand from under his cloak, he released his grip on Barabbas and stood. "There'll be another day when you won't hear me coming. And it will be your last."

Barabbas sprang to his feet and glared into Reuben's face. "Then make your first thrust kills, Reuben. Because if you don't, I'll see that you never get off a second."

"Traitor," Reuben spewed as he headed back to the home where Rebekah waited.

Barabbas watched him for a few moments, then looked back up the hill toward the rabbi. A small group clustered beneath Yeshua. Barabbas envied the rabbi. At least in his suffering, Yeshua was not alone. Counted as good as dead by his mother, deemed a traitor by his comrades: Barabbas started plodding down the hill. He set his course: not into the city, but toward the south and east, and the path that led to New Damascus and the dwelling of Abraham.

* * *

Julius reckoned it must be close to the third hour of the afternoon. He couldn't be sure, as clouds and blowing sand had nearly obscured the sun's position. Only a few hours before, it seemed they would soon be off this hill. Joshua died close to noon, followed minutes later by the second prisoner. But Yeshua: Yeshua still hung in agony, attended by those gathered beneath him. Hannah. Mary. The disciple who had come with Mary. Even Simeon and Naomi remained.

The extra guards who arrived in the wake of Nathaniel's murder had left more than an hour ago. With only a few bystanders rather than the usual crowds of gawking onlookers, Julius deemed no threat remained. They were more than glad to follow Julius' order to return. The original execution detail bunched close together against the wind. With only one prisoner alive, and one small group standing vigil, there was no need for even one of them to stand guard anymore.

"*Eloi eloi, lama sabbachthani!*"

Mary clutched at her son's feet. "I'm here, my son." In the God-forsakenness of his cry, Mary offered herself as assurance that he was not abandoned, not by the one who gave him birth.

Yeshua's cry burned in Simeon's ears. After his brother's execution and his father's desertion of family, these opening words to one of King David's songs had become the single enduring creed of what was left of Simeon's faith. Abandonment by God rang true to his experience of life. But now, hearing those words uttered by the one he blamed for their imposition upon him, and having watched the death of a father who abandoned him, Simeon could not contain himself: "I'm glad you finally feel what you brought into our lives!"

"Simeon!" The voices of Hannah and Naomi converged in shocked outrage.

Simeon might have said even more, but for Mary. Mary left her place beneath Yeshua and walked to Simeon. Tears filling her eyes, she placed her hands on his shoulders. "It's me, and my husband, who deserve your condemnation. It was our choice, not my son's, to leave without warning. Don't hold this against Yeshua. He was only a child. And now, he's dying. My son's dying! Please, Simeon, forgive me. . ." Mary's voice trailed off.

As she spoke, Simeon held his arms stiffly at his side, trying to resist a surge of emotions that had festered since Bethlehem. But when Mary sought his forgiveness: Simeon, who only days before had beaten her son in his cell, slowly lifted the arms he'd used to pummel Yeshua, wrapped them around Mary, and drew her gently against him. And then came words from so deep within, at first it seemed to him as if another spoke them. "I'm sorry, Mary. I'm sorry you suffer. I'm sorry – sorry your son suffers." Simeon lowered his face onto the top of Mary's head. They held on to each other for the sake of a life one held dear, and the other no longer hated.

"It is finished."

While Yeshua's words did not come with the same strength as his earlier cries, they were still loud enough to be heard by the five gathered below him. And by Julius. Afterwards, a rattling noise came from inside Yeshua's throat, his chest heaved, and he became very still.

Mary edged toward the cross, supported by Simeon on one side and Hannah on the other, with Naomi and John close behind. "Yeshua? Yeshua?"

Her seeking went unanswered.

Julius picked up one of the spears brought by his men and walked directly before Yeshua, taking off his helmet and bowing in Mary's direction. "Woman, I am no Jew. But if ever there was one worthy to be called a true son of the god you call Elohim, Yeshua was that one." Mary, voice and spirit stripped raw by seeing her son die, could only nod at Julius before succumbing to groans and wails for her dead child.

"The spear," Hannah asked in a hushed tone, "why?"

"My duty. I have to verify his death. Please, all of you, look away." All but Hannah and Simeon followed his advice, and Julius made a quick thrust upward below the ribs of Yeshua. At once, the fluids that had filled his lungs and drowned Yeshua as he hung on the cross flowed out, along with blood from the piercing. Julius saw no movement in response. Death was certain.

Julius turned to Mary. "There's no more you can do here. I was informed earlier that a member of the Sanhedrin, Joseph from Arimathea, has offered a tomb for your son's burial. He and a friend wait a short distance from here, and will take your son there."

"And my husband?" asked Naomi.

Julius had not had opportunity to tell Hannah the news about Nathaniel, and this did not seem the time. However, he did have one thought regarding the Sopher. "Your uncle holds high office in the Temple, Naomi. I'll see that your husband's burial place is provided by the Sopher."

Naomi brushed aside a tear. "Thank you, centurion, for tending to that."

"It's the least I could do, for all that's been done you ... to all of you." Taking Hannah aside, he lowered his voice: "I'll meet you in Bethany once I'm done with my duties."

The mourners of Yeshua and Joshua started down Golgotha's slope. As they did, two men ascended the same path to the crucifixion site: Joseph, and a Pharisee named Nicodemus. Yeshua's body was removed from the cross and carried away by the pair. That done, Julius had Joshua's body taken down. "His remains go to the tombs kept by the Sanhedrin for their members." To preclude any questions, Julius added: "Part of the deal struck with Antony."

Julius accompanied his men to the burial place of Joshua, so that he might pass on its location to Hannah. But before going to her, Julius had another task. Dismissing the detail under his command once they entered the city, Julius headed toward the caravansary of Ishmael.

CHAPTER LX

Naomi and Hannah and Simeon sat at the dining table in Nathaniel's home. On the way back from Golgotha, Mary had invited them to join her in Bethany where she lodged. Naomi told her she first had to confront Nathaniel over his complicity not only in Joshua's and Yeshua's executions, but going all the way back to the massacre in Bethlehem years ago. Hannah and Simeon tried to persuade her to delay doing this, given the rawness of having just watched her long-estranged husband's crucifixion. But when Naomi insisted this day of all days was the one when truth must be told and Nathaniel must be held to account, her children resolved to stand by her and add their own voices. But the rising tide of anger and resentment that propelled their steps from Golgotha to Nathaniel's home crashed headlong against the words of the servant who greeted them at the door. Face ashen, he simply blurted out: "They've killed him."

"Killed who?" Naomi asked.

"Your uncle, the Sopher. And now, I don't know what I'll do. The Temple guards ordered me to have the house readied for a new Sopher, once Caiaphas makes that decision. But will he want me to stay on, or will —"

"How did it happen?"

Simeon's question interrupted the servant's fretting, and in doing so reminded him that, until any changes did result, he remained responsible for the running of this household and its hospitality. "Please, excuse my rambling. Come inside." They followed the servant, who brought them to the main table. "I'll bring water and wine. The khamsin must have you thirsty."

As they walked in, Simeon asked. "What do you know of Nathaniel's death?"

The servant pulled out a chair for Naomi to be seated, and then for Hannah. "All the guards would tell me is that he was murdered by unknown assailants. They weren't specific as to where, only that it was near the temple in some passage."

Simeon pictured the scene in detail. He'd traveled that way many times – as had Nathaniel. Was he going to meet with the procurator, perhaps to betray another? It didn't matter. Without explanation, Simeon uttered: "so be it."

The servant didn't understand the meaning of Simeon's words, nor was it his place to question them. Now that the guests were seated, he added: "I don't know your plans, but Nathaniel had arranged the Passover meal for this evening. You are welcome to stay for it."

In the day's turmoil, it had escaped Naomi that the Seder was tonight. On their walk here, she was determined to speak her mind and then leave. But with Nathaniel gone, and her children now with her: "Yes, thank you. My children and I have not shared this meal for a long time."

When the servant left, Naomi grasped the hands of Hannah and Simeon. "I may have spoken too fast about the Seder. You both may need to be elsewhere."

Simeon and Hannah looked at their mother. Simeon was first to speak. "I've no more important place to be this night. And it's been too long since I sat at Seder. With you."

Hannah put her arms around her mother. "My place, too, is with you. But first," she added, "I need to go to Bethany and let Mary know we won't be joining her tonight. And to leave word there for Julius, as to where he can find me. But I'll be back in time for Seder." She kissed Naomi and started to leave.

"Wait!" Simeon rose from the table. "I'll not have my sister walking alone. This storm darkens the sky already, and by the time we get there and then back it will be near sunset."

"But that would leave mother alone here."

Naomi stood. "I can help the servant with the Seder meal preparations. It'll give me something to do, for my family – and it wouldn't be right to leave Mary wondering. Please, go."

As Hannah and Simeon embraced their mother together, the servant entered the room. He marveled at how a hard man like Nathaniel could generate such a loving family.

* * *

Inside the caravansary, a lad was on his hands and knees, scrubbing the floor. Julius recognized him as the stable boy whom Ishmael used to send messages. Julius knelt by him.

"I'm busy," the boy muttered with his face down, focused on the stains made by Ishmael's blood on the stone floor, "and the inn's closed. Go away."

Julius reached down and placed a hand on the scrubbing brush. "Not so long ago, Ishmael had you ask me about a friend from Tyre named Nabal."

The boy looked up. He recognized the man with the short beard whom Ishmael had sent him to this week. And he remembered Ishmael saying later how this man was the best friend he had. "I'm sorry, sir. But Ishmael, they've –" His words faltering, he lifted the brush for Julius to see its bristles soaked red. "Murdered him, sir."

Julius would have liked to pound the wall, or put a dagger into the heart of the killers. Instead, he gently patted the lad's shoulder. "You know, old Ishmael would not allow just anyone to carry his words to others. He must have liked you."

"I liked him, too. Even when he got gruff." The words of the boy came out in laughter tinged with sobs.

"Well, to be honest now, he got gruff with me more than once. Just his way of showing affection." Julius glanced around. "Where might his nephew be?"

The boy's head dropped again. "He's taken the body out to be buried. Told me to get this place cleaned up as best I could while he was gone, so he can reopen before dark."

"I'd say you're doing a good job." Julius reached under his coat, took out a handful of coins, and handed them to the boy. "I owed Ishmael some money. It seems you're next in line."

"Shouldn't his nephew be the one?"

"No, he's got this inn. Besides, I think Ishmael would want you to have this."

"Really?"

"Absolutely." Julius stood and headed toward the door, then stopped and looked back at the boy. "Don't you ever forget Ishmael. He was as good a man as I've ever known."

"Yes, sir! And by the way, I know his nephew told me to get rid of it, but do you remember Ishmael's apron?"

"I certainly do."

The boy reached underneath a table and pulled out the apron. "Would you like it?"

Julius studied it. He'd never seen Ishmael without it. Had he been here when the body was taken, he'd have insisted the innkeep be buried in it. But that was now too late. "I do quite a lot of traveling, so maybe you should keep it. For the both of us."

"I will, sir. And like Ishmael used to say, I'll never wash it!"

Julius smiled. "You keep that tradition. He'd like it." Once outside the caravansary, Julius started out for Bethany.

* * *

The disciple called John met Hannah and Simeon in the street. "Mary is resting, but she did leave instructions to welcome you, Hannah. And your mother, will she come later?"

"Actually, not. We're going to have Seder together, as

a family, in Jerusalem, So I won't be able to stay very long myself. And John, this is my brother. His name is –"

"Simeon," offering his hand to John. "My name is Simeon."

"Please, both of you, come in."

As Hannah stepped into the doorway, Simeon paused. "I'll join you later, so I can wait outside for our friend." Hannah nodded and went inside while Simeon watched the street. The wind had died down, and the air began to clear of dust and sand, though the heat lingered under clouds still thick from the storm. Simeon figured an hour or so remained before needing to set out, in order to be at the Seder table before sunset. His wondering whether Julius would arrive before then ended when he saw him walking up the street, no longer in the uniform of a centurion. Simeon waved, and Julius joined him under the porch of the house.

"Hannah's inside, with Mary. But before you go in, you need to know about Nathaniel."

Julius held up a hand. "I heard the news. The Antonia sent word of it to Golgotha. With all that you and your family were dealing with, I couldn't bring myself to add that to the mix."

"I understand," Simeon replied. "Though when we heard, I can't say it grieved me."

"Nor me, Antony."

"Simeon," he interrupted in a clear and firm voice. "From this day forward, Simeon."

The declaration triggered memories in Julius: of a young man wanting to flee his past, of a legionnaire's induction that came with a new name, and of a son standing this day beneath his father's cross. "Then Simeon it is."

At that moment, Hannah and Mary stepped out of the house. Julius stepped up to Mary. "My lady, for what I've done this day, and years ago in Bethlehem, I regret the day I was borne. You, and your son, and Hannah's family, and all the others, deserved none of this. None of this." Julius would have continued, but his throat choked further attempts to speak. He lowered his gaze, ashamed to look at the faces and lives he'd wounded.

As a result, Julius didn't see Mary reach her hand toward him, and gently touch his chin, which she lifted so their eyes could meet. "I will say to you what I believe my son would have said: whatever came to be in your past, what matters is this day. Today, you spared Simeon from being his father's executioner. Today, you showed kindness to me when others cheered my son's agony. And as Hannah confided to me: you risked coming to Jerusalem to protect my son's life, even though he wouldn't let you. Hear me out, Julius: In all these things, you acted for others, not self. And that is the core of love. What you do tomorrow, and the day after, and all the days you may yet have: don't waste their time in regret. Fill their time with actions of love. And as for that past that burdens you: my son forgave today. Forgave *you*. Julius, please, forgive yourself."

As she spoke, Julius focused on Mary's eyes. What struck him most was how her words and their sentiment flowed through them as much as her voice. Julius felt overwhelmed: this mother who should be grieving her son chose in this moment to turn her presence to him. Julius allowed Mary's words, and eyes, to wash over him. Through him. Hannah had described to him the release she experienced when her raging at Yeshua by Galilee's sea had been transformed by him into a deep sense of peace. Julius had always been grateful that Hannah found deliverance from her past, partly out of the conviction he had gone far beyond any such possibility in his own life. But now, Julius looked on Mary as Hannah had once looked on Yeshua. Clasping her head in his hands, he brought it forward until their foreheads touched.

No one had a sense of time's passage under that porch. Not Julius and Mary, who leaned into one another; not Hannah, who wept; not Simeon, who wrapped one arm around his sister's waist while placing his free hand on Julius' shoulder. When John came out to see if they needed anything, he stopped in silence. While he didn't know what had transpired, it reminded him of times when Yeshua had broken through to someone, and life had changed. John whispered a prayer of thanks that such times could still come. Even on such a day as this.

* * *

The night brought no relief from the heat. Low clouds had rolled in from the Great Sea once the khamsin died down. They blanketed Jerusalem, shutting out light from moon and stars, preventing the day's heat from dissipating into the sky.

All of which made for a difficult trek for Judas out of the city and into the grove at Gesamani. As he walked in the dark, he rehashed the events and conversations that eventuated in the kiss. There could be no doubt: Judas had been used by Nathaniel, by the Zealots of Judea, and likely even Jacob, who'd assured him time and again the rabbi would be safe. But Yeshua was not on his way back to Galilee, disgraced but alive. Yeshua was dead, crucified like the worst of criminals, a form of death that Torah declared to be cursed by God.

Cursed by God. Judas looked up – for what, for who, he no longer knew. There was no light above, only darkness. Then again, unlike the times when he would listen to Yeshua: there was no stirring of light, or hope, within. Darkness prevailed inside as well.

Judas fumbled at the rope he'd bought shortly before the markets closed for the Passover Sabbath. He knew he overpaid, but it no longer mattered. The coins given him by the Sanhedrin for his kiss had already exacted their toll, and he'd no desire to cling to them. He wished to be rid of it all. Spotting the fixed arm of the grove's olive press mechanism, Judas tied off one end of the rope. He looked up again: this time, not for light, not for any sign that might convince him otherwise; but this time, for a stout branch in reach that could bear the weight he could no longer bear. Once found, he coiled the rope and tossed it over, then grabbed its dangling end. There was enough length in the rope to tie a knot remembered from childhood. The branch jutted out sufficiently close to the stone pressing wheel, so that Judas now climbed up and then out upon the stone's edge and cinched the loop tight around his neck. Checking the slack left in the rope, and the distance to the ground from where he perched: Judas judged his feet would not reach the ground once he stepped off. "None of this was meant to be, Yeshua!" he shouted. "You could have heeded Jacob, none of this would have happened!" Judas teetered on the edge of the grinding wheel – "Why! And why me!" Judas leapt – after a snap, the night was still once more.

* * *

"Water! Bring me water!" Pilate's screams roused him from what had become this night's recurring nightmare. Sitting straight up, he tossed off the covers and strode to the door, throwing it open and shouting: "Hurry! I need water! And a basin!" In a few minutes, footsteps clopping down the hall were followed by a servant's entering the room with a full pitcher and basin. "Put them there, on the stand beside the bed. And fetch towels as well."

As the servant hurried off for the towels, Pilate began to rinse his hands, then rubbed them hard together underneath the water. He kept at it until the servant returned. Pilate grabbed the smaller washcloth brought with two towels, got it wet, and scrubbed his hands

"Procurator, what's wrong?"

"Look at this!" Pilate lifted his hands from the water and held up his palms.

Outside of a slight redness, the servant saw nothing.

"Well, what do you say?"

"Excellency, your hands appear fine."

"Fine? You fool! Can't you see my palms are pierced clear through?!"

The servant thought for a moment. To contradict the procurator could prove risky. "Oh, yes, now I see. Maybe the candle flickered when I looked before."

"Well then, get me more water! And this time, see that it's hot! And another cloth for washing." As the servant left, Pilate swabbed his hands on the larger towel. "By damn! What's wrong?" Taking up the washcloth again and soaking it, he resumed scrubbing each palm.

At sunrise, when the Antonia's chief steward came on duty, the night servant met him in the corridor that led to Pilate's residence. "Sir, I fear the physician is needed. Since midnight, the procurator's been washing his hands over and over."

"What?"

"He claims the palms to be punctured. But I've seen them, and they're not. The more he washes, the angrier he becomes. Besides that," he continued, lowering his voice as if Pilate might somehow hear, "for the last hour, he says someone named Yeshua has done this to him."

"Before I bother the physician, I'll need to see for myself." The two strode down the corridor and saw the door to Pilate's room left open. The steward peeked inside. Pilate was vigorously working the washcloth between his palms. But instead of clear water dripping into the basin beneath his hands, the steward saw the water to be stained deep red with blood.

Turning to the night servant, trembling, he ordered: "Get the physician. Now!"

CHAPTER LXI

It had been well after dark when Barabbas reached the outskirts of New Damascus. On the journey from Golgotha, his thoughts fixated on his mother's disowning of him as well as Reuben's threats. It seemed to Barabbas he had no one left to turn to save Abraham. But as the flickers of lamplights in the stone abodes of New Damascus came into view, he considered that even Abraham might not welcome him. Harsh words spewed the last time they met. Then, Abraham disclosed that the rabbi Yeshua he followed was none other than the child whose parents fled Bethlehem and gave no warning of the impending slaughter. And today, hadn't Abraham's beloved rabbi just hung on a cross that should have impaled Barabbas? Deciding he couldn't face Abraham at the end of this tortuous day, Barabbas spent the night in a cave sometimes used by the Zealots to store weapons and supplies. Its darkness afforded little rest.

And now, Barabbas watched as Abraham poured water into a cup for the son of Rebekah and Elias. Little had been said since Barabbas pounded on the door shortly after dawn. When Abraham opened it, he put his arms around the haggard figure he first came to know as a young boy back in Bethlehem, then stepped back. "Please, wait here in the shade. I'll fetch water."

As Abraham retrieved pitcher and cup, remembrances of yesterday chilled him. Still in Jerusalem for Passover, he had stood among the crowd in the Antonia's courtyard for Yeshua's trial. When Pilate announced they could choose to spare Barabbas or Yeshua, but not both, Abraham faced an impossible choice. Would he cry out for the rabbi he believed to be Messiah, or would he shout on behalf of the boy-become-man who was the closest thing in his life to a son? In silence, he shed tears for both, then left. He couldn't bear to see the rabbi's death.

When Abraham returned, Barabbas downed two cups of water, then slumped forward. "My life's over. I might as well have been the one on that cross."

Abraham moved his chair closer, stirring up a bit of dust as its legs drug across the ground. "Don't say that. As long as you have life, there's always potential for good."

Barabbas smirked. "Good! Really? Is that what your rabbi taught? Look at the good it got him! Yeshua's potential is dust and ashes. Death seals all, Abraham. Can't you see that?"

Abraham clasped his hands together. "Yesterday was a hard day, for us all. And yes, the good Yeshua brought to this world, to me, was met with a Roman cross. Not to mention the condemnation of many an Israelite. But I tell you, Barabbas: even in this, in spite of this, the Almighty will have the final word. The Holy One is Lord, even in death."

Barabbas shook his head, then flung his emptied cup against the stones of the porch wall, scattering shards of kiln-dried clay everywhere. "Abraham, please! Do the children interred in Bethlehem's cave, and my brother, breathe again? Does my father take up his carpentry tools and carve wolves for his son once more? Do those students you saw slaughtered by the Temple porch, do they study Torah again? Or do they, like all the rest, like your Galilean dreamer, rot in the ground? You live in a fool's world, Abraham!"

"If that is so, Barabbas, why do you seek an old fool when your life unravels?"

The eyes of Barabbas flashed, and in a single motion he sprang to his feet and lifted Abraham underneath his armpits off the ground: "I've had my fill of your fantasies! Your rabbi still bewitches you from the grave, just as he's ruined my life, taken my family from me!"

"He's done no such thing, Barabbas! If only you would –"

Abraham's words ended with Barabbas tossing him against a wooden pole that supported the awning. As the cloth fluttered down on top of Abraham, a red stain formed where it came to rest on his head. Panicking, Barabbas pulled up the cloth to see how badly he'd hurt the man who'd given him shelter and food as a youth during his training in Torah and Zealotry.

"Abraham. Abraham?"

The older man opened his eyes. Looking at Barabbas, he smiled. "I forgive you, my son."

"No. No!" Barabbas turned and stalked out the gate. Abraham's words echoed ones he'd heard invoked by Yeshua on Golgotha. Then, forgiveness of enemies sounded like the height of folly – worse yet, blasphemy, when directed to Roman executioners. But here and now, the weight of forgiveness by Abraham, whose blood he'd just spilled, was too much to bear. "No!" His shout echoed off the ridge and down toward the Salt Sea. With nowhere, and no one, left for him: Barabbas set out for the wilderness beyond the Jordan.

* * *

Julius ascended the steps leading to Nathaniel's home. As he stood on the porch next to the main door, Julius recalled his first stay here. It was the night that Kohath and his band of Sicarii came to assassinate Nathaniel, the night that Julius and his troop put the assassins to the sword. Julius briefly considered whether that had been a mistake. On the other hand, though he didn't know at the time, Hannah had been inside the house as well as her mother. At least some good came of that night. Julius knocked on the door.

Moments later, a servant cracked it open to see who came on the morning of Sabbath. The stranger had the look of a Roman, like others who'd often showed up unannounced to fetch the late Sopher. "What do you want?"

Before Julius could reply, Hannah slipped beside the servant. "This is a friend of mine."

The servant bowed and opened the door. As Julius stepped in, Hannah brushed her cheek against his, on one side and then the other. "Welcome, Julius." Taking his arm, she walked him down a hall and in the direction of the courtyard.

"Is Simeon here?"

"No, he left before dawn. He said he was going to speak to the tribune about retirement from the Legion, and get started on whatever needed to be done to accomplish that. But he promises to return first thing tomorrow morning. Simeon wants to make a quick journey to Bethlehem, as do I, to see our brother's resting place. In the afternoon, we'll return and go with my mother to bring burial spices to my father's tomb."

Where the corridor opened to the courtyard, Hannah pointed to a bench in the courtyard where a woman sat alone. "My mother wanted to speak with you. Just the two of you."

"Without you? Are you sure?"

Hannah nodded. "I am. Just so you know, I've told her about us. About everything." Hannah squeezed his hand. "Go to her. I'll wait inside."

Julius straightened his robe at the neck, took a deep breath, and walked to the bench. Naomi didn't look in his direction until he stood directly in front of her and bowed.

"I'm Julius, my lady."

Naomi studied his face: a face familiar from yesterday at Golgotha; a face she tried, but couldn't place, from an alley long-ago in Bethlehem. "And I am Naomi. Sit by me."

Julius took a place on the bench. Turning his head to look at her, Julius noted she kept her gaze straight ahead. He wondered what would come next.

* * *

Having been summoned by Rebekah's host in Bethany, Jacob now stood dumbfounded at her announced intention.

"Are you sure about this, Rebekah? Bethlehem is your home, and that of Elias!"

Rebekah continued to gather the clothing she'd brought to Bethany. "I have no home there anymore. Elias will always be remembered for his courage. But Barabbas will never be forgotten for turning his back on our cause. And I will not live there under his shame."

Jacob knew the martyr's widow had a will as strong as any of the men he led. "If this is what you truly want, then so be it."

"And it won't be a problem to find a place in Galilee to live out my days?"

"Any number of the brothers in Galilee would count it an honor to provide you home, Rebekah. You are the widow of Elias."

"But I'm also the mother of Barabbas, Jacob."

"And I was a friend to him, practically a brother. If any blame you for his desertion, they'd need to blame me more." Jacob thought back on the times he and Barabbas had shared: some in friendship, some in fighting, some in remembering martyred fathers. Those times were over. "For me, as you said for yourself: Barabbas is as dead. You lost a son, and I a comrade. But I swear: you'll have a home in Galilee. And from this day forward, I will be to you as a son."

"Thank you, Jacob." Rebekah brushed a tear that had begun to form, then resumed stuffing clothes into a sack. "Once I'm through here, I'll need to leave for Bethlehem. Today. Once there, hopefully I can find a cart to pack what remains."

Jacob took the sack from her. "Rebekah, I'll see to it. Let me tell the brothers here what's needed. When I return with cart and donkey, we both can be on our way to Bethlehem. And come tomorrow morning, you and I will set out for Galilee."

* * *

"My daughter tells me you were why she gave up whoring."

Naomi's bluntness took Julius aback. "Hannah already wanted to do so. I was just fortunate enough to be in a position to help make that possible."

Naomi kept her eyes forward. "You, centurion, make many things possible. You arranged my husband's resting place, when you could've not bothered over a stranger."

"A stranger to me, yes. But Hannah's father . . . and your husband. As I tried to say yesterday, awkwardly, it was the least I could do."

At these last words, Naomi turned to face Julius.

"Do you say that because of Bethlehem, centurion? I don't remember your face from that day, but Hannah told me you were there. When my son was murdered. When my husband cowered. Does your "least I could do" arise out of what you made possible that day?"

Julius wished he could leave. But Naomi deserved the truth. "It does. And not only for your son's death in Bethlehem. At Nathaniel's urging, I arranged for Simeon to enter the legion and take another name. Another loss imposed on you, for which I bear responsibility."

"Indeed you do." After a long silence, Naomi resumed. "But others share its guilt as well. What Joshua did, and did not do, in that alley ate away at all of us, but especially Simeon. Nathaniel wanted to be rid of my son. And I," Naomi's voice began to break, but she pressed on, "I failed to be strong for him. To stand up to Nathaniel. To assure Simeon he needn't carry his father's guilt. That would've been the least I could have done, centurion. And I failed Hannah, too, blaming rather than believing her about the rape. I helped drive her into that life. If it weren't for you, she might still be selling herself. Or, she might not be. At all. . ." Naomi moved her gaze straight ahead again, covering mouth and nose with hands moistened by tears.

Julius sat quite still for some time, searching for words that finally found voice. "You didn't fail, Naomi. You have the courage that brought you to this house yesterday to confront Nathaniel. You have a daughter and son who've returned to you. And love you. You didn't fail, Naomi. Hannah and Simeon are living proof."

Naomi took a handkerchief and daubed the corners of her eyes, then stood and looked down at Julius. "For Bethlehem, centurion, for my son David: I hate you." She paused, letting her last words ring in both of their ears. "But for saving Hannah, and sparing Simeon yesterday: a mother thanks you for her family's safekeeping." Placing her right hand on Julius' head, she intoned: "May Elohim bestow his mercy on you, mercy which I will never be able to give you."

Julius absorbed the full weight of Naomi's words, then stood. "It is mercy enough you'd even speak to me, Naomi. Mercy enough."

Naomi nodded, and the two slowly walked from the courtyard back into the house. Back to Hannah.

* * *

It was mid-afternoon when the cart led by Jacob, with Rebekah seated inside, reached Bethlehem. Few others had been on the road from Jerusalem, as it was still Sabbath. Rebekah and Jacob both rationalized that their circumstances justified travel that would normally be considered a breach of Torah. Besides, who would dare challenge the widow of Elias and the leader of the Galilean Zealots?

By early evening, the packing of the cart with Rebekah's belongings was almost complete. She knew many things would need to be left behind, not only because of the cart's size but also the uncertainty about what space would be available to her in Galilee. Rebekah's choices weighed values based on sentiment as much as utility. Cooking pots and utensils would not be difficult to obtain, so few of those were taken. But nowhere in Galilee could she find furniture crafted by Elias. She and Jacob carried the storage chest he'd built for her as a betrothal gift, her name carved into an olive plaque on top, and placed it in the bottom of the cart with the lid open. Rebekah then filled it with items either too fragile or too important to be left loose in the cart. A large platter that was a wedding gift. Elias' favorite carving knife, the one he used the day of the massacre to defend his family. Rebekah's wedding dress. The woolen blanket that she and Elias slept under – and that then kept her warm in the nights after his death. But the most precious cargo nestled inside a small cedar box lined with fleece: a small lamb that Elias carved for Levi, still showing the stain of Levi's blood. Rebekah ran her fingers over the lamb before placing the cedar box in the chest, and shutting it tight for tomorrow's journey.

As Jacob lashed a chair and stool to the top of the cart while Rebekah held a lamp for him in the growing darkness, a figure approached. Rebekah shifted the lamp to cast its light in that direction, and recognized the face to be that of Rabbi Joachin.

"Rabbi." Her greeting came with a short bow.

"Rebekah, I'd not heard you were back until one of the widows informed me." The rabbi paused to look at the man on the cart. He didn't know him, though the frequency of Zealot visitors to Rebekah led him to assume he was one of them. "And it's wonderful news about your son, spared from enduring the cross. You must be filled with joy."

Rebekah never had been impressed by Joachin. Still, his misreading of the situation was understandable, and she'd no desire to explain it any further. "You cannot begin to imagine."

"If I might ask, though: the cart? Are you preparing to sell these things?"

"No, rabbi, I'll be moving to Galilee. I leave tomorrow."

For a moment, the rabbi was at a loss for words. The

earlier news of Barabbas' release had caused him concern: what if he were to return to Bethlehem? Would he lead his raids from here? Might the Romans hold the village responsible for this Zealot's actions? Now, with Rebekah leaving: would Barabbas take over her house and make it the center of operations? As the town's rabbi, responsible for the community's welfare, he needed to know such things.

"So, are you leaving in order for Barabbas to have your home?"

"No, rabbi, I am not. And he will not."

Her last words puzzled the rabbi, who took note that the man on the cart had gotten down and now stood next to Rebekah. "But what will become of your house?"

Jacob had heard Rebekah speak before of this novice of a rabbi, whose gift was for study but little else. "What concern is it to you, rabbi, how Rebekah disposes of what belongs to her?"

Joachin's resentment at a stranger questioning his role and standing in the village spilled out: "Who are you to tell Bethlehem's rabbi what my concerns for the community should be?"

In an instant, Jacob stepped before the rabbi, their faces mere inches apart. "I am Jacob, son of the martyr Judas, leader of the Zealots in Galilee. And I am Rebekah's right arm."

Joachin's eyes lowered to the ground. The reputation of Jacob carried beyond Galilee. "I meant no offense. I just wondered what would become of Rebekah's home."

Rebekah had also been wondering about this since deciding to move. The moment seemed opportune to broach the idea that had become her focus. "Rabbi Joachin is right to ask about this, Jacob."

The zealot stepped back, a move eliciting a distinct sense of relief in Joachin.

Rebekah continued. "I remember talk in the synagogue of securing a caretaker for the cave: to ensure its upkeep as a memorial for the dead, and to serve as a guide to its pilgrims."

Joachin nodded. "Those conversations are ongoing. Some have even contributed to a small fund to someday make that possible."

"My husband and my son rest behind those stones," the carving of the lamb packed away flashing through Rebekah's mind. "So, Rabbi Joachin, what of this: the synagogue can have free use of my home. To house the caretaker. Perhaps to provide lodging to any who journey here to see the martyrs. My husband's carpentry shed could store whatever tools or supplies beyond those already there that might be needed to keep the cave in good condition."

"Rebekah, this is extraordinarily generous. Are you sure?"

"I am. And since I'm taking but a few things, you'll find the house well stocked with cooking utensils and other goods that will allow someone to move in without much to add."

Rebekah felt Jacob's hand rest on her shoulder. "This is a righteous act, Rebekah. The memorial is a holy place, deserving care and preservation of its story."

"May Elohim be praised!" Joachin interjected. "And the Almighty reward you for this. I promise, we at the synagogue will see this comes to pass. Bless you, Rebekah, bless you."

"Come by early in the morning, rabbi. I'll show you what is here, and can sign whatever document the synagogue needs to transfer ownership. Then Jacob and I will be on our way."

Jacob extended his hand to the rabbi. As Joachin clasped it, Jacob drew the rabbi toward him and lowered his voice. "See to it this happens, and soon. The brothers in Judea will keep me informed on your progress. I'd hate for Rebekah to be disappointed. And if my return becomes required to hasten any delays – well, that's not something you or I would want. Understood?"

Joachin sputtered agreement and returned to the synagogue, his stomach churning at the thought – and potential consequences – of facing a displeased Jacob. The rabbi Joachin swore to himself that a caretaker would be found and in place before the next pilgrimage festival: the Feast of Weeks, which occurred seven weeks after the first Sabbath following Passover. Or, as more and more Greek-speaking pilgrims named it for its passage of fifty days: Pentecost.

CHAPTER LXII

Shortly after sunset, and with it Sabbath's end, an older man stopped outside a house in Bethany. Hoping the directions proved correct, as darkness would complicate any further searching, he knocked on the door.

Inside, several of the women scooted closer to Mary, while John stood and left the circle. There'd been rumors that the Temple police might hunt down Yeshua's supporters after his execution. John wished he'd not left his fishing knife behind with the nets when he first followed Yeshua. Then again, the memory of the garden arrest came to mind, and the rabbi's words there to put down rather than take up weapons. John leaned against the door. "What do you want?"

"I've come to see the mother of Yeshua."

John glanced back at Mary, then asked, "Why? And who are you?"

"My name is Nicodemus. Along with an Arimathean named Joseph, I took the rabbi's body from the cross. I came to tell Mary of the tomb's location."

"Please, John," Mary said as she rose, "let him in."

John pulled back the wooden lock bar and swung the door open. "Come in." As Nicodemus stepped inside, John poked his head out to make sure the visitor had come alone.

Nicodemus approached the woman who'd stood when he entered. "You are Mary?"

"I am."

The visitor dipped his head. "Good woman, I'm deeply sorry for your loss. For the loss that is all of ours, truly. Your son was a righteous teacher."

"You knew my son, then?"

"I did. On an earlier pilgrimage he made to Jerusalem, I sought him out. At night." Nicodemus paused to gather the words he labored over on the way. "When I sat in the Sanhedrin this week, I could do nothing, nor could Joseph, to sway what had already been decided. But we had to do something, anything. So, Joseph provided his own tomb for Yeshua's resting place. And I brought linen and spices to give the rabbi, your son, a proper burial. We wanted you to know that, and to tell you where his tomb is."

Mary looked up at Nicodemus. His long grey beard reminded her of her husband's toward the end of his life. "Thank you, Nicodemus. And give my thanks to Joseph. I was told my son's body would be taken for burial, and I'm grateful you tended to the preparations. But, would you excuse me for a moment?" Taking a lamp from the table, Mary walked into another room. Nicodemus thought Mary might have been overwhelmed, needing time and privacy to regain her composure. But she returned shortly with something in her hand.

"I brought this from Galilee. Even before we left, my son spoke of suffering and death." Mary unclasped her hand, revealing a small glass vial. "He continued to speak of Jerusalem in those same terms all along the journey here. And then, with the arrest . . . and Golgotha. . ." Mary found words escaping her as she stared at the vial and as her tears began to flow.

Nicodemus stared at the glass, but understood no connection between it and the grief of Yeshua's mother. "May I ask, Mary, what this vial is to you?"

With her free hand, Mary motioned for the women and John to move closer. "The day before we fled Bethlehem, two Persian Magi came to Yeshua and me in a stable, the cave that now entombs the innocents of Bethlehem. The Magi brought gifts to Yeshua and professed him to be the Promised One of God. Gentiles were the first to confess Yeshua as

Messiah."

Still processing that revelation, Nicodemus blurted: "And this vial, is one of the gifts?"

"It is." Mary carefully pulled the stopper out, brought the vial to her nose and inhaled. After all these years, its bittersweet scent still blended traces of green wood right after it's been cast into a fire with the pungent earthiness of moistened soil.

"May I?" inquired Nicodemus. Mary lifted the vial for him to smell. "Myrrh," he said without a moment's hesitation. "The same as Joseph and I used to prepare your son's body."

Mary replaced the stopper. "Tomorrow, with your directions to the tomb, I will take this and anoint my son's body."

* * *

Naomi and Hannah watched as the servant cleared the last of the dishes from the evening meal. The women had offered to help, but he would have nothing of it. "The two of you have enough on your minds, what with the Sopher's death to grieve." Neither woman clarified the grievings that truly weighed on them: for Hannah, of Yeshua and her father; for Naomi, of all the tangled memories of life with and apart from Joshua. "If you need anything else before retiring, let me know. Otherwise, I'll have breakfast prepared for you in the morning."

"Would it be possible to have the meal ready at first light?" Hannah asked. "My brother will be arriving then, as we hope to get an early start for our visit to Bethlehem."

The servant bowed. "Certainly. And I'll pack fruit and bread for the three of you to take."

"Pack only for two," Naomi added. "I'll be staying here. When my children return in the afternoon, the three of us will go to the cemetery for prayers."

"Very good. I'll see that tomorrow's dinner will be enough for guests, in case you invite others join you afterwards in remembering Nathaniel over a meal."

"Thank you," Hannah replied. "Breaking bread with others in such times can be a genuine comfort." She left unspoken who'd be remembered, and who would not.

"Yes," Naomi added, "thank you."

"Then rest well, and Elohim grant you peace." Bowing, the servant turned and left.

The women sat quietly at the table for some time before Naomi broke the silence.

"I hope you and Simeon don't mind my not going to Bethlehem. I want to save my strength for when we go to your father's grave."

"Not at all, mother. If it weren't for Simeon assurance we'd ride there rather than walk, I'd stay too. But given all that's happened these past two days, we just felt a trip to Bethlehem, and the cave, was fitting. Even necessary. So much of our lives trace there, for good and ill. And what, and who, we grieve today. All from Bethlehem."

"All from Bethlehem," Naomi repeated, lingering on the breadth of that truth before adding, "even your centurion, who stood by while David was struck down."

Hannah knew this conversation couldn't be avoided. "Yes, even Julius. I can't deny his part in Bethlehem. But I also can't deny I've forgiven him."

"Forgiveness is one thing. But love him? How can you do that, knowing what he did?

Hannah took hold of her mother's hand. "I came to love him before I knew what he did."

"And when you found out?" Naomi implored. "That didn't change your heart?"

"When Julius confessed his guilt, I was furious. I even grabbed a piece of wood and swung at him. In that moment, I would have gladly struck him dead for what he did to David. To all of us. But I missed. And we parted ways. Ironically, that same night, I found forgiveness with Yeshua – not forgiveness for others, certainly not Julius, but for myself. For what

I'd become. For all the hatred I'd carried that made me into that person."

"Oh Hannah, child," Naomi squeezed her daughter's hand. "You're not, not anymore."

"And why I'm not is the forgiveness Yeshua helped me to accept. It was only over time I found it possible to extend that forgiveness to Julius. And what I discovered in doing that, to my surprise, is that I'd really never stopped loving him."

"In spite of his role in David's death?"

Hannah grasped her mother's hand tighter, and spilled out other words she needed to say. "For years, mother, I thought I'd stopped loving father. And I was sure you had as well. But on Golgotha yesterday, when the husband and father who let David be torn from our arms, and then cowered when he might have avenged his son's death, when he hung on a cross: you called out his name, assuring him he was not alone. And then, you said you loved him. You loved him in spite of David's death. In spite of all those years. You still loved him. . . As I still love Julius."

Mother and daughter held on to one another. The glow of a full moon's rise shone through from the courtyard. "You are wise, daughter. And gracious." Naomi sighed. "To be honest, my heart and tongue had no such grace when I spoke to Julius today."

"Before he left, Julius told me what you'd said." Hannah's smile when she said this caught Naomi off-guard. "He appreciated your frankness. And I, your entrusting mercy toward him into the hands of God, when you couldn't offer it yourself. Because that's how it was, and in more ways than I care to admit, still is, for me. At first, I could only ask God to forgive the ones, Julius included, I wasn't ready to forgive myself. But like so much else, forgiveness begins with small steps, the ones we're ready for, if we are ever to take up the harder ones."

"Then may God guide both our steps. And may I learn

from a daughter who's become her mother's teacher." Naomi and Hannah rose from the table and made their way toward the rooms where each slept. "Tomorrow will be a long day for us both, Hannah. Sleep well."

"You too, mother. And may God provide the coming day some fresh gift for its facing."

* * *

While Hannah and Naomi slipped into their beds, Julius approached the destination of his evening trek. Earlier in the afternoon, after his conversation with Naomi, Hannah had invited him to go to Bethlehem in the morning with her and Simeon. Julius declined, uneasy at the thought of intruding on their time at the cave where their brother David had been buried along with all the other victims of Herod's massacre. But all through his dinner at the caravansary, Julius sensed a peculiar draw to go to Bethlehem, and to the cave. Alone. As he considered why, a web of possible reasons knotted his gut and spoiled his appetite – though he couldn't sort which held more truth for him. Was it to confront the enormity of what he'd done years ago? Or was it to attempt some far-too-belated regret? Was it to rage against Herod, as if that might bring some diminishing of his own responsibility? Or was it . . .?

No clear answer presented itself, save to set out for Bethlehem tonight. Julius paid Ishmael's nephew to fill the wineskin he would take, then stuffed bread and meat left from his meal into a cloth sack. Julius didn't want to draw attention to himself, especially in Bethlehem, so he decided he'd travel the six miles on foot. On his way out, he found the stable boy and gave him an extra coin to see that his horse was fed and groomed for the night and morning.

A nearly full moon provided more than ample light as he left Jerusalem through the Joppa gate on the west-leading way, then turned south at its junction with the road that led to Bethlehem. It took the better part of two hours for Julius to reach and partially ascend the ridge a mile or so northwest of Bethlehem. The night's chill was deepened even more by the memories conjured in this particular place. More than thirty years ago, he had encamped in this very spot with a detachment from the Antonia. Concealed in its rocks and hollows, they waited for the coming afternoon to swoop into the village and carry out Herod's carnage.

With Bethlehem in sight, Julius tried to remember what he felt on that long-ago night. He recalled urging his men not to look at the faces of the next day's victims, to avoid anything that might cause hesitation in their assigned task. But now, peering across at the moonlit village, the faces were all too clear. Hannah's. Simeon's. Naomi's. Even the face of Lucius, who brutalized that family by killing its youngest and disgracing its father and husband, only to be struck down later with the same callousness that slaughtered Bethlehem's children. As Julius tried banishing those faces out of his mind, another face came into focus. It was as if the face of Yeshua loomed over the whole of Bethlehem, and this ridge, and him. The face of the one who'd inexplicably disclosed in Gesamani his knowledge of Julius as the centurion in charge of carrying out Herod's murderous plan for Bethlehem. The face of the one who escaped execution under Julius' command in this place, only to be crucified as Julius stood guard at Golgotha. Yeshua.

"YESHUA!" Julius' shout echoed off the hillside. He wondered: had Yeshua's name been shouted into the night that followed the slaughter? Or did those shouts only name Bethlehem's other children: in anguish, in outrage, beseeching some God who'd saved one child but not theirs? Julius imagined the voice of Naomi shouting "David" into the bleakness of that darkness: with no answer forthcoming, no comfort for her grief. Nothing to undo what Julius and his troops had inflicted on her. On Hannah. On Simeon. On them all.

"YESHUA! Is this what you wanted? For them? For me?" The only answer for Julius' outcry came in a silent sky that absorbed more light than it shed. Wrapping himself in the blanket brought from the caravansary, Julius laid down in hopes of sleep. As he closed his eyes, Julius envisioned the cave that Hannah had described to him several times: the one used by her father as a stable, the one she played in as a child with David and Yeshua, the one that now entombed her brother and the other victims of Herod's insanity – victims of Julius, who followed orders he knew to be obscene but still obeyed. Such thoughts, and Julius' wonderings as to why he felt so drawn to Bethlehem and its cave, prevented any respite that sleep might provide. The only thing Julius could hope for in his restlessness was dawn's earliest hint, and with it enough light to find and enter the cave. And then? Julius didn't know what *then* might bring. But this much was sure: he would go to Bethlehem's cave, and he would face its truth. His truth.

* * *

Another could not sleep this night. Rebekah took pains not to wake Jacob as she left the house. She needed no lamp to illumine her steps, and not just because of the full moon's light. Rebekah had taken this way countless times before from her home to the cave of the martyrs.

Stepping through the entrance, Rebekah could make out the remnants of the cave's former use as a stable: the worn slats and timbers from troughs and stalls, a pitchfork and shovel covered with dust. Walking past the artifacts, she headed further back into a passage that once went deeply into the hillside, but was now blocked by a wall of stones. A small oil lamp sat beside it, its flame kindled every evening by one of the synagogue elders to make sure the martyrs were not engulfed in darkness, without remembrance. Kneeling by the wall, she stroked the stones the way her hands once caressed the head of Elias, and Levi – and Barabbas.

"Husband, take care of our Levi. I can't stay here any longer. The son who survived your fate has become a coward, no better than Joshua, who turns from avenging your and Levi's death in order to live in disgrace." The stroking of Rebekah's hand became more of her squeezing at the cold rock. "Maybe, if you were still here, it would be different. He would be different. But, I have failed you. And him. If only you'd still be here, husband! But now, no one is left. And I must go." Rebekah pressed her lips against the stone, then stood and walked back toward the home that had once been hers, that had once been theirs, but no more.

CHAPTER LXII

"WHA –" Julius sat straight up, an unexpected stretch of deep sleep having been rudely interrupted. He felt his forehead to make sure it hadn't been a dream. It was no dream – his fingers were wet. Julius opened his eyes to see the cause. When he bedded down, the night sky had been clear. But now, while the sun had not broken the horizon, it was bright enough out to see clouds enveloping the ridge. A fine mist filled the air, dripping off the overhang above him. Julius held his hands out, letting them be lightly moistened. As he did so, his thoughts left Bethlehem far behind, all the way to his childhood, when warmer weather inland pulled in such air from the Great Sea across to the village he grew up in. Back then, he loved its relief from summer's stilting heat. The mist felt especially refreshing after the scorching wind of the khamsin only two days prior in Jerusalem, on Golgotha. Golgotha had reminded him of the khamsin's raging on the day when he and his troops swept into Bethlehem.

But now, today, Julius relished the coolness of the mist on his hands. He closed his eyes, brought his hands up and massaged his face with this morning's moist gift. For a moment, it was if he was a young boy running through the grassy fields near his home, dampened by the sea air's arrival, soaking his legs up past his knees, even splashing his face the faster he ran.

Julius opened his eyes. The clouds seemed thin, almost as if lit from within by the predawn's soft glowing. Light enough, he thought, to travel the mile or so across to Bethlehem. But first things first. He took out the remnants of last night's meal and ate, washing them down with a single swallow of wine. He would have had more, but he wanted his mind clear when he stepped into Bethlehem's cave. After rolling his blanket and tying it onto his pack, Julius cinched his belt and drew the hood of his cloak up and set off for Bethlehem.

* * *

"Are you sure you want to leave now? If we wait for another hour or two, these clouds will lift, I'm sure."

Rebekah made a final adjustment of what had been the cloth sheltering her porch being used to cover her belongings on the cart, then clambered onto the bench Jacob rigged on the front of the cart. "No, the longer we wait, the longer we'll be traveling in the heat of the day."

"So be it." Jacob mounted his horse while holding on to a tether rope attached to the ox pulling the cart. "Remember, let me know when that bench gets old. You're welcome to take my horse, and I can walk."

"And I can walk a ways, too, Jacob. But let's be off."

Jacob pulled on the tether and gave his horse a soft kick with his heel. Both horse and ox stepped forward, and the journey to Galilee began. Rebekah glanced at the passing homes as they made their way through Bethlehem. Some sheltered friends, some sheltered parents whose children lay still in what had been Joshua's stable. Waiting until later would have allowed more goodbyes to be said. But in Rebekah's mind, what words needed speaking had already been said, and she wished to hear no others.

The last of Bethlehem's dwellings had soon been left behind, and the road stretched north into the distance. The sun's rising brightened the way its rays sparkling the still descending mist. Through the glare, Rebekah could barely make out a solitary figure walking toward the road from the west. Rebekah presumed it to be some shepherd, wandering back to the village for more supplies. The glare, and the years, hid recognition of the face that belonged to the

Roman who'd reared his horse to cut off any hope of escape for her and her family the day of the massacre.

* * *

Barabbas cupped his hands, dipped them into a pool fed by one of Jericho's springs, and splashed its waters onto his eyelids and cheeks. It felt refreshing, a welcome start for this morning after sleeping on the ground near this oasis. Through the night, and again now, Barabbas thought back to his last trip to Jericho. Then, he came to assassinate the Roman who'd killed his father and brother in Bethlehem. The remembrance allowed him to momentarily relish the elation of revenge finally enacted. But, as had been the case too many times last night when Barabbas longed for sleep, that elation sank under the weight of its cost: arrest, torture at the hands of the Romans, martyrdom stolen from him by another dying in his place, the terms of his release. But worst of all, his mother's response to it all: not gratitude that he would sacrifice pride and face in order to save her life, but a despising of him as a coward. He splashed water on his face again. This time, it didn't refresh, but stung.

And with the sting, Barabbas felt a hand on his shoulder. "Sir, is that you?"

Barabbas rubbed the water from his eyes and turned to see who this woman was. She held a water jug, half-full. A woman speaking to, and touching, a man in public – he thought she might be one of the town's whores, who serviced Herod's guards or even his entourage.

"You don't remember me?"

Barabbas studied her face. There was something vaguely familiar...

"Aricea. I work at Rome's outpost here." She sidled up closer to him. "You know, I was the one who gave up Lucius to you."

His eyes widened – it was her!

"I'd heard you were arrested, Barabbas." Others gathered at the spring to draw water stopped what they were doing and stared when they heard that name.

"No, you confuse me with another!" Barabbas said loudly.

"I'm not confused! Not at all. You're Barabbas!"

Barabbas glanced around. The crowd was murmuring, and one woman ran in the direction of two soldiers patrolling nearby. Barabbas had hoped Jericho would be large enough for him to blend in, at least for awhile: to gather supplies with what little money he brought, at least to figure out where he might go next. But Aricea spoiled all that.

"You're wrong," he shouted as he stood and began to leave. "I'm not Barabbas!" He could see the woman standing with the soldiers, and she was now pointing in his direction. Barabbas had no choice but to break into a sprint toward the Salt Sea, and its eastern shore even more desolate than the west. As he did, not knowing if he could elude whatever patrol would doubtless be dispatched his way, Barabbas realized his abandonment was complete. For now, Barabbas had abandoned his own identity. A man without a name. Without a family.

* * *

Julius had a rough idea from Hannah's stories of the cave's location in Bethlehem. She remembered being told the soldiers streamed in from the north, and how the family headed from their home away from the increasingly terrifying sounds. So, Julius reasoned, the cave would have to be somewhere in Bethlehem's southern quarters. As he walked into Bethlehem on a spur from the main road, he was grateful the village was relatively small. Perhaps, he thought, a villager might assist him on the way.

What he didn't expect was the resident who came racing up at him, sling in hand. Julius stopped, and the child whipped the cord of the sling round several times and took aim. At that moment, a man leapt out of a door and shouted, "Benjamin, no!"

But it was too late. The lad let loose the stone in the

sling, and it whizzed by Julius' head, missing by less than a hand's length. The boy bent down to get another rock to hurl, but the one Julius took to be the boy's father caught him by the arms. "No! You could have hurt this man!" Taking the sling from the boy's hand, he gave him a firm swat on his backside. "Go inside!" The child ran, crying, to a woman who now stepped out of the same house. As Julius watched, the boy's attempt to get a hug received instead a wagging of a finger in his face, before she took him by the hand and led him inside.

"Sir, I am very sorry!" The man now stood in front of Julius and bowed low. "My son is too spirited at times."

Julius put a hand on the man's shoulder and laughed. "Your son, was it Benjamin? For one so young, he's a knack for that sling."

"Again, I'm very sorry. My brothers and I are shepherds, and I've just started teaching Benjamin the use of a sling." The father's lips parted in a smile. "He's better at it than I was at his age. But still, a stranger should not be greeted in such a way. My name is Judah. Is there anything I can do to make this up?"

"Actually, Judah, there is. A friend told me there's a cave here that serves as a memorial to the martyrs of this village, the ones killed at Herod's command."

"Then peace to you, pilgrim. I would be happy to take you there. Wait here while I tell my wife." Judah went inside the house, where Julius could still hear Benjamin crying, and then returned. "It's but a short walk."

The two set off. Judah asked Julius his name and where he came from.

"Nabal. Originally from Tyre, lately of Jerusalem."

On hearing of Tyre, Judah asked: "I've heard that Tyre is mainly Gentile. Are you one of those we call a God-fearer?"

Julius pondered how to answer that honestly. "How the one you call Elohim would judge me, I wouldn't venture a guess. But your people, and traditions, I have always tried to respect."

"Well, Nabal, I'm a shepherd. Because of that, some of my own people hold me in lesser regard than even a Gentile. So I am certainly not the one to pass judgment on you or anyone."

Julius stopped. "You are a man who looks out for strangers, even Gentile ones. There's no cause for anyone look down on you, Judah. And if they do," Julius added with a wink, "you set that sons of yours loose with sling in hand to teach them a lesson!"

Judah looked at the stranger. This man spoke more truth than some of the synagogue goers who often tried to ignore him. "Thank you, Nabal. And just a few more steps," he added as they resumed walking, "and we'll be at the cave's entrance. You know, it started out as a stable."

"Yes, my friend did tell me that."

In a few moments, Judah stopped beside an outcrop of limestone that revealed an opening to the cave. "This is the place you seek. Would you like me to go in with you, or would you rather have time to yourself and your thoughts?"

"Thank you for asking, Judah. But I think I'll go on my own from here. I do appreciate your showing the way."

Before walking home, Judah reached out his hand, "God go with you, then."

"Judah, my being a Gentile, if I shake your –"

Judah grasped Julius' hand. "I'm regularly told that being in the fields with my sheep leaves me unclean. I'd just as soon endure that judgment for grasping the hand of a friend."

Julius smiled and shook Judah's hand. "For what it's worth, I'd venture that you are a true son of Israel, more than a few I've known in Jerusalem." Julius entered the cave.

* * *

Naomi and her two children stood on the front porch of Nathaniel's residence. At the base of the steps leading down to the street, Simeon had tied two horses brought from the Antonia. Simeon hugged his mother, then picked up a satchel containing the food that the servant had prepared for their journey and slung it over his shoulder.

Hannah kissed Naomi on the cheek. "I promise, we'll be back shortly after noon."

"Not to worry, Hannah. There'll be plenty of time left to go to Joshua's grave. Please, take whatever time you need with... with our David." These last words caught in Naomi's throat, and brought tears to both her and Hannah.

Simeon placed a hand on each of their shoulders. "We will, mother. And soon enough, once my papers come through, you and I will return to Bethlehem for good, as we discussed."

Naomi nodded, then stepped back. "And Hannah, you're still set on not returning to Bethlehem to live with us?"

This, too, had been part of the conversation at breakfast. "There's so much uncertainty for me right now. I still would follow the way Yeshua taught, but with him dead, I don't know what that might mean. And Julius – I love him, and I know he loves me, but, I don't know."

Simeon eyed his mother and sister. "Let me get this off my chest, to both of you. Twice, Julius acted on my behalf with no benefit to him. Years ago, when I sought refuge in the legion. And two days past, when he took my place at Golgotha. I'll not stand between the two of you if that's your choice, Hannah. And as for Yeshua: after being with Mary at the crucifixion, I wish I'd known him as you did, Hannah. So whatever you choose there, you've my blessing."

Hannah took Simeon's hand. "Thank you, brother. Truly."

Naomi's mind filled with the words that passed between her and Hannah last night. About Joshua. About forgiveness. About learning wisdom from her daughter. But for the moment, she could not bring herself to offer such acceptance of Julius as Simeon just had. "Travel safely." Naomi then stepped inside and closed the door behind her.

For a moment, Simeon and Hannah stared at one another. Then, wrapping one arm around her shoulder, "She needs time, Hannah. And we need to be on our way." Together, they walked down the steps and mounted the horses, then set out for Bethlehem.

* * *

Julius stood still, allowing his eyes to adjust from the brightness outside to the cave's darkness. Some light did angle in from the entrance, revealing the remnants of the stable that Hannah once played in. Further ahead, Julius could make out the turn of the cavern that, as Hannah had described, led to a wall that entombed the innocents. As Julius reached that juncture, the light from the entrance quickly dissipated, augmented by the flicking of a lamp ahead. A few more steps, and the wall came into view. To Julius' surprise, what also came into view was a figure kneeling at the far corner, where the stones of the wall butted up against the side and ceiling of the cave. Julius considered leaving, not wanting to disturb the vigil of whoever this was. Yet, he had come all the way from Jerusalem, and –

"Please," spoke the one who knelt. Julius could see nothing of the man's face. The hood of the stranger's cloak was drawn fully over his head, obscuring any view that the lamp's light might have revealed. "The place is large enough for us both."

"As you wish," Julius replied, taking a seat by the wall, the lamp between them.

"Have you been here before?" the stranger asked.

"No. At least, not to the wall. I was in Bethlehem once, but before this memorial. And you, is this your first visit?"

Julius heard a long sigh. "Second. My father brought me here years ago. He wanted to show me this place, so I'd remember these innocents all my days."

The irony of it struck Julius, He'd spent nearly thirty years trying to keep these innocents out of his memory. Out of his dreams. Those thoughts were interrupted by a scraping sound, as the stranger twisted the top of a clay jar and then lifted it off, followed by the crinkling of a leather scroll being unwound. The stranger turned his back slightly to Julius and lifted the scroll to his side, so that the lamp might better the writing on it. As he did, he began to quietly read.

Julius could not make out what was being said. "Forgive me, but the scroll you read, what is it?"

"The names of those who rest behind these stones." The stranger continued to speak too softly for Julius to hear.

"Please, sir. I don't wish to impose, but might you read those names that I may hear?"

The stranger lifted his head slightly. "Have you come here to remember them?"

In the solemnity of this place, and the anonymity its darkness offered, Julius considered: perhaps, at last, honesty had nothing to lose. "Remember them? Most of my years have sought to forget them. But yes, today I come to remember them, and my debt to them I can never pay."

The stranger resumed the litany of names, now spoken loud enough so Julius could hear. It was then that Julius noticed something that unnerved him. The stranger was rolling the scroll back up, putting it next to the jar – but still naming the innocents!

"Sir, I think you've been here more than once. You know these names by heart."

The stranger made no reply to Julius' comment, but continued with the litany, only louder. "Levi, son of Elias and Rebekah. Elias the carpenter. Rachel the midwife."

Julius felt his body tremble as the voice grew in familiarity.

The stranger turned to face Julius directly and drew back the hood from his cloak. "David, son of Joshua and Naomi. Brother of Simeon and Hannah."

"YESHUA!" Julius gasped for breath. "How . . . I watched you. . . Yeshua?"

Yeshua moved over beside Julius. "You are not the only one in debt to these. My whole life was lived in their debt."

"You?"

"I lived, but these innocents died. In my place. I could never pay that obligation, save by honoring them with my life. And to reveal the God who doesn't snatch life from such ones, but who receives them. The God who seeks us to live in a way that never forfeits such lives again."

"But, I was the one who came here to take these lives."

Yeshua grasped Julius' head between his hands. "And ever since, you have not just lived in regret. Your life has changed. I've seen that. Through Hannah. In Gesamani. At Golgotha. Accept the forgiveness God holds you in, Julius. Leave your guilt at this wall. For good!"

Eyes closed, Julius leaned into the feel of Yeshua's hands on his temples. A sensation of pressure overwhelmed Julius – not a pressure brought by hands squeezing too tightly. Rather, for Julius, it was of pressure released, flowing outward from him into the rabbi's hands.

Time for Julius suspended in that flow.

In time – he didn't know much had passed – but in time, Julius attempted to speak the gratitude welling up inside. "Yeshua, thank you!" Opening his eyes, he saw – nothing. Nothing but the wall, and the lamp, and the opened clay jar with the scroll rolled up beside it. "Yeshua?" Julius looked around in the cave, and back toward the entrance. "Rabbi? Yeshua?" No answer. No sound. Julius leaned back against the wall of the innocents. "Yeshua. Alive."

* * *

Simeon and Hannah walked their horses through Bethlehem. All these years, and the streets still seemed familiar. Familiar, and dreaded. Within sight of the cave's entrance, their focus was suddenly broken by a voice calling out.

"You there – please!"

They stopped, turning to see a man hastening in their direction. Hannah had noticed him earlier, standing in the synagogue's doorway as they passed. As the man drew near, and his features became clearer, Simeon recognized him as the rabbi who presided over the funeral of his grandmother a few months ago. He told Hannah, so that she would know his identity.

On reaching the pair, Rabbi Joachin reached his hand out to Simeon. "Yes, I thought I recognized you. You're Deborah's grandson, right?"

"I am. And this is my sister, Hannah."

Joachin didn't bother to acknowledge Hannah. Other matters raced through his mind, triggered by his conversation with Rebekah last evening, and now –

"And not only Deborah's grandson. You would be the son of Joshua the innkeep!"

Simeon stared hard at the rabbi. He didn't know what to make of his tone, and even more he didn't appreciate the rabbi's ignoring of his sister. "I am his son, and Hannah is his daughter. And if I may ask of you, Rabbi: why is any of this of interest to you?"

"Did you know your father's former stable is a memorial to the victims of Herod's massacre?"

Hannah remembered comments her mother recently made about this rabbi: the kindest word used was "naïve." Joachin might wish to proceed as if she weren't there, but Hannah wouldn't give them that pleasure. "Are you so obtuse as to think that only those who live in Bethlehem know of the memorial? It's why Simeon and I come today. Our brother lies there!"

Hannah's rebuke caught Joachin off-guard. The only other woman who dared talk to him like that was Rebekah – and as with Rebekah, Joachin stammered in retreat.

"Why no, of course, the memorial is well-known, I just thought, well, no offense."

Simeon shook his head. "Again, what's your interest

in who our father happens to be?"

"The stable. By law, it still belongs to your family, though the synagogue has been saddled with its upkeep for years. And its use as a memorial requires labor and monies to attend to its maintenance."

"You expect our mother to repay this?" Hannah's tone grew even sharper.

"No, not repay. Up till now, Rebekah helped fund its upkeep. But she left this morning, to live out her days in Galilee. Now, I know your mother has been in Jerusalem of late. But seeing you here this morning, Simeon, would you have an interest in returning to Bethlehem? To be caretaker of the memorial: which is, again, by law, your family's property and responsibility?" Joachin did not reveal Rebekah had signed over her home for use by a caretaker. If Simeon accepted, he could stay in his mother's home – and, Joachin imagined, the synagogue could have free use of Rebekah's home and any income it could provide. "Besides," Joachin blundered on, "your serving as caretaker might mitigate your father's disgrace here."

Hannah would have launched a volley of epithets learned from her seafaring clients in Caesarea – but before she could open her mouth, Simeon had sprung forward, lifting Joachin by his robe and pinning him up against a wall: "You never knew my father, so never slander him in my hearing again! Rabbi or not, you'd regret it." Simeon let go of the robe, and Joachin roughly slid down against the wall till his feet touched the ground. "Yes, I'll return. I'll be caretaker of the wall – but not for you. For our brother David. Understood?"

"See here," Joachin sputtered, "I only meant to say this would be a chance, an opportunity, for you, for your mother –"

"I heard what you said. But if you ever speak of my father that way – and if you ever ignore my sister like you just did –" Simeon jammed a finger into Joachin's chest, "just don't."

Joachin, heart pounding, bowed. "Please, Simeon. And Hannah. My apologies if I've misspoken. But I must be getting to work. I'll see that the elders are notified you'll be caretaker. Thank you." Joachin beat a hasty retreat to the synagogue.

"Caretaker?" Hannah asked. "Are you sure?"

"For David, and all the others there: yes. And if the rabbi is right about Rebekah leaving, I won't have to face her hatred of me again for joining the legion."

Hannah nodded. "Trust me, you're not the only object of her spite."

Simeon smiled. "Yet another bond between us, sister." Then, more seriously, "But we're not here for the rabbi, or Rebekah. We are here for David. And the stable is just ahead."

The last of the journey's steps now taken, they tied their horses to a post outside the entrance. Hannah found herself wishing Julius had come, though she understood why the one charged to carry out Herod's orders didn't. "Are you ready, Simeon?"

For Simeon, the moment reminded him of times before combat, when even the best of preparations can't remove the uncertainty of what will come to pass. "Our brother's gone long enough without us." Holding each other's hand, they entered the cave.

CHAPTER LXIII

"Julius!" Hannah could not believe her eyes. "You said you didn't want to come here!"

Still sitting with his back against the wall, Julius looked up at Hannah and Simeon. He didn't know if he should stand, or even could stand, much less how or where to begin his words.

Simeon picked up the lamp beside the wall and held it to Julius' face. "Are you alright?"

Hannah sat down, a mix of bewilderment and worry and anger rushing through her. "Why did you come alone? Without me?"

"Last evening, after I left you, I felt compelled to come here. Alone. To face this wall, and my part in its erecting."

"But you didn't have to face it alone," Hannah countered, "I would have come."

"I know, Hannah. But I realized, if I was to finally confront what had been done here – what I had done, and what that did to me – I needed to come here on my own."

"And did it help?"

Julius glanced toward Simeon. "Please, sit with us. What I have to say, both of you need to hear." Simeon obliged, then repeated Hannah's question. "Did it help, Julius?"

Julius wondered if his experience of its help would be believed – COULD be believed. But, he couldn't answer their question without revealing it. "It helped. That is to say, he helped."

"He?" Hannah leaned back. "Who, Julius?"

"When I arrived, there was someone already here, by the far end of the wall. I considered leaving him his privacy, but he'd heard me enter and bid me join him. Which I did."

"The two of you talked?"

"Only briefly, Hannah, at least initially. But then. Things turned to this jar, and scroll, next to me"

"What about them?" Simeon asked.

"He took the scroll out of the jar, and after unwinding it began to read. As he did, it became clear that the scroll listed those killed in the massacre."

"I do remember mother talking about such a record kept, Simeon, though I never saw it."

"Nor I. But Julius, was that all there was to it? How did reading the scroll help?"

"As I said, he knelt at the far end of the wall, and I sat where we are now. When he began reading the names, his back was to me, the hood of his cloak pulled up. But then – " Julius raised his hands and pressed them against his temple, much like had been done to him before. "Then he put away the scroll, but continued to name the victims as if he'd memorized them."

Hearing this, Hannah reasoned that the man may have spent time at the memorial before, committing these names to heart. But before she could ask Julius if that were so, he resumed.

"Before he named your David, whom he identified not only as the son of Joshua and Naomi, but also as brother of Simeon and Hannah – just before he said your names, he turned his face into the light and pulled back his hood." His heart now pounding, Julius gripped the shoulder of Hannah with one hand and that of Simeon with the other: "Yeshua!"

"What do you mean 'Yeshua'?"

"I know it's impossible, Simeon, but the stranger was Yeshua!"

Hannah began to tremble, while Simeon roughly brushed Julius' hand away. "What is wrong with you, Julius!

Yeshua is dead. Buried. It's over."

"I swear, it was Yeshua."

"More likely, your imagination conjured up this delusion," Simeon spewed, "to soothe your guilt for carrying out Herod's orders that day!"

"It was no delusion. As for my guilt – no question, that's what brought me to this wall, and what I probably would have carried away with even greater burden." Julius turned to look at Hannah. "But for Yeshua. He took that from me, Hannah, as I remember your telling me how he did the same for you, by Galilee's sea."

"Stop it, Julius! Don't mock my experience by inventing one of your own. I saw Yeshua on Golgotha, I saw you thrust your spear into his side to prove he was dead! I saw, Julius, I saw! And you claim him alive? Even if he were, why would he come to you? Why to one who never believed anything I ever said about him, or who I held him to be, or could have been, until you Romans crucified him!?!" Whatever remained for Hannah to say dissolved in guttural moans.

Hannah's fury evoked Julius' remembrance of her reaction when he first revealed his role at Bethlehem; the night she cursed him, and Yeshua. The night he fled from her, and in truth from himself. Julius resolved not to flee either again.

"I have no clear answers to your questions, Hannah. What you say of my attitude regarding your beliefs about Yeshua is deserved. But believe me, the last thing I would ever do, especially now, is mock your experience of Yeshua's forgiveness. It changed you. And in doing so, your love for me that wouldn't give up began to change me."

Julius leaned toward Hannah. "All I am saying is: by this wall, Yeshua came to me. Not as an apparition. Not as a ghost. But as the rabbi we met in Galilee, the rabbi whose first teaching we heard was about forgiving enemies. Which is, in plain truth, what I was. As to why he might come to one such as me: you're right, I didn't believe what you said about him . . . but I did listen. And I recall your saying more than once that following him demanded trust. Trust in him, and the God who sent him. Trust when things didn't make sense at the time. I'm no scholar, Hannah, but maybe that's the answer as to "why me." It would be one thing to trust the impossibility of his being alive when such a word came, say, from Peter. Or Mary. But what greater trust might be required to believe such news when it comes from one like me? An unbeliever. A Gentile. A Roman, counted by your people as an enemy, with good cause."

Simeon shook his head. "Trust? The man's dead, Julius. Same as David. Dead."

Hannah drew her knees up to her chest and slowly rocked back and forth. "It sounds like you've finally found a measure of peace, Julius. Even if what you saw, or who you thought you saw, was an illusion: I am glad for you." As she rocked, other words came to Hannah's mind. Words that Yeshua had spoken on the way to Jerusalem: not just the ones about the suffering and death that awaited him there; but something about rising, words none of the followers grasped. "Julius, if you are right about Yeshua – how could that be?"

Julius shook his head. "How, I've no idea. All I can say is, Yeshua came to me. If he'd not been here, I wouldn't be as I am now. I swear, Yeshua lives."

"I can't believe it, Julius. But if you're so convinced," Hannah declared, "then the one who should be told is Mary. And if you feel this strongly, I'd be willing to go with you."

"And what of our mother, Hannah? We're supposed to go with her to our father's grave today." Simeon stood, glaring at Julius while asking Hannah, "Or is that no longer important?"

Hannah rose to her feet and put her arms around Simeon. "Simeon, of course I'll still go with you both to the grave. But would you leave Mary in the dark if this somehow were true?"

Simeon recalled how Mary looked and felt on Golgotha two days prior. "Fair enough, sister. If you think his tale, foolish as it is, might bring comfort to her." As Julius stood, Simeon stepped close and pointed a finger at his face. "But take care, Julius. Mary's suffered enough. Don't force your claim on her. Let her decide whether the impossible can be trusted." Lowering the finger, Simeon added, "You and Hannah can take the horse I came on. He's the stronger of the two. When you've spoken with Mary, bring Hannah back to Nathaniel's."

Julius then held out his hand. "Thank you, Simeon."

Simeon clasped it and squeezed. "He wasn't here, Julius. He's in a tomb."

"For what it's worth," Julius replied, "if I were in your place, I'd say the same."

* * *

The three traveled together until the junction outside of Jerusalem's main western gate. While Hannah and Julius continued north, Simeon turned east and rode through it into the city. Passover pilgrims starting on their homeward journey added to the usual press of crowds in the narrow streets, slowing Simeon's progress. He'd originally thought of taking the horse back to the Antonia before returning to Nathaniel's house. But already delayed by the throngs, and not wanting to make Naomi wait any longer, Simeon went directly to the house. After hitching his horse on the street below it, he walked up the stairs onto the porch and knocked on the door. Instead of the servant, the door was opened by Naomi. "Simeon, I was starting to wonder." After kissing him, Naomi stepped out onto the porch and looked down the stairs, then out to the street. "Where's Hannah, I thought she'd be with you?"

"Let's go to the courtyard and talk."

As they walked through the house out into the courtyard, Naomi grew anxious. Had something happened with Hannah? Would she not be coming with them to Joshua's tomb?

"Here we go," Simeon said, pointing to a bench shaded from the sun.

As Naomi sat with Simeon, her worries flooded out. "There's something wrong, I know it. What aren't you telling me about Hannah? Why hasn't she come with you?"

"Please, mother, give me a chance to explain. First, there's nothing wrong with Hannah. She'll be coming, I would guess within the next hour or so. And secondly, I have some news I think you'll like."

"What would that be?"

Simeon took his mother's hand. "At breakfast, we talked about your returning to Bethlehem. And how, once my release from the legion came through, that I hoped to join you."

"Yes?"

"This morning, as we made our way through Bethlehem, Rabbi Joachin spoke to us. Actually, to me."

"About what?"

"The elders at the synagogue have decided to hire a resident caretaker for the memorial. And he asked me if I would consider it, especially since the property remains our family's."

"Really? What did you say?"

"I said I would." Simeon lowered his gaze. "I've not been much good to my family, even before I left for the legion. But now," Simeon moved off the bench to kneel before Naomi, "Now, I can do something. If you would, I could stay with you and see that you do not want. And, taking care of the memorial, I can do something for David. Finally."

Naomi could not help but smile. "I would like that, Simeon. I would like that very much."

"Then it's settled," he replied, rising enough from the ground to kiss Naomi.

As soon as the kiss ended, Naomi asked. "There's still the matter of Hannah. Where is she?"

Simeon sidled back onto the bench next to Naomi. "In

Bethany. With Julius."

"Julius? Did you meet him on the way back or something? Hannah said he wouldn't be going to Bethlehem with you."

"It's a long story, mother, at the core of which is something utterly preposterous. But to begin with: when we got to Bethlehem and entered the cave, we found Julius there, by the wall."

"What! What business did he have there, of all places?"

Simeon thought to give his own perspective on that, but decided otherwise. "For that, you'll have to ask your daughter. Or Julius."

"I certainly will! But why are they in Bethany instead of here?"

"They, at least Hannah, will be here soon, as I said. As to Bethany: that's what stretches belief. Julius must've had some dream, for he said Yeshua had been with him at the cave."

"What! Has he lost his mind?"

For the life of me, I don't know what to say. All the time I've known him, Julius has always been level-headed. And smart. But this? I can't explain it."

"Can he?"

"Only that he's convinced."

"What of Hannah? Does she believe this nonsense?"

"At first, she took as much offense as I did, if not more." Simeon considered his next words carefully before speaking. "But my sister, and your daughter, deeply loves Julius. As to whether she believes him or not? She did follow the rabbi, so I'd venture she wants to."

Naomi stood and walked over to one of the vines growing up the wall. She picked off one of its leaves and studied it, then let it drop and flutter to the ground. "Until I stood on Golgotha and saw your father two days ago, I'd not given any thought to what even the remnants of love can make someone want to believe again." Simeon got up and stood by his mother as she continued. "Julius may be on a fools' errand in our eyes, but who knows what Hannah's love will lead her to see? I just pray she'll remember she is always loved here."

"She will, mother. She will."

* * *

Julius and Hannah could have entered the same gate as Simeon, as the way through Jerusalem and on to Bethany would have been shorter in distance. But even the usual number of people on its streets and alleys would have slowed their travel considerably, not to mention the pilgrims remaining in the city from the just-completed Passover celebration. With that in mind, Julius and Hannah skirted Jerusalem to the north and west, until they intersected and set out on the Jericho road. After climbing up its ascent of the Mount of Olives, they descended into Bethany. It was almost noon as they neared the place where Mary lodged and dismounted.

"Julius, are you sure you want to do this? I mean, are you prepared for Mary and the others to reject your story?"

"I suppose as much as I can be."

"Mary is a kind woman, but the offense she may take as Yeshua's mother – not to mention Peter, and the others, hearing such a claim by someone outside the circle, who is also a Roman. And after what was done on Friday. . ." Hannah's voice trailed off.

Julius stopped and took Hannah's hand. "Whatever happens will happen. But I must –"

"Hannah! Julius!"

The sounds of their names called out startled them – especially since the voice belonged to Mary, who stood in the front yard of the home she'd been staying in. Julius and Hannah walked the remaining steps to the low stone wall in front of the house, with Julius pausing to tether the horse to it. As he finished, Mary came out and hugged them each, followed by a hushed: "Have you heard? My son, some have claimed they've seen him." Julius and Hannah stood speech-less. "Three of the women left early this morning to prepare his body. I, I just couldn't, not after seeing him at Golgotha. I told them I'd come later, when their work was done. But when they returned, they said he'd had spoken to them."

Hannah judged from Mary's face that she remained un-convinced by the women, as did Hannah of Julius. "But what do you say, Mary? Do you really believe them?"

"I thought they must have been confused, or mistaken someone for Yeshua. I wanted to believe, but . . ." Mary stopped for a moment, peering back at the house. "Peter had finally rejoined us last night. When Salome and the others re-turned from the tomb, he and John told them to get a hold of themselves. That it couldn't be, and they'd prove it by going to the tomb."

"Did they?" Julius asked, wondering how all this might impact what he came here for.

Mary nodded. "They went. And when they came back, the confusion only grew. For they found no body. And now, the twelve argue over the meaning of that: whether it was stolen, or moved, or something else. The only thing they agree on is that the women must be wrong. But Salome as-sures me that they saw my son." Mary's eyes filled with tears. "I want to believe them, but how can I? Except for John, the men blame the women for raising hopes that can't be."

Julius looked at Hannah, and felt her hand take his as she whispered, "Tell her."

"Mary, all the way here, I've pondered how I could tell you what brought us here."

"Tell me what, Julius?"

"Last night, I journeyed to Bethlehem, alone. I stayed outside the village until early this morning, when I went to the cave. To see the memorial wall."

Mary softly mouthed, "Yeshua's birthplace."

"Another was already there when I arrived, kneeling by himself in the dark. In time, he opened a jar beside the wall, and took out a scroll."

"The names of the martyrs," Mary offered, "Joseph told me he read them to Yeshua, when he brought him there years after we'd left."

"After unrolling the scroll, by the light of a lamp between us, this stranger began to read the names. But then," Julius paused to wipe away the lines of tears beginning to streak his face. As he did, Mary brought her hands up to cover her mouth and her eyes widened. "Then, he set the scroll down and continued to name them. And he turned to look straight at me, his face now revealed by the lamp's glow. It was Yeshua, Mary, it was your son. Alive. At that wall, he named those innocents who once died in his place. And in their presence: he forgave me. Of all people, Mary, he forgave me. So trust me: the women speak the truth. Your son lives."

Mary took her hands from her mouth and clasped those of Julius. "May Elohim be praised! I believe you, Julius! My son! Thank you!"

Hannah wrapped one arm around Mary and nestled her head against the shoulder of Julius. "As do I, Julius. I believe you."

In that street: children still played, merchants and customers still haggled, workers still paused labors for noonday meals. And these three clung to one another, in shock and in joy at what had dawned this morning in Jerusalem ... and in Bethlehem.

EPILOGUE

Years ago in Bethlehem, the birth cries of three women pierced a clear night sky that canopied Bethlehem. Now, on this night, other voicings – and silences – rose up from those same three mothers, and from their children, and from the centurion bound to them all.

In Emmaus, Rebekah fussed with her sleeping mat in the guest room. Jacob had found lodging for them in the home of a Zealot sympathizer who often shared the profits of his carpentry shop with those needing supplies or weapons for forays against Roman patrols. When they first arrived, the man showed Rebekah his shop, having been told by Jacob that she was none other than the widow of Elias the carpenter, the martyr from Bethlehem. She could see there, and from the platters used at dinner, that the man had some skills – but nothing like her husband's. Even the tools used were not of the quality Elias employed. Then again, sitting on the edge of the sleeping mat, wondering how poorly it compared with the one in her home, Rebekah couldn't help but think: at least this man's wife has him by her side. Old resentments of having to live in solitude all these years smoldered, and they in turn brought to mind her son: reared to be a Zealot chieftain, now a coward running from his own shadow. Rebekah laid down, and soon could feel the bumps of the packed dirt floor beneath the mat. Had she been wrong to leave Bethlehem? And why had Elohim turned his face against her by taking Elias? Rebekah pulled the coarse blanket over her head, as if to not give God the satisfaction of seeing her tears.

Above the east shore of the Salt Sea, Barabbas sat on a ledge a hundred or so feet above the waters. A large column of rock, brine-crusted where waves splashed against its base, rose up just offshore. Barabbas had watched the sun disappear into the water beyond it, the sky splashed in oranges and yellows before yielding to darker hues, and then night pocked here and there with stars and only the hint of a moon not yet risen. He knew he should keep moving, in case pursuers from Jericho still tracked him. But where would he keep moving to? A breeze descended from the eastern mountains, chilling the air. Perhaps, Barabbas thought, the dilemma of his moving on was no longer "where" but "why." Was it refuge he sought, or simply an end to all this? He peered over the ledge. In the dark, the waters were not so much seen as heard, washing against the rocks on the shore. If he were taken into custody again, the tortures of the Antonia might be repeated. Or worse. For him. Perhaps even for his mother. Looking again over the ledge, this way would at least be swift. There would be the impact, one terrible moment. Then, nothing. "Yeshua!" he screamed. "Why didn't you die in Bethlehem, and leave us be? Yeshua!"

In Jerusalem, Naomi settled into her room for the night. The best, and hardest, part of the day had been going to Joshua's tomb, her children at her side. Words and emotions long sealed inside at last found venting. Joys and longings for what once had been. Regrets and anger over lost years and relationships. And, in the end, wishes for husband and father finding some measure of peace. Naomi gazed out the window, down at the courtyard, knowing it would be her last night here. Tomorrow, she and Simeon would return to Bethlehem, for good. That Hannah would not join them pained her. But her daughter had made this choice for love, and that was a choice that had once been Naomi's, as the best of today's remembrances at the tomb reminded her. Reclining on the bed, Naomi whispered prayers of thanks: that Simeon had been restored to her, that Hannah would not be alone, and that David might soon feel the touch of his mother's hands through the stones that sheltered his resting place.

In the Antonia, Simeon saluted Glaucus and left the tribune's office. Discharge papers in hand, along with a small advance of the donative that would soon be dispatched to him: Simeon couldn't' remember the last time he'd felt such joy! Normally, any release from the legion's service in Jerusalem would have to be approved by the Procurator. But given Pilate's mental frailties triggered by Yeshua's crucifixion, Glaucus had acted on his behalf. Simeon was a free man. He couldn't wait to tell his mother in the morning before they headed to Bethlehem. The only hitch in tomorrow's anticipation would be saying goodbye to Hannah. And Julius, if he were there. Simeon still couldn't grasp what had come over Julius. But: he loved his sister, and she'd been a follower of Yeshua herself. Maybe the delusion of his rising might not harm them.

In the courtyard of Nathaniel's residence, Hannah and Julius talked late into the night about the future, their future. Julius had told her he'd understand if she wished to join her mother and Simeon in Bethlehem. But Hannah declined, saying she wanted to live out her days with Julius, ideally somewhere close to other followers of Yeshua. They both recalled Mary's declaration that she intended to return to Nazareth, and that others of the disciples spoke of returning to Galilee. Hannah suggested Julius' villa in Tiberias as their home. It was an easy journey to Nazareth, and the towns on the shore of Galilee's lake where several of the disciples lived. Hannah had come to cherish the waters of that lake: waters that reminded her of the retreat she once found in the waters of the Great Sea by Caesarea; waters, too, that Yeshua had poured over her in baptism after he'd healed her. "Please, Julius. Let it be Tiberias for us. We can leave tomorrow, when Simeon and mother depart for Bethlehem." Julius put his arm around Hannah's shoulder and pulled her close.

One final night alone in Ishmael's caravansary, and then he'd return in the morning. To Hannah. To Tiberias. To the rest of his life. "So be it."

In Bethany, Mary drifted into sleep. Nights without rest since Golgotha had caught up with her, even with the incredible news brought by the women and then Julius. Or, perhaps, that news and its joy allowed her to finally embrace rather than dread the night. As she slept, a dream pieced together like a mosaic. Colors and shapes formed into the stable where she'd birthed Yeshua. Sounds filtered in, the welcome noise of children. Yeshua toddled about with David, Hannah holding each by their hands. Saul and Levi tumbled in the straw. By the manger stood the midwife Rachel, smiling as she watched the fruit of her labors at play. Joseph strode into view, taking Yeshua into his arms and swinging him in a circle, then setting the boy down with his friends while he sat next to Mary. As Joseph held her, Mary nestled her head against his chest. Too soon, it seemed, the shapes and colors of her dream blurred, while its sounds grew distant. Mary's longing to stay in that scene grew to the point of tears. But looking up, she saw Yeshua, not as a toddler but as he had become. He lifted his mother to her feet. "Everything's going to be alright." Yeshua drew her close and kissed her forehead. "I will always be in your life. And you in mine." Mary awoke. The night remained. But in place of its dread: peace.

As for Yeshua, the other of Bethlehem's children? A trader from Jericho arrived in Bethlehem nearly thirty years after this night with an odd story. He told the aged caretaker of the village's memorial to its slain innocents about an old hermit he'd befriended on his travels between Jericho and the Edomite territories east of the Salt Sea. On his last trip through, the hermit neared death and insisted the trader take something to Bethlehem's memorial for him – which the trader now handed to the caretaker, an old man named Simeon: "The hermit, called himself Saul, said it belonged with his brother. And that if it hadn't of been for someone called Yeshua, it would've been dashed on the rocks, along with him, years ago." Simeon looked down: in his hand nestled the carving of a wolf.

Made in the USA
San Bernardino, CA
22 June 2020